Also by Robin Hardy
THE WICKER MAN (with Anthony Shaffer)

THE EDUCATION OF
DON JUAN

a novel by

Robin Hardy

WYNDHAM BOOKS • NEW YORK

Library of Congress Cataloging in Publication Data

Hardy, Robin.
The education of Don Juan

I. Juan, Don—Fiction. I. Title.
PZ4.H27188Do 1980   [PR6058.A6754]   823'.9'14   79-22340
ISBN 0-671-25335-2

For my sons
Jeremy, Alexander, Dominic and Justin

Acknowledgments

To Joan Littlewood, the distinguished British stage
director, I owe the original encouragement to write
this book. Many others have helped in various ways,
among them Caroline Hardy, Kim Waller, Bernard Breslauer,
Robert Lasky, Joan Packard, Pamela Peabody,
and my mother, Veronica Hardy.

In Lawrence Freundlich, my editor, I have been
fortunate in finding a kindred spirit.

I am grateful to them all.

Contents

Haschich Fudge—A Receipt

In Morocco it is thought to be good for warding off the common cold in damp winter weather and is, indeed, more effective if taken with large quantities of hot mint tea. Euphoria and brilliant storms of laughter; ecstatic reveries and extensions of one's personality on several simultaneous planes are to be complacently expected. Almost anything Saint Theresa did, you can do better if you can bear to be ravished by *"un évanouissement reveillé."*

Take 1 teaspoon black peppercorns, 1 whole nutmeg, 4 average sticks of cinnamon, 1 teaspoon coriander. These should all be pulverized in a mortar. About a handful each of stoned dates, dried figs, shelled almonds and peanuts: chop these and mix them together with about a cup of sugar dissolved in a big pat of butter. A bunch of *cannabis sativa* can be pulverized. This along with the spices should be dusted over the mixed fruit and nuts, kneaded together. Rolled into a cake and cut into pieces or made into balls about the size of a walnut, it should be eaten with care. Two pieces are quite sufficient.

—From *The Alice B. Toklas Cook Book*

1
The Conception of Don Juan

Morocco 1921. Spain, having already lost her empire in the Americas, embarked on the pacification of her colonial possessions in Morocco. Some days before Don Juan was conceived ten thousand Spanish troops, under General Fernandez Silvestre, were surrounded and massacred by Berber tribesmen under Abd-El-Krim. The disaster was so great that, for a time, Spanish officials refused to believe it.

On the day Don Juan was conceived, as on every other day, his mother, the duchess, took a bath. She always had the water drawn in the first cool of the afternoon. It was a ritual both she and Ayesha, her Berber maid, enjoyed. The big zinc tub was placed in the middle of the duchess's bedroom, well away from the chinks of evening sunlight that penetrated the closed shutters and patterned the tiled floor with little regiments of light. Like every other Spanish gentlewoman of her generation, the duchess abhorred the effect of sunlight on a woman's skin. Spaniards, once conquered, and for so long ruled by the dark-skinned "Moor," would breed in themselves a European pallor and pinkness if they could, would exorcise from their blood, if they might, all strains of what they considered the Moorish pollution.

Ayesha was born scarcely darker than her mistress. For the Berbers are the ancient Caucasian race of Morocco, conquered, like the Spaniards, by the great Arab invasions that long ago swept a missionary Islam across North Africa and Spain to the very foothills of the Pyrenees, and then receded, like a spent tide, till Christian Spaniard and Moslem Moor faced each other malevolently across the Straits of Gibraltar.

Unlike her mistress, Ayesha had played naked in the sun as a baby, had helped her brothers mind their father's sheep in all weathers. She held herself very erect, her body sculpted by her robe as she strode along the flagged and shuttered passages of the Moroccan fort, carrying a gourd upon her head, making the twentyfold journey needed to fill her duchess's bath with water drawn from the well pump in the kitchen.

Both women, absorbed in the pleasant anticipation of a half hour of intimacy ahead, tried to shut out from their consciousness the sights and sounds of the male world around them. Spain's vainglorious colonial adventure in Morocco had brought them together, but until this day, the day of Don Juan's conception, they had never spoken to each other of anything outside their female cloister.

The duchess slowly took off the afternoon dress in which she had just presided over a painful meeting at the Melilla Club with the distraught wives of the senior army officers. She hated noise and panic, and she had persuaded her husband, the civil governor, to talk reassuringly to them. The women's petition for the immediate evacuation back to Spain of themselves and their children the duke had torn up contemptuously. He had spoken to them of duty to king and fatherland, of the need to show the natives that the wives of Spanish officers were confident of their husbands' victory. He reminded them that the rebel leader, El Krim, was a simple savage leading a rabble of bickering tribesmen. Whereas the Spanish army was a modern twentieth-century force. The duke's speech was punctuated by the not-too-distant sound of artillery fire.

His most reassuring words, however, had been those with which he had left them. He had said he had no compunction in taking his wife back with him to their summer home in the fortified village of Monte Aruit, far nearer to the front than the safe port of Melilla.

In the motor car on the dusty road back to Monte Aruit, he had read her a telegram from the king. "Glad that General Silvestre has at last had the eggs to attack." Her husband had apologized for his Bourbon master's metaphor, but the duchess had been unoffended, turning over in her mind, instead, the curiosity that something as female as an egg (*huevo*) should have become a Spanish word for testicles. The duchess was, she admitted to herself, feeling distinctly "broody."

Waiting for Ayesha, it took the undoing of nearly sixty tiny buttons to open both bodice and sleeves so that she could step, like a gorgeous, plump dragonfly, from the chrysalis of her dress.

Letting it fall to the tiled floor and stepping delicately out of the little circle of crushed chiffon, she waited expectantly in her spencer and petticoat, her whalebone stays, and her silk stockings for the ministrations of her maid.

The Berber woman, carefully avoiding collision with the hurrying messengers and soldiers who thronged the corridors of the fort, carried her burden of water upon her head, moving with a quicksilver grace, molten and feline. She knew, all of Spanish Morocco must have known (with the exception of the Spanish civilians), that her countrymen, the Berber tribesmen of the Rif Mountains, were close to driving the Spanish "Army of Africa" into the sea. But her thoughts concentrated on the young duchess, upon the familiar image of her pale, plump beauty immersed in the cool well water. The war was, as ever, the affair of the men; of her brothers, the tribesmen; of her mistress's husband and of his Spanish soldiers. Ayesha's whole young life had been filled with the ebb and flow of Spain's attempts to occupy Morocco and her countrymen's wars of insurrection, and their endless internecine strife. She was conscious of the men's doings only as an animal whose first anxiety is nurturing keeps watchful track of the predators around it.

The only males who really claimed her entire attention for a minute, as she carried her last gourdful of water into the duchess's bedroom, were two whiskery pink-and-white creatures who stood talking to the governor in the anteroom of his apartment. In loud, unmeasured tones they spoke (to her ears) a strident foreign tongue that she had learned to hate. It was the language of secrets between the duke and the duchess. "Not in front of the servants" was the only English phrase she fully understood. She noticed with surprise not only that these two men were angry, but that they made no attempt to conceal their emotion from the duke.

In the duchess's bedroom Ayesha clucked her tongue, half disappointed and half contrite that her mistress should have had to remove her own afternoon dress, a task she privately viewed as the prologue to a familiar drama in which she and the duchess were the only players. Since they never spoke during this ritual, had never discussed it, Ayesha could not know for certain whether the duchess regarded it in quite the same way as she did. For her mistress's role was entirely passive. She left every detail, every cue in the play, to her maid. In a sense both women were at once players and spectators, protagonists and audience. For they found ways of giving each other signs of pleasure; intimations, sometimes, of a gentle rapture. Anything more explicit would have broken the spell.

The duchess stood watching the dust-flecked rays of sunlight that fed the golden pattern upon the tiled floor. She half-listened to the sound of approaching rifle fire and thought that if her stay in Morocco was soon to end, her only regret would be the loss of Ayesha. She felt her maid's strong fingers taking the pins from her hair and endured the pleasurable pain of twenty brisk strokes of the hairbrush, drawn from each temple. Ayesha always stood behind her for the hair.

To complete the undressing, the maid placed herself before her mistress and the duchess gazed into the middle distance, careful never to catch her servant's eye. After the petticoat had been removed, the spencer was drawn over the duchess's head with a brisk movement, gently facilitated by her very slightly raising her arms and inclining her head. Ayesha watched the soft pale breasts as they settled after the disturbing friction of the departing spencer. She knelt beside her mistress to unlace her stays, ease free her suspenders, and remove with deft and practiced hands her beige and silken stockings. Circumspectly, Ayesha rose again to her feet when it was time to hold her lady's hand, lending her balance while the duchess herself unfastened, and dropped to the floor, her own lisle drawers.

Spreading a huge turkish towel on the bed for her mistress to lie upon, Ayesha took soap and water from the gourd and proceeded to lather the duchess's body until no fold nor arbor on her plump person remained innocent of those cleansing fingers. The duchess closed her eyes during these ministrations, allowing only a faint "click click click" to escape her slightly parted lips. She suffered herself to be turned over and manipulated gently, but firmly, like a fish on a slab, as her servant scrubbed her skin to a pink glow with a soft brush. Then came the cool balm of the bath.

The duchess lay in the bath, her dark hair carefully draped over the back of the zinc tub, concentrating on the tactile pleasure of the hard well water coolly burning her scrubbed skin. She tried to shut out the raised voices in the anteroom down the passage. But the bald, uncompromising English phrases came through. They brought back unpleasant memories of the English boarding school she had so recently attended. The curious British needed always to be taking some form of *action*, like their exhausting enthusiasm for games. The vulgar search for meaning. As if God's will were not enough.

She knew that Ayesha was waiting for the smile she always gave her when the cool water had finally restored her equilibrium. She gave it now as her maid retrieved the scattering of soiled clothes from the floor. But something in the tone of those alien voices made them both listen to the men—the duchess with an increasingly disturbed attention, her maid with an undisguised grimace of dislike at the sound and for the very noise of male anger, which she easily discerned without comprehending the words.

"I repeat, Duke, what in tarnation are you going to do? Hell, man, nothing you have told us indicates that you have the ghost of an idea how you're going to get out of this trap."

The duchess recognized the voice. It was Piggott, the American correspondent from the New York *Tribune.* She remembered he'd introduced himself, with some self-importance, as an old friend of ex-President Theodore Roosevelt. The duke had remarked afterward that this was the president whose favorite word was, appropriately enough, "bully"—and who had provoked a war with Spain in the hope of acquiring not only the Philippines but also Cuba and Puerto Rico. Now she could hear her husband's voice replying, icily polite, hiding his impatience under layers of good breeding.

". . . I have not heard today from General Silvestre. I must remind you that I am the *civil* governor. Both the general and I report to the high commissioner in Tetuan, although I am, naturally, in direct contact with the king. Military matters, however, are outside my sphere."

"Supposing you *never again* hear from General Silvestre?"

The duchess recognized the voice of Tom Gaitskell of the London *Morning Post.* She remembered a face perpetually flushed with liquor, a white walrus mustache stained half-yellow with nicotine. She considered him unusually repulsive, even for an Englishman, but she had heard that he spoke fluent Arabic as well as the Berber dialect. Before the duke could answer the Englishman, he was interrupted by an explosion of words from the American.

"Stop dreaming, fella! You're clinging to a bridgehead, your backs to the sea. Tetuan is five hundred miles away by steamer. Your king, if he happens to be minding the store in Madrid and not balling some French whore in Montpellier, is still thousands of miles away. In our opinion you'll never hear from General Silvestre again. Right, Tom?"

"All the information I have from the tribesmen is that Silvestre's army was ambushed and surrounded yesterday in a classic mountain killing ground. If he's not already dead, he'll certainly wish he was by now."

"They had ten thousand men!" It was the duke's voice now, uncomprehending, cold, determined to turn away from the meaning of their words. "You are not able to tell me any of this officially? You are relying purely on the words of some treacherous tribesmen who want us to panic!"

"I can't tell you officially, Duke," came the Englishman's voice. "But I believe it to be true. Have you or the commander of the garrison here had any communication from General Silvestre's army today? A wireless message, a dispatch rider—anything?"

There was a long silence. The duchess could hear herself breathing while she listened for her husband's answer. When it came, it was the grandee of Spain making clear the dismissal of his two visitors.

"It is not our policy," he said, "to discuss military matters with the foreign press. Now if you'll excuse me, my equerry will show you out."

She heard them protesting as they left the anteroom. The American shouted, "Cut it out, Duke! Cable Tetuan and get them to ship you Colonel Francisco Franco and the Foreign Legion. That's the only outfit you've got that's worth a damn—that has any chance of holding Melilla."

"And get this whole bloody garrison the hell out of Monte Aruit right now, if it isn't already too late!" yelled his English companion.

Their footsteps clattered on the flagstones as they were hurried away. The duchess was surprised to see her husband appear almost immediately in the doorway of her room. He had never, in her experience, entered her bedroom before without first knocking, and indeed, waiting for her clear invitation to enter. Ayesha hurried to drape a towel around the duchess's neck and over the entire tub so that her mistress looked as if she were wearing a gigantic bib.

He did not speak but simply gazed at her face as if committing it to memory. The duke was a fifty-five-year-old man, a little gnarled and bent before his time, a courtier who would have preferred to be a priest and had been condemned by his sovereign to become a proconsul. He looked bleakly at the twenty-year-old wife he would have much preferred not to marry had she not brought him one of the largest dowries any industrialist in Spain could afford to give a daughter.

"Did you hear what those people said, my dear?" asked the duke, in English, signaling his wife, in this way, that he wished to speak "for her ears only."

"Of course. They must be deaf, those two, they speak so loudly," answered the duchess. "Was what they said true?"

"Oh yes, absolutely true, I should think. It will be another military disaster. Silvestre is an idiot. Thank God I didn't appoint him. He was the king's man, you know. The Bourbons could never choose good people. Never."

"When are we going?" asked the duchess, wondering already what she could bear to abandon if asked to pack and leave in a hurry.

"Go?" asked the duke vaguely, as if he hadn't really considered the matter. "Well, you know we have seven thousand troops here in the Monte Aruit. I hardly think we need to go scurrying back to Melilla, whatever those fellows say. However, if you'd feel safer there, my dear, I shall quite understand. It's such a pity that there's really no one suitable with whom you could stay, although the Castros would be all right. They'd certainly be very flattered. Naturally. I could order the car in the morning. Tonight that road might be a little dangerous."

"Whatever you wish, Jesus." The duchess used her husband's Christian name rather self-consciously, not because it was the name of the Saviour (which is a not uncommon "given" name in Spain) but because her use of it always reminded both of them of the tragicomedy of the fifth night of their marriage.

For the first four nights of their honeymoon in Florence, he had found consummation quite beyond him. On the fifth he had decided perversely, and to his subsequent mortification, to imagine that the innocent girl beside him in their marital bed was St. Catherine of Siena herself, dreaming of stigmata and longing to embrace the corporeal body of her beloved Saviour. For some reason this fantasy had worked. Held fast in his pajamaed arms, the little duchess cried his name aloud in pain and alarm as she received each ducal thrust, thereby exciting him to the first wholly spontaneous sexual frenzy of his life. The memory of her agonized cry as she yelled, "Jesus, Jesus, Jesus!" was enough to excite him still. Indeed, without his encouraging her to call his name aloud he was still quite powerless to possess her as a husband should (to use his own confessional phrase).

"What about us?" asked the duchess, still in English, smiling reassuringly at the rather injured-looking Ayesha as the maid fussed around the bed preparing it in case the duke was seized with a rare fit of desire for his young wife. For he so rarely disturbed her toilet otherwise, having his own suite on the other side of the anteroom.

"They do not *choose* people like us for a post like this," said the duke obliquely, responding perhaps to some more urgent question in his own mind. "They are lucky to have me devote my time to such a thankless task."

"No, I mean what will *happen* to us?" asked the duchess.

"If you stay or if you leave, my dear?" The duke tried to hide a note of impatience at the obtuseness of his child bride.

"If we stay. All that gunfire one hears . . ." She wished only to be reassured. She had never known the duke to be wrong in any material matter.

"A few skirmishes outside the walls of the fort. Remember those seven thousand good defenders. I hear they are sending some aviators from Melilla to drop bombs tomorrow. We must select a good position to watch the show!" The duke's equerry was calling to him from the anteroom in polite but urgent tones. He prepared to leave, giving the duchess an encouraging smile, like an uncle who has promised a languishing child a visit to the zoo.

"Jesus! Just before you go . . ." There was a breathy hesitation, more than a hint of embarrassment, in the duchess's voice.

"Yes, yes, my dear. There is much to do, you know," said the duke, pausing at the door nervously, as if he had a premonition of what her question would be.

"I followed the doctor's advice. You remember our discussion with him about my temperature?" She spoke confidently, knowing the business of begetting an heir to be important to him.

"I'm very glad, but forgive me. This is not the time for this discussion!" The duke made a gesture which somehow encompassed all the harassed affairs of his fast-diminishing colony.

"I just wished to tell you that tonight would have been propitious. I prayed this morning to the Blessed Virgin for our success."

"I'm sure the Blessed Virgin will bear with us," he said, and upon this mildly sacrilegious note the civil governor of Spanish Morocco left his wife's bedroom to face one of the greatest colonial disasters of modern times.

When the duchess turned to Ayesha, she found her looking out of the window. It was a Moorish window placed high in the wall with an iron lattice across the outside and shutters within. To see out of it

Ayesha had to stand on the cherrywood coffer in which were kept the duchess's petticoats.

"Ayesha!" called the duchess quite sharply, unused to her maid misbehaving in this distracted way, and she swaddled and abandoned in her bath.

At the sound of her mistress's voice, the Berber girl leaped from her perch and hurried to help the duchess from the tub. Ayesha's face was for the moment expressionless. But whatever she saw outside had, together with the duke's visit, quite broken the spell of their intimate charade.

"I hope the duke will come to me tonight," said the duchess, speaking again in Spanish. "It may be better if you make your bed in the anteroom," she added, referring to the fact that Ayesha's straw mattress was normally laid at the foot of the duchess's four-poster bed, an Emanueline wonder in rosewood from Portugal. The duke never came to lie with the duchess unless she had expressly invited him—he might have been a devout Orthodox Jew, so great was his fear of being defiled—but she felt confident that her invitation had been sufficiently specific.

"This is no time to be making babies!" said Ayesha gruffly, patting her mistress's body dry with the turkish towel.

"What do you mean?" asked the duchess, more disturbed, if anything, by Ayesha's tone of voice than by what she said.

"You don't know what happens when one of our tribes defeats another in battle. Be glad you have no children for them to torment. You want to hear?" It was not really a serious question, but Ayesha conjuring up for herself some hideous childhood memory.

The duchess shook her head vehemently.

"No, I don't want to hear. That sort of thing gives me bad dreams. One must conceive, you know, feeling placid, having only good, sweet, kind thoughts. It is important for the baby. What kind of man he will become."

"You *want* a man child?" Ayesha sounded astonished. Then, seeing the hurt surprise in the duchess's eyes, she added, "Of course. Everyone does!"

"Don't you?" The duchess was quite incredulous. "When you marry, I mean?"

Ayesha stared at the duchess. At the girl to whom she was part nanny, part servant, and part lover; even if her love had to be expressed in the subtlest of ways, never declared. She thought of what the duchess's marriage really meant. The protection of a famous name for a woman already cocooned by a great fortune. An occasional mating, with procreation as its only purpose. On her straw mattress in the anteroom she heard no evidence of pleasure. But neither had the duchess evidenced any disgust. Sex for her was like "the curse," a necessary evil for the suffering of which a woman was rewarded with the incomparable "joys of motherhood," or so, at least, it had been advertised. Marriage to a Berber tribesman was, naturally, beyond the duchess's imagination.

Ayesha at the age of six had been repeatedly raped as a captive of sharifian troops "pacifying" her tribe and at eighteen had been put aside by a husband who had beaten her incessantly for sullenness and barrenness. That same Ayesha had no desire for marriage, and, curiously, if she had any slight desire for a child, it was for the child of her mistress. Her love for the duchess encompassed and comprehended her mistress's longing. But of these things she had never spoken to the duchess, who knew nothing of her history and had never asked. It had been enough, when Ayesha had been employed, that she could launder and sew and iron, that she looked clean and neat and spoke halting but serviceable Spanish.

"You look tired," said Ayesha, not answering her mistress's question about children and marriage but preparing the bed for a late siesta, the duchess having been on the road from Melilla at that sacrosanct hour. The duchess perceived vaguely that her questions had disturbed Ayesha but had no inclination to pursue the matter. She allowed herself to be wrapped in a peignoir of cool shantung, and lay down to rest.

Ayesha shut tight the shutters, excluding most of the growing clamor of gunfire and shouting from outside. She hurried away to find her brother, who, being part of the civil governor's personal guard, was usually on duty at one of the entrances to the inner fort. She noticed, in passing, that the duke's rooms were empty, though ordinarily, at this time of day, his valet would have been laying out his evening clothes and drawing his bath. The anteroom and passages were quite deserted. No guards, no messengers, no soldiers or equerries. Ayesha hurried along, her bare, callused feet flapping on the flagstones, her silver ankle bracelets jangling as she half-ran toward the distant staircase that led to the main entrance of the inner fort and its guardroom. She paused only once, and then to peer out through a tall, thin "lookout's" window.

In the bright evening sunlight she looked first at the surrounding hills. Normally a uniform purply green with outcroppings of gray rock, these hills manifested an eruption of tribesmen, most of them in dun or white robes. They surged, like lava, toward the outer walls of the fort.

The defenders moved like tiny mechanical mice on the catwalks of the fort's defensive wall. The staccato firing that came from them seemed to make no impression on the advancing horde. Down below in the marketplace of the little fortified town, the scene reminded her of an ant's nest maliciously disturbed by the probing stick of a child. Soldiers, seemingly without military formation or purpose, mixed with a melee of shopkeepers and tribespeople, who, friendly to the Spanish, were working or sheltering in the fort. Their horses, sheep and goats added to the throng. Inching its way through the crowd, the civil governor's car was approaching the inner fort with his personal standard and the royal flag of Spain drooping rather disconsolately from the little silver flagpoles on the fenders. It was only a few minutes before sundown and a terra-cotta light bathed the whole scene, making the anguished center of Monte Aruit seem about to melt away.

Ayesha ran down the stone staircase to the inner fort's main entrance hall. The administrators' offices that surrounded the hall were deserted, except that of a comptroller, where a crowd of furious, frightened tradesmen kept up a shouting match with an equally scared but drunken Spanish quartermaster. Ayesha emerged through the gate of the inner fort into the fetid, dusty atmosphere of its courtyard, where the guardroom of the governor's guard was to be found. The outer gates to the courtyard had been barred and were guarded by Spanish soldiers. Some twenty Berber governor's guardsmen, disarmed and shackled together, squatted in the middle of the courtyard, ringed by armed Spanish troops. Among them Ayesha at once saw her brother. She attracted his attention and called to him in their own dialect.

"Hasaan! Why have they done this?"

"They're so shit-scared they can't think straight anymore. They don't trust us." He used the slang of their family and village as well as the dialect of their tribe.

"Is that good or bad?" she asked.

"Maybe good," he said, shrugging. "Almost everyone will die here tonight. It's a question of how one dies. If the Spanish decide to shoot us, at least it will be quick. You know El Krim."

"Where is the duke?" she asked him unemotionally. Death had been their familiar since childhood. They had faced more atrocious enemies.

He motioned with his head toward the guardroom. She could see dimly through the open door that a conference of Spanish officers was in progress.

"There is some good weed in my locker!" shouted her brother. "See if you can persuade the ball-less wonder"—he used all of Spanish Morocco's nickname for the duke—"to let you bring me some. 'A last request.'" He drew mock tears down his cheeks and mimed to her how she should appear as a supplicant. Just then the Spanish soldier who was covering him with his rifle kicked him hard in the shoulder to stop his talking.

As Ayesha crossed to the guardroom, the gates to the courtyard were being opened slowly by some twenty Spanish infantrymen under the command of a lieutenant. The combined weight of these men was needed to hold back the huge crowd of panic-stricken people outside and to admit the civil governor's staff car.

Ayesha watched curiously while two staff officers emerged from the back of the car escorting an old Berber tribesman, unarmed, but with his chest crisscrossed with bandoliers. He stood in the middle of the courtyard, his arms on his hips, refusing to move further, while the two rather effete-looking staff officers appeared as confused as two dowagers with an awkward debutante, asking him first in Spanish and then haltingly in Berber dialect to follow them to the duke. Seeing the guards, his countrymen, squatting chained, a few feet away from him, the old man cleared his throat and spat venomously in their direction.

Then he raised his head and shouted in Spanish over the silence that had fallen in the courtyard, "Where is the representative of King Alfonso of Spain, the enemy of the Moroccan people?"

The duke appeared at the door of the guardroom, shrugging off the restraining hands of some officers who clearly felt he should not answer this imperious summons from a mere tribesman under flag of truce.

While the duke crossed the courtyard to treat with the old man, Ayesha walked, with that certain anonymity that women in Morocco share with dogs, toward the guardhouse door beyond which were the lockers of the governor's guard. The money both brother and sister sent home to their family was kept here, awaiting some safe courier, and she had a key she always carried on a little chain around her neck. Here, as she rummaged among their few valuable possessions, she found a half-kilo package of the good weed.

The duchess lay on the edge of sleep, her hands gently tracing the contours of her body, remembering Ayesha's touch. It was in the duchess's nature to receive. Money, care, security, status. All that there remained for the duke to give her was a child. It had never been her role to *give*, so that she would hardly have known if it was in her nature to be giver. No real opportunity had ever presented itself. Nor, in consequence, had she ever spared much thought to those people who had endowed her with their bounty or their love. It was, to her, as if God had created every person of importance in her life expressly for her benefit. For all she knew, or very much cared, they were folded away, like Potemkin villages, when she had passed by. Yet for some extraordinary reason her "native" maid—for that is how she thought of Ayesha, feeling quite liberal and adventurous not to have brought a Spanish girl with her—the personality of her native maid had impinged upon her consciousness in a quite unexpected way. Having known neither feelings of romantic love nor experience of pleasurable sex, she was at a loss to account for an emotion which kept conjuring up thoughts of Ayesha, which left her physically bereft without her.

To her surprise the duchess found herself considering Ayesha's body. The sandalwood smell of her skin, the strength and suppleness of her back, glimpsed through her robe, as she walked under her burden of water. She tried to imagine, very tentatively it is true, touching Ayesha as she, herself, loved to be touched. She wondered, for an instant, if she might, by some caress of hers, be able to change the expression in those agate eyes. But chiefly, as she allowed her imagination to travel in those uncharted places, she found herself hoping for more of Ayesha; that strong, smooth sand-brown face next to hers. Considering the Berber girl's full pink lips, with the faint cast of Africa's bluishness about them, fig-blue, she pined suddenly for those lips to be close enough to taste. Knowing, in her dream, that she was dreaming, as one sometimes does, she had a fearful sense of how illicit her desire for Ayesha must have been. Fearful screams seemed to surround her and sulfurous explosions turned the whole world red, so that the fearful demonology of her Catholic childhood, including Beelzebub and the pale horseman himself, seemed to be summoning her to hell to atone for the fearful sin she had committed. But what was the sin? Surely not lust? Was this thing with Ayesha *lust?* Lust in the heart, quite as serious, they said, as consummated lust . . .

A crumbling, continuous explosion, like the herald of an earthquake, awoke her, shaking the closed shutters like a strong wind. And the room was filled through the chinks of the shutters with an etched pattern of fiery light. Above the sound of the explosions

outside came the sobbing, squealing of humans dying slow, interminable, bestial deaths; deaths most men would shrink from inflicting
upon beasts, although such scruples are rare in North Africa.

The duchess, finding herself alone, desperately hoping that she
was still in the grip of nightmare, suddenly saw a figure approaching
through the infernal pattern of light, and, almost sobbing with relief,
recognized Ayesha. Her maid carried a lantern and a little tray of
mint tea and cakes.

"Is that our aviators bombing the rebels?" asked the duchess,
remembering the duke's last words. "If it is, it sounds too *awful*. I
certainly don't want to watch it!"

"The battle continues," said Ayesha simply. "For the time
being. I brought you these. I made them myself. The cooks have all
disappeared. The duke wishes you to stay here this evening." All
these statements were more or less true. The duke's equerry had
noticed Ayesha before she had left the courtyard and had asked her to
relay his message.

"You are breaking it to me that the men have no time for us this
evening?" asked the duchess, trying to speak lightly, wanting to be
reassured that nothing was quite as frightful as it seemed.

"Madam, no one explains these things to servants. What would
we understand?" Ayesha sounded guileful, and both women knew it.
"Please eat these cakes," she added, smiling encouragingly at her
mistress, "I made them specially."

"Oh, that noise is so dreadful. Is that sound human? Surely that
must be animals they are slaughtering. I know that you're Moslem,
Ayesha, but I do think it's *barbaric* to bleed those poor creatures to
death." The duchess munched at one of the cakes and sipped mint tea
as she spoke.

"Do you know anything of bees, madam?" asked Ayesha gently
of her duchess. The first time she had ever raised a subject outside
their daily domestic weal.

"The worker bees. The male drones. The queen bee. Yes, a
little. Why?"

"My mother once told me a story," began Ayesha. "Trying to
make me less frightened, I suppose. Trying to make something seem
natural that I found terrifying, horrible. She wished to put something
in my mind that would make me strong enough to survive. . . ."

"Oh dear, I do hope you're not going to tell me something
horrible. Ayesha, these cakes are delicious. You must make them
more often." The duchess settled back in her pillows with a sigh.

"It was at a time when many strange soldiers came to our village.

They chased us. At first I thought it was a game. That I was a tiny queen bee as my mother had suggested and they were the drone bees. I must try and run faster than they. The one who ran fastest might be destined to catch me. She did not tell me what would happen then. But she did say that they, the drones, would all die, even the one that caught me. Only I would survive. For I was the life of the hive."

"Why do you tell me this? I feel wonderful tonight. As if inside this room we were traveling in time. Maybe in the morning I can take you down the passage to show you the garden of our house in Málaga, where I play as a child. I mean *played* as a child." The duchess gave a great pealing laugh.

"I would like to see it," said Ayesha.

"I'm so hot. Please open the shutters, Ayesha."

"There is much smoke in the air. It is better not. I will rub you with cool water if you like? There is still some in the gourd."

"Yes. Oh yes, yes. Yes, yes, yes, Ayesha. That's a wonderful idea."

The duchess struggled out of her peignoir and lay naked across her bed, rolling from side to side, laughing to herself.

"Why don't we do this every night?" she said as Ayesha returned with a sponge gently saturated in cool water.

Her maid cooled the duchess without, balmed her breasts, watched her nipples harden like the emergence of tiny pink snails, saw the restless opening of her thighs, and felt her urgent embrace. "Aren't you hot too?" the duchess murmured and lay giggling wide-eyed as she watched her lover undress and join her strong brown body to her own soft and melting self.

"What do you mean that you have no rose? *Rien pour aroser avec?*" she giggled much later, using her schoolgirl French. "How can you bear to be without one, when you can make my rose bloom so *beauti*fully? Where did you learn to call it that? When you can make me . . . I've never felt that before." She knew she hardly made sense anymore. "It's awful to lose yourself so. But I love it. I love it so."

Ayesha had not so far lost herself in pleasure as to have missed the telltale sounds from outside the inner fort. She had taken the precaution of bolting all the doors to the duke's apartment from within, excluding not only the duke but any equerry who might wish to shelter there. From fire she felt relatively safe. The entire edifice of the inner fort was constructed of brick and mortar and stone, even the floors. Virtually every building that could burn in Monte Aruit was already ablaze when she had brought her very special fudge up from the deserted kitchen in the basement.

She had stood at the "lookout" vantage point at the top of the stairs and peered down into a hell more truly frightful even than that image a Spanish Jesuit had managed to inculcate in her sleeping mistress, having nightmares down the passage. The military had not allowed the duke to accept the terms of surrender offered by El Krim's emissary. The tribesmen had scaled the walls half an hour later and the killing had begun. Most of the troops left behind at Monte Aruit, Ayesha knew, were recruits fresh from Catalonia and considered too raw to be taken on General Silvestre's ill-fated advance. Her brother had told her that some of them didn't even have bolts or firing pins on their rifles. Many officers had gone to Melilla for the opening of a Kursaal casino and not returned.

She could see these poor Spanish youths running with the goats and the tradesmen, the women and the children, like rats trying to escape a burning field of chaff, only to be picked off one by one by the whooping tribesmen, who had almost ceased by then to use their guns but worked like artistic butchers with their knives, mutilating women, castrating males of all ages along with the animals of the same sex, slitting noses, gouging eyes. Letting atrocious pain and shock bring death. Reveling in the chance to cause, in a few hours, as much misery to others as they felt, perhaps rightly, their whole lives would encompass.

While her duchess had, beneath her triumphant gaze, slipped by degrees into a bliss she knew to be entirely of her causing, while her duchess sobbed her pleasure into pillows already drenched with their sweat, she, Ayesha, had heard the hammering and calling of the duke beyond the anteroom door. But that had been half an hour ago. Since then there had been silence. Now there was the sound of more people beyond the anteroom. They were firing, probably at the locks.

Ayesha took the duchess in her arms and whispered in her ear, "Now, you will do exactly as I say?"

"Yes. Anything," said the duchess, her surrender to her maid's will now complete.

"We will hide under the covers and lie quite flat, quite still," said Ayesha, manipulating her mistress as she spoke.

"Is it the duke? I hope it's not the duke," whispered the duchess.

"Shh," said Ayesha, knowing that they were there in the room.

When they pulled the covers off the bed, she saw that there were seven of them. Young Berbers, their clothes soaked in blood. They looked exhausted. Elated but exhausted.

Ayesha spoke to them in their dialect. She spoke to them at

once, the instant their eyes registered the fact of the two young and naked women.

"Whatever you like. For as long as you like. My friend is Spanish, but I'll tell her your pleasure. Just don't hurt us. And please protect us from the others. We want to be only yours," said Ayesha.

For as long as men have sacked cities and villages and reveled in the loot and the rapine, so long have women made similar speeches. Sometimes it has saved their lives, sometimes not. Fortunately for women, "man born of woman" is not always entirely without pity, is bequeathed, along with his genetic heritage of cruelty and lust, a concomitant sense of gentleness and protectiveness toward the sex of his mother and his sister and his daughter.

Their desire for the duchess was intense. Ayesha had only to suffer their attentions when their impatience to possess the duchess again seemed likely to lead to violence. Then Ayesha would suggest she do for them what she had taken a beating for rather than accord her estranged husband. To the duchess they seemed like figures in a dream, beautiful and brutal, but somehow an extension of Ayesha herself. When Ayesha commanded her she obeyed, turning, bending, caressing as Ayesha indicated. Ayesha described them as beautiful to her, as fish who would swim into and out of her, as drone bees who would limp home to die when she had sucked them dry.

They were, consequently, not men to the duchess, but creatures in Ayesha's dream, that dream in which she, the duchess, was privileged to play a sublime part. She was Life, Earth Mother, fecund SHE deity, known by many names, who came from the pagan belief that lay not far from the surface in Ayesha's Berber culture.

No woman is impervious to the attractions of triumphing over man, even a woman so long passive as the duchess. Under Ayesha's direction she felt herself both willing sacrifice and fatal priestess.

She felt no surprise when the shots rang out that killed her lovers one by one.

Tom Gaitskell and Jonah Piggott stood in the doorway for an instant, as the last Berber fell, still erect and glistening, to the floor. Then the two men rushed forward and wrapped the duchess in a blanket, and, calling to Ayesha to don some clothes and follow them, prepared to leave the apartment. The duchess screamed that she could not leave unless Ayesha was close to her, unless Ayesha held her hand.

"Of course, dear lady. Of course," murmured Jonah Piggott.

"El Krim has given us a pass to take you out, duchess. You'll be

absolutely safe—we'll take you straight to the hospital in Melilla,"
said Tom Gaitskell.

"What about my maid?" said the duchess. "I can't leave without
her."

"I'll tell them she's my mistress," said Jonah Piggott gallantly.
The duchess was back in her own world. She had only to ask.

She had also conceived a son.

2

In the Arms of the Loving Creatures

The great progress made may perhaps deceive us into thinking that
everything possible has been done for children.

—Maria Montessori, in 1914

With the light came the noise. If birth is but a sleep and
a forgetting, it could not have seemed that way to the newborn Don
Juan. His mother, the other principal in the drama, wept and
protested at the renewed pain of being stitched. Ayesha, furious at
having been excluded from the delivery room by the Spanish doctor
and midwife, was insistent that the baby be put entirely into her care.
The absent duke's relatives, his loyal tenantry, and his servants
crowded loudly in the anterooms and passages outside the duchess's
bedroom. Not since the birth of the unfortunate duke himself, more
than fifty years before, had the great, gloomy castle on the banks of
the Guadalquivir River in Andalusia known such excitement.

Carried by the triumphant Ayesha, the little don made his first public appearance. His lungs, only for minutes used to their appointed function of breathing air, now inhaled the heavy scents of the ladies, his aunts and cousins, the fragrant and acrid tobaccos smoked by his male relatives, the rich garlic and wine smells on the collective breath of the privileged tenantry. He did not cry, and although he regarded their blurred shapes through a single beady eye (the other having been inadequately ungummed by the impatient Ayesha), he managed to make a certain impression on the crowd. At eleven pounds he was large for a newborn baby, his pale-olive skin was silken-smooth and barely blotched by the extravagant exercise of being born, and his dark hair was abundant enough for a tenant to shout, "God be with him, he is ready for the barber!"

If the duchess's mother had not died in her daughter's infancy, she might well have preempted the role that Ayesha assumed on the day of Don Juan's birth. She would surely not have found it necessary to display his masculine parts like tiny trophies to the crowd. But in the extraordinary circumstances of this child's birth, his noble relatives were prepared to accept such unorthodox behavior. It was fully understood that this simple Berber woman had helped save the duchess's life. No word of her mistress's multiple rape had ever been breathed by the two gentlemanly war correspondents. Neither the duchess nor her maid had ever discussed, in retrospect, the happenings of that terrible night. The male child being displayed to his relations was, therefore, the duke's undoubted heir, and some small gratitude was due to Ayesha for all that implied. A noble line would continue. The great wealth the duchess had brought with her to her marriage would now pass on through her son to benefit the future of the estate.

The duke's absence was so macabre and unusual a circumstance as to have, by mutual consent, been put out of everyone's mind; at least, until the "event" of the birth of his heir should be over. The war correspondents had not spared the world, to the fearful humiliation of the Spanish people, their description of how the defenders of Monte Aruit had surrendered and died. Every noncommissioned officer and enlisted man and civilian had been butchered. The surviving officers, including the duke, had been stripped naked and chained before being marched off to imprisonment in the Rif Mountains. Apart from a huge demand for ransom, nothing had been heard of these captives since. His relatives, who remembered how delicate and ascetic a figure the duke had always been, wondered how he could survive the rigors of so frightful a captivity at his age. But no news had yet come of his death. In toasting the baby, quite a few of the guests in the castle that day believed they were actually toasting the new duke. They were wrong.

In the early years of his life, Don Juan saw, felt, heard, smelled, and tasted women to the exclusion of almost anything of his own gender. In his first year, each time he awoke, his wet nurse, Maria, a strong Andalusian peasant girl with a figure like a stone-age votive offering, all hips and breasts, a small head and tapering prehensile legs, gave him of her inexhaustible supply. Her own baby had been stillborn a week before Don Juan's birth, and she was kept "in milk" at Ayesha's insistence until past the child's fourth birthday. Her milk was, of course, by then only a "supplement" to his diet, but Ayesha believed strongly in its prophylactic properties. If germs were believed to be around, the little boy was offered nothing but Maria's breast until the danger of infection was past. Maria's own diet was strictly controlled for the same reason. She was forbidden anything that might "taste" her milk. The Berber woman, a peasant herself, treated Maria like an indulged cow.

The duchess, who had so strongly desired this child, was not equipped by either experience or the custom of her class to look after him. In the first month, when she risked her figure by sharing the chore of suckling her son, it gave her a certain physical pleasure but ultimately bored her. She would have liked to be able to read aloud to him at once, to be able to go shopping for amusing little clothes for him, but he still, in the heat of the Spanish summer, wore no more than his diaper. He was like a longed-for doll that somehow failed quite to come up to expectation. She had other preoccupations. The castle, accessible as it was to her husband's relatives, proved very uncongenial. To be in Spain at all meant that she was expected to take a constant interest in the freeing of the prisoners, whereas she was utterly indifferent to the duke's fate.

Physically, she was in love with Ayesha, in love for the first time in her life. Intellectually, she felt starved in Spain and longed to pick up again, in Paris, the chance to live the broader, more stimulating life she had glimpsed there when at her finishing school, Les Cygnes. In heart and mind she considered the duke to be dead. Like his relatives, she could not imagine how he could survive.

She had seen her husband naked and shackled in the courtyard of the inner fort, standing with the other officers among the stinking piles of butchered corpses. He hadn't seen her as El Krim's guards hurried them toward the correspondents' car. She had been appalled, at the time, that her only cogent thought had been that she had never before seen the duke naked and would probably now always remember him that way; a plucked, gaunt chicken whose ganglia reminded her of suspended offal.

Ayesha was in many ways father and mother to the infant Don Juan. She it was who taught him to walk, who came and comforted him when he cried, carrying him to his mother's bed, the bed in which she herself slept almost every night. When his emerging teeth hurt him, her fingers caressed his little sex, distracting him from his pain with the strange sensation.

Years later he could not remember the order in which all this happened. Whether Maria had still been with them when they started to travel. Whether he was four or six when they had lived in the huge suite at the Hôtel Crillon in Paris. But he remembered, all his life, Maria's big melon breasts and the milky smell of them, the long hard nipples and how it pleased her when he nibbled at them with his little teeth.

"Not too hard! What do you think I'm made of, cork? Yes, like that. Like that. Like that."

It was at the Crillon that he started to learn to read. His mother had taught him to recite the alphabet in French and in Spanish as soon as he could talk. At the age of six, he could read a hundred or more words in both languages, although he sometimes confused the two tongues. Beside her on the huge feather bed, surrounded by the elegant, uncomfortable Louis XVI furniture, he liked to snuggle into his mother's cushiony bosom, follow the words in the book as she read to him, and join her in the world he had never so far visited, the world beyond the foyer of this grand hotel, beyond the ride by chauffeured Delage limousine to and from the Bois de Boulogne.

In the *Fables* of La Fontaine she taught him to see the creatures in the stories as people he would surely meet, that when he recognized in some man, soldier, courtier, or financier the character of Reynard the Fox, it would be well to remember how Reynard acted in the fable and be warned.

In after years Don Juan learned that his mother lived in hotels during those years to spare herself the ordeal of Ayesha's cooking. Brought up on French food in her father's more-international-than-Spanish household, she hated the saffrony, overspiced cookery she had found in North Africa. In the close domestic relationship she shared with her "companion-cum-servant" Ayesha during Don Juan's infancy, it would have been hard to deny the Berber woman some part of the ordering of the kitchen in their own home. Hotels were a perfect solution.

The little boy became, long before he was ten years old, an *amateur* of hotelkeeping. The laundry rooms, the sewing rooms, the stillrooms, the wine cellar, and the attics where the servants slept—all these he frequented. In this way he made the first male friends of his life. A porter called Laurent who worked at the Hôtel du Cap at Antibes, in the South of France, was the first man Don Juan ever saw shave. It came as an astounding discovery that he would one day grow hair all over his chin and have to scrape it off each morning. Indeed, he did not entirely believe that Laurent was not the exception that proved the rule until the duchess and Ayesha assured him otherwise.

It led to one of those small "landmark" happenings in a child's life that stick in some key part of the subconscious, regulating, affecting, and directing his actions long after. In this case Don Juan "consciously" remembered the conversation, or thought he did.

"If I have a beard like Laurent, will I have a voice like that, gruff and sort of furry?"

His mother laughed, but Ayesha looked at him very seriously. They were sitting on the rocks below the hotel, watching the swimmers in the *plage*.

"My poor Juan," said his mother. "You will be a man like your father. What did you think? Of course you will be big, hairy—not too hairy, I hope—and have a deep voice. Perhaps you will have a baritone. That is attractive."

"Will my *petit choux-fleur* (Juan used their pet name for his sex) become all big like those of the men over there?" Don Juan pointed to some young men in the newly fashionable tight bathing shorts.

"Don't point, Juan. It's very rude," said the duchess, about to change the subject. But Ayesha interrupted her.

"Perhaps bigger. The bigger the better. It is the principal weapon of your tribe."

"Ayesha, please!" said the duchess in mild remonstrance. It was, she had always heard, better to answer a child's questions. But Ayesha had so many "barbarous" ideas.

"Tribe? What's that? What's that?" asked Juan. "What's my tribe?"

"A tribe is a group of people who must defend themselves against the tribe next door. Sometimes they *hunt* separately, but they must come together if they are to defend what belongs to them. Like my Riffi people against Spain. Men and women are two tribes. You belong to the men. For now you stay with us and hear our secrets. But one day you will have to go and join the men and you will forget."

"What secrets do I know?" asked the child, thrilled that he knew something as valuable as a secret, worried that he might forget it.

"Our mysteries. You know some of them. But I will not remind you what they are."

"That's not fair. I'm still part of your tribe!" protested Don Juan, feeling, for the first time in his life, excluded.

"No, an honored guest, darling!" The duchess contradicted him as reassuringly as she could. "And we adore you!"

"Of course we love you," said Ayesha, catching the duchess's warning look. ."But that has nothing to do with it!" she added with finality.

His mother took him into the sea for his swimming lesson, and he went on wondering about what they had said as he watched members of the two tribes bobbing about in the waves.

During these years he must have heard that the duke, his father, had finally been ransomed and freed. Much later he learned that the "old man" (for that is how he emerged from El Krim's prison) had spent nearly two years in a Madrid hospital before returning to spend most of the remainder of his life a semi-invalid at his castle in Andalusia. There, in due course, Don Juan was to visit him and try to learn to be his son.

The duchess certainly visited her husband in the hospital in Spain soon after his release, and several times thereafter. It is not known whether he asked for his son to be brought to him then; presumably he did. Nor has it ever been possible to form an opinion as to whether the duke really believed some seed of his had impregnated his young wife; or whether she or the Berbers had ever told him of her rape. However, he never, by any word or act, repudiated Don Juan as his son and heir. That his stupidity and moral cowardice had been largely responsible for the duchess's near death she is known to have reminded him, using it as an excuse to continue to live apart from him in France. Whatever passed personally between the couple, their legal agreement of separation is a matter of public record. She retained custody of Don Juan until he should be old enough to be prepared for his confirmation into the Roman Catholic Church. A financial settlement involving undisclosed amounts returned the control of the duchess's marriage portion to her father, in return for which the duke accepted an annuity. What pressures were brought to bear by the duchess and her father to achieve so unusual a result in Catholic conservative Spain can only be conjectured. But the fact that her father was a strong financial supporter of the new dictator Primo de Rivera (King Alfonso called him "my Mussolini") may have had something to do with it.

At about this time, the duchess moved her household into the Hôtel Raphaël on the Avenue Kleber in Paris, taking the whole top floor. The management had agreed to allow her to carry out certain refurbishings and to hang her own pictures. In the main reception room, her salon, she hung a collection of paintings inherited from her mother. They included two Goyas (from the Horrors of War period); a Velázquez portrait of a Hapsburg monarch with a chin like a bowsprit; a Murillo of two young musicians at a Bacchanal playing for an unseen crowd but entranced with each other; a pair of Tiepolos, cartoons for a chapel roof, where the theme was to be the Ascension; and a huge Turner landscape of the Port of Cádiz at the very instant of sun-up.

Don Juan, on first entering this room, was so moved to childlike wonder at the pictures that he sat quite still and silent, gazing about him for half an hour. For the next month, he continued to ask his mother questions about the paintings. She told him Goya's life story, but he demanded to know every fact she could tell him of the war in which the "horrors" he painted had occurred. Visitors to his mother's salon were greeted by a seven-year-old who behaved as if he were the proud curator of a gallery giving voice to a spontaneous art lecture. Meanwhile, Don Juan himself had started to draw, and went on drawing for the rest of his life.

As the duchess became more and more established in Paris, she ventured out into the great city discovering, and herself being discovered. She took Don Juan to visit Marie Laurencin and watch her at work, first with charcoal, drawing one of her graceful, noseless little girls. Then adding the paint, it seemed to Don Juan in retrospect, by a series of the simplest smudges—some pink, some white. He was fascinated, but thought she had entirely ruined the drawing. Here the duchess met Adrienne Monnier, the proprietor of one of the most famous bookshops in Paris, La Maison des Amis des Livres, and her friend Sylvia Beach, also a bookseller and the publisher of Ulysses. These women knew almost every writer of consequence in France, Britain, or the U.S.A. Through their enlightened sapphic circle, she met Gide, Cocteau, and the Spanish painter Picasso.

From her frequenting of the two bookstores, a stream of volumes flowed into the salon, and some, specially selected, into the schoolroom in the Hôtel Raphaël. For it never occurred to the duchess, at this time, to send Don Juan to school. She herself saw to his early education, reading him, in French, Jules Verne, Émile Zola, Victor Hugo, and Alexandre Dumas. From these authors he was obliged to learn not only the basics of the French language, but also history and geography. Arithmetic was a subject the duchess believed quite unsuitable for young children. She herself found it impenetrably difficult and was afraid to tax Don Juan's brain at too early an age.

The duchess's relationship with Ayesha had started to change. Having legally separated herself from her husband and regained the indulgent guardianship of her powerful and generous father, she felt herself to be a more or less emancipated woman. Ayesha's role as both protectress and amanuensis was at an end. The duchess was bored with a love affair that offered no intellectual stimulus. Nothing but the fading pleasures of Ayesha's increasingly desperate passion kept her from sending the Berber woman—where? Since there was no immediate answer to that question, things continued, for a time, as they were.

On a night of the duchess's return from Spain after a prolonged absence, Ayesha went with the chauffeur to meet her at the Gare de Lyons. Don Juan awaited them, reading, in his mother's bed. He had never, so far, been expected to sleep in a bed alone. If he had not slept with Maria, now long since returned to Spain, he had slept with his mother and/or Ayesha. Occasionally he had been left to sleep with the duchess's laundress, Odile, and had hated the experience. The woman reeked of disinfectant soap, and her hands were rough, nor had she the faintest idea of how to caress a small boy to sleep.

When he heard the women coming down the passage toward him, he could sense the strain in their familiar voices. Someone else was with them. Don Juan remembered that his mother had engaged a French maid for her trip to Spain. This other person must be she. His mother was talking in Spanish. "Good night, Ayesha. We can talk about it in the morning."

He couldn't hear Ayesha's muttered reply, but when his mother came into the room, she was accompanied only by the new maid. Don Juan was too absorbed in the pleasure of his mother's hurrying toward him and kissing him to take notice of the new woman. After the hotel porters had arrived with the cabin trunks and the suitcases and departed, and Sylvie had been formally introduced to him, he started to examine her with an attention that he was to accord every new female he would ever meet.

Sylvie, sensing this, looked at her mistress's seven-year-old son, looked at him squarely and returned his gaze, smiling to reassure him that she was friendly Sylvie, a girl who wished she were a *midinette* for a couturier, sewing in an attic with a dozen other girls all chatting and gossiping, but who knew she was lucky to be the duchess's maid.

Sylvie saw a well-made little boy sitting, apparently naked, in the bed, the covers pulled up to his waist. His slightly olive skin had a curious sheen to it, almost like the gloss on a chestnut, so that his slim body looked like a carving in some soft, warm-colored wood. The face was as sensual as any face she had ever seen on a man or a woman, let alone a child. Under a mass of too-long, dark, curly hair were eyebrows of sooty black and wide eyes of green flecked with brown. His mouth disturbed her. Although not out of scale, it was already a man's mouth, on the face of a little boy. The lips, full and strongly outlined, had the faintest tinge of blue to them, reminding her of figs, still unripe but promising to be luscious. To her dismay, the child's eyes above the man's mouth seemed to read her thoughts. He did, and he wondered how his mother could possibly prefer her to Ayesha.

"Sylvie, you can unpack all these things tomorrow," said the duchess in French. "Draw me a bath. I'll be going straight to bed afterward."

"Will Sylvie sleep with us?" asked Don Juan in the same language.

"No, she won't," answered his mother, almost sharply, in Spanish. "Now be quiet and read your book till I come to bed!"

"But where's Ayesha?" he asked in Spanish. "Where's *she* going to sleep?"

"In her own bed. I'm surprised you haven't explored the whole apartment yet. Ayesha has two rooms of her own, you know."

"I know," he said almost tearfully, hating the idea of a new order. "But why do we have to sleep alone? I *like* having her with us."

"*Silencio!* Be quiet till I come to bed!" said the duchess as Sylvie emerged from the steamy bathroom to undress her.

Don Juan watched the familiar sequence. He felt sorry for Sylvie. The poor girl had no idea of the ritual. Where was the cream that was rubbed into his mother's thighs where the stocking suspenders left their mark? How could her stockings be removed delicately unless the undresser knelt on the floor? But his mother made no complaint. She dismissed Sylvie before even putting a foot in the bathwater. Was that an implied rebuke? Don Juan wasn't sure.

Lying in the dark, after his mother had come to bed, he wondered how they would sleep without their lover. He sensed her wakefulness, how she seemed to be breathing shallowly so that she could hear all the sounds in the nearby rooms.

"Are you waiting for *her* to come to us?" he whispered.

She turned to him and hugged him to her breast. He kissed her cheek gratefully and was surprised to find warm tears, tasting faintly salty. *Their* tears tasted the same as his own. *They* were the same in so many, many ways it was hard to tell when they were suddenly going to surprise you and be different. The mystery here was why his mother had sent Ayesha away when she plainly needed her. His mother did not answer his question.

"Shall I go and fetch her?" he asked.

Again silence. But this was a silence he understood. It meant "yes." He almost fell from the bed in his haste, and ran for the door only to be stopped by his mother whispering loudly and complicitly, "Juan! Shh! Quietly!"

It did not entirely surprise him to find Ayesha also in tears, although he had never seen her cry before. He did not speak, for he could think of nothing to say. He simply kissed her and pulled at her hand. She came without questioning, without coyness or bitterness. She followed him gratefully, but with a quality of terrible resignation. He always remembered how she was that night. The intensity of the two women's feelings awed him. Their complexity he would only be able to guess at in retrospect.

At first it seemed as if things would be once more as they had always been. Ayesha lay between him and his mother, kissing her carefully as a cat licks a recovered kitten. He knew that for a time they were still weeping, but then Ayesha started to weave what Don Juan thought of as "her magic," kissing the duchess in that secret place which always started her on her journey of delight.

In past years Don Juan had dozed through Ayesha's pleasuring of his mother. The cries and sighs were comforting to him. The urgent trembling and the sweet smell of musk that told him it was ending reassured him. These warm, loving creatures with their magic and their pleasure cared for him, cherished him, were his world. It did not seem strange to him that Ayesha clearly derived *all* her pleasure from her *power* to create languor and bliss in his mother. That was the way the little universe of their common bed was ordered. Afterward, Ayesha's soft hands and warm mouth savored his own little body, drew any lingering aches away from him, and turned him on his tummy to join his mother in a deep sleep. It was the last time he was to know such contentment in his mother's bed.

In the morning he was awakened with a start. His mother was up and dressed in her peignoir and it was still not quite light outside. She was awaking Ayesha.

"You must go to your room now."

"Why?"

"I don't want Sylvie to find you here. Please, Ayesha."

"What?"

"Ayesha, please! I was weak last night. But we can't go on like the old days. Juan, too. He must sleep in his own room."

"Why?" Ayesha almost shouted. Shocked, awake, and more frighteningly angry than Don Juan had ever seen her, she leaped from the bed, grabbing the duchess by the wrists. "Is Sylvie to replace me? Has she been sleeping in my place? Don't lie to me. Don't dare lie!"

The duchess shook her wrists free and struck Ayesha on the breast and shoulders, hammering with her fists and shouting, "How dare you! Sylvie's my maid. As you were, and don't you forget it! Now get out of here! Go to your room!"

Ayesha looked at the duchess for a measurable instant. As if she needed to read something in her face or mind. Then she left without a glance behind her, closing the door quietly enough.

Shaking, the duchess sat on the bed beside her little son and looked at her reddening wrists. She walked over to the door and opened it a crack, listening. She went to the bathroom and soaked her wrists in cool water, took some tablets, and came and lay down on the bed beside Don Juan. It was his turn to ask the question.

"Why?" He whispered it.

"One day I will explain. When you're older," she said.

He found himself crying. What had happened frightened him terribly.

His own prospect of banishment to the cold impersonal little room down the hall was bad enough, but Ayesha was more than half his life. He wanted to go to her and console her. To reassure her that he loved her even if his mother had gone mad. Each time he made a move to go, his mother's hand restrained him, and a new hardness and determination in her face deterred him. In the end, he lay back exhausted by the emotion that had seized him, and slept until Sylvie came with the breakfast tray and opened the curtains.

The French girl was a morning babbler—something Don Juan had not met with before, and, like everything new involving a woman, it held his attention.

"*Bonjour*, Madame la Duchesse, it is a marvelous day outside. The Cabinet is at each other's throats again. Poor France! Spain is so stable under their good king. They have sent baked eggs for young Monsieur Juan. He eats an English breakfast, this one. That is why he looks so big and strong . . . ."

She plumped up the bed pillows. Don Juan speculated on the exact shape of her breasts under the black poult dress. The nipples would be small if they were like her mouth. Pink, perhaps, like the noses of little mice. He shuddered delicately and addressed himself to his eggs.

Nothing Sylvie had said seemed to require an answer, and the duchess, who was already used to this aimless chatter, simply opened her newspaper and nodded her thanks. The girl left after giving a slight curtsey at the door and intoning a cheerful *"Bon appétit."*

The duchess hardly touched her coffee or brioche, and soon rang for Sylvie to come and dress her. Don Juan she sent to Ayesha to be dressed in his jodhpurs for a riding lesson in the Bois. The child found her room empty, and an envelope on the bed. It was addressed to his mother in the childlike hand Ayesha had learned when his mother had taught her to read and write Spanish while he was still a baby.

His mother called the police as soon as she had read the note. But it was too late. Ayesha had ended her life as quickly as she conveniently could, throwing herself under one of the incoming commuter trains at the Péreire Métro station.

The suicide of a parent—for that is what Ayesha's death amounted to for Don Juan—is such a cataclysmic event as to leave traumas that continue over a long period in a child's life. It is certain that he never wholly forgave his mother in his heart, although his reasoning excused her soon enough.

One immediate effect of the event was to make him determined to face out the horror of sleeping alone. He refused to talk to his mother for days, except in monosyllables—reading the books she gave him in the schoolroom, going to his riding lessons and his Swedish drill dutifully enough, but obstinately refusing to come to her room.

In a perfectly conscious act of faithfulness to the "martyred" Ayesha, he kept a photograph of her by his bed and tried to think of no other woman, although he longed for the nearness of a female body. At night it helped him to face his fear of "someone" lurking in the closet or under the bed or behind the curtains to know that his mother slept as coldly alone as he. More than once he went to Sylvie's room to make sure that she was not with his mother.

No simpleton, Sylvie understood the reason for his visits. A kindly girl from Évreux in Normandy, she talked to this curious, lonely little boy of her home, of her younger brothers and sisters. Without any direct denial, she found a way to convince him that she had never taken Ayesha's place, that she was simply his mother's maid. She became his friend.

The duchess grieved over Ayesha's death because she felt an extreme guilt mixed with a genuine, a deep, sense of loss. Don Juan's attitude was as bitter a blow and as difficult to bear as he intended it to be. Teaching him and watching his inquiring mind develop had been as rewarding as anything she had been able to do in her life. His capacity for an absorbed, total affection for those he loved had been her constant delight. Nor had she minded sharing that love with Ayesha. Now she felt quite desolate.

3

In Search of the Goddess

Most *average* children are capable of learning to read at the age of four. Particularly if isolated from their siblings. The gifted child will be deducing, inventing, forming propositions soon after. Mozart and Menuhin performed music with distinction before adult audiences by the time they were seven. William Pitt the Younger, a British statesman who rallied the European alliances that defied Napoleon, went up to Oxford at the age of fourteen, was Chancellor of the Exchequer at twenty-two and Prime Minister of England at twenty-four. His sometime fiancée Mlle Necker, later Mme de Staël, argued impressively with Voltaire at the age of eight. . . . But all this, of course, was before radio and television.

—Nibor Ryadh, *The Gifted Child and Mass Communications*

Perhaps it was no coincidence that Henrietta Muloch chose this moment to make what she subsequently referred to as (frank in this as in everything) "my move." The duchess had met

Henrietta at Les Cygnes when they were both being "finished," each according to her fashion. It had been clear even then that Henrietta was destined to prowl the Sapphic world. She looked rather like her countryman Douglas Fairbanks, Sr., perhaps a little narrower in the shoulder, possibly a trifle broader in the beam, but essentially a swashbuckling figure with a profile so aquiline, a head so proudly held, that she reminded people of a heraldic beast "rampant."

When they had met at school, their slight friendship had encompassed introducing each other to writers of their respective countries. García Lorca was swapped for Jack London, both in French translations. Henrietta, a free spirit, whose family owned a chain of newspapers in the Midwest of the United States, hoped to become a foreign correspondent, a wish that was dashed because she was prepared to work only in Paris.

Too much money prevented her from ever working at anything but the serious business of knowing how alive she felt. But her life was as full as if she had held down several jobs. In a typical year she painted scenery for Diaghilev and fell in love with a young ballerina. She went to readings of Gide and Cocteau and Reverdy. She eased the way for the flood of American literati then invading Paris. She nursed an unrequited passion for Josephine Baker, posing as a Swedish prince at her stage door in the hope of "getting to first base" with her.

When the duchess had appeared in Paris Henrietta had called on her, had then seen Ayesha and decided she had no alternative but to wait. The two dined together from time to time after the duchess felt sufficiently in tune with Paris, and her husbandless self, to seek out a new circle of friends. Henrietta was careful not to invite her into her demi-world of *grandes lesbiennes*, lest she be frightened of totally estranging herself from her Spanish relatives. But Henrietta saw in the duchess the first woman with whom she might be content to spend the rest of her life.

The death of Ayesha was not widely reported in the French press, but within hours Henrietta sent a tactful note and offered her services in any capacity in which she might be useful. The following week she took Don Juan to the races. It was on the day the duchess had to attend the inquest and later escort her friend's coffin to the Gare de Lyons for its long journey back to the burial ground in Axdir, Morocco, where the imam had promised to bury her under the proper Moslem rites.

Communicating in French, the boulevardier heiress from Minneapolis took Don Juan to a Longchamps paddock and introduced him to the intricacies of "form," filled him with her enthusiasm for fine horseflesh, and entirely seduced him to her own passion for placing bets at long odds. They lost a fair amount of her money and returned full of mutual admiration. She liked his quick little mind, although she was appalled at his total ignorance of the simplest arithmetic. He frankly admired her style, her panache, her gaiety.

"I hope you don't mind my being personal," he said, prefacing his admiration with the approved formula his mother had taught him. "But you remind me of Jo in *Little Women*. Only you are a million times more . . ." He searched for the word, while she looked at him amazed. *"Chic!"* he finished in his slightly sibilant alto voice.

"Thank you, Juan," she said, laughing. "I've always rather liked Jo, although she was always doing the silliest things."

"I'd rather hoped she would go off and become a general. Very disappointing," said Don Juan, pleased but surprised when she gave a neigh of laughter at this apparently ordinary remark.

Henrietta enjoyed herself hugely talking to this sagacious seven-year-old, whose conversation showed so clearly what the duchess had been forced to admit, in a moment of *mea culpa*—that Don Juan had scarcely ever met another child, certainly never "played" with one.

His reading was impressive for a boy his age, although she thought *Little Women* a bizarre choice on the part of the duchess and said so. He explained that so few English and American books were available in French or Spanish translations. *Little Women* was an exception, but his mother had read it in the original, he added, showing some pride in her linguistic ability.

This short conversation set off a train of thought in Henrietta Muloch's mind which was to change Don Juan's life swiftly. What he needed, the American woman decided, was to be raised, insofar as it was not already too late, as a *child*. And a *boy child* at that. He needed a good old-fashioned governess who would teach him the three R's so that he could go to school like a normal kid. It would do no harm if the governess was English so that he could gain another language in the process. Helping organize such an arrangement would give her both the opportunity and the time to seduce the duchess.

It was to prove easier to seduce the mother than to find an appropriate governess for the son.

In a sense the duchess had, for a long time, been looking for a new mate. Culturally and temperamentally she was inclined to marriage. She wished to lean on another person. To be relieved of all responsibilities in her life except those she had some special interest in or desire to retain. Intellectually she was a late evolver; her mind having traveled extensively in her reading, she was now developing a desperate craving for good talk. Physically only a woman could satisfy her. Ayesha had seen to that. Emotionally the link to Ayesha had remained strong, but it had weakened steadily as the duchess had recognized her other needs. Here was the answer to Ayesha's pathetic "Why?" and to little Don Juan's bewildered "Why?"

In the end Henrietta had only to "take charge" of things. She suggested buying a house now that Ayesha's death had released the duchess from the threat of couscous and sheep's eyes. She personally tutored Don Juan in math while searching for a suitable governess for him.

The duchess was so grateful for these initiatives, so admiring of Henrietta's confidence, of her energy and flair for living, that she was not long in leading the tall American to her bedroom and closing the door behind them. It is some measure of the discretion with which Henrietta soon organized their joint household that Don Juan was hardly ever to see his mother in bed with her lover, and never to sleep with them.

Only in the matter of governesses did Don Juan present a problem to the new regime.

"Do you realize that he has looked at every woman we have interviewed as if her were considering her as a mistress? It makes them very nervous to be looked at that way by a child, even a child as charming and persuasive as Juan. Perhaps particularly because of those qualities of his."

Henrietta was explaining the problem to the duchess.

"But he is only seven years old," said his puzzled mother.

"Exactly. Imagine what he could be like at nine!" said Henrietta.

"So have they all turned the job down?" asked the duchess incredulously.

"Far from it. Several found him enchanting. But he found *them* wanting," said Henrietta. "A matter of their hands. Or the cast of their eyes. In one case he didn't like the poor woman's voice. You must speak to him. These were all highly qualified people."

When Tabatha Truscott arrived she came highly recommended. There was a letter from George Moore, and another from Elizabeth Bowen, both writers known to Henrietta and both Anglo-Irish, as was this much-praised Tabatha. She came for her interview in the elegant salon on the top floor of the Raphaël as if she had just walked in from the bog on a windy day. Her complexion was russet, like an apple that has weathered on the bough. Her red hair stood up and away from her high-domed forehead like a frizzy halo (Henrietta was reminded a little of Colette). Her long-skirted suit was made of such heavy Irish tweed that the seat and the elbows and the knees all bulged where they had taken the strain. Her brogues were sturdily sensible, and her reddish hands clutched a music case bursting with papers. Henrietta and the duchess took in all these details with slight dismay, but Don Juan looked at her eyes, which were large and of an intense lapis lazuli blue, and smiled.

"Look at her eyes, Mother," he said in Spanish. "She is like Titania, the Faery Queen in the story. I expect she has crushed wings under all those funny clothes. But you can see from her eyes that she knows *everything.*"

"What does he say?" asked Henrietta irritably. She rather resented private conversations in Spanish.

"He likes Miss Truscott," said the duchess. "Please forgive him, Miss Truscott. He is given to saying rather personal things to ladies, so I encourage him to say them in an anonymous Spanish."

"That's quite all right, Duchess," said Tabatha. "If you'll forgive me for saying so, Juan, you remind me a bit of Ariel. No, that is not quite right either. There is something Dionysian about you, *rex quondam rexque futurus.* Once a king, and a king to be. But if I come to teach you, I will find out who you really are."

"It is difficult to see how you can resist a proposition like that, Juan," said Henrietta, laughing.

Don Juan said nothing, but looked at his mother with eyes that spoke his total consent. He was so hugely attracted to Tabatha as a personality that he was terrified she would, for some grown-up reason, be refused him. He wished to take her away and explore with her without a further instant's delay. Nor had she in any way aroused his sexual curiosity. In that he felt, without even considering the matter, of course, as neutral, as naturally friendly as he felt toward Henrietta. The duchess, who noticed this in her son, attributed it, with a typical Latin bias, to the fact that both women were "Anglo-Saxon."

So Tabatha stayed and Tabatha filled his waking hours with new ideas. So that he always went to bed pleasantly tired, and alone. These were the halcyon days of experimentation in education: Dewey, Rudolph Steiner, Montessori, and others were as fashionable as the fox-trot. The duchess asked Tabatha to describe her "method."

"I try to help Juan to solve riddles, Duchess. I start with himself. It has not escaped his notice that he is locked, along with his skeleton and all his working parts, inside his skin. How did he come to be there? Why is he there? Will he, can he, ever escape? Or must it all end in a box?"

"*Dios.* That sounds a little macabre for little Juan, Miss Truscott," said the duchess.

"Not at all. The whole of biology, mythology, religion, science, and history follow logically from these questions as surely as the chain reaction that will ensue when they finally split the so far immortal atom."

"I see," murmured the duchess, not seeing at all. "But surely we must think of his future responsibilities. I mean, science . . ."

"Not a proper subject for a Spanish grandee, Duchess?" Tabatha laughed. "Prince Henry the Navigator, a neighbor of Juan's Andalusian ancestors, doubled the known world. Prince Rupert of the Rhine helped found the Royal Society in London, still the greatest forum for scientific thought in Europe. Even Spain must eventually totter into the twentieth century. But I'm afraid his future career is set. He draws like God."

"I would not mind his being an artist," said the duchess defensively. "But I hope you will not denigrate Spain to him."

"He has too much Spanish *hubris* to ever let me do that. No, we will speak of how Spain may be saved by his generation. Later. We have not yet 'got there," as they say in the classrooms. It is early times yet. We are starting, logically enough, with the Genesis myths. I'd like to take him on a trip to Ireland."

"The Garden of Eden?" The duchess laughed outright, and Tabatha had the grace to smile.

"You can get nearer to Europe before Christ in Roman Catholic Ireland than anywhere else I know. It's a good place to begin. I have a cottage in Galway. He'll be quite safe. The 'troubles' are over, you know. At any rate, for the time being."

And so, learning English with a lilting Anglo-Irish accent, Don Juan spent the summer with Tabatha Truscott in Ireland, while the duchess, delighted to be entirely free for the first time in her adult life, went with Henrietta Muloch to cruise with Nancy Cunard on her yacht.

Before his trip to Ireland, Don Juan's knowledge of the natural world was largely what he had gleaned from the kitchens of a number of grand hotels. He knew that wild strawberries appeared in July, that truffles were sniffed up by pigs in the Périgord, that caviar was the roe of the virgin sturgeon and came from the Caspian Sea. He knew by heart the cuts of meat from a pig, although he had never seen the live animal. He could name all the different cheeses made, respectively, from the milk of a ewe, a goat, and a cow, but the creatures themselves he had only seen from the windows of the Blue Train en route to the South of France.

On the drive to Cherbourg, where Tabatha and he took a tramp steamer to Cork in the Irish Free State, he started to learn the names of trees. It was May, and they wore their new young leaves.

"Will we meet these same trees again in Ireland?" he asked her.

"Oh yes. They will become old friends. For each tree has a special meaning. In the days before the saints came to Ireland, they lent their names to an alphabet. But you must be patient. We will be meeting the sea birds next. If we are very lucky, we may see an albatross when we get into the Atlantic. There's a famous poem about him and dozens of myths. . . ."

The little boy who sat in the Pullman car of the Cherbourg Express listening entranced while his red-haired Faery Queen recited "The Rime of the Ancient Mariner" was on his way to that part of his childhood when everything suddenly started to come into a sharper focus. Encouraged to challenge every riddle he found in his path, he found that often the answers themselves posed further riddles but that he was hopelessly hooked on the game of unraveling them.

He was sure that Ireland would be the enchanted realm of long-dead kings, and seeing it through Tabatha's eyes he found it to have all the aspects of an epic tapestry. On the very first Sunday she proposed to take him to Mass in the local village church. She knew he had not been in a church since his baptism and had not expected to go again till it should be time for him to be prepared for his confirmation by his father in Spain. The duchess, in her subconscious profoundly Catholic, believed her "sin" to be unconfessable, and like many of her faith, felt that there was plenty of time to repent. Never having been taken near a church by his mother and never having previously heard Tabatha discuss religion, Don Juan was both surprised and intrigued by her proposal.

She set the stage for him by explaining the ritual he was about to witness. A priest dressed as a woman was by the magic of the Christian God going to turn wine and bread into the blood and flesh of a man called Christ, considered by many to have been a god, who had been executed nearly two thousand years ago. He would do this on a sacrificial table or altar. The villagers Don Juan had seen in the street and the shops would all be in church and they would file up to the altar and eat this sacrificial meal, which they called a "celebration." There would be singing and a lecture on morals.

In the event, Don Juan found the whole show rather boring. Although Tabatha had started to teach him the rudiments of Latin, he couldn't begin to follow the long incantations in that language. The sermon was fun because the priest singled out Tabatha Truscott as the kind of person—mocking, godless, and atheistic—who would try the patience of any Christian community. Tabatha had taken care to sit at the back and had spent much of the service whispering her explanations to Don Juan. After the denouncement, she was noticeably quieter, although she made no attempt to leave.

When the congregation filed out of the church, Don Juan was surprised to find that the priest shook hands with Tabatha in a friendly enough manner and, on being introduced to him as "Father Carroll, the scourge of the ungodly," spoke very kindly.

"Did she tell you it was a cannibal feast, then, boy?" he asked Don Juan.

"Well, I expected to see a good deal of blood!" said Don Juan truthfully to a roar of laughter from the priest.

"The miracle takes place in the mouth, doesn't it, Father?" said Tabatha in much the same tones as an English missionary might tax a Papuan aborigine on ancestor worship. "Wine across the tongue, sticky gore in the intestinal tract?"

"That's right, Tabatha, and it takes a good Irish Catholic to digest it! Will you send the lad over to see me so I can have a little 'equal time'? I hear he's one of ours."

"I will not!" Tabatha's indignation was only slightly mock. "Isn't it enough that this church is built on the very site where the worshipers of the Triple Goddess Brigit kept her eternal fire?"

"It's now St. Brigit's Church, and the light in the sanctuary is never put out; can you complain about that?" retorted Father Carroll, smiling.

"He's saying that nothing has changed in Ireland except that there is now a male trinity where once there was a female one."

"It is the same in Spain," Father Carroll said complacently. "Man is made in God's image, and most good women are glad of it, Juan. Come and see me and I'll tell you more."

Genuinely furious, Tabatha Truscott dragged her charge away, leaving Father Carroll and a little knot of his parishioners laughing together at her discomfiture.

"The last laugh will be with us when they find out that God is a woman," she confided to Don Juan.

During the early summer of showers and sunshine, of scudding clouds trailing their shadows over the green hills, Don Juan learned to be with other children. Tabatha sent him to play with the children of a neighboring farmer, a boy a little older than he and twin girls of his own age. He had now turned eight.

The first time he met Maire and Siobhan, the blond, rather moon-faced twins, his desire to undress them was instantaneous. He felt quite weak at the thought of their double nakedness. He stared at the fine, fair hair on their legs, which seemed to peter out altogether on their inner thighs. His eyes strained to see that soft, smooth grotto when they sat and he could peer up their skirts. He hated the navy-blue bloomers that hid their little crotches in a cul-de-sac. If Tabatha noticed his preoccupation, she gave no sign of it at the time. She asked the farmer's children to explain everything that happened on the farm to the little Spaniard from the city. It was a dairy farm, with a small piggery attached. They showed him the feeding, the milking, the bull serving the cows, the castration of the little boars, and the early hay-making.

In the meantime, there were long bicycle trips so that he could see the shape of the original Ireland, before the priests came. They visited the barrows of kings and the stone circles where the sacred rites were held. Standing high on the long deforested hills, he could see here and there the residue of the great oak forest that had once covered most of Western Europe, the oaks sacred to the Irish druids. He learned the significance of the seasons in the old religion and how Christianity had incorporated almost every ritual or symbol of pagan times in its new liturgy. She taught him how the days got their names. Sunday for the great life-giving deity in the sky. Monday for the moon goddess—the same Brigit, whose color was white, as the dress of a bride is still. She explained not only the meaning of the days of the week, but of the months of the year, how Janus, the two-headed god, had given his name to the first month of the new year, and so on. He listened to Tabatha Truscott and half-recognized who and what she was when she told him that in the days of the old religion, it meant death for a male to witness female mysteries.

"What mysteries?" he asked, insistent in his questioning, as always.

"A mystery is a secret, my dear," answered Tabatha. "Only a few do I know. That is the price of my 'civilization.' Others are buried in my tribal memory, in that of every woman, I truly believe."

"When Ayesha and Mother wore a towel between their legs, Ayesha told me that was a woman's mystery. But I know all about that! It's something else, isn't it? The twins up at the farm are just little girls, but there is something about them. I can't stop thinking about them," he admitted, smiling.

"You're sure you don't just want them to take their bloomers off for you? That then the mystery would be over?" asked Tabatha gently, laughing at him.

"It might be just the beginning. I'm not sure," he answered seriously. "Do you really believe God is a woman?"

"I for one am sure that Brigit lives. Not St. Brigit, who they don't even pretend was an historical person, but Brigit of the Golden Hair, the White Swan, the Triple Goddess. Her name hardly matters. I just feel her to be the eternal Bride and Mother. Not God but the one real Goddess. I have, I suppose, as much right to believe in Her and believe myself to be Her priestess as that Father Carroll, nice enough man that he is, has to believe in all that looted mumbo-jumbo stolen from my pure faith!"

"Does she look after boys as well as girls?" asked Don Juan, feeling, once again, as with Ayesha and her tribes, excluded.

"Of course. She herself had a son. He had many names in many places. One of them was Dionysus. Like Catholicism it is a religion involving two important figures. A mother and a son. Very much a religion for both sexes.

"We could ask the twins over for tea tomorrow!" she added, changing the subject suddenly. "Would you like that?"

"Oh, yes, please!" said Don Juan, wondering if one of her "secrets" was the reading of other people's minds.

"The day after tomorrow is the summer solstice, the longest day of the year," she said. "I want to make it a holy day for us. We'll picnic up at Bridie's Circle on the hill. I'd like to take the twins, but their father has so much for them to do around the farm these days. They can come to tea and spend the evening tomorrow, if you promise not to stay up too late. We'll be getting up very early the next morning to get the first glimpse of the sun up there."

It was raining and Tabatha had to visit a sick cousin in Cashel that day, so Don Juan spent his time reading Mallory on King Arthur ("Think of him as more than a king, perhaps as a god," his mentor had said) and writing a long letter to his mother describing all the beautiful and wonderful things he had seen and heard under the tutelage of Tabatha Truscott. When he went down into the village to post his letter, he met Father Carroll at the post office.

"Is Tabatha Truscott being good to you then?" he asked the boy.

"Yes, sir, thank you," said Don Juan politely.

"Teaching you about the old religion, I suppose. Do your father and mother know that, I wonder?" he asked, still speaking quite kindly.

"I've just posted my mother a letter telling her all about it," answered Don Juan. "We're going up to the stones to watch the sunrise for the summer solstice. I'm afraid Miss Truscott wants to be a priest too, you see," he added, trying to break this news as gently as he could to Father Carroll.

"Is that a fact? Is she then?" said Father Carroll noncommittally, but clearly not all that surprised. "Well, she's had a very sad life, poor lady, so we must be charitable, mustn't we?"

"Sad?" echoed Don Juan, really surprised. "She doesn't seem sad to me. Why should she be sad?"

The priest looked taken aback at Don Juan's question.

"Why, she'll have shown you the remains of the big house, surely?" he asked.

"No. What big house? Where?"

"It's up a long bit of a drive the other side of the river. There's not much to see now because the fire burnt it to the ground. Her Da and Ma died in the fire. She was lucky to escape. They were terrible times. People here didn't know what they were doing. Shooting and killing and burning. But that's all over now, Juan. Not many of the English have stayed. But those who do, like Miss Truscott, are welcome, now Ireland's free. Sure enough."

"You mean people *here* lit the fire?" Don Juan was incredulous that the easygoing villagers he'd met could have deliberately burned Tabatha Truscott's parents to death.

"Yes. It was before I was priest here. But I couldn't have stopped them. Not at all. You should get herself to teach you a bit of modern Irish history, and then you'll understand."

"But *why?*"

"They were English, boy! They were big landowners, and Protestant! They were the Ascendancy. Get her to tell you about Cromwell and William of Orange. The Truscotts came here in Cromwell's army."

"D'you think she hasn't told me about it, sir, because it makes her unhappy to talk about it?" asked Don Juan, feeling the burden of so much inside information about Tabatha Truscott.

"Sure enough," said the priest, recognizing the implied reproach. "Maybe you'd better wait and see if she talks about it first. It's good to be hearing herself's happy. Everyone in the village feels badly about what happened. God have mercy on us—now that it's too late, and all."

So Don Juan made no mention of his meeting with the priest when he next saw Tabatha. But when he returned to her house and still had it to himself, he looked at the family photographs he'd seen in her room. There were snapshots of people who could easily have been her parents with a younger Tabatha Truscott. There was also a photograph of a grand house whose colonnades reminded Don Juan of the drawings by Palladio that hung in the passage of the apartment in the Hôtel Raphaël in Paris.

At evening milking time the following day, Don Juan went to help the twins and their brother clean out the cows' stalls after their father had done milking. Then the twins came home with him to high tea, as the Irish call it thereabouts. A meal of potato bread and eggs and bacon and fruit cake and potato cakes all washed down with milk or strong Indian tea, well sugared. It was the older brother's night for catechism class, so he couldn't come, and the twins promised to save him some potato cakes, a special treat when Tabatha baked them.

When the children got to the house they found it decorated as for Christmas with sprigs of mistletoe hanging from the ceiling and candles burning. She had bought lots of gramophone records in Cashel, and played them Irish jigs and catchy show tunes and fox-trots during their meal. She allowed them all to drink a little raw cider to toast the summer solstice. Maire and Siobhan had no idea what the occasion was, but they enjoyed the tea hugely and, in constant fits of giggles, gave themselves up to the novel pleasure of being alone with "the luvly Spanish boy with the eyes," as they called him privately and in frequent discussions with envious little girls in the village. For Tabatha Truscott, having served them their tea, had left them alone in the kitchen.

"Why don't you play sardines with them, Juan, and kiss in the middle? That's what all the mistletoe is for, remember?" she said before going up to her bedroom to listen to the radio.

The first game was one of hide and seek, with the whole rambling house at their disposal. The first person to find the hider had to hide in the same place. Since the best hiding places were in cupboards, that often meant a tight, squashed-up pair of hiders. Hence "sardines." This gave Don Juan plenty of scope for squeezing up to each little girl in turn. To his surprise and relief, they seemed anxious to squeeze back. Sardines was a very popular game because it separated the twins and allowed each girl license to squeeze and cuddle in a way she was still too shy to do in front of her sister. In between they played kiss in the middle, much like the old game of pig in the middle, only with kisses as penalties. Don Juan wanted to kiss them as he had seen Ayesha kiss his mother in the half-light of their bedroom in Paris. But something told him that that would frighten them. They started by letting him kiss them on their flushed cheeks. But he soon insisted on finding their lips and they became even more excited and giggly, returning his embraces with long kisses, allowing his questing tongue to explore theirs until the unkissed twin shouted, "My turn, my turn! It's not fair, you've had much longer than I had!"

"Back to sardines?" he suggested, longing to go a step further and feel up inside their thighs. Squealing and shrieking, they went on playing the game until, it being his turn to hide, he decided to get under the covers of his own bed. Feeling hot and flushed with the cider and longing to be naked with the twins, he took off all of his clothes except his underpants, turned out the light, and crawled under the covers. Maire, who found him and slipped in beside him, at first froze when she felt his almost naked body. But he put his lips gently to her mouth, and she, feeling his hands softly describing her whole body, whispered breathlessly in his ear:

"Herself's got to get undressed and all, if I do? Isn't that the way of it?"

"Yes, of course," he said, adding, "That's the rule of the game."

Siobhan was so surprised and envious when she found them that she almost shouted at her twin:

"Who said *undressing?*"

"He did!" said Maire. "We all have to. It's the rule of the game."

"It's silly!" said Siobhan huffily.

"If you undress too I'll let you both put your hands inside my underpants," said Don Juan, looking at them both in the soft light from the passage. Ayesha had caressed him since he was a baby. He assumed it was a desire these girls might share.

"Who wants to feel you? Disgusting!" said Siobhan.

"Disgusting, is it?" retorted Maire. "Who said they'd like to give it a kiss and all?"

"I never!" said Siobhan.

"You did too and all. You bet me sixpence you'd be the first to do it," said Maire.

"Yes, and we agreed it was a mortal sin," said Siobhan.

"Listen to her. It was you who said we're too young for it to mean anything, so it couldn't be a sin! You said that."

"If you *both* kiss me there, I'll kiss you—in the same place!" said Don Juan with considerable bravado, having searched unsuccessfully for the right word in English.

They both stared at him, astonished.

"We haven't got the same place, silly," said Maire.

Don Juan slipped his hand under the elastic of her bloomers where it rounded her pale little tummy. He let his index finger slide down till he felt the soft little cleft. It felt shiny-smooth as a nectarine where it divides to take the stalk. She gave a little "Oh!" but she didn't move or resist.

"I'll kiss you both there," he said. "If you'll do the same."

The twins stared at each other, searching for their usual trust in one another.

"Oh come on," said Maire. "you know you want to. Neither of us is ever going to tell. You know we never tell."

So it came about that when Tabatha tiptoed down the passage she saw the three children entirely naked on the bed. The two little girls' heads were stooped over Don Juan's midriff.

She knocked at the door pretending she couldn't see anything in the half-light.

"Are you children in there?" she said loudly over the continuing din of her radio down the passage. "Time for the twins to go home."

The little girls had plunged over the side of the bed and Don Juan had hidden himself under the covers the moment they heard Tabatha's knock.

"We're playing sardines, Miss Truscott. *On sort tout de suite!*" Don Juan shouted back breathlessly, losing his English in his panic that she would come in and turn on the light.

Father Carroll had driven the three boys home from his catechism class. The twins' brother, Sean, was the last, and he parked his old Morris runabout in the farmyard and accepted the farmer's invitation to a glass of Guinness stout before going home to bed. After taking leave of the farmer, who, like Tabatha, was listening to his radio, he walked across the farmyard to his car. He could hear the twins' voices coming down the lane and paused to listen to them. For priests, who know that none of their congregation ever speak unguardedly in front of them, unless it is in the confessional, there is considerable temptation to eavesdrop.

"Do you really think she saw us?" asked Maire.

"She musta!" said Siobhan.

"But she couldn't. She'd have half-killed us if she'd seen us. She'd have told our da, for sure," said Maire.

"The second I took my mouth away from his thing I saw her. She was sort of peeping," said Siobhan.

"Did you like it? I liked it," said Maire, giggling.

"Yes, I liked it. But I'd die if anyone knew we'd done it," said

Siobhan, and both twins squealed with excitement at their adventure. Then, seeing the dark-suited figure in the farmyard, were suddenly quite silent.

"Evenin', girls. Have you been to a party then?" asked Father Carroll's voice from the darkness near his car.

"Yes, Father," they chorused nervously, recognizing his voice.

"Where was that?" He sounded kindly. They thought perhaps he hadn't heard what they'd said.

"At Miss Truscott's. A party for Juan"—they pronounced it Ju-one. "She's taking him up to the hill tomorrow," said Maire, forgetting why, if she'd ever really known.

"Oh, yes. The boy told me he was going. And what kind of games did you play at the party? Something about your mouth and his *thing,* did I hear you say?" He spoke the last sentence in the kind of roar he used in the pulpit to denounce any and all the sins of Sodom and Gomorrah.

"Oh, no," sobbed Siobhan, terrified. "He musta heard'n us."

"You girls will go straight to your mother right now and tell her everything that happened. D'you hear me?" he shouted at them. "Herself will tell your da, and himself will tell me. Now I warn you, one pawky little lie and I'll know it. Don't think the Devil doesn't take little children to hell. He loves to put them in eternal hellfire. D'you know why? Because he hates innocence and purity. If you're not absolutely innocent and pure, he's got you. But we can still save you if you tell the truth."

Father Carroll followed the twins as, screaming and sobbing with fear, they ran into their home.

The following morning Tabatha Truscott's alarm clock went off at two-forty-five. She had calculated that sunup by the stones on the hill would be at five minutes to four. She woke Don Juan and told him to wash and dress and come down the hall to her bathroom, where she had a task for him to perform. She washed her body with particular, almost ritual, care and wound her hair into a tight bun. Then she took a pot of blue liquid and a brush and started to paint her body blue. When Don Juan arrived at her bathroom door, he was astounded to find her naked and already painted quite blue from her forehead to her shins. She hardly glanced at him as she continued to paint every reachable surface of her body.

"Don't stand there with your mouth open, Juan," she said. "You're not shy. I saw you last night. I've known since I met you. I want you to paint my back, where I can't reach."

She handed him the pot. The blue stain dried almost instantaneously on her rather freckled, slightly sagging skin. Her buttocks and hips seemed disproportionately large as his artist's eye followed the brush over her gluteal curves.

She sent Don Juan off to have a glass of milk and some sandwiches that she had laid out for him on the kitchen table, while she got dressed.

They set off to walk across the fields to the foot of the hill. Don Juan, who still felt sleepy and hollow inside in spite of the sandwiches, had a strong urge to giggle at the sight of Tabatha carrying her usual music-case handbag, dressed in her baggy tweeds (Midsummer Night in Ireland is not all that warm), with what, in the dark, looked like a minstrel's blackface giving the whites of her large eyes a glittering luminosity. She appeared, he thought, quite comically theatrical. As they tramped across the dew-sodden fields, clambering over stiles and through gaps in hedges, he wondered how a woman so proud of her sex could make herself look so silly. He thought of her pointing out that Father Carroll dressed in lacy women's clothes to say Mass. Why hadn't that been equally ridiculous? But it wasn't. He felt a little disloyal at this thought. It was part of his observation of adult life that every now and then they did something entirely ridiculous from a child's point of view. He'd learned not to point it out. Besides, he had experienced few boring days with Tabatha Truscott. In his eyes, she had earned her right to go a little mad on the "longest day."

As they struggled to the top of the great rounded old hill, he could see the dark humps of the stones. They looked like a group of sentinels after a long, hard watch, some lying prone, some leaning, some standing upright. Tabatha had been so concerned that she might have misjudged the time of sunrise that she half-ran up the last hundred yards to the crest of the hill, where the stones were set. In sharp contrast to her normal habit of continuously regaling him with information, no word that was not absolutely necessary had passed her lips since she had awakened him. To her obvious relief, they arrived in the center of the great circle of stones while it was still dark, although a pale-blue light had started to outline the hills to the east. The wind chapped their cheeks and hands as Tabatha, laying her music-case hold-all on the ground, surveyed the stones, calculating from their layout the exact direction in which they should prepare to greet the newborn sun. Content that her calculations were right, she selected a huge flat stone that lay in the path of the deity's first rays of expected light. Don Juan was beginning to bang his hands together against the cold when she turned to him and spoke in her usual kind, informative voice:

"Now, Juan, we can't have you getting cold. Have a little drink of this and it will warm you up no end."

She produced a thermos, from which he gratefully drank a mixture of hot milk and some sweet burning liquor that made him cough but nevertheless warmed him so that his limbs felt almost weak at the joints. She watched the sky continuously, looking occasionally at her watch. Suddenly she almost barked at him.

"It's time to undress! We must both undress at once. Hurry. The timing is everything, I'm sure. Oh, how lucky we are that it's so clear."

Don Juan watched her start to undress in a frenzy of hurry, throwing her clothes aside, not bothering where they fell. He struggled out of his own, hoping that he wouldn't have to stand around naked for too long in the wind, but feeling a little sleepy and relaxed nevertheless from the drink she'd given him.

"You can sit on the stone now, Juan. Facing me," she said, towering over him, her breasts like pendant sacks, the rather protuberant belly looking, in the cold light, like the flesh of a blue whale.

"It's, it's a bit cold. Must I?" asked Don Juan, wondering why adult games tended to be so desperately uncomfortable. This was worse than going to Mass.

"Must, Juan! It's coming!" she shouted, throwing him back on the stone with a skull-numbing crack. Dazed, through a haze of encroaching blackness, he felt her hand grab his sex. She was yelling in triumph, and he saw, bright as lightning, the sun reflected on a knife in her hand. His bowels seemed to melt, his breath to cease, within an instant of total fear. Then she was moving back and away from him as if she were being lifted in the air.

Two uniformed Guarda officers clad incongruously in gym shoes held her between them spread-eagled and yelling, her woaded body mauve in the warm sunlight. Taking off his coat, Father Carroll ran forward to the half-conscious child and covered him.

4
The Revolutionary's Handbook

He has shown strength with his arm,
He has scattered the proud in the imagination of their hearts,
He has put down the mighty from their thrones,
   and exalted those of low degree;
He has filled the hungry with good things and the rich he has sent
   empty away.

—Luke 1:51-53

Normality is what the child needs," said Henrietta. "A good, firm English nanny, school, routine, three square meals, plenty of fresh air and sports. That kind of thing!"

She was standing in the saloon bar of the station hotel, a large pink gin clasped firmly in her hand, talking to Father Carroll, who sipped at a Guinness.

"And don't forget his religion!" said the priest sharply. "I was shocked to find, when I went to chat with the little fella in the hospital, that he had no notion of the Ten Commandments. Not at all."

"Religion," echoed Henrietta reassuringly. "Of course he must have religion. I'm a Protestant myself, I'm afraid, so please forgive my ignorance. Is he too young for us to get him a confessor?"

"Sure and he's not confirmed yet," said Father Carroll. "No, he needs instruction. It's a pity it'll have to be from a French priest. I'd rather see him taught by a good Spanish Jesuit—there's no nonsense about them, y'know."

"Instruction he shall have, Father. A Spanish priest is an excellent idea. How d'you think he's looking?"

They both glanced through the door of the bar into the residents' lounge, where a rather morose Don Juan, his head swathed in bandages, sat reading H. G. Wells's *The War of the Worlds*.

"Better! It's a miracle he's there at all. They say he'll have headaches for a while, but that's to be expected. The concussion was quite severe."

"What of the woman? Barking mad, I suppose?"

"Oh yes. I went to see her once they'd calmed her down. In a straitjacket, she was. Poor soul, she was still a bit blue around the edges from the woad. It was as I thought. As soon as she saw me she shrieked, 'He was the ideal sacrifice, a brilliant, beautiful child, the descendant of great princes!'"

"What was all that part about the twins? Your wonderful letter was so explicit, but neither the duchess nor I could make out how the twins came into it."

"She as good as gave the twins, two lovely eight-year-old girleens, to himself the night before the sacrifice. To satisfy his young lusts. Part of the pagan ritual."

"How horrible! When they're all such babies," said Henrietta. "But did one of the twins *tell* you?"

"She did that," said Father Carroll grimly. "One of them told me that she was sure that *herself* was watching the orgy. That was the clue I needed, because I already had my suspicions."

"Simply terrific you've been, Father," said Henrietta for the tenth time, at least, since she'd arrived that morning to collect Don Juan from the hospital and take him back to Paris. She looked at her watch impatiently. They said the trains were always late in Ireland, but she had been standing in the bar of the station hotel with Father Carroll for over an hour of "announced" delays. The "announcements" took the form of the stationmaster coming in from time to time and ordering himself a Guinness. He would then tell anyone interested where the train had got to. "It's at the water tower at

Ballydon." "The race meeting at Cashel was late startin', so the train's to wait 'n' see."

"Wait 'n' see?" A puzzled Henrietta echoed this announcement.

"The driver or the guard maybe needed to see the closing prices for the first race," explained Father Carroll. "The betting is the curse of the country. Next to the English."

Eventually the train came. Just before getting into the carriage after Don Juan and the luggage, she turned to Father Carroll and handed him the first of two envelopes.

"This," she said, "is for whoever will now be trustee for Miss Truscott. These are her back wages. She does seem to have taught Don Juan the most excellent English. It would be a final kindness, Father, if you see it gets into the right hands."

"I will, that," said Father Carroll, simply, eyeing the other envelope.

"And this," said Henrietta, "is a present to your parish from the duchess. We spoke to the cardinal on the telephone, and he felt quite sure you'd accept a new window for your lovely church. The enclosed check, I'm told, should enable you to choose an artist in stained glass of real merit. Oh, an Irish artist, of course." She paused to make sure that she remembered all of the details of what they had decided would be an "appropriate" gift of thanks for Don Juan's delivery. The church's patron saint? Ah, yes, St. Bride. "The duchess would like the window dedicated to St. Bride, who she feels must personally have been looking out for the kid."

A green flag was waving, a guard's whistle blowing, and Henrietta climbed into the carriage feeling she had done rather well. Looking back to receive the priest's thanks, she was surprised to find him gazing at her with an expression of dismay. He was saying something, but the huffing of the steam engine and the moving of the train obscured his voice. She waved at him and put her head back into the carriage to escape the billowing smoke. Whatever it was he had to say, it could hardly have been important.

"Cheer up, Juan," she said to the little boy at her side. "Only two days' travel and you'll be back in civilization."

The moment they got back to Paris, religion was taken care of by Don Juan himself, much to the surprise of both his mother and Henrietta. On the journey back from Ireland, three railway and two boat-train changes long, he remained uncharacteristically silent and morose, only answering Henrietta in monosyllables. In a later age it might have occurred to someone to take a child who had been molested and nearly killed by a madwoman straight to a psychiatrist. The best Henrietta could do was: "You've been through a bad scrape, poor little boy. Now get it out of your mind and think about what you'd like for Christmas." But Don Juan was in a continuing state of shock and, like any other eight-year-old, he was saving all his questions and doubts for his mother.

She was in the middle of preparing for a party when they arrived at the Avenue Foch from the Gare du Nord. Don Juan was uncertain about his new home. He had been looking forward to the familiar rooms and faces at the Raphaël. To be sure, his mother kissed him and hugged him when he arrived, but she had the guest list to discuss with Henrietta, and he stood, on the edge of tears, listening to her talking about all the plans for the evening, trying to swallow back the sobs that rose in his throat.

" . . . Natalie Barney is coming, so I can't ask Gertrude Stein and Toklas, they don't get on at all. Colette can't come, but Elizabeth de Gramont can, thank God. Sylvia Beach and Monnier, of course. Coco Chanel, yes. Romaine Brooks, yes—"

"What about the men?"

"No men. D'you think that's a mistake?" asked the duchess anxiously.

"You're damned right I do. It's all very well for Natalie to have her Isle of Lesbos parties on the Left Bank," said Henrietta. "But this is the Seizième. It's far too sleazy and tacky to have a brazenly sapphic party in this part of town. Besides, it's too boring not to have any men. All those dykes bitching at each other."

"Oh, Henny, what shall we do?" The duchess was distraught.

"Get on the electric telephone, dear, and start calling. See if Fitzgerald's in town. I hear Zelda's in the sanitarium—"

"I want a priest!" gulped Don Juan, his eyes starting to fill in spite of his efforts.

The two women looked at him in astonishment. He repeated his demand. The only person in recent history who had been consistently kind and concerned about him, if severe over his moral lapses, had been Father Carroll. The Irish priest had told him, before Henrietta had arrived, that at all times of crisis and doubt he should seek out a Catholic priest and ask his advice.

"The funny little Irish priest has been talking about religion to him," said Henrietta.

"Mother's terribly busy, darling," said the duchess, distraught, trying to focus on her son. "But there's a church just round the corner. St. Honoré d'Eylau, I think it's called. Daisy de Blonnet got married there. The curé was quite old, but rather sweet. A face like a peeled walnut. . . . Oh, Juan, mustn't cry. It breaks my heart to see you cry. You *never* cry, darling. What's the matter?"

The duchess was on the point of feeling really maternal toward Don Juan, not just performing her role as she had when he'd arrived. Henrietta, acting, no doubt, on an instinct over which she had little control, moved to cut short the duchess's sudden absorption with her child. It was not so much that she felt jealous of Don Juan, but she feared where any excessive interest the duchess might show in her son would lead. Perhaps an abridgment of her own relationship might follow, and this thought panicked her.

"I know what," said Henrietta brightly. "I'll take him right around there, and we'll see if we can find the curé. Then you can make those telephone calls. I promised Father Carroll we'd take him to a priest. He needs to be able to talk to a *man*. Don't you, Juan?"

Don Juan just stood there and sobbed, nodding his head.

His interview with the curé, when it was finally arranged, was rather a success. The old priest, the Abbé Lemoine, was a social cleric, certainly. His "clientele," as he called his parishioners, were, many of them, well-to-do bourgeois, and members of the nobility, old and new. The worldliness these contacts had instilled in him, listening to their confessions, counseling them in times of crisis, made him an almost ideal listener to the problems of this sophisticated and troubled little boy. As they sat together in the fustian comfort of his parlor, he encouraged the still-weeping child to tell him everything. In an act of intuitive felicity he took the child's small hands between his and waited quite patiently for Don Juan to speak. The child looked at the old man's hands and was reminded of a drawing by Dürer he'd seen in a book. The warmth and the stillness of them calmed him.

He told the abbé everything, about how he missed Ayesha, of how he had been happier in his time in Ireland than ever before. He insisted that Tabatha Truscott was not mad, but really believed in her goddess, but he simply could not understand why she had wanted to mutilate and kill him. He really believed that she liked him. Could it be that any woman might suddenly turn on him and want to kill him? Henrietta perhaps?

"Do you believe in God?" asked the abbé when Don Juan had finished.

"Yes, I do," said Don Juan. "He saved my life. He is stronger than the great White Goddess—her goddess."

"My child, God is ineffable, beyond something as trivial as sex."

"Man is made in God's image, Father Carroll said. Man is male. Is me. Like me. What about women, then?"

"Woman is simply the other side of the male coin. Part of man. Made from Adam's rib. You have read the story in the Bible?"

"Tabatha read it to me. To laugh at it. She called it church . . . something about a goose?"

The abbé lost touch at this point and looked bemused.

"Propaganda," remembered Don Juan, saying the word in English and going on. "She laughed at the whole story. Adam and Eve with no navels . . . "

"It is meant for very simple people, that story," said the priest. "Miss Tabatha was no doubt raised a Protestant. They rely too much on their interpretation of words from the Bible, those dear lost souls. It is the church that must interpret God's message as I shall for you, my poor child. I wish to give you instruction on God's love for you and what you must do to deserve it. But while that is not complicated, it will take time. Meanwhile, let me put your mind at rest. God loves you. There is only one God. But there is also, never doubt it, a Devil, the evil one. He it was who possessed the woman who tried to kill you, filling her with his evil—"

"Is it possible that the evil one is her goddess?" asked Don Juan excitedly.

The abbé paused before answering. The power of females for evil was for him part of the whole Christian tradition. Their evil was expressed in their sexuality, their power to arouse men. Christian marriage, with its proposition that procreation is God's only purpose in making His creatures sexual beings, bridled and disciplined woman's innate sensuality. Clearly the frightful happening the child had experienced (the bald facts confirmed in a note from the duchess) had made him fear that there was something essentially evil and threatening in all women. Perhaps the child's immortal soul would be safer if he continued in his belief? The abbé himself accepted as an article of faith that the "ordering of women" by men, by male institutions such as the church and state, was God's will. Why was this so unless one believed in an alliance between female nature and the evil one, the alliance symbolized by the story, in Genesis, of the fall, where the serpent and the woman conspire behind man's back?

"When there is evil in woman," he said finally, "it is part of her inheritance, expressed most often in her temptation of men to be impure. That is why we revere the Blessed Virgin—because she was entirely pure."

"Is that power to tempt men one of woman's mysteries?" asked Don Juan.

"It is one of God's mysteries that he created her thus," said the abbé.

So, for the moment, was the matter fixed in Don Juan's mind.

He took instruction from the curé and enjoyed it. He felt armed with this new dogma to face his life as a hostage in the women's camp. Not that he felt hostile to the women in his mother's household. On the contrary, he liked them all in varying degrees. But he had for the first time a sense of his own uniqueness. He did not now need to go to the men's tribe, although he looked forward to the day when he would go to stay with his father, the duke. He believed that he of himself formed a man's tribe in his mother's household, he and his mentor, the old curé; that his newfound religion was a talisman against those mysteries of the women that never ceased to attract and intrigue him.

Because, however, the Abbé Lemoine had no experience of a child as sexually experienced and motivated as Don Juan, it never occurred to him to utter anathemas against dalliance with women that he could hardly have imagined a child of eight would contemplate.

In the next three years, Henrietta fulfilled many, if not all, of her vows concerning normality for Don Juan. An English nanny appeared. Because it is the custom for English nannies to take the name of the family by which they are employed, a small crisis arose when nanny found she couldn't pronounce the duchess's name. She seemed an excellent choice for the post, being plain to the point of hideousness, so when she said, "I don't know that I could accept a post where I can't say me own name," Henrietta had to solve the crisis by offering Muloch as an alternative. Nanny Muloch she became. Don Juan liked her, warts and all.

They sent him to school at the école normale primary school in Neuilly with the children of people whom Henrietta dubbed, in her democratic American way, "just plain folks." Considering Neuilly was then a smart residential quarter on the west side of the Bois de Boulogne, his fellow students weren't that "plain," as the lines of Lasalles, Rolls-Royces, Hotchkisses, and Daimler Benzes, along with the duchess's Delage, waiting at the school gate indicated. Don Juan was at once popular with his fellow students, both boys and girls. Rather tall for his age, he easily won all his early battles with his male contemporaries. This, combined with his above-average intelligence, gave him a natural ascendancy over the others. The girls found themselves rather in awe of him. His already evident physical beauty and his disconcerting awareness of their femininity attracted them and made them feel curiously vulnerable and excited when he was around. At first, however, he was very careful with the girls. Henrietta had taken him aside and given him a warning.

"Now let's get this straight from the start, kid," she said. "Those girls are off limits to you. The first time we hear of you trying to get into their little panties, it's off to Jesuit boarding school for wayward boys. Understand? We love you, but don't say I didn't warn you." Don Juan was impressed with her seriousness.

They had moved into a six-floor town house, what in Paris, that city of apartments, is called an *hôtel particulier*. Situated on the Avenue Foch, it was large enough to give a whole floor to Don Juan and his nanny: a nursery, a bedroom and bathroom each for him and Nanny Muloch, and Nanny's kitchen and sitting room. The servants' rooms were immediately above, and the duchess's and Henrietta's suite was immediately below. Then came a huge salon occupying one complete floor, while below that, on the ground floor, was the dining room, the library, and cloakrooms for guests. In the basement were the kitchens and a sitting room cum dining room for the servants.

Most of the house was furnished in the ornate style of the Empire. It had been built for a cobbler's son who had become a marshal of France under Napoleon. Its extravagant, slightly vulgar elegance suited Henrietta's taste perfectly. The duchess's taste was reflected only in the paintings. She had become a patron of the later impressionists and the cubists. Picasso, Matisse, Fernand Léger, Gris, Braque, and others were to be found everywhere in the house, except the salon, where her collection of classical paintings had been enlarged with the help of the London dealer Duveen and on the advice of the American art savant Berenson. She discussed art with her son on an almost daily basis, and in this, if in little else, she helped influence his taste and mind.

Don Juan spent as much time in the library as he could. The books there were his best company in what became one of the loneliest periods of his life. He ate all his meals, except dinner, with Nanny Muloch in the nursery. If he had been an average little boy he would still have been rather old to be supervised by a nanny at the age of eight, but it was precisely to check his precociousness that she had been hired. Armed with the comfortable verities of her kind, she was less than stimulating company for Don Juan. He passed time by collecting Nannyisms, as he called them:

"Time waits for no man, Master Juan, hurry or you'll be late for school."

"No's a little word we never say, Master Juan. Eat up all your rice pudding, the goodness is all in the skin."

"Manners maketh man, Master Juan; never *ask* for the sugar at table. Always offer it to someone else first."

"If you don't take that look off your face, Master Juan, the wind will change and you'll look like that for the rest of your life."

The little boy said his prayers each night now, kneeling by his bed while Nanny Muloch let out his bath and filled his hot-water bottle. Ave Maria. Pater Noster. He said them both out loud, liking the sound of the Latin words.

He watched Virginie, the nursery maid, in her white starched apron, her budding breasts trussed in with safety pins, her pale Parisian face under piled-up auburn hair. Very soft hair, this, always escaping her hairpins and coiling down the nape of her rather delicate neck. Her lips were rather thin, but she had, Don Juan thought, peeping through his fingers as he prayed, the most enchanting little pink tongue, which she used as other people used hand gestures to express dismay or pleasure. She would spill some of the hot water as she poured it into what Nanny called his "hottie." Out would come the tongue, long and rather pointed. For an instant he saw a chagrined tongue vowing to be more careful. At fifteen, she was by far the youngest servant in the house, and he had at once struck up a friendship with her, listening to interminable stories she loved to tell about her large family and the special and wonderful characters and sayings of her many brothers and sisters.

When Virginie had gone upstairs and Nanny had turned the lights out and gone to her rooms on the other side of the staircase, Don Juan would get out of bed. Listening first for Nanny to settle down, he would then steal upstairs. Virginie would be waiting for him in her tiny bedroom, already in her nightgown. Not for hours would the other servants come up to bed. In whispers the two children, hardly disparate in their mental ages, would talk for hours. It was with Virginie that he first practiced what he had so often heard and half-seen Ayesha do with his mother, and it was Virginie who first gave him the pleasure he had sensed in Ayesha of knowing the power to physically delight another person.

He had learned the Ten Commandments. He realized that this was *almost* fornication, but he also knew that he lacked the power as yet to fornicate. His conscience was therefore clear.

The pleasure she gave him as she curled and twined her chameleon tongue about his still-small person became, as he learned to relax and receive it, a beginning to trusting woman once again.

Not on every night did he visit Virginie. Sometimes she kept the hours of the grown servants, of Sylvie, the ladies' maid, of Armand, the butler, of Boris and Valéry, the pederast cooks, and of her superior, old Yvette, the parlor maid, and waited on them all when they themselves were entertaining in the servants' hall. But on those evenings when he slept with her, she always awoke him at first light so that he should be in his bed when Nanny opened his door with her morning "Get the sand man out of your eyes, Master Juan!"

This arrangement, so satisfactory to boy and girl, so helpful in calming his adventurous spirit when it came to the many delicious little females at school, objects of his desire who had been declared, so forcibly, "off limits" by Henrietta, this most innocent of Don Juan's relationships, ended as a result of an indiscretion by the well-meaning Sylvie. Since the ladies' maid's own room, under the eaves of the big house, was next to that of Virginie, she had long been privy to the conspiracy. Being fond of Don Juan and knowing more of his history than the other servants, she had decided to keep her mouth shut about the matter. She was a *barvarde*, a chatterer, but not necessarily a gossip.

It was the invariable routine of the household when Don Juan was not going to school that, having breakfasted in the nursery, he would be taken to his mother's bedroom to discuss his program for the day. Nanny always left him after she had heard the duchess's response to her knock on the door.

"Come in!" the duchess, or sometimes Henrietta, would call. Nanny *never* went in. What employers did in the privacy of their own bedrooms was their business. It was neither her place nor her inclination to intrude.

"Master Juan, Duchess!" she always announced loudly before leaving him to enter by himself. Perhaps this was a precaution so that her employers could be warned that a child and not some sophisticated stranger, the shah of Persia or the president of the Republic, for instance, was about to enter.

On this occasion, both Henrietta and his mother were in bed, their breakfast trays still athwart their knees, while Sylvie was laying out the duchess's chosen wardrobe for the day.

"Ah, Juan, my poppet!" said the duchess as he went to receive her kiss and be pecked by Henrietta in turn. "You must advise me,

you with your artist's eye. Is that pink organdy too *jeune*, too young,
for your old mother?"

"Really," interrupted Henrietta, laughing. "How can you expect
the boy to answer that question? That's not a matter of artistic taste.
The color, perhaps."

"I do think it looks a little like a bridesmaid's dress, if that's what
you mean," said Don Juan. "Where are you going to wear it?"

"To Longchamps. Coco Chanel did it for me. 'You'll look like a
charming butterfly,' she said, 'among all those horsy people.'"

"But you're a moth, Mother. An elegant, beautiful moth. Surely
never a butterfly," said Don Juan.

"Oh!" said the duchess, rather taken aback.

"I think you're way over your head now, Juan," laughed
Henrietta.

"Well, it's true," said Don Juan, not at all put out, "that you
can't go mothlike to the races, either. What about that . . . oh, it
was so fabulous . . . that gaucho suit that Jacques Lanvin made for
you, with the broad-brimmed Spanish hat and the veil?"

Sylvie had dragged the costume out of the closet as Don Juan was
speaking, not being able to resist adding her opinion.

"The organdy is not with your personality, madame. This is
much better. Don Juan is quite right about the beautiful moth. He
understands you. Like his mother he is a person of the night." She
paused in her babble imperceptibly, regretting her words, and hurried
on, hoping they hadn't been noticed. "But the gaucho costume is
perfect. The scarlet sash and madame's dark hair—"

"But I've already worn it," protested the duchess.

"That was for Ascot last year. Never at Longchamps," said
Henrietta, staring at Don Juan speculatively.

"Yes, that's right. But didn't the papers here, or one of the
magazines, show photographs? Do you really like it, my treasure?"
The duchess, half persuaded, squeezed her son's hand, asking for a
final reassurance.

"Unless there's something else I haven't seen?" said Don Juan,
trying to broaden the conversation, acutely aware that Henrietta
seemed to have picked up Sylvie's unfortunate remark.

Henrietta said nothing further at the time, but for more than a
month he avoided going up to see Virginie, explaining the circumstances to her in a private moment.

Three days after they had resumed their nightly pleasure
Henrietta walked into the little maid's room and caught them in such

extreme disarray that Don Juan guessed she must have been listening at the door. So great was their surprise and shock that Virginie's tongue remained outstretched long after Don Juan had managed to cover his loins.

"You'll pack your bags at once, mademoiselle," she said. "I want you out of the house within half an hour. You are absolutely forbidden to speak of this to anyone in this household if you wish to leave here tonight with any money. Juan, put your clothes on and go to your own room. I'll see you as soon as I've finished with Virginie. Do not on any account wake Nanny!"

It was obviously a prepared speech. Virginie dissolved into a weeping, terrified child, begging Henrietta to take pity on her, saying she had been so lonely, declaring that Don Juan had insisted on the sex, that she was the victim of seduction, but that, anyway, he was too young for them to have really "done anything terrible."

Don Juan, knowing there was nothing else to do, went downstairs to await his fate.

When Henrietta finally came to his room, it was to be matter-of-fact and cold, rather than hectoring. In a way this frightened and chastened Don Juan far more than if she'd shouted at him.

"I don't suppose you know what a 'dirty old man' is?" she said, speaking to him in French but using the English phrase. "But I'm sure you can guess. Both revolting and pathetic. And that is what you will be one day. If you go on like this. What have you to say for yourself?"

"I'm sorry for Virginie. It was my fault—"

"It sure as hell was your fault," said Henrietta. "That was a shifty thing you did. You took advantage of the poor little bitch. She's gone home to her parents, with Sylvie to see she gets there. I'm waiting for you to explain, Juan."

"I, too, am lonely sometimes," said Don Juan, wondering why he felt no tears coming, no real emotion. Loneliness was all he expected. He knew that, except in his relation to the opposite sex, he probably preferred it. In a sense, Virginie had betrayed him, but he felt no real surprise.

"That's not a good enough excuse, Juan. Haven't we told you to bring back kids from school to play here? Anytime. All you have to do is ask." Henrietta was, as she herself would have said, over her head. She knew it and she realized that Don Juan knew it.

"We don't have much in common out of school," said Don Juan.

"I'm not surprised. Nine- and ten-year-olds don't usually chase little girls. As far as I seem to remember they downright despised little girls."

Don Juan said nothing.

"All right. You can go and discuss this with your mother if you like. But so far I haven't told her. I warn you that she may simply decide to send you straight to your father if and when she hears, feeling that he's the person to discipline you. But I want to spare her pain and anxiety. You'll have to go to your father next year anyway, as you know. Do you want to tell her?"

"No—I'll do whatever you say, Henrietta," said Don Juan quickly. He had always been realistic enough to know that Henrietta's was the fairest kind of discipline he could expect. She wasn't really interested in him as a person. That he understood. She concerned herself with the duchess's interest, such as it was, in her son. He knew, too, that his father had quite specifically refused to be concerned with a young child. His mother had told Don Juan as much. The preparation for confirmation of his son and heir the duke considered to be his duty. Raising children was woman's work. Don Juan knew he would not be welcome if he came too early and in disgrace.

"I think that is sensible of you, Juan," said Henrietta. She went on, "We will not mention this matter to your mother. I shall tell her that Virginie was caught with a 'follower' in her bedroom. It is no more than the truth. Sylvie dotes on you, so she'll say nothing if I explain that it would distress the duchess needlessly. You're too old for Nanny now. I suppose you always have been. You can eat with us in the dining room except when we have grown-up guests, so we'll be able to keep our eye on you. This is your last chance. One more lark like that, and it's off to the Jesuit boarding school for you till it's time to go to Spain, d'you hear?"

"Yes, Henrietta," said Don Juan.

"I must say. Now that we've got that off our chests," added Henrietta with a hint of a smile as she left his room, "that girl's tongue was quite *extraordinary.*"

Henrietta understood Juan quite well. As a mature lesbian, she had developed that uxorious tendency Gertrude Stein had desired and experienced in Alice Toklas. But as a girl her "crushes" had been numerous. The duchess had been one of the few attractive fellow students at Les Cygnes to whom she had not made some more or less physical advance. But then she had perhaps always been in love with the duchess from the beginning, and frightened, as she put it, to chance her arm. Moreover, Henrietta was one of the very few people who knew, at that time, of Don Juan's early nurturing as part of the hothouse relationship of the duchess and Ayesha. Nor was it in Henrietta's nature to be morally censorious. She always attributed her long exile from her native Midwest to a very low threshold of toleration for hypocrisy. When she warned Don Juan that he would one day become a dirty old man, she really meant that he seemed undiscriminating. Henrietta was certainly a snob and could simply never have found a servant, however prodigious her tongue, attractive.

Of the eighteen months that remained to him of his life with his mother, Don Juan contrived to make the most. He prevailed on Henrietta to keep Nanny on but to give her a smaller role in his life. He liked the old woman, and if his remaining chaste helped to keep her, it was worth the effort. Perhaps the greatest single influence in his temporary reformation was his maternal grandfather, the Catalonian industrialist from Barcelona.

The old gentleman, tall and imposing in his appearance, always wore pince-nez and spats and tweaked Don Juan's cheek with a plump, ringed hand that smelled of snuff. Both the duchess and Henrietta adored him, and his visits were the occasions of elaborate preparations. Dinner parties were given for him with guests never otherwise seen in the house on the Avenue Foch. Politicians and their fixers, soldiers and businessmen and their lady wives. Marshal Pétain, the hero of Verdun, currently minister of war, was the guest of honor at a dinner the duchess gave for her father, which took place soon after the debacle in Virginie's bedroom. The little boy was allowed to meet the guests in the salon before they went down to the dining room. The duchess had taught him to bow to the ladies, taking their hands and just brushing them with his lips. An abbreviated bow, a mere nod of the head, was appropriate when being introduced to the gentlemen. He was to answer any question asked of him with a well-thought-out, gracefully phrased reply ("Try and make it memorable, but still respectful"), but not to chatter, remembering that people only asked children questions out of politeness to their parents, never out of any real interest.

It was at dinner that Don Juan's grandfather, who spoke French well but with a sibilant Spanish inflection, was introduced to the Abbé Lemoine. Don Juan watched them curiously from a distance, knowing that he was a likely subject of conversation, but they were interrupted by the arrival of the Marshal of France. When it came his turn to be introduced to the nation's hero, Don Juan was understandably nervous.

"And do you plan to be a soldier?" Pétain asked the little boy.

"No, *mon maréchal*, I hope to be a priest."

"His dear father had the same wish," said the duchess. "But he had to do his duty."

"Quite so, my boy. Your duty must be sacred to you," said the marshal, with which he moved on.

Henrietta passed Don Juan a moment or so later. Smiling, she gave his ear a little pinch.

"Liar!" she said.

"Well, I could hardly have said I wanted to be a painter. Not in the middle of this group!" said Don Juan, slightly aggrieved.

His grandfather came and visited him next morning while at breakfast with Nanny.

"I would like to speak alone with my grandson," he said politely to the old woman in French.

"Nanny doesn't speak a word of anything but English, on principle," said Don Juan, and so they all sat down around the table and the old man and the boy conversed in Spanish.

"I have to go back to Barcelona today. We have a strike on our hands there in one of our factories. Those damned anarchists! You made a good answer to the marshal last night, Juan, even if it was a lie," said his grandfather.

"I'm rather ashamed of that. I don't like telling lies. But what does one say? Tinker, tailor, soldier, priest?"

His grandfather gazed at Don Juan with keen, calculating interest. Obviously this boy had inherited a disproportionate supply of his own excellent genes. What a favor he had done the duke to offer him a little rich new blood to mix in with his watery blue stuff. The lad had brains and looks. A spell in the diplomatic world would be a perfect prelude to his taking over the control—a grandee of Spain could not concern himself with actual management—of the great industrial complex that he had decided to bequeath him. He asked the boy in great detail about his studies and what was planned for him.

"It is I who will take you to your father when the time comes," he said at last. "The abbé tells me that he believes you will be a very worldly man. That is not a betrayal of your confidences. He has made an assessment of your character. Is he wrong?

"No," said Don Juan simply.

"I suspect you have inherited much from me, Juan. You are the son I have never had in wedlock. I am a man of strong passions. But it is important for people like us to channel all this energy. Into a cause, perhaps, or into some great enterprise, as I have done. I tell you this because your father is a good man but a dry man. He has very little juice. You are his heir, of course, but don't forget you are also my heir."

"Thank you, Grandfather," said Don Juan, impressed, wondering briefly about his out-of-wedlock uncles.

"Henrietta has also told me, in the strictest confidence, naturally, about your little affair with the maid. I don't blame you. It shows you have spirit. But while you are living in your mother's household"—the old man's voice hardened—"I strictly forbid any more of these adventures. When you are out of school you can have all the women you want. A gentleman must always respect his wife, that's my rule. Otherwise he must please himself, that's obvious. But one more transgression while you are still here and you will have to deal with me."

"I understand, Grandfather," said Don Juan, reflecting that his grandfather was likely to provide his best passport into the adult, masculine world.

Don Juan's resolution to be good till he left his mother's house had already been made before his grandfather had added his own strong voice to that of the Abbé Lemoine and Henrietta. That Nanny should also, in the end, prove an influence was unexpected. She was to produce a book that profoundly interested him in a rather surprising way.

Don Juan's reading in the library had always been eclectic. Works by Humboldt and Darwin were followed by a book on the Bauhaus and a biography of Diaghilev. The short stories of Turgenev and P. G. Wodehouse alternately made him cry and laugh, while Maeterlinck's life of the bee enthralled him. He found a collection, belonging to Henrietta, of Karl Marx's articles for the New York Tribune and thought how different they made nineteenth-century history seem after what he'd learned at school. Nanny, who came to fetch him up to supper one night when a Sapphic ball in the salon precluded his dining with the grown-ups, remarked, "You'll get funny ideas reading all those books, Master Juan." "Funny" meant "odd," meant "bad," in her parlance.

"What d'you mean, Nanny? You told me you always read when you go to bed. 'Can't get to sleep without it,' you said."

"That's always the same book, dear. That is *the* book." They had arrived in the nursery, where the new nursery maid, Solange, was laying out their meal.

"How can you bear to read the same book over and over?" he asked, amazed, and trying not to look at Solange.

"Because it is a book with all the *answers* that I need in it," said Nanny, speaking a little stiltedly, as if quoting from an evangelical tract; which, perhaps, she was.

Don Juan had given over all his attention to looking at Solange. She had been engaged only a few days before by Henrietta, who had been anxious to employ someone as little like Virginie as possible. Solange was extremely fat and had the faintest squint in her blue eyes behind thick goggle glasses. Her mouth was small, and she seemed to keep her tongue in its proper place.

Don Juan was almost sure that no man could ever have touched Solange. He wondered how she would be with the first person who undressed her, unleashing that huge bosom into his lap. Faintly he could make out where the nipples sat beneath her serge dress, under her apron. They must be the size and shape of nectarines to show through all that material.

"It's the most beautiful book in the English language," Nanny was saying.

Don Juan forced himself to concentrate on Nanny, but failed. Solange was in his bedroom; he could see her through the door, bending over his bed as she turned the covers down for the night. He imagined bare those thick haunches and wide buttocks and nestling in between them that soft, tight fold.

This is absurd, he thought at once. I *must* ignore her. Nanny was talking of a book. The Bible, obviously, from what she had said. How could the language of the Bible be so extraordinary in English? The monkish dog Latin of the Abbé Lemoine's to-be-learned-by-heart texts was rather ordinary and frankly boring. The catechism in French was pedantic and monotonous. The Bible had, of course, been ignored by the abbé. Don Juan forced himself to look at Nanny, and found himself intrigued by her enthusiasm.

"Can I look at it after supper? It is the Bible, isn't it?" he said.

"You are a clever cat, aren't you? Yes, it's the New Testament. I don't care for the Old. It's somehow sort of *foreign.*"

"I thought God was English," said Don Juan teasingly.

"You mustn't joke about it, Master Juan. But yes, in the New Testament He does seem sort of English. It's all about 'fair play,' you see."

She showed him some of her favorite passages after dinner. "Consider the lilies of the field. They toil not, neither do they spin," he read, and said to her, smiling, "That is the most beautiful invitation to stop working that I can imagine. May I read the book?"

He read the New Testament in the Authorized Version, utterly absorbed, for two days. It was the time of the New Year holiday, and he had little else to do. Nanny was so delighted at his interest that she had gone off to the English-language bookshop, called Shakespeare and Company, on the Rue de L'Odéon, to buy him his own copy. To his mother and Henrietta, when he saw them at his morning audience, he made excited announcements of what he'd discovered in the book.

"It's all about revolution," he said. "No wonder the Abbé Lemoine and all our priests never let anybody read it."

"Nonsense, Juan. Of course it isn't. You've been reading that awful Marx book of Henrietta's," said the duchess.

"It's easier for a camel to go through the eye of a needle than for a rich man to enter the Kindom of Heaven. Aren't we rich? Doesn't that worry you?" Again, he was half teasing.

"That's not aimed at us, dear," said the duchess. "He was talking about all those moneylenders in the temple. Jews, of course."

"They're all Jews, Mother," said Don Juan, laughing.

"Not Jesus. Never say that. That's a terrible slander!" Centuries of Spanish Catholic dogma and anti-Semitism reinforced the duchess's determination on this point.

"He does tell people to give away all their possessions and follow Him," said Don Juan. "The English and American Protestants—have they done that, Henrietta?"

"You're misinterpreting it, Juan," said Henrietta from behind her *Herald Tribune*. "There are tens of millions of Americans raised on that book, and they ought to know. No one is about to give anything away, unless it's 'something' for charity. 'Something' is a hell of a long way from 'everything,' I can tell you. Now don't be childish. It's not like you."

Don Juan sensed an edge of genuine annoyance in Henrietta's voice, and realized that only the truth could so irritate her.

Next morning he brought the book with him. "I promise not to go on being boring about this book," he said. "But if this isn't a call to revolution, what is?"

He read them the Magnificat, the Virgin Mary's great song of triumphant motherhood with its prophecy for mankind. When he had finished he closed the book and looked at their faces, sleek and well fed against the damask pillows. They seemed faintly embarrassed, as if he had let off wind.

"She's saying that she *rejoiced* that the mighty had been put down from their seats and the poor exalted. That the hungry had been filled with good things while the rich had been sent empty away," he repeated.

"Doesn't it say somewhere 'Give to Caesar the things that are Caesar's'?" asked the duchess, puzzled and bored by her son's new interest.

"Yes, it does, Mother," said Juan. "But I don't know what Caesar has got to do with it."

"Sounds as if you've decided to go into the church after all," said Henrietta, amused in spite of herself.

"It's very possible," said Don Juan wickedly. "I'm off to ask Father Lemoine a few questions he's been avoiding!"

"That girl Solange has turned out rather well," said Henrietta, apropos of nothing in particular, after Don Juan had left the room.

The night before he left for Spain with his grandfather, Don Juan climbed the stairs to Solange's bedroom.

He had controlled his desire to be with her by developing his religious dialectic with the Abbé Lemoine and his unwilling mother. Solange he had only spoken to in terms of admiration. Seeing her taking linen from the cupboard, he would say, "Your figure is extraordinary. I would love to hug you." Solange always reddened when he said such things, answering nothing but "Monsieur Juan!" He was sure, however, that she liked what he said, because he found her watching him when she thought she was unobserved. If their eyes met, she blushed and turned away.

Poor Solange. It was true, Don Juan's guess that she had never been touched by a man. Acutely aware of her squint, she had eaten nervously and too much all her life. She thought him a beautiful boy and wished he were a man. He aroused a maternal interest and attraction in her that was as sensual in its way as if he could really have been her lover. She knew the history of Virginie and guessed that she had been chosen because Henrietta thought her too plain for Don Juan.

On the night she first heard him come into her room, it was already very late, and she had been asleep for hours. The other servants and, indeed, the whole household were already in bed and asleep. But she knew, at once, that it was he, standing barefoot in the dark room, listening to her breathing.

"Monsieur Juan?" she whispered.

"Yes," said Don Juan, not moving.

"What do you want?"

"To be with you tonight," said Don Juan simply.

There was a long silence from the bed.

"Come," she said. "Just for a cuddle and a squeeze. Then you must go back to bed."

He slipped in beside her and felt the large warm mass of her enclosed in a flannel nightgown. She calmed his searching hands with her strong peasant arms, pinning him gently beside her. Then, undoing the neck of her nightgown, she gave him one huge breast with its tangerine-sized nipple to suck. To his surprise and slight shock, it was ringed by sparse but wiry hairs. She smelled dank with stale sweat. "Now you must go back to bed, little boy," she said after a few minutes, kissing him with garlicky breath.

Don Juan lay in her arms for a moment, feeling her body stirring with those nervous movements he knew to be desire. There will be other bodies like this when I am a man, he thought. That will smell of the kitchen, of hard work, of too little soap, but still the smell and feel of woman is irresistible. She was pushing him gently from the bed. He kissed her bravely on the mouth, breathing in the acrid odor and liking it because he tasted her lips too. Then, thanking her courteously, he left.

5
Shades of the Prison House

The surface of our country constantly decays, but never the depths.

—Canovas on Spain

After the farewells at the Avenue Foch, he drove with his grandfather to the airport at Le Bourget outside Paris. Don Juan had seen pictures at the cinema of Lindbergh landing there at night after his famous flight from America; tens of thousands of people, swept by searchlights, as they engulfed the tiny aluminum airplane. Flying was still, in 1932, both romantic and hazardous, and Don Juan was excited at the prospect.

The two-engined Douglas in which they flew contained fifteen seats and was capable of a speed of two hundred miles an hour flying at an altitude of eight thousand feet. Don Juan learned of these statistics from a brochure tucked into the "sick" bag he had been given by the steward. His grandfather sucked alternately on a little bottle of oxygen and a flask of brandy. En route he lectured Don Juan on the anarchy that had threatened Spain since the end of the monarchy and the establishment of the Republic, a year before.

"Ultimately," he said, "we will have to depend on the army. But the army is still unprepared."

"Who will prepare them?" asked Don Juan.

"*We* will help arm them at least," said his grandfather.

"Arm them?" Don Juan realized he had no idea *what* his grandfather presided over.

"I see your mother has told you nothing about the products that keep her in some luxury. She is right. Women should know nothing of these things. It doesn't concern them. We produce, *inter alia*, the finest rifles, mortars, machine guns, grenades, and mines. Of course, that is just a small part of our activity. We make steel in Toledo. We mine copper and lead and zinc near Rio Tinto. In Barcelona we help build ships and have our factories for making arms and perambulators, milk churns and surgical instruments. I do not share the feelings of Nobel, who wishes to apologize for being an arms manufacturer. I contribute to peace and to war, like everyone else."

They stayed at the Ritz in Barcelona, where Don Juan's grandfather kept a permanent suite. It was the first time that he had been in Spain (since babyhood), and one of his grandfather's secretaries took him to see the sights, Gaudí's Church of the Sagrada Familia, the bull ring, and the smart shops. Spanish, a language that he had spoken, since Ayesha's death, principally with his mother, was all around him, together with the unfamiliar Catalan dialect. It felt strange, as if he had heard these voices before, knowing that not to be the case.

Next day his grandfather took him to the factory where arms and perambulators were made.

"Those men are mostly Andalusians. Redder than hell, most of them," said the old man, conducting the boy past the rows of identical machines, each, it seemed to Don Juan, attended by an identical man.

"People from your province, Juan, one of the poorest in Spain. Come to make a good wage here in the city. They look docile enough here. But believe me, every one of them belongs to the Anarchist Union, CNT, and every one is capable of being a bomb-carrying revolutionary. Remember that. It will take the army to keep them in their place."

The workers looked straight into the faces of their employer and his grandson. There was pride, if not active defiance, in their eyes.

All of them seemed to have their heads covered, with cloth caps. A few, Basques perhaps, wore berets.

Don Juan had for years thought of himself as French; in that he forgot that he was born Spanish for he felt entirely Parisian. To be faced now, suddenly, with his Spanishness and to be marching beside his dapper, quicksilver grandfather among people who were supposed to be, in an even more intimate sense, *his people*—this was hard to digest. He looked at the workers under their cloth caps with their often hollow cheeks and bad teeth, their dark complexions and day-old beards, as people gaze at distant cousins unexpectedly encountered, searching for some hint of common identity.

"A villainous-looking lot, wouldn't you say?" said his grandfather as they emerged.

"But they're my people, you said." Don Juan was confused.

"A lot of them *belong* to you is what I meant. Or would have in feudal times," said his grandfather. "There must be three thousand people like that who are workers on your father's lands. A few are tenant farmers; the rest do piecework for your father, which means that much of the time they're unemployed. Many come here to work in the factories. They're not popular with the Catalans—too dark-skinned, too Moorish. Scratch any one of them and you'll find an anarchist. But their labor is the cheapest we can get, and even with the unions and the strikes, it's worth having them."

After lunch they flew from Barcelona to a military airfield near Seville in the old man's private plane, a twin-engine Fokker with five seats. The plane flew at around four thousand feet, and Don Juan was allowed to sit up by the pilot, where he could observe the physical geography of his native country. It was a clear June day, with only some slight cirrus cloud far above them. At first the landscape was relatively green. Then the prevailing color of ocher in the land below proclaimed its aridity for hundreds of miles as they flew over the Ebro River and southwest toward La Mancha.

"That is where Don Quixote is said to have come from," shouted his grandfather over the roar of the engines. "He thought it was virtuous to live on acorns. You can see why that may have been necessary. In Spain we make a virtue of our poverty because we have no choice."

Don Juan nodded and thought about his grandfather. What was it about this old man who did him nothing but kindness, who spoke to him without any condescension as if he were almost an adult? He wanted to like him, and yet he knew that he was somehow repelled by him. Watching the shadow of the plane undulating over the rocky terrain below, he tried to analyze this feeling. Was it perhaps some condescension on *his*, Juan's, part that made this so? Had he been raised as too rarefied a Parisian to accept the provincial aggressiveness of his industrialist grandfather? The old man seemed to be saying: "You are part of me. These are *our things* of which I speak." Don Juan wasn't at all sure that the teaching of Nanny's book wasn't too fresh in his mind to accept being a capitalist, a rich man-to-be. But he also sensed the absurdness of these feelings. He had always known that he was the heir to a great name and, judging by his mother's mode of life, considerable wealth besides. One did not, of course, ask to be born into great good fortune, but it seemed churlish to despise aspects of it if you found you had experienced pleasure accepting the whole.

They were met at the military airport by a number of officers who were friends of his grandfather's. An impromptu conference took place while Don Juan was shown around the warplanes in the hangars.

The drive to the duke's castle at Guadal took over three hours. Traveling in the duke's commodious Daimler, which had been sent to meet them, they were somewhat insulated from the terrible condition of the road. All the way his grandfather gave Don Juan a running commentary on the ills of Andalusia.

"You have heard of the lemming? A volelike creature that at irregular intervals multiplies and heads in a mad rush to the sea, where vast numbers pointlessly drown themselves. It is like that with these people. They are stirred up by foreigners, anarchists from Italy, communists from Russia, and so on, to revolt against the natural, established order of things, the landowners like your father and the priests. They burn a few churches and kill some of the shopkeepers to whom they owe money. They set up some pathetic, naive new order of their own to run the villages themselves. The government sends troops. The ringleaders are shot and once again, for a few years, there is quiet."

Don Juan looked out of the car window at the landscape outside, at the occasional groves of cork trees half stripped of their spongy bark by the harvesters, at the rambling plantations of olive trees, their shimmery, silvered leaves tokens of life in the harsh, stone-strewn hills. From time to time they passed a village, its buildings clustered together like molluscs on a rock, or a small town where the doorways of the houses looked like the dark mouths of barren caves in the low evening sunshine. It seemed to him that this journey was like revisiting the eighteenth century, as he'd seen it in paintings. They passed no other cars, although they did see one ramshackle bus, but for the main part the peasants walked or rode donkeys, and carts were pulled by mules and sometimes oxen. The men had the same faces as the workers he'd seen in his grandfather's factory; the women seemed to be all swathed in dank shapeless black, as if in mourning for their very lives. Again he saw dignity in these faces, even pride, but no joy.

"What starts a revolt here? Is it only the foreigners?" Don Juan asked his grandfather.

"Not always. It can come from a drought. From some specially imposed tax. A raising of rents. Or because the price of things necessary to them, like candles or cloth or salted fish from the coast, suddenly rises. Then their everyday misery that you can see with your own eyes becomes an *intolerable* misery." The old man gave his explanation without a hint of emotion in his voice, as if he were describing some entirely natural phenomenon like the ocean tides.

"Don't you pity them?" asked Don Juan curiously.

"Since they do not pity themselves, why should I pity them? They have put hate in the place of self-pity. You think perhaps that they desire what a French peasant might want—a bicycle, a radio, new furniture, more clothes? That is not what these anarchists want. They would like a world with no landlords, no rich, no bourgeois, no priests, no God, no police, no soldiers, no money, no marriage, no prostitutes, no alcohol, no tobacco, no coffee—yes, you may laugh, even coffee is a vice to them—and of course no government."

"What do they believe will happen then?" asked Don Juan, amazed.

"Then barren hills will become green. As in the Garden of Eden, there will be effortless plenty when the forces of evil—that's us—have been wiped off the face of the earth." The old man laughed aloud at the fantastical-sounding quality of what he had just said.

"It sounds very beautiful—for them!" remarked Don Juan, smiling, wondering if his grandfather was teasing him.

"I heard one of their rabble-rousers outside our factory in Barcelona shout, 'We look for a new world. It must come from the moral resurrection of our class, for we, *compañeros*, have never been contaminated by greed or by luxury!'"

"It sounds like a religion," said Don Juan.

"You are a bright boy," said his grandfather. "It is a religion, and we cannot afford any pity for these people. They are fanatics who want to destroy our whole civilization."

Don Juan was impressed by his grandfather's words, in spite of his feeling of discomfort at the evident hate the old man felt for the

Andalusian peasants who, he could not forget, were *his*, Juan's, *people*.

"It is strange that they should not want to simply share in what we have," he said, and suddenly dreaded the responsibility of one day being a great landlord in this hostile country.

The sun was setting behind them when the old man first pointed out the castle in the distance. It seemed to perch like a petrified dragon with a thousand scaly castellations on a promontory over the Guadalquivir. The tiled roofs of a small town formed a terra-cotta bracelet around it, fastening it to the river.

As they drove through the town in the dusky blue light, there was, to Don Juan, a reassuring number of relaxed, cheerful people abroad, some of them in uniform. Nor, to his relief, were all the women dressed in black. Outside one of the buildings he even saw some girls in brightly colored shawls. He thought them dramatically beautiful with their glossy black hair, like his mother's, and their heavily made-up eyes.

"This is the garrison town for the Guardia Civil in the area. Hence, I suppose, the bordello," said his grandfather.

So those few girls in colorful shawls were whores, thought Don Juan, and was fascinated.

The castle was approached up a winding cobbled road that led directly to the Moorish keep. The drawbridge still crossed a twenty-foot-wide chasm below which was a moat fed from the river. The gates on the other side were wide open to receive the Daimler, and, to Don Juan's amazement, what seemed like a small parade was drawn up in the courtyard beyond.

In a panic, Don Juan said to his grandfather, "Which is my father? I don't recognize anyone there from the photographs!"

"Your father never leaves his apartments, Juan. I told you he is not a well man. These are the town notables, and the senior servants, who naturally want to greet us," said his grandfather, putting on his pince-nez and brushing some snuff from his lapels.

Don Juan was overcome with the fact that these people were all smiling and clapping. As the Daimler came to a halt a photographer aimed his elaborate black box at the car door, waiting for them to emerge. They were handed out of the car by a graying man in a black coat and striped trousers who looked to Don Juan distinguished enough to be the president of the Republic.

"This is Garcia. The majordomo," said his grandfather, introducing Don Juan. "Excellency!" intoned Garcia, looking Don Juan straight in the eye, as a master sergeant regards his young lieutenant.

Garcia then took over the chore of making the introductions. His grandfather pushed Don Juan ahead of him with a "Go on, boy. It's you they want to meet. You're heir to all this. I'm just the duchess's father."

Garcia announced the name of each person as they went along the receiving line as if he were conducting a roll call of King Arthur's knights instead of introducing a rather threadbare set of provincial notables and senior servants.

"Father Anselmo Gonzalez, rector of the Church of the Virgin Mary of Andalusia! Pablo Iglesias y Moro, mayor of Guadal! Colonel Francisco Mesa y Morato, commander of the Guardia Civil! . . ."

To these people Don Juan was a revelation as he walked politely down the line, looking them gravely in the face as if he found each person intrinsically interesting, which indeed he did. They knew him to be between ten and eleven years old, yet he was as tall as, or taller than, any local lad of fourteen. His dark-brown, not black, curly hair had recently been cut short; his greenish eyes, under their sooty brows, were very steady in their gaze. Quite unconsciously, it seemed, he was possessed of considerable presence. A woman certainly would have noticed his mouth, but there were no women to welcome him.

Among the senior servants, the following persons particularly held Don Juan's attention as people with whom he would spend much time:

"Pío Mella, groom to Don Juan!"

"Rafael Farga, valet to Don Juan!"

"Fermín Azorín, steward to Don Juan!"

Don Juan looked at these three young men, none of them much more than two inches taller than he, and wondered how he could endure so much masculine society after the surfeit of women that seemed natural to him. He hoped there were a few females inside the house, but he was to be disappointed. There were none.

Garcia asked him if he wished to speak to the assembly before going into the castle. Don Juan's grandfather tried to restrain the majordomo from making this request, believing that the boy would be understandably overwhelmed by the ordeal of so unexpected a public appearance. But he need not have been concerned.

"Thank you for greeting me so kindly," said Don Juan. "I am looking forward to getting to know you all much better. I'm sure you'll forgive me now because I'm most impatient to see my father."

There was immediate clapping, and both Don Juan and his grandfather had the pleasure of knowing that he had made an excellent impression.

The castle proper—that is to say, the thirteenth-century Moorish palace within the castellated walls of an even earlier Moorish fort—had been entirely renovated and largely reconstructed in the reign of Queen Isabel. Its interior was like a large Victorian mansion.

Garcia assigned two liveried footmen to show Don Juan and his grandfather to their separate apartments. Valets and stewards accompanied them. Before bowing them on their way, Garcia announced, as if informing plenipotentiaries of a forthcoming audience, "The duke looks forward to receiving you in half an hour, as soon as you have refreshed yourselves from your journey, excellencies."

Don Juan found his apartments huge and airy, with a view over the river. The castle seemed to have remarkably modern appointments, considering its great age. There were big electric fans suspended from the ceiling which turned with an endless tucketa-tucketa noise.

The castle had been built before the invention of passages, so that to reach his bedroom, Don Juan had to pass from the great oak doors that marked the entrance to his domain through an anteroom, a dining room, another anteroom, a living room furnished as a study, full of books, and another anteroom, which gave off finally to his bedroom, which formed the corner of the east tower of the castle. Next door to this was a commodious bathroom large enough to contain a squash court. He had paused for an excited moment in the library. There were books in English and French as well as Spanish there. Some of his very favorite books were laid out on a writing table to greet him.

"Would your excellency like to take a bath?" asked his valet, who, together with the steward, had accompanied him on the tour of his apartment.

"No, thank you, Rafael," said Don Juan, smiling at being treated in this grand way. "I think I'll just have a pee and wash my hands."

"Farga, excellency. You must call us all by our family names. It is the custom."

"Would you like something to eat and drink, excellency?" asked the steward. "Dinner with your father will be at half past ten."

"Do you have any rice pudding?" asked Don Juan, wondering if the hated dish Nanny had given him so often existed in Spain. But both of the men looked totally blank.

"We have rice, perhaps . . ." began Azorín.

"Oh, no, I'm delighted you haven't got it. I had it for supper almost every evening at Mother's house. How about some fizzy lemonade and some bread and butter with strawberry jam?"

"Yes, excellency. At once," said Azorín, and hurried off to fetch Don Juan's favorite food.

Half an hour later Garcia himself was leading Don Juan and his grandfather up a winding stair to what had been the principal refectory of the castle in Moorish times and was now the duke's living room, known in the household as the Blue Room for the cool blue Moorish tiles that covered the walls and even the ceiling.

The five minutes before entering his father's room was one of the single most frightening stretches of time in Don Juan's life. Childlike, he had shut from his mind the reality of going to greet this totally strange human being to whom his relationship was supposed to be so intimate and close. Only when he heard Garcia's distant tread coming through the anterooms of his apartment to summon him to his father did it suddenly take on a fearful, an urgent, reality. Unaccountably, his bladder had urged him back to the bathroom.

Now the doors to his father's room were before him. Garcia went ahead, standing in the open doorway and announcing them, bowing as they passed him. And there he was, sitting in a chair by a log fire. A log fire in June? thought Don Juan, forcing himself to concentrate on the man in the chair.

The duke was a skeletal figure in a dressing gown, his slippered feet propped on a footstool. Wispy untrimmed white hair framed a face as pinched with pain as any Don Juan had ever seen. He held up two clawlike hands swathed with bandages at the wrists to welcome his son, and spoke with a voice that was surprisingly strong, coming from so ravaged a body.

"Dear God. You are almost a young man. I have missed the child!" said the duke, urging his son to approach him. "Pepe," he went on, addressing his comparatively youthful father-in-law, "you should have told me how fast he was growing. I hold you responsible," he added with a thin laugh.

Don Juan walked to his father and for once in his life found no words. From this ruined man's loins I came, he thought, how incredible it is. But this man has been incredibly ill, a prisoner of war, a sufferer for our country. I must put revulsion out of my mind on that score alone. He has still-black hairs growing from his nose and ears. How extraordinary. But he is my father, and I must greet him properly. Kiss him, I suppose.

"May I kiss you, Father?" asked Don Juan politely, taking one of the old man's outstretched hands.

Perhaps there is some emotion in the dry old stick after all, thought Don Juan's grandfather as he watched the child's marvelously expressive mouth kiss the raddled cheek of the duke. For he saw a glistening in the old courtier's eyes at the touch of those warm lips.

"Sit, sit!" said the duke. "Sit, Pepe, my dear fellow, over there in that comfortable chair. You sit here by me, Juan. What will you take? I never drink, so I have no idea what people 'take' these days."

"A little champagne!" said Don Juan's grandfather.

"Some grenadine, please," said Don Juan, finding his voice. "With some ice, if that's not too much trouble."

"Some hot water for me!" said the duke to the waiting Garcia.

While Garcia was ordering their refreshments the duke asked them not a thing about the outside world, but spoke only of health, principally his. It had clearly become an obsession.

". . . one doesn't want, naturally, to dwell on one's privations in El Krim's prison, but to live in shackles for years . . . My wrists are covered with a black tar—extraordinary stuff—it insulates one's still-raw flesh from the bandage, you know. It'll never get better, they tell me, but the tar mitigates the pain a little. It is the same with my ankles, but there the problem is circulatory, you know. They are still as swollen as when the steel bit into my flesh. Extraordinary, isn't it? The doctors fear clotting in the blood, of course, so I never touch salt. Just the opposite problem for poor Alfonso's children. All those bleeders he had. Got it from Queen Victoria. Through the female line. Do you know what they call that disease, Juan?"

"Hemophilia, Father. Didn't the czarevitch have it?"

"Good boy. The czar got it from his mother, Queen Victoria's daughter. There is not much you can do with a bleeder except blood transfusions . . ."

Don Juan and his grandfather left the duke's room after half an hour of clinical monologue in order to go and dress for dinner. The old industrialist invited his grandson to come and talk to him while he changed, and took the precaution of dismissing the hovering valet before he spoke of what was on his mind.

"You may have wondered," he said, referring to the duke, "why neither your mother nor I have spoken to you of him very much."

"Does he ever talk of other things?" asked Don Juan. "He couldn't always have *sounded* like that."

"Certainly not. The man who married my daughter was one of the most urbane and influential men around King Alfonso. His imprisonment has destroyed him. Out of respect for the man I knew, who is also your father, I must tell you that the old man you met is only the mangled body of your father that somehow survived El

Krim's prison. His mind is, of course, hopelessly impaired. But that is not to call him mad. We didn't wish to tell you this. You had to come to this conclusion yourself."

"He never once asked me anything about *me*," said Don Juan, bemused. "And yet someone must have taken the trouble to order books that would please me for my study. How did he know?"

"He doesn't and he didn't. Look, Juan, I wish to keep secret what I have to tell you. For a long time we negotiated with El Krim for your father's life, not just for his release. To raise the huge sums needed, money had to be borrowed against the security of your father's lands. Since your father had only recently redeemed his lands from crippling debt with the money from your mother's dowry, I decided to handle the negotiation with El Krim myself. We got the duke freed at immense cost. I settled an income for life on your father, but I, in fact, own this castle and all its lands now, in trust for your mother and for you."

"Does my father know this?" asked Don Juan.

"He understands that there was what he now calls 'lawyer business' that took care of the debts and that leaves him in peace. He doesn't want to know anything else."

"Who else knows?" asked Don Juan.

"Your mother, of course. Otherwise only the lawyer, Mendoza, who is my agent here. Mendoza hires the servants and pays them. The caciques * here—they help run the political side of things—he pays them on our behalf. But it would cause trouble among the 'anarchists,' which is many of our tenants, if they knew all this belonged to me, the Catalonian industrialist, and not to the poor wounded duke."

"So Mendoza got my books," said Don Juan, beginning to see the whole pattern of things.

"Your mother asked me to arrange it. Mendoza was my agent." His grandfather smiled.

"Did he arrange that there should be *no women* either?" Don Juan asked his grandfather reproachfully.

"No, Juan, your father no longer likes women around," said the old man.

Don Juan almost laughed aloud. In Paris Henrietta had been his surrogate father. Here, Mendoza, whom he had yet to meet, was to stand in for his mother.

* Political agents of the government.

They met at dinner, an elaborate meal during which footmen stood behind each chair and Garcia magnificently presided.

Mendoza had been invited at the request of Don Juan's grandfather. He seemed to Don Juan both obsequious and rather sly. He treated the duke with elaborate ceremony and then paid real attention only to what Don Juan and his grandfather had to say. However, the boy himself found it hard to focus on the duke's conversation and eat a meal at the same time. The duke had been carried into the dining room by a hefty footman, who deposited him and arranged him at the head of the table. He talked ceaselessly about catheters and enemas, bedsores and the vicissitudes of his circulatory system. He directed most of this at Don Juan, who was seated on his right, without much expectation of an answer. Perhaps ill-advisedly, Don Juan made an attempt to respond in kind.

"I suppose, Father," he said brightly, "that the hot water you drink helps your digestion. Being forced to sit so much must make the digestive system rather . . ." Don Juan was wondering whether "lazy" or "sluggish" would be the better word when his father interrupted him.

"It is unlikely," said the duke, pouncing on the subject, "that you will ever have a better opportunity than I to study the human digestive system. Pepe, Mendoza, this will interest you . . ." He summoned the attention of the others, who had been discussing the rising cost of repairs in relation to rents. "Did you know that a man can be opened up and have his intestines, yards and yards of them there appear to be, taken from his body and fried on a brazier and still be alive?"

"It was the 'drawing' part of the ancient punishment of being hanged, *drawn*, and quartered, was it not, Duke?" said Mendoza, toying with his bull's-tail soup.

"Quite so," said the duke with a slight frown. He was long unused to conversation as such. "El Krim's people knew more about what you could do to an eviscerated live human being than if they'd been trained surgeons. One wonders if a training in the thresholds of pain would be useful in clinical work . . ."

Don Juan tried to shut out his father's voice and concentrate on the food. He had never thought that he would long for one of Nanny's high teas, with its wholesome starch, but the bull's-tail soup and what followed seemed a dismal augury of what was in store for him in Spanish cooking.

The duke was carried out after the fruit course. Don Juan went to kiss his father on his way to the door, but was relieved when the old man waved him away.

"I don't believe in too much kissing, Juan. We all have germs. Can't help it. But one must try not to share them around. I enjoyed our chat. You do your mother great credit. You look quite extraordinarily robust for a boy of your age. I, myself, was always delicate. My chest, you know . . ."

"Aren't you in a draft there, Jesus?" asked Don Juan's grandfather.

"Yes, perhaps I am. Get on with it!" squeaked the duke to his bearer, and they were gone.

The meal had been cleared, and the two adults sat drinking brandy while Don Juan, fighting off sleep, sipped his favorite "fizzy lemonade."

"Mr. Mendoza would like to outline the plan we have made for you, Juan," his grandfather was saying, sniffing at his snuff. "When I say 'we' I mean your mother and I. It is Mr. Mendoza who will see to everything. He is acting as our 'executive' in these matters."

"Thank you, Grandfather," Don Juan said, and looked at Mendoza curiously. On short acquaintance, he infinitely preferred Henrietta. But he had joined his own tribe now, and for better or worse, he must learn to like it.

"First let me say, Don Juan, what a privilege it will be to serve you. You are clearly a boy of great gifts. We are truly fortunate, those of use who can play a humble part in preparing you for your inheritance," said Mendoza.

So this is a courtier, thought Don Juan. He smiled his encouragement to the lawyer opposite, catching, for an instant only, his grandfather's eye. The old man was watching him carfully.

"You will be prepared for your confirmation while you are here," said Mendoza. "The bishop of Seville will confirm you in the castle chapel so that your father may be present. You will be prepared by Father Gonzalez. A Mr. Whitticker has been engaged through the well-known educational agents Gabbitas and Thring, of London, to be your tutor—"

Don Juan burst out laughing. Mendoza hid his irritation behind a questioning smile. His grandfather frowned.

"Gabbitas and Thring! Please forgive me, Señor Mendoza, but they sound like crooked lawyers in a novel by Dickens."

Neither Mendoza nor Juan's grandfather had any idea what the boy was talking about, but they detected an erudition appropriate in a grandee of Spain, and were mollified.

"Mr. Whitticker and his wife have arrived and moved into one of our houses in the town. I hope you find your body servants satisfactory. I engaged them myself. Please report any complaint you have to me at once."

So they will be your spies, thought Don Juan. He thanked his grandfather and Mendoza and said good night. Garcia bowed him out, and he found Farga and Azorin dozing in the first anteroom to his apartment. The business of being undressed, like his mother, by another person irked Don Juan, but he decided that there would be time to change things later. He slept a boy in a man's world, at last, and dreamed of women.

For the first three months there were so many new impressions to be absorbed that Don Juan could hardly find the time to think of that sex from which he seemed to have been so completely emancipated. That they were out there with their smooth cheeks and gentle voices, their dark hair and pale Spanish bodies, was certain. But he glimpsed them only occasionally.

His mornings started with a cup of coffee and some rolls brought to him by Azorín. Farga laid out his riding clothes but had soon been persuaded to let him dress himself. In the courtyard the Daimler waited to take him to the hunting lodge eight miles from the town. There Mella cared for the horses, two Arabs and half a dozen assorted hunters imported from England and Ireland. To Don Juan, who had learned to ride in the Bois de Boulogne in Paris, the freedom to gallop in the Andalusian countryside was a revelation that made him wonder how people like his mother could bear to live their entire lives in cities or resorts.

Whereas Don Juan remained both distrustful and, as a result, slightly distant from his valet and steward, he soon realized that Mella, a wiry Andalusian with a small farm of his own, had been chosen principally for his consummate skill with horses. He was not the servant type. In the first months Don Juan must have asked him a thousand questions about his people, their customs, their superstitions, their fears and hopes. Mella answered honestly but carefully. Don Juan realized that it would take time for his groom to trust him.

By ten o'clock each day, Don Juan was back at the castle and in his study to spend the next five hours with Mr. Whitticker. This first Englishman in Don Juan's life was to have a profound and quite unforeseen influence upon him. He was the kind of schoolmaster who saw all of education as a series of stories. The story of the atom was part of the story of evolution. The story of evolution was also the story of man's climb to preeminence in the world and perhaps, ultimately, in his galaxy. He made Don Juan look backward with Stefan Zweig, Carlyle, and Gibbon, forward with Jules Verne and H. G. Wells.

He wore linen suits that he thought appropriate to the climate of Spain, and always managed to look like an ill-laundered, unmade bed. He chain-smoked the cheapest Spanish cigarettes and, between paroxysms of coughing, spoke English in a whole series of voices and accents that he thought appropriate to the story of the moment. He was, as a schoolteacher, perpetual theater, and Don Juan treasured every moment he spent with him.

While most of the time they worked together in the beautiful study overlooking the Guadalquivir, the tutor insisted that when it came to science, they should have a proper laboratory. Don Juan, who had an instinctive dislike for math, and, by extension, science, tried to suggest that Mendoza would never agree.

"You're wrong there, Johnny," said Whitticker, who had called a delighted Don Juan this from the very first day they met. "You haven't cottoned on to who Mendoza is. He's Machiavelli, and you're his student prince. D'you think if there's a chance to teach you necromancy and all the black arts he's going to pass it up?"

He was right, and the laboratory was built in one of the old dungeons into which water rats had once swum to torment the prisoners. The moat was far lower now, and the portcullis gave a view of the water birds that raised their chicks there. Here Bunsen burners hissed, retorts bubbled, and Whitticker relived with the enchanted Don Juan the great discoveries of the past.

"Imagine, Johnny, Lavoisier's surprise when out of that hideous brew came something useful. . . . Madame du Châtelet knew how to do this one; she wasn't always play-acting and carrying on with Voltaire, you know. She spent a good deal of time with old Newton in London—that was after the apple fell on his head—and when she came back to Paris . . ."

But once school was over, Whitticker was suddenly shy, like an actor taking off the mask, like a joker suddenly without the protection of his cap and bells. With a "Well, my missus will be waiting. Good day to you, Johnny," he was off. Don Juan had once probed into his past and his family life. Whitticker had been discouraging.

"I'm a simple man, Johnny. A Yorkshireman or worse, as they say. Not a gentleman. My family is an ordinary family. What else is there to say?" An Englishman's sense of class and place. An Englishman's privacy.

Don Juan lunched with his father. It was an agonizing meal carried on in pointless splendor. Occasionally the boy would use a stratagem to try to discover something about his father or mother that, in a direct question, would have produced a blank stare. The circumstances in which this man had married his beautiful, languorous, vulnerable mother boggled his mind, and he attempted, by indirection, to broach the subject in the middle of one of his parent's tirades on infection.

"Father, I understand your feeling about kissing being a source of infection. How do you think married people ought to cope with that problem?"

"Don't think that germs are the only problem there, my boy," said the duke grimly. "Few things are more debilitating than the sexual act. I hope you will discuss this with Father Gonzalez. Chastity is the great prophylactic. If it had not been for the need to have an heir, I should never have troubled your mother, never. My brain was certainly less acute after my marriage. I knew it would be. But one has to make these sacrifices in our position, don't you know . . ."

During the hour of the siesta, Don Juan sometimes slept, but more often he sat at the bathroom window, where he had a small telescope set up. From the vantage point of that particular window he could survey the neighboring houses and streets and thereby circumvent, to some degree, one of Mendoza's most positive interdictions. He was forbidden the town. Only when he drove through the streets to the hunting lodge did he see the population and catch sight of womankind. He always took the precaution of dismissing Farga or locking the bathroom door before "making his observations," as he thought of it. Here he had to find, vicariously, the small sexual pleasure available to him in those months.

There was one particular row of houses where the backs of the upstairs apartments faced only the river and, by coincidence, the tower from which Don Juan viewed them. There were three houses in this row which must have been among the most well-to-do in the town. One of them he knew to be Mendoza's house. The front of it had been pointed out to him by his driver on his way through the town. By watching the back through his telescope at this hour of the day and occasionally at night, he felt he was getting to know its inhabitants by sight.

Mendoza, he discovered, had a wife whose hair hung down to her waist when she took out her pins at night or at siesta time. A modest lady, she always undressed, even in the presence of her husband, behind a screen which was placed by the window. Since the window faced only the river and the apparently shuttered window of Don Juan's bathroom in the castle tower, she stripped naked, unknowingly, for Don Juan's telescope almost every afternoon. Don Juan did a number of sketches of her over the first few weeks after he had made this discovery.

At first he found the looking-downward perspective hard to handle, but slowly he mastered it. Hardest, perhaps, was a large hooflike mole on her belly which always looked like a blob until he found a way to shape it to the roundness above her abdomen. He found painful the absence of her smell, and missing the sound of her voice. When she raised her arms to don the voluminous nightgown she always wore to bed with her husband, he longed to taste the outthrust pears that were her breasts. On one of the upper floors of the same house there were tiny rooms where the Mendozas' servants slept. Through one of these windows he witnessed for the first time the sexual act. It was a hot day at the siesta hour, and the couple he guessed to be the Mendozas' cook and his wife were in the room. The cook sat facing the window, fanning himself. His wife came and kissed him, undoing his fly and unfastening and removing his shirt, kissing and being kissed all the time. Don Juan was moved by the sight of them, and when she finished her gentle arousing and sat astride her husband, the boy looked away with tears in his eyes. He had known that it would be beautiful, and it was. He closed the shutters and put away his telescope. He never looked again, knowing that he hated the role of voyeur.

From six to eight each evening, Whitticker returned to the castle, and the day's studies were resumed. The Englishman admired Don Juan's drawings, and encouraged him to do a batch each day for them to discuss. He particularly encouraged the boy to illustrate his daily essay. "You must draw, Johnny, because you have the gift. I don't know enough to criticize you. But if you illustrate the things we discuss it'll help you remember, because you will have 'visualized' the event."

Don Juan, who had hidden the drawings of Mendoza's wife and placed the guilty telescope in a window facing the river, produced the sketches one day for Whitticker's consideration.

"You did that from life," he said at once. "Some time ago, I suppose, when you were in Paris."

Don Juan grunted. He could not bear to tell "the lie direct" to Whitticker.

"But she looks Spanish. I almost feel as if I've met her," said Whitticker. "She reminds me of one of Goya's nudes. I suppose French women are similar."

"It's Mendoza's wife!" Don Juan blurted out, and explained how he had come to draw her.

The Englishman looked at him with a sad smile on his face.

"Will you confess this to Father Gonzalez when you've been confirmed?" he asked.

"I suppose I must," said Don Juan.

"He'll want you to destroy these," said Whitticker. "It's a pity, because they're among the best you've done. A good likeness of the face too, I'd say, although I hardly know the lady. I'll keep them for you if you like."

Don Juan was glad to have something to give this man he so admired.

"Take them," he said. "I'd like you to have them. I can confess that too, can't I?"

"Yes, you can," said Whitticker at once. "When is your confirmation to be?"

"On my name day," said Don Juan. "I'll be nearly thirteen."

In the evenings before dinner Don Juan went each day to the castle chapel with his father to pray or to a service conducted by Father Gonzalez. The duke and his son sat in an enclosed screened box near the altar rail for these services. Don Juan always felt like the prisoner at the bar in illustrations of French police courts by Daumier. The remainder of the congregation was made up of all the household staff, led by Garcia. No one was ever excused.

Afterward Don Juan sat alone with Father Gonzalez and rehearsed his catechism or read aloud from the lives of the saints while the priest gave a commentary.

The experience of the holy life in his father's household dulled Don Juan's religious fervor for the Most Catholic and Apostolic Church which had been kindled by Father Carroll and kept alive by the Abbé Lemoine. But the teachings of Nanny's revolutionary Bible stayed with him. He saw all around him dire need for revolution. The relevance of the New Testament to life around him seemed endless. *Quis habet duas tunicas, det unam non habenti.*

Don Juan ate alone every night in the dining room, a book propped up against a candelabrum. His only conversation was with Garcia—indeed, it was against the protocol of the dining room to address a footman direct except in an emergency such as soup spilling on one's fly. When he spoke to Garcia it was always of the food.

"Garcia!" Don Juan would exclaim.

"Excellency?"

"Is there some God-given rule why we must eat an omelette which resembles desiccated shoe leather every single night for the second course?"

"What would your excellency prefer?"

Don Juan's nostalgia for his mother's table would then prompt a small outpouring. "I'd like a soufflé made with cheese or fish, or some *quenelles de brochet*. There are pike in the Guadalquivir, I believe. The cook might consider scrambled eggs in the English style, done with a little cream and butter," he added, remembering his favorite among Nanny's high-tea dishes.

"The cook is Spanish, excellency," said Garcia reproachfully. And there the matter always had to rest.

Before going to bed, Don Juan wrote his nightly essay for presentation for Mr. Whitticker the following day, and almost invariably concluded it with some illustrations in pen and ink or sometimes in conté crayon or watercolor.

After bathing and a final cup of hot chocolate, he dismissed his servants and went to bed. He found it pointless to dismiss them earlier, since they slept on sofas in the anterooms. Don Juan had long since understood that, in addition to their other duties, they were his guards.

He slept well after his full days and nearly always dallied the night away in the arms of Mendoza's handsome wife. The dream, for a long time, was always one of pleasurable caresses, of watching Ayesha, who inexplicably was always there, linger with her inventive mouth between the lady's thighs. In the gentle paroxysm that followed, Ayesha disappeared and Don Juan found Mendoza's wife kissing him passionately till he woke. On one memorable night sometime after his twelfth birthday, the dream changed and Ayesha was, for some reason, absent. Without waiting for such preliminaries, he found himself entering the Spanish woman. How he could hardly tell. But when he woke the sheet told its own tale. Don Juan was man. Boy still, but in this important particular, *man.*

If the pattern of his days remained the same, Don Juan found a subtle change in the atmosphere of the countryside when he went on his morning rides with Mella, his groom.

They had always started each day with a canter over the heathlands that ringed a shallow valley where the soil was poor but irrigation work had improved it. This land, which ran for nearly ten miles in an east-west direction, was fed by flash floods when the rains came. It was all part of the duke's estate, and the workers for some forty miles around found most of their employment there. But it was, and always had been, *destajo* (piecework). From the time that Mendoza had first taken over the management of the estate soon after the duke's return from captivity, there had been an increase in investment on the land. There had been ditches to dig, water catchments to be constructed on the gentle hillsides, stones to be moved, and so on.

The first time they had ridden around the area, Mella, prodded by Don Juan's questions, had said, "It is better now, excellency. Before, people died of hunger. Now, if there's a bad harvest here, people have money to buy salted fish in the town."

"What has changed, then?" Don Juan had asked.

"The duke, your father, has made work for people's hands. So there is a little money. God be with him, excellency!"

But in the second year of Don Juan's sojourn in the duke's castle, the boy noticed that the projects had stopped. Painted on the walls of the duke's barns and warehouses was ¡Viva el anarquismo! Men were leaving every day from the familiar huts he passed on his rides to try to find work in Barcelona, for there was no longer work on the duke's estates. The children combed the fields and the sparse woods of the region for roots and nuts to eat, and their mothers, some of whom were still employed in the fields, had joined a trade union inspired by a woman from Málaga called Belén Sárraga. Her name was everywhere on the sides of buildings, even on the walls of churches.

Don Juan remembered what his grandfather had told him and wondered if the "lemmings" were about to march once again.

One day he and Mella rode into a village where Don Juan had been used to stop and water his horse and buy cool goat's milk to drink. Mella usually stayed on his horse, keeping watch over his charge but talking to the old men of the village. On this occasion a group of young men suddenly appeared and pelted Mella with stones. He tried to duck the missiles, shouting to Don Juan to mount. The boy was quickly in the saddle, but not before Mella had been hit in the temple. *"Los malos, los perversos,"* they shouted at the groom. Don Juan, seeing that Mella was dazed, grabbed his rein and, digging in his heels, managed to get both horses out of the village and with Mella reeling but still "up."

The groom recovered enough for them to be able to ride to Mella's own little farm three miles away. They were still five miles from the hunting lodge, but Mella, bleeding from a gash on his forehead, was half blinded by his own blood.

Don Juan had never been very close to the farm before. When he'd asked to see it as they rode by, Mella, in his taciturn way, had always said it was "an unsuitable place for your excellency." He had added that his wife was a woman of uncertain temper.

Now as they approached and Don Juan dismounted and tried to help his half-fainting groom to the ground, a woman rushed out of the house already keening as if her man were actually dead. She pushed Don Juan violently aside and, still moaning and crying, half-carried her husband into the farmhouse. When Don Juan approached to see if she wanted him to fetch a doctor, she simply came and spat at him, giving the sign against the evil eye. Then she slammed the door in his face. Someone had painted on it ¡Viva el anarquismo! Almost more shaken by this woman's evident hatred than by the stoning of his groom, Don Juan rode back to the hunting lodge at a gallop. After unsaddling and seeing to his horse, he ran to find the waiting Daimler.

He said nothing to his driver of what had occurred, but told him to stop at the house of the lawyer Mendoza. It is doubtful if the driver would have stopped anywhere else on Don Juan's order except the castle itself. But he pulled up outside the house and handed Don Juan out and rang the doorbell for him. Don Juan was horrified to find that he was shaking now and that his teeth had started to chatter. He had once before been the victim of shock, after his dreadful experience with Tabatha, so he recognized the symptoms. The door had opened and a maid appeared. He heard the driver say, "His excellency wishes to speak to Señor Mendoza." He saw someone else coming toward him. Someone curiously familiar. But her long black hair was piled on top of her head, and he had never seen her from this angle before. Then as fast as she appeared she seemed to recede. He had fallen in a dead faint into the arms of his driver.

There was a marvelous scent of woman, a sense of things female about him, when he awoke. He could see little because he was in a curtained four-poster bed. But the sheets had that dear, that too long unfamiliar, smell, and the lace on the pillows was further evidence of their presence. Don Juan inhaled and was happy. He went straight to sleep.

When he awoke again it was to the sound of voices. The bed curtains were open. A man whom Don Juan recognized as his father's doctor was examining him and talking to a very concerned Mendoza. Mendoza's wife sat on the other side of the bed and held Don Juan's hand. He listened to what the two men were saying, but took advantage of the fact that they clearly thought him semi-conscious to get a good look at the woman who had for so long slept with him in his dreams. He saw that she had a mouth even more sensitive and naturally red than his perspective through the telescope had been able to suggest. Her eyes were unexpectedly blue, with charming little laughter lines at the corners. He looked at them carefully, committing them to memory, when she suddenly became aware of his gaze. For an instant or two she returned it, looking into his greenish eyes with their searching, sensual expression. She found his look not only disturbing, but astoundingly "familiar."

"The driver can give no explanation whatsoever," Mendoza was saying.

"He has all the appearances of being the victim of shock. But I find his pulse quite normal now, considering the injection I gave him at lunchtime," said the doctor.

"He is awake!" said Mendoza's wife, catching her breath as she found that he was gently caressing the inside of her hand with his fingertips.

"Don Juan, tell us what happened," asked Mendoza. "You came here asking for me. Why?"

"I really can't remember," said Don Juan, searching for some way to protect Mella, to make it possible for him to go back and find out what was really happening among the "lemmings." He remembered something Mella had once warned him against. Mushrooms he'd seen on the heathland.

"I did eat some mushrooms. Perhaps I was feeling ill from them . . . ?"

"Ah! Mushrooms. That is more than possible," said the doctor, as if everything might now be explained.

"I think I came to your door to ask you to call the doctor," Don Juan said to Mendoza, relieved that his lie was working so easily.

"Quite right. Quite right, Don Juan," said Mendoza. "Thanks be to God you're better. Please, never touch any food outside the castle. One cannot be too careful."

Don Juan looked at the screen across the room by the window. He could see the river beyond and, high up on one side, the jutting east tower of the castle and his shuttered bathroom. He had not watched her in the flesh for months. Now that he had met her, inhaled her scent and made her aware of him, he would watch again.

Mendoza took Don Juan into the castle himself. It was clear that the boy felt quite recovered, but the lawyer wanted to reassure himself that the duke had been given no alarming news of his son. They met Whitticker in the courtyard.

"Don Juan had a slight accident, Mr. Whitticker," said Men-doza. "It may be better if we excuse him his afternoon lesson today."

But Don Juan said, "I'm quite all right, thank you, señor. I seem to have slept half the day! I promise to be careful in the future."

In their study Don Juan explained everything, making a story of it in the Whitticker manner. When he had finished he asked the Englishman simply: "What does it mean?"

"Couldn't Mendoza give you a better answer than I?"

"I didn't ask him."

"I see. Or rather, I don't see, because Mendoza's your man," said Whitticker cautiously.

"I don't really like Mendoza. I realized after the driver had rung the bell that I couldn't very well *ask* without also *answering*. And something told me that the Guardia Civil will take revenge on that village if I tell on them. So thank God I fainted. I've known that village now for two years. They've got absolutely nothing. Only a few of the men even have shoes. Kids my age live on berries, yes, and mushrooms. Mella showed me the good ones they eat. You know, the hatred in those people's eyes made me feel sick, sick to my stomach, physically sick."

"Poor Johnny. The accident of birth can be such hell. That above all makes me question a God with such a macabre sense of humor."

"Meaning?"

"If you'd been born in the fourteenth century, who would you have liked to be?"

"Froissart, out of the fray. Always on the sidelines. I'd have done my own illuminations, too."

"Oh, Johnny, you're a bloody marvel. My thought was such a boring thought. Tutor to boy prince: 'What would you have liked to be in the fourteenth century, sir?' Answer: 'Please, sir, a knight, sir. All that lovely armor. Gorgeous damosels tying favors on my codpiece, oops!' 'Not a laborer, serf, or villein, not then or ever, Boy Prince?' asks the tutor. 'Oh, no, sir. Now I'd like to be a stockbroker prince, sir, or an executive prince or even a salesman prince. I can see that is the future.' But you, Johnny, see that it's all going to end in tears for boy princes. You see that the laborers, serfs, and villeins are still, against all the evidence, hoping for the millennium when the shirtless ones inherit the earth. You guess, as I do, that it may just be about to happen here. You think you may be able to get away with being a contemporary Froissart, sitting on the sidelines and recording it all in word and sketch."

"You think I'm incapable of taking sides?" said Juan, half sad, half angry.

"You took a side when you were born. Or it was taken for you. You have too much to lose by going over to the other side now. As you have seen, they don't want you. Also, your side may still win. They're remarkably resilient, you know."

"Can't I be a neutral Froissart?"

"Froissart wasn't neutral. He was noncombatant. That's different."

Don Juan sat in thought for a moment, and his thought was quite childlike for once.

"I'd love to be an entirely free person," he said. "Owning nothing. But books, of course. Millions of books."

Whitticker roared with laughter, but when he finished, Don Juan was looking at him very straight in the eye.

"'And where do you stand, tutor?' asked the boy prince," said he.

"I don't stand. I teach," said Whitticker warily.

"All right. Teach me why there is no more work for thousands of people who depend on us."

"That's a sentimental way of putting it. Those people are not your property."

"If they were really serfs, they would have a *right* to depend on us. I see. Then if we are such undependable employers, why don't they just go away? Emigrate to the Americas? If they are free?"

"Because as Andalusians who have lived here for thousands of years, they believe that the land they live on—and they pay rent to you for that privilege—is really their land. They believe that the land you sometimes pay them, by the hour, to tend is really their land. They hope that if they wait long enough, it is *you* who will emigrate. As the landed Russians did at the time of their revolution."

"How would they live if we were gone? Would it be like Russia?"

Whitticker took a folded piece of paper out of his pocket. "Would you like to see one of their broadsheets? They're all over town," he said.

Don Juan read it:

We demand: The abolition of all class.
             The social and economic equality of both sexes.

In order to achieve this we further demand:
> The abolition of individual property and abolition of the
> right to inheritance.

We desire: Equality of education for children of both sexes.
> And for all children an equality of food supply and
> social position.

We are the enemy of:
> All despotism.
> All authority and form of State.

We refuse:
> All revolutionary activity that has not for its object the
> direct triumph of the workers' cause against capital; for it
> desires that all political and authoritarian organs of the
> state be reduced to mere public services.

We declare ourselves:
> To be godless, atheistical.
> To desire the substitution of science for faith and of human
> for divine justice.

"It's the Sermon on the Mount without God," said Whitticker. "In England we don't plan to go quite so far. But then we never do."

"So that's where *you* stand, tutor," said Don Juan wryly, still trying to visualize the new world the broadsheet conjured up. Then childish again: "It's not fair that you don't trust me when I trust you."

"Working-class by origin, guv'nor," said Whitticker in his best Yorkshire. "Educated thanks to the likes of you. School founded by the Webbs. Lord and lady, only you wouldn't know it, guv'nor, if you didn't listen to them talk. Scholarship to Oxford. Socially unacceptable, so had time to get a good First. Trade unionizer by profession. But want to write about revolution. Get Gabbitas and Thring to place me in a tutoring job in Spain. Find agreeable post with student prince. Am fast becoming seduced by bourgeois values."

"I see. I see," said Don Juan, thinking Whitticker's life sounded marvelously exotic, relieved to understand, at last, what he really faced as his father's heir, wondering what Mendoza's answers would have been to the same questions. He asked Whitticker this.

"Mendoza is neither stupid nor intentionally cruel," said Whitticker. "He is a straightforward capitalist doing the best he can for the estate. When he was put in charge here he saw a need to invest in modernization. So he invested and modernized, and for three or four years that meant plenty of work. Now the period of investment is over. The estate should be more profitable. His next investment, out of profits, may be in a Barcelona factory. Then the jobs will be *there.*

That's how it works."

"But you think that's wrong?"

"Yes. I believe that the means of production should belong to all the people, and that means you, me, and everyone, including Mendoza—and let's not forget Mendoza's wife," he added, knowing how to distract Don Juan's attention from an otherwise endless discussion.

Next morning Don Juan was driven out to the hunting lodge as usual. The Daimler dropped him and went off to wherever the driver went while the young excellency was amusing himself by galloping about the countryside. He would be back in two hours. Don Juan stood alone, listening. The hunting lodge was shuttered and never used. He had never been inside the stucco building. The stables were behind and out of sight. If Mella was not there he would have to make an important decision. From facing the possibility of that decision he hesitated. He walked around the building and saw two youths who helped Mella clean out the stables, but no Mella. He asked them about his groom, and they said he was sick. Their eyes were quite blank with concealed fear.

While Don Juan knew himself not to be rash, except when it came to women, he was beginning to find that physical danger, far from repelling him, actually rather attracted him. Emotional shock, such as he had experienced the previous day, could undo him temporarily. All his life he must arm himself against it as best he could.

He chose the fastest hunter in the stable, an Irish bay gelding which, at sixteen hands, was a little bit big for him, and did the saddling up himself. The stable lads watched him go, and Don Juan glanced over his shoulder once or twice to see if anyone was following him. But he was quite alone on the heathland until he made the turn that would take him to Mella's farm. Long before he got there he heard screams. They were staccato and spoke of instants of intense pain.

The screams had ceased when he arrived at the farm. There were some infant children sitting quite still, as if petrified, in the yard, and a snorting and snuffling from the small piggery Mella kept out back. The groom's horse was grazing in the paddock where Don Juan had left it. It had not even been unsaddled, and one of its legs was entangled in a rein so that it hobbled about on three and a half legs. Two other saddled horses were tethered nearby. The farmhouse door with its defiant slogan was firmly closed.

Don Juan dismounted and walked toward the door. Forcing

himself not to hesitate or even, as his upbringing urged, to knock, he
opened the door. Three faces turned to him in intense surprise. Two
male faces, feral with beady eyes, now frightened, and a female face.
On hers the astonishment showed through a layer of agony. Mella's
wife was suspended by her hair from a beam in the ceiling; her arms
were free to take the weight, as she now did. Two Guardia Civil, the
male faces, stood at once and advanced on Don Juan. One, clearly
the senior, made to push him from the house.

"Excellency, you must leave," he said, and the boy knew, with
relief, that they recognized him.

Don Juan, for the first time in his life, played his appointed role
as grandee of Spain, and played it instinctively.

"Where is my groom?" he bellowed, as if he didn't care about the
woman's pain.

Hearing a tone of voice they understood, they immediately made
way for him, pointing to a bed at the back of the room. Mella lay
there half conscious with fever, a bandage over his eyes. His hands
were tied to the bedpost.

"We are questioning this woman, excellency. It was necessary to
tie him up. But he is very sick."

"Then untie the woman and get out," said Juan. He thanked
God he was taller than they. It added to his authority.

"But excellency, this is a police investigation," said the spokesman.

"These are my servants. Speak to Señor Mendoza, our lawyer, if
you wish to question them, or get an order from a magistrate."

"She is a red, excellency. She is organizing the women on your
land to strike," said the younger man of the Guardia. "We just want
to know who the other organizers are. She is too stubborn to tell us."

"Take her down!" he shouted. "D'you think I'm interested in
your wretched work? Take her down and get out." He was astonished
and excited to realize he enjoyed shouting at them.

Shrugging and grumbling, the Guardia did as they were bid. But
they made no attempt to untie the woman's hair (of the usual waist
length common to young peasant women), but took a kitchen knife
and hacked at it till she was free to fall to the ground. Don Juan
would have liked to ease her from the beam as she unclutched her
cramped and bleeding hands. But he knew he must show no pity. He
intended that the Guardia should see him as they expected him to be,
a spoiled-brat aristocrat concerned for his servants as property, as
one would be concerned for a dog and bitch of some value.

They went, banging the door, leaving the moaning woman

squatting on the floor, running her bleeding hands over her mangled hair. "My hair, my hair!" she cried.

The boy who had so successfully brazened it out with the Guardia Civil now was at a total loss as to what to do next. He untied Mella's hands, but he saw the man was too sick to speak. His head had been bandaged with torn strips of rag, but it had started to bleed again. The skin of his face, what Juan could see of it under a day-old stubble, was like pale dough, and his mouth was gummed closed with mucus. Touching him, Don Juan was appalled at the heat of his body. He went to fetch some water. Finding some in a bucket, he put his handkerchief into it and went and squeezed the moisture into Mella's mouth, cleaning away the viscous effluent. The woman was standing beside him, looking hopelessly at her man, and then, like a wounded bird that just sits and quivers, she looked again at the swelling, shredded palms of her hands. Sobs came retching up from her guts, and, clutching her elbows into her stomach, she started to howl like an animal. Don Juan thought he might calm her if he could get her to sit. He found himself shouting, "If you'll only be quiet, I want to go and get the doctor!"

It worked. For an instant. Then she grabbed Don Juan with her bloody fingers and pulled him to the bed. Mella, who hardly seemed to be breathing now, was covered with a blanket. The woman pulled the blanket back. At first Don Juan couldn't understand what he was seeing. She was shouting in his ear: "With their rifle butts they did it!" Mella's body was clothed in a sweat-soaked pajama top. The bottoms were missing. And then he saw it and felt himself about to be sick. The man's loins were smashed into a bloody pulp.

The boy rushed out of the house and stood fighting back his bile and breathing in great drafts of air. Suddenly she started to keen again. He supposed and hoped that poor Mella was dead. What else was there to hope?

I am twelve and a half, thought Don Juan, and I am almost a man already. Where did my childhood go? I can't walk back in there because I don't know what to do. I can't not go back in there because he was my friend. I don't suppose death will seem like anything extraordinary. Not after the last five minutes. But will anything at all ever be the same? I mean, am I me in this skin around these bones, or can I escape from me and be someone else before it's too late?

He went back in a dream to see the dead man. He was still, totally still; otherwise he looked the same, except his body seemed to be settling, diminishing. Her noise continued, and he watched her for a moment without hearing, as if he were looking at a kinematograph without the pianist's accompaniment. How totally she feels this, he thought; it is as if she is letting her whole life out of her mouth like gas escaping from a balloon. But, in spite of that, she looks like a survivor. She will have life enough left to go on.

Bending, he kissed her hand, exactly as he had done at his mother's receptions on the Avenue Foch. It was a completely reflex action. He at first thought it ridiculous, but as he left, he realized it was natural, part of who he really was. He rode away.

Don Juan was sitting in his study an hour later drafting a letter to Mendoza, informing him of the groom's death and the manner of it. Tears kept coming to his eyes, and he blinked them back, hoping Whitticker hadn't noticed them. But the Englishman's calm helped him nevertheless.

"There has been a revolt near Rio Tinto," said Whitticker. "It's serious. The strikers have threatened to destroy the installations. They're sending most of the Guardia Civil from here. They leave tonight in supposed secret. The bourgeois Republic, predictably enough, seems to be doing no better than the monarchy or the dictatorship."

"I'm not going to say anything about the stoning in the village, but why do you think they stoned him and not me?" asked Don Juan.

"Because they are sworn not to harm children, women, or old men. It is part of their creed," said Whitticker.

"But why him? He was one of them. His wife certainly was. They say she's a union leader," said Juan.

"Because he had so far lost his pride as a man to be a servant, your servant," said Whitticker. "Anyway, you won't need another groom for some time. Soon they will all be on strike. The moment the Guardia is safely away."

"The day after tomorrow is my confirmation. Do you think they'll cancel it?" asked Don Juan.

"I shouldn't think so," said Whitticker. "Strikes are Mendoza's problem. You fellows and the church are above all that, surely?" he added teasingly.

The following morning, while Don Juan was having his break-fast, Farga came to say that Garcia wished to speak with him. Never before had the majordomo come personally to his apartments, and Don Juan was curious to find out what could be thought important enough for such a break with custom. When Garcia arrived, Don Juan had the forethought to dismiss Farga, who was hovering about the place.

"Excellency, I am most grateful for your seeing me personally at this hour. Something of importance is occurring today. Your grandfather and the bishop of Seville are arriving this afternoon for the confirmation service. They, naturally, will be given the two guest suites, leaving us with no guest rooms in the castle. This place was built as a fortress, not as a hotel."

"Yes, of course, Garcia," said Don Juan. "You are not *consulting* me about all this, surely?"

"Excellency, these matters are left in my hands," Garcia assented. "I consult only with Señor Mendoza in the case of any difficulty, since the duke prefers not to concern himself with such things."

"You have a difficulty now?" asked Don Juan.

"Yes, excellency," said Garcia, pained to admit any deviation from the norm. "Señor Mendoza has asked that his wife might also stay here. He makes no such request for himself, naturally."

"His wife?" Don Juan was genuinely astounded.

"As your excellency knows, no woman has been in this castle since your noble mother last left for France," said Garcia. "The duke would be most disturbed to hear of the presence of a woman in the castle. Naturally, Señor Mendoza is quite content that his wife should take all her meals in her room."

"Garcia, you are going too fast for me. *Why* does Mendoza want his wife to stay in this castle for my confirmation? I hardly know the lady."

"Quite so, excellency. But the people believe her to be a witch. There is a rumor that all the workers and tenants on the duke's lands are soon to march into town, and that, among other things, they intend to burn her. The occupations of the town have happened many times, particularly before we had the Guardia Civil stationed here. This time, the CNT have proclaimed a strike against all the landowners in Andalusia to coincide fraternal action with the strike at Rio Tinto. It was on the radio last night, excellency."

"But a witch, Garcia. Señora Mendoza is a sweet, gentle lady. Why do they think that?" Don Juan was bemused.

"I cannot imagine, excellency. Of course, Señor Mendoza runs the estates. But in my humble opinion, he is hardly a man to be managed by his wife. It is inexplicable!" said Garcia.

"Do you really think my father would object to a woman here? In such circumstances?"

"Excellency, your father will not have a she-cat in the castle. He believes that females represent a kind of doom for him. Whether from infection or what, I cannot say. Your excellency, knowing his father as I do, surely understands?" Garcia was extremely embarrassed to be discussing the duke with Don Juan.

"Did Mendoza ask you to come to me?"

"It pains me greatly to deceive the duke. I could not think of doing it without your consent—"

"—and connivance."

"Yes, excellency." Garcia was chastened by the word.

Privately Don Juan could scarcely believe his good fortune. She would be accessible at last. He would be able to visit and talk to her. He was doing Mendoza a favor and his father was not to know. What about his grandfather? Don Juan was not at all certain that he wanted his grandfather to know that he had connived at bringing a beautiful woman into the house and deceiving his father. It was important not to seem eager.

"Well, Garcia, we must make the best of a bad situation. I understand your dilemma perfectly. She will sleep in my room, and I will sleep in my study. Naturally, I don't wish my grandfather or the bishop to know that I am deceiving my father. But nor will you or Mendoza want them to know."

"Certainly not, excellency," said Garcia. "I think Señor and Señora Mendoza will think it most generous of you to be giving up your room in this way. And if your excellency will forgive this allusion to your extreme youth, I can see no possible taint to the lady's honor that a child of your age should be sleeping next door to her," said Garcia, and after expressing this convoluted and extremely Spanish sentiment, the majordomo bowed and withdrew.

Don Juan's morning ride would in any case have been canceled that day, because the Daimler had been sent to meet his grandfather and the bishop. Mendoza arrived forty minutes later with his wife, and while Garcia was supervising the installation of such light luggage as she had brought in Don Juan's bedroom, the lawyer commiserated about the death of Mella. He had reported the whole matter to the commander of the Guardia Civil with the most rigorous complaint. Meanwhile, he had to make the strike his first priority.

"Last time they occupied the town for a week," said Mendoza. "It was before my time. They elected a new council from among the working people and the surprising number of artisans and even small shopkeepers who supported them. They issued a utopian manifesto. Damage to property was slight, but they murdered the two Guardia Civil in the town. That was before the government sent us a garrison. They vandalized the church, and they burned the priest and the mayor on a huge bonfire in front of the castle gates. This time they have threatened to burn me and my wife, who they say is a witch. Someone even wrote a note saying, 'If you want her to be safe, send her to the castle.'"

"Why cannot you stay with your wife?" asked Don Juan, hoping for a negative reply.

"It is not possible. I am the leader here. We have still got a reasonable number of Guardia Civil in town. Eight in all. Three will be at the castle gates. Two we have sent to escort your grandfather and the bishop. They will join the remainder at the barracks. And that is where I must be, with the notables, the mayor and so on. We have extra guns in the armory there, so there should be nothing to worry about. The government is sending reinforcements."

Whitticker came at his usual hour. They did no schoolwork, but sat in the study talking about the strike. Don Juan had closed the doors to the intervening anteroom between study and bedroom so that Señora Mendoza could not hear any of Whitticker's alarmist opinions. Besides, he wished to discuss the extraordinary news that the people thought her a witch.

"If they don't believe in God, how can they believe in witches?" asked Don Juan.

"It takes a long time for one religion to supersede another," said Whitticker. "There is always some of the older religion left behind. Belief in witches is part and parcel of Christianity. There are services for the exorcism of devils, as you must know from your confirmation studies."

"You said that they have sworn not to harm women," said Don Juan.

"It's part of their catechism, Johnny," said Whitticker. "None of them will copulate while they are on strike. Nor will they drink or smoke or mention God's name, because that, to them, is a curse, and strikes are holy. But just like the Puritans of old, who used to say the Ten Commandments daily, which included 'Thou shalt not kill,' they, too, can burn a witch."

"But she's nothing like a witch!" said Don Juan, still amazed.

"You mean no pointed hat and broomstick?" said Whitticker. "But you're forgetting the other tradition about witches. That they are very beautiful women who retain their beauty."

Don Juan smiled. "Through a pact with the Devil?"

"Exactly," said Whitticker. "What one wonders is how they *know* she's a witch."

"Some mischief-maker has told them. Denounced her!"

"You're getting very warm, Johnny, lad," said Whitticker. "Boy prince shows aptitude. But with application will improve still more."

"Mendoza is the real target?" Don Juan hazarded.

"He must be," said Whitticker with certainty. "Remove Mendoza and this estate will, for a time, become ungovernable. What an opportunity!"

Don Juan looked at Whitticker with great curiosity. Here was the cool Froissart who, while partial to one side, certainly, watched the game from the sidelines. They went on discussing the fascinating contradictions of the anarchist movement until it was time for lunch.

Whitticker was leaving as Azorín came through with Señora Mendoza's lunch tray. "Glad to see you're making the lady comfortable, Johnny," he said, and was gone.

The bishop and Don Juan's grandfather arrived in the afternoon, driving through empty streets past shuttered stores. The town was apparently deserted. Don Juan was glad to see his grandfather and, after kissing the bishop's ring, helped Garcia show the guests to their apartments. Whitticker never appeared for the evening lesson, the first time he had failed to do so. Dinner with his father and the guests was more tiresome than usual. Everyone went early to bed.

Don Juan had his bed made up on a sofa in the study and dismissed the servants to the outer anteroom. It was barely midnight when he knocked at the bedroom door. He had changed into a pair of shantung pajamas the duchess had sent him for his birthday, and he shivered slightly in the cool air of the windowless anteroom, but really more from anticipation. He had rehearsed his role in his mind. He would be apparently insouciant to her as a woman; otherwise he might as well be entirely honest. He was a boy starved of feminine society who wished to keep her company for a while.

She came to the door clutching her peignoir around her. He was relieved to see that all the lights were still on. She could not have been asleep.

"Dear Don Juan, I declare! You've left everything you need in this room? I'm so sorry to have displaced you!" she said in the bantering tone women use to boys, but which is not wholly innocent of flirtation.

"Señora, can you believe that you are the first and only Spanish lady I have met since I came to the castle from France?"

"You have left nothing behind here that you need?"

"Nothing!" he declared, smiling. "I simply want to talk to you. Were you already in bed? I see you were. Please get back into bed and I'll sit beside you as you sat beside me when I was in *your bed.*" Don Juan managed to make this juxtaposition of their beds sound extraordinarily intimate. Theirs was a bedroom acquaintance.

She got back into her bed, contriving to smile at him in a maternal way. There could be no harm in a pleasant, playful chat with this charming boy who would, after all, probably sooner rather than later be their duke and employer.

He leaped onto the bed and did not sit, but lay full length beside her, his chin cupped in his hands, gazing at her in a way that was at once childlike but also intimate and sensual.

"My mother is the only Spanish woman I have known intimately, if you see what I mean," Don Juan began.

"They say she is extraordinarily beautiful, your mother," she said, wondering where this was leading.

"Yes, she is. But quite different from you. I'm sorry, but you seem to me to be quite unique," said Don Juan, enjoying the luxury of examining her face in detail, this face he'd drawn so often, had kissed countless times in his imagination. She gazed back in amazement at a boy with a man's, a lover's, expression.

"What is your name? Your Christian name?" he asked in his alto, even now just becoming baritone.

"Isabel. Don Juan, you're a naughty boy. You sound quite romantic."

"Not romantic, Isabel. Nostalgic. I'm far too young for romance. What I miss is the warmth of my mother's embrace. When I lay in your bed and found the scent of you there, it was so wonderful. It reminded me of her bed."

How beautiful to have a son like that, she thought, for Isabel Mendoza had, as yet, no children, but then she had been married barely eighteen months. How pleasant, she thought, to have a boy like this one day to hug and caress. To be able to tousle his hair, those soft springy curls of his, and to feel lips like those kissing your cheek in a boyish way: what a wonderful emotion to have. Not faintly threatening, as the love of a man always seemed to her to be. Although that too was exciting with Mendoza. But the gentleness that this promised, the candor, the sharing of secrets.

Don Juan laid his head on her shoulder. "You don't mind, do you? Isabel. Isabel!" Juan rolled it on his tongue. "Name of queens."

"The last Isabel of Spain was a very wicked queen. She had far too many lovers!"

"Do you think it's a matter of quantity?" he asked her quite sincerely, raising his head and looking hard into her blue eyes, as if warning her it was a game where any prevarication would be instantly detected and pounced upon. "Too many surely means just some would do nicely."

"I could never take a lover!" she said firmly, wondering whether she meant it.

"You're not sure, really. I can see that," he said, and laid his head back on her shoulder. "I should think you'd be safer mothering and being friends with a boy like me. Don't you think?" He looked into her eyes again and laughed at her surprise. She liked his laugh.

"My feet are cold," said Don Juan. "My mother always warmed my feet with her hands. Of course, I was shorter then. Perhaps you could warm my feet with your feet. Will you?"

So there it is, she thought. He wants to get into my bed with me. What can happen, except that I'll feel his hard little body against me and perhaps like it enough to forget that horrible threat out there. Perhaps he'll want to hug a bit. What harm?

"In you get. And let's feel those feet," she said in a brisk maternal way.

To her surprise he first rushed around the room turning out lights and then leaped into bed as if he intended to stay. The foot-warming exercise became a vigorous game of "trap the foot" until, breathless, she laughed, "Stop! Stop! You win!" She smiled at her companion in the dark, in his bed, in his castle. How lighthearted, how beautiful. Like a brother but not a brother, much more exciting than a brother. Not as big as Mendoza, but as tall as many men.

Don Juan curled in her arms for a moment, content to lay his head, like a son, on her shoulder, on her breast, nuzzling there, breathing in the scent of her skin, feeling through her nightgown her warmth, her softness, the contours of her body.

She kissed his brow, and very slowly he sought her mouth. Instinctively he knew he must seek it indirectly. He brushed with his lips the bare rise in her breast where the neck of her nightgown parted. Was it kiss or accident—how could she tell? But her breath was held shallower in expectation. He kissed her neck. The softest of filial kisses. More the murmur of breath on the skin than a kiss. Then in the dark she knew his mouth was within a scintilla of her cheek, his breath warmed her skin, and he lay quite still. Still, still in her arms. She thought she could hear her own heart. And still he lay still.

Mendoza, Mendoza. She must think of Mendoza. When she changed into her nightgown behind the screen in her bedroom, it was always "Hurry, darling, I want you. Oh, why can't you just throw off your clothes as I do and get into bed?" "Like a whore?" she always asked, quoting her mother, making him wait for it, keeping his respect but excited at his urgency just the same. Then getting into the bed, the bit she never quite liked, seeing him there all hirsute and hard, his virility evident and thrusting. But wanting time now for gentleness before the hardness. Never, somehow, had he either understood that or wanted it, but just grabbed, hard hands on her arms, pulling her to him, poking into her nightdress and feeling her breasts—like prodding melons in the market to test their ripeness, she always thought. The scissor movement of Mendoza's legs that parted hers, neat the way he did, like a well-practiced drill, then his thrusts, his hard-breathing, grunting thrusts, immediate and urgent. "Relax, darling, relax." Forcing into her before she had really melted. Some pleasure always in the dying thrust itself, warm and effulgent. Some pride in feeling him spent and relaxed, watchful at last of her face, of her eyes, which, thank God, he found unreadable, of her lips. Then it was, always, that he finally kissed her a bristly, grateful kiss before returning to his day, leaving her to her siesta.

In the dark the boy's mouth had moved. His breath now warmed her lips. Was this a kiss? His mouth traveled over hers. She felt her own lips quite marvelously alive, as if they played host to fireflies. But still his body lay still. His mouth moved on, gentle and moist, like very fine rain, upon all the surfaces of her face, her brow, her cheeks, her eyes. Even as she moved her face to offer him some new place to kiss, she asked herself, Is this a game, a gentle, wonderful game of which I have been ignorant? Played perhaps by mothers with their sons in sophisticated France? What response should I have? Perhaps if I kiss him as I wish to, as I want to, as I would, it would confuse him. But then he is not in bed with his mother. That he must *learn!*

The divine mischief of it was too tempting for Isabel as she gave him her neck, her ears, her throat, her chin. He cannot know how this game makes me, who is not his mother, feel. But he must be made to know. As the child that plays with fire must burn a little to understand the danger.

Isabel sought Don Juan's mouth. Sought it with such a kiss to give that Mendoza had neither felt nor, perhaps, deserved. She gave him the kiss it had been her dream to give a lover. The fireflies that Don Juan had ignited on her lips moved through her whole body now as she found his mouth, urgently found his mouth and tongue. But as when a wave, rolling toward its breaking point in shadow, is suddenly, in the instant of exploding, lit by brilliant sunshine into foam, so her sudden mad desire met in the man-boy an illuminating passion that quite banished from her mind all thought of mother, game and boy, but fastened her to the now surging man with whom she lay.

As she sank entirely under the spell of his extraordinary kisses, even those cries of caution that still called to her from somewhere in the wings of her mind were drowned out. He whispered that he would kiss her whole body. She consented utterly.

He *had* to kiss her whole body. She yielded everything to that mouth. Even the ugly hoof-shaped mole on her belly; she was moved to tears almost to feel him kiss it.

All this, and she had still to feel his hands.

For his fingers had started their long-learned magic, and she was sinking, dissolving, not caring that he seemed no longer to be wearing his shantung pajamas, frantic to feel with her hands the man who made her burn and glow and weep and melt like this. How is it possible, she almost screamed, that all this is new to me?

Some other woman Don Juan would certainly have disappointed that night. But Isabel could have been created expressly to take his virginity. To her he was unalloyed delight. Nor, as long as she lived, could she ever believe that she was the first. But that's how it was.

A great noise awakened them. It was just before dawn. Together they rushed to the bathroom window, which gave a view of part of the town. The Church of Our Lady of Andalusia was burning, lighting up the surrounding homes and the throngs of peasants who seemed to engorge every street and alley.

Don Juan kissed and left Señora Mendoza, grabbing his shantung pajamas and running to his study to dress. His valet and steward, also awakened by the noise, had just found his study empty and gaped at their young master.

"Stop staring at me, you idiots!" shouted Don Juan. "Can't you see I've just been to the bathroom? Throw me my clothes, Farga. Azorín, go and wake Garcia if he's not already up. They're burning the church. It can't be too long before they're on their way up here."

Don Juan met Garcia on his way down the staircase to the courtyard.

"Is my grandfather up, Garcia?"

"No, excellency. He's on the river side. I'm going to wake him."

"Tell him I'm going up to the tower above the keep, where I can see what's going on."

"Yes, excellency. Be careful not to expose yourself to some madman with a gun."

"If the Guardia Civil haven't got the drawbridge up every one of us will have to worry about worse than that!" Don Juan shouted as he ran out into the courtyard. But the drawbridge was up, the guards watching through peepholes, their guns at the ready. He climbed the cramped stone spiral stair to the tower over the Moorish keep and emerged onto the battlement, sixty feet above the gaping moat, which the drawbridge usually spanned.

The narrow lane that led down to the town from the castle entrance was still empty. But the tower of the church was burning merrily. Don Juan wondered about Father Gonzalez and remembered that he had slept the night in the vestry of the castle's chapel, so as to be on hand for the confirmation, siege or no siege.

The noise from the town was colossal—the screaming of iron being forced as locked shutters were prized from their sockets with crowbars, an occasional fusillade from the distant police barracks, a rolling hum of people on the move punctuated by the shouters, both the threateners and the frightened.

Don Juan's grandfather joined him just after dawn broke, toiling up the staircase behind Garcia. Both of them were followed by the bishop, a youngish man for his office at fifty-five, but, Don Juan thought, very beady and dyspeptic.

"If only it were enough to excommunicate and anathematize them," the prelate sighed, watching the now collapsing spire of the church. "But next year if there's a drought they will follow the sacred figures around the fields and genuflect and cross themselves and pray." He was referring to statues of the Virgin and certain saints fitted with mechanical arms for ambulatory blessings.

"You can no more excommunicate the lot of them," said Don Juan's grandfather sympathetically, "than I can permanently lock out all my workers. It puts one out of business."

"D'you think they'll try to get into the castle, Grandfather?" asked Don Juan.

"I doubt it. They've never really hated the duke. I'm told the poor man's misery appeals to them. Fellow feeling. Very Spanish, that," said his grandfather. "Mendoza's got enough men and arms to take care of himself. They'll mess up the town a bit and then the army'll get here or they'll send back the guards from Rio Tinto, although I do hear things are a bit critical there at the moment. I spoke to the minister of war last night on the telephone. He promised reinforcements by tonight at the latest. There's nothing they can do to hurt *us*."

"Well, here they come," said Don Juan. Like liquid flowing up a pipe, a solid mass of strikers was now moving up the narrow roadway toward the precipice where the drawbridge normally spanned the moat. They carried with them huge cardboard posters held high. Don Juan was reminded of newsreels in which the great heads of Marx and Lenin wobbled over processions in the Soviet Union. But the pictures on the vast placards were too extraordinary to be believed at first.

One was a huge picture of Mendoza wearing a pair of antlers on his head. The picture of him was a photograph. The antlers had been drawn, cut out, and nailed onto his head.

Then came an eight-foot enlarged photograph of a drawing of a naked woman. Of Isabel Mendoza with her hoof-mark mole on her belly. Don Juan's heart sank as he recognized his own drawing.

Finally—and there was a roar of laughter from the still-moving crowd as this was raised—a picture of Don Juan himself, full-face, taken, he remembered, by a local photographer on his birthday.

"Bring out the witch! Bring out the witch!" they were shouting.

"She is not here!" shouted back Don Juan's grandfather, showing himself on the battlement, peering down from between the castellations.

It was then that Don Juan saw Whitticker. He stood next to a thin, steely-looking woman in a red dress, a woman who held a large megaphone.

"The woman who has put a curse on us all, forcing her husband to deny the people their right to work, is a witch. What is more, she has seduced the heir to the dukedom. The boy who stands beside you, *compañero,*" she shouted up at Don Juan's astonished grandfather, "is even now hiding the witch in his bedroom. Ask him if this drawing of her shamelessly displaying Satan's own hoof is not *his drawing*. Ask him, child that he is, if she has not put her spell on his body, forcing him to make love to her like a man!"

The old man turned to Don Juan, to Garcia.

"Is this true?" he bellowed, and both stared back at him speechless.

"Excellency, Señor Mendoza asked for his wife to be brought here," said Garcia. "For safety *because* they said she was a witch. It had—had—had . . ." Poor Garcia was going to add the words "to be secret," but he couldn't force them out.

"It's true, Grandfather, that she's in my room now. But a witch! You can't believe—"

"Of course I don't think she's a witch, you idiot. But don't you see it doesn't matter? This is primitive thirteenth-century Spain. Their chief enemy was Mendoza. And they've ruined Mendoza. If he and she don't kill themselves from shame, they'll still have to leave.

You're such a clever boy, and yet you've been used by someone far cleverer. Who? Not Garcia?"

The majordomo let out a shriek of dismay.

"No, no, Grandfather. It was the Englishman. My tutor. He's down there beside the woman with the microphone."

Don Juan leaned over the battlement, pointing out Whitticker to his grandfather. The crowd was quiet, sensing the drama going on up in the tower.

Seeing them from below, the Englishman shouted up to his pupil. "Sorry, Johnny, we're on different sides, you see. I'm no bleeding Froissart. I was a ruddy Trojan horse. This is the missus, by the way. Don't think you'd like her. One of your typical Spanish fanatics. Still, that's the future, so never say I didn't warn—"

"Bring out the witch!" yelled Señora Whitticker in an incongruously cultivated Catalonian accent.

"Bring out the witch!" all the crowd yelled. Except Whitticker, who wore the expression of a man who, out of politeness, is joining in a native war dance but feels rather foolish just the same.

Don Juan felt as if his bladder were going to betray him. His grandfather had turned from the battlement in disgust and had motioned to the bishop that he intended to descend the stair, saying, "I want to question that woman for myself."

There was then a fusillade of guns in the distance, growing louder, and down below the ritual shouts had turned to screams. Don Juan darted forward to look down at the crowd. Something was happening far behind the people choked into the lane. It was making the people behind them push. They were pushing, pushing, in panic, being forced on from behind.

With shrieks of terror the people in the front were propelled forward toward the moat as a piston is pushed up a cylinder. They simply swept over the edge, falling in all kinds of attitudes, some spread-eagled backward, some head first, some finding time to jump.

Don Juan saw Whitticker go, and Mrs. Whitticker beside him, among the first.

"There go the lemming horde," said his grandfather's voice from beside him, and, to his horror, he heard the old man shouting with laughter.

6

In an All-Male World

Speak roughly to your little boy
And beat him when he sneezes
For he can very well enjoy
The pepper when he pleases.

—Lewis Carroll

Afterward Don Juan was to feel that the punishment had
been far too severe for the crime he'd committed. But at the time,
when the sentence was passed and he'd been given a chance of
appeal, it hadn't seemed quite so bad. For his part in the disastrous
events of his confirmation day, he was sent to complete his education
at an English public school, as that perverse race chose to call their
private academies for boys. His grandfather, who had read *Tom
Brown's School Days* in translation, chose Rugby College as an ideal
reformatory. At Rugby, he was reliably informed, there were still cold
baths in winter and frequent canings and other more exotic forms of

corporal punishment to make a man a man. A man among men. On appeal from the duchess, Don Juan was allowed to go to the English public school of his choice, there being a yearbook which listed all these institutions and gave their specialties in sports and, more occasionally, the arts. Leafing through this rather uninformative tome he found a school called Deerhurst College in Buckinghamshire. As was the case everywhere else, sports dominated the curriculum. For instance:

· "Michaelmas Term: Soccer, Field Hockey, the Deerhurst Pit Game, Badminton, Squash, Fives, Fencing (Epée, Foil, and Saber), Boxing, Coursing, Cubbing, Shooting, Falconry, Running, Golf, Rugger can be arranged. . . ."

Much farther down the list of Deerhurst's activities, Don Juan spotted that immediately after mention of "A well-equipped machine shop" came "Dame Serena Partinger, D.B.E., R.A., the distinguished artist, conducts a weekly life class." Don Juan knew it seemed a slight enough thread to *their world,* but he was hooked. They sent him to Deerhurst.

He spent a couple of months in Paris at the house on the Avenue Foch preparing for his new life as an English schoolboy, taking an exam for Deerhurst at the British Consulate General and being sent suitable clothes, on approval, from London's Army and Navy Stores. If anything, these activities were a relief from the cross-questioning of his mother and Henrietta.

"What I don't understand," said Henrietta in one of the endless postmortems they conducted into the 'first communion day fiasco,' "is why the bishop refused to confirm you."

Don Juan looked appealingly at his mother. He really thought he'd explained enough for this, at least, to be obvious. But she was agog to hear his detailed explanation. It was little comfort to him that they thought the whole affair hysterically funny, so that he could hardly get through any rehearsal of it without their dissolving into helpless laughter. He knew that they had already dined out on the story with huge success and were mad for any embellishments he could offer them. They were giggling now as they waited for his answer.

"A hundred and fifty-four people had landed in four feet of muddy water and several were killed by the fall or drowned—" began Don Juan.

"One does see the problem. The Spanish are not a tall race," interjected Henrietta. "But how did that affect the bishop? It was, surely, too early for a requiem Mass. A mass requiem Mass . . ." She dissolved into hysterics again.

"Hush, Henrietta. We're being very wicked, and Juan is right to be shocked at us," said the duchess.

"Shall we say," said her son miserably, "that the bishop found me not to be in a state of grace."

"On account of the adultery?" asked Henrietta, genuinely curious now.

"Couldn't you have made a general confession?" asked his mother.

"But I had to be confirmed *before* I could make a confession. Also, adultery is a serious offense in Spain. Grandfather had to get me out of the country before Mendoza decided, or the state decided—"

"To prosecute *you*, child?" Henrietta was incredulous. "What, at your age, could you have possibly done to the poor woman? A little slap and tickle such as you had with poor Virginie?"

"She was the one who would have been prosecuted! I would have been the chief witness," he almost shouted, for here his burden of guilt was heaviest. "For seducing *me*, a child, a minor. In addition to the adultery, it appears that is classed with some kind of rape in Spain. Seven to ten years in jail you can get for that! And you're forgetting the witchcraft charge. The bishop took that a lot more seriously than you might expect. He insisted on personally examining the birthmark on her tummy—"

"The birthmark in the shape of a hoof," murmured Henrietta. "It is really too delicious. Did he think she'd given herself carnally to Satan?"

The way they treated the matter made him hate himself the more. It would be a long time before Don Juan regretted a seduction. But Isabel had been monstrously wronged by fate because of him. The last he heard was that the bishop had imposed a fearful penance on her. But what it was he had never heard or dared to ask.

It was also some time before he got over Whitticker's death. Being one of the first to fall, the Englishman was drowned beneath the weight of the others. Don Juan received a letter from him the next day. It had been found in his home with a stamp on it ready for posting:

Dear Johnny,

 I don't see why you should ever forgive me for temporarily making a farce out of your life.

But laughter and ridicule are the weapons that are to hand here, and you surely understand that we had to destroy your family's power if we could. You've seen enough to know what is at stake for the wretched people of Andalusia.

The moment I saw the drawings I knew it could be done. That you could be trusted to do the rest. I pushed things along by writing to Mendoza. But you'd have found a way to have her sooner or later. You can't help it. Try not to let the people who see that in you make use of you as I did.

This is your affectionate tutor's last serious advice to Boy Prince.

I hope that even in betraying you I've taught you something useful.

See you on the barricades. "Up the post office," as they say in Ireland.

Whitticker.

Thomas Cook and Son, the British travel agents, was one of the many companies that kept the English preeminent in "service" industries. This admirable company ran a courier and surrogate-father service for parents who, living outside the British Isles and wishing to send their children to English private schools, could conveniently forget about them till the revealed horror of the next school holidays loomed up again and their young returned to them.

Two days before Don Juan was due at Deerhurst, a Major Clifton Barnet, Royal Marines, Ret., appeared at the Avenue Foch to fetch him. He closeted himself with Sylvie in the old nursery and checked the school's list of required clothes. Finding that Sylvie had not been instructed to sew name tapes into each garment, he sat down and helped her.

Meanwhile Don Juan ate his farewell lunch with the duchess and Henrietta in quite high spirits. They had just heard, through the ubiquitous Gabbitas and Thring, who had negotiated Don Juan's entry to Deerhurst, that he had been awarded a scholarship as a result of his examination results. G & B observed, in their letter of congratulations, that while Deerhurst had a special "house" for scholars, the duchess might prefer not to accept the scholarship. In which case, they added, *inter alia*, Mr. Trubshawe's house had a vacancy.

"Always these ambiguities. Do you think they're suggesting that we *don't* accept the scholarship?" the duchess asked Henrietta. "It says I have to send them a telegram."

"Of course you mustn't accept the scholarship 'financially,' darling," said Henrietta, "but they can't come right out and say that. I believe the 'scholars' house' at Eton is a kind of ghetto."

"You mean *Jews?*" The duchess was amazed.

"No, I mean for the clever proles. Not a place to make *friends,*" said Henrietta, whose grandfather had been a penniless fur trapper.

Don Juan paid little attention to this conversation, to his subsequent regret. He had heard nothing good of English food, and the cooks had made him a wholesome, nourishing meal that day. A Mirasol pâté of pork and veal, followed by a *velouté cressonière,* followed by sweetbreads braised in Madeira wine accompanied by artichokes *à la clamant* (with peas). A wholesome Camembert and a good endive salad rounded out the condemned boy's last square meal for some time to come. He was to dream of that repast at Deerhurst as he had dreamed of Mendoza's wife in the castle.

The journey to Deerhurst was entirely without incident. Major Barnet efficiently handled everything, and they collected, before they left Paris, a veritable caravanserai of students bound for Britain. Don Juan spent his time watching women, and when there were no women of interest to watch, he read a book that Henrietta had given him for the journey. He was always asking her about America, and she suggested this book, a collection of articles by a journalist called H. L. Mencken, as a good place for someone interested in her country "to start." It explained both why she didn't live there and why she sometimes longed to go back. In Don Juan, Mr. Mencken inspired a lasting desire to go and see the place for himself.

They stayed overnight in a "children's hotel" in London, and next day Major Barnet delivered Don Juan and his luggage to the school train at Paddington Station, finding his housemaster, Mr. Trubshawe, who said, "Oh, yes. Hullo. Glad you made it," and then seemed to forget about him. Major Barnet gave the boy some pocket money.

"Well, you're a lucky chap," he said in parting. "One of the best schools in the country. They say you can always tell a Henrician anywhere. See you at half-term," said the courier, and was gone before Don Juan could discover what he meant.

Don Juan looked around at the faintly patrician crowd of English parents, inevitably more mothers than fathers, and for the first time gave some thought to the English as people among whom to live. The England their writers such as Smollett, Fielding, Dickens, the Brontës, and Kipling conjured up was rather appealing. Roustabout England, the England of the gallant, humorous poor, romantic England, the English as empire builders. He had never read Austen,

Thackeray, Trollope, Henry James, or Galsworthy, so the people on the railway platform were strangers to him. With their prevailing pink-and-white complexions, with their rather angular faces and pale eyes, long necks, and large, reddish hands they didn't look like the characters he expected to see.

A woman standing near Mr. Trubshawe (perhaps Mrs. Trubshawe?) seemed typical. Her tweed suit was well enough cut, but it could have been designed expressly to hide her figure. Her hair seemed unfashionably neither short nor long, but squeezed into a series of unattractive "rolls." It was a concierge's hair style. And yet, as Don Juan considered her, she might be quite beautiful naked. The color of the hair was corn-blond and clearly her own color. It must curl prettily at the confluence of her marvelously long, well-shaped legs. How sad that she was wearing those mannish shoes and frightful lisle stockings.

It was, as he remembered it later, his last wholly pleasant moment of reverie for a long time.

"Trubshawe's new boys!" a voice nearby proclaimed. "Trubshawe's new boys here!"

A bespectacled youth of about eighteen in a frock coat, winged collar, and white tie, carrying an ebony walking stick under his arm, stood near a carriage door. He summoned them, and when they had gathered, all of them, he ticked off their names on a little list he held discreetly in his hand.

"Now get in. First two compartments. Yes, you can say goodbye to your parents, but hurry. You have a great deal to do," he said.

Once the train had started he handed them each a mimeographed piece of paper. Then he spoke:

"I am Cooper. B. J. C. Cooper. Remember that. I'm the prefect in charge of newbugs this term. God help me. You look a singularly ill-favored bunch. I should think probably the worst we've ever had by the look of you." He laughed humorlessly as he said this. "Before I have to speak to you again, I expect you to have learned what's on the Newbug's Bumph by heart. It's an hour to Maidenhead— that's the school station—so get those snotty little heads down to it."

He left them alone.

The paper consisted of a short résumé of the history of Deerhurst. Its full name was Henry VI's School at Deerhurst, founded for the sons of indigent gentlemen, veterans of the wars in France and Burgundy. There followed a complete list of the school's present ushers (as the masters were called). No one seemed to have fewer than three initials before his name, and most hạd five or more afterward.

Col. P. A. L. Fisher, M.C., D.S.O., M.A. (Cantab), Headmaster. And so on. Don Juan looked in vain for some key to the code of letters that strung out after these names. It was obviously absurd to try to learn all this in an hour, and he intended to say so if Master Hooper made an issue of it. Instead, he tried to sort out the people who would be relevant or interesting to him personally.

R. A. Trubshawe, T.D., M.A. (Oxon), Housemaster, the House by the Pit. And under "Trubshawe's House Prefects" he found that B. J. C. Cooper stood quite low in the order of their seniority. S. St. J. Martin (Captain of Fives) was "head of the house." Don Juan hoped he would be an improvement on Cooper.

While the new boys were studying the paper—and all were so cowed by Cooper's words that they had done nothing else since the train left the station—other, older boys came running down the passage to gape at them and make comments.

"God, they look awful," said one.

"There's a dago and a yid in here, by the look of it," said a red-haired boy, pointing first to Don Juan and then to a boy sitting opposite him. "They're scraping the bottom of the barrel this year."

"Hey, dago, what's your name?" said the red-haired boy, aiming a kick at Don Juan's leg, but missing. Don Juan told him his name.

"Funny name! Even for a foreigner," said the red-haired boy. "Tell us, where are you from, greaser? Father a Maltese brothel keeper?"

Another boy said, "*Cave!* It's Bloodnut and the Poodle!"

The boys crowded around the new boys' compartments at once stopped their baiting while Mr. and Mrs. Trubshawe appeared. Don Juan noticed his bald head and understood the nickname. He greeted these boys by their Christian names, as did she, but neither addressed a word to the new boys.

"Hullo, Nigel, didn't see your father at the station."

"The regiment's gone to Palestine, sir."

"Really? Nasty business, that."

"Reckon the Queens will sort them out, sir."

"Hope to see you on the colts this season, Peter," said Mrs. Trubshawe to one of the others.

And the housemaster and his wife were gone. The baiting then continued until they reached Maidenhead Station. Don Juan wondered whether he had enough money with what Mr. Barnet had given him to take the next train back to London.

As they approached Maidenhead, Cooper reappeared.

"You're damned lucky, you frightful little beasts," he said. "The test of your Newbug's Bumph has been postponed till tomorrow. Now get out. The last one into the bus gets to be *my fag.*"

The ten little boys in the two compartments fell over each other grabbing their raincoats and the pathetic little parcels their mothers had given them to take to school. Don Juan, who was half a head taller than any of them, and the only one with a broken voice, stood aside while they ran to the bus.

"Decided you want to be my fag?" said Cooper, slightly surprised at the size of this thirteen-year-old.

"I haven't the slightest idea what you're talking about," said Don Juan.

"Good God. You're not Irish, are you? You don't look Irish," said Cooper, distracted by Don Juan's slight Irish accent, learned from Tabatha and never quite lost in the time with Whitticker.

"No. I'm Spanish," said Don Juan, looking at him levelly.

"You'd better do all your jacket buttons up. Newbugs aren't allowed to have any buttons undone. One button undone is a first-year privilege. Two second year. Open when you're a senior."

"How childish!" said Don Juan, and walked at his own pace down the corridor, across the platform, and onto the bus. He was aware that Cooper had met something outside his ken, outside the rules of the game he was playing. Looking at his face as they walked side by side, he could see the petulance of a bully nonplussed. He knew he was the wrong size for the hazing that was inflicted on the others. Just because they were little and homesick, they could easily be terrorized. He would be attacked for his olive skin and his dark hair just because he was alone, in a minority, or different. These people had declared their intention to try to humiliate him in every way possible. But he put aside the thought of walking out on it. This his grandfather had meant to be a punishment. Poor Isabel had no choice but to accept the bishop's imposed penance to add to whatever other unhappiness she now suffered. He must prove that he could take this too.

In the next twenty-four hours, he was effectively introduced to the prison in which he was to serve his sentence. The House by the Pit where Mr. Trubshawe's boys lived was a Plantagenet building to which a rudimentary form of plumbing had been introduced some time in the nineteenth century. There were forty-two boys and three toilets unenclosed in any way. Don Juan assumed this was to prevent the juniors in their misery from having the privacy to hang themselves. While the older boys had separate tiny studies, everybody slept in a series of fourteenth-century dormitories without the benefit of any form of heating. The fireplaces had not, he was told, been used since the eighteenth century, when some prefects had playfully roasted a junior to death. It seemed an article of faith to these British, as dear as their hatred of foreigners, that any form of heat where you slept could be fatally debilitating.

Washing was done in two ways. At six o'clock when a bell rang all boys, except prefects, who were deemed clean by virtue of seniority, left their beds, stripped naked, and ran down two flights of stone stairs to take a fifteen-second cold shower, timed by a prefect with a stopwatch. No one seemed to use soap under the shower. Nor was there any pretense that it had any purpose other than its shock value. In winter the first boy down had to break ice from the shower nozzle. Back in the dormitory there was cold water in china bowls on rows of wooden washstands. Here soap was provided.

They then dressed in the clothes prescribed for the day, but normally corduroys and sport coats, and, donning short black academic gowns, left the building for the ten-minute walk to chapel. Since it had occurred to no one in Paris to inquire about the religious denomination of the school, Don Juan now found himself regularly attending Anglican services almost identical, except for the language (less Latin, English instead of Spanish), to those Catholic services he had attended at the castle. He told no one about his Catholicism, and it occurred to no one to ask. In fact, one of his few pleasures in those bleak days was the language of the prayer book and the Authorized Version of the Bible. The felicities of these books alone seemed to him to have justified the English Reformation.

Breakfast, after chapel, was the first of three appalling and inadequate meals provided during the day. It consisted of porridge so thick and lumpy as to require chewing. Bread made in the school bakery tasted of nothing and had the texture of moist flannel. It returned throughout the next two meals. Eggs, scrambled beyond recognition, boiled bullet-hard, or fried in an oil that smelled of axle grease, followed. There was tea and milk. Lunch was nearly always stringy stew followed by boiled rhubarb and powdered custard. The alternatives were worse. Tea (the meal) would consist of American baked beans and jam or potted paste to go with the leftover bread from the first two meals. There was cocoa to drink and, of course, tea.

New boys were given a room that contained ten desk-cum-cupboards. It had no other embellishment whatever, no curtains, no pictures. Here they studied after class. From here they ran to fag for the prefects. While each prefect had his own assigned fag, whose daily duty it was to clean the older boy's study, press his clothes, clean his shoes, make up his fire, and prepare his teatime meal, all fags could be called upon at any time to do some service like fetching their books from a classroom or running an errand.

If the prefect was homosexual, there was nothing to stop him from seducing his fag except the will of the latter. If the fag strenuously objected, he might be excused, for there was almost bound to be another fag who would consent. However, the pressure brought to bear on young boys by this system was very great. The more severe the prefects, the more grateful these children were when they were offered a sudden kindness. Don Juan was assured by everyone that an appeal to Trubshawe would only mean a beating for "sneaking." Very probably from Trubshawe himself, who would be unwilling to believe a boy he had appointed could abuse his power.

Officially, in this school, active homosexuality was frowned upon. In practice it flourished. Semi-official was the "raffle," always held at the end of the second week of the Michaelmas term. The new boys were told of it as if they were whores in an obscure competition. The prettiest boy was transferred to the winner. Cooper, the winner, got the sweet-faced Latimer as the prize.

While all the boys below the rank of prefect could be beaten by any prefect, the housemaster had, in theory, to give his consent. Since the boy who was to be beaten had no right of appeal to the housemaster, and, indeed, never saw him till long after the punishment had been carried out, it was a heavily abused system. The British, a Germanic people, had rules for everything. Pajama bottoms were worn for canings. A three-yard run was the limit for the boy with the cane. Twelve strokes was the maximum. Six were usually enough to make a child howl with agony. No beating on the hands was allowed. Used in British Jesuit schools, it was considered popish and foreign.

Classes and lectures were the only escape a boy had from this intolerable round of discomfort, ugliness, and pain.

From a distance the pile of buildings that made up Deerhurst College was picturesque, even beautiful, if you included the Elizabethan chapel. But inside, the residences were corrosively ugly. Chipped glossy green and brown paint covered the stone walls, down which condensation poured moisture throughout the winter. There were no pictures. Bare light bulbs lit the dormitories and passages. A strong smell of faulty plumbing, disinfectant, and inadequately washed boy hung about the place so that the inmates tendd to seek the outer air, however cold.

In addition to hundreds of initials and names, the new boys had to learn the arcane language peculiar to the school. Some of its origins were clear, others obscure. Don Juan, whose English vocabulary was greater than that of most of his British contemporaries, found it both fascinating and repellent. His fellow students just learned it and accepted it.

Years later when he tried to remember the words, he could recall only the most expressive, nearly all unpleasant, the origins of which he'd come to understand.

Begens:	A lavatory (big ends?).
Bumph:	Paper. From bum paper—lavatories again.
Peach:	Young catamite. From the love song of the Sikhs: "There's a boy across the river/With a bottom like a peach."
Oick:	A lower-class person. From the sound a pig makes.
Budgen:	A lower-class person. Originally "boot john."
To Jew:	To cheat. Anti-Semitic.
Wog:	Wily Oriental Gentleman. "Wogs begin at Calais" was considered a joke. But mainly used for Arabs.
Dago:	Dark-skinned person. All Latins, Greeks, and Levantines.
Greaser:	Jews, wogs, and dagos were all also greasers.
Roundhead:	A circumcised male.
Cavalier:	Uncircumcised male.
Bugger:	Any homosexual.
Camp:	Homosexual characteristics.
Hearty:	An incurable heterosexual.
Tart:	A girl. No better than she ought to be.
Skivvy:	A servant girl.
N.O.C.D.:	Not our class, dear.
To blub:	To cry.

"Fag" did not then mean "homosexual." "Gay" still meant "happy," "jolly."

In their first week, all the things were done to the new boys that "were done to us when we were new boys." The middle group of boys, fifteen years old or so, committed these mild atrocities, and were allowed to do so by the prefects, it being "only fair" that everyone have a chance to join in the tormenting.

The larger boys invaded the new boys' dormitory at night and kidnapped them one by one. One game was to take them and force their heads below the level of the water in the toilet bowl. When their struggles became desperate, the chain was pulled, flushing the toilet and giving them a moment of air till it filled up again. To be held through four flushings was considered "reasonable," five "going too far."

Someone explaining this to Don Juan as he fought to fill his lungs with air after the ordeal said, "Fair do's, d'you see?" and added, "Perhaps it's the sort of thing a foreigner could never understand."

Don Juan discovered that it took a long time to get to know boys from other houses, since he met them only in class or on the soccer field, which in spite of the high-flown list in the yearbook was the only sport he had time for his first year.

It was part of the system that a new boy should make friends and common cause with the other "newbugs" in his house. For the first time in his life, Don Juan found himself spending a good deal of time with other boys of his own age. He was the senior among them by virtue of his scholarship, and their desks and beds were arranged in order of their academic seniority. It was the only privilege he ever saw given to brains while he was there. In fact, he was so far ahead of his fellows academically that the school had been obliged to place him for nearly all subjects in classes inhabited by fifteen- or sixteen-year-olds. But that touched his everyday life at Trubshawe's not at all.

He learned all there was to know about his nine fellow new boys within days, and in spite of his manifest "foreignness" became their leader. He described them in a letter to his mother and Henrietta which he had to submit to Mr. Trubshawe for censorship. It was the first time he had actually sat alone with the housemaster, although he saw him each evening in the refectory at "house prayers." It was also the first time he had heard his Christian name used in a week.

"Sit down, Juan. Hope you're settling in all right, what," said Mr. Trubshawe.

"Sir!" said Don Juan noncommittally, bursting to speak out, but mindful of his grandfather.

"I think you've brought your letter for me to see. We only do this for the first half-term with new boys, what. In case they're unhappy in some way and there's something I can do to help, what."

The "whats" weren't quite questions. Don Juan supposed they meant "D'you see?"

"Oh dear, oh dear, dear, dear. D'you usually write to your mother in French?"

"No, sir, I usually write to her in Spanish. But I'd heard I would have to submit the letter and I thought you might prefer French."

Trubshawe was gazing at the letter, clicking his tongue and occasionally sucking his teeth.

"She has no Latin, I suppose?"

"No, sir."

"No Greek? No, of course not. It'd be modern Greek. No good at all. And of course, no, ah, English, what?"

"Her English is excellent, sir. She went to school here."

"Really, Juan. Then write to the dear lady in English. My own field, as you ought to know, is physics. I should get you to go and translate it. What have you said?"

"Well, I speak of my nine fellow new boys, sir."

"Read it to me. Translate as you go along."

" 'Parsons-Purefoy is a tall boy with huge ears and feet and hands to match. He is much disturbed by his parents' divorce and keeps wondering about circumstances which might bring them together again. I hope you and Henrietta never give me that kind of trouble.

" 'Then there is Caldwell Minor. His brother is a prefect, but apparently it is considered socially unacceptable for them to speak to each other. Caldwell Minor is sturdy, fair and blue-eyed like a Doré drawing of the young Siegfried.

" 'Tebbets wears thin-rimmed glasses on a face which at thirteen and a half already looks fiercely 'entrepreneurial.' He is the only one who does not seem ashamed to have origins in industry. In this case, his father is in the 'beerage,' as they call the *petit-noblesse* whose fortunes are founded on the national drink. He has a passionate interest in motorcycles.

" 'Masters-White-Masters is the first person I have ever met with a triple-barreled name. He says that it is all explained in a yearbook called *Burke's Landed Gentry*, but apparently has never read the entry himself so he has no idea why the Whites had such a passion for the Masters.

" 'Portarlington is a cousin of the Duc de Choiseul and goes to stay at Bercy-le-Duc sometimes in the summer. We speak French and

of things French together, although his accent is appalling. His father
sits in the House of Lords and is, he says, a fascist. I had no idea they
had them here. It appears they dress in Boy Scout trousers and wear
black shirts. He is very upset because his bed is next to Manley-
Cohen.

"'Manley-Cohen is, you will be amused to learn, the son of an
Anglican bishop who leads "the Christian mission to the Jews." He
thinks Portarlington's anti-Semitism quaint and keeps saying that he
thought Fascism was invented to give the educated lower middle class
something to do. He has a beautiful treble voice, and is said to already
be a certain soloist for the choir.

"'Horder is born to be a farmer. He is an entirely red person.
With a thick little body and nails bitten down to the quick. Only his
hair is black and looks as if it had been clipped with shears. Tiny feral
eyes move between rather chapped cheeks, and he is always looking
out of the window, as if he expected nature to do something rash in
his temporary absence.

"'Griffith is Welsh and very sensitive about it. The English tease
the Welsh without ceasing. It's "Taffy is a Welshman, Taffy is a
thief." Do you remember in *Henry V* all that threatening to make
Fluellen, the Welsh officer, eat his leek? He has a Welsh accent,
which he confided in me his parents have sent him here to lose.

"'Latimer is a dormouse. If he could sit and hide in a teapot he
would. As it is, he tries at all times to find protective coloring in the
landscape, hoping not to be noticed. He is the only one of us so far to
have been beaten. He was given six strokes of the cane for putting
boot polish on his prefect's, Cooper's, gray trousers. Clearly he used
the boot brush by mistake for the clothes brush. He cried himself to
sleep and must now eat standing up. He has the face of an anguished
little girl.

"'Lastly, you have this Spaniard, a dago greaser whom they call
Big One. It is a pun on his name and refers, I suppose, to his height.
Tell his grandfather that his solution to the problem of "the affair of
the day of the first communion" seems a just one, but by no means
lenient.'

"I end, sir, by sending my mother my love. May I post it, sir?"
asked Don Juan when he'd finished.

Trubshawe was looking at Don Juan in a rather abstracted way,
as if he hadn't quite heard him finish and was still listening, or,
perhaps, still *not* listening. Actually he was thinking: He's a
handsome devil. Thought he was when I saw him on the soccer field.
Moves well. Beautiful legs. These dagos grow up much too fast. It's

the sun, I suppose. Sort of hothouse effect. But a beautiful boy, this. When I first saw Stephen St. George Martin, he struck me that way. Beautiful boy. Rather like a perfect plant. I'm glad I made him head of the house.

"D'you know anything about chrysanthemums, Juan?" he asked.

"I'm afraid not, sir," said Don Juan, puzzled by this question. "I mean, the imperial flower of Japan, of course."

"I grow them under glass. A lot of work. Usually see them about Christmas."

"That must be an exciting moment, sir. May I post the letter?"

"Good letter, if I may say so. You might add a post script."

"Sir?"

"Tell the duchess we hope that she will find time to visit us one day. One looks forward to meeting her, what."

"Thank you, sir."

So there it was, thought Don Juan. The housemaster is a semi-educated idiot. What else could he be? What had he expected? A sort of Dalai Lama contemplating the spiritual values of Britain behind that green baize door to his study, with the temporal cane kept ever ready in the corner? He was all of a piece with the rest of this prison. Mediocre, philistine, ugly and boring.

The worst past, Don Juan became accustomed to the place up to a point. The point was that he had to find some way he could keep in contact with the outside world. Trubshawe's had a house library, but apart from eight volumes of P. G. Wodehouse, all of which he got through in the first three weeks, there was nothing to read except books by minor British authors called Sapper and Dornford Yates. Don Juan tried them, found them funny in the wrong places and deplorable otherwise.

"That swine Goldstein has got hold of that lovely girl. He's not fit to kiss the hem of her skirt. Damn it, Berry, we've got to do something. Ask Benson to get out the Bentley; I think I've got a plan . . ."

The scholars' house was reputed to have a proper library, but it was out of bounds to others. Indeed, the scholars were treated rather as if their scholarship were a communicable disease. Don Juan met them in class and found them socially indistinguishable from his friends at Trubshawe's, apart from being, naturally, rather cleverer. He planned an orgy of book-buying with Major Barnet at half-term.

Fagging seemed, at first, to be less frightful than he had expected. His prefect, H. A. L. Springer, had been a noted peach in his day, and was still known as Bum Springer because of the way he moved his arse when he walked. He was in the classics sixth and considered the brightest of the prefects, but thought very eccentric because he called himself a socialist. It was when Springer's study door was closed and the prefect lounged on his bed, while Juan swept and polished and made tea and toast, that the latter learned how the power structure of Trubshawe's house worked.

"Speak to me, bright eyes," he would say while Don Juan, having arrived from his own dreadful tea meal, prepared something a little better for Springer. "Are you going to give your old aunt a little something today?"

"What do you have in mind?" Don Juan answered as he always answered.

"Oh, you are a wicked boy. You know what I'm just dying to have you do. I'd order you a whole hamper of goodies from Fortnum and Mason's, caviar, champagne, the lot, if you would. You're quite the best-looking thing to happen around here *ever*, as far as I'm concerned!"

"Springer, please!" said Don Juan.

"I know, I know, you're saving it for those perilous slits. You're an incorrigible hearty. It's written all over you."

"And aren't you being a little unfaithful to Braddock? Head of the school the year before last, wasn't he? Parsons-Purefoy told me, and he got it from an unimpeachable source, if you'll forgive the pun."

"I will. It's quite funny. Stephen Martin, I suppose. Purefoy's his fag. What about beautiful Braddock?"

"He's up at Trinity. You hope to join him for his last year there."

"Stephen's such a gossipy bitch," said Springer vehemently.

"Is *he* camp, too?" Don Juan was surprised. Martin exuded masculine energy and clean-cut virtue.

"Not really, dear. Not like Cooper or me. Of course, he's had this long-standing affair with Bloodnut. Even the Poodle adores him. He'll end up a married queen."

Don Juan, who by this time had the kettle on the boil and two muffins toasting on forks propped up in front of the small coal fire, stopped work long enough to look at Springer and see if he was joking.

"Perhaps I shouldn't have said that. Oh, you're terribly *discreet*, aren't you? I mean, I don't think he ever does anything with Stephen. I should think it's *almost* platonic. Probably just a little stroking now and then. *You* know."

"Is that why Martin is head of the house?"

"Of course. Studies next door to each other at the end of the passage. In and out Martin creeps. I mean he is a creep. He's captain of the creeps. They talk about chrysanthemums and run the house together. I'm sure Stephen sees far more of Bloodnut than the Poodle does. She only gets him in bed, poor old thing."

"I rather fancy her," said Don Juan, smiling.

"That's the most revolting thing I ever heard," said Springer with conviction.

The first of three bells rang for prep, the in-house study period. Don Juan hurried to put out Springer's favorite jams, to carve him some York ham from one of the Fortnum and Mason hampers, make his preferred Darjeeling tea, and slice into oblongs the toasted crumpets which he would dunk into soft-boiled eggs that were already decapitated, and cradled in little Meissen egg cups. Springer liked things just so, he had explained to Don Juan, and his fag, who had probably been better served than anyone in the house, found ironic pleasure in this unaccustomed role.

"You're an old-fashioned treasure, Big One. Give us a kiss before you go off to prep."

"Better go and have a cold shower, Springer. Isn't that the British cure for unrequited love?"

"Beast!" said Springer, already enjoying his high tea. "I suppose I'll have to make do with that sadist Cooper."

"He's taking prep tonight."

"He comes along *later*. You should see what he wears under those crimson pa-jams of his. An appalling leather jock strap and this bicycle chain around his waist. He really is too frightful, but he's all I've got. Poor me!"

Prep was a short interval of escape for Don Juan. Since he was usually able to do his homework in half the time allotted, it gave him blessed leisure to read. He had found Kipling's *Plain Tales from the Hills* in Springer's study and borrowed it. The men in it were characters straight out of his dormitory playing at being grown-ups in British India. Not surprisingly, they spent their lives hovering perilously on the edge of the "reality" precipice. Every now and then one would fall off. He wondered which of his companions would be the first to tumble. Don Juan looked around at his fellow new boys diligently studying in the baleful presence of Cooper, who sat facing them at the prefect's desk fingering his cane, as a nun says her beads, and reading a motorcycle catalogue. Don Juan, whose own childhood had been so desperately unnatural, felt deeply sorry for these companions of his. Molded in this caricature of a classical education, they were being prepared to combine the worst of Athens with the worst of Sparta. A state built on the economic slavery of hundreds of millions of people around the world under the rule of a democracy, wedded to the principle of endurance and physical excellence at the expense of the intellect. And yet, and yet there must be more to these people, far more, and he could not forget Whitticker.

Eventually half-term came, and Major Barnet took him to London for the weekend. They made straight for Hatchard's, the famous bookshop in Piccadilly, and bought ten pounds sterling worth of books, after which Don Juan went to The Children's Hotel, excused Major Barnet, and retired to his room. The major had not considered it his duty to censor what his charge was buying. He could not imagine a Deerhurst duke-to-be buying anything improper, nor Hatchard's selling anything "unsuitable." Wilde, Firbank, Beerbohm, Shaw, Ford, Galsworthy, Strachey, Woolf, and Huxley were on the list Don Juan had gleaned from Springer and his classroom masters as likely to enlighten him further on the complex nature of the English. He could not wait to begin. At one o'clock in the morning, however, his eyes aching, he decided to go for a walk. Since the point of The Children's Hotel was that they checked the coming and going of their young guests, he was obliged to steal out through the empty kitchen and via the back door.

He walked through the gaslit streets of Mayfair, hazy in the perpetual fog then fed by millions of coal-fired chimneys. Like lines of indolent sentries the prostitutes of London patrolled the streets of this, the richest four square miles in the British Empire. Walking in his overcoat, its collar turned up, Don Juan was tall enough to be a potential customer, and he was regaled with the ritual offers as he passed the ladies by. "Hullo, luv, like a nice time?" "Come and take the weight off your feet, handsome."

He looked at them curiously. He had never considered pros- titutes before. There were a few on the Avenue Foch at home in Paris, but he had been too young to even think of them except as an odd phenomenon of adult life. He'd heard that they were usually lesbians, a fact that seemed more understandable to him than it would to many adults. Accustomed to consider each and every woman because each separate one represented for him a separate little universe, a being perhaps waiting to be explored, a person whose heart and mind and body held puzzles Don Juan found it hard to ignore; accustomed to view women in this way, he somehow had never included prostitutes. They were not part of the *territoire des autres* he wished to visit. A group of three of them were standing near a large well-lit building, probably an embassy. He could see their faces from comparatively far, even in the fog. One was tall and blond, teetering on high heels. She looked well fed and forty. Another was short and dark, perhaps French. She wore quite a well-cut tailored outfit. The third stood in their shadow, and he could not easily see her except that she had big, jutting breasts under a blouse of imitation silk. But by now he could hear them. They spoke French to each other with rich Norman accents.

"Hullo, *mes belles*," he said in French as he approached, intrigued to see their reaction. They looked at him, still in shadow, surprised at his greeting, disposed to be welcoming. Then his face was lit by the same light as theirs, and he saw that the one with the big breasts was quite young, her youth presumably her stock in trade, since she was far from good-looking. "My God, but how he is young," said the blonde. "I hope you are not looking for a piece of ass, my child. Because the police in this country . . ." She shook her fingers expressively.

Don Juan found he had not changed his mind at all about them. But as people from the country he thought of as his own, he was anxious to chat. He asked them about the region of Normandy from which they came. It appeared that they had all been born within twenty miles of Rouen. They discussed English cooking, and he amused them hugely telling them about what passed for food at Deerhurst. The older women did the talking and the young one just watched him impassively. He was curious about their all standing together. The blonde explained.

"A John approaches. Maybe he is looking. One can usually tell by the speed they walk. He slows down as you did. Now he has to choose. Perhaps he speaks to Lilliane"—she indicated the short, dark woman. "Being English, the approach is usually shy, embarrassed. A short question: 'How much?' 'Two pounds,' she says. One doesn't want to start at one's lowest price, you understand. 'What do you have in mind, though?' she asks. Sometimes, very rarely, he will say, 'I wish you to do this, in this way or that, et cetera.' For the most part they let us suggest: 'You can have it French or straight, or half and half.' I do not wish to tell a boy like you what these things are exactly, but you can imagine, I daresay. He may say, 'Yes, I will, at this price or that,' or he may hesitate. It is then that we can start to make little offers. For instance, we suggest the excitement of an orgy. 'You could have me and Berthe, here, together,' Lilliane says, 'for only one pound more. You can have a marvelous time. Berthe is only eighteen. Two weeks ago she was still a virgin.'"

"Is that true?" asked Don Juan, laughing.

"No, it is two years since she lost her virginity, and she is actually just seventeen. But that is too young to be admitted."

He had been puzzling about their relationship, and something in the way Berthe looked at Lilliane gave him a clue.

"Mademoiselle is your daughter, madame?" he hazarded, speaking formally as he might in his mother's salon.

"Yes, monsieur," said Lilliane, surprised.

"And you, madame," he said, turning to the tall blonde. "You and Madame Lilliane are *together.*"

They looked at him and all laughed.

"My name is Céleste, monsieur. You are right. One must admit it."

Just then a couple of men were approaching, and Don Juan, anxious not to interfere in their business, said a cordial good night and left them, starting to walk back to his hotel. He had walked only a hundred yards when he heard running feet behind him. He turned to see Berthe, who seemed literally abashed now that she had caught up with him.

"Would you like to come home with me?" She said it quickly.

"But I have no money, just a few shillings," he said.

"No need for money," she said simply.

Don Juan looked at her plain peasant's face with its gappy teeth and slightly acned cheeks disguised by a dusting from the powder puff. It was a more childlike face than that of any of his friends at school, and in its way more innocent, in the sense that the absence of experience of the world or even knowledge is a kind of innocence.

She took his hand and they walked quickly for about half a mile, till the streets were less well lit. They entered a block of apartments built for the deserving artisans of the 1890s, close to Mayfair, where their services would be needed.

Until the front door of the tiny flat had closed behind her she hardly spoke. Then she said:

"Would you like a cup of tea?"

She said it in French, the language in which they all had been talking in the street. But it seemed incongruous enough for Don Juan to laugh.

"Don't you like tea?" she asked.

"Yes, yes I do. Thank you very much," said Don Juan, looking around the apartment after this formal exchange.

It was just two rooms. A living room full of cheap furniture and a few stuffed toys, besides a number of hideous religious pictures of saints and the Virgin Mary in her Roman Catholic incarnation. Beyond it a bedroom with a large bed in it, but little else. He used the bathroom and saw a portable tin bidet, on little metal legs, such as one saw in maids' bedrooms in France.

They drank their tea together sitting on the sofa in the living room. She was as shy as if he had been courting her. He wondered quite where to begin in this, his first encounter with a female who sought him rather than the other way around.

"Have you been with a girl before?" she asked.

"Yes, oh yes," said Don Juan, laughing.

"You're lying. You're too young," she said.

"Is your mother joining us?" he asked.

She looked as if he had hit her.

"You *want* her?"

"No. But I wanted to know if we are going to be alone."

"Yes. Quite alone."

She got up and went to the bedroom and got out of her clothes, put on a robe, and came back to him.

"What would you like?" she asked.

"I'm not sure."

"It's your first time. I told you," she said triumphantly, and seemed pleased.

"All right," he said. "In a way that's true."

Instantly she smiled. It was a charming smile. True, it showed a little too much of her gapped teeth, but it made him aware of her eyes, which were nicely spaced and suddenly, strangely trusting. She acted now like a bossy little girl who had, for the first time in her life, been allowed to organize the games at a party.

"First you must let me undress you," she said.

He stood for her to approach him. Touched and, at last, attracted by her earnestness, by her unexplained happiness, he stooped to kiss her lips. She dodged him neatly, but gave him a coquettish smile.

"That comes later, monsieur," she said.

"My name is Juan, Berthe. Won't you call me that?"

"If you wish it," she said, and smiled at him again.

She had taken off his overcoat and jacket and started to undo his shirt when she found him watching her face intently. She looked up squarely into his eyes. She found his face marvelously beautiful. In the gaslight while he was talking to her mother and Big Céleste, she had examined his face. Never had she seen someone she actually wanted to be alone with before. Someone fresh and beautiful and with no experience of "the game." Because of the circumstances of her life, it had been impossible for her to be attracted by men. They were work and money, and for her mother, very rarely, they represented a little excitement or perhaps amusement. But for her, never.

"Why did you ask if my mother was joining us?" she asked, suddenly unsure of herself.

"I wanted to be alone with you," said Don Juan truthfully, in that he certainly had wanted nothing from Lilliane.

"D'you want to know how it works with us, her and me?" she asked.

"Tell me."

"We bring a John back here. She makes him pay for both of us. She says I am her young friend. Then she sells him the *pièce de théâtre* that we offer. I am to be the *bon bouche,* what the English call the 'king's lick,' for the jam left on the spoon. Maman undresses the John. Herself she undresses just down to her stays, for she is no longer young. But she is very skilled. She has creams and lotions, and she kneels by the bed and arouses the John. Then I come into the room entirely undressed, and I lie there. I do nothing. Maman has finished with him, and he turns to me. All the time she is saying, 'She is so young, so innocent, two weeks ago she was in a convent.' To him I speak no English. In French I say, *'Mon dieu! Quel horreur!'* And if Maman tells me to I cross myself. I look at the ceiling. It is always soon over."

"I see."

"I never bring anyone here by myself."

"Thank you," said Don Juan. "Are you going to play your mother's role? Or can we just be *us?"*

"As you wish," she said.

"How about as we both wish?"

"Then it is right that I undress you." The bossy little girl at the tea party spoke again.

"Good, and it is right that I kiss you from time to time while you do it."

They looked at each other. He saw the most vulnerable of girls, knowing that she was without defenses since she was without experience of emotion. She saw only his beauty and the kindness and the gentleness in his eyes, the softness of his mouth. The chameleon, the natural lover of women, in Don Juan knew instinctively that sensuality would scare her if it came too early, and that, with her, there might never be a time for passion.

She who had shut out of her mind so many bodies, muscular bodies, pale stringy bodies, fat hirsute bodies, white bodies, black bodies, clean bodies, perfumed bodies, and smelly bodies, unpacked this, her special present to herself, in a kind of awe.

Out of confusion at her emotion, she talked: "Maman is staying with Céleste tonight. She often does, but, of course, they have to have separate apartments." His shoulders are wide and perfectly smooth, she thought. He is the palest olive color, like our men from the Midi in France. His chest is hard and broad, and the nipples are so small, so neat and pink. His hips are wonderfully narrow. It is all quite beautiful, as I knew it would be.

In the night that followed, she tried to do what she had seen her mother do. She imagined that she had snared a young saint in her net and that she must anoint him and serve him as his beauty and his sanctity deserved. Not even under the influence of Don Juan's kindness could she imagine that he felt an iota of the emotion she felt for him. So she would not let him be the lover, only the loved, and because he only half-desired her, he was marvelously content as she added her own delight and desire to her mother's considerable lexicon of "tricks."

He awoke at dawn to see her walking naked from the bed to the window to let in a cat from the fire escape outside. He looked at her back as she stretched up to close the window again, and watched the dimples distend above her broad, firm buttocks. He saw her turn, holding the cat against her large, too large breasts, and then he watched her loins as she moved, and, for the first time with her, knew unalloyed desire.

He stretched out and pulled her gently toward him.

"Again? You've come so many times," she whispered as she dropped the cat to the floor.

Now he kissed her, without another word, finding her at last quiescent, as people are in the hours at dawn. Now he found ways to ignite her, and she, still happy with the knowledge of how she had served her saint, consented to be served, laid down all the defenses wrought by too much self-knowledge, found feeling where before there had been fear, and suddenly, shouting, gave up her hold on any reality except his possession of her. Don Juan heard that shout and felt it coursing back from deep inside her to tintinnabulate inside his brain.

How ineffably good to be he!

The second half of the Michaelmas term at Deerhurst found Don

Juan growing steadily in confidence. He had decided that if what these people admired was sporting prowess, it was a pity not to use the advantage of a good physique and a naturally well-coodinated body. On the soccer field he made the "colts eleven" with ease. He was a fast dribbler and a good kicker, with excellent control of the ball. He grasped at once the necessity of being able to place the ball accurately when kicking a pass, and he was as fast as anyone in the school in the thirteen-to-fifteen age bracket. He even played wing on the Trubshawe house team once, promoted from reserve because of another's injury, and was congratulated by Mrs. Trubshawe as he came off the field.

"Jolly good, Juan. Did you play in Spain at all?"

"No, Mrs. Trubshawe."

"I suppose they do play in Spain. Or is it just bullfighting?"

"They do. But bullfighting is still more popular. Have you ever watched a bullfight?"

"I couldn't. Those poor horses."

"But the bull. What about the bull?"

He thought she saw in her mind's eye the swinging balls where the Spanish believe masculine courage is stored, that it was in woman's nature to be excited to see male challenge male to the death.

"It seems a little different with the bull," she said, sensing, with a mixture of mild alarm and astonishment, that this boy was looking at her and *considering* her as a woman, considering her woman's thoughts. To her surprise she found a faint and unfamiliar murmur in her body as she looked back at him and turned the talk to football once again. What an amazingly beautiful male face he had. Its contours already hardening. The hair that seemed to *spring* from his head into those curls. She did so hope he wouldn't join the "camp group," as she thought of them. So often the best-looking boys did!

As is so often the case with a new schedule that is imposed upon a person, it can seem onerous and intolerable until he has had time to subject it to analysis, to the kind of natural time-and-motion study that people impose on their work when they are trying to find space for leisure. During the second half of the Michaelmas term Don Juan had organized his life so that it was possible to look around outside Trubshawe's house to see what, if anything, Deerhurst had to offer. Dame Serena's life class, the bait which had made him choose this particular prison in which to serve his sentence, was at last accessible.

He found that it occurred in a gothic cottage called the Art

School on Sunday afternoons from two till four. Although many prefects kept their fags busy at that time, Don Juan prevailed on Springer to excuse him. Dame Serena, a woman of about fifty, looked more like a caricature of a fortune-telling gypsy than Don Juan would have thought safe for her if she didn't want people offering to cross her palm with silver. He heard that she had spent much of her life trailing along after the raggle-taggle gypsies and she painted nobody else, unless one included their horses. Usually the women were portrayed bare to the waist, had snarls on their faces and remarkably cheeky little tits. Don Juan was told that Deerhurst had obtained Dame Serena's occasional services in return for allowing her to graze her horses, and quite often her gypsies, on the college's ample pastures. She lived in a cottage nearby.

When he arrived to sign on for her course, he found six boys, of assorted ages, drawing the school gym sergeant in a muscular pose. Dame Serena took one look at Don Juan and said, "What a head. What carriage you have, bucko. D'you ride?"

"Yes, I ride, Dame Serena," said Don Juan politely, faintly embarrassed by her personal remarks.

"Got any drawings with you?"

"Nothing, I'm afraid."

"Afraid, eh? Pity you've picked up that dreadful English phrase. I call us the 'sorry people.' Terribly sorry. Dreadfully afraid. Cut it out, bucko. The language doesn't call for it, so you don't need it. Try drawing *me* as I correct the others' work. If I like your drawing I'll tell you what I can teach you."

Don Juan, as always, saw the woman inside the clothes, and that was how he drew Dame Serena. Under her bandanna, her weathered face, handsome, with its prominent bones, the skin a little stretched where the sun had bleached it, the hazel eyes squinting slightly as if in perpetual sunlight. Below, the woman's sloping shoulders were held well back to counterbalance the thrust of the heavy breasts. A thickening waist still gave little hint of producing too much belly, and wide hips were supported by what were still a good pair of legs. Her arms were as weathered as her face, and her hands ended in stubby, abbreviated fingers. She moved with the fluidity of a natural rider. He drew her three times in twenty minutes, and had time enough to rough in her clothes and hachure in their texture a bit before she arrived to look over his shoulder.

"Oh, bucko, you and I are going to be friends. But for the next year you're going to hate me. You'll have to start with plaster casts. I'll tell you one thing, though. Your line is as good now as it will ever be. Rowlandson would have praised that line. It's your grasp of anatomy that's still at fault. But we'll get to that."

"You mean I can't start drawing from life right away?" Don Juan was disappointed.

"Listen, you see my body through my clothes. Excellent. But you must also learn to look at a person's muscles under their skin. And then again, the bones on which those muscles are strung. That I can teach you. The plaster casts I want you to draw are essentially physical-relief maps of how the muscles are placed in relation to each other."

Don Juan enrolled.

He no longer had to submit his letters home to censorship, and he wrote both to his mother and to his grandfather telling them most of the truth about Deerhurst. He complained, however, only about the food, which they expected. From then on, occasional food packages arrived containing somewhat impractical notions of his mother's, like caviar and truffles. His grandfather wrote back giving him the news of his father—nothing had changed—and telling him that he and Juan March, another industrialist, were certain that there would eventually have to be a military government in Spain. Don Juan guessed that they planned to help install it.

In one of the many rituals dear to everyone at the school, the new boys were asked to tea with the Trubshawes, two by two. The housemaster and his wife lived in a building that was an extension of the House by the Pit, joined to it at Mr. Trubshawe's study, which had unique access to both.

Don Juan went with Portarlington. They knocked at the appointed hour on Mr. Trubshawe's door, and from the moment he opened it and ushered them through into his house, everybody pretended that the two boys were not inmates of the prison but rather social acquaintances who were more or less welcome.

"Ah, Juan, Percy, good to see you. I think Verena is ready for us," said Trubshawe.

They went through to a drawing room of stultifying gentility, with pictures of dogs on the walls and a large number of live canines of various breeds all over the furniture. They were introduced to Mrs. Trubshawe as if they had never met.

Portarlington at once spoke to the dogs and about them, and clearly made an excellent impression on both the animals and their owners. Don Juan was left to praise the sponge cake when it appeared, which he was able to do most sincerely.

The conversation turned to the boys' parents. Don Juan thought wryly, as the tortuous conversation proceeded, how tiresome the modern trend toward divorce and separation among parents must be to housemasters and their lady wives.

"What is your father interested in this session, Percy?" asked Mr. Trubshawe. "I understand he's very active in the upper house?"

"Palestine, sir. He thinks we should send all the Jews there."

"Indeed, how interesting, like Mr. Hitler," said Mrs. Trubshawe, as if sixpence in the income tax were being discussed.

"No, Verena, Mr. Hitler wants to send all his Jews *here*," said her husband.

The Trubshawes and Portarlington laughed loud at this, as loud as it is considered genteel to laugh in such circles in England.

"Very good, sir!" said Portarlington. "I must remember that one, to tell my father."

"I saw a picture of him in the paper last week with, I think, your mother, and Sir Oswald Mosley," said Mrs. Trubshawe, including everyone in her conversation, as a good hostess should. "Juan, they were doing something terribly brave, I thought. They were marching into the slums, where the Jews and the dockers have been giving all that trouble."

"Oh, that wasn't Mummy with Daddy," said Portarlington. "That's his new one. Mummy's raising pigs on Offa."

"Where's Offa?" asked Don Juan, mildly interested.

"Inner Hebrides. You're going to have to bone up on your British geog, Big One," said Portarlington.

"Big One?" said Mrs. Trubshawe. "Is that your nickname, Juan? You certainly are very, very big for your age. I didn't realize Spaniards could be so tall."

"My grandfather is six foot six," said Don Juan. "As a matter of interest, are you all Fascists?"

"Oh, dear, dear, dear, dear," said Mr. Trubshawe. "Juan, in England we never discuss people's politics."

"I see," said Don Juan.

"Or religion," added Mrs. Trubshawe, being pleasantly informative. "I mean, you said how nice the cake was, which was very sweet of you. But we never, I mean never, talk about food. It's like making a personal remark."

"I see," said Don Juan, wondering what they *did* talk about.

"As a foreigner, how could you have known?" added Portarlington, for he liked Don Juan and wanted to be supportive.

Don Juan was sitting next to Mrs. Trubshawe on the sofa. He felt now even more than he had on the football field an awareness of her body. He noticed her gently powdered smell and marveled at the skin of her cheeks; like faintly brushed peaches they had a kind of luster that came, he supposed, from the constant application of cold, damp air in this frightful climate. She, in turn, was, to her surprise, conscious of the body of this foreign boy sitting next to her with his outrageous eyes watching her face. She, who was never conscious of people's bodies. Never if she could help it.

"Does the duke often have time to leave Spain?" Mr. Trubshawe was asking of Don Juan.

"Never," said Don Juan.

"Big estate, I imagine. Keeps him terribly busy. I do see they have had a little bother with the workers over there lately, too. It's the same everywhere. No one is satisfied these days."

"No, they certainly aren't," said Don Juan, grimly thinking of conditions in Trubshawe's house.

"I hear your mother lives in Paris," said Mrs. Trubshawe. "How can she bear the noise? Those taxis."

"Paris quite suits my mother. Henrietta—she's my mother's lover—always says that any long absence from Paris makes them increasingly desperate, like fishes out of water."

The silence that followed this remark was soon displaced by a determined prattle, intended to preclude Don Juan from having a chance to say anything further.

"Honestly, Big One," said Portarlington as they reemerged into their prison and ran down the passage to prep. "You are batty. How can your mother's lover be a woman? Anyway, you can't talk about sex at a tea party. The lavatory is where we talk about that kind of thing here."

Occasionally there were school holidays. The Ascension of the Blessed Virgin Mary (or the B.V.M., as she was known on the school calendar) was one of them. Don Juan was invited by Parsons-Purefoy to accompany him on a long walking tour of nearby parish churches in pursuit of his hobby, which was brass rubbing. The English boy understood the architectural history of these buildings. Don Juan liked the way he greeted each church they came upon as he himself might greet the sight of a beautiful woman.

"By George, Big One, look at that clerestory. Isn't it magnificent? You can see from the sanctuary that the nave started off being Norman. And that reredos is very fine, too, don't you think?"

Don Juan made sketches of the churches while Parsons-Purefoy searched the floors for brasses. His enthusiasm for the search and his delight at his finds never faltered.

"Oh, wizard show!" he would shout. "You've got to come and look at this one. D'you see, the boy children and the girl children all separated like that? The girls are usually on their mother's side, the boys on their father's. D'you think they made a mistake? I've never seen that before. How wonderful if it's unique and I've discovered it!"

Don Juan looked down at the formalized drawing-in-brass of an Elizabethan knight and his lady, both in attitudes of prayer, their adult and younger children in miniature rows beside them. Frantically excited, Parsons-Purefoy was unrolling the paper he had brought with him over the brass and getting to work with a lump of heelball to trace the image.

"I'm afraid it may have been rather boring for you as a foreigner," said Parsons-Purefoy as they hurried back for the evening chapel service in honor of the B.V.M. "But to us, I mean to me, those churches are our whole history. Their records are the most reliable evidence we have of who we are, and they were built so lovingly, you can tell; when people *really* lived their lives by the church bells and their feast days, they felt they had to put together the most beautiful stone . . ." He paused, searching for a word.

"Stone *inspiration* of how they felt?" ventured Don Juan.

"Yes, yes, something like that." Parsons-Purefoy's eyes shone. It was wonderful to have found someone who shared his pleasure. He had guessed Big One wouldn't scoff.

"That was fun today. I almost forgot all about this frightful place," said Don Juan as they approached Deerhurst.

"Do you hate it that much?" asked Parsons-Purefoy.

"Don't you?" asked Don Juan.

"Yes, I do. But when you think what it must have been like in the trenches, we're pretty lucky, I suppose. That's what my mother said. Dad was in the trenches," said Parsons-Purefoy. Don Juan laughed out loud.

"I wonder if it has occurred to your mother that your father had this *and* the trenches," he said.

"Rupert Brooke had both, and look what beautiful poetry he wrote. I mean, I think 'There is some corner of a foreign field that is forever England' is such a wizard poem. That's how I'd feel if I had to die abroad."

Don Juan shivered. "Let's hope you never have to."

A week later Don Juan and Griffith and Masters-White-Masters were washing up in the fags' pantry. Suddenly Griffith stopped what he was doing and was very still, listening.

"Hey, Big One. M.W.M. D'you hear that?" he said in his still-

Welsh intonation that Don Juan found rather attractive.

Don Juan listened. Some girls' voices were singing in a foreign tongue. They were pretty, clear voices, descanting as if they had been trained for a choir.

"Girls. Where the hell?" asked Don Juan, fascinated to think there were girls in the House by the Pit and he had never seen them.

"They're singing Welsh. I've heard them before. They work in the kitchen," said Griffith.

Together Don Juan and Griffith forced open the normally closed pantry window, which was of frosted glass, and found themselves looking straight across an area into the house kitchen. Two dark-haired girls in white overalls were scouring pans and singing as they worked.

"But they're no older than we are," said Don Juan, rather surprised.

"School-leaving age is fourteen for the oicks, y'know," said Masters-White-Masters.

"D'you know the song?" asked Don Juan of Griffith.

"Yes. It's a song from the valleys." He repeated the lines.

"Let's sing it to attract their attention," said Don Juan.

"What if someone catches us?" asked Griffith.

"What if they catch us? It's not a crime," said Don Juan.

"All right," said Griffith.

"I'm not going to sing in bloody Welsh," said Masters-White-Masters. "You must be joking!"

"Just a minute," said Don Juan. "Mine's going to be the one on the right, the one with the snub nose."

"You wouldn't *touch* one of those Welsh skivvies, would you?" Masters-White-Masters was appalled.

"If I'd known they were there, I would. Where do they sleep?" asked Don Juan.

"A bit N.O.C.D., isn't it? Asking where the skivvies sleep?" said Masters-White-Masters.

But Griffith had started singing, and Don Juan joined in.

The girls heard them almost at once and looked across the area, where the boys' faces were somewhat obscured by the steam from the washing-up water. The snub-nosed girl opened the kitchen window.

"So who's the Welshman?" she called quietly. It was clearly against her rules to talk to the boys. Her accent, to Don Juan's ears, was most musically, prettily Welsh.

"I am," said Griffith shyly.

"And I'm learning the language," said Don Juan. "What are your names?"

"I'm Blodwen. She's Gwynneth," said Blodwen.

At which both Don Juan and Griffith let out shouts of pain and somebody closed the window, leaving Blodwen and Gwynneth alone in their kitchen again.

The three new boys turned to face Cooper, who had taken a cut at the back of their legs with his cane. They had forgotten that his study was across the passage from the pantry.

"You know it's strictly against school rules to talk to skivvies. Not house rules, school rules. You could get a capital beating for this," said Cooper, his face reddening. "But I suggest you accept my punishment."

"I didn't know it was against any rules," said Don Juan.

"Ignorance of the rules is no excuse," said Cooper grimly. "Well?"

"What's a capital beating?" asked Don Juan.

"Junior common room. Your head goes under the common-room table. All twelve school prefects get a ten-foot run at you. I think you'd better accept my punishment." Cooper got redder and redder.

"All right, Cooper," said Griffith.

"I didn't do anything," said Masters-White-Masters. "It was them."

"If you aren't careful you'll get twelve for sneaking," said Cooper.

"It's true. He didn't want anything to do with it," said Don Juan.

"D'you accept my punishment?" asked Cooper.

"Yes, Cooper," said Masters-White-Masters, on the edge of tears. "But it's not fair."

"Right, *twelve* for you," said Cooper.

"I'll take the capital beating, because I don't believe you," said Don Juan.

"I'll see you in your dormitory tonight," said Cooper, as if he hadn't heard Don Juan's last words.

The dormitory had been the scene of innumerable beatings since the beginning of term. Three strokes with the gym shoe was usual. Six strokes of the cane had been awarded to everybody at least once. No one yet had been given twelve. At least half of all the beatings had been given by Cooper, whose special preserve was the discipline of the new boys. As the term had gone on, Don Juan had noticed that his demeanor when he beat a boy was becoming more and more frenetic and vicious. His normally pale face would become quite lividly red as each stroke went in. Evidence of the efficacy of his work with shoe and rod could be seen at shower time, when the pale bottoms of the British boys showed a crisscross of red wheals. It was Portarlington who pointed out that on Don Juan's bottom the stripes were blue and slightly brown.

At each beating, whether of himself or one of the other boys, Don Juan always felt on the edge of total rebellion. Try as he would to think that these brutalities were what his grandfather had in mind for him to bear, he could not get over his revulsion for, his growing hatred of, the smug ignoramuses who presided over this degrading institution.

They were in their pajamas and getting into bed when Cooper arrived. He was wearing his winged collar and white tie and held under his arm the black silver-tipped walking stick Don Juan had last seen him carry at the station on the first day of school. Part of the technique of the beatings at Deerhurst was speed. The victims were given little time for thought once the cane arrived.

"Griffith!" shouted Cooper, pointing to the "beating table," so called because it was under it that the victim placed his head and was forced to straighten his knees. Its other function was to hold the boys' brushes and combs.

Taking far more than the statutory three yards, Cooper swung at the bending Griffith six times. A purple-faced Griffith ran to the lavatory. The refuge of that semi-private place was allowed for the victim to collect himself and be spared the shame of being seen to "blub."

"Masters-White-Masters!" shouted Cooper.

Don Juan liked this boy less than any of his fellows, but he watched him with pity and resentment on his behalf. This child, weaned onto snobbery and prejudice with the withdrawal of his mother's milk, was quite white with fear. Cooper had probably sensed the coward in him and got great pleasure from punishing him excessively as a result.

"Straighten your knees, damn you!" yelled Cooper at the trembling boy. On the eighth blow Masters-White-Masters emptied his bladder. Cooper, whose face was a blur of frenzied concentration, his veins standing out in his neck and temples, continued to twelve without noticing the trickling flood at his feet till he had finished.

"Oh, my God! You filthy little beast!" Cooper shouted at the poor boy, who stood now stooped and sobbing. "Go and get a mop and clean this up!" Then he looked over to Don Juan.

"The housemaster will see you in his study! Now! Latimer!" he said to his fag. "You left some work undone in my study. Get down there and finish it."

Don Juan went downstairs and along the passage and knocked at the housemaster's door.

"Come in," said Trubshawe's voice. Don Juan went in. Trubshawe had his cane in his hand already. "Bend down," he said. Don Juan bent. Trubshawe gave him six cuts of the cane. "Now get out," he said. Don Juan got out.

Don Juan had the feeling of intense burning in both his buttocks and his face and an after-pain that made him wince as he walked back along the passage. He stopped outside Springer's study door and opened it.

"Can I come in?" asked Don Juan.

"Yes, but close the door quickly behind you. What do you want?" There was not a trace of Springer's usual camp in his voice. And he clearly knew about the beating.

"Is this entire place insane?" asked Don Juan. "Or am I the mad one?" He was so angry that he could scarcely speak, and while there were tears in his eyes, they were tears of humiliation.

"We're mad, angel. Not you. But what can we do? If we have the imagination to see the madness and badness of it all, we don't have the courage to fight it."

"I want you to come with me to the headmaster tomorrow."

"Because of Cooper?"

"Yes."

"Angel, I can't do that. I'll talk to Cooper if you like. I know he's getting more and more manic. But Trubshawe will never, never go against a prefect. The headmaster would *never* see us. And it would *ruin* me here. My parents expect me to go up to the varsity from Deerhurst, and I owe it to them to do so. What's that?"

From Cooper's study next door came a repeated whimpering cry.

"Is he beating Latimer again? Why isn't Latimer in bed?" asked Springer.

"He had to come down to finish off something he hadn't done, poor little thing," said Don Juan.

"Wait here a minute," said Springer, and walked fast from his study into the passage, flinging open Cooper's door.

Don Juan heard Cooper's furious voice. "What the hell do you want? Feeling jealous?"

But Springer remained in the passage. "Stay right where you are, Latimer," he said.

"Stephen!" he called loudly down the hallway.

Don Juan heard Stephen Martin's door open. "Yes?" came his voice.

"Come here a minute," said Springer.

"You bastard, Springer!" shouted Cooper. "You vengeful little queen! D'you think we don't know what you get that little dago to do with you?"

Don Juan could hear Latimer's steady sobbing now. Stephen Martin had passed Springer's door and was looking into Cooper's study.

"Are you all right, Latimer?" asked Martin's voice.

Don Juan could hear no reply.

"Then pull up your pajamas and cut off up to bed," said Martin.

"And keep your mouth shut, if you know what's good for you," said Cooper.

Springer said, "I think we'd better go and discuss this with Bloodnut."

"Oh, come off it," said Martin. "I've got a rather good bottle of wine open. Come on, both of you. The children are all in beddy-byes. It's time for us to relax."

It was the leader of the pack speaking. Diplomatic, confident that everyone would follow his line.

"Why did you have to hurt the poor little beast so?" Springer was saying to Cooper as they walked down the passage. Don Juan was grateful, at least, that his escape was being covered. When he heard Martin's study door close he went out into the passage and started to run.

Up in the dormitory he found Latimer buried under his covers. Masters-White-Masters was lying in his bed, crying and hiccuping his sense of injustice and resentment. Don Juan walked straight over to Latimer's bed and gently pulled back the covers to talk to the steadily crying child.

"What did he do? Did he beat you again?" asked Don Juan.

Latimer shook his head.

"Tell me. I'm going to the headmaster tomorrow."

Latimer looked terrified.

"I won't use your name, if you don't want me to. I promise. Do you trust me?"

"The others are listening," said Latimer.

"So they are. But they won't tell, either. Will you?" Don Juan asked the others loudly. The others all gave voice to their agreement.

"Well, he makes me do all sorts of things. But he hardly beats me anymore. So I don't mind. I mean I don't mind at all. He can be terribly nice, Cooper can. You'd be surprised. But tonight he was in a kind of state . . ."

The boy stopped talking for an instant. Then he brought out one of his hands from under the covers and gave a little squeak of fear. Don Juan saw that it was stained with blood. "You'd better go to Matron," he said, speaking of the wizened old female who gave them cod-liver oil every day and to whom they went if they felt ill.

"But I can't. What will I say?"

"Tell her you've been raped," said Juan quietly. "I'll go with you."

But the child refused to go.

"Is there *anyone* here who likes this school?" asked Don Juan. But he knew the answer. They'd talked about it often enough. There was a predictable silence.

"No one. But you're stuck with it. As I am," said Don Juan. "But has it occurred to you that if we all stood together and refused to be beaten, there's damn little they could do about it?"

"But they'd pick us off one by one," said Manley-Cohen. "As they did you and Latimer tonight."

"That's true," said Don Juan. "What we need to do is soften them up in advance. Make them think it's not worth it. In my country we invented the guerrilla war. That's how we threw Napoleon out of Spain."

"I thought we did that," grunted little Horder, who was seldom heard from. "The duke of Wellington?" he murmured, wondering if he'd got the right war.

"Oh, shut up, Horder. What does it matter? A guerrilla war is a great idea," said Caldwell Minor. "And I'll tell you just how to get at that bloody brother of mine. Burn his asinine stamp collection and all his leering pin-up girls in his study fire. Each of us could do something like that."

"But good God, they'd kill us all the next day," said Masters-White-Masters.

"It would be a showdown," said Don Juan. "Like a strike. But if they couldn't blame any one more or less than the others, they'd have two alternatives: to negotiate with us, or expel the lot of us. That would be a hard thing for Trubshawe to do, and as a result he'd almost certainly lose this house. I'm still going to see the headmaster tomorrow. Horder, I might need your help."

"Me?" Horder was much surprised.

"What would destroy chrysanthemums? Which wouldn't be too easy to trace."

The dormitory went to sleep that night smiling at Horder's five different foolproof ways of killing chrysanthemums stone dead. Breaking into the glass house and peeing in all the pots was everybody's favorite.

Next day, on the way back from afternoon class, Don Juan stopped at the headmaster's residence. It was the day before the Deerhurst pit game (a sixteenth-century ball game played in a muddy pit), and everyone was watching the ludicrous rehearsal for its entertainment value. The Beak (as the headmaster was known) had a small secretariat that functioned in two front rooms of his house.

His secretary seemed surprised to hear a *boy* ask to see the headmaster.

"You have to have a chit from your housemaster and arrange an appointment. What's your name?"

But even as Don Juan was giving his name, knowing that the whole idea of seeing the Beak was, probably, as a result useless, the man himself came into the office and saw Don Juan.

"Who are you?" he asked, and on being told, said, "Come in, come in!" and, to Don Juan's amazement, shook him by the hand.

They went into a drawing room cum study of some size. The furnishings were more comfortable than elegant, but Don Juan noticed that the pictures were good, if you liked the contemporary British School. There was a de László of a beautiful woman over the chimney piece, a person in mauve and violet with that marvelous flesh coloring which is the real glory of Englishwomen.

The headmaster followed Don Juan's gaze. "My wife," he said. "I've heard from Dame Serena that you yourself have real talent," he added. With which he introduced his other pictures. There was an Augustus John of himself in an open shirt, holding an ax. Don Juan looked from painting to subject approvingly. The slightly bull head of a physical man who was nevertheless a dandy. The choice of pose was an almost transparent comment on the headmaster's evident narcissism. He had a magnificent torso, which his perfect tailoring and John's revealed flesh made equally clear. There were a Carrington sketch of Keynes, an Alfred Munnings of horses fretting for the start at Newmarket, and some woodcuts of artisans at work by William Morris.

Don Juan was offered a chair to sit in and some tea or a glass of sherry "if it isn't too early for you to sip at a thimbleful of your national drink?"

Don Juan thanked him and asked for "fizzy lemonade, a nursery taste I don't ever expect to grow out of"—he said it just a little grandly, finding his host's ironical style infectious.

"Happily for you, my daughter drinks it," said the headmaster, rummaging in his drink cupboard. "Now, before you tell me the reason for this visit, there is something I have to say to you. At least three of the ushers who teach you have mentioned you to me, speaking very favorably. A really good scholarship to a first-class Oxbridge college seems on the cards for you if you keep at it. Secondly, I hear from Trubshawe that you're the most promising new footballer his house has had in years. I will make no promises, but the life of a school prefect here can be very pleasant. What you are about to tell me, I suspect, may not be pleasant."

The gloved hand, thought Don Juan. I wonder, can I trust him? But not much point in being here if I don't.

He told his story as clearly and briefly as he could, benefiting from the fact that he had been rehearsing it all day, and he contrived not to mention a single name. He made of Trubshawe's house a neat parallel to a city-state reigned over by a fairly benevolent but negligent tyrant, the housemaster, who ruled through an oligarchy, the prefects, who maintained their privilege by the systematic terrorizing and exploitation of the house's proletariat, the fags.

"Forgive me for interrupting you," said the headmaster. "But can you see *no* virtue in the system? Because if you can't, I shall think the less of you."

"I know the 'advertised' advantage is that if a person knows what it is like to be exploited, then he will think twice about doing it to other people."

"Quite an important 'advantage,' wouldn't you say, for an oligarchal class that is being sent abroad to govern five hundred million people?"

"But surely, sir, my experience at Trubshawe's house demonstrates the exact reverse. This little oligarchy seems to be saying, 'I have been exploited, ergo, I will exploit!'"

"They should say, 'I have learned a lesson in the responsibility of power. I will never forget it,'" said the headmaster.

"Isn't that rather hoping for the best in human nature, sir?"

"Good heavens, no. I'm a firm believer in original sin. It is hard to imagine a schoolmaster who could think otherwise. You are forgetting the figure you call the negligent tyrant and whom I refer to as a benevolent despot. He is the key to this thing. His job it is to protect the proletariat from a rapacious oligarchy. His role to warn and advise the oligarchy."

"With respect, sir, it seems that this is a perfect system if you are planning to send the successful housemasters abroad to govern your colonies. Meanwhile the negligent despots wreak havoc here in England."

The headmaster looked at his pupil for a long moment before he spoke again.

"You are a brave boy to argue against success. The British Empire is the most efficient and, I venture to add, enlightened despotism since the end of the Republic in Rome. But I have understood what you have to tell me. The city-states must answer to me, and I will not tolerate a tyranny any more than I can refuse to uphold the rule of law."

Don Juan perceived that this was the response for which he had come. He could expect nothing more specific. The preservation of face was a trick the British must have picked up in the Orient. He rose, thanking the headmaster for the fizzy lemonade.

But just before he opened the door to leave through the outer office, the headmaster said, "Trubshawe's a physicist, as you know. In trying to modernize a school like this, one has had to advance people of that ilk. I hope you enjoy the holidays."

Don Juan arrived in Paris just before Christmas to find Henrietta gone to America to spend the festive season with her family. He found time to drop off a present at Berthe's apartment while he was in London, mystifying Major Barnet by diverting the taxi taking them from the school train to the boat train, via the dingy block of council flats.

His mother's life with Henrietta was a balanced one in that they had many heterosexual friends together. Alone she gravitated toward a total reliance on the Sapphic world of Paris. Don Juan was, as a result, included in little of her activity. They had their tête-à-tête each morning. His mother telephoned to order him tickets for this concert or that theater, even to make sure that, if she knew the artists involved, he had a chance to go to meet them after the performance. But her own life was spent in a whirl of intimate dinner parties, séances, and encounters. She explained it to him in these terms: "You know, darling, that I adore my Henrietta. But ever since dear

Ayesha died I have never been free in my own right. The world being what it is, everyone wants to take advantage of Henrietta's absence. To see if I can be wooed away. Even men we know have called me with invitations. I am enjoying it all enormously."

"Oh dear, you're not going to abandon Henrietta?" asked Don Juan, genuinely anxious.

His mother smiled. "Never. And I hope she never abandons me."

"I shall write to her and tell her I miss her and she should hurry home," said Don Juan firmly.

He luxuriated in there being no bells in the morning and no cold showers, and in the consistently delicious food. The cooks were quite overwhelmed by his praises and his constant visits to the kitchen. By common consent he took most of his meals in the library among stacks of books on England. He had already read the Anglo-Irish Shaw and Wilde on the English at school. He now read Marx and Engels on the English and Madame de Staël and Maurois and Stefan Zweig. He read Henry James and Mark Twain on the English. They remained, to him, a baffling race. For all the rationalizations his headmaster and others had made, he decided that they responded as a people not to rhetoric nor to reason, but to a kind of national osmosis of feeling. For all their mongrel origins, they had the profoundest of tribal instincts. That, he decided, far more than their insularity, was the important thing to know about them.

He promised his mother faithfully to seduce none of the maids, but she forgot to mention her guests.

On the occasion of Réveillon, which for the French is a larger celebration than Christmas, the New Year was to be rung in with an enormous masked party at the house on the Avenue Foch.

They came, that night, disguised as toreadors, hussars, mendicants, paladins, marshals of France, executioners, aviators, bishops, knights and so on, but women every one. There were also columbines, milk maids, princesses, fairy queens, medieval damosels, and other feminine personae. Don Juan watched them arrive, walking in groups up the staircase to the salon, their masks hiding their identity. But even from his oblique vantage point, looking down from the nursery landing, he recognized quite a number of them. This was the party Henrietta would never have permitted and the duchess had always longed to give. The servants had been given the night off, and his mother had hired blacks and Arabs as waiters and dressed them in costumes she had rented. Turbans and caftans, galabias and fezes, curled shoes and yashmaks, the staff serving sherbets and champagne and tiny thimbles full of cocaine to her guests, who looked like the cast of *Scheherazade*.

Don Juan had been invited to a party of young people at the house of American friends of Henrietta's, an invitation which ordinarily he would have relished; it was so rare for his mother to think of arranging for him to meet children of his own age. But ever since he had been privy to the arranging of this party, listening to her animated telephone calls, watching the arrival of the costumes, hearing her audition the musicians, he had felt bitterly the exclusion that had led her to go so far as to get him invited elsewhere.

Now she was gathering her guests in the salon. The mandolin players that had been her final choice had started to play, and he went to her bedroom to telephone his regrets to the Americans, claiming a migraine.

His plan for the evening was vague, but he knew that the erotic possibilities of posing as a lesbian at such a party were too great for him to resist. Besides, in no other way could he hope to evade his mother's discovery.

From Henrietta's cupboard he chose a black satin trouser suit that Coco Chanel had made for her years before. He tied a piratical red scarf tightly around his head and then considered the androgynous result in the looking glass. His features had already the lapidary cast that shows a man emerging from the soft contours of a boy's face.

A Pierrot's mask, face-fitting and black, helped hide this face. Still it left visible a mouth that would be extraordinary on a female. How to disguise it? He thought that a smaller mouth painted in lipstick upon his own, the reverse of what a clown uses, might work. He tried a Clara Bow mouth, so popular back in the '20s. He no longer recognized himself.

The salon, when he entered it an hour later, was lit by hundreds of candles. At one end he could see his mother, looking both dramatic and beautiful in the crimson dress of a Spanish dancer, her opulent bosom very white and partly obscured by the fine screen of her black mantilla. Don Juan wandered for a while, almost un-noticed, among the throng of guests. A *citoyenne* of the revolutionary period asked him to dance, but he simply smiled his refusal. He drank a little champagne and inhaled the sweet smell of hashish, which many people were smoking, some in cigarettes, others in pipes. He was looking, a predator searching for the perfect prey. The hunter, unnoticed, in the very middle of the unwary game.

Then he saw her. She looked almost as young as he, but Don

Juan supposed that she was actually about eighteen. She wore the full red trousers of a Zouave trouper and a velvet embroidered waistcoat to match over her otherwise bare torso. Her hair was chignoned to a soft, tapering little curl at the nape of her neck. She had the slightly pouting expression, Don Juan thought as he watched her, of a nymph by Bellini. Indeed, everything about her was delicately carved, the slightly flared nostrils, the exquisitely miniature ears like little pink shells fresh from the sea. Would they taste of salt? he wondered. She was leaning forward to hear what an obese and incongruously broad-bosomed Napoleon was sayin to her, and it made her waistcoat open sufficiently to show Don Juan her boyish breast. Only the budded nipples gave tiny, swelling evidence of her femininity.

Her neighbor, the emperor, seemed to be making an elaborately phrased proposition to her. She responded by laughing and shaking her head, by looking around her as if for more congenial company, and by those little shrugs that in young French girls used to mean "No!"

Don Juan circled around so that he could approach her from behind. He bent his mouth close to that wonderful ear.

"I am the spirit of the old year that in sixty minutes or less must die," he said. "Will you spend that time with me? And take what remains of me with you into the new year, like a posy pressed to your heart that will not even be there in the morning when you come to press it in a book for memory."

She turned to look at Don Juan's face, peering at his eyes through the slits in his mask. His poetic proposition she accepted without comment, the spirit of Sappho being so clearly abroad.

"What a strange voice you have!" she said, adding, "Let's dance!" thinking that would at least rid her of the importunate Bonaparte.

Now, dancing was not something of which Don Juan had the remotest knowledge. But he led her to where the mandolins were playing and held her, praying that the music would do something easy, something his feet could manage. They played a balalaika, which is not, in a normal sense, a dance. Somehow he found that its rhythms, long and elliptical, allowed him to lead her gently through the crush on the floor. His hand held her back gently under her waistcoat and traced the rhythm of the song, like the beating of a bird's wing, upon her spine.

Her eyes half closed, she felt the rhythm and the caresses together giving music to her feet and a certain languor to her limbs. She considered the girl in whose arms she found herself. Amazingly strong arms. There was something so remarkable about her in every way that she listened to the stream of whispered words in her ear and watched the glittering eyes through the mask, giving herself over to the fantasy that, like Cinderella's coach, this dark figure would simply disappear when the clock struck twelve. She thought that the pleasure she started to feel as that marvelously subtle and accomplished hand made love to her back might yet be far, far greater if she followed the suggestion in her ear that they climb the stair together and hide in a place known only to the dark stranger until it was midnight. Her curiosity, the undoing of more women than there are grains of sand on the beach, led to that gentle nodding of the head which, in those days, with French girls meant "Yes."

Dozens of guests were already sitting on the stairs as the Zouave and Don Juan climbed them. Many of these were already embracing and fondling each other. Others were wandering about on the third floor, near the duchess's bedroom, looking for dark corners and places where they could have more extravagant embraces.

Don Juan led the Zouave through to the service staircase and ascended to where Nanny's old bedroom stood empty.

The door closed, and they stood in the light from the Avenue outside. Already the fireworks had started, in the distance by the Eiffel Tower, and their colored lights warmed the dark room as Don Juan gently kissed her ear.

"I shall remember this," he whispered, "when I am gone, as the 'year of the ear.'" He felt her become limp in his arms, her strength slowly flowing out of her, as he lit her face with gentle kisses and, with the palm of his hand, teased her breasts to hardness and to fire. He laid her on the bed, and under his hands her body flowed, not a writhe which would have been pleasurably impatient, but an arching of the back, an offering of her torso, as a cat arches to be stroked. Again and, similarly, again. But always he returned to her ear, breathing into it and listening as one does for a pebble falling down a well. And the sound came back as he knew it would from deep inside her, and the flowing was no longer of her back, but of her red-trousered thighs. Arching again, like the cat. Offering. He undid the drawstring of her Zouave trousers and traced, in the virtual darkness, a line from her neat carnelian navel to a surprise.

She was shaved perfectly smooth. Perhaps she had used some depilatory, but she was as hairless at the mount of Venus and beyond as was her cheek. Don Juan guessed that a shade about to work magic, and leave the world like a shadow stamped out by light, doesn't express surprise. He discovered, not without an instant of searching, the entrance to her other ear, the tiny echo in her well, and within instants found he had to hold fast her hips while the smooth plateau of her belly, the distant hillocks of her breasts, moved in great undulating sweeps while she cried, "Oh, no, no, no! No, no, no!"

Meaning no, I adore it, as in yes, it is too much. Don Juan soon tasted her nectar, and had to struggle with himself not to play the man. For that, his delicate sense of honor told him, would be carrying this delicious deception too far. That, not to put too fine a point on it, would be rape. He distanced himself. He prepared to make his promised disappearance true. "If I stay," he whispered, "I will become a pumpkin."

But she, for the first time, struggled to kiss him, to lean down and find her lover's mouth. Her kisses were frantic, and she sought her lover's breast. Now, in an instant, she *knew*, there was no breast; thrusting her hand between his legs, she *knew*; ripping apart Henrietta's satin trousers, she *saw*. And screamed!

His mother was not pleased. Guests, that holiday, had to be added to servants on a growing list of people he promised not to seduce.

7
Don Juan Has a Pyrrhic Victory

Soon I began to find a mass of the strangest surprises, the most monstrous facts awaiting me at every step. And it was only later, after I had been some time in the prison, that I realised fully the exceptional, the surprising nature of such an existence, and I marvelled at it more and more.

—Fëodor Dostoevski, *The House of the Dead*

In an agonizingly short time, Don Juan found himself back on the train to Deerhurst.

He had managed to visit Berthe early that morning, being unsure he would not find Lilliane entertaining clients before that hour. The women were alone by then, as he had hoped. Lilliane had made tea for them and left them together on the sofa in the living room while she went back to bed, closing the door behind her. They had made love comfortably and quietly, without much passion but in token of renewing their friendship. Mostly he let her talk about her tiny world, guessing she had saved these things to tell him against the possibility of his keeping his promise and returning.

On the train there were the familiar faces, but when they had sorted themselves out the new boys in Trubshawe's house found they numbered only nine. Latimer was missing. At the last moment, just as the train was about to leave, a bowler-hatted man thrust a small boy into the carriage and a porter struggled to put two cases and a tuck box * in after him. Don Juan and Parsons-Purefoy, who were in the corridor at the time, helped him. The train's whistle was blowing and the steam engine was already huffing itself into its departing lurch.

"This is Peter Kabanda!" shouted the bowler-hatted man. "This *is* the Trubshawe house carriage?"

"Yes, sir!" shouted back Parsons-Purefoy. "We'll look after him."

Then he and Don Juan stared at Peter Kabanda. He was quite black.

Before prayers that first evening Mr. Trubshawe made an announcement.

"It grieves me very much to have to tell you that, ah, Gordon Latimer died during the holidays. In his place we have the crown prince of Kabanda, who will be known by the name of his, ah, country, as Kabanda. We will now say a prayer for Gordon Latimer. . . ."

Don Juan and, indeed, all his fellow new boys found themselves staring from time to time at Cooper. He had not terrorized them on the train. In fact, they had not seen him on the train.

As Don Juan spent his first evening back on duty in Springer's study, he heard what his prefect described rather bleakly as "the background to this beastly news story." It appeared that Latimer had hanged himself from his bedroom cupboard the day before he was due to come back to school.

"They got hold of Kabanda as a replacement pretty quickly," said Don Juan when he had got over the shock of Springer's news, although something about Cooper's demeanor at prayers had half-prepared him for the manner of Latimer's death.

"Oh, we're going to have quite a few of *those,*" said Springer. "It appears the Colonial Office is sponsoring half a dozen darky princes to the better public schools. Apparently they've got them at crammers in London, 'straining like greyhounds in the slips.'"

* A tuck box is a vital piece of schoolboy luggage in England. Made of wood, it is two feet square and contains 'tuck' = sweets = candy.

"Springer, what must a *bad* public school be like?" asked Don Juan bitterly.

"I know, angel! Cooper," said Springer miserably.

"To hell with Cooper. Bloodnut is ultimately responsible. For all the dressing up in winged collars and strutting about with canes, Cooper and you and Martin are just seventeen-year-old boys. Even if you're getting away with the equivalent of murder."

"Shut up, Juan. That's enough. Just because I'm a poncy old queen and lark about with you, don't you dare think you can talk like that to me. If you don't like this school, my advice to you is 'get out.' Go back to anarchic Spain and let us run things our way. We'll muddle through. You'll see."

Don Juan went on cleaning the study in silence. Why quarrel with one of the few people at Trubshawe's who had a glimmer of humanity? Before he left for the evening, Don Juan said, "I'm sorry, Springer, I went too far. I know you stopped Cooper that night."

But Springer avoided his eyes. "There's an inquest tomorrow," he said. "You won't see any papers in the house library till it's over. You can guess what we're all wondering."

"If he left a letter?" said Don Juan.

"That's right," said Springer grimly.

For the next two days Don Juan watched the oligarchy sweat it out at Trubshawe's house. Springer was right. There were no papers. Normally the *Daily Telegraph* and the *Times* were in the library daily. On the afternoon of the second day, in an agony of suspense, Don Juan took a circuitous route back from a gym class and stopped at Dame Serena's cottage. She was pleased to see him, but mildly surprised.

"Dame Serena, d'you have a newspaper?" he asked, realizing that this question might raise several in her mind that he hardly knew how to answer.

But she simply said, "Come in," and he walked with her to a large, cozy kitchen with a dutch door opening onto her paddock. Two donkeys were nuzzling their heads through the upper half of the dutch door.

"These are my 'donks,'" she said. "Both jacks, and the randiest things on four legs. We made the mistake of putting them out to stud and then entering them in the Donkeys' Derby. Both of them got themselves a jenny to mount right there on the race course. The owners of the jennies were furious, of course. Ah, here's the paper. It's only a rag." She handed him the *Daily Mail*. "But what you're looking for is there. It's on the second page." He looked at her, his turn to be surprised, and turned to the page.

Deerhurst Boy, Inquest

Truro, Cornwall. The inquest took place here today into the death of Gordon Latimer, age 14. On January 23rd, the day before he was due to go back to school at Deerhurst College, the boy allegedly hanged himself with his prep school tie from a hook on the back of a high nursery cupboard. There is no suggestion of foul play. The boy's father, General Sir Peter Latimer, Ret'd, gave evidence today.

"He was very happy over Christmas and New Year," he said. "About ten days ago he seemed to become depressed, however, but would give no explanation. I asked him if he was unhappy about going back to school, but he denied it. I told him to try and be a good chap and cheer up. He seemed quite all right the night before this happened. It is a terrible shock to my poor wife and I."

The general himself went to Deerhurst, as did his father before him. In her evidence the boy's mother told the coroner that he had had some trouble with his entrance exam for Deerhurst but that they had all been greatly relieved when he was accepted.

A spokesman for the school expressed their sympathy with the parents but had no further comment to make.

The coroner issued a verdict of suicide "while the balance of the boy's mind was disturbed."

"Balance of mind disturbed?" asked Don Juan.

"It's a formula to get the poor lad planted in consecrated ground," said Dame Serena.

Before he left, she asked him if he would consider posing for her. She'd asked the headmaster, and he'd agreed, subject to the consent of Don Juan's parents. "I'd like it to be a portrait of the whole Don Juan," she said, addressing him with curious formality. "But first do *you* agree?"

Don Juan was enchanted with the idea and said so. It seemed to him, and this he did not say, a marvelous opportunity to get away from Deerhurst and the Deerhurst people. It would also excuse him some fagging, as did all such extracurricular activities. He gave her the duchess's address.

Next day the papers were back, and there was an air of evident relief amongst the prefects, particularly Cooper. Don Juan, however, had used their moment of uncertainty to encourage his troops in the dormitory. Everyone agreed to protect Kabanda from being subjected to the usual indignities, and everyone helped him with his new boy's bumph. Only Portarlington and Masters-White-Masters called him a nigger to his face in the first few days, and the others made both apologize.

"I don't know why you chaps are more protective to him than anyone is to Big One and Hezekiah," said Masters-White-Masters, using their nickname, for Don Juan and Manley-Cohen. "I mean, Big One is a jolly decent dago and Hezekiah is a splendid yid, so why can't Kabanda get used to being called a good old nigger, if that's what he is? And, I mean, he is, isn't he? What *does* one call him— 'you super chocolate-colored fellow'?"

Horder did what the boys usually did when they wanted to deflate one of the others: he went up behind Masters-White-Masters and, putting his hand through his legs, grabbed his balls and pulled hard. His victim, quite helpless to retaliate, screamed and squeaked and whined every time Horder gave his balls another tweak.

"Speaking of name-calling," said Kabanda, laughing, "'Masters' reminds me of a pig. Little piggy eyes, pale hair on a pink body. That's what we niggers call you chaps, y'know, behind your backs. Pigs."

Portarlington was appalled. "Pigs. But the king. I don't mean your father. I mean *the king*. Surely *he* didn't remind you of a pig?" King George V had just died and was still being mourned.

Don Juan watched for Kabanda's answer curiously. His father, the king of Kabanda, must have foreseen moments like this in his son's life. He had always been a tributary of the British. Had he trained his son to be a diplomat?

"His majesty had too much hair on his face to be like a pig. I had tea with him last year, and he reminded me more of one of your English hedgehogs. Terribly nice animals, I've always thought those," said Kabanda, fully aware that having tea with the king of England was the single most impressive thing that could happen to an English person. And these boys were not easily impressed. There were three lords in the house, of whom Portarlington was one, and sundry other honorables, and even Don Juan was the heir to a dukedom—only foreign titles, of course, hardly counted. But to have broken bread with the British monarch conveyed real manna upon a person. No one called Kabanda nigger again.

Don Juan's career at Deerhurst continued to be successful. He played soccer for the school colts and was considered the best right wing they'd had in years. Finding most of his classes congenial, he supplemented the gaps in what his teachers had to tell him with his own reading. He read the papers after the Latimer incident more regularly, examining the *Times* daily and trying to follow what was happening to the cause of the anarchists in Spain. During this period of his life, Don Juan found the scene in Mella's farmhouse pricked his memory like a sore boil. In a curious way, he unconsciously linked that terrible scene with the night of Latimer's rape by Cooper. The two events were catalytic, no doubt, in his evolving desire to be a revolutionary.

He read the leaders in the *Times* that prophesied civil war in Spain. The paper hoped the middle class might be saved from red revolution by the military. "Maintaining Order" and "Protecting Property" were the catchwords the British press used. They meant the property and order of the middle class. No other "property" or "order" seemed to matter to them.

Don Juan wondered what the Whittickers of England thought. He never met them, of course. He was insulated from their world as securely as were all their fellow Englishmen who went to Deerhurst.

He had never ceased to love Whitticker even though he recognized the callousness of his betrayal. Perhaps the fact that the Englishman had lost his life because he supported what Don Juan believed was a just cause kept his myth alive for the boy. When Don Juan was not dreaming of making love to the Zouave or to Berthe or to Blodwen or, most violently and often, to Verena Trubshawe, he sometimes dreamed of the day Whitticker came into the study in the castle and started the lesson with a hilarious imitation of Queen Victoria:

"You see, Johnny, when she got an idea into her head, blind pit ponies couldn't drag her away from it. For some reason she thought coroners were horse butchers. Anyway, picture, Johnny, this line of Victorian gentlemen, big spade beards, stovepipe hats in their hands, waiting while this little all-dressed-in-black baggage moves down the receiving line. No sign of feet. From the receiving line, rather like a piano stool wheeling along with a skirt on it. She is introduced to this cove. Someone says, 'This is the coroner of Birmingham, ma'am.' She refuses to speak to him or to extend the gloved hand. They drag him away. He's kicking and screaming. He doesn't understand. That's the way, you see, Johnny, with the use of arbitrary power. There's usually nothing *to* understand about it except that it's arbitrary."

And Don Juan woke up to realize that it was a dream memory only, and his eyes filled with tears.

The daily grind in Trubshawe's house continued to turn up its rash of beatings. Anstruther, only a second-year man, walked on the prefects' lawn. Three strokes. Manley-Cohen scorched Caldwell Major's flannels. Three strokes. Horder was late for prep twice. Six strokes. Big One was caught trying to get into the servants' annex. Twelve strokes.

The duchess had given her consent to Don Juan's being painted by Dame Serena. She hoped that they might have a reproduction of the painting for the Avenue Foch.

Dame Serena had decided to paint Don Juan, as she always called him now (when she didn't call him "bucko"), in the barn-cum-studio behind her home. In this rather bare space she stood at an easel, her back to a vast carpenter's table on which she mixed her pigments and made the frames for her canvases, stretching the cloth herself and covering it with sisal. She had a Spanish hidalgo's saddle set on a trestle next to a stove. She wanted Don Juan to sit with one leg curled over the pommel, the other supported by his foot in the stirrup. His left hand was to take his weight and grasp the back of the saddle. His right elbow was to lean on his right knee, and he was to look straight at her, which meant leaning his head slightly forward. It was to be an equestrian portrait, and she proposed to put the horse in later.

He had brought his riding clothes with him, assuming this would be the costume she would want him to wear.

"I think I'll just have you in your boots," said Dame Serena.

Don Juan stared at her.

"You're joking!" he exclaimed.

"I'm not, bucko," she said. "Since the moment I saw you, I've thought how marvelous you'd look. You're at an age where the length from the top of your hip to your thighbone is the narrowest part of your body. Between your knees and your neck, that is. You're well muscled, bucko, but there still isn't an ounce of fat on you. You'll look as patrician nude as anyone I ever saw in the ermine."

"Did you ask my mother that? Or the headmaster?" Don Juan felt tricked and suddenly resentful.

Dame Serena looked at him amazed.

"Do I hear my ears aright, bucko? Little Blodwen tells me you've tried everything to get into their annex. I'm not surprised. Nor is she. That's who you are. But now when I want to paint you naked, it's 'Have you asked Mummy? Have you asked the Beak?' Hypocrite!"

He knew before she finished how right she was.

"I'm not allowed to say I'm sorry, am I?" he asked ruefully.

"Just this once," said Dame Serena.

"Couldn't I just be naked?"

"Oh, Don Juan, are you afraid that you'll look like no more than a young stud?" she asked.

Don Juan said nothing.

"No boots," she said at last, with decision. "Just the whole of Don Juan, feet and all."

He took off his clothes quickly, feeling slightly self-conscious and wanting to get it over with. It wasn't, after all, as if, like a nurse or a doctor, she were taking no particular notice of his body. She was going to record every detail of it. He kept his back to her as he slid off his underpants, forgetting his recent stripes, and was reminded only by her exclaiming, "Juan, love! What have they been doing to you?"

Her voice was curiously, unusually feminine in its timbre, and he craned his head back, trying to see his own buttocks.

"They take pride in their work," he said.

"Your poor arse looks like a tram station. What was it for?" she asked.

"Wanting to see more of Blodwen."

"I see," she said, laughing. "Then we must outwit them."

Among other current offenses: Tebbets caught using the prefects' lavatory, the one with doors. Three strokes. Cloudy steals a pot of jam from the kitchen. Six strokes. Portarlington fails to turn up to cheer on the first eleven against Eton. Six strokes. Caldwell Minor is caught trying to dodge the cold shower. Six strokes. Kabanda, now Cooper's fag, is caught sampling his prefect's sherry. Six strokes. Parsons-Purefoy has his brass rubbings confiscated by Cooper for working on them in prep. He also gets six strokes.

Like the tax on tea in Boston, or the maggoty food on the battleship *Potemkin*, the brass rubbings of Parsons-Purefoy did it.

The scene in the dormitory was the usual one while they waited for Cooper. Parsons-Purefoy rubbed some methylated spirit into his buttocks, let it dry, then washed away the telltale smell with soap and water. He was ready, when Cooper arrived with the black walking stick, to take his beating. Cooper thrashed at him in his usual manic way, but slipped on the fifth stroke and fell. The whole dormitory shouted with laughter. Cooper was shaking when he stood up, and Don Juan noticed a dribble of saliva trickling from his mouth. For the sixth blow he took a six-yard run and broke his stick. Parsons-Purefoy, gasping with agony, managed to straighten himself fast, wanting to speak before Cooper left the room.

"Can I come and collect my rubbings now, Cooper?" he managed to ask. But Cooper left without seeming to hear him.

Kabanda ran over to Don Juan and whispered, "He's burned the rubbings. I made up his fire in his study after prep. He came in and made me put them on the fire!"

Parsons-Purefoy was in too much pain for the next ten minutes to be told the bad news. When he heard it he couldn't believe it.

"He must have been ribbing you, 'OK,' he said to Kabanda.

"I don't think so. Where I come from, to burn the images of the dead is considered a very poor show indeed," said Kabanda. "I asked him if he was sure. 'Burn the bloody rubbish,' he said, 'or I'll tan your nigger hide for you.' You know Cooper, that's the way he talks."

Don Juan was watching Parsons-Purefoy carefully. Suddenly he started to cry. In a way, Don Juan was reminded of the woman keening when she first saw Mella wounded on the horse. It was a cry of unbearable loss.

"Turn out the lights," ordered Don Juan. He was obeyed instantly, and all the boys were very quiet. Don Juan used the dark to put his arms around Parsons-Purefoy.

"I started it with my father," sobbed Parsons-Purefoy. "When we were still all together. Before he went off. We used to do it every Sunday, he and I. He taught me all about how to date the churches. I'm being allowed to see him next holidays. I've got such a tremendous collection now. I mean, he'll be awfully impressed. And now, and now . . ."

The child's wail started again, and he sobbed into his pillow while Don Juan kept his hand on his shoulder.

"Now listen, everyone," said Don Juan to the dormitory at large. "From tomorrow, we go on strike. No fagging. None. If there's to be a beating, they'll have to drag us to the beating table by force."

Shouts of "Wizard!" and "That's keen, Big One!" greeted Don Juan's announcement.

"But what do we say?" asked Horder.

"Nothing," said Don Juan.

"When they shout 'Fag'?" asked Portal.

"You don't run. You don't hear them," said Don Juan.

"When they say 'What is it? What's wrong with you?'" asked Portarlington.

"You tell them it's a strike."

"But strikers have to have a list of demands," said Manley-Cohen.

"Well, don't we have them?" replied Don Juan.

"No more name-calling," said Kabanda.

"No more beating," said Masters-White-Masters.

"No more fagging," said Horder.

"No more destroying other people's property," said Don Juan.

Hooray! Hooooraaaay! Raah! It was the classic British cheer. It was a loud, liberated, not-caring-who-heard-them kind of cheer. Don Juan remembered reading somewhere that the sustained cheering of the British was like a lion's roar. These cubs were roaring, all right, and it was good, at long last, to hear them defiant.

Caldwell Major, the duty prefect, burst into the dormitory, turning on the lights.

"What the hell are you little beasts doing?" he shouted.

"Get out!" they all yelled in unison. "Get out of here!" And in a body they ran toward him, pushing him out into the passage and slamming the door in his face.

"Have you all gone mad?" he shouted through the door.

"Go to bed, Donald!" his brother shouted back. "We'll see you in the morning."

"I'm going to the housemaster unless you open that door," said Caldwell Major.

"Can't keep order, eh, Donald?" shouted his brother. "You'll never make a great big school prefect if you can't keep order."

There was silence.

"I've warned you, if there's any more noise I'll go to the housemaster," said Caldwell again.

"Shh, everyone," said Don Juan, sensing they'd won the first round. They went to bed, and he didn't come back. Far into that night they excitedly planned their action.

Next day the strike began in earnest. The prefects came to the common room and yelled for their fags, but no one moved. They sat at their desks and read schoolbooks, as had been agreed.

Cooper was the first to test their determination. He stood over Kabanda, who bravely pretended to be learning Latin verbs.

"Have you gone deaf?" he shouted. "Move your black arse and get into my study. You've got *six* coming. In ten seconds it will be *twelve*."

Silence.

"Now it's twelve," said Cooper grimly.

Kabanda sat. Cooper grabbed his ear and jerked the boy to his feet.

"Don't you dare touch him!" shouted all the others in unison. "Let him go!"

Cooper looked around, astonished. But he grabbed Kabanda by the scruff of the neck, determined to beat him then and there. He only managed to move a couple of yards before they were on him, freeing Kabanda and hurling Cooper out into the passage. Then they all returned to their desks.

Ten minutes later every prefect in the house was back, and each one dragged his own fag back to his study except Springer, who simply stood in the common room and looked at Don Juan with resignation.

"So you're refusing to fag, angel?" he asked very quietly.

"Yes. Nothing personal against you. But we've all had enough," said Don Juan, and told Springer about the brass rubbings.

"I've been waiting for this," said Springer. "It's *you*, isn't it, who put them up to it?"

"Looking for a ringleader?" asked Don Juan, smiling.

"You've always misunderstood me, angel. I'm with you. Not just because I fancy you. Anyway, I'm not sure I do anymore. But because in the long run your side is going to win."

Don Juan looked at the slightly acned handsome face of Springer, with his mocking eyes and his boyish fringe of yellowish hair. Of course, he thought, the would-be gentleman socialist politician. The anarchists, he knew, disdained to use such people, but he saw no reason not to test Springer's good faith.

"We have a manifesto," said Don Juan. "It has to go straight to the housemaster. Will you take it with me?"

"Does it mention the rape of Latimer?"

"Yes, it does," said Don Juan.

"All right," Springer said slowly. "But suppose all that beating going on now cows the others? Makes them give up?"

"It won't," said Don Juan hopefully, for this was indeed the dangerous part of the scheme. "Anyway, it's quite illegal. Trubshawe's supposed to approve all beatings like that. I'll bet he hasn't. But if you really want to prove you're with us, you'll go along the prefects' corridor and try to stop it."

"It'd be quicker to go straight to the housemaster," said Springer the politician.

And so they went.

Having taken the plunge and gone to Trubshawe's office, Springer proved worthy of his role. Not for nothing was he the senior classics scholar in the school and head of the debating team.

"I think a situation has arisen that requires your personal intervention, sir," he said to the surprised Trubshawe, who couldn't think what Don Juan was doing at Springer's side.

"Good heavens, ah, Harry, what?" asked Trubshawe.

"Have you just authorized the beating of every fag in the common room?"

"No, certainly not. What have the little wretches been doing?"

"They are being beaten without your permission, against school rules, sir," said Springer. "I expect you will want to stop it at once. Then I have something else to say to you." He opened the study door for the unwilling Trubshawe.

In Stephen Martin's study the head of the house was wrestling with Parsons-Purefoy, who was refusing to bend over in the approved way.

"What are you doing, Stephen?" asked Trubshawe.

"He refuses to be b-beaten, Billie," said the head of the house, inadvertently using Trubshawe's pet first name.

"Have you permission to beat him?" asked Springer.

"What the hell d'you mean?" shouted Stephen Martin, at last letting go of the struggling Parsons-Purefoy.

"I'd like you to come next door, sir," said Springer, moving the housemaster down the passage, where the yells and howls spoke eloquently of what was going on.

In the end, all the fags were sent to the common room and all the prefects except Martin were confined to their studies.

"Just while we sort this thing out," said Trubshawe.

Back in his study the housemaster irritably asked Springer to explain to him and to Stephen Martin what on earth was happening. Don Juan was made to stand outside and wait. He didn't mind. He knew Springer was committed.

"What on earth has gone wrong with the fags?" asked Stephen Martin.

"It's a strike, and I'm supporting them," said Springer. "Cooper has just gone much too far. That boy outside the door and every fag in this house knows that Latimer was raped. You and I knew it, Stephen, and you refused to come to the housemaster when I asked you."

"That's not true. I told you, Billie. Don't you remember?" said Stephen Martin, now suddenly a very frightened boy.

"No, I certainly do not, Martin," said Trubshawe, warning his favorite by using his surname.

"You knew about it, Billie. Don't pretend," said the head of the house.

Trubshawe's bald head was scarlet with anger. "Go to your study and stay there till I call you," he said to the head of the house. "And send that boy in as you go out."

When Don Juan concluded their list of grievances, Mr. Trubshawe was still desperately wondering what the implications of all this were for *him*. He had not particularly wished to be a housemaster. But Verena had wanted it because it meant social advancement in the academic community; it also meant more money, particularly since it was the housemaster's wife who had the lucrative job of supervising the house catering, receiving a budget from the school for the purpose. He didn't really want to hear what the dago boy was saying any more than he'd ever wanted to involve himself with his charges' lives.

"Well, what a pickle this is, isn't it, what," said Trubshawe, looking up at them, his face bleak and baffled.

"I have a suggestion, sir," said Springer.

"Yes? Yes?" Trubshawe almost said, "Anything!"

"May I speak to you alone, sir?"

Don Juan was asked to withdraw.

After an evening of confusion in the House by the Pit in which Springer took prep and house prayers were canceled, they all went to bed with no knowledge of what was going to happen.

At breakfast the following morning the housemaster appeared, and while everyone stood waiting for him to say grace he made an announcement.

"There are to be some new arrangements in this, ah, house," said Trubshawe. "The headmaster has agreed to our conducting an experiment that I have proposed to him. There will be no more fagging or corporal punishment in this house. First-year boys will have a program of general household tasks to perform after tea. All the house rules remain the same, but punishments will consist of extra tasks or work to be done in a boy's spare time. Springer, whom the headmaster has today appointed as this house's second full school prefect, will outline the new arrangements to the house after prayers this evening."

But if this were not sensational enough news for the boys of Trubshawe's house, there was more to come. Halfway through breakfast the observant Kabanda noticed that Cooper was nowhere to be seen. It did not take long for news to filter down that he had been fired and sent to the sanatorium to await transport home.

Don Juan had the good sense not to begrudge Springer his coup. Whitticker had taught him enough to foresee it. Without Springer their little revolution might never have been successful. As it was, his time at Deerhurst continued to become pleasanter with each passing term.

In the Easter holidays his mother was with Henrietta in New York, so he stayed for a month at The Children's Hotel in London. The rules were that he had to be in by eight-thirty unless someone was taking him out. Since he spent almost every day in bed with Berthe either making love to her or reading, he hardly found this restrictive. In the early evenings they went to see the latest "talkies."

He found Berthe warm and uncomplicated. She had very little to say except that she adored him, and almost every day she found some new and recondite way of making love with which to entertain him. From her he learned the felicities of popperbeads and crepe hand-kerchiefs and the strenuous art of the free-fall entry. She was so afraid that her simplicity might bore him that she beseeched her mother to dredge up from her bottomless experience new games to play with Don Juan. It was in the end her mistake, because he liked her, alone of all the women in his life so far, not for passion but for peace and quiet. He did not care that perhaps ten customers possessed her every night. She assured him that she had started to enjoy her work and could simulate with them what she really felt with him. She was wise enough to understand that he would have minded if he thought her unhappy.

It was never in Don Juan's nature to be a reformer any more than he was, in any strict sense, a moralist. His brand of revolutionary spirit meant only that he had a keen sense of injustice. (Revolutionary "dogma" always bored him.) He had the *imagination* to compre-hend and feel the injustice being done to others, but it was his tragedy that this imagination rarely extended to the women he left behind.

The summer term made Deerhurst appear unexpectedly beauti-ful. Great chestnuts, elms, and oaks softened its hard contours and made it look like a village in a sylvan glade. Early in the term the headmaster summoned Don Juan to his presence. Dame Serena, who felt a little guilty taking up a good deal of the boy's time with the portrait, and hearing that he hated cricket, had asked the Beak if Don Juan might be excused games for the summer term so that he could concentrate on his drawing.

"I think Dame Serena has taken a fancy to you," said the headmaster.

"That's very kind of her," said Don Juan, assuming there were no sexual implications.

"She's admitted to me that she's painting you in the buff."

"Yes, sir," said Don Juan, swallowing, thinking, How indiscreet of her!

"She's an important artist in my view. Perfectly proper for her to be painting you that way if you consent. Wouldn't want her submitting it to the Royal Academy for their summer show, however. 'Deerhurst Boy on Saddle.' Might shock all the ultra-fastidious. Not sure that the governors of the school mightn't kick up a fuss."

"Did you say that to her, sir?"

"Yes. I said, 'My advice to you, Dame, is to keep that picture for ten years, and then they'll be ready for it at the academy.' In any event, I insisted on the title of the painting being 'Gypsy Boy.'"

"You've seen it?"

"Yes. It's got a long way to go, of course, but I like it very much. I'm disturbed, however, that she has not been quite straightforward with your mother."

"My mother is scarcely an 'orthodox' personality, sir."

"That was my impression. My wife takes *Vogue.* There were pictures of her New Year's party. What an exquisite house she has!"

There was a pause while the headmaster gazed at Don Juan with a twinkling, conspiratorial eye. He is determined, Don Juan thought, to show that in this backwater of provincialism he, at least, is a man of the world.

"So how are things at Trubshawe's house now?" asked the headmaster at last.

"Much improved, thank you, sir. Mr. Trubshawe and Springer seem determined to make their experiment work."

"What fundamentally has changed as a result, do you think? No need for metaphor."

"Racist prejudice continues. An atmosphere that is hostile to any intellectual activity continues. Spiritually it is a wilderness. Aesthetically it is a desert. The food is insultingly bad. But there are now good things. People are friendlier and more relaxed now that the endless threat of pain is gone. The younger boys have recovered their sense of dignity. Without fagging there is time to have a little more fun. Homosexual love comes naturally to those who are so inclined. It is no longer a matter of coercion."

The headmaster suppressed a desire to laugh at Don Juan's solemn, sententious indictment of Deerhurst as an institution. He decided to "dine out" on the young Spanish grandee's opinion of his school. It could be very funny in the telling.

"And yet you haven't asked your mother to remove you?" He asked it with a straight face.

"No. My grandfather sent me here as a punishment. I accepted it as just. It is a matter of honor. Besides, there is much here that I enjoy very much."

"A matter of honor. How Spanish, Don Juan!" The headmaster mocked him now.

"Yes, I sometimes think we make our 'honor' as absurd as you do your 'spirit of fair play.' We hide a great deal behind these national totems." But Don Juan had a feeling that he had been pompous and was embarrassed.

"Dame Serena thinks it 'only fair,' if you are giving her free time for the sittings, that we let you off your compulsory cricket. I've arranged that for you with Trubshawe," said the headmaster.

"Thank you very much, sir." said Don Juan, genuinely grateful for the boon of being spared the world's most boring game, as he saw it.

"I don't suppose the dame will try to seduce you. Anyway, Trubshawe tells me that he is going to tell you the facts of life a trifle early. We usually wait until after the fifteenth birthday."

Henrietta had rather belatedly arranged for some Scottish friends of hers to have Don Juan to stay for the half-term holiday. The earl and countess of Stow and Lauder she had met crossing to New York on the French liner *Normandie*. The earl was one of the most noted collectors of rare books in Britain, a trustee of the British Museum, and had literary interests that often brought him to Paris and sometimes to New York. Sitting together at the captain's table, she had spent a happy five days discussing books with the earl and food with the countess, a rare Briton who knew what she was eating and appreciated, as did Henrietta, the stunning fare served up by the *Normandie's* incomparable chefs.

This cultivated and gregarious couple had two children of about Don Juan's age. Their son was a year older and at Eton, while their daughter was virtually the same age and at Eton's female equivalent, Rodean School for Girls.

The earl, driving his own car, fetched Don Juan from Deerhurst and, after stopping at Eton to collect his son, Giles, they all drove on together to Brown's Hotel in London, where the countess and her daughter, Juliet, were already installed.

Don Juan thoroughly enjoyed his weekend with Giles and Juliet. While both children rather liked their schools, much to Don Juan's surprise, they were mercifully reluctant to talk about them. On the first evening, the earl took them to see a vaudeville show with a then-celebrated pair of comics called Flanagan and Allen. The show was marvelously bawdy in a pleasantly Rabelaisian way, and the audience was a genuine cross section of the British public who roared with laughter, in common, at jokes which Don Juan would have imagined most of them far too prim to enjoy. It was, he supposed, a residual part of the British character that the eighteenth-century novels of Fielding and Smollett led one to expect, but in which the ushers at Deerhurst seemed remarkably lacking.

They had an excellent dinner afterward at the Café Royale, and the children were allowed to sit up till one o'clock in Giles's room discussing the show and laughing a great deal until the earl came and sent them off to bed.

All through the evening Don Juan was conscious of Juliet, but not of any desire for her. Her feminine presence was enough after the famine he endured at Deerhurst. She was pretty, with auburn hair and crinkly, laughing brown eyes, but she had no detectable sexuality. He wanted to see her again and be friends, but no more than he felt this about Giles.

The next day they went to the British Museum with the earl for a privileged tour of that great institution. Don Juan found that Juliet shared his wonder at the Elgin Marbles, and from that point on they talked more and more of painters and sculptors they admired, both classical and contemporary. That evening they all saw Noël Coward in *Present Laughter* at the Adelphi. Don Juan loved the Coward play and saw in it a welcome evidence that the English could laugh at themselves, reassuring after the smugness of Deerhurst.

On Sunday they all went to St. Paul's Cathedral for the morning service and heard the boys in the choir sing Stanford's *Magnificat*. Then, after a delicious lunch at the Savoy Grill, Giles went with his parents to watch a cricket match while Don Juan and Juliet journeyed by bus to the Tate Gallery to see the Turners. Don Juan had never seen any canvas by this greatest of English landscape painters except *The Harbor in Cádiz*, which now hung in his own mother's salon in Paris.

Moved to the edge of tears by those vast canvases, he wandered in a daze. Apart from the genius of Turner's vision of nature, of composition, of the very textures of atmosphere, Don Juan was stunned by the technical miracle of Turner's total mastery and understanding of light.

"While nothing about his pictures is in the least photographic," said Juliet afterward, while they were having fizzy lemonade and rock cakes in the Tate's tearoom, "don't you think he sort of foresaw what the camera can do?"

Don Juan suddenly loved her earnestness as she asked this question, so that he half-pretended not to understand her, to make her open up and give more of her view.

"I'm not quite sure what you mean," he said encouragingly.

"Well, those scenes in which the sun is so bright you can't look at them with the naked eye, the camera can sometimes see. I do photography at school, and we've done experiments exposing into the shadowed detail, letting the rest almost burn out. He did that with paint long before the camera was invented."

"Yes, he did. He also seemed to foresee something like a wide-angle lens, although I think other painters did that, too."

"You mean those paintings which took mirrored distortions and copied them?"

"Well, yes. But ever since Van Eyck, painters have changed lenses, as it were, in the view they give us of the world. Sometimes they seem wall-eyed and sometimes myopic in comparison to normal vision. I mean, I've sometimes wondered why the movies don't develop the convention of a triptych to tell some kinds of stories . . ."

It was her turn to continue the conversation only half-listening. Juliet had sometimes found the male sex rather disappointing. A romantically minded child, she had been raised on Walter Scott and J. M. Barrie and Robbie Burns and had only recently started to prefer the mocking Burns, or, rather, Burns in a mocking mood. The men in the modern world around her, with their hideous three-button suits and oiled short hair, seemed an unattractive lot in comparison to the males of literature and her imagination. She had noticed from the first moment she had seen him that Don Juan was a quite exceptionally good-looking boy. But she had kept fearing conceit in him, that he would act as if he knew that he was good-looking, and she had, in her feminine self, been on guard against liking him too much for fear that this was so. But by the time they had arrived at the Tate together, she had begun to be certain that she had a "crush" on him.

Now watching him as he drank another fizzy lemonade as if it were a rare and delicious champagne, and talking about how Turner affected him, she realized that it was not conceit that made him so sure of himself with women—rather it was as if he considered them all his "natural" companions, as no British boy, including Giles, ever did. She remembered, too, there being tears in his eyes when he had first seen the scope and breadth of Turner's work. She was moved to find such emotion in a plainly masculine person. But Juliet believed it to be proper for *her* to hide her own emotions.

In the romantic world of poetry and fiction, where her only experience of males lay, there was a strict rule of law. A girl was always *surprised* by masculine admiration. She only *consented* to be admired with reluctance. Her heart and mind must be relentlessly wooed, preferably in verse. Once won, she must be *true* until death. It was both edifying and frightening, this game, and traveling back on the bus with Don Juan she was wondering whether he "admired" her and what she could possibly do to make him think along those lines.

"May I write to you?" asked Don Juan formally as the big red bus swung around Sloane Square.

"Yes, I suppose you could," replied Juliet, hoping not to sound too enthusiastic.

"Do you promise to write back?" he asked.

"If I like what you write," she said, laughing at his surprised face.

"I take it, Lady Juliet, that news of cricket scores and my feats of scholarship won't suffice to make you take out your mauve writing paper with the bunny rabbits on the envelope?" Don Juan mocked back.

"Your news, Don Juan, will have to be cosmic and couched in something more inventive than iambic pentameters if you expect an answer on anything as elegant as loo paper," she said sharply, smarting under the suggestion that she used schoolgirl's writing paper.

"We're doing the love life of the slug in biology," he said. "If it turns out promisingly, perhaps a madrigal on the subject? Something you and the other girls in the dorm could sing to with lute and viol da gamba? I rather see the rest of them all a bit on the plump side in their nighties and you looking ravishing—"

"Be quiet, Juan, people are listening," said Juliet, giggling, as their neighbors on the bus, with their neutral English faces, stared at the two exuberant young people.

They looked at each other in silence thereafter, smiling at each other with their eyes, sensing that something pleasant and irreversible had taken place between them. And yet Don Juan, tremendously though he liked her company, did not yet think of Juliet as *woman*. Although only half aware of it, he was, for the first time in his life, held by an awakening platonic love. Fortunately Juliet as yet only comprehended romantic love; the erotic variety was still beyond her ken. So all was well between them.

Back at Deerhurst, Mr. Trubshawe's sex talk proved as memorable an interview as Don Juan was ever to have with his housemaster. Tea was on hand to smooth the way on this prickly subject.

"Ah, Juan, I hope that you like China tea. It's something of an experiment Verena is making."

"Delicious, sir."

"You're a big chap. Voice broken, I notice."

"Yes, sir."

"Noticed any emissions? Stains on the sheet. Wet dreams?"

"Yes, sir."

"Worried you a good deal, I dare say?"

"No, sir. I imagine the school laundry can cope . . .?"

"Of course. I don't want you to worry about it. It's your seed, you see."

"Yes, sir."

"Incidence of an erect penis when you're awake. Had any of that?"

'It has happened, sir."

"Awfully embarrassing, I know. The thing to avoid is touching it. Concentrate on something abstract. A logarithm, acrostics, pose yourself a problem in simple calculus. I found that to be efficacious myself."

"Why, sir?"

"Because you know by fiddling with it you can actually stimulate yourself into an ejaculation of the spermatozoa. And that is, of course, very wrong."

"Wrong?" Don Juan was incredulous, but managed to sound simply ignorant.

"Wrong, Juan. The sin of Onan. If you've missed that in the Bible I'll give you the verse and you can look it up, what."

"I remember it, sir. Scattering his seed. My English has improved since then, but I used to think of him as a careless farmer."

"Really? Most amusing," said Trubshawe with only a hint of a smile. He hoped the dago wouldn't interject too much. He hated giving sex talks and tried to make them brief.

"Yes, well, of course, to scatter your seed is against God's will, what. It must be saved strictly for procreation in marriage."

"Except the emissions at night."

"Yes, the best way to think of those is this. God has made this wonderful arrangement in our testes. Balls, you know, what. Rather like a bathtub they sometimes overfill, then out comes some of the water through the overflow."

"The emissions are simply overflow?"

"Exactly. Take no notice. Perfectly normal."

Mr. Trubshawe went on to describe the basic anatomy of the human female, for which he had a handy chart. The egg of a married woman and its eventual union with a live spermatozoon from her husband, with God's blessing, was the end of the saga.

It was over. But Don Juan could not resist asking a question.

"When one is married and finally inserts onself into the woman. Is that pleasurable?"

"Oh yes, a beautiful experience. Worth waiting for, Juan."

"Pleasurable for her?"

"Perhaps not at the time. But she is doing God's will, as we men do in waiting. Then children are a great joy for her if she is blessed with them. Women are more spiritual, of course. That is their nature."

Don Juan used some of his newfound leisure to help Parsons-Purefoy restock his brass-rubbings collection. He also learned to play tennis, a game at which he soon found himself more than proficient. Springer, an excellent player with whom he now had an easygoing friendship, had undertaken to teach him the game. He considered it paying off a political debt to Don Juan. For while the other prefects had, resentfully, to make their own evening meals in their studies and press their own clothes, Springer was entirely in charge of making the new system work. The head of the house had become irrelevant, and, for all practical purposes, Springer reigned in his stead.

Dame Serena's picture gathered detail and texture, and Don Juan found it harder work than he had imagined to maintain that stance of straining virility which his portrait required. One day he arrived for his sitting to find Blodwen in the kitchen having tea with Dame Serena.

Now Blodwen, of the snub nose, came from the hills of remote Dyfed in Wales, where thousands of her countrymen spoke no English at all. She had about two hundred and fifty words of the language, most of which had to do with kitchens where she worked. Her letters to and from home, her songs, her hopes, and her dreams were all in Welsh. She was saving to go home and continue her education in night school, her ambition to marry a Welsh schoolteacher.

At Deerhurst she and Gwynneth were under the supervision of

the female cook at Trubshawe's house, and they lived in the servants' annex. They had every other Sunday off and half a day off a week; neither could they take together. Their board and lodging were free, and they tried to save money out of a pound a week in pay. Three million people were unemployed in Britain at that time, a disproportionate number in Wales.

In spite of Dame Serena's efforts to promote conversation between them, the Welsh girl was very shy in Don Juan's presence. He came from the other side of the kitchen door to the refectory, where they were raising demigods, if Cook was to be believed. He was also *boy,* and while she spent many of her waking hours thinking about boys, a real, live, breathing, staring, speaking one was a bit intimidating. Moreover, to her confusion and wonder, she knew that this boy had endured six strokes of the cane for speaking to her through the window and another twelve for trying to come to see her in the annex. His face reminded her of an illustration in a storybook of Llewellyn ap Llewellyn, last true Welsh Prince of Wales, as a boy. A dark Celtic prince was how he was described, hero of heroes and the last of his line. Awed by Don Juan's presence across Dame Serena's kitchen table, she could only expect an answer in monosyllables. But finally Don Juan made an unexpected breakthrough.

"Are there giants in your part of Wales?" he asked.

"How did you know?" she replied.

Now, Don Juan did *not* know. He had expected her to bridle at being teased in this way, and, he hoped, giggle and make some saucy answer.

"If there were giants left in Europe, where else could they be?" he managed to ask seriously. Dame Serena looked at him as if to tell him she was keeping the score.

"That's true, but very few people here have ever seen him. Cook thought I was lying when I told her. But she's English. You're not English?"

"No, I'm Spanish. Is he always there, your giant?"

"Of course, he's on the hillside, isn't he?"

"I see," said Don Juan, mystified.

"Our minister is always sending people up to cover his . . ." She paused and giggled. "His ceiliog with turf and that. Then in the night we creep up and uncover him again."

Dame Serena shouted with laughter at this anecdote, and Blodwen heaved her little shoulders in delighted giggles. Don Juan was mystified.

"Have you ever seen an animal rendered on a hillside by taking away all the earth from a chalk-based hill?" Dame Serena asked him.

"I've seen photographs of a huge horse like that somewhere in England, executed by Bronze Age people, I believe," answered Don Juan, starting to understand.

"Right. There are many of them all over the British Isles. Several are of men. None, as far as I know, of women. A man on a hillside who is eighty feet long can reasonably be described as a giant."

"His ceiliog?" asked Don Juan, who had guessed the meaning but watched to see the girl blush. Her olive skin and the bright brown eyes of a doe with dense, long lashes to match reminded him of what he had heard of the dark Celts, a race quite distinct from the English with their Germanic build and occasionally Norman coloring.

"Oh, no, noo. Don't tell him," said Blodwen, blushing now right to the tip of that nose which Don Juan found so adorable.

"How much turf does it take the minister to cover it up?" asked Don Juan.

"It's almost as long as this room," admitted Blodwen shyly.

After tea Dame Serena and Don Juan went to the studio and Blodwen set about scrubbing the kitchen floor, for which the dame paid her the going rate of a shilling to put toward her savings. Don Juan thought the girl's little lean body in its cheap Woolworth's dress extraordinarily touching. She aroused in him a feeling of tenderness as well as desire, and this new emotion occupied his mind as he stripped for Dame Serena and went and took up his pose.

"I like the way you look today, bucko," said Dame Serena. "Giving you a sniff of that filly has put some juice back into you."

"I suppose she's a virgin?" he said.

"No reason to think otherwise," said Dame Serena. "D'you want her that badly? Ah, yes, I can see that you do."

Slowly brushing his thigh as it stretched itself, the ceiliog of Don Juan saluted the thought of the lovely snub-nosed Blodwen.

"If you want to woo her, you can meet here whenever you like. But I'll not pimp for you, bucko. Now, what are we going to do about Don Juan rampant?"

"I shall think of logarithms and acrostics. Bloodnut uses calculus, but that's beyond me."

He stared across the studio toward the door that led to the kitchen. He was trying to conjure up numbers when something moved. It was Blodwen, standing, quiet as a cat, watching him, thinking that in the deep shadow by the door she was invisible. Don

Juan pretended that he hadn't seen her, but he was more aroused than ever by her presence.

"Are you painting 'it' at this very moment?" he asked the Dame.

"No, no, don't worry about it, Juan. I'm doing your thigh where it loops over the pommel. Particularly difficult because of the foreshortening."

"Have you ever painted the Beak?" he asked.

"Yes. How did you guess?"

"Like this?" he said, not wishing to answer her question.

"No, but bare to the waist. It's upstairs in my bedroom."

"Have you ever painted a man like this before?"

"Oh yes, several of my Romany men."

Don Juan knew the girl was there watching, her dark eyes like those of an alert animal staring, amazed and fascinated, at the world outside the safe forest.

"Did you actually paint them as I am now, rampant?" he asked.

"Yes, oh yes. While I painted furiously away, I kept them like that for hours, talking. Of what we'd done and we'd do. I was, and I suppose I still am, a very different female creature from the charming Blodwen. If she's a virgin you'll need to be tender and very gently take her where you want her. But I always needed to fight over it. Like a recalcitrant and high-bred mare. I like a man to be like a stallion. Literally. I like to stoop for him and feel his hairy belly on my back, to have him biting my neck and shoulders. I could never stand a caress. The good, hard ceiliog of a strong, mean man, that's my Valhalla, bucko. But I see I'm not helping matters."

"Oh, I wouldn't say that," said Don Juan, thinking of Blodwen still lurking by the door. "Could I take Blodwen up to see the paintings in your bedroom? The painting of the gypsies and of the Beak? That's where they are, I take it?"

"Yes, but I think they would shock her, frighten her, even," said the dame.

"Maybe so, but I'd like to take her there *now*." Don Juan's voice was raised enough so that Dame Serena sensed that he was projecting it to someone else. She looked around and saw the suddenly embarrassed girl, who ran from the room.

Don Juan was off the saddle and had slipped on his trousers.

"Please let us be for an hour," he said, running across the studio.

"I will—I have plenty to do here. But promise me you'll be gentle. And don't forget to look in the drawer beside the bed. I don't want any accidents!" she shouted after him.

He found her, an entirely blushing girl, even her arms and neck had reddened, kneeling on the kitchen floor, trying to restart her scrubbing.

"I couldn't resist it," she said when he knelt by her. "I don't know why. Not just to see a boy naked. I've got brothers, you know. But I wanted to see *you*. She told me that's how she was painting you. I couldn't believe it, see? She's such a strange woman. I thought maybe she fancies you. I didn't want that. I don't know why . . ."

He knew that she would go on talking until he kissed her, so he took her still-red, rueful little face in his hands and did so. She kissed him back and went on kissing him with frantic nuzzling kisses, as if she feared they might be all she would ever be allowed. Then she broke away, looking fearfully at the kitchen door.

"She might come here any minute."

"Not for at least an hour. She made me promise to be gentle."

"She said that? Isn't she a strange woman?"

"She's Welsh."

"But she's an artist, see, that's why she's different."

For so long Blodwen had thought about this moment when she might be with *him*. Talking to *him*. No one else there. A chance she'd thought could never come because he really did seem like a demigod to her. The most beautiful and perfect of boys, whom this rich lady artist was painting stark naked. Talking about men as if they were horses. Amazing. It was like a tall story told in a pub. But much better because here *he* really was. Touching her. Kissing her. Wanting to make love to her. Her mum would kill her if she knew she'd made love to a boy who hadn't promised to marry her. She wasn't a prude, her mum. "You have to do it sometimes," she had said. "But get them to propose first. Then there's *the breach of promise* if they try and wriggle out of it." But this was a schoolboy. Tall as a man, almost, but not yet fifteen. He couldn't ask her. How could he? But she wanted him to be the first one. This chance had taken a long time to come, and he might not ask her again. And she did so want him to be the first one. "Save it for your husband if you can," her mum had said. But what good was that if all your life you wished you'd given it to a boy who looked like a god and had taken so much pain to be with you?

"Have you seen upstairs?" he was saying.

"No, just the kitchen. It's a wonderful house, though, isn't it? Hot and cold in the sink. Indoor privy."

"Let's go and look upstairs," he was saying, adding, "She said we could."

So she followed him in a happy dream up the stairs, admiring the appointments on the way. All the pictures. Chintz curtains. Carpets everywhere. She was glad of those. His poor bare feet. She kept looking at his body, wanting to run her hands over it quickly before he disappeared. Because all of this, she was sure, might end at any moment.

Don Juan led her along the corridor of the upper floor and peered into several rooms, wondering which was the dame's. There were two single guest bedrooms, and then at the end of the corridor he opened a door into a huge bedroom which must have taken up half the area of the house. They entered it together and Blodwen gasped. Don Juan had known what to expect, and yet he was surprised. He knew the sort of pictures of men that Springer kept locked in his desk. These were not, at first sight, so dissimilar. But then, as he looked at them, he saw the difference. Stubbs, the great eighteenth-century painter of horses, had shown the nobility of the beasts, their enormous pride. Here was what Dame Serena had caught in the men she painted. The beast who is so proud, so utterly confident of the marvel of his manhood that he stood before her like a stallion sniffing the air, watching for his mare. Don Juan was abashed to realize she had seen the same thing in him.

"Let's not stay in here," said Blodwen, overwhelmed by the sheer aggression to the senses of the pictures on the walls, pulling Don Juan back toward the passage. He left her for an instant, shielding her eyes, and ran to the bedside table and opened the drawer. The familiar packages that Berthe had so handy were there. He took one and hurried his little Welsh girl to the first guest room they came upon.

She let him undress her, feeling like the beggar maid to King Caphetua; another of her favorite fairy stories, with the wonderful illustration of the king in his marvelous armor and the beggar maid in a dress shiny and tight like a snake's skin, a dress she'd have loved to wear for him. She could hardly bear for him to look at her imperfections once she was bare. Her left breast that seemed a little bigger than the other, the hair under her arms, when she knew from magazines she'd seen that there were women, rich women, who shaved themselves there and on their legs. Probably he'd be making comparisons.

And indeed he was. How extraordinary, he thought, to be with a woman who has not one single artifice about her body. She is as clean and original as an aboriginal Eve. She smells faintly of *she*. That most wonderful of scents to Don Juan's senses. Her body is that of a child-woman, formed for its function but not yet shaped by its use. He held her by the hips and asked her to look at him, but she could not take her eyes from what she saw as her imperfect self. She felt about to cry. She covered her breasts with her arms and pressed her thighs close together, closing herself off from him.

He came and stood behind her and took her to the window, enclosing her in his arms as he did so. The sunshine bathed them both and he whispered, "Let me see the sun touch your breasts. There, do you see how beautiful it is, your breast? How golden the sun makes it? Why d'you hide it? Is it because with you I'll be the first one? And I am, aren't I?"

"You are. You are," she said emphatically, turning to him, forgetting her shyness and her shame, finding him bare again, as he had been on the saddle, feeling him kiss almost every inch of her, from her head to her toes. But now she felt so weak that she could hardly stand.

He took her to the bed and did things to her body with his mouth and hands, his chest, his thighs, that were new and more extraordinary and magical than any mere caress of which she'd even dreamed. He did things that she would have feared, or found, perhaps, unnatural, had it not been *he* who did them.

At first she felt the muscles of her loins stiffen as they were invaded by his inquisitive and passionate tongue, experimenting as a musician does with a stringed instrument and drum, finding pitch and frequency, making a music in her body that blotted out for her the room, the bed, the world, and left only the blooming and throbbing of her rose, that made her hover in a marvelous new limbo between the unknowable and the beyond caring. That place where a woman new to love, like Blodwen, feels that only her tight hold on a slim thread of reason is saving her from falling into a fearful but tempting oblivion.

Trusting Don Juan, she finally let go, found her loins thrusting and melting, heard her own voice crying and speaking, felt his lips now on her cheeks and ears, her breasts crushed to his chest and, straining her open thighs toward him, knew at last the pain and bliss of his possessing thrusts. Agony so mixed with pleasure and triumph that, as she clung tight to him, struggling to regain her senses, she wondered how she could ever bear to feel his body leave hers, now at long, long last it was there.

He pulled the covers over them, and together they stayed, attached and content, resting and loving, loving and resting, till Dame Serena brought them both a cup of tea.

The summer term wound its way pleasantly enough toward its close. Springer and Don Juan entered the house tennis doubles competition and did well. Mrs. Trubshawe played with Stephen Martin as her partner, and Don Juan thought she looked at her most desirable in tennis clothes. He could see now that her breasts were high and large, and they swam viscously as she moved.

"I know what you're thinking, you beast," hissed Springer. "Concentrate on your game and think of Spain, dear!"

On July 15, 1936, the Spanish military rose in rebellion against the Republic of Spain. Perhaps the key ideological war of the twentieth century was under way. While it is remembered as the Spanish Civil War, it involved, before it was finished, regular troops from Italy and Germany and confirmed the demoralization and cowardice of the governments of all the major Western democracies, particularly Britain. The *Times* of London became daily reading for Don Juan for the rest of the term, and he listened to the newscasts on Springer's radio whenever he got a chance.

Next evening Mr. Trubshawe arrived at house prayers in an unusually jovial mood. After they had all intoned the final ". . . as it was in the beginning, is now and ever shall be, world without end, Amen," he made an announcement:

"The headmaster and ah, I have surveyed this, ah, experiment we have been making in the House by the Pit and feel that it has been, ah, interesting. However, it does seem to us that it is rather *unfair* to the boys who will be prefects next term and who in their day had to fag to deny them the privileges that are traditional here. Tradition's the thing. None of us have been very happy with the suspension of beating in this house. Again, it doesn't seem quite *fair* that a boy in another house at Deerhurst can be beaten while a boy here at Trubshawe's can get away scot-free with only some extra work for the same offense, what. It's a matter that has been discussed with the governors of this school. Their consensus on the matter, the headmaster tells me, is that we should keep up these traditions.

"There are people in the country, lefties and people of that kidney, who think that blood sports should be banned, that the House of Lords is anachronistic, what. The point I'm making is that this school is supposed to make a boy into a 'chap.' A real 'chap.' It's good for him to go through a little hell now and then. From the beginning of the next term things will be as they always were."

The enthusiasm of the sixteen-year-old boys who would succeed the outgoing prefects the next term was considerable. Several clapped. All the prefects except Springer wore broad smiles, as if vindicated in some way. Only Don Juan and his fellow first-year boys had that sick feeling that comes when an apparently bright victory turns into a tawdry defeat.

Don Juan was in Springer's study the following evening listening to the news from Spain. Andalusia remained in the Republic's hands, but the rebels had taken Cordova and were still fighting over Seville. In the countryside, however, the anarchist militia was gaining the upper hand over the Guardia Civil, who had, for the most part, joined the rebel army.

The main items of news were over when he felt Springer's hand on his shoulder. He turned and saw the older boy's eyes, inviting, proposing, and unexpectedly vulnerable. Don Juan sat quite still, wondering what, if anything, he felt. Springer had been, in many ways, a remarkable friend to him. Together they had fought a campaign and almost won a little war. He felt not an iota of desire for Springer, yet he couldn't but like him a lot. Before, he had managed to turn Springer's advances into a joke because they were master and servant. He had the privilege of that distance. Now, as friends, it wasn't as easy. Finally, there was the curiosity factor. When Springer's lips approached his he didn't flinch or move away; he simply waited. He felt himself being kissed; he felt Springer's hands on his body. He knew at once that he loathed it, that for him the smell of man was not so much repellent as wrong. Not in any moral sense, but in that it did not fit with any instinct he had.

Gently he disengaged himself. "I'm sorry, Springer. It's as you always say. I'm an incorrigible hearty."

"I know, angel," said Springer, sighing. "I'm afraid Braddock won't be waiting for me either."

"Good heavens, bum, love," said Don Juan, slipping into his friend's camp argot. "There's a whole circusful of queens up at Oxford. They'll light fireworks when handsome old you arrives, you know they will."

"Don't talk like that, angel. It doesn't suit you," said Springer.

And they remained firm friends.

Among the end-of-term events was the Latin dissertation contest, which occurred on the next day. Don Juan knew his Latin prose was less impressive than his obvious ability to be articulate in public. Nevertheless, the headmaster, who had for the last term been teaching him Latin composition, encouraged him to enter. He had planned to do a Ciceronian piece, *"Honor virtutis praemium"* ("Honor is the reward of valor"), as a small private joke between himself and the headmaster. But the news the housemaster had announced made him change his mind, although not to tell the headmaster he had done so.

The Anglo-Saxon mores and habits of mind that had prompted the housemaster's speech reminded Don Juan of the book that Henrietta had given him to read on his first journey to Deerhurst. It was called simply *Prejudices* (Fourth Series), and was written by H. L. Mencken, the writer whom Henrietta most recommended as giving a true picture of America. Mencken had much to say about Anglo-Saxons in general in this book, referring to the English in a way only a knowing cousin could.

The competition was held in the school's principal assembly room, known, for some long-forgotten reason, as the Roman Baths. It was actually Jacobean, its decorations the work of Inigo Jones, but its lines of Doric columns supporting a frescoed ceiling with a hideous painting of the conspirators waiting with their daggers for Julius Caesar, which may have led to the assembly's old cognomen.

Virgil, Ovid, Horace, Sallust, and Seneca were declaimed in front of the whole school. The competitors stood to one side of the stage where the judges sat on a rostrum, the headmaster at their center. The competitors were given no lectern, for they were presumed to know their speeches by heart. Don Juan was the only junior among the competitors. When, third from last, he walked center stage before the whole school, a fourteen-year-old who looked a mature sixteen, a foreigner who, against all the odds, was clearly destined to be one of the school's winners, he commanded close attention.

"Quales naturas, O illustri magistri, clarissime cerno in genere hominum qui Anglici-Saxones dicuntur? Statim duas qualitates praecipue eminere confirmo. Alteram singularem atque desperatam, ut videtur, infirmitatem habemus: imbecillitas innata quidquam difficilem facile et ꞁrecte conficere, sive contagionem separare, sive cantum scribere. Altera mollitia mira terroribus metibusque est— brevi, paterna timiditas.

"Sane generi promptissimi et felicissimi timiditatem assignare, mentem in ridiculum vocare; tamen credo iustam inquisitionem historiae me probare. Maxima pars rerum grandiorum fortitudinis quas lactentes scholiis admirari docentur—id est, res gestas generis et non facinora disiuncta hominum singularum, qui certe plerumque partim alii progeniti—adeo principis virtutis omnino indiguerunt. Cogitate vel, O professores, res prosequentas duorum magnorum amplificationem imperiorum, et Britannicum et Americanum. Num utnum actum quisquam animum sincerum atque constatiam elicuit? Minime vero. Utrique imperii primo constructi sunt fraude et caede inermos indomitos, et posthac spoliatione nationes sine amicis et infirmos. . . ." *

When, after five more minutes, he faced the Roman Baths with a bow, the eighty percent of the school who didn't really understand Latin well enough to follow any of the dissertations clapped him as they had the other competitors. The headmaster looked in front of him into the body of the hall, absorbing the colossal insult to his pride in being a judge of boys. He had been sure that the freedom of Dame Serena's house and studio would buy Don Juan's loyalty in spite of the need to restore Deerhurst traditions to Trubshawe's house. But Don Juan's stupid sense of honor had come first, as he might have guessed it would. The boy would have to go. Independence strong enough for such an act of defiance in an intelligent fourteen-year-old was bad enough, but once he was older, even if denied, as he must now be, any part among Deerhurst's principalities and powers, he could be exceedingly dangerous.

That night after the lights had been turned out, Don Juan felt quite lightheaded at what he had done. The adrenaline still pumped in his veins, and he had no desire for sleep. Slipping on a pair of trousers and a shirt, but remaining barefoot, he walked down the darkened stairs and passages out into the night. The annex where Blodwen slept was beyond the kitchen block, sheltered and by itself in a clump of trees. He had been caught before when he tried to get into the building, by the cook coming back late with some friends from the pub. The door, however, was not locked, then or now, and Blodwen had told him exactly how to find her room.

---

* What, illustrious masters, are the characters that I discern most clearly in the so-called Anglo-Saxon type of man? I may answer at once that two stick out above all others. One is his curious and apparently incurable incompetence—his congenital inability to do any difficult thing easily and well, whether it be isolating a bacillus or writing a sonata. The other is his astounding susceptibility to fears and alarms—in short, his hereditary cowardice.

To accuse so enterprising and successful a race of cowardice, of course, is to risk immediate derision; nevertheless, I believe that a fair-minded examination of its history will bear me out. Nine-tenths of the great feats of derring-do that its sucklings are taught to venerate in school—that is, its feats as a race, not the isolated exploits of its extraordinary individuals, most of them at least partly of other stocks—have been wholly lacking in even the most elementary gallantry. Consider, O teachers, the events attending the extension of the two great empires, English and American. Did either movement evoke any genuine courage and resolution? The answer is plainly no. Both empires were built up primarily by swindling and butchering unarmed savages, and after that by robbing weak and friendless nations. . . .

It was Don Juan's misfortune that a perhaps more serious tragedy was in the air that night. Verena Trubshawe had been out to play bridge with some other housemasters' wives, but one partner had been unable to join them, so they broke up early. She had come into the house to find no one there and her husband's study empty. Remembering that all the lights seemed to be out in the prefects' studies, she wondered where her husband could be. Accordingly, she wandered into the main corridor of the House by the Pit, a thing she very rarely did, particularly at night.

Ten paces took her outside Stephen Martin's study, and out of curiosity she opened the door and turned on the light.

Wanting, at all costs, to block out what she had seen, she had run the whole length of the corridor and out into the fresh air.

Verena Trubshawe was not in the least surprised. But she would just have much preferred not to *see* it. She had for a long time had plenty of similar grounds for leaving her husband, but it had never occurred to her to do so. After all, none of the boys he'd liked ever stayed around long enough for anything much to happen. Once, one of them had nearly come back to Deerhurst as a junior usher. She had told Trubshawe that she could not stay if that happened, and somehow the young man had changed his mind.

Frightful though being Mrs. Trubshawe was, in some ways, it had its compensations, from Verena's point of view. In the small pool of Deerhurst she was somebody. Nobody knew about her husband's illicit activities. In an age when a semi-educated middle-class woman had a dearth of alternatives, she had opted for security.

Standing, breathing in the cool air of the summer night, she saw a boy come out of the house and set off toward the external entrance to the kitchens and the servants' annex beyond.

Walking quietly along the grass edge to the cricket pitch that skirted the House by the Pit, she followed the figure until she saw him enter the annex. By that time she knew whom she was following. Don Juan had impinged on her consciousness sufficiently on the tennis court for her to recognize the way he walked, the way he carried himself, and the cast of his profile as he opened the annex door and appeared, for an instant, silhouetted against the light.

In the mood that she found herself, hating Trubshawe, feeling self-pity for the humiliating half-life she had chosen to live, she felt resentful of the beautiful boy who so determinedly went out to take what he wanted. Her normal reaction would have been simply to alert her husband to this gross infringement of the rules and forget the matter. For why should she feel pity or understanding when she lived under rules herself which were quite as onerous and would last the rest of her life? But on this particular night she felt the liberation as well as the pain that the powerless onlooker feels. And something about the very sight or thought of Don Juan stirred her senses. She wanted to delay reporting him. She wanted to watch.

Poor Blodwen remained in Don Juan's memory long thereafter inextricably connected with voyeurism. He had exploited Blodwen's curiosity to win her. Now Verena Trubshawe's curiosity was to conclude the matter.

But in the first minutes that he spent with Blodwen that night he was, of course, quite contentedly unaware of being watched. He woke his sleepy Welsh love by putting the side light on by her bed. He had taken off his clothes in the dark and stood beside her, warning her to be quiet.

Verena Trubshawe stooped to look through the keyhole, and she saw him and saw the girl's face alight with pleasure and desire. She heard him say "Blodwen vach!" ("darling!"), as the Welsh girl had taught him.

Blodwen whispered, "Juan bach, Juan bach, Juan bach" to him, kissing his ceiliog, and then Don Juan faced his scarred posterior to Verena Trubshawe's point of view and Blodwen's legs rose up to take him. The girl's pleasure, which she saw and heard, excited Verena Trubshawe even as it enraged her. She flung open the door, determined that she too would *feel* something that night, if it was only righteous indignation and the humiliation of the two naked children. She physically hauled Don Juan off the Welsh girl, shouting:

"Stop fucking her, will you? Stop fucking! For fuck's sake, stop fucking . . ."

She couldn't prevent herself shouting and repeating that unique Anglo-Saxon word. It continued to stream out of her mouth like the gasps from an epileptic. Cook appeared and Gwynneth and the groundsmen and the handyman, while poor little Blodwen hid under the sheets and Don Juan struggled into his trousers.

Don Juan was summoned from his dormitory at six o'clock next morning by the head of the house. He was told to dress in his pajamas and over them to put on his trousers and shirt. Half an hour later he found himself in the sanatorium, a separate building mainly used to isolate epidemics like mumps and chicken pox. There followed four hours of waiting in an examination room, during which he was ignored completely by the nurse, who didn't even offer the usual cup of tea. So far, Don Juan had been told nothing of what he was to face, except that the head of the house, when questioned, had not denied that it was to be a capital beating.

The arrival of the doctor at ten o'clock to examine him confirmed his worst fears. The state of his heart was checked, and his blood pressure. His buttocks were cursorily examined to see that any previous stripes he might have received were not infected, and that he did not suffer, as many boys do, from sore boils on the behind. He was found to be caneworthy. "Nothing wrong with you" were the only words the doctor said to him.

The head of the house came and collected him and took him along to the school prefects' common room at twelve o'clock. Don Juan's thoughts were of his grandfather and of Blodwen. As they made the ten-minute walk from the sanatorium to the college, Don Juan kept on asking the head of the house what would happen to her. Finally Stephen Martin was tempted to reply, although it was clearly not "the rule" to do so.

"I should think they'll send her to some whorehouse in Cardiff. I wonder if you've got a disease? Anyway, forget about her. We sent her packing this morning. Mrs. Trubshawe saw to it personally."

It had been in his mind to put up a fight rather than accept their punishment, but in the same way that he had grieved for Isabel and had accepted his grandfather's sentence, he now saw the beating that he must suffer as some atonement for the misery his little Welsh Blodwen vach was undergoing as she faced the world disgraced and alone. He was determined that he would show them Spanish pride. That if they had failed to feel his contempt in his dissertation, they would feel it now.

When he came into the school prefects' common room he almost laughed aloud at the absurd panoply that had been assembled to punish one boy. Thirteen school prefects, including Springer, stood in gowns and mortarboards, winged collars and white ties, striped trousers and tail coats. Each held a cane. They stood in two lines, making a corridor to the low common-room table. The head of the school, whose privilege it was to wear a carnation in his buttonhole, now replaced Stephen Martin at Don Juan's side.

"You will receive a capital beating. You know why?" asked the head of the school.

"I know why," said Don Juan calmly.

"You will take all your clothes off except your pajama trousers."

Two prefects came forward to manhandle him to the table as was the custom, having taken his clothes and thrown them into the corner of the room.

"Please," said Don Juan. "I can get there by myself."

But they dragged him just the same, forcing his head under the table, kicking his legs straight. Behind him he heard a slight commotion, and looking back through his legs he saw that Springer was walking backward toward him and that, in a sharp movement, he had broken his cane on his knee.

"Bum, for Christ's sake, what the hell are you doing?" asked the head of the school.

"I will not take part in this piece of hypocrisy, this childish judicial crime. At least a quarter of the people in this room have been buggering each other silly for the last four years, and we're going through this savage charade because he fucks one willing little girl—"

"Bum, are you mad?" shouted Stephen Martin. "This is a capital beating, not your bloody debating society."

"Get him out of here," barked the head of the school, and three of the prefects pulled the protesting Springer from the room.

"Sorry, not fair to keep you waiting in this way, old boy," said the head of the school to Don Juan's bottom.

And the beating began. Each prefect took a twenty-foot run at Don Juan. Each was allowed two runs. But they took it in strict turns, "going in" in order of seniority. Oh, their love of ceremony, from coronations to this squalid little scene, how it protects them from reality, thought Don Juan, just before the first burning pain hit him. He had been allowed to empty his bladder before leaving the sanatorium, but he feared dreadfully that he would suffer the humiliation of being unable to control himself. Thought of this carried him through the first eight blows, until nothing but excruciating pain filled his every sense, his whole shrieking nervous system. The longer run meant that the cane actually bit into the flesh, sometimes cracking the skin itself. After the eighth cane had struck, almost every succeeding blow was hitting flesh already whealed and often raw. The agony was making him retch, but with the retching came a merciful receding of consciousness. He did not faint, but he forgot where he was, trying to gasp in air in the intervals between blows. Suddenly there was shouting behind him, and he felt water, stinging cold water, and trying to keep himself taut and from falling, he slipped. On the floor his consciousness at once returned, the excruciating pain and the sight of Springer, standing at the door, wielding one of the college fire hoses.

"Run, Juan," he was shouting. "Get out of here!"

And Don Juan, clad only in his pajama trousers, his backside, bleeding and raw, showing through the tattered material, ran down the main college stairs, out across the quadrangle, and toward the headmaster's house. The only thought in his mind was, I must go and see my grandfather and tell him that I have endured my punishment and consider myself free. The headmaster has had his revenge, he thought; now he will have to show me that he is capable of being civilized.

Don Juan knew that it was the tradition for someone who had received a capital beating to be patched up in the sanatorium and sent from the school the same day. No pretense was ever made that the beating was intended as *remedial* punishment. It was intended simply as revenge upon those who mocked Deerhurst and its penumbra of tradition. He doubted very much if the headmaster ever saw these boys. Their parents would be summoned to take them away.

He burst into the outer office, making the appointments secretary scream. The Beak opened his door and saw him.

"I'm not going to see you, Juan," he said coldly, disguising his hideous embarrassment as best he could. "Telephone Trubshawe, Miss Penrose," he added, his voice almost squeaking.

"But he's bleeding, Headmaster," said Miss Penrose.

"Is he?" cried the headmaster. "Not on the carpet, I hope. Better call the sanatorium. Have him taken there at once."

"I want to go home to Spain!" said Don Juan, trying to hold back tears as the pain and throbbing increased.

"We've cabled your mother in France to have you fetched, dear," said Miss Penrose, trying to telephone the sanatorium.

"No good," said Juan. "She's in America with a friend. I want to go home to Spain. Please call Major Barnet at Thomas Cook."

The head of the school and Stephen Martin, both dripping wet and bedraggled, came into the office.

"Well, Keith, well, Stephen!" shouted the headmaster. "You seem to have bungled this one extravagantly! Go and change. I want to see all school prefects in my study in half an hour."

"But sir, Springer's gone off his rocker—" started the head of the school.

"Go, you're making idiots of yourselves and me. Get out!" barked the headmaster.

Before leaving the office to enter his civilized sanctum, the headmaster turned to Don Juan.

"You will not be coming back here, Juan," he said. "But this, at least, will teach you never to commit the 'unpopular crime,' wherever you may be. Miss Penrose, call Thomas Cook and ask for them to arrange for Don Juan to be taken straight to his family in Spain."

8
Rebels Versus Revolutionaries

All Madrid was astir in the warm summer night, loud with the
rumble of lorries stacked with rifles. For some days the workers'
organisations had been announcing that a fascist rising might take
place at any moment, that the soldiers in the barracks had been "got
at" and munitions were pouring in.

At one o'clock in the morning the government had decided to
arm the people, and from three o'clock the production of a union-
card gave every member the right to bear arms.

It was high time, for the reports telephoned in from the
provinces, which had sounded hopeful between midnight and two
o'clock, were beginning to strike a different note.

—André Malraux, *Man's Hope*

It is not in children to look back when the currents of
their lives are running fast. Nor, unlike Lot's wife, did Don Juan have
any special temptation to do so. Only when the horror of Deerhurst as
an institution began to fade in his memory did he start remembering

with pleasure the personalities of his friends there. Dame Serena, that lover of horses and men, for whom real live satyrs ought to have existed. Horder, the farmer; and Portarlington, the forgivable snob; and Kabanda, who, through his African prism, saw the whole of Deerhurst as theater of the absurd. Manley-Cohen, who shook off the anti-Semitism constantly thrown at him as a puppy dog shakes off water. Parsons-Purefoy, that rare creature, an Englishman with soul, who managed to get a message to the sanatorium just before Don Juan left, which read, "We will fill up those flower pots in your honor next term. Good luck from us all."

The image of his friends having a secret pre-Christmas bacchanal in Bloodnut's glass house, arcing their little riddles into every precious chrysanthemum pot, was, indeed, a delicious fantasy, to which he occasionally returned.

When Major Barnet arrived to collect Don Juan from Deerhurst, he viewed his assignment with some perplexity. The office of Don Juan's grandfather had cabled from Barcelona that their boss was in Seville, care of the Hotel Bristol. When Major Barnet and Don Juan arrived in London after a journey in a wholly reserved first-class carriage, so that the suffering Don Juan could lie full length on his stomach, they found that Thomas Cook had received some precise instructions. Don Juan's grandfather was now at an address in Biarritz, near the Spanish border, visiting Juan March, his fellow industrialist. His grandson was to be brought there at once. After a visit to the dispensary at St. George's Hospital to change the dressings on Don Juan's battered bum, they drove straight to Croydon airport, south of London.

Here a chartered Dragon Rapide, piloted by a Captain Bart, flew them to Biarritz, after refueling at Cherbourg. The thoughtful major had a mattress put on the floor of the aircraft so that Don Juan was not compelled to try to stand up, an anyway impossible task in so cramped a plane.

In Biarritz there was a message telling them that they should go straight to Seville, signaling their time of arrival. Since it was by now nighttime, the major decided to keep the plane and proceed again in the morning. Meanwhile, hearing that the British ambassador to Spain, Sir Henry Chilton, had retreated with most of his staff to the French border town of Hendaye, Barnet telephoned to him for up-to-date news of the military rebellion, particularly in relation to Seville. He was told that Quiepo de Llano, the commander of the *carabineros*, had seized the city for the rebels, and that the embassy expected that the army would soon control the whole of Spain. Reassured, Major

Barnet, who was on the side of armies everywhere, kept to his plan of flying to Seville. An attempt to telephone Don Juan's grandfather at the Andalusia Palace Hotel was foiled by the inability of the French telephone operator to get through. He therefore sent a cable advising of their expected time of arrival.

The Seville airport, when they arrived at eight in the morning, was quite deserted, except for the inevitable *pareja*, the pair of Guardia Civil, and some workers at the refueling dock. There were no taxis. Don Juan, lying on the floor of the aircraft, had not seen what the pilot had pointed out to Major Barnet, that a large number of small fires seemed to be burning in the suburbs of Seville. The major, assuming that a chauffeur would be meeting the boy with a car, saw no reason to alarm Don Juan by mentioning the matter. Faced with no one at the airport to meet them and no obvious form of transport, Major Barnet showed the initiative which had long since made his company a byword in the travel business.

Leaving Don Juan with the pilot while the plane was refueling, he rented a bicycle from one of the *pareja* and returned half an hour later, driving an ancient Ford truck which, from the smell of it, was normally used for transporting hogs or cattle.

Asking the pilot to wait for him, the major, with Don Juan kneeling on the seat beside him, set out for Seville, cradling in his lap Baedecker's guide to Spain (1929), open at the map of the city. What the German authors of that admirable compendium had been unable to foresee was that on this 21st day of July 1936, almost a third of Seville was inaccessible, because militia loyal to the government held out there against the attacks of Quiepo de Llano's forces, composed of the Guardia Civil, elements of a regular-army artillery regiment, and cadres of the fascist Falange. Major Barnet drove down the Avenue of the Two Theresas, which, according to the map, turned into the Calle de los Capuchinos, from whence it was only eight city blocks to the cathedral, opposite to which was situated the Hotel Bristol.

Long before he reached the Capuchinos turning he was aware that the streets were unnaturally empty, and Don Juan had drawn his attention to two burned-out churches. Then came the explosions. In front of them and beside them, the road was erupting and hurling flame and cobblestones and dust into the air.

"Hold on tight, lad!" shouted Major Barnet over the roar of these explosions. Don Juan felt himself thrown sideways as the major put the vehicle into a skidding turn and headed up a side street.

"The bastard I bought this heap of a truck from might have mentioned these fellas were still carrying on with their barney in this way," said Major Barnet, peering ahead at what appeared to be a barricade of furniture across the street. "Get down on the floor, lad, we're going through this," said Major Barnet, putting his foot hard down on the accelerator and joining Don Juan on the floor. A noise like a high-powered sewing machine seemed to be stitching into the metal of the old Ford's cab, while glass showered down upon them. There was a lurch as they penetrated the barricade and then a loud cough from the engine as the vehicle stalled. The truck freewheeled until it finally crashed to a halt, traveling by this time at no great speed.

"You all right, lad?" asked Major Barnet.

"Yes. I think so," said Don Juan.

"Then lie still till we see what mood these chaps are in!"

They could hear people shouting and running toward them.

"I think I'm going to just speak English," said the major, whose Spanish was, in any case, that of a halting Berlitz beginner. "I suggest you do the same." Someone kicked open the offside door and peered in. Don Juan found himself looking at a gun pointed at his head by a murderous-looking civilian, a man who looked as if he had been painted gray.

"We're English. *Inglés, señor,*" said Major Barnet's voice over Don Juan's shoulder.

About ten other armed men and a couple of women had gathered around the cab of the smashed Ford, all as gray-colored as the first, only their eyes showing pink and white and brown between gray lids. The major handed out his passport, which they all examined curiously and discussed for a minute or two, only to be distracted by renewed shelling twenty yards away, close to the breached barricade.

"Get out, *compañeros,*" the man pointing the rifle at them ordered.

Don Juan climbed laboriously out, his cramped limbs hurting him almost as much as his still-throbbing, aching backside. Four men and one woman had remained to discuss what should be done with them while the rest dispersed back toward the barricade.

Don Juan tried to take in the scene around him. He had an irresistible impression that this was an elaborate theatrical set in which he and Major Barnet found themselves standing midstage. Beyond the barricade through which they had just driven, swirling smoke from the shelling darkened everything to a blur. Back there, he thought, is the audience. Back there is the right side of the looking glass. While here, around where he stood, some brilliant art director, like Diaghilev's Benois, whose sets he'd seen at the opera in Paris, has wrought a dust-covered hell, painting in hell's authentic color—*gray*. Half the chorus lay as limp as if they had been made of dough, one draped over a curbside, another hitched by a still and spastic arm to a railing, yet another blotted onto a wall as if hurled like a gigantic ball, his (her) blood congealed in the sun and the dust, three of them, rictus-grinning, half-sprawled by a doorway. There were too many of these for him to take in. The tenement apartment buildings, once five stories high, reminded him of so many collapsed hayricks, stretching out their charred roof timbers to the sky like burned fingers. And everything, every pebble and stone and person, was gray with the dust from the erupting explosions that never seemed to cease.

What these countrymen of his said Don Juan never knew. Only the noise and the sulfurous smell of cordite filled his waking senses. His will seemed to have left him. They were pushing and pulling them, the major and him, along the street. There was a building outside which smashed barrels littered the area as if a giant and demented cooper had stamped about in a rage. Inside, they found themselves propelled among the huge archways of a wine store, the barrels in here still intact. Perhaps twenty women were tending nearly a hundred badly wounded men. Don Juan was left beside the major, gaping around him, while their escort talked to some armed women who stood at the entrance to a cellar staircase.

Don Juan, whose infant consciousness had been fed on the images of Goya from the moment when he had first seen them in his mother's salon at the Hôtel Raphaël, recognized all around him the continuous and authentic passion of his race, that passion which was like the endlessly rehearsed dying of Christ. The wounded lay on mattresses, on tables, and on the bare stone floor, and from them emanated a murmuring of pain that made Don Juan think of the pain of animals in traps. It must be infinitely more terrible to be pinned down with your agony like that than simply to be walking around, like him, aching but free to move; free to dodge, perhaps, the next horror he might face.

He had time, too, to study the women. Working women, mostly black-garbed, in Spain's eternal mourning that they all wore. In their impassive, melancholy faces, their eyes seemed to draw on that well of love and hate that they all shared like a secret and sacred source from which they found the will to mate and procreate, the strength to try to share and alleviate the pain of hard and bitter lives, the courage to face out their constant "familiar" Death, wearing his drab uniform.

The women guards held the cellar doors open for Don Juan and the major, and their escort pushed them down, so that they had to run not to fall. Below, in the pitch-dark cellar, a main must have burst, for the floor was a foot deep in water. The doors at the head of the cellar stairs banged closed behind them, and the sound of heavy locks' being turned and bolts' being driven home followed.

Splashing about, trying to find their bearings, they became aware at once that they were far from being alone.

"Who are you?" said a rather refined Castilian voice.

Major Barnet lit a match quickly. Peering around him, he said in his halting Spanish, "Barnet's the name. Major. British. This is my boy, um, John."

The faltering light lit up about a dozen people sloshing forward to get a closer look at the newcomers, their shadows looming and lumbering about on the vaulted ceiling. They stood among serried ranks of huge barrels, piled up to the roof and too high to permit them to get out of the water and use them as seats. Don Juan could see that their fellow prisoners were not workers. Some wore suits, their collars turned up against the damp. Others were women in print or plain dresses. They looked like housewives of the middle class culled while out shopping.

When darkness returned they continued to talk, Don Juan asking occasional questions in Spanish, using an assumed English accent, respecting the alias the major had given him.

"Who exactly are our jailers?" he asked after the major had explained that they had just arrived from England.

"The UGT, the Socialist Trades Union," said a man's voice.

"People of the lowest sort," said a woman's voice.

"It has been a total revolution. The Anarchists of the CNT, the Trotskyists of POUM, and the Socialists of the UGT. The Popular Front, as they call themselves, have declared war on religion, on property, on everything," said a dry, high male voice that Don Juan thought he identified as that of a professorial-looking figure seen in the flickering matchlight, standing quite close to them and holding his shoes and socks in his hand, as if wading at the seaside.

"I thought the *army* had rebelled," said Major Barnet, genuinely bewildered.

"The army rebelled against the Republican government," said the professorial voice. "But the government is being taken over by the Popular Front in order to fight the army, the church, and the eternal Spain we all love."

"I'm sorry to seem stupid," said Major Barnet. "But if the

government did not represent the church, the army, or the Popular Front, then whom did it represent?"

"One does not wish to insult a gentleman from England," replied the professorial voice pedantically. "But the government represented the majority in a disastrous democratic Cortes modeled on the English Parliament. It represented people of the center, such as rule in England, señor, conservatives, liberals, socialists of the non-Marxist kind. But it is they who have given that mob up there their guns."

"Those swine in the Cortes were always quarreling," said a woman's sharp voice. "They were making way for the reds to take over. It was all planned."

"That is not true," said the refined Castilian voice. "It is the army's rebellion that has done that. Even if those creatures up there kill us all, and I believe they will, one must tell the truth. It is the army and their fascist allies that have brought us to this."

"Oh, God, oh, Blessed Virgin," said a woman's voice. "Has it occurred to none of you that any one of us in here may be an informer? That for what we are saying we're almost bound to be shot? All shot."

There was a long and uncomfortable silence. Everyone concentrated on listening to what was going on upstairs, but could hear virtually nothing except the scrape of footsteps and the muffled moans of the wounded.

Major Barnet started to inspect the walls of the cellar, lighting matches and looking for possible air vents. He found nothing which looked at all promising for would-be escapees, but in climbing up the barrels he managed to put his ear to the ceiling. His toehold was precarious, on the upper lip of the lower of two five-foot-high barrels, and he had to jump down with a huge splash, extinguishing his match.

"I think you could get up there, John," he said to Don Juan in English. "I could hear their voices pretty clearly with my ear to the ceiling. You could hear them clearer still, if you catch my meaning."

With the major's help and one of the Spaniards holding a match to light the way, Don Juan managed to squeeze himself up between the top of the barrels and the ceiling, so that he could comfortably put his ear to the vaulted roof.

At first there was very little to hear, and he reported the fact. The constant to-ing and fro-ing of feet he supposed was the women moving among the wounded. The occasional shouts and cries were consistent with the fearful wounds he had seen exposed when he was upstairs. But eventually another continual, if staccato, sound started to impinge on his ear. It had a metallic popping to it and started to grow louder. He reported this too.

"Is it gunfire? Rifles, not artillery?" asked the major.

"Rifles. I'm sure it is," said Don Juan after considering the sound once again.

"What will the reds do if their enemy gets as far as trying to storm this place?" asked Major Barnet of the others, lighting a match both for emphasis and to watch the expressions of his companions.

"Kill us first," said the woman with the dolorous voice, whose face was that of a stricken Magdalene.

The others agreed, wading about so much in their panic that they sent large ripples lapping among the barrels.

"Then we must make ourselves a barricade. There are three light bulbs in the ceiling which light from outside, I imagine. We must smash those. Anything to gain us time," said the major.

So while he organized some of the men into smashing the lights and tumbling several of the barrels into the water and half-floating them to the foot of the cellar stairs, Don Juan kept his ear pressed to the ceiling.

There was no question that the rifle fire was getting nearer and nearer. He could hear the echoing of the defenders' guns in the room above. They were, no doubt, firing through the windows and doors onto the street by now. He kept up a running commentary to the major in English.

"Tell these people," the major shouted to Don Juan, "to get as far from the steps as they can now! Tell them if the door opens to lie down in the water. Just to keep their mouths above so they can breathe. Whoever comes down those steps may just be firing as they come. Try not to present a target, tell them!"

Don Juan translated as best he could in mock English-accented Spanish, worried that the relatively sophisticated words he had to use might make them suspicious. But they were impressed by the major's calm but urgent authority, and they backed obediently away into the far corners of the cellar.

Don Juan could hear, now, an entirely new pattern of sounds developing in the huge room above. The defenders were shouting, yelling. He could hear them clearly. "¡Viva los Trabajordes! ¡Viva el anarquismo!" And more distantly another cry: "¡Ariba España!" He could make out the expended shells from a machine gun rattling on the floor above.

Then the doors burst open. A woman's voice cursed the unexpected darkness. Two people ran down the stairs and started to fire around them in the dark. There were some screams from among the barrels, but whether from fear or bullets' hitting home Don Juan could not tell.

The noise above was increasing to a crescendo, and everyone could hear it plainly now, for the huge steel doors at the top of the stairs were ajar. A sudden commotion among the two people firing in the dark now occurred. Someone, probably the major, Don Juan thought, had jumped them. One was floundering in the water and the other, after loosing off a bullet that punctured a barrel quite near Don Juan's ear, had turned and run back up the stairs. The doors were being slammed shut again. They heard the locks turning and the bolts being fastened anew. A steady stream, as of a dozen faucets running, attested to the damage done the barrels.

"Anyone got a match?" came the breathless voice of the major, struggling at the foot of the stairs.

After about thirty seconds a match illuminated the scene. A youngish man, obese to the point of looking bloated, held it. The major restrained one of the female militia who had admitted them to the cellar. He had her arm forced halfway up her back.

The fat youth hit her full in the face with his pudgy fist, snapping her head back.

"Hey, stop it," said the major in English. "She's a bloody prisoner."

In all the accruing horror of the situation, Don Juan could not help grinning from atop his barrels. The major's going to try to teach this lot the rules of "fair play" to prisoners, he thought. These English! How I hate to love them. But sometimes one must.

The fat youth paid no attention. "Tell us what's happening up there, whore!" he shouted in her face. "Or we'll drown you like a rat!"

Don Juan could see, as the youth struck another match, that she had a beaky, aquiline face and her nose was streaming blood from his blow. He was appalled by the look in her eyes. They swiveled about like those of a trapped animal wondering where death was coming from, hoping to see the blow first, hoping against all the odds to evade it. He wondered, even then, how a woman could put at deliberate risk something as precious and unique as her person, her progenerating and eternal person. He had assumed that they did it only to protect their young, their homes, or even their men.

She shook her head and would not speak. The major turned her away from the youth, sheltering her with his body. Then the big noise came. The noise so piercingly frightful that it stilled everyone's movement in the watery cellar. Don Juan could hear hundreds of shots ringing out in the room above and the running of heavy feet against a cacophony of shrieks, of bellows of fear and pain.

"The fascists are up there now," cried the girl the major had disarmed. "They're killing everybody. They always kill everybody. Why do you think we tried to shoot you? Because they will shoot us, all of us! You fascists aren't human. You are like wolves. You take our labor. Our health. Our children. Our lives. *¡Viva el anarquismo!*" she shouted, as if she were leading a charge instead of being imprisoned in the grip of Major Barnet from suburban London. Don Juan loved the passion in her voice and thought at once of Mella's wife and wondered how, on this day of all days, he had forgotten her.

The yelling and the shooting were as loud as ever up above. But now another almost more dreadful sound came—that of many women in infinite pain and extremis.

The major had asked the men Don Juan thought of as the professor and the Castilian to take charge of the prisoner while he mounted the stairs to hammer on the steel doors.

Don Juan half-knew what would happen and shouted to the major, warning him in English, "They're going to drown her!"

And indeed, while one of the women continuously lit matches, they converged on her from all over the cellar. The fat youth grabbed her hair and jerked her bodily from the restraining arms of the Castilian and the babbled remonstrances of the professor. He thrust her head under the water, and the rest leaped on her, trampling her thrashing body down and shouting, "*¡Ariba España!*" until nothing stirred below the surface of the water.

The major stared at them from the foot of the stairs as if he simply could not credit his eyes.

The steel door at that instant opened, and a number of uniformed Falangists ran down the steps with their guns at the ready. Everyone in the cellar except the major and Don Juan made the fascist salute and shouted, "*¡Ariba España!*" The screaming of the women in the room above continued.

When they trooped up into the light, Don Juan faced a sight which he at once knew he must try to blot out. These images were so strong that they seared his eyes and drummed at his reason. The major, still shaking with fury and shock from the murder of his prisoner, could only gape slack-jawed and try to pull his charge toward him to cover the boy's eyes.

The wounded were dead. All of them. Mostly with bullet wounds right between the eyes, that efficacious place where the slaughterer of cattle places the humane killer on furry brows. Their pain, at least, was over.

But the women—those soothers and sufferers in black Don Juan had noted before being thrust down into the cellar. They were not dead. Perhaps a hundred young gallants of the Falange were systematically carving the initials UGT and CNT into their brows. Those already mutilated were half-stripped of their clothes. Don Juan was aware of a dozen simultaneous rapes occurring, but one face, close to him and livid with pain, was that of a woman of about forty, forced face down across the body of a dead militiaman whom her ravisher was using as a bolster. Her eyes she managed to keep open, and she looked up at the passing parade of freed prisoners, determined to get them to look back at her and thus have a glimpse of hell that would never leave them.

Out in that gray street again, the absence of explosions made of the phantasmagoria left by the battle a curious impression of still life, left slightly out of focus by the lingering pall of dust, like one of those cunning nineteenth-century daguerreotypes that, if struggled with long enough, will yield up an uncanny and unreal effect of three dimensions. Looming out of this scene, becoming swiftly more plastic and real, was a speeding Hispano-Suiza roadster. It stopped with difficulty, the external hand brake having to be applied, and two Spanish officers emerged. One was exceedingly dapper and wearing a rather bibulous grin.

"Quiepo de Llano!" he said, introducing himself to everybody and saluting the still-soaking ladies in the print dresses. There was instantaneous applause, as if this dapper, tipsy general had personally rescued them from the brink of death. His aide, a fat and flustered officer who looked as if he had been scared incontinent by the general's driving, struggled to get the details of what had happened to the prisoners in the cellar. He also, in the hearing of Don Juan, asked one of the Falange officers to get his men to leave the wretched women with their dead. The Falange militia were needed to help quell stiff resistance still going on near the railway yard.

The hubbub of everyone talking simultaneously made it difficult for Major Barnet to make himself heard. But speaking loudly in English, he eventually commanded the attention of the general himself. The freed prisoners then eulogized the major for his behavior during their confinement. General Quiepo de Llano may or may not have been able to speak English, but on this occasion, rather like the major himself, he seemed to feel that if he spoke loud enough in Spanish he would be understood. He therefore bawled his congratulations to his English brother-in-arms while Major Barnet shouted his need to know the whereabouts of Don Juan's grandfather. Since he understood that this grandparent was one of the two richest men in Spain, someone must know of his whereabouts.

Both Quiepo de Llano and his aide, having received the major's message almost simultaneously, turned at once to Don Juan.

"But you should not be here!" said the general. "Your grandfather told us that he cabled Juan March's house in Biarritz, saying you must be taken to Burgos."

Don Juan translated for the major, who produced from his pocket, by way of reply, the cable received in Biarritz.

"Seville. Andalusia Palace Hotel. Says so quite clearly," said the major in Spanish.

"Ah, but that must be the cable he sent before General Mola asked him to go to Burgos," interjected the aide.

"He is now in Burgos?" asked the major wearily. "Perhaps this is a stupid question, but can I telephone him?"

"Of course. We have the American Telephone Company here. If I wish to I can pick up the telephone to the Republican minister of war in Madrid and tell him what an asshole he is," said the general.

After a breathtaking ride in the Hispano-Suiza through the corpse-strewn streets, they were at General Quiepo de Llano's headquarters. Half an hour later Major Barnet was talking to Don Juan's grandfather in Burgos. Meanwhile Don Juan read in the Seville newspaper of the atrocities committed by the government's people against priests and property in Barcelona.

"Bring the boy to Burgos," said his grandfather.

"There will be someone at the airfield, sir?" asked Major Barnet.

"Of course. I'm sorry you didn't get the second cable. But this is going to be the capital for a few days till we take over in Madrid. I had to be here. May I speak with my grandson?"

"Hullo, Grandfather. So your army's done it!"

"Thank God, at last," said his grandfather. "What did you do to Deerhurst?"

"I was always too old for Deerhurst, Grandfather. But I have been punished, as you intended. Tom Brown's school days are far from over."

"Well, you will learn much if you stay with me for a while. We will see our dear Spain reborn. *Adiós.*"

Don Juan was about to ask, "Which Spain?" but his grandfather had hung up.

The general's aide drove them out to the airfield and seemed less harried in the absence of his colorful superior. It turned out that his Berlitz English was better than the major's Berlitz Spanish.

"Is it a deliberate policy to kill all your prisoners and wounded like that? To have all the women raped?" asked the major, still seething with anger and disgust at what he'd witnessed.

"I'm sorry you saw that," said the aide. "As a professional soldier, it makes me sick. But it is necessary!"

"Good God, why?"

They were heading out of Seville past the Square of the Catholic Monarchs, toward the Isabel II bridge. On their right, smoke rose from the area around the station, and the clatter of gunfire persisted. The aide paused not to consider why—he knew the "justification" well enough—but to find some way to communicate it in English.

"The workers and the peasants are very many, and we, the rulers, we are few. That is why they must fear us. Isn't it?" he said at last.

The major made no reply. In India alone Britian ruled over three hundred million people with a few thousand civil servants and some tens of thousands of white troops. He saw little difference between Spanish peasants and Indians. But one didn't shoot them like that. It just wasn't done.

"Who controls the territory between here and Burgos?" Don Juan asked in Spanish as they approached the airfield.

"It is about three hundred and fifty air miles to Burgos," said the aide. "Not until you get over Ávila—that is, about two hundred miles northeast—will you be over our territory again. Around Seville we control only about a ten-mile radius. We wait for General Franco with his Army of Africa to come and relieve us. Within a few weeks, of course, all Spain will be ours."

Half an hour later they were airborne over the Republic's territory.

Captain Bart, their pilot, had been anxious to take off; it was only when the Dragon Rapide was in the air again that he had time to question the major, whose face and clothes were still caked with gray dust.

"You and the boy look as if you'd been playing tag in a cement yard," he said.

"A bit sticky there for a while," said the major. "All these people seem to have gone stark, raving bonkers, if you ask me."

"They acted a bit queerly at the airfield while you were away," said Captain Bart. "Came and asked if it was General Franco's plane.

Terribly excited. All jabbering and waving their arms the way they do."

"He's the general they hope is going to relieve them," said Don Juan, who was listening from his prone position on the floor.

"I know," said Captain Bart. "Some people have hired him another of these Dragon Rapides from Croydon. Captain Jebb's been flying it all over the place for the last ten days. Took Franco from the Canary Islands, where he has been in a kind of exile, I understand, to Morocco. Now he and his Army of Africa are on their way to Spain to help the rebels, so they say."

Flying by the map, watching the physical terrain below, Captain Bart set a course northeast for Burgos. They left the Sierra de los Santos to the east of them, misty blue in the afternoon heat. They passed over the town of Azuega. To the west the Sierra del Pedrosa cast long shadows as the sun started its slow decline. For a while the six-thousand-foot high Mount St. Inés obscured the sun, for Captain Bart was flying at half that altitude.

They were accustoming their eyes to the shade when the cabin seemed to be torn, as if by a hacksaw. Bullets were shattering the perspex windshield, and one had fractured Bart's jaw. He managed to put the plane into a dive. The major held Don Juan down with one of his hands, and he alone saw the assailant, a single-engine Breguet fighter in the colors of the Republic. It made no attempt to attack them again, but circled overhead while Captain Bart landed in a field, spitting out blood and broken teeth as he did so. They had landed on some moorland pasture where sheep grazed, enclosed by occasional low stone barriers.

A couple of minutes later the Breguet itself landed nearby, just as the major had extricated the speechless pilot from his shattered cabin. Two goggled officers ran toward them, brandishing revolvers.

"You are our prisoner, general!" they shouted at the major in their excitement, and then were much crestfallen when they realized their error.

"But it is General Franco's plane. Who are you?" Major Barnet explained quickly, demanding, as he did so, that Captain Bart be flown straight to a hospital in the Breguet. The Spanish airmen, embarrassed at their mistake, agreed at once, and within a minute or so the Breguet had taken off and was heading for Villaneuva, the nearest town with a hospital in the Extramadura region. One of the airmen remained with them to escort them to the nearest township.

Don Juan had, perhaps, more time to reflect on the full implications of what had befallen them than had the major, who had been concentrating his energies on looking after Captain Bart. He, Don Juan, was a citizen of this Republic. He was also of the class that were the chief targets of the revolutionaries' murderous ardor. But ironically, he knew beyond any doubt that he could not be on his grandfather's side, on the side of the Spanish military. His decision to be on the side of the revolutionaries was of long standing. Perhaps it had started before the incident in Mella's farmhouse. It had certainly been reinforced by the years with Whitticker and confirmed during his incarceration in that academy of class and race hatred, Deerhurst.

More than most people Don Juan was always aware of his daemon. An occurrence as fortuitous as this one, that spared him having to struggle with his grandfather, could not be ignored. But in order to take advantage of it he had to fully consider his options.

To stay with the major meant that this brave, excellent (if dull) Englishman would do everything to get him across the lines to Burgos and his grandfather. He would want to do that out of duty, because that was the kind of man he was. In addition, however, it was what he was being paid for doing and was expected to do.

Don Juan could confide to the major his plan to join the revolutionaries. But what plan? He had as yet made none. And how could the responsible major ever agree, let alone understand?

He could simply steal away by himself at the first opportunity without telling the major, and make his way home to the castle. There, at least, everyone knew that it had been he, however inadvertently, who had ruined the hated Mendoza. He set some store by the fact that the anarchists had always proclaimed that they killed neither women nor children nor the very old. It would be a chance to be with his father in whatever state an ailing duke would have come to in the now revolutionary Republic. He hoped to get the anarchists to accept him as one of them. He would come, after all, with no possessions. His trunk and tuck box had gone by rail and sea to the Avenue Foch. He had only a suitcase and almost no money. He felt himself, as they say in the church of would-be communicants, to be in a state of grace.

He couldn't have known that the decision would be made for him—that in the new freedom he had so long desired a great many decisions were going to be made for him.

As they entered the small town of Zalamea de la Serena, dusk was closing in. Some local worthies with shotguns came and escorted them to the town hall, where there was a telegraph but no telephone. While the air force officer used the telegraph to his headquarters, a group of five men and one woman led the major and Don Juan into a room furnished as a council chamber. The men with shotguns remained at the door.

"What is this?" asked the major a little testily. It had been an exceedingly hard day. His Berlitz Spanish, however, hid his growing anger from the assembly.

"We are the committee of control here, *compañero*," said an old man with a leonine head who appeared to be their spokesman.

"Tell them, please, Don Juan, that we are with the air force officer. That we were shot down in error. You know what to tell them, lad."

"Don Juan?" said the leonine head curiously. "You are Spanish? What is your full name?"

"Is this a police station?" interrupted the major, suddenly alarmed at these questions.

"We are the committee of control here. Every locality in the Republic has one now. The Guardia Civil are no longer." He drew his forefinger graphically across his throat to show what had happened to them.

The major rose to leave, determined to try to bluff their way out of the hands of these people whom he thought of as officious yokels.

"You will give us your identification," said the leonine head, signaling the men with shotguns to bar the major's way.

A little later, to the major's horror, it became clear that the committee's power locally was almost absolute. The air force officer came and spoke to them as if he were giving evidence for their consideration.

"My feeling is," he said, "that if, as you say, the boy is Spanish, then you must dispose of him as you decide. He has landed in your pueblo. The Englishman I feel is the responsibility of the air force, as is the pilot we have taken to hospital. As a foreigner, he must be free to leave with me so that we can deal with the matter of the plane. The major has also just come from Seville, and headquarters wishes to interview him—I will not say interrogate, since he is our guest."

The committee considered this disposition of the "guests," voted on it, and endorsed it as the proper course of action.

A vehicle came to fetch the air force officer and Major Barnet. Close to tears with anger, the major was forced to take leave of Don Juan. Three local men half-carried the furious Englishman to the waiting vehicle, where they handcuffed him to the waiting air force officer, giving the key to the driver.

Don Juan had time while all this was going on for a good deal of further reflection. These people do not kill children, he kept telling himself, not because he felt any great fear but because he had long since convinced himself that he believed in their credo, and hoped not to be disillusioned. They will allow me to take the place proper for a boy of my age in their revolution, he reasoned. I did not ask to be born who I am. If they are just, they cannot hold it against me. Thinking this, Don Juan took some paper and a nibbed pen from the council table and started to record the nightmare impressions that remained with him from Seville.

When the committee returned, he shouted, *"¡Viva el anarquismo!"*

They stood in the doorway, smiling among themselves.

"We are socialists, my boy," said the leonine head.

"I didn't shout that because I wished to please you, but because it is what I feel. My region of Andalusia is surely not so far away. You must be aware that we are all anarchists there?"

"Even the heir to a dukedom, raised on the fat of other people's land, boy?" The leonine head was testing him with this question as they all sat down again at the council table. The woman among them, a fat, jolly-looking creature with a large birthmark on her forehead, started to look at his drawings, showing them to the others.

"You did these?" she asked in wonder while the others examined them.

In answer he took the pen and paper and drew the leonine head. It was probably the most brilliant quickly executed likeness he had ever achieved. The old man's face he rendered literally as that of a lion, an old king of the cat family, his mane a little tattered, his whiskered face pugnacious and confident, as if he had just completed a jungle-quelling roar.

The committee was both amazed and deeply impressed.

"Learning to be a duke in England you have had time to become an artist?" asked the leonine head, looking now at the sketches of the massacre and rape in the wine vaults made from Don Juan's memory.

"I was *sent* to England. I wish to go to my home and ask the *compañeros* there to let me learn and serve with them. I believe they will accept me. My father is an old and very sick man who has not knowingly harmed them. Even if he has, have I not the right to start my life with a clean slate? I believe that I am an anarchist, and I wish to be an artist, to spend my life interpreting man, nature, and the universal truths for my fellow men through my art," said Don Juan, feeling gloriously Spanish and free making this grandiose speech.

They might have voted his right to go home there and then, but for their horrified fascination with the drawings and the events they portrayed. He nearly asked them if the atrocities of Barcelona, reported in the Seville press, had any basis in truth, but decided wisely that he had talked enough. They had accepted his quixotic speech as just that. The speech of an adolescent boy inspired by the Spanish spirit of Don Quixote. Only when they found themselves deep in conversation about the state of things in Seville did they realize that the boy had so far remained standing, that they had not thought to offer him a seat. He seemed to be swaying slightly, and, indeed, Don Juan felt increasingly faint.

"Please sit," said the woman.

"I can't sit," said Don Juan in a matter-of-fact voice.

"Some reason?" There was the faintest hint of class suspicion in the leonine head's voice.

"No, not at all," said Don Juan hastily. "It's just an injury. It will soon be better, but for the moment I cannot sit!"

"Injury? Today in Seville?" The woman turned to the others suddenly. "What monsters we are. Think what this child has been through today. And a plane crash. Yet here we are, a socialist inquisition!" She turned to Don Juan, who had thankfully sunk to his knees. "We are new to all this, *compañero*, you see. We are police, judges, lawmakers, everything. Often we don't have time to think."

"It's quite all right," he said, smiling at her. "But I am very tired. Is there somewhere, an empty jail cell perhaps, where I can sleep?"

"We have no empty jail cells," said one of the other *compañeros* sadly, as if it were one of their chief problems, which indeed it was.

Just then they were all genuinely distressed to see the boy sink to the floor. The woman, who was a midwife by profession, lifted his lids and saw that he was more asleep than unconscious.

"Carry him to my place," she said, and then added, "Wait, let's first take a look at this injury of his—he may need the doctor."

They craned over the table as she loosened his belt and slipped his trousers down to reveal the layers of cotton wool that cushioned his raw buttocks. Gingerly she lifted the edge, and they saw the crisscross of wheals, purple and scabbed from bleeding.

"They did this to him in Seville? Fiends!" said the woman.

"Quick, fetch Thomas, the photographer," said the leonine head. "What perfect evidence of the deep perversion of the bourgeoisie."

"But he never mentioned it," pointed out one of the others.

"He is a young Quixote. He is all pride," said the woman, turning over in her mind the best salves and balms to use on the behind of this extraordinary guest. Wondering what bed linen, which pillowcases, which towels were good enough for his use. Considering which of her daughters to displace from the family bed so that he might sleep there.

When Don Juan awoke the next morning, two swarthily pretty girls in their teens and a boy of about nine were watching him.

He was lying on his belly, his head protruding slightly over the mattress, and he felt stiff in every limb, stiff between the legs. He was dressed in somebody's nightshirt, and he could feel that his bottom had been elaborately dressed. He smiled at the two girls, who looked immediately abashed and lowered their eyes. Their brother ran down to tell his mother that the young hidalgo was awake. Don Juan was, at that instant, seized with a cramp in his calf. Giving a shout of sudden pain, he leaped out of bed, grabbing at his leg.

The girls were terrified, partly by his unexpected antic and partly by his alarming puissance, suddenly aimed at them in this way like Don Quixote's lance. They too ran downstairs to tell their mother that the hidalgo was not only awake, but up. Don Juan was himself again.

A little later in the day he was riding the country bus route on his way to Guadal. In addition to his passport, he carried a letter of recommendation and identification from the committee of control at Zalamea de la Serena explaining that he had been tortured by fascist hyenas in Seville, could not sit down, and was on his way home.

It was a complicated journey, and they had written it all down for him. From Zalamea de la Serena to Cabeza del Bucy was the first leg of the trip; then he had to change onto the "big bus" to Pozo Blanca. This bus went via the "cities" of Balalcázar and Hinojosa del Duque to Pozo Blanca. There he had to make a final change onto a bus which would take him, via Montoro, to Guadal. Touchingly, the committee of control, which he subsequently discovered had already shot more than a dozen bourgeois families in the neighborhood, had taken up a collection for his journey. They knew he had money, but told him to keep it in case "your family is not there to greet you." The leonine head even advised him against sending a telegram to inquire after his father. His anarchist friends would think this bourgeois caution if they intercepted the letter, which was likely. He must arrive like a true *compañero*, saying, "I am here, this is my home. If my father lives I am glad. Otherwise my castle and lands are yours, dear *compañeros*. Till them and give me what I need to eat and follow my vocation as an artist."

On the first leg of his journey he began to see more of the process of revolution going on around him. Like yeast it was at work, feeding on itself, enlarging its hold on the people as they experimented with what seemed to many a dreadful freedom.

On the way to Cabeza the bus stopped many times. Peasants, farmers, workers, and professionals such as veterinarians and school-teachers all used the bus. Produce and luggage traveled on a rack on top; livestock such as chickens and ducks and rabbits traveled inside, suspended in bunches by their legs from the overhead handrail or cradled in women's laps.

Where once the conversation might have been of stillborn calves, of aphids in the olive groves, or of some unique happening like the birth of triplets, death now danced on everybody's lips. Don Juan, standing always as the bus jerked and lurched its way along the potholed road, listened to his fellow countrymen as he had never been privileged to listen to the commonality of folk before. That they believed some kind of millennium was upon them was very evident. Sometimes he asked a question, risking their sharp glances at him for his outlandish accent.

In some beautiful pastures edged with willows, they all craned out of the windows to watch the shooting of three men and a woman. They had just made their scheduled stop in a deserted village five hundred yards behind them, where only one old man had mounted the bus. The shooting was being attended by all the villagers, dressed as for a fiesta. Someone was singing to a guitar, but the bus's overheated diesel engine was too loud for them to hear the song.

"What was that about, Granddad?" they asked the old man.

"The priest, his housekeeper, his brother, and the housekeeper's son."

"Ah, yes. 'The gang,'" said a woman in a head scarf, nodding her head knowingly. The whole bus seemed to agree, as if the unfortunate four were endlessly duplicated all over the province.

"Do you think there are *any* good priests?" Don Juan asked her.

"Oh, yes. There are some," she said thoughtfully. "One I know, no one would touch a hair on his head. He lives up at Nenín, in the mountains. You know Nenín?"

Don Juan shook his head.

"It is hot as hell up there. They quarry slate. Father Olande, that's his name, is a saint. God help me, I know there is now no God, but that is no reason why there should not be saints. Everyone in Nenín must carry water up from the valley. He takes his turn. No doctor, naturally, for twenty miles, for no one has any money. He is the best midwife, they say, in the province. He lives as they do. Only he never drinks. Never smokes. No housekeeper taking bribes for favors. That man has never touched coffee. A saint."

The people around them on the bus agreed.

"But he asks them to believe in God?"

"For such a man, they are glad to do it."

He had to wait overnight at Cabeza. After a charred omelette at the newly named Largo Caballero Inn (called after the socialist leader), Don Juan wandered through the town, thinking that it would take more than a revolution to reform Spanish food. An egg, after all, was innocent of exploiting anyone. It deserved better treatment. In the warm evening air he took part in that pleasant ritual of Mediterranean countries, the evening "parade." The women and girls walking arm in arm at a leisurely pace. The old people sitting outside their front doors, watching everybody. The men, walking at a slightly faster pace, hunting for a girl's eyes with theirs, turning to devour every inch of her retreating body after she had passed them. The girls adept at seeing the men in the periphery of their vision so that they could consider them without appearing to have looked at them. Like the others, Don Juan gazed at the unmarried girls, seeing in their collective virginity, thus on tempting display, a quite irresistible challenge. As for them, by the time he had walked past them all once, there was not a girl in Cabeza who could not have identified Don Juan from a blurred passport photo.

Before returning to the inn, Don Juan paid a visit to the church. The front doors were nailed up with planks across them, but the side door to the vestry was missing entirely, and he walked in. The pews had mostly been chopped up for firewood and carried away. The marble altar looked as if a sledgehammer had pulverized it, and above, scratched with a charcoal brand, was Dante's legend from the gates of hell, "Abandon hope all ye who enter here." Above that again was a window which had survived the vandals. A Christ with an elongated El Greco face suffered up there. For what? Don Juan wondered. For this desecrated building? For the Church of Spain, which had so long desecrated His faith? For the Spanish people walking arm in arm outside, lost to His love, looking only for their own?

Walking back toward the vestry door, he saw the entrance to a crypt. Peering in, he saw a single tomb. A white marble effigy of a woman of the eighteenth century lay, her hands crossed over her breast, upon a granite catafalque. He descended the stair, wondering how it was that the ambient light of moon or town could reach this dark place. Inside, it was clear that probably the same hands that had smashed the altar had been at work here, too. Behind the white marble lady, tombs were let into the wall, as in a catacomb. These had been smashed open from both inside and above the outer wall of the church, so that there was a huge hole in the roof and wall of the crypt, letting in the light.

Looking at the marble figure, he was reminded of a short story his mother had read him as a child. Written by Gustavo Becquer in the 1860s, it was the quintessential gothic Spanish story. A French officer of the Napoleonic period was quartered in a deserted Spanish church. Then, as now, a more or less atheistic regime prevailed. In the church the Frenchman found the effigy of a beautiful woman at the stone side of her knightly husband. One evening the officer introduced his comrades to her during a drunken party, telling them he found her more beautiful than any woman of flesh and blood in Spain. Agreeing with him, they said, half in jest, "Be careful, the knight will hear you." In the end, the officer dashed his wine into the face of the stone knight and tried to steal from the marble lips of his wife a kiss. Just then the officer collapsed to the floor, his face smashed and bleeding. Don Juan remembered well the last lines, which he had asked his mother to repeat because their frightful finality made him shiver. "As their friend sought to put his burning lips to those of Dona Elvira, they had seen the knight raise his fist and strike the officer down with a fearful blow of his stone gauntlet!"

Don Juan smiled at this memory. How quintessentially Spanish that story is, he thought. Passion and purity. A life for a kiss. He looked at this Dona Elvira (there was no inscription) and wondered about her in life. Her lips were overfull and her nose slightly crooked, so he imagined that the sculptor had not lied about her, and he found the wide-spaced almond eyes quite compelling. He thought of how, when making love to a woman, he had found it hard to tear his gaze away from her eyes when, by his agency and at his bidding, she left him for some inner place where he could never follow. He had looked for her return, welcoming her back with his eyes. As his remote ancestors had welcomed their women back from the celebration of their mysteries, asking no questions.

He kissed the marble lady respectfully on the ringed right hand that crossed her breast. To a married lady he didn't feel his homage was excessive. But in Don Juan's mind, that kiss became inevitably a whole sequence of warm woman with almond eyes, a full, open mouth, warm, sweet breath, saliva, a questing tongue, the nibble on his lip of sharp little teeth. He shook his head clear of this storming reverie and found himself looking at the back of her tomb. Here the grave robbers had done their work, too. Where the granite catafalque had been hacked away a lead casket protruded. Its lid had been prized open, and the skull inside stared out, looking over Don Juan's shoulder. Shreds of her shroud remained, and Don Juan could see that her hair had been red and that her little teeth had indeed been sharp.

Voices echoed from the church, and as he left the crypt for the vestry door he saw a couple embracing by the altar.

The resumed bus journey next day seemed endless. It started at seven, and by the time he had waited for connecting buses and then continued, it was dusk when he finally got off the bus on the outskirts of Guadal.

The deeper his journey took him into Andalusia the more evidence there was that they were entering anarchist territory. Far more shops were shuttered or gutted than in semi-bourgeois, socialist Cabeza. Churches he saw from the bus had been razed with a fearful fury, the fractured figures of the saints put on display outside to try to show that whatever manna they had possessed was gone. In this way, Don Juan remembered Tabatha had told him, the early Christians had dealt with the idols of their pagan predecessors.

Outside Guadal and along the road hung huge signs painted on bunting. "God is dead." "Protect women, children, old men, trees, and animals!" "Down with alcohol, tobacco, and coffee!"

He asked a man on the bus what he might expect in Guadal.

"They haven't finished off the Guardia Civil yet," the man said, shaking his head.

"How long have they been fighting?" asked Don Juan.

"Since July the twentieth, I should think. That's when we managed to kill most of them hereabouts. But Guadal—that's a hornets' nest full of the bastards. And they've got that damned castle."

Ominously the bus skirted the edge of the town, and when it stopped the boy was the only person who got off.

Don Juan was, as we have said, rash when it came to women. But in no other respect was he foolhardy. Enjoying life, he cared to stay alive if he could. That being said, he did not fear death, although he was wary of pain. Such religion as clung to him after his experiences with both Catholics and Anglicans was really a conviction that all the metaphysical reports he required from life were not yet in. Hell seemed a distinct possibility, but he was prepared to defy it. Heaven he hoped to find on earth. That the key to it, for him, lay in women—even, conceivably, in a singular and entirely unique woman—was the chimera he followed. Standing on the empty road outside the town where he was born, he faced for the second time in forty-eight hours the fact that he might soon be dead. But some instinct told him that if he could bring himself to walk straight up to his father's castle and leave the rest to fate, why, then his future would continue to be extraordinary. He was never one to court the banal.

The firing he heard almost at once. It became louder or fainter, depending on the angle of the street down which he was walking in relation to the castle. The monolithic stone structure he was obliged to think of as home dominated the whole town in a way that he had never considered in the days when he had spent his life within it.

Eighty percent of the shops were smashed up in some way. Painted legends scrawled on walls or shutters explained why. "Pepe gave no credit to the poor." "Pablo's scales were always wrong." Bodies lay about the street. Many lay where they had been defenestrated, below the windows of attics where they had, no doubt, been hiding. Don Juan recognized in most of the victims a common factor—soft-looking hands, bellies that had long been full, faces that, even in death, still looked smug; surprised, some of them, terrified, others, but these expressions sprang from a smug mold shaped by a lifetime's expectation of plenty.

Hanging by one leg from the balcony of his smart town house was the little town's only doctor, his face black and bloated in death. He who had attended Don Juan at Mendoza's house. Don Juan, who was obliged to hold his nose as he passed him, was fascinated to see that his wrists and hands which dangled almost to the sidewalk were still furnished with the rings he had worn in life, still wore his Swiss gold watch, while his French cuffs still sported a pair of flashy platinum cuff links. Two feet from his face, where he must have had ample leisure to read it while he died, was a notice lying flat on the sidewalk. It read:

"You never left your house to come to the bedside of the poor. You used the gift of learning you had exclusively for money. If there is a purgatory, be glad we shortened your days in it. Long live liberty. Down with fascism!"

Passing through the square outside the school, Don Juan saw the bodies of two Jesuits exposed near the children's entrance. A placard lying across them read simply, "They lied." Don Juan was reminded of Browning's poem about the betrayal of the confessional.

As Don Juan walked he kept expecting that someone would come up to him and say, "I know you. You're the duke's son." But those few people he saw scurrying about the streets moved as if they were defying some curfew, like mice when they suspect a cat lurks in a room. And all the time the cacophony of the guns grew louder as he approached the castle.

At one moment there was nothing to see. The next moment he could see it, almost all. He had emerged into the Alfonso XII Gardens. The row of houses opposite included the one in which the lovely Isabel had once lived. The castle loomed immediately behind. The narrow roadway to the castle drawbridge also had its entrance opposite. In the middle of the garden about three hundred men were involved in the labor of constructing out of wood a wheeled tower clearly designed as a siege engine to be hauled up to the moat and cantilevered across it so the besiegers could get onto the battlements. People, presumably Guardia Civil, shot at the builders from time to time from the same vantage point from which Don Juan had watched poor Whitticker plunge to his death with the lemming horde.

Don Juan decided that there was little point in buttonholing someone at this point and saying, "Take me to your committee of control!" Busy as they were, he might easily be shot in a fit of absentmindedness.

So, using his suitcase as a pillow, he stretched out on the thin grass, on which a notice still warned against walking. It had been another long day for someone unable to sit. He lay on his side and watched them light bonfires by which to continue their work of construction. The firing from the tower above the keep had stopped. Don Juan wondered if it was from lack of ammunition.

Close to sleep, he forced himself to consider the problem of his father. Did he love the duke? The answer came as it often had before. "I have never known my father. His mentality has been hopelessly impaired ever since I first saw him. Ergo, how can I possibly love him?" That they might well kill the old man in one of their spectacularly nasty ways was something he must try to face. He cast his mind back to the corpses he'd seen in the streets. Had any of them been *old* men? He couldn't recall any, but he had avoided looking too closely at most.

He awoke shivering and damp in the heavy dew to see that the siege-engine maneuver had started. They had set fire to the whole row of houses that backed onto the Guadalquivir, starting with their roofs; and the castle was lit up against the indigo sky like an ogre's fortress in a silly symphony. The sixty-foot tower weaved about as they slowly wheeled it to the roadway up to the castle. The hundreds of men pulling and pushing it sang as they worked:

> *"Son of the people, your chains oppress you*
> *This injustice cannot go on!*
> *If your life is a world of grief,*
> *Instead of being a slave, it is better to die!*
> *Workers,*
> *You shall suffer no longer!*
> *The oppressor*
> *Must succumb!*
> *Arise*
> *Loyal people*
> *At the cry*
> *Of social revolution."*

The bell in the still-standing belfry of the ruined church pealed out, and all the inhabitants of the town started to fill the gardens, cheering on the men with the tower as if they were a soccer crowd whose team was on the attack. Agonizingly slowly the tower lurched up the narrow roadway.

Don Juan jumped up and ran to join the crowd, feeling caught up now in their enthusiasm. The song made him see again the dead Mella and his battered body, his wife hanging by her hair from the beam in the farmhouse ceiling. He saw that again, and he joined in the song, fumbling for the words, but roaring them out when he found them.

"Here come the committee. Here comes Inés herself," said someone, and Don Juan looked around to see a group of people led by a woman. It was the strongest, most handsomely beautiful woman's face he had ever seen. She wore her hair in a long plait, scraped back from features that carried the everyday lines of life that any thirty-five-year-old woman must carry. They were lines *of* pain, *from* pain, they could have no other source; but they gave a meaning to her face itself. He adored her face and longed for her on sight. In a night of fire, when salt was in the air, she had for him, for the whole crowd who turned to her, the very effulgence of power. They roared. "Inés. Inés. Inés. Viva. Viva. Viva. Viva Inéz!" And her eyes laughed in that superbly tragic face, and she held high a German Mauser gun, and in a voice Don Juan had never forgotten, shouted, "They shall not conquer us!"

He could not now, for an instant, doubt that it was *she.*

Mella's widow transformed. The female union organizer, now leader.

The crowd was making way for her and for the rest of the committee of control, and Don Juan lost sight of them almost immediately.

For a few minutes there was a pause in the excitement while the tower was inched forward, its great metal wheels shrieking and scraping on the cobblestones. Don Juan meanwhile stared at the battlements to see what, if anything, the Guardia Civil's response would be. There was as yet no sign of the defenders. Now the tower was in position, and with a great, groaning creak it was collapsed across the moat, coming to rest at a forty-five-degree angle a few feet below the battlements. A mighty hammering followed, which the townspeople said was wedges' being driven under the tower's base to make it solid for the anarchist militia to climb. And climbing they already were. Don Juan thought they looked from a distance like the pupae of dragonflies moving up brightly lit reeds.

Now he saw, as one does sometimes, something of great importance happen with that shock of recognition which made him think afterward that he had known it was coming. Small figures appeared on the battlements with buckets. Seconds later liquid fire was raining down on structure and men alike. The pupae seemed to curl in the flame and drop away. Two Maxim machine guns now poked their wicked snouts through the castellations of the castle and poured bullets onto the densely packed people at the base of the blazing wooden tower.

Don Juan had watched the lemming horde on the move once before. He hurried to get to his suitcase on the other side of the gardens before, like a lapping tide, they started to flow back into the open space anew. The yelling of the crowd, as they fled, made Don Juan's mind numb. He stared at them as they streamed by him, hoping to see Inés. It didn't seem possible that his daemon could have meant him to find her like that, then snuff her out. But equally he feared that if she had been anywhere near the base of the tower when the assault started, she was probably dead.

He started to move against the wave of people running toward the town, shouldering his way forward. Taller than the others. Looking constantly for Inés.

It cannot have been more than a minute later that Don Juan

found himself alone, walking across the Alfonso XII Gardens, carrying his suitcase. The row of houses still made an enormous bonfire a block long when the anarchists' pathetic wooden tower, or all that remained of it, crashed into the castle moat. As he approached the entrance to the narrow road that led up to the castle, Don Juan saw that there were many trampled bodies on the ground. But some were still alive, those who hugged the side of the road.

He had already reached halfway to where the road ended in the sharp drop to the moat when he found her. Her back was forced against the wall, and she clutched her stomach where a dozen running feet had trampled her. She was alive. Hers, he was to discover, was probably the hardest stomach in Andalusia.

"I am the duke's son," he said. "Do you remember me?"

She was still fighting to breathe, but she stared at him, amazed. "The boy?"

"I have grown."

"But you're tall as a man. Taller."

"Almost fifteen. I want to join you."

"You? Never!"

"Why?"

"Because you are *you!*"

"I see," he said, deflated, crouching beside her, looking up at the battlements, where there had been no sign of Guardia Civil for several minutes.

"I have never been able to thank you for that day. What you did," she said at last, and he wondered whether she meant that "thank you" was difficult for her.

"I have always remembered what they did. It is one of the reasons I want to join you," he said.

They heard the sound of motor vehicles' being started on the other side of the drawbridge.

"We must get away. Quick," she said.

But she was too late. In the first instance, she overestimated her ability to straighten her body after the pounding it had received. And the ominous rattling of the block-and-tackle mechanism that lowered the drawbridge had started. There seemed to be no other survivors as near to the drawbridge as they, but farther off some of the injured and wounded were trying to move away. Instinctively Don Juan pressed himself over her body, pinning her closer to the wall. One of the Maxim guns up on the tower started its blatter, raking among the injured, who struggled to move away. Long before the drawbridge finally slid down with the rumble of a giant anchor, all the painfully moving figures had been accounted for, sinking back, spun around, or falling headlong like abandoned marionettes.

In the course of the long war that was to follow, Don Juan was to hear many of its arcane and beastly sounds. But two truckloads of Guardia Civil driving off that steel drawbridge and the few yards of cobblestones that followed onto what was literally a roadbed of human bodies, some, at least, probably still alive, remained unique. Within a short space, the mire of blood created by the first crushing wheels caused the rear wheels to lose some of their traction. Inés and Don Juan were showered in blood as the truck passed, crunching and grinding its way down the incline.

"Where is your gun?" he hissed at her.

"Under me."

"Shall we try to make it across the drawbridge?" he asked.

"Yes, *compañero*, but . . ."

"But?"

She was exercising all her bruised muscles, checking them out.

"If we get inside I shall start killing."

"Not the servants?" Don Juan thought of Garcia and the others.

She gave a small bitter laugh.

"Most of the servants are already dead. We gave them the privilege of climbing the tower first. They knew the castle. No, everyone but a man called Garcia joined us on the first day of the revolt. So. Are you coming, *compañero?*"

But still Don Juan hesitated. "Garcia and my father are old men," he said.

"I know. We don't kill old men. You can trust me," she said.

They peered up at the tower above the keep. No one was in evidence, but above the distant sound of the Guardia Civil's guns terrorizing the town and the occasional crashing of timbers and walls in the blazing houses along the banks of the river, hovering above these sounds they could hear singing from inside the castle's keep.

> "Arriba *battalions and conquer*
> *For Spain has begun to awaken*
> *Spain united. Spain great.*
> *Spain free. Spain arise.*"

"'The Cocksuckers' Hymn,'" she said, using the English word. "Are you ready?"

Don Juan nodded.

"Keep close behind me," she said, and they started to run.

Their feet all slippery from the puddles of blood, they made it across the drawbridge before a uniformed man of the Guardia Civil detached himself from the doorway of the keep. She shot him economically with three bullets before he could get his finger to his safety catch. She kicked open the old porter's office of the keep and sprayed bullets inside as she kicked. Three off-duty Guardia Civil in their underwear had been setting out their bedrolls for the night. They subsided into them, crumpled in a series of improbable postures. Inés listened. A toilet was still flushing behind a small door at the back of the room.

"Come out of there backward with your hands on your head or you're dead!" she shouted at the door. To Don Juan, "Keep a watch out on the courtyard, *compañero.*"

He did. Standing at the porter's door. Watching the familiar landscape of his home. Wondering how he could think of this cold, lifeless place as home. But watching intensely. Straining to focus into the shadows. Nothing moved. There was no other sound except Inés's voice behind him.

"Come out slowly. Stand right there. How many more of you are in the castle?"

"None. They're all in the town."

"Who else is here?"

"The duke. Garcia. He sleeps near his master."

"Put your tongue on the table."

"Oh, no!"

"Would you rather put your cock?"

"No!"

"Do it!"

Don Juan heard a squealing, grunting sound. Glancing around, he saw that she had impaled his tongue to the table with her knife.

"*Compañero,* come and tie this man's hands. Use one of their belts. Hurry."

He did so.

"D'you know how to raise the drawbridge?"

"I've seen it done. It's just a block and tackle. It takes two men, though."

"That's what I heard," said Inés, going to the porter's telephone. Lifting the receiver, she asked for a number.

"It's Inés," she said when somebody answered. "I'm in the castle."

A doubting, probing question came back.

"No, they haven't got me. But I know you can't be sure of that."

Protestations the other end. She cut them short.

"Listen, we're going to raise the drawbridge. When the trucks try to get back they won't be able to. Then you'll know for sure I'm in charge here. Find a way to close off the narrow approach road behind them when they return. Use the fire engine. Then I'll get them with a Maxim gun from above."

Together Inés and Don Juan hauled the chains of the block and tackle that slowly raised the drawbridge. It was hard work.

"Why didn't you kill the man . . . the man with the tongue?" he asked.

"We may have further use for him. A punctured tongue is painful, but not disabling. At least he's suffering."

"D'you think your friends believe you?"

"No, they can't be sure. Inés might have her breaking point. Who knows what the Guardia might be doing to me if they had me alive in that porter's lodge. D'you want to know?"

"No."

"Bourgeois sentimentality, *compañero.*"

"I'm very attracted to you."

"You're a boy."

"I am not yet a man, it's true. But I manage."

"It's true you dishonored the tyrant's wife. I remember now. I'll try you out if you like. We'll see if there's enough man in you for me."

It was the simplest, most disconcerting seduction of Don Juan's young life.

Up on the tower above the keep Inés examined the Maxim guns anxiously. One had been left loaded, with a belt of some one hundred and twenty bullets unexpended. The other was unloaded, although there was a box of ammunition beside it.

"Our communist allies have had training from the Russians. We have only manuals. Mostly stolen. I think this is a cooling device here."

She talked as she rather laboriously loaded the other gun. Don Juan was impressed at her methodical way with these deadly machines. It was one of his weaknesses that anything much more complicated than a mousetrap panicked him. He was always convinced he couldn't handle it till he'd forced himself to try. In under half an hour they were both reasonably sure they could fire the guns.

The shooting in the town had died down, and Inés was worried that the committee had had insufficient time to collect themselves, particularly when faced with the need to try to contain the Guardia Civil.

"Won't they think it a little odd that firemen who ignored the burning of the whole street should suddenly be driving their machine toward the castle?"

"The fire station is on the other side of the road from the burning houses of the bourgeois. Manuel, who is on the committee with me, is the chief fireman. They have only to drive across the gardens to block the approach road."

For a leader who had just suffered a spectacular defeat, Inés had remained extraordinarily optimistic. This time luck was on her side.

When the Guardia Civil came back they were singing the Falangist hymn and sounded drunk. The driver of the first truck, bumping once again over the anarchist dead, saw that the drawbridge was up only just in time to stop clear of the moat. But the driver of the second truck, which was simply following the leader, having had no warning of this sudden halt, slammed right into the first truck, sending it into the moat. By that time Inés had started to fire her Maxim gun, telling Don Juan to hold his ammunition in reserve.

She had a perfect field of fire and the advantage of surprise. The few guards who managed to get down from the open truck, seeking cover, stumbled and slipped in the bloody mess underfoot. She used Don Juan's gun to pour bullets into the cab of the second truck, where she couldn't see the driver. But by this time its fuel tank had exploded and the whole area was ablaze. She had killed every man of the Guardia Civil in under a minute, not a difficult feat with a gun that fires six rounds a second.

The fire engine never came.

About five minutes later, however, the Alfonso XII Gardens started to fill up with people waiting expectantly to hear if the Guardia Civil were indeed, as the rumor now had it, dead.

Don Juan had by this time gone to his father's apartments and found Garcia. He looked much older than he had remembered him, although it had been only eighteen months since he had last seen him. The old majordomo was visibly shaken by the sudden apparition of a blood-soaked Don Juan. He thought for an instant that somehow, in the turmoil that was Spain, the heir had actually been killed, that here before him stood his dreadful ghost. But Don Juan's words reassured him.

"I have come home, Garcia. There has been a battle outside. But I am not hurt."

"Thanks be to God, excellency," said the butler, crossing himself.

"How is my father, and how are you?"

"The duke is, alas, bedridden, excellency. But otherwise well. These recent events have overexcited everybody, but, as for me, I find civil war does not agree with me." Garcia managed a thin smile.

"The anarchist leader Inés, a former tenant of ours, has just captured the castle. She has assured me that neither you nor my father are in any danger. I will come and see him in the morning."

"Yes, excellency," said Garcia. Nothing the aristocracy did or said ever much surprised him. A wholly sane aristocrat he had never met.

"Oh, and Garcia—please don't call me 'excellency.' Those times are over. We are all equal now."

"I understand perfectly, excellency."

When he came down to help Inés lower the drawbridge he found that she had dragged the bodies of the Guardia Civil into a neat row. The man with the brand-new hole in his tongue had had his throat cut. He had not been needed and was not worth a wasted bullet, in her view. She was an essentially tidy revolutionary.

They picked their way through the carnage on the approach road with difficulty. The skeleton of the Guardia Civil's truck still burned. It was impossible not to tread on bodies.

At the end of the road the committee of control hovered, seeming uncertain and divided. The crowd themselves moved around looking rather tentatively at the road from the castle. When they all saw Inés there was a wave of applause, which soon petered out. She waited until she had reached the members of the committee of control, who came forward to meet her. "The castle is ours," she said quietly. "All the Guardia Civil are dead. I wish to suggest that an armed guard be put on the castle. Not for what is in it, but because I have promised this young *compañero* who helped me capture it that his father and Garcia will not be harmed. Tonight the dead must be retrieved. Tomorrow we can decide everything else."

The committee of control was so stunned by her news that they found it difficult to take in. Only the equally extraordinary appearance of Don Juan made it explicable. They assumed he had been inside the castle and betrayed it in some way. It was part of their instant democracy that Inés's proposal had to be voted on at once. They agreed unanimously to do as Inés suggested, their own excitement at their victory at last taking over.

Inés left them to address the crowd.

"*Compañeros*, the enemy are all dead. The castle is not ours. But no more is it theirs. What need have we for a castle? Now all Spain must kill the enemies. So that we and our children can be free with the sacred land itself to live in peace. Now you have many dead to bury. It is the next task."

Before she had finished they were weeping and cheering. Manuel, the fireman, a tall, burly man with a bull neck, came and put his hand on her shoulder. It was a possessive hand, used to resting there.

"Sorry about the fire engine," he said quietly, "I was so sure it was a trap. The tower—you remember how I said it would burn too easily? You were so sure it would work. It doesn't matter, Inés. We all make mistakes. You're tired. Let's go to bed."

She removed his hand gently enough.

"Not with you, *compañero*." She breathed it at him like a blowtorch. "Not tonight or ever again. You have no *faith*. If we believed in God we would say a miracle happened here tonight. That boy there has more balls on him than you, *compañero*."

At this Manuel's eyes bulged with anger and his lips blubbered. He lifted his large, hairy hand to hit her. The crowd who had been watching her seemed to stop breathing. For all their atheism, a woman like Inés acquired a kind of sanctity in these people's eyes, rather like a nun. It was ingrained in them. To hit her would be an extraordinary act, like sacrilege.

"If you touch me I will kill you," she said.

He knew she meant it, that even if he killed her first the crowd would get him. He turned away.

9

Fighting for the Effortless Acraria

Revolution . . . is the idea of justice. . . . It divides power
quantitatively not qualitatively as our constitutionalists do. . . . It is
atheist in religion and anarchist in politics: anarchist in the sense
that it considers power as a very passing necessity.

—Pi y Margall, *La Reacción y la Revolución*

Her room, when they finally reached it, was on the top
floor of a tannery in one of the poorest parts of town. It had, as a
result, an odor of leather that clung to everything. Even the blankets
smelled of leather.

"I have not been here for a long time," she said to Don Juan.
"That coward has a place over the fire station. It was what the
bourgeois used to call 'central.'"

She had lit an oil lamp, and now rummaged on a large table
covered with tattered books and pamphlets. Producing a couple of
bottles of wine, she turned to him.

"There is water in the street if you want to fetch it, *compañero.*"

She stared him straight in the eyes.

"I'd rather have wine."

"Aren't you going to ask for a glass?"

"I would rather take it from your mouth, or give it to you in mine, as you prefer."

"Give it to me in yours. Your mouth is a marvel, *compañero.*"

He gave it to her.

Touching her was like suddenly making contact with an active volcano. She literally seethed in his arms as she sucked the wine from his mouth. Her hands tore his trousers open and clutched, feeling him as a blind person does a face, committing it to memory.

"Oh, that is good, *compañero.* As marvelous as your mouth. What life it has! I must have it now. Afterward we can talk. But now, now . . ." She ripped off her blood-soaked shirt and trousers. Her only underclothes were a pair of British seaman's drawers, which she likewise shucked off in seconds.

She saw his wounded buttocks without asking where it had happened.

"Good," she said. "A little pain for you will be distracting. This is my night. Tomorrow will be yours."

Don Juan was dazzled by her nakedness, in the time he had to take it in, for she was, from her armpits to her thighs, almost covered with tattoos. Her boat-shaped breasts and dark, chewed nipples reminded him for a fraction of a second of the children he had seen outside her farm.

Her mouth sucked and kissed at his body in an agony of impatience, and when he took her she guided him as a steeplechase jockey does his knowing horse. "Harder, *compañero,* harder, harder. Let me feel how strong you are, *compañero.*" And then she shouted and yelled as if she were riding through hell with the four horses of the apocalypse. She showed him the inner rhythms of her body, beating a tattoo on his poor buttocks like a drummer at the charge, making him yell like her. When she put her tongue in his ear, she seemed to be drawing ribbons through his brain. Her comings were like avalanches, when she wrestled with him, her eyes tight shut, her breath singing like a steam whistle, her thighs working till at last she was done. But done for Inés meant only that the volcano was merely on bubble for an instant. A space between eruptions.

Don Juan never once thought of poor little Berthe that night, but without her he would never have been man enough for Inés. As it was, she aroused in him such incessant, insatiable desire that he drove her finally to hammer on the bed for breath and surcease, as a wrestler asks for quarter.

He fell dead asleep in her arms, and she found herself laughing, hugging him to her like a prize and laughing. He heard her and thought, She has some secret I am too tired to ask about, and now I shall never know.

He saw his father the next day and found it a depressing experience. The duke sat in his bed looking like a plucked chicken, stubbly with growths of unexpected hair peeking from under his pajamas. Only his voice remained strong, if a little hoarse, for he was, if anything, more voluble than ever.

"It seems a pity, my dear boy," he said to Don Juan, "that you should have grown so large. It is very weakening for a person to overgrow as you have. A Spaniard should be five feet, ten inches. No more. In this climate it is most unwise to grow farther than that."

"Don Juan looks remarkably healthy, your grace," said Garcia kindly. "Perhaps he has his maternal grandfather's excellent constitution."

"Oh yes, now he looks healthy enough. But wait awhile. By twenty he will be feeling a need for extra sleep. He will have to fight off a continuous lethargy. It is a well-known problem. My advice is to do everything you can to stop growing. They say that avoiding protein is wise. I believe something of that kind was recommended to your dear mother," the duke concluded, staring at Don Juan, wondering, perhaps, why his own genetic pool had contributed so little to this boy's appearance.

Afterward, in a conversation with Garcia down in the deserted kitchens of the castle, Don Juan discussed what was to be done with the duke in view of the uncertain temper of the town. Garcia, who was a Catalan, coming from a country district near Barcelona, was anxious to get home to his family's farm, where he would feel more secure. Don Juan's grandfather had asked him to stay at the castle, however, and had spoken to him over the telephone from Burgos almost every day since the revolt of the army had sparked off the revolution of their tenants, the Andalusian anarchists. Don Juan proposed that they put through a call to his grandfather, and within an hour the connection was made for them. Don Juan spoke first, greeting his grandfather with the news that he was at the castle.

"I'm relieved to hear you're still alive," said his grandfather, rather as one might say he was pleased to hear the weather was fine. "Major Barnet called me and told me what happened. He and the pilot will be all right. Everyone is being very polite to foreigners. Their help is going to be needed if this goes on."

"Garcia would like to go to Barcelona as soon as possible. The anarchists killed all the Guardia Civil last night, so the siege is over."

"I wondered how you got through!" said his grandfather. "Do you think that you or the duke are in much danger there at the moment? They've imprisoned the relatives of so many of us. Young Primo de Rivera is in prison in Madrid, I hear."

"I don't think we are in danger at the moment. But if Garcia goes, who is to look after the duke?"

"It can't be long before Franco and the Army of Africa get there. But I see that something must be done. Let me talk to Garcia."

In the end it was arranged that Garcia would take the duke to his family's farm until "this trouble is over." Don Juan agreed to accompany them. The old man would need lifting into and out of the car. Although he never knew what his grandfather had offered Garcia for this risky enterprise, it must have been a considerable sum. It was arranged that Don Juan would also stay at the farm for the time being. Garcia had agreed to pass them off as relatives, an elderly lunatic and his son. Don Juan told neither his grandfather nor Garcia that he had no intention of staying at the farm. It seemed simpler and kinder to have them worry about one thing at a time. However, Garcia was not entirely deceived.

"You did not tell your grandfather of your sympathy for the Republican cause, excellency," he said with some reproach in his voice.

"I will soon, Garcia. It is hard to tell him such a thing over the telephone, don't you think?"

"Perhaps. But eventually it must be done, excellency. It is not honorable for you to do otherwise. However, I fear that the journey we face may change your mind about your political allegiance."

The closing up of the castle and preparing for the duke to leave took about a week. During that time Don Juan split his time between helping Garcia in the daytime and being with Inés at night. He wished the nights were longer than the days.

Inés bestowed passion on her lover with the limitless zest she brought to being a revolutionary and a consistency of style. In between making love she engaged him in bouts of dialectic, dredging up from a magpie collection of half-digested reading bits of Rousseau and Proudhon, Bakunin and Jesus Christ. In the early hours of the morning, Don Juan would sponge the stale sweat from their bodies and listen to her declaiming, with an excitement that was wholly infectious, on how they now had the chance to build their utopia.

She was scornful of the fact that Garcia and Don Juan were locking away everything of value before they left the castle.

"D'you think, *compañero*, that we wish to have what the duke had? What is there about him to show that possessions or titles have made him the least bit happy?"

"Inés, there are happy dukes and unhappy dukes, I'm sure of it. Possessions have very little to do with it. A man like my poor father who has lost his mind and his health is naturally unhappy. You can't say that he is unhappy simply because he's a conservative monarchist. Or that you are happy simply because you are an anarchist."

"It is easier to be content when you have the soil to till, nature to watch over you, and no possessions about which to trouble yourself."

"Wouldn't you be happy to be the possessor of beautiful paintings that every day would give you pleasure?" he asked.

"I have them!" she said, shouting with laughter and undulating the mermaid on her belly. She had already told Don Juan that while in hiding from the Guardia Civil across the border in Gibraltar, she had taken up with a tattoo artist.

"But seriously," she added. "That was my idea. I know he wasn't our Goya. But he was a beautiful man, a Genoese. On the night he gave me my mermaid, he had made me for the first time put out of my mind what they did to my Mella. Beside you, *compañero*, he was a poor, simple person, but his gifts were all over my body when I had to leave him, and inside me he had made me again into a whole woman."

"Why did you *have* to leave him?" asked Don Juan, pitying the man who, having found Inés, should have to lose her.

"They needed me here. Everyone knew what the military planned to do. It was always a question only of *when.*"

He traced with the sponge the dolphins that sported on her shoulders, the eruption at Mount Etna that straddled her spine, sending lava to her hips, and the Genoese sailor's vision of Gog and Magog, who stood guard on either buttock, to the straits of his desire. But it may have been, Don Juan reflected, that his predecessor had placed the giants there as a warning, for Inés could never be taken from the rear. He ran the sponge down those torrid shallows between the giants' feet, squeezing the cool water into the crevices so that she arched her back in pleasure. Thinking he had overcome her reluctance, he dropped the sponge and knelt behind her, grasping her molten hips and starting to pull the giants toward him, when, with a shout of "No, *compañero,* never do that!" she somersaulted out of his arms and turned to face him, her arms raised in a wrestler's challenge.

"Take me looking me in the eyes, if you will, *compañero,"* she said. "And if you fight well your reward will be my reward. But never come from the back. We are not animals to bend for one another."

Reluctantly, warily, he lunged at her waist, hoping to carry her to the bed again in one deft move, but she had him almost instantaneously in an arm lock. Their wrestling bouts were more exciting to her than any other foreplay she could imagine. Don Juan had long since abandoned with Inés the intimate caresses learned from Ayesha and since. She fought as long as her body would let her. When he finally hugged her ribs so tight that her arms flailed uselessly, she was steaming hot and her pelvis sought him in a frenzy of anticipation.

She shouted in his ear, "Good, *compañero!* Good, Good! Quickly, now . . ." Folding her legs around his waist, she impaled herself urgently, and he had her standing, staggering around the cluttered, leather-stinking room like a couple of novelty dancers at a carny.

Her husband, whom he had so admired in life, they did not, for some time, discuss. He out of a delicacy of feeling that instinctively told him that if she wished to speak of her marriage, she would have given him some sign. She because she was more afraid of the past than of the future.

In Don Juan Inés saw a boy-man who was somehow free of the class labels that her training as a revolutionary made her affix to all too many of the people with whom she came in contact. He was, she accepted, technically an aristocrat. But he saw himself as an anarchist, however little he was really suited to that austere political confession. Others were easily slotted into the ranks of class enemy or friend, bourgeois or worker. Don Juan was none of these. He was a marvelous exception to her rules, and she felt free with him to be her (nonpolitical) self.

Her husband had been the other exception in her life. To him she had brought the dowry that her well-to-do parents had allotted for their cleverest, most promising daughter, in a marriage to a man from the privileged class that served the grandees of Spain. She became almost a bourgeoise by marriage. Mella, a groom and expert in horseflesh, like many of the tradesmen in town belonged secretly to the societies called the *candiles* for their secret meetings in candlelight when the message of Bakunin, Farga Pellicer, and others would be discussed as the early Christians may have discussed the Gospels in the catacombs of Rome. Pellicer's ringing phrase became the chief slogan: "We wish the rule of capital, state, and church to cease and to construct on their ruins anarchy, the free federation of free associations of free workers."

Both Mella and Inés had been sent to schools founded in Andalusia to combat the church's teachings that poverty and oppression must be suffered in this life, that people must wait for their reward in the next, and the even more hated Catholic doctrine of original sin, with its cynicism about mankind. The anarchist schools taught that Eden was there, waiting to be possessed, if the church ceased to pollute men's minds and the state became man's servant, not his master. They were taught equally to despise Marxism and communism as a deathly authoritarianism carried out by a race of *fonctionnaires.* Much of what they believed made sense to Spaniards raised in the cruel countryside of Andalusia. It soon became a religion for Inés, who brought to it a passionate commitment.

While her husband served the duke and tutored Don Juan in horsemanship, she went out into the valleys and among women workers in the fields and continued the organization that had been started by Belén Sárraga, the female labor leader from Málaga—an organization aimed at lessening the sixteen-hour day and raising the sixty-centimo wage paid for it.

If Mella had been an ordinary man he would not have found it compatible with his principles to be groom to the son of a duke. But in him Inés knew she had found a spirit too big for the narrow strictures of their anarchist faith. Horses and the people who rode them well were part of nature's plan to him. The duke had beautiful horses, and Don Juan rode them well. To Inés her husband was Spain itself, the bravery, the simplicity, the special *hubris* that is Spanish pride, the innocence of malice that was Don Quixote's. She mourned him before he was even injured, because such people are fated. She had canonized him in death after the fashion of her race. His name was too sacred to be mentioned lightly. She spoke of him to Don Juan once only.

"It is my fate, *compañero,* to die for anarchism. I hope that I will be able to die as *he* did, defying the enemy. I hope it is no trivial death."

On the day before Don Juan was due to leave for Barcelona, he was called before the committee of control together with Garcia. They were given the papers that had become tantamount to passports between the self-governing communities of Republican Spain. While much of the country was controlled by their allies, the socialists and communists and the ever-bourgeois Republicans, who remained nominally the government, Barcelona was under anarchist rule, the largest city ever to have such an experience. The committee announced to them that it had decided to commandeer the duke's car for their use. It would take their dear *compañera*, Inés, to Barcelona to represent them at the congress of the CNT (the Anarchist Trade Union). They had decided, however, to allow the car to transport the duke and his son, Compañero Juan, and Garcia (no *compañero* he) to their destination en route. It would, on its return to Andalusia, be converted into an ambulance.

So they set out together on the following day, Garcia driving with Inés beside him, her machine gun in her lap. Don Juan sat in the back with the duke, for whom a kind of cot had been contrived. Because the glass partition remained in position, the duke, though he shrank from Inés whenever she came near him, felt comparatively secure. It was not her revolutionary violence that he feared, but what he described as "those germs women carry to which men are seldom immune."

Their journey took five days—the first three of them on the way to the Mediterranean coast at Valencia via Jaén, Baeza, and Ubeda, then skirting the wastes of La Mancha via Villacarillo, Albacete, and Requena and so to the sea at Valencia. At Jaén the people were murdering a Jesuit and his mother with great ceremony, the task being given to a militiawoman. It was the first test of their rather grand car on crowds venting vengeance on the rich and privileged. Children hammered on the windows and kicked the tires when the car was slowed in traffic. But Inés looked what she was, a revolutionary leader. Waving her gun at staring, hostile crowds, she would give the clenched-fist salute and they, thinking the occupants of the car were being taken to a place of execution, saluted back and cheered.

"Long live liberty! Down with fascism!" they shouted.

At night they slept in sleeping bags at the roadside, except the duke, who stayed in the car. He left it only when Garcia and Don Juan carried him to a stream to wash him or perched him precariously on a portable commode that they had brought with them.

Passing through a village near Albacete on the third day, they attracted the attention of a crowd conducting executions in an outdoor skittle alley. The local committee of control stopped the car, and after looking at Inés's papers still seemed suspicious. Half a dozen monks were awaiting their death, their heads bowed in prayer.

"If you are who you say you are, you will not mind killing one of these vermin for us, *compañera.*"

"Certainly," said Inés, and without further hesitation she went over to one of the monks and shot him with a burst of three bullets. At which Garcia instantly crossed himself. Some of the crowd, seeing this, rushed to the car to pull Garcia out. But his door was locked from the inside.

"These three are to be tried in Barcelona!" shouted Inés, telling Garcia to drive on. The committee members, who hadn't seen Garcia cross himself, restrained the crowd, satisfied that no Nationalist could shoot a monk.

The duke, witnessing this scene, became totally incoherent for the remainder of the journey. Garcia never again spoke to Inés, and answered her only if it seemed absolutely necessary. Don Juan reasoned to himself that the monk's life had certainly been the price of Garcia's life and probably of his own and the duke's as well. He would anyway have died, but probably more unpleasantly at the hands of the crowd.

The duke and Garcia they left at the latter's family farm. It belonged to two older brothers as well as to Garcia and was a great whitewashed rambling affair in the middle of a fertile valley not far from Mortorelli. Garcia said his farewell to Don Juan with a finality that only partly had to do with the perils of the times. It was clear to him that the duke's heir was the lover and supporter of a murdering female twice his age. He could no longer call this brilliant boy he had loved and revered, as if he were the hope and the future of his own family, "your excellency." Don Juan had been right. All that was over.

"I shall pray for you, Don Juan," were his parting words.

The boy left the duke still gibbering.

During the next two years Don Juan served as a militiaman in a company under the command of Inés. He donned the uniform while in Barcelona. She introduced him as her "batman," which everyone took to be a kind of joke. While she joined in the conference of the CNT leaders, he walked the corpse-strewn streets. At night the city was full of music and excitement. Government was being carried on by tram drivers and factory workers from his grandfather's factories, now expropriated. Trucks rolled out of the city at all hours, carrying the middle classes off to their places of execution, beautiful places where they could reflect, amid scenes of natural grandeur, on the puny, petty nature of their bourgeois lives.

"Look at this, *compañeros*," the executioners would say. "You see how you have wasted your lives? Anyway, don't worry about death. It is a little thing."

For the anarchists the glory of nature was like the face of God.

Guadal, and the castle with it, fell to the Nationalists under General Varela on September 28. The Republicans, under General Miaja, regrouped their chaotic army on this front, partly in the province of Jaén. Here, in a mountainous region, Inés took command of a force of five hundred anarchist militia, most of whom had been friends or neighbors from Guadal. In the Andalusian plains to the south of them, the Nationalists were in control. She was given the task of holding a pass leading north and protecting a south-eastern access to New Castile and Toledo and, ultimately, Madrid.

From the fall of 1936 until the spring of 1938, Don Juan and Inés lived a life of almost humdrum calm and domestic felicity in the Morena mountains, considering the militia was holding part of the front line in one of the most vicious wars of modern times.

The Madrid front was attacked by tens of thousands of Moroccans, Carlists, Falangists, the German Condor Legion, and Mussolini's Italians; it was bombed by German Junkers; and, finally, its entire working class, men, women, and children, defended the city, sallying forth in city buses to throw back the enemy. But nothing happened on the Jaén front.

From Barcelona, El Campesino ("The Peasant") led the militia of the anarchists, the communists, the socialists, and the Trotskyites in offensives against the enemy. In Jaén, the orders from above were to be watchful.

On May 31, 1937, the International Brigade, men of many nations fighting for the Republic, broke through the Nationalist lines at San Ildefonso. On the Jaén front there were almost no foreigners, although some of the militia under Inés thought of Don Juan as foreign. Nor was there any action.

Most of the militia men and women were billeted in farmhouses or barns or abandoned churches. Inés and Don Juan lived in a windmill and converted one of the upper rooms into a studio where he could paint when it was not his turn to be on guard duty or out on patrol. His subjects were villagers or their children and, whenever she had time to pose for him, Inés herself.

Living all together, without priests or police or any other kind of authority except that of the government of the Republic far away in Madrid, the anarchists at last had a chance to try to realize in practice the theories on which they had been raised. No one smoked. Even Inés gave up wine. If they were going into action, such as a probing patrol down into the Nationalist-held valley, they abstained from sex. Otherwise, love was free. The ideal was to have a *compañero* living with his dear *compañera*. But no one was to have the sense of *owning* anybody else. Everyone was at liberty to move on. Money ceased to be used among them. Their pay as militia was paid into a central account controlled by Inés. They had a store, and from it people took what they absolutely needed, no more.

In the marvelous future described by Don Quixote de la Mancha, people live contentedly on acorns. Generations of Spaniards had competed in their pride as to how little they needed to survive. The anarchists, part of this tradition, lived on mountain air and little else as the war wore on. By 1938 just about the only food available was lentils and chick-peas, washed down with a little goat's milk.

As lean as a couple of whippets, Don Juan and Inés spent their spare time in an argument that grew more elaborate and vehement as the days passed by. It started with eggs. On one of her patrols into the Nationalist plain, Inés had liberated some hens from their bourgeois owners. They were erratic layers, but what they produced was, to Don Juan, a blessed variant from the pulse family of vegetables. Each day on which they were honored with an egg, he would solemnly spend up to an hour preparing a dish worthy of the event.

He managed one day, scrounging for ingredients, "baked egg Savoy." Inés watched, fascinated, but with mounting disgust, as he separated a white from a yolk, leaving the yolk in the eggshell. With a fork he beat the white with a couple of tablespoons of cream skimmed from the goat's milk, adding salt and pepper until the mixture was frothy. Having no butter, he pounded an onion until the oil from it had separated and then sieved it away, giving himself fat for a baking dish. Fanning the charcoal under the hot plate, he slowly warmed the dish till the onion oil had melted, and then added the whipped egg-white mixture, stirring as the amalgam cooked, bringing it to a creamy consistency. Now he took the dish from the fire and dropped on the egg yolk. He covered the dish and allowed it to bake for six minutes, after which he revealed his tiny flan to Inés.

"You are a glutton, *compañero!* Such an effort for something that will soon be in your alimentary canal! That is obscene! It is bourgeois!"

Saying nothing, he divided the already small dish into two minute portions on separate plates.

"Please try it while it's still hot. I'm not sure the white has risen enough," said Don Juan, handing her one of the portions.

"You can have my portion. I like an egg to be plain, as nature intended."

"You sound like a priest," he said.

"A priest?" she shouted.

"The dogma of an egg. 'Nature intended it to be natural. Amen!'" he intoned, descanting his voice.

"Be careful, *compañero.*"

"Oh, was I about to blaspheme?"

"Nature *is* sacred. How can you reverence her perfection if you try to alter it?"

"I'm surprised that doesn't suggest itself to you when you kill one of nature's creatures."

"I have never killed except in the ultimate defense of nature." Inés was furious.

"Has it occurred to you that someone down in the plain can be having this selfsame conversation, only using God's name as you use nature's?"

"That is blasphemy," she said. "You dare to compare to nature that conspiracy of superstition and ignorance you call God. God whom you have never seen or touched. God who, if He existed, would, I presume, have saved the monk I was forced to kill, have saved the bishop of Jaén and the thousands of His priests we have justly slaughtered. You compare God to the glory nature shows us in these mountains, in ourselves now we are here?"

"All right, Inés, but then nature created this dish," he said, almost swooning with pleasure at the first mouthful. "It made the marvelous arrangement of separate yolk and white and created goat's milk with cream that can be skimmed. Nature put the oil in the onion and nature gave us salt and allows us to pick pepper. Nature gave me those faculties of invention and skill of which Shakespeare spoke when he remarked, 'What a piece of work is a man!' And if God and nature turn out to be one, I shall not be surprised!"

"You have a priest's love for your belly," she said sharply.

"My belly is indeed a lover of good food; what it cannot stomach is half-baked, naïve dogma."

"You used to accept our anarchist ideals! You used to." She said it almost in tears, as a bourgeois woman might say, "You promised to go on loving me. You promised!"

"I accept them still," he said sadly. "I hadn't counted on them turning into a religion. . . ."

In this way discord came to Utopia in the Sierra Morena. As Inés neared her spiritual passion she became more and more puritan

and exacting. She told Don Juan one morning when she awoke that
she had dreamed of the blessed day when the company would need no
food, when, because of their oneness with nature, the earth would
feed them through the soles of their feet, as it passes its life-giving
juices to the trees through their roots.

She took to walking barefoot after this and told the company of
her "vision."

The only major military action which occurred near the Jaén
front during the entire war came in the spring of 1937 at the
sanctuary of Santa Maria de la Cabeza near Andújar, thirty miles
from their idyllic valley. Here more than one thousand of the
bourgeois from Andújar, together with some hundreds of the Guardia
Civil and Falangists, had shut themselves up in the mountaintop
sanctuary many miles, in fact, behind the Republican lines. The Jaén
front being what it was, these people were ignored for nine months,
until they thought it only honorable to declare themselves at war
with the Republic. Madrid finally ordered a siege, and ten thousand
militia were gathered in the area. Inés's company was not, so far,
affected, being needed, as the orders from the ministry of war always
said, "to be ever watchful."

However, a considerable time elapsed and the ten thousand were
quite unable to take the stronghold, which was gallantly defended
under the inspired command of a Captain Santiago Cortés. Meanwhile the Nationalist planes, flying from Córdoba and Seville, were
perfecting the new art of dropping supplies in small areas from the air.
Thousands of kilos of food were dropped successfully into the
defenders' lines, and it looked as if they could hold out indefinitely.

Inés and her company heard all of this on the radio, and she
became increasingly impatient at this "dishonor" the Republic was
suffering by being unable to reduce this impudent fortress.

"There can be only one reason we have failed there, compañero,"
she said to Don Juan.

He was painting what he planned to be a major full-length
portrait of her in their studio-cum-bedroom in the windmill.

"What is that?" he asked.

"Our people are afraid to die!"

"Try to stay still," he murmured. "Fear of death is a natural
reaction if you're a half-trained mob facing professionals who can
shoot straight."

She knew this to be the problem, and held her pose well enough
for the next few minutes. Don Juan was painting her in heroic mien.
On his canvas, she seemed to be leaping straight up in the air, one

arm raised, and holding a machine gun. Otherwise she was adorned only by her brilliant tattoos. Dragons lit her thighs, their yawning mouths breathing fire toward the single place where her otherwise hard body seemed tender and vulnerable, and on her breasts, the prows of galleons yawed as she stretched. It was a difficult pose to hold because she had to stand on her toes and be "reaching" all the time.

"We have been training for six months now," she said at last, relaxing her pose. "D'you think you're ready to face professionals?"

"It depends on what they know in relation to what we know," he said. "We're certainly pretty good at shooting and looking after our guns. But you've ignored a lot of what those manuals say about taking cover, about presenting as little target to the enemy as possible, and about camouflage."

"Camouflage is a kind of cowardice," she said vehemently.

"The British thought that when they refused to stop wearing red coats," said Don Juan. "It helped them lose the American colonies."

"In the days of chivalry you would have been an armorer or a gravedigger," she said with contempt.

"How romantic you are," he said wonderingly.

"You're right. It's an incurable national disease!" she agreed bitterly, and then, after resuming her pose, "Tonight we take a vote in the company. I want to ask the ministry to transfer us to the siege at Santa Maria."

They arrived at night. A convoy of trucks had rattled all the way from Valencia to transport them. Rain was deluging down, and for the last ten miles the trucks had taken almost all day in a sea of mud. It had been intended that they join in an attack planned for the following morning, but that assumed that they would have arrived the previous day. Somewhat to Don Juan's surprise they were met by a quartermaster who had actually reserved an adequate number of tents for them, although their floors were not covered by groundsheets. The quartermaster apologized. Rain was something people prayed for in this region. The cultivators of olive trees would be grateful.

The company was grateful to be under cover at all after eight hours in open trucks. Soaking, they slept sitting on the muddy hillside, stacked back to back, only their heads and shoulders and backs slowly drying under the tents, their bottoms immersed in a muddy stream.

Inés went straight to a company commanders' meeting and took Don Juan with her as her messenger. The headquarters, where this meeting took place, was a farmhouse with a number of outbuildings, around which hundreds of supply mules were bivouacked, looking very forlorn in the pelting rain. The smell of these creatures' wet hides and of their dung seemed strangely reassuring to Don Juan. He had a fellow feeling for the mules. It would be an exaggeration to say that his commitment to the cause of the Republic had faded. But he knew that he, like the mules, was following reluctantly in the wake of this army of zealots and amateurs. He did not dread an unavoidable death in action. He agreed with the anarchists when they said that death itself was "a little thing." What appalled him was the prospect of a death thrust upon him that would be quite ridiculously vainglorious.

Finding shelter with the other messengers in a leaky barn, he took out a British infantry handbook that Inés had acquired with some difficulty, made him translate, and then largely ignored in their training sessions. Organizationally she had followed the handbook rather literally. The company was divided into platoons, and each platoon had mortar or machine-gun sections, where available equip-ment allowed, and rifle sections. There was a signaler in each platoon. She herself had a headquarters platoon with riflemen, a signaler, stretcher bearers, and a messenger, Don Juan. They were armed with First World War rifles of British manufacture, bolt-actions that took a clip of six bullets, heavy but accurate up to a range of two hundred and fifty yards. All the section and platoon leaders, and Inés herself, were elected to their commands.

When in defense, she believed in following the book and taking cover. The handbook's dictum for what to do when coming under fire from the enemy—their infantry should get down (illustrated as throwing oneself flat), crawl (on one's belly), observe (see where exactly the enemy's fire is coming from), and fire back—all this she regarded as arrant cowardice and what you would expect of the bourgeois British. Don Juan thought it seemed both logical and sensible. But since he had been chosen as messenger because he was the fastest runner in the company, there seemed little prospect of his putting it into practice.

One part of the attacking procedure Inés had particularly liked. It was that when preparing to charge the enemy and after fixing bayonets, it was thought essential to scream as loud as possible, terrifying the foe, and then "to put on your killing face." It was a pity, Don Juan reflected, thinking affectionately of his mistress's wild and colorful body, that she could not charge stark naked. He made the mistake of mentioning this foolish fantasy to Inés as they walked back to their lines.

"It is a wonderful idea, *compañero*. I had already intended to wear no shoes when we go in. My feet are getting marvelously hard. We are to join the attack at first light. Let us find a dry place to make love. It is an old legend, but I like it, that a woman should be full of sperm when she goes into battle."

"Perhaps it comes from our Spanish belief that the seat of all courage is in a man's balls."

"You mock me so, *compañero*. Whatever happens tomorrow, I must tell you that tonight, and for a long time since, I have loved you. You are not one of us. But you have a quality and a strength that is as eternal as ours. I hope I don't have to live without you."

And on this somber note they made love with a fierce and fatalistic joy in the company of some mules, all standing under an olive tree.

The rain stopped during the night. An hour before dawn Inés mustered her company and led them to their place in the order of battle. A force of five thousand militia was to try to break through the defenses at a place on the mountain where the walls of the sanctuary had been thoroughly breached by shelling and bombing and where the defenders had made a redoubt from the rubble. They advanced up the hillside in open order, Inés at their head, the whole company spread over two hundred yards from flank to flank.

At first they made their way through sparse olive groves, already too high up for the trees to be strong and bushy. Then they came out into the open, where the only greenery was the occasional mastic tree, some cactus, and thorn bushes that tore at their legs, try as they would to avoid them. Inés walked steadily on her bare feet, unflinching.

Now they could see the redoubt curling down from the breached walls of the sanctuary like a tongue. It was lit by the gray light in the sky, still too early for the sun.

They had been ordered to march in silence, to avoid, where possible, treading on sticks that would make a noise as they snapped. The nearer they were when the defenders saw them, the more the element of surprise at this hour, when man's resistance is at its lowest.

Soon there were no more plants, only rocks in their path. They could, by now, make out the separate stones that piled up to form the redoubt. On their right flank a company of UGT (socialist) militia from the city of Jaén could be heard breathing heavily, having difficulty keeping pace with Inés's men.

Still no shot had been heard. Don Juan, marching almost

alongside Inés, passed on her whispered order to release their safety catches. Every gun had a bullet already in the breech, bayonets long since affixed.

He strained his eyes to see if he could see the face of a defender, the muzzle of a gun even. Nothing. Lacking that human dimension, in this now treeless landscape it was hard to know how close they were. But the lack of any enemy to see . . .

A hundred or more faces. As many guns firing. The smoke seen before the ragged trail of bangs heard.

"Hold your fire!" shouted Inés.

The faces disappeared.

Don Juan looked to left and right. Everyone seemed to be there. Still advancing. But then he glanced backward. Half a dozen of the company lay either still or moving only tentatively.

He watched ahead now. Frightened to blink. Straight ahead. Where the faces had popped up before. Always advancing.

"Fire next time, *compañeros*. Take careful aim and fire."

This they had rehearsed many times. Inés had likened it to shooting rabbits among the rocks. The animal looked at you as you approached him. You stopped, aimed, and fired in one continuous motion.

The heads came up. Don Juan sought a single face, brought up his rifle to his shoulder. Get him in the sight before he gets me. Steady the arm. Watch for the kick. *Squeeze*—don't pull—squeeze the trigger.

The sound of his shot was lost in the automatic fire from Inés's machine gun.

The head in Don Juan's sight looking startled. A red blur on the side of his skull.

Remember to reload. Reload.

Heads had all gone down again. They were forty yards away by Don Juan's estimation. And advancing almost at a run.

Inés had flung off her shirt.

"Chaaaaaarrrge!" she shouted. And the screaming started as they pelted over the rocks, the redoubt seeming to loom out to meet them.

Oh God. Oh God, thought Don Juan. There are the faces. And they're rapid-firing. The hands working the bolts as fast as they can. But they'll need another clip after six shots, surely? But a number of Mauser machine guns have joined them. Pumping lead.

He could hear their bullets now. A whirring sound. Too late for us to fire. We're charging now. Twenty more yards.

He glanced to his right. No Jaén company. Few of Inés's company.

Inés, quite bare now. Pants kicked away. A slight fold in the flesh at the waist as she ran, firing from the hip, spraying the bullets at the fascists.

Don Juan's rifle butt knocked as if by a sledgehammer. The rifle out of his hands. He slowed. Turned. Stooped to retrieve it. Skidded on the still-muddy rocks. Lost balance. Put out an arm to save himself. But fell hard.

There seemed to be twenty members of the company now crouching in the rocks. The rest lying about. Quite still. But far behind, another line of Republican infantry advancing up the hill. Poor bastards.

He had his rifle. The butt shattered. He turned to face the fire. It couldn't be long now. Might as well get it over with. "It's such a little thing, *compañero!*" they always said.

Inés had made it onto the redoubt. On the wall of it. No faces around her. But then arms pulling her down. He went on running toward where she had disappeared.

Shells were landing. Weren't they supposed to precede the charge? To keep the enemy's heads down? How difficult to remember.

A noise seemed to be closing down Don Juan's brain. He felt his breath leaving his body. Like a giant blow to his solar plexus. Simultaneously a curiously slow-moving ball of flame was unfolding in front of him.

General Quiepo de Llano spoke in his nightly news program on the radio from Seville that night. He told his audience in exultant tones how ten thousand Republican militia had attacked Santa Maria de la Cabeza in waves and been beaten back. It was the war story of the day. As an example of the barbarity of the enemy that faced the fascists, the announcer told the story of the attacker who had appeared in the guise of the Whore of Babylon, stark naked and painted like a savage from head to foot. "On this hillside sacred to the living memory of the mother of God, our heroic forces have beaten back the hordes of the Antichrist led by the Abominable Whore herself! *¡Viva España!*"

A radio was playing in the redoubt, and the defenders cheered this news of themselves. Lying in the dark where he had lain all the sunny day, Don Juan could hear clearly the familiar intoxicated tones of Quiepo de Llano. None of the three succeeding lines of attackers had got as far as the redoubt. No single attacker that day had actually stormed the redoubt as had Inés. He tried not to speculate on the manner of her death, nor on the even more horrible possibility that she might be alive. Almost certainly she had died the death she would have wished. Her children, who had hardly seen her for years, would be proud of her. Don Juan was proud of her and regretted he had never found a way to really match her love with his.

He knew that if he stirred in daylight it would invite a bullet. Once he had fought some breath back into his lungs after the bursting shell had knocked him flat, he knew that he had suffered no serious injury. He spent the day trying to exercise his muscles one by one, flexing first his toes inside his rope-soled shoes, then the muscles of his calf, and so on.

During the night he crawled painfully, and then walked, his way back to the Republican lines. He found fewer than fifty survivors of Inés's company, and slept alone and long in a tent now dried by the sun.

The next day he and his demoralized and bewildered *compañeros* watched the arrival of the Thirteenth International Brigade. First came the Franco-Belgian battalion called for Louis Michel, then the Tchapiaev batallion, a polyglot group of Czechs, Hungarians, Romanians, and others. The Henri Vuillemin battalion was apparently entirely French, while the Mickiewicz batallion was Polish. Don Juan was amazed to hear that this brigade had consented to be led by a Spanish general called Gomez, and almost as surprised when he heard that Gomez was only a *nom de guerre* and that the leader was actually a German communist by the name of Zeisser.

No officer attempted to reorganize the rumps of the anarchist militia at this stage. Don Juan found food at the canteen tent and plenty of time to watch the International Brigade prepare for its assault. He wished Inés could have seen them and learned from them. But he saw no more action. The final battle, when it came, he watched from a distance with a group of Inés's company who had agreed to go up after and retrieve Inés's body and bury it themselves with some kind of fitting ceremony. Ten thousand trained men took part in the assault, and its result was a foregone conclusion.

Very few of the male defenders survived, and some of these were noncombatants. The women and children were taken down to a tent prepared by the Red Cross for their care after the rigors of the siege.

They found her in the redoubt. Her body had literally been torn limbs from trunk, the torso and head mutilated so viciously that it was hard to imagine the human original. It took some time to find and assemble among so many other corpses, but they carried her remains away in a sack. Don Juan could find no tears for her, only an aching emptiness in himself now that he knew for sure that she was dead. He felt like a husk, without hunger or thirst or pleasure or pain or hope. If loving meant someone's becoming an extension of your life, a daily marvel who nourished body and soul and imagination with her life and her hope, then he had loved her.

They buried her the same evening, not able to find a spare coffin, using the same sack in which they had carried her down the mountain. When they asked Don Juan, as the most educated among them, to say something—not a prayer, of course—he remembered a book he had once read with Whitticker. It had been written by a Spaniard Whitticker rather admired, surprisingly a priest called Father Juan de Mariana. This text, taken from his *De Rege et Regis Institutions of 1599*, Don Juan had been made to use as the subject of an essay in answer to the question "Is the real interest of the church always compatible *only* with the status quo?"

In deference to his lost Inés, for whom he now invoked these famous lines, he substituted the word "Nature" for "God." Also in deference to her, he added "women" to "men" in the text.

"'It is a duty of humanity,'" he said, "'for us to open to all men and women all the riches which Nature gave in common to all, since to all she gave the earth as a patrimony, so that all without distinction might live by its fruits. Only unbridled greed could claim this gift of nature, appropriating as its own the foods and riches which were intended to be the property of all. In a Republic in which some are overstuffed with riches and others lack the very necessities, neither peace nor happiness can prevail.' For these ideals our elected leader and dear sister, Inés, fought and died."

They nearly all said Amen, and some crossed themselves, not noticing, perhaps, that they had done so.

"You still thinking of her, *compañero?*" one of them asked Don Juan as the remains of Inés's militia company were being divided up into small details to do guard duty in Jaén. He was taken by surprise at the question, preoccupied as he was with the terrible void he felt within him.

"Yes," he replied. "I was wondering why they should take such bestial vengeance on her body."

"They are credulous, *compañero*. They believed she was the Devil's Whore."

"I think it was simply because she was a woman, and braver than the rest of us, braver even than they."

10
Interval in Eden

How shall we kill this old, this long Remorse
    which writhes continually
And feeds on us as worms upon a corse,
    Maggots upon a tree?
How stifle this implacable Remorse?

—Baudelaire

Once a Carthaginian city, conquered for Rome by Scipio the African, and once the royal capital of the forgotten kingdom of Taiga, Jaén had, by the time Don Juan came to do his duty there, slept through a thousand years of provincialism. It slept still.

In a large, airy town house off the main square of St. Francisco, he and a number of other militiamen detailed as part of the garrison of Jaén were billeted. Don Miguel de Cayuela, the owner of the house, had been shot the same day that they had murdered the bishop of Jaén, Don Manuel Basulto Jiminez, with his sister before an audience of thousands. A woman of the militia called Freckle-face had been the specially invited executioner. But that had occurred near Madrid, where people were more excitable and demonstrative than in sleepy Jaén.

Three unmarried sisters of Don Miguel lived in the house, all of them in their fifties. His widow was bedridden with Parkinson's disease. The only surviving daughter, Teresa, was fifteen and had, before the rising, been promised to the church. The late Don Miguel's sons were fighting for General Franco somewhere in Extremadura. The only male member of the family living in the house was Commander León de Cayuela, a former naval officer under the monarchy and the late Don Miguel's twin brother. He had somehow survived the first months of terror after the rising, and was now confined, like the rest of the family, to the top floor of the old house, where once the servants had slept.

Teresa de Cayuela had lived the life of thousands of other Spanish girls of her class. From the day in babyhood when she had realized that she was a girl, different from boys, destined for a female's life, she had accepted, without hesitation, the limitations and the privileges of her gender.

She learned, when still tiny, to sit with her legs close together, her little girl's dress pulled well down over her knees. Her voice she modulated, whenever she remembered, as a little girl should. Her mother taught her sewing, the care of linen, and deportment. She learned how to supervise both cleaning and cooking in the household, understanding that whether in a convent or in marriage, her dowry would be quite sufficient to spare her the actual performance of menial tasks. The nuns' school had taught her to read and write in Spanish and Latin. She knew her catechism by heart, and had enough knowledge of arithmetic to manage household accounts. The nuns had also taught her of the history of the church in Spain. Her country had, as far as she knew, no other history worth knowing. Early on, for some never wholly explained reason, there had been the age of saints. Opportunities for martyrdom abounded. Then there had been the Christian kings' wars against the Moslem Moors. The Christian Spanish conquests of the Americas and the achievements of the missionaries in converting millions of miserable heathens. The church's expulsion from Spain of the Christ killers, the Jews. Catholic Spain's valiant efforts against the heresies of the Reformation to the north. The church was Spain. Revolution against the church had destroyed the state of Spain as her family understood it. Teresa prayed several times daily for the Nationalists' victory.

Before the war was over, when she was thirteen, the nuns had been so pleased with her simplicity and meekness and, perhaps, with the prospect of the dowry of one of the richest heiresses in Jaén that they had told the bishop of their belief that Teresa had a vocation. He had passed on this glad news to Don Miguel and Dona Maria, his wife. The child herself was informed in due course and told to give thanks in her prayers for this benediction.

It happened that the news coincided with a series of small events in Teresa's life that, taken together, made her greet it with less joy than everyone expected.

The stark gray dress she had to wear to school each day she had begun to hate, as she hated her black wool stockings, as she loathed the tight braid that imprisoned her hair and the bandage that her mother made her wear to suppress her budding breasts. It was not that she had any urge to be immodest; quite the contrary. But it had always seemed part of the absolute promise of being female, to be set against the lost freedom to run around and shout like a boy, that she would have the chance one day to look beautiful. Not to adorn herself—that might be too vain, even sinful—but at least of herself to be an adornment in the world.

She had been taught never to look at or touch her own naked body, to keep it covered even when she washed. Her mother had shown her how to contrive all her ablutions under a huge sheetlike shroud fastened at the neck, which shielded her body, as she washed it, from her own eyes. But her face and her hands and her feet she looked at with extraordinary attention. The looking glass in her bedroom had been confiscated because her aunts had noticed that she lingered in front of it when one or another of them was waiting to take her to school. Vanity had been declared her besetting sin in the household. Yet still she found ways of seeing her reflection—in windowpanes, in the knobs on the silver taps in the bathroom. She gloried in the luster of her dark hair. She knew that her eyes were among the largest, with the longest lashes, of any girl in her class at school. The length of her fingers was another pride; her nails, which she kept scrupulously clean and carefully shaped, had cuticles she pared daily. The toes of her feet were as long and evenly spaced, slightly, pleasingly spatulate, as any feet she had seen on religious statues or paintings, where feet were almost always bare.

To confine these beauties forever in a nunnery, to cut her beautiful hair and always to have to hide her lovely feet, seemed too cruel a thing to ask of her.

And that was before the first tincture of blood appeared on her nightgown.

Things male had also impinged on her consciousness at about

that time. Before that, men had seemed like a separate genus altogether. Like an extremely superior breed of horse. There had been a foreignness about them which she had been taught to find faintly repellent. Their scratchy faces and hairy hands. Their deep, loud voices and noisy feet. The strange arrangement they had for going to the toilet that necessitated having a special place set aside for them downstairs and away from the women's bedrooms.

Teresa had been taught from the earliest age that the world, in almost every detail, was, for all practical purposes, in the hands of men. Morally speaking, however, the lives women led redeemed the world. In God's recognition of the selflessness of their motherhood and in the efficacy of a pure woman's prayers, through the intervention of the Blessed Virgin Mary, the safety of the race depended. That was why, they told her, and told her often, a girl should always look to her immortal soul, that spotless balance sheet she tended, for the good of her family and the world, at least as much as for its promise of paradise for her own insignificant self.

But as she grew from girlhood to adolescence, she found in the world around her that there were two values at least as compellingly interesting to her as goodness and sin. They were beauty and ugliness. "The values of vanity," her hideous aunts would have said.

Sounds, shapes, colors, both natural and contrived, started to be sorted in her mind into the harmonious against the cacophonous, the pleasing against the ugly. A cornice in a room pleased or repelled her. The way flowers sat in a vase compelled her to arrange them to the symmetry her eye demanded. The sound of a Gypsy street singer might move her to tears, and the splendors of nature when she went into the countryside affected her as she imagined a lover must affect a woman in love.

For by now she had heard of *love*. It was spoken of in whispers at school. It was extolled by the Gypsy singers. Her mother had even mentioned it as an emotion that grew between men and women in marriage. But that had sounded somehow different.

Before her first bleeding, no one had mentioned the matter of sex to her. She had long since known that babies were formed in a woman's body. There could be only one channel by which they were born into the world, and it did not seem surprising that a woman should bleed thereafter. But to be bleeding in her girlhood, to be bleeding while still unmarried and not yet a mother, seemed extraordinary and frightening. Sure that it was the result of her sinful vanity, she kept the matter secret, stealing napkins from the dining room and living in a turmoil of fear and secret washings.

Then had come the rebellion and the revolution. The frightful month when the whole world seemed about to end. The nine nuns who taught school hanging together by their angularly snapped necks, like a rat catcher's haul, suspended from the school flagpost. Her aunt had covered Teresa's eyes too late to spare her that supremely ugly sight. Home to find her father gone, her brothers fled, only the commander, her uncle, hidden, they said, on the roof.

For a fearful twenty-four hours she had lived in the appalling fear that her bleeding had some frightful prophetic significance for the entire community. Her whole childhood, after all, had been filled with stories no less extraordinary. The stigmata of a dozen saints were the sign of miraculous powers. Was it not logical that this insistent bleeding from that part of her which her mother had made seem most shameful, never to be touched, never to be seen, could be the sign of Heaven's fearful displeasure? With her. With her family. With the world.

Curiously, it was the commander, the only man left in the family, who reassured her. She was sent up to the attic with food for him. The servants had all left, but the commander was a popular and kindly man, and they didn't betray him to the mobs in the street who were still hunting for bourgeois victims.

She sat to talk to him while he ate, trying to get him to explain to her why *he* thought these mad, inexplicable things were happening in their sleepy city of Jaén, with its eternity of history, with the millions of God-praising prayers it had offered up over the years in its cathedral and its many other churches. How could He have permitted it?

The commander said it was the fault of men, not God. Man had made the church in Spain in his own image, not God's.

She had no idea what he meant, but was so relieved that he seemed to sincerely believe in his explanation that she burst into tears.

"I thought God had sent me a terrible sign!" She blurted it out.

"What sign?" he asked skeptically, half amused at her intense expression. A lifelong bachelor, he had always liked women more than he desired them. For Teresa he had a real affection. She filled a gap in his life.

"I have been bleeding. Please don't ask me where. I am so ashamed."

He told her very gently that every single woman had bled since Eve had been cursed for offering the apple to Adam.

"Is it because it is a curse on all of us that my mother makes of those parts such a secret?" she asked, blushing deeply to be discussing these things with her uncle, but determined to know.

"If God had cursed you all with a cloven hoof instead of a right foot you would have made that a secret, wouldn't you?"

"What a horrible thought. Yes, I'd wear a special shoe. We all would, I suppose," she said thoughtfully. "If we have such a curse from God, how has he cursed men?"

"The mark of Cain, my dear," said the commander simply. "My sex is, as you see, a gender of inveterate killers."

The next months, which brought the news of her father's death, followed by her mother's extreme sickness, were months of constant change in Teresa's young life. The aunts had to learn to cook and to clean the large house. The churches remained closed, but the banks reopened, and, to a surprising degree, the surviving bourgeoisie returned to near-normal lives. The commander continued to receive his pension from the Republic, which made such matters a point of honor, stressing as they did the government's legitimacy as the constitutional and elected successor to the monarchy.

The bands of murderers had been ordered by the various trade unions, to which they belonged, to cease their activities, and comparative peace had returned to Jaén.

Nine months later the battle at Santa Maria de la Cabeza brought floods of militiamen from other parts of the Andalusian front through Jaén on the way to the siege. When the battle was over, the town was garrisoned with a battalion of militiamen, and for the first time a billeting sergeant came to the house off St. Francisco Square.

The commander, who was, in any case, confined to the house by order of the local committee of control, received an order to move the whole of his family to the top floor. Twenty anarchist militiamen occupied the rest of the house. Among these was Don Juan.

Teresa saw him on the first day the militia arrived. He had a mule on which was packed a great pile of canvases wrapped in burlap. The aunts, who were with her at the window watching the arrival of their uninvited guests, insisted that the canvases must be booty from some church or mansion that the "murdering thief" had probably looted.

"He might be a painter," said Teresa, looking at his face as he worked at untying his load from the mule. "He looks like an angel."

"Remember, Teresa, that Satan himself was an angel before he fell from heaven," said the commander, overhearing this conversation and teasing her. Since their conversation in the attic, he had become more her father than her real father had ever managed to be.

Don Juan had contrived to find himself a new job in the militia. The rump of Inés's company had returned to the valley they had previously guarded. Don Juan had been offered a job as interpreter with the International Brigade, but the local committee of control in the province of Jaén decided they wanted to keep their militiaman interpreter for themselves, against the return of the foreign troops. He therefore had to go to Jaén as soon as he had collected his things from the windmill. No one seemed to notice the mule he took for his journey, which he made on foot, taking ten days in all. The mule was prepared to be a beast of burden, but refused to be ridden. It was the kind of compromise that Don Juan understood, and they had a contented journey together.

Teresa saw very little of the militiamen on her trips up and down the stairs or to and from the market with her aunts. She kept her eyes down, and if they sometimes brushed the "dead hand" against her body, it puzzled her but she pretended not to notice.

The aunts, however, talked about the militiamen incessantly. The damage they had done to the stairs. Their unspeakable language. The smell of these peasants who couldn't even use the bathroom properly. They complained, too, that the militiamen looked at them lasciviously. Teresa wondered how her aunts knew in what way they looked at them if they had never met their gaze. She never looked into their eyes. She had been told not to do so. Lasciviousness, too, puzzled her. She asked about that.

"They want us, you ninny," said her oldest aunt, who, at fifty-nine, looked as if she had been cured like a ham.

"Want?" asked Teresa, bemused. "What for?"

"Hush, my dears," said the commander. "This is not a suitable conversation to have before the child."

And so, just for the moment, the subject was dropped.

But Teresa started to think about the militiamen. Their physical presence in the house started to assert itself. She began to apply to them those unconscious aesthetic tests by which she now measured everything. In the courtyard behind the house they washed their clothes, using the well pump outside the kitchen and the washboards, tubs, and mangles once used by the servants, still used by Teresa herself when the militiamen were away on duty. Stripped to the waist, their shoulders, seen from above, could easily be sorted into the ugly and, yes, surprisingly, the beautiful. She didn't like the neck and back all matted with hair, nor did she care for the back that seemed like a monolith of bull-like flesh. There were some whose backs were marvels of beauty as they worked. She felt her own narrow, sloping little shoulders and admired the beautiful back of the youth she thought of as the artist.

He must have ached with working at the washboard on his shirts, for at that moment he straightened out and looked up, catching Teresa's eyes and holding them. All the admiration she had ever craved since she had first examined her own reflection was in his gaze. She knew without any possibility of doubt that he thought her perfectly beautiful. Since in her innocence she had no real idea why the rule of the lowered eyes had been made, Teresa took her time in examining his beauty. His eyes had a color it was hard to fathom at that distance, but they were set wide in his face, and his mouth seemed to be a kiss; he was making it shape like a kiss. His hair, which was long and curly, he brushed from his forehead the better to see her. The man's body he had was more wonderful naked to the waist than she could have imagined, an extraordinary pattern of opposites to her own body, sometimes felt but never seen. The breast hard and flat-looking and strong where hers was round and bluntly pointed. The belly above his belt flat, with a thin line of hair, where hers was a smooth, soft, rounded mold. His hips were narrow. Why did it touch her to see how narrow they were where hers were wide? His legs in the tight denim trousers seemed long, and if there was some hateful arrangement locked in there, it seemed to be tucked safely away, lining the side of his leg, perhaps. She regretted that there must be such a part of him, because if he were entirely bare it could not, she felt sure, fail to abridge his beauty.

He made a gesture for her to stay where she was and ran into the house. She knew he would be coming up the stairs to see her, that it must be quite wrong to go to meet him halfway. But there were aunts about on the top floor, and no one was paying her any attention. She felt, as she took each successive step down, as if she were walking toward some nameless fate both welcome and terrifying.

His feet coming up the stairs were both light and fleet, as if he scarcely needed to touch the steps to reach her. And then there he was, standing no more than a meter away from her, more gloriously alive than any being, human or celestial, she had ever imagined, breathing a little deeply, catching his breath from the run and speaking.

"Your name is Teresa, isn't it? They told me there was a beautiful girl in the house. But they find so many women in the town beautiful I've stopped looking around when they say, 'Hey, look at that one. Isn't she something?' You know the way they do. My spirit soared when I saw you!"

"What is your name?" she asked, storing his words like treasure inside her.

Don Juan told her his name was Whitticker, taking his dead mentor's name as so many revolutionaries took the names of the men who had inspired them.

She smiled. "I am Teresa," she said, and turned and walked back up toward her family's apartment. She clutched the whole encounter to her. His looks, his action in running up to meet her, his words. She could not have borne to prolong the meeting. It was for her already too perfect to tempt the fates by asking for more.

Don Juan watched her go.

He understood, he thought, her sudden shyness and found it charming. But he could never have entirely understood her inno-cence. If he had been raised in Spain among sisters he might have done so. He watched the childish legs in their woolen knee socks below the woman's hips. He saw her extraordinary hand upon the stair rail. But she moved as if she had no knowledge of her own body, as if she were as virgin to herself as she would be to him, and that he found both remarkable and irresistible. The thought came of joining her on a voyage of discovery—of herself!

He never doubted that it would happen. To _pursue_ this one would frighten her. He must let her find him. Encouraging her. Making it easier for her. Letting her discover more of herself each time she saw him. Till it was time to take her. To take her little by little. To amaze her with her own capacity for bliss. Gently weaning her from her innocence into womanhood. Don Juan felt confident that it would be like that.

He could not, as we have said, gauge the totality of her innocence. It was quite outside his experience.

Unlike his fellow militiamen, he had no bridges or public buildings to guard. He reported each day to the committee of control, to whom he was Whitticker, the interpreter _inglés_. They thought of him as English, although his true identity was known to the committee. Usually there was nothing to do. The Jaén front remained inactive. Sometimes foreign visitors came, and Don Juan accompanied them on whatever tour had been planned, translating from French or English.

This work gave him time for painting and drawing, for going to the city's indifferent library and gleaning what he could. The committee of control also gave him access to the libraries of the cathedral and its school.

Listening to the stories and superstitions and songs of his fellow militiamen, he became interested in their origins. Those trains of thought which Tabatha had awakened in him as a child, and the successive teachings of both Roman Catholics and Anglicans kept alive, were with him still. Even the millennialism of Inés, with her mystical belief in the coming of an effortless Acraria, formed part of a gigantic puzzle that was never far from his thoughts as he transposed and reorganized the pieces, looking always for some gigantic but essentially simple meaning that he felt certain was only just eluding him.

In this frame of mind he approached the seduction of Teresa.

He had claimed for himself a room that no one else wanted. It was a long, very narrow room with a high window facing north at one end. The door came halfway down one wall, and he had wedged a bed into the narrow end opposite the window. It had formerly been the linen closet and ironing room.

Here, late at night, he brought the chance seductions that his easy life in Jaén brought him. Shopgirls pretending to their parents that they were staying with friends, widows, and others, but never virgins or whores. He drew and painted them all after he made love to them, leaping from their reluctant arms, trying to record in crayon, in ink and watercolor, a look of eyes and mouth, a tone of flesh, the attitudes of hands, the angles of legs still moving in the aftermath of love. He made no special effort to find these women. They seemed all around him in the city. Like a constellation of distant and mysterious stars, they created a firmament he could never cease exploring.

It was not that he ignored their souls as he possessed their bodies, but he became always more convinced that they were informed and illuminated by one great all-pervading soul—a soul that in no way diminished their individuality as persons, but that, like the concept of the Holy Spirit itself, was immutable and yet endlessly divisible. It seemed to him that when they left him, transported within themselves in his arms, they visited some sacred grove of their universal female spirit, a place too sacred to speak of when they returned to him in his linen-closet studio. It must not be thought, however, that Don Juan was never refused by women. It happened often enough. Perhaps not so often as if he had been devoid of charm or looks or gentleness and modesty of manner, and taking into account that he never ceased *considering* women wherever and whenever he met them. But this consideration often led him to the conclusion that they were in love with another, that for one of a myriad of reasons they would not welcome his company, let alone his love. Another thing that may have limited the number of rebuffs he received was the fact that "the taming of Kate" was not in his nature. He was a seducer, it is true, but he had no taste for conquest, nor for women who enjoyed the game of being conquered.

One afternoon, a month after their encounter on the stairs, he waited for Teresa on her return from the market with one of her aunts.

"So many packages, ladies," he said. "Please let me carry them upstairs for you."

The aunt hung firmly on to her packages and marched by without even acknowledging him. Teresa let him carry hers, but could not bring herself to speak to him. Her throat was full, and somehow her voice would not obey her when she tried to thank him at the top of the stairs. But she saw the little note he had tucked into the package of flour that she carried.

She read it secretly, brushing the paper with her lips before opening it, as if to ensure that it held a token of love.

> I have so much to say to you, so much to ask you. It will take days, weeks, and perhaps far, far longer.
> I want to make a journey with you, in the linen room, a journey in search of true love. Can you take to doing your ironing there? I know you now do it on the landing at the top of the stairs while your aunts are having their siesta.
> I kiss your hand, señorita, reverently, in homage to your beauty and your grace and your innocence. Also because it is the most perfect hand I ever saw.
>
> Juan Whitticker

Poor Teresa was beyond conversation at dinner that night. It was her turn to read to her bedridden mother afterward, but she did it so badly, perpetually losing her place, that her mother excused her early. She read and reread the note before she went to sleep. What kind of journey could he mean? Would his voice take her there, all alone with him in that narrow, tiny room? She knew that for her there need be no journey to love. For her it would be enough to sit and watch him, to hear him speak to her. Love was there. Love was this feeling that already consumed her. She felt breathless at the thought of that. How would she be when he was there in person?

He stood in a smock by his easel next day when she scratched at the door and came in at his bidding. She was carrying some linen to be ironed.

He put down his paints and came straight toward her, lifting her hand and kissing it gently. She took in his tall figure, his bushy curly hair, the vigor and the laughter in him. It all made her feel small and insignificant, and the feeling of his hands as they touched hers made her whole body tremble. The kiss itself was so exciting an event that she closed her eyes and went on feeling it after his lips had left her skin.

"Teresa!" He was speaking to her. She looked into his face and saw that his eyes were green flecked with brown, like pools she had seen where silvery fish occasionally darted in the depths.

"Please sit down, Teresa. I want you to tell me what you think of these." He held a chair for her politely while she sat down, and then disconcertingly sat at her feet opening up one of half a dozen folders that were stacked against the wall. It was covered in marbled green paper and fastened on three sides with black linen threads, which he now untied.

She tucked her legs well under her, forcing her skirt as far over her knees as it would go. She had undone the usual braid that tied her hair on the way down the stairs, and it hung now, a glossy mane, to her waist. It was still agonizing her that she had done this immodest, vain thing when he placed the first of his drawings before her. The sight of it made her heart thump so that she made a little sound that came out as *"OH!"*

It was her face. The face the looking glass would have shown her if she were allowed to look into it. It was impossible that she was really as beautiful as he saw her. But the emotion she felt at his having remembered every detail of her face and recorded it in this way kept her speechless still.

"OH!" she said again, but it was all she could manage.

"But I've got your hair wrong. How stupid I am. It's beyond belief and imagination, that hair of yours."

He was looking up, trying to fix this new facet of her in his mind, smelling her freshly washed hair, inhaling the delicate "she" smell of her with it, longing to touch her, to nuzzle her whole body.

He showed her other drawings he had done of her, many of them drawn, covertly, from life, as she herself worked at the washboard in the courtyard. She looked at them, amazed and confused. He had caught her figure so exactly, it was as if he saw what she could only guess at herself, the actual contours of her body. The place where posterior met thigh, the weight of her breast, held in by her blouse, weighed as if he had held it. For all this seemed to show through the clothes in which he drew her, and undeniably her clothes were there.

"Please let me hear your voice, Teresa," he said at last.

"I love the drawings. I wish, I wish I could show them to the commander."

"But you cannot. Is that it?" he asked gently.

"Oh, no. He would think . . . I don't know what he would think."

"It is a pretty voice. I should like to hear it read aloud, that voice."

"My mother likes me to read to her. It sends her to sleep," she said.

"It does?" He looked her very straight in the eyes, his whole face on the point of laughter. Her childish mouth, on the upper lip of which was the softest down, trembled as if it had forgotten how to smile, and then the smile came first to her large, serious brown eyes, suddenly crinkling them and transforming her whole face into that of an enchanted and happy girl-woman.

"It does. It does. I read a paragraph and her lids start to droop. So. I read a page and her eyes close entirely. So. 'I'm awake, child,' she murmurs to me if I stop. I read another page and there is a gentle snore, 'gngngn aah.' Like that. Then I can close the book."

Don Juan laughed at her little story, loving the confiding, breathless way she told it.

"It is hot in here," she said, feeling her cheeks to be crimson.

"I can open that window," he said. "But I lit the stove in case you really wanted to iron. The irons are still there by the ironing board. I've had no reason to move anything in here, except the linen, of course."

"Of course," she said solicitously, like an anxious hostess. "There is so little room for all your things as it is."

She had risen from the chair, and he with her, and they stood looking at each other, done with words for the moment, marvelously content to be together. But she soon started, feeling with a rising panic that this stillness between them, this allowing him to admire and caress her with his eyes, was almost certainly one of the forbidden things between man and woman.

It was so intensely pleasurable that this must be so.

"It must be wicked for us to be like this," she said, loving it so and hating having to make this declaration.

"How can it be wicked? You are as innocent as if this were the Garden of Eden!"

"Innocence," she said seriously, "is something I've never quite understood. I mean, I don't think I'm wicked, you understand. But I try to make myself look pretty. I'm guilty of pride. If there are black olives left over from lunch and no one has noticed them, I nearly always manage to gobble them all up. That's gluttony, you must admit. I laugh at the way my aunts walk in the market, as if they were pursued by unpleasant smells. That's levity and something else wicked, I'm sure," she added.

"You seem far gone in sin," he said. "I'm surprised the floor doesn't open, revealing Hell and all its demons at your feet."

"You mustn't laugh at me," she said. "I want you to explain why you call me innocent."

"Well, if I'd known all that, I might not have done so," said Don Juan, wondering now if she were teasing him. "But I know that it is no sin to look at you. Or for you to look at me. To tell you the truth, I'm not at all sure that there can be sin between a man and a woman, because they are what they are. I mean I believe that cruelty is wrong and betrayal of trust is wrong and selfishness is wrong and jealousy and covetousness are wrong. But for a man to be a man to a woman or for a woman to be a woman to a man, I cannot see how that can be wrong."

"But that is lust," she said.

"And you have never felt lust?" he asked.

"I don't think so. Unless being happy just standing with you, talking to you, is lust. Do you think that can be so?"

"No, that is innocence," he said, unable to restrain a laugh.

"Is that, then, what it was like in the Garden of Eden? I have heard of the story, of course. The beginning of the world. But it isn't taught in our catechism, you know."

"Yes. Eve and Adam walked in the Garden quite naked together and felt no shame. It doesn't say whether they loved each other. But they were innocent, that is certain. According to the story, it was the serpent who tempted the woman into destroying their innocence."

"They walked *naked?*"

"Yes. God made them clothes only later. After they had eaten the forbidden apple from the tree of knowledge of good and evil. Until then it seemed natural to them to be naked. After all, animals wear no clothes."

"But babies. They had babies from that nakedness?" said Teresa, wondering at her daring in discussing the sinful subject with this beautiful man.

"Not according to the Bible. They only had babies *after* God had given them clothes."

"That is the most curious thing I ever heard," she said. "Are you positive?"

"Next time you come and see me I will have a Spanish Bible here. We will read the text together. Before that I will draw you again with your hair down, and, perhaps, your feet bare. The beginning of seeing the whole Eve."

"My feet?" She had stopped at the door. She still held the unironed linen, had probably forgotten that she held it.

"Yes. Sit again for just a minute and let me look at your feet. Please, they are so long and narrow. The toes must be perfect. You are not ashamed?"

"No," she said, sitting. "Even the saints are always painted with their feet bare. Mine are just feet, though!" she said, aware at once of the sin of false modesty.

He slipped off her flat-heeled, but well-made, cordovan pumps. She wore no stockings under them, and he saw at once the perfect alignment of her long pink toes, the moon on every perfect toenail showing pale and distinct, framed by infinitely soft little folds of flesh. He ran his hands under her insteps, making the feet arch and stretch, as if offering the delicate morsels of her toes to his lips. He kissed both feet gently. Of one simple toe he made a metaphor for his most extreme desire for her. He touched its tiny rounded end with the tip of his tongue.

Watching his head bend toward her feet, she felt his kisses, she felt particularly his tongue's soft touch echoing strangely in her body. He was looking up at her again. Into her eyes, as if he saw the echo of his kiss there, affecting her eyelids, causing an involuntary tremor. He replaced her shoes and went with her to the door.

"May I kiss your mouth, innocent Eve, before you go?" he asked.

"How can you ask me that? When we are clothed? Once they were clothed, you said, *then* they had babies," she said, remembering the story, watching his mouth, wondering how it would feel; warm and strong, no doubt, against hers.

Don Juan knew that young bourgeois girls in Spain were often told that to be kissed on the mouth could make them pregnant. Since everything else was hidden from them, he supposed it was not surprising that they half-believed it. It fascinated him that she had taken the Adam and Eve story to suggest that nakedness was itself a kind of prophylactic.

He kissed her hand instead. She slipped away from him, running up the stairs and taking from a cupboard, en route, a pair of sheets she had previously ironed, leaving the unironed ones in their place and praying to the Blessed Virgin to forgive her the sin of deception.

By the next time she visited him, they had exchanged several notes. He had named a day, a week ahead, and she had been disappointed at having to wait so long.

When she entered the room again, however, she immediately understood the delay. The place was transformed. Plants of all kinds were everywhere. Ferns and flowers and miniature palms. And on the walls he had hung bold poster paintings of tropical gardens full of wonderful trees and creepers, birds and animals. The stove was lit, and the room was warm, like a hothouse.

She stood for a moment taking it all in, registering the wonder that all this had been done for her. She who received useful gifts on her name day, who occasionally had some special present of clothes from the aunts, to whom, sometimes, her uncle, the commander, had given something frivolous like a locket or a pair of tiny earrings: for her this beautiful youth had created a Garden of Eden where together they could play an elaborate and loving game. An innocent game, he had promised her in his last note. She could not resist the tears that burned in her eyes. She was sure she had never been meant to be so happy. With her father dead and her mother mortally sick, her brothers in constant danger, how could she be so happy?

And yet he had also promised in his notes never to kiss her on the lips, which seemed to confirm the danger she believed such kisses held.

He served her a drink of fruit juice that tasted like nectar; then he sat on the floor in front of her, removed her shoes, and after kissing each toe in a most extraordinary and wonderful way that made her whole body shiver, he placed her feet in his lap and opened the Bible at the first chapter of Genesis.

His voice with its strange, slightly foreign accent was a well-modulated baritone, the very timbre of which seemed to strike chords in her not entirely dissimilar to that curious physical feeling that came when he kissed her toes. She thought he seemed to have brushed them with his tongue and to have even given the gentlest of pressure from his teeth, although she believed that this had been her imagination. (It was really too strange a thing for him to have done, otherwise. But blissful to have imagined.) Having his strength, his warmth, touching her in so intimate a place made other places, more intimate still, tingle and seem unexpectedly viscous and warm. She felt a curious throbbing between her legs and tried to listen to his voice.

"'And the Lord God planted a garden eastward in Eden; and there he put the man whom he had formed. . . .'"

She suddenly realized that she had no exact idea of how God had formed man. This man who read to her he had formed with a pleasing voice, more pleasing than any voice she knew. Some men's voices had a growl in them like the sound a dog gives off when its hackles start to rise. She hated and feared that sound. In the month of the killings, the streets had been full of such voices. But this voice had light and shade. Laughter and pathos stood in the wings with this voice, always ready for their part. And this voice came from a mouth that seemed to her to be the source of pure magic. Yes, she longed to know exactly how God had formed *this* man. It was not a knowledge God had kept from Eve about Adam. Of him she had seen every secret place, known every tiny, God-created detail.

As if in answer to her growing curiosity, it was then that she felt a stirring in his lap, beneath the soles of her bare feet. And that stirring that seemed to come from a fifth, an unseen, limb within his trousers made her throb the more.

"'And the Lord God caused a deep sleep to fall upon Adam, and he slept; and he took one of his ribs, and closed up the flesh instead thereof;

"'And the rib, which the Lord God had taken from man, made he a woman, and brought her unto the man. . . .'"

Don Juan paused, looking up at Teresa. "I have thought many times," he said, "of seeing you come to me in that way. Naked, innocent, waiting for all of life to begin."

He looked such a tender, loving Adam that she wished for it too. But her poor little body was so inundated with strange emotions that she was relieved that he returned at once to the text.

"'And Adam said, this is now bone of my bones, flesh of my flesh; she shall be called Woman, because she was taken out of man.

"'Therefore shall a man leave his father and his mother, and shall cleave unto his wife: and they shall be one flesh.

"'And they were both naked, the man and his wife, and were not ashamed.'"

Don Juan closed the book and stood up. "If I will be your Adam, will you be my Eve?" he asked.

"You promise not to kiss me on the lips?" she asked in turn, meaning "Yes."

"I promise," he said. "I must tell you that that is not how babies come to be conceived. But I promise."

Teresa heard his promises, and they were all that mattered to her. Perhaps it was true that vanity was her besetting sin. But why else had God made her beautiful if it was not to please her Adam? At fifteen a girl does not reflect that this incomparable boy may be the first of many. Indeed, in the little world of upper-class Jaén, the chance to meet such another as Don Juan was, in reality, extremely remote. But such considerations were subconscious if they existed at all in Teresa's mind. She *wanted* to be his Eve. She wanted to be the first Woman, the unique unadorned God-creation, that this Adam ever saw.

"Will you turn your back?" she asked.

"I will first make my scar," he said, and slipping out of his shirt, he took a paintbrush and drew the scar on his flesh where his missing rib should have been. "Now I shall lie as if in sleep. Giving God time to entirely create you."

Don Juan went to the bed and, standing with his back to her, undid his belt, letting his trousers fall to the ground. She found that the slimness of his buttocks held her gaze as she took off her dress; so slim were they between his narrow hips that she imagined that if she touched her thumbs together and spread her fingers, she could have actually held his bottom. Extraordinary. But what lay the other side of his hips was still as unknown to her as if it were the far side of the moon. She knew only that her feet had felt it to be astonishingly alive. He lay now on the bed, his back to her, seeming infinitely relaxed.

Teresa stood now in her petticoat, a garment she had been taught to change without looking at herself. Of course, she had seen her own body, to glance at from the perspective of an owner between the change of shifts, but had never, ever seen it reflected since she had become a woman. His eyes would be her first mirror. He would have to tell her what he saw.

Slowly she drew off the petticoat. Her breasts had a certain weight. She saw, with concern, that the nipples hardly protruded, but rather lay recessed in their neat and swollen aureoles of pinker flesh. Her stomach, between her broadly rounded woman's hips, was a soft plateau. The fringe of dark and curling hair that sank like a dart to be lost between her thighs alarmed her. Its very furriness awoke in her memory her mother's warnings of evil in those parts. She examined her delicate arms, innocent of muscle but firm and mercifully hairless, likewise her long, straight legs. If he liked not this Eve, it was too late now for her to change. She hid behind the plants where they were thickest and called out to him.

"God's work is done. I hope you like it," she said.

He turned and saw her, but only parts of her, through the foliage.

"Are you going to come to me?" he asked her gently.

"Yes, but it is very hard for me. Be patient. I am so frightened of seeming ugly to you."

"The mirror must tell you that you are not ugly. Through your clothes I could see that you were not ugly."

"I do hope not. But please tell me what you see. You with your artist's eyes. It isn't vanity. But curiosity. I have never seen myself in a mirror."

He wondered how this half-glimpsed little goddess could have been kept from a mirror for so long and at the endless philistinism of Christianity as people chose to live it.

"Gladly," he said. "Walk toward me, Eve. Hold your head high. For you are the first of women, once known as the Mother of All Living. Before the God that created the man who invented you; before that you yourself created God."

But she wasn't listening to his words. "Tell me, tell me," she said, "what you see!" She had emerged from the plants slowly.

"I see a neck and shoulders that remind me of Aphrodite Calipocus, goddess of love and most perfect of women. Your 'breasts are like two young roes that are twins which feed among the lilies. Thou art all fair, my love. There is no spot on thee.' I quote one of your descendants, Eve, a certain Solomon, a king whose knowledge of the beauty of women has probably never been surpassed. But if you want only the opinion of your still-untutored Adam, then know that I feel quite faint from your loveliness. You will have to come and sit next to me and let me kiss it all, except, of course, your lips."

She stood still before him, only a meter from the bed. She was looking at him. He had forgotten that she might never have seen a man before, entirely naked.

"Is that the snake? Are those the apples?" she asked, staring, fascinated.

"Yes," he said simply. "In this garden I believe they are."

"I felt the snake *stir* under my feet while you were reading."

"He wished to see you. He was telling me so," said Don Juan. "I hope you don't find him ugly."

"No, not ugly. But so strange. He lies there as if asleep upon your leg."

"Touch him and he will wake."

"Really?"

She put forward her perfect hand, and with the tip of one long finger caressed the head of the snake. Almost at once he stirred.

"Later," said Don Juan, "he will want to be kissed. There are few things he likes more."

She did not demur. His body seemed to her like a new and inexpressibly valuable possession. She would certainly wish to examine it minutely. To kiss what he wished kissed. Except, of course, his mouth. But she saw how Eve was tempted.

"It is forbidden to pick the apples?" she asked.

"Forbidden."

"They are stranger than the snake. And not, if you'll forgive me, quite so beautiful."

"They say that a woman can learn to see their beauty. Like all fruit they are very vulnerable."

"Yes, I see that they are, Adam. That's true, and it's rather sweet." Her single finger traced a line now from his neck to his wrist. It was a proprietorial finger. "You look so strong with your broad shoulders and your muscled arms. It's sweet that you should have those delicate fruit. They surprise me more than the snake. Oh, look. He seems to have raised his head now. Look, Adam, he is asking a question."

"It is always the same question."

"Oh, tell me!"

"Quidni?"

"Latin. I know *Quidni?* It means 'Why not?'"

"That is the question the snake always asks."

"Why not what?"

"Why not pick the apple, Eve? Among other 'why nots.'"

She looked down at him, wondering already, now that they had been like this together, how soon he would ask her to marry him. It could not be for years, of course, with the war. But they would have an *understanding*. When she saw how he looked at her body, how his eyes seemed to grow wide with wonder when he looked into hers, it could not surely be very long before he asked for that. Such happiness would not stop now that it had begun. And even Teresa realized that it had scarcely begun at all, that she still stood on the threshold.

But the next part was starting. He had begun to touch her.

His hands felt only her waist, drawing her back onto the couch, but it made her shiver. She found herself on her back on the bed beside him. His shoulders and chest loomed over her, making a muscled delta of his torso, and at its root the snake, hard as a spear now, brushing her thigh with his questing head. She felt for the first time that languor which robs the muscles of their power. It did not, at first, stop her shaking, this languor, as his hands skirted her breasts, making them feel bereft, and settled in upon her neck, the back of her neck, where her spine seemed to balance her head; there his fingers worked to stop her shivering. And there they worked while the mouth she longed to kiss closed her eyes and traced the smooth contours of her brow and bellowed tiny sounds into her ears, so that her whole brain seemed to fill up with wave upon wave of color and sound and sensation. But beyond everything the throb between her legs never ceased. It was as if it were a rhythm that came with his very presence.

As long as his mouth was dangerously near to hers, that long she clung to some sense of where she was and of what he did to her. She did not dare respond for fear of tempting him to suddenly undo her with a kiss upon the lips, and she pursed her mouth shut even as she absorbed the myriad of delights his hands were bringing. Only as she felt him start to kiss her breasts, kneeling astride her, the snake tracing moist patterns on her belly, only then did she allow her mouth to open, did she draw in the gulps of air she needed to feed the convulsions this ferment in her breasts ignited. And the throbbing seemed so strong now between her legs that she was forced to move her pelvis this way and that to stop herself from shouting. Why should she wish to shout? Was it just joy? Perhaps that was it.

She could feel her nipples leaving her body. He seemed to be drawing them out in tiny spirals. And the spirals wound all the time. Back down into her guts. The spirals joined in the throbbing she now moved her hips frantically to quell. She knew he was there by the smell of him and the feel of his mouth and the ever-tracing snake. But for now she knew she had to leave him on the outside and look in on herself. It was like revisiting the moment before her soul had entered her body.

Don Juan watched her go.

Seconds later he found the soft purse between her thighs, and with his tongue undid the coral latch and there fed among the lilies.

"Open to me, my sister, my love, my dove, my undefiled. For my head is filled with dew," said Don Juan, borrowing King Solomon's words for the second time in as many hours. And she opened and he kissed her slowly into that warm delirium from which only the slowest of returns is possible.

But her mouth remained chaste. And his snake he deliberately refused to answer, though it throbbed *"Quidni? Quidni? Quidni?"* incessantly for hours after she had dressed and gone upstairs to dream.

Throughout the rest of 1937 and most of 1938, Don Juan continued what he thought of as his "education" in Jaén. He spoke to his grandfather from time to time on the telephone. But secretly. It would have cost him his life if the committee of control had known. He corresponded with Garcia until the increasing success of the Nationalist armies in the north made it evident that the Republic would be split into two. The duke survived. But his always tenuous hold on reason had snapped, probably forever.

He wrote his mother a monthly letter, always adding a lengthy postscript for Henrietta. They had rarely left New York City since 1936, and the house on the Avenue Foch remained shuttered and empty. They wrote regularly, chatty, amusing letters giving him some perspective on the world outside Spain. And they sent books. He always asked for more books. He never once mentioned the civil war, the battles he'd been in (such as they were), or local politics. He used his correspondence entirely to keep abreast of art criticism, new books and the discovery of interesting old ones, and politics in Europe as a whole. American politics hadn't seemed relevant to the world outside the U.S.A. since the failure of Congress to ratify the Versailles Treaty.

When the duchess, who was stoutly pro-Franco, asked in one letter, "Is it true that La Pasionaria kills priests by tearing their throats out with her teeth?" he answered, "Of course, but she always adds seasoning—do you want the recipe for *prêtre tartare?*" Henrietta, on the other hand, was pro-Republic; she agonized over Guernica and spoke bitterly of the nonintervention of the lily-livered Anglo-Saxons, by which she seemed to mean the English. He wondered if they argued in bed each morning when the newspapers brought news of the war with their breakfast.

The invaluable Thomas Cook acted as his mailing address in Barcelona and forwarded his letters on to Jaén. Among the first post to reach him after he settled in the city was a letter from Juliet. It said:

Dear Juan,

We were so frightened when we heard that you were somewhere in Spain but that even your family had lost track of you. Do send all your news. Quickly. I can't wait.

Giles tells me that he heard from some boys that you were sacked from Deerhurst. It must have been for something fearfully wicked, because Giles won't tell me. He said something about "those Latins are too hot-blooded for English public schools," but he said it enviously, so please don't be offended.

I do worry a bit that you might have been fired for kissing one of the headmaster's daughters there, but I don't quite see how any of them could have been there in term time, so it is a *mystery*.

Why didn't you tell me that you paint frightfully well yourself? Your Aunt Henrietta (she is your aunt, isn't she? Mummy wasn't quite sure) told Daddy that you draw divinely and are going to be a painter.

Giles isn't sure whether he wants to be a bookmaker or a pilot. Daddy says it's rather difficult to be a bookmaker if you're Viscount Foxburgh like poor Giles. I mean can you see him on

the racetrack where he's got his little stand with all the odds
chalked up under a sign saying "Trust Honest Lord Foxy"?
Anyway, he makes book at school, and I expect Daddy will let
him become a pilot. There's talk of his going to the Royal Air
Force for a bit when he leaves Eton.

I don't have a photograph of you, as you know, and most of
the other girls who write to boys do. So could you send me one?
Taken in a good light without a hat on so that I can see your eyes
and your hair.

Oh, Juan, I do like you so much it's rather painful.

With lots of love,
Juliet

Many similar letters followed, and he wrote to her rather
faithfully every week. He talked to her about Spain and the Spanish
character. In his letters to her he tried to rehearse some possible
solution to what he called in *1066 and All That* style "The Spanish
Question."

He explained his adherence to the anarchists and the Republic
in terms of what he understood of his country's history. Her letters in
reply became noticeably less schoolgirlish. He assumed that she had
gotten over the British female's fear of betraying to her male friends
that she might be equipped with brains.

At the time of Munich she wrote a most eloquent letter
describing her shame for her country and their race. By that time
British equivocations and cowardice in dealing with Franco, Mussolini, and Hitler had brought that once proud nation to the nadir of
its own self-esteem and to the open contempt of the rest of the world.

So far as his education was concerned, he tried to complete in
Jaén what he believed Deerhurst would have attempted to teach him
in the way of Latin. He designed himself a program of reading in
French, English, and Spanish that covered a good deal of European
and world history, literature, and philosophy. His math was painfully
deficient, and he made not the slightest attempt to improve it. At
Deerhurst he had entered the first sparse thickets of calculus, but
balked at entering the wood. His science all had to do with war. He
hoped never to find a gun he couldn't figure out how to use. Don Juan
wished to survive the civil war, and while the Republic still held his
allegiance, he had long since lost any passion for its cause.

Communism seemed to him to be the capitalism of the hypocrite
fonctionnaires, a world run by ruthless and successful concierges.

Socialism was, of course, Christianity put into practice. Which tended to mean government by pedagogue. Like all political movements which appeal to intellectuals, it had become dangerously factionalized. Its supporters were as fond of compromise as they were of splitting hairs. They seemed to function like a perpetual minuet, parting and joining, joining and parting.

Don Juan had discovered that temperamentally there was much of the anarchist in him, yet he had no real taste for the life that the creed imposed. But his heart remained with them always, and for Inés he still sometimes wept.

A war fought by a government drawn from such an improbable alliance as these three parties presented was surely doomed to failure and defeat, or so Don Juan soon concluded.

The women of Jaén who had entered his life continued to multiply each night. Widows, unhappy wives, schoolteachers and nurses answered the snake's *"Quidni?"* in the affirmative. But only Teresa ever saw him during the day.

Don Juan often painted when she was with him, listening to her prattle about her family, about the school that had now reopened with lay teachers. She loved to exercise her power over the snake, but always spoke of it as if its life were quite separate from that of Don Juan himself.

For instance, he might be cleaning his palette. She, tired of sitting naked on the bed, swinging her legs, and talking of her aunts' latest collective idiocy, would run and kneel in front of him, unbuttoning him. She would take out a snake who might well be sleeping, resting from a bout with a lusty widow, or an insatiable almoner, and did not always leap to ask his parrot question. Making of him a sandwich between her breasts, she loved to watch him stretch himself until she could hold him with her mouth and lead him and a mildly protesting Don Juan to bed.

So total was her freedom from fear of pregnancy (they had so far never kissed on the lips) that she was more relaxed than any very young girl to whom Don Juan had ever made love. She had learned much in a year of sex, but still had no idea of the real cause of conception. As the war went on and Don Juan sensed that the time would soon come when he must leave her, he decided that it was his duty to tell her the truth. She herself finally gave him his cue.

"What does it remind you of?" she asked one day, taking a tiny fingerload of the creamy white frappé from her tongue and swallowing the rest as she always did.

"Chilled absinthe." Don Juan pondered. "No, it is too viscous, I suppose. The ancients, you know, found the crushed white berries of mistletoe similar. Perhaps that's why they kissed under it. To be fruitful. Sympathetic magic, you see."

Teresa looked at him curiously. "Fruitful?" she echoed.

"It contains the seed of those apples you squeeze and caress so deliciously."

She looked at him appalled, and leaped from the bed.

"¡Dios! I've swallowed it. I've been swallowing it for months."

"That's all right. It won't do you any harm. I haven't so far died from the taste of your honey."

And he told her the whole truth about impregnation.

She let him finish. For almost half a minute she sat quite still, her eyes filling with tears. Then she leaped up, shouting at him and grabbing her clothes.

"You've made a fool of me. I thought you loved me. I hate, hate, hate you!" She dressed as she spoke, looking as beautiful as he'd ever seen her as she spat out her words.

"But don't you see, you're still a virgin," said Don Juan, trying not to laugh.

"I see now. If you're telling the truth, I see. But I feel so stupid. Such a silly ignorant child. And I was so proud that I was a woman."

"You are a woman!"

"Am I? I don't know what I am. Why, oh why, couldn't someone have told me? Why couldn't you have told me?"

"Because you were so sure you knew the truth. From our game of the snake and the apples, of Adam and the honeycomb. It would have taken away the charming innocence. Now there will be fear mixed with the pleasure."

"You must have thought me so simple! A cretin!" she said bitterly.

"Nonsense. It is only ten thousand or so years since our ancestors understood any direct connection between the sexual act I described to you and conception. To this day there are whole peoples, such as the Eskimo, who see no exact connection. If you had been living when this very town of Jaén was part of the Carthaginian Empire, your mother would probably have insisted that you impale your hymen on the stone phallus of a god in the temple—long before you gave yourself to mortal man. Why? To make you fruitful. And you'd have believed her. Every girl did. Would you be surprised if hundreds of thousands of present-day Spanish girls like you went into marriage totally ignorant of the truth?"

"No. But you should have told me!"

"I have told you!"

"I was so happy. I thought we were really lovers."

"We were. We are."

"You must have laughed at me so much. When I said, 'Promise not to kiss me on the mouth.' Oh, I could kill you!"

Dressed now, she looked superbly fierce and Spanish, her black hair starting in unruly waves from her head, her cheeks burning. And now he could no longer stop himself from laughing, although something in her face should have warned him. She came at him like a cat, clawing at his eyes, his cheeks.

"Don't dare laugh at me!" she screamed. And if ever he doubted that she was fully woman, that doubt disappeared now as he tried to defend his face and body from her nails. She went on yelling as she pursued him around the room, knocking over plants and collapsing the easel.

Trying to cover his eyes and protect his loins from her blows, he heard a commotion on the stairs outside and a hammering on his door, which out of precaution they always locked. It was a time of day when a few of his fellow militiamen, those who were sleeping after night duty, might be in the house. Otherwise only the aunts and the commander, whose siesta hour it was, would be there.

Suddenly she ceased her attack and said in a terrified whisper, "It's my uncle. I can hear his voice!"

Don Juan could feel blood hot on his face from her gouging nails, and the corner of his eyelid felt torn. It sounded as if a crowd had gathered outside the door. And the hammering continued. "What do you want?" he managed to shout to them.

"Teresa, are you in there?" came the commander's voice.

"You must go to him at once," said Don Juan, pulling his painter's smock over his bleeding face. But she just stood sobbing, and giving every now and then a great keening wail.

Don Juan opened the door. The commander brushed past him and half-carried his niece from the room. The militiamen who were off duty and who were standing with the aunts, all gawping, burst out laughing at the sight of his face. The aunts hurried their niece upstairs while the commander turned to Don Juan.

"Rapist! Degenerate! Defiler of innocence!" he roared.

"Oh, come off it, graybeard," said one of the militiamen. "She's been coming to his room for months. Lucky bastard. Her pants must be as hot as mustard, that one."

"Maybe she found out how he spends his nights," said another.

"Hey, Whitticker, compañero. You're not going to look so pretty for a while."

And they went on in this vein, laughing and milling around Don Juan, handing him wet towels and a little cognac to clean his wounds, as good buddies in armies always do when misfortune has befallen one of the tribe, a misfortune that could easily be theirs some other day.

But the commander, whom they ignored, had run upstairs with a purposefulness that, if anyone had paid attention to it, would have put them on their guard. For less than a minute later, he stood at the head of the staircase and aimed his naval officer's revolver straight at Don Juan's head and squeezed the trigger. Some cognac had just been dabbed on the clawed cheek, and the burn of it made him jerk back his head, saving his life as the bullet shattered the landing window behind him. The militiamen dived into the large bedroom opposite the linen closet. Don Juan himself just missed being caught by the next bullet as he threw himself backward into his room. The older man was coming down the stairs now, taking them two at a time, when, to Don Juan's horror, he saw two of the militiamen come out of their room, firing their rifles as they came. There was one more shot from the commander's revolver, but it went wide; he must have been falling at the time.

The two militiamen stood in the doorway looking down at the floor, and when Don Juan joined them, he saw that the commander had rolled almost to their feet. He was not yet dead, but one of their bullets had got him in the throat, and blood came from his lips and nostrils in little bursts.

"I promise you, Commander," said Don Juan, "that your niece is still a virgin."

He was not quite sure why he told the commander this truth, except that he thought, perhaps, that it might ease his death to know his family's honor, as he saw it, was intact. It was not, in any case, possible to tell whether the commander heard or not, but he stared at Don Juan, an unblinking stare that continued for so long to hold the boy's eyes that one of the militiamen had to jog him to look away.

"He is already dead, *compañero*," he said. "It is never good to look too long into the eyes of the dead."

It took only forty-eight hours for Don Juan to be authorized to transfer to the anarchist militia headquarters in Barcelona for reassignment. The committee of control in Jaén had Teresa de Cayuela examined by a doctor before dismissing the aunts' charge of rape against Whitticker, but they saw every reason to grant his request for a transfer. No charges were brought in relation to the commander's death. His possession of his revolver could have earned him a death sentence if it had been known.

He saw Teresa only for a few seconds in the corridor of the city hall as she went to give her evidence to the committee of control. He had just finished telling them that Teresa was still a virgin, but that he and she had a tender and romantic relationship. He knew how to talk to Spanish anarchists and socialists of love. They were ready to greet Teresa when she came to them as if she were Juliet and they all Capulets. He had used his eloquence to remind them that the clammy hand of the church had blighted enough young lives in Spain, that Teresa was the victim of the church's ignorance and prejudice and, yes, Don Juan admitted it, his own young and selfish desire. When he saw her in the passage, guarded by her posse of aunts, she looked at him beseechingly. "Take me away from here. Don't leave me to rot without your love or your laughter or your imagination," her look said. And then they took her into the council chamber and he went to prepare for his journey to Barcelona.

Could he have stayed? He asked himself that question sometimes when he thought of Teresa. If he had been prepared to ask for her hand in marriage it might have been possible. But he was partly responsible for her uncle's death. In Spain it is hard for young people to wed against such odds. Beyond that was the question, Did he love her? Don Juan loved her as much as he loved womankind itself. No more, no less. He believed himself right to leave. He thought it his duty to leave. But in a small corner of his heart where Teresa had found a niche, there he hated leaving.

He arrived in Barcelona on April 15, 1938, only days before the Nationalist forces reached the Mediterranean at Castellón. His journey had been neither hazardous nor particularly uncomfortable, thanks to the funds his grandfather made available to him via the Union des Banques Suisses. Their telephone conversations during this period led the old man to hope that his grandson might yet see the error of his ways and come over to the Nationalists. But Don Juan was filled with self-hatred, and maybe the melancholy that this mood imposed upon him communicated itself to his relative as dissatisfaction with the Republic's cause.

He had decided to try to purge himself in battle from the feeling of guilt he felt over the commander's death. It was as if he wished to put to the test that curious certainty he had always felt as to his own immortality. For he was too intelligent not to notice the accruing debris he was leaving in his wake.

In armies and in war it is always hard to get anything absolutely logical to take place. A man volunteers, thirsting for the enemies' blood, and he finds himself counting sacks of beans in the supply depot while congenital cowards who urinate at the backfire of a car are sent to the front line. Gideon's host was almost certainly beset by similar problems. No army in the history of warfare, however, has been more bizarrely organized and led than that which the Republic fielded between 1936 and 1939. While all that has no place in this story, suffice it to say that Don Juan was not finally able to join an anarchist battalion at the front until December 14, 1938, when he reported to Colonel Marny Perlmutter at his headquarters not far from Seo de Urgel, less than twenty miles from the frontier between Spain and the tiny independent principality of Andorra.

They sat and ate canned gefilte fish that had accompanied Don Juan in a package the colonel's mother had sent her son from the faraway New York borough of the Bronx. This plus nearly a month's mail occupied the colonel for the first half hour of their meal together. A gaunt-looking Gypsy girl of about twenty cooked for the colonel, making them acorn coffee when they had finished the gefilte fish.

"So why did they send you to me, kid?" he asked kindly, putting away his letters and facing his guest across the rude kitchen table that was almost the only piece of furniture in the ruined cottage where he made his headquarters.

"I hope to be of some use," said Don Juan. "I can shoot straight. I can use Mausers, Brownings, Brens, Maxims, M.G. 34s and a few others. I took a course while I was in Barcelona. I've seen action on the Jaén front."

"No shit, kid. I thought you guys spent your time pissing in the wind down there."

"I was at Santa Maria de la Cabeza," said Don Juan with dignity, wondering if these battle references were really necessary.

"Yeah. I was with the International Brigade myself then. That was the Thirteenth, wasn't it? Fuckin' Hun Zeisser in command. They've all gone home, those guys. Did you know that?"

"Yes, I heard."

"Well, what are you doing here? You're a limey. All the other limeys got the hell out when Uncle Joe Stalin pulled the plug on aid to the Republic."

"I'm Spanish. I went to school in England."

"Spic, huh? Good-looking kid. Don't let those guys out there catch you bending too often. They'd cornhole anything that moves, those guys. Been up here without any female ass one hell of a long time. Still can't figure why they sent you."

"For that matter, Colonel, what are you doing here, since the International Brigades have pulled out?"

"Nowhere much to go. Ever heard of the Wobblies?"

"No."

"Union back in the States. Some of us were Trotskyites. A few like myself, anarchist. We were the last hope of the true left in America. All gone down the tubes now. The capitalists' unions, the AFL and the CIO, shot, blasted, dynamited us out of existence, and they got their stuff from the company store."

"You could go to France. The left isn't dead there."

"My *mujer* here is another reason to stay," said the colonel, jerking his thumb at the Gypsy. "She gets on my tits with her long face, and she can't cook worth a shit, but she's the goddamnedest earthiest broad I ever sacked up with. D'you know what I mean? Earthy. I get that *mujer* of mine on the mat and I think she's going to suck my skeleton clean through my cock with her ass."

The colonel was a big, balding man who looked as strong and as fit as any human being Don Juan had ever met. He'd heard that some Americans had an alarming habit of confiding their personal life stories to total strangers, and rather hoped the colonel would spare him further details. He did, however, eye the tall, thin Gypsy woman with an added interest.

"Can I go with one of your machine-gun sections, Colonel?"

"Sure can, kid. The big one has got to be along real soon. Don't know what Franco has been waiting for. Except he's such a cautious little runt."

"You think they'll attack soon?"

"Sure. I give it three months, six at the outside. And then— d'you speak any French?"

"Yes—it's really my first language."

"Well, that explains it, kid. That's why they sent you!"

"I see," said Don Juan. Headquarters was assuming that interpreters would be needed to negotiate the crossing into France of the defeated Republican armies. So it really was almost over, this war.

On December 23 the Nationalist armies attacked from the Mediterranean south of Barcelona to the French frontier in the Pyrenees, north of Seo. At first Colonel Perlmutter's battalion had an easy task fighting back against columns of fascist infantry and light tanks that tried to advance through valleys where the anarchists had commanding fields of fire from their prepared positions on the hills. Don Juan's machine-gun section spent the whole of January 1939 in four-hours-on, four-hours-off watches from a single hill position, with redoubts of sandbags and rocks below them and steep escarpments of rock at their backs. Bombing from German Heinkels and strafing Italian Fiat fighters kept their heads down intermittently, but never for long enough to prevent their decimating any Nationalist force trying to advance down the valley below them.

Barcelona fell on January 26, but by that time it was a ghost town, and virtually all the working-class population were clogging the roads to the French frontier. Resistance by the Republican army in the north had effectively ceased as they followed their civilians into exile. In all, a quarter of a million Spanish Republican civilians and another quarter of a million Republican troops had crossed into France by February 10, 1939.

Don Juan and his dwindling number of comrades held their positions until February 4. On that date the indefatigable Colonel Perlmutter spent most of the night touring his defensive positions.

Don Juan was asleep when the colonel entered their redoubt. Perlmutter's *mujer* followed him like an insubstantial shadow, sitting or standing at a fixed distance from him, never letting him out of her sight but always effacing herself, avoiding the light from the fire around which the off-duty militiamen had been sleeping.

Bone-tired after almost six weeks of continuous defensive action, they took a little while to rouse themselves for what the colonel called his "bull session." He spoke Spanish so badly that they sometimes laughed aloud as he scrambled improbable idioms and metaphors together, trying not to lose the flavor of his own salty brand of English when he talked to his troops. But on this night he asked Don Juan to translate for him.

"Fellas, this is like we was having our last locker-room bull session before the final football game of the season. I think we have played good football. I'm real proud of you guys. I bet you're the best bunch of spics I ever hope to meet. But the season's over, see. And our league has lost. Not your fault. Nor mine. Certainly not the fault of all the guys who've given their lives these last weeks up here. Now as you probably know, fifteen miles up the road from here there's this cockamamie little country called Andorra. It's like solid mountain from here to there, with snow all the way. Here are half a dozen maps of the area, and these compasses come from some five-and-ten-cent store, but they work. As far as I'm concerned, you're free to go. My order to you is . . ." He paused, looking around at their faces, as Don Juan finished translating. "My order to you is 'Dismiss.' You're mustered out, fellas."

There was a questioning mutter from the militiamen.

"We thought you said something about a 'final game,'" said Don Juan.

"Yeah. I said that. I'm going down into that valley tonight killing fascists. Our side still holds Madrid and a helluva chunk of central Spain. As far as I'm concerned, the war goes on even if it's as good as finished here. There are a helluva lot of krauts in those columns down there. I can hear them on the squawk box, schnelling and achtunging. Nazi bastards! Anyone who wants to come with me, that's okay. But it won't make a hill of beans difference to the war, or I wouldn't have dismissed you. Get it?"

Only two of them decided to go with the colonel. He shook all the rest by the hand when he said goodbye. He hadn't expected anything else. Don Juan was one of the two. He made the decision without any deep thought on the matter, but reflected on it as they walked single-file down the snaking path to the rendezvous point from which Colonel Perlmutter's last "football game" was due to start.

Was this what was known as a suicide mission? he wondered. If so, why was he on it? He had no desire to die. But he also had been prey, as we have said, to deep feelings of guilt and doubt about himself. He could not but believe, as so many people do when very young, that he was immune to death. He knew that this belief was absurd, but he clung to it just the same. Perhaps following the colonel was a kind of Russian roulette that he had half-determined to play with himself when he came to the front. A way to face the dead commander's side and give them a fair chance to shoot at him as close to as the militiamen of Jaén had fired. He felt a need to expiate his sense of having participated in a murder—participated if only by being the direct, if unwitting, cause of it.

Snow had started to fall heavily, and was lying even in the valley, where the enemy column was dug in, its vehicles bivouacked far enough back down the road to be out of range of Colonel Perlmutter's field of fire. The very first faint light of dawn, reflected by the snow, threw the whole area into sharper focus than the colonel had expected at that hour. After reaching the rendezvous point, he greeted the eight volunteers who had gathered there and immediately surveyed the enemy's positions through his night glasses. Then he gave them his game plan.

An hour later, traveling by a circuitous route through the hills they knew so well, they had reached a point only a hundred meters from the fascists' bivouacked transport. They had seen some sentries in the distance on the road, and there were two weary figures, stamping their feet every few minutes to keep warm, guarding the vehicles. But attack was clearly the last thing the fascists expected. The two sentries had their throats noiselessly cut by Marny Perlmutter himself while the others watched him moving stealthily among the vehicles, ready to give covering fire if either sentry raised the alarm.

All this occurred sometime before that great American invention, the self-starter, was in general use. But nor, as a result, did the vehicles have ignition keys. In the cold weather it took half an agonizing hour to crank-start three of the trucks while adjusting the hand-controlled gas and air levers, the number of vehicles the colonel had decided to use for his operation being partly dictated by the number of his volunteers who could drive. Don Juan was not one of them.

The trucks were open American Fords. The colonel had armed his men with three Bren machine guns, one to each vehicle, and carbines for ease of handling. They also had twelve hand grenades apiece. He and his *mujer* went in the lead vehicle with a militiaman driving and another in the back with Perlmutter, who himself was going to fire the Bren gun. Don Juan was in the second vehicle. Its Bren gun they had mounted on the roof of the cab, while he stood in the rear aiming it forward. The third vehicle, similarly equipped, followed.

Since the parking ground was to the rear of the fascists' dug-in positions facing what had been Perlmutter's defensive line, his plan was the simple one of attacking them from the rear as he traveled up the road in his three captured vehicles. He had the element of surprise on his side—surprise that he should be attacking at all, let alone from the rear.

Looking back on it afterward, Don Juan realized that the whole battle lasted less than five minutes, and perhaps a hundred men died during that time. The images of the battle remained with him, nightmarish and unreal, so that he sometimes wondered later whether he had dreamed the whole thing.

Once they had turned onto the road in the two-inch-deep snow, they saw a guard detail doubling toward them, disturbed, no doubt, by the unexplained starting of the vehicles. Colonel Perlmutter killed them all, in one long burst from his Bren.

In less than thirty seconds the convoy came upon some hundred low two-men tents. A few people roused by the gunfire had started to clamber out of them. The three vehicles halted now and trained their machine guns on the fascist soldiers struggling like larvae out of their small canvas enclosures. Don Juan burned his hands changing magazines, so hot did his gun become with firing. No one in the tented camp stood a chance, but Colonel Perlmutter stayed at the killing of them for too long. For the fascists from the forward positions down the road started to direct machine-gun and mortar fire on their vehicles. A lucky mortar bomb took out Perlmutter's third truckload, the one behind Don Juan, hitting near the gasoline tank and blowing it apart in two blasting explosions that left only a skeleton of blazing metal.

The blast knocked Don Juan and his companion in the back of the truck off their feet, the Bren gun slipping off the cab and down onto the road. Too late, Colonel Perlmutter ordered his two remaining vehicles forward, aiming them straight down the road, where the fascists had now had plenty of time to be ready for them.

Don Juan pulled himself upright. Peering over the cab of the truck, he could see Perlmutter firing in a wide arc ahead of him; his *mujer* was beside him with clips ready for reloading. On the sides of the road, an avenue of machine-gun and rifle fire was being poured into his vehicle. Don Juan saw Perlmutter fall, and then the Spanish woman beside him must have simply pulled the pin from a grenade and kept holding it, for she was at the very center of the next explosion, followed once again by the truck's gasoline tank exploding in a second bang that spread flame over both sides of the road for such a distance that he could see several of the fascists blazing from head to foot, running uselessly from the explosion, shrieking eerily as they went.

Don Juan saw no more of this, for at that moment the driver of his own vehicle, whether out of fear or because he was hurt, put the truck into a skid that turned it violently around by one hundred and eighty degrees. It came to a crashing halt with its front wheels in a ditch, throwing Don Juan out into the soft snow. Looking to where Perlmutter's truck had been, he could see only a wall of flame, with men trying to aid the screaming soldiers who had been engulfed in the burning gasoline. Although his shoulder ached abominably from his fall, he seemed to be otherwise intact. His companion in the back of the truck had disappeared. Both the men in the cab had gone through the windshield. One was clearly dead, and the other unconscious, with hideous head injuries. Don Juan started to run through the snowdrifts, away from the road and toward the hills. Dawn was still half an hour away.

Under the Cabinet of the Mistresses

> Chloe's hair, no doubt, was brighter;
>   Lydia's mouth more sweetly sad;
> Hebe's arms were rather whiter;
>   Languorous-lidded Helen had
> Eyes more blue than e'er the sky was;
>   Lalage's was subtler stuff;
> Still, you used to think that I was
>   Fair enough.
>
>   —Dorothy Parker, *Renunciation*

Don Juan arrived at what he considered his home on the Avenue Foch in Paris at the beginning of March 1939. Apart from an interminable and painful walk through snowdrifts to Andorra, he had been spared the fearful sufferings of his fellow Republicans, most of whom were incarcerated for many months in primitive and disease-ridden refugee camps in southern France. Don Juan simply telegraphed his mother and telephoned his grandfather. At once the wheels of privileged accommodation started to whirr. Thomas Cook rented him a chalet in Andorra until his papers were ready for him to reenter France. Henrietta and the duchess went so far as to cancel dinner engagements, parties, theater seats, and weekends in the country and sailed almost at once from New York to open their Paris house for the return of the prodigal.

For his seventeenth birthday the duchess planned a party, and in the meantime she and Henrietta and Sylvie, the ladies' maid, and the cooks, Boris and Valéry, and the rest of the staff awaited his return with impatience.

"Poor boy. It seems likely that he will be covered with spots," said the duchess to Henrietta on the morning of his expected arrival. "One worries, too, about his manners. It's been almost a year, do you realize, since he's seen *anybody*. Wandering around with all those ruffians. He must be an absolute Caliban by now."

"I realize that we must start thinking about his education!" said Henrietta.

"But he's too old for school. Who would take him?"

"He was too old for school at thirteen, darling," said Henrietta with asperity. "The problem now is going to be getting him into a university. Here in France, without taking the baccalaureate exam, there's no way. He'll have to spend months and months with tutors."

"Oh dear, how boring. If only he had decided to be a fascist."

"I know what you mean, darling. Why would a fascist duke need an education?"

"Please, Henrietta. Not today. I've promised not to reproach him over his extraordinary behavior. Isn't that enough?"

For Henrietta, it was, indeed, enough. Don Juan would never know how much he owed his family's tolerance of his behavior to Henrietta. She had written eloquent letters in his behalf to his grandfather defending "youth's impetuosity" in Don Juan. He had shown spirit and originality, she argued, rather than good sense. It wasn't his fault his tutor, Whitticker, unbeknown to anybody, had been a dangerous revolutionary. To punish Don Juan further (as if Deerhurst hadn't been punishment enough) for being influenced by his tutor's ideas would be injust. His grandfather was inclined to agree.

The Thomas Cook courier brought him from Le Bourget airport, as promised, in plenty of time for lunch.

When she heard the doorbell, his mother went so far as to go and meet him in the hall. She saw a clear-skinned young man as tall as his grandfather, well over six feet, with the kind of face that would have made Michelangelo pause. There was no trace of boyish softness left. The mouth, once rather too large, had come to perfectly proportioned terms with the rest of the face, remaining the most expressive of mouths. The eyes were, as they had always been, beautiful, humorous, and wise. She recognized him first from his eyes.

It is true she saw him with a mother's indulgent eye, but then, for a number of obvious reasons, she was oblivious to the total impression of sexuality that he conveyed to most women. It was an impression of which he, himself, was unconscious. He had been born completely without any sense of competition with other men. He therefore rarely considered whether they were in any way different from him, a difference noted almost universally by others.

To the party they gave for his birthday the *tout Paris* of 1939 came. In that spring and summer, while Hitler was preparing to invade Poland and Mussolini to war with Greece, while the appeasing governments of Britain and France drew the last line beyond which they said they were not prepared to be pushed, the Parisians, like most Europeans, hoped that the fascist nemesis would blow away if they ignored it. That summer everyone with any money to spare, which was about a third of the population, had a defiantly good time.

For Don Juan's birthday party, two black American dance bands, then so popular in France, played fox-trots, sambas, rhumbas, and occasional Charlestons (at Henrietta's special request) until five in the morning. While there was inevitably a coterie of the hostesses' lesbian friends, they had gone out of their way to ask lots of young men and women in their early twenties, for to have asked teenagers for the sophisticated and war-weary Don Juan never occurred to them.

"Try this evening, darling, just to play the host," said his mother, in one of the most comprehensive, maternal lectures she ever gave him. "There will be two hundred women here tonight. Think of this as I do when I go to see the spring collections. It is unwise to order from Chanel until one has seen what Rouff or Molyneux has to show. See what the season seems to be offering. But wait till you have been to another five or six parties and formed a better picture of what appeals to you. Then start choosing what is to divert you this year."

She was speaking to him over lunch on the day of the party. Don Juan was at table with Henrietta and his mother while pandemonium reigned outside the dining room as moonlighting stagehands from L'Opéra temporarily transformed the decor of the duchess's classic house into something that Benois, the designer, described as a Night at the Alhambra.

"I have decided that I am in love," said Don Juan with a straight face, knowing that this announcement would cause a mild sensation.

"Of course you are," said Henrietta, making light of the matter to hide her concern. "I was perpetually in love at your age. Too frightful, it was. I could hardly sleep at night because of the dreadful pain of unrequited passion."

"I do hope it is some *midinette* with a sound knowledge of birth control," said his mother, making them all laugh.

"Please!" said Don Juan, enjoying his teasing and looking as soulful as possible. "This is platonic love. We write to each other, and each letter I receive from her makes me more convinced that she must be the girl I will ultimately marry."

"Oh, God, how inconsiderate you are, Juanito," said his mother. "These *quenelles* Boris makes are so delicious, and now you've quite taken my appetite away. Marriage?"

"Tell us! Tell us!" said Henrietta impatiently.

"Her name is Juliet Fitzjames. Hers is the innocence and the good sense I have come to adore."

"Not *little* Juliet? Stow and Lauder's daughter? That sweet, darling child? I absolutely forbid it, Juan!" roared Henrietta.

"A mere correspondence. I have one of her letters here. May I read it?"

"If you must," said Henrietta, wondering what would be the fastest way to warn her Scottish friends.

"'Dear Juan,'" he read. "'I am sorry that your side seems to have lost in Spain. I bought a hammer-and-sickle flag at the Russian bookshop on Museum Street and carried it around all day when I heard your army had finally had to leave Spain. I would have bought an anarchist flag if I could have found one. What are they like? I imagine something very impressionistic, a veritable *explosion* of color, with a flame in the middle representing "life."

"'Daddy was making a speech in the House of Lords that day, and Giles and I went to listen. He denounced all our enemies, but not as vehemently as I should have liked, but he did make some rather splendid phrases. Lord Perth—he's our man in Rome, an arch-appeaser—he described as being a man "so credulous that if a smoking bomb were brought to him in his morning eggcup, he would be like to tap it complacently with his spoon." He got quite a lot of "hear, hears," but I cheered and waved my flag. Everyone stared!

"'Oh, Juan. I'm in despair. Mummy says that you have a very "odd" reputation. There is no "swear" in the English language worse than "odd," as you must know. So that when I asked whether you could come to stay with us this summer, she said "absolutely no." Oh, how will I ever see you again now? You will meet hundreds of girls in Paris and forget all about this mousy English schoolgirl.

"'Please send me a very reassuring letter. I'd like to hear that you plan to summer at the monastery on Mount Athos in Greece, where, I understand, even hens are considered a feminine intrusion.

"'With love from Juliet.'"

"She sounds adorable, if quite ridiculously under your influence!" exclaimed his mother.

"Her mother is absolutely right. I feel very responsible," said Henrietta. "I cannot think of anything more disastrous than you two getting together until she's old enough to take care of herself."

"When will that be?" asked Don Juan, laughing.

"Oh, when she's about eighty, I should think," said Henrietta firmly.

At his birthday party Don Juan behaved in an exemplary way. For once his mother's advice seemed to him wholly sensible. But quite apart from that, he was so dazzled by the women the *tout Paris* fielded at his party that the very thought of spending time choosing some particular delight for further and better knowing seemed ridiculously premature. He therefore admired and amused, he conversed with and danced with, virtually every female at his party, causing, quite literally, a sensation.

The deluge of invitations that he received after the party persuaded the duchess that she had provided for Don Juan's entertainment for as long as he should wish to stay in Paris. Talk of his joining a university in the fall had petered out, since he seemed, academically speaking, to be interested only in going to the Beaux-Arts, which had readily accepted him after seeing his portfolio. Thomas Cook had, not without difficulty, recovered all his possessions from Spain.

His mother and Henrietta left him a small staff (not including Boris and Valéry) and the house on the Avenue Foch, themselves returning to America to summer in Locust Valley, Long Island. They had asked Don Juan if he would like to join them, but the women of Paris, still under review, as yet unsavored, were too limitless an attraction. The women of America, after all, he had never as yet seen.

Don Juan was indeed intoxicated by what Paris had to offer that year. Englishwomen, he had found, lived a life of licensed freedom in a profoundly masculine country; part of their charm was that under their often mannish clothes and assumed masculine attitudes, they lurked warm, soft, giving, and often beautiful. The contradiction was of itself exciting to Don Juan.

Spanish women, he found, *reserved* their passion as a Catholic priest reserves the host in the tabernacle. Before a Spanish woman decided to give herself, she peered through a lattice at the world, still profoundly Moorish in this way. The moment she decided to *give*, she was capable of great passion, but without much humor, without much light and shade to her.

In the Paris he found so full of immediate promise that summer, he saw women who, for all their lack of legal and constitutional emancipation, were at the very core of human life, were its inspiration, its electromotive force. It is true that there were many dull, drab, shrewish, and boring women in Paris, as everywhere, but Don Juan was destined to meet very few of these. Of the generality of the women he met, the following can be said: They awoke each morning confident, in bathtub and on bidet, that they were by definition desirable, and more than that, indispensable, to the well-being and happiness of their menfolk. They dressed for the splendid and invigorating battle of life each day, anxious to spare the world nothing of what was *woman* about them. They set off each morning as if for a unique meeting with a lover. For even if they currently had none, who knew around which corner he might lurk, the new one, waiting only to be bowled over, struck dumb, maddened with sudden desire? The possibility was as ever present to these women as the risk of the common cold in an English winter.

A French woman of this kind has not changed. Then, as now, she was prepared for those accidents from which a woman's happiness so often springs. Suppose *he* stops to kiss her hand? The hand must have skin so silken-soft and fragrant that thoughts of its potential caresses will not leave him all day, may never leave him. The luster and scent of her hair, as he hands her into her car, will blot out all thought of work and make him take the afternoon off, the year off, or leave his mistress, his mother, his wife. The sight of her figure as she comes through the revolving door of the restaurant must drive from his mind any mild irritation that she is an hour and a half late. He will sense by the way her clothes sit upon her underclothes of what exquisite silk the latter are made. From the subtle scent of her he will sense, or believe he does, what is mere perfume and what the scent of her own flesh, the latter infinitely more intriguing because unique. French women are not, on the whole, *naturally* beautiful; they need artifice, as an actor needs a script.

Having reached man where he lives, as a male, she is now ready to confound him in the department of the intellect. She will invariably be better read than he, better informed. It is true she has more time than he, but also true that she rarely wastes time, any more than she neglects her mind.

Her education, at the time of which we speak—that is, the dying days of the Third Republic—need have been no worse than that of her brothers. And over her Anglo-Saxon sisters in America and England she had the advantage that she was not always being told that men hated women with brains; on the contrary, she was being encouraged to be as mentally aware as she was physically attractive. It was only from *action* that French society discouraged its women, never from thought. Their influence on affairs had always been immense.

Don Juan never slept alone from the day his mother and Henrietta left again for America until the day he arrived in the South of France the following June of 1940. He avoided any regular mistress, he sought out no particular woman above all others, but from the many who made plain their desire for him, he chose a certain few, all of them women who seemed to be beyond the ordinary in beauty and talent and brains.

Moving in the great world of de Mouchys and de Rochefoucaulds, of Orléanses and Bourbons on the one hand and of the raffish crowd who studied at the Beaux-Arts and took out showgirls, *midinettes,* and models from the fashion houses and female students on the other, Don Juan soon had three women who would have shared their beds with him every night if they could, but aware that he had committed only a small part of his hectic life to them, made do with all of their handsome Spaniard a fraction of his time.

He thought of it as his Eclectic Year afterward, and vowed that if he ever had a son, he would recommend the age of seventeen for the parallel enjoyment of a number of marvelous women at the same time. (In Jaén his nights had been filled with a *sequence* of women.)

There was Mireille Benoit, who worked in the sideshow of the permanent circus of the Foire d'Orsay. She was a girl of the working class from the Batignolles section of Paris, a daughter of a trade-union official, and her aspirations all centered around poetry.

To earn her bread she spent each day in a comfortable open coffin with fourteen sleepy snakes of various breeds. She wore for this work only a small snakeskin cache-sex; otherwise she was made up with an unearthly pallor and a mock stake through her heart, from which trickled some glutinous blood made from egg white and cochineal. Her only duty was to occasionally roll her eyes as the lines of paying viewers filed by the glass case in which this remarkable exhibit was kept. In a good eight-hour day she could easily compose and memorize a passable sonnet and make a reasonable living.

Don Juan had heard her one evening reciting her verse publicly in a café off the Boulevard St. Michel, and found her voice the most musical and enchanting sound he had so far heard come from human lips. It was a cool voice, but husky, capable of sounds with such texture to them that they moved him much as might an intimate caress. He had taken her out to dinner and astonished her by remembering most of her verses and discussing them minutely with her.

In her bed he asked her to speak lines of hers he liked as he loved her. It pleased him to listen to her voice change slowly with each stroke of his body. It pleased him, too, to find some lines she could repeat again and again in her lovely fibrous tones, listening to the sound melt away as it turned into the abstracted expression, in sound, of the sensations he gave her. To make her wait for him, when she was ahead of him in love's race, he would ask her to try to speak poetic images for every nuance of her feelings, clinging to reason till they were ready to drive words from both their minds, surrendering entirely to sensation.

She thanked him once for never asking her whether she made love to her snakes. No other lover had ever failed to be curious on this point. Don Juan did not tell her that it had occurred to him that this might be so. Because he had never asked this question, she pressed upon him the information that a snake's tongue had for her tiny rose the perfect rhythm, opening her petals with an extraordinary switchblade precision, but that, curiously, the pleasure it gave her was of a shivering, *cold* kind.

"It makes me shiver so excessively in the end that I *jouisse*," she said, using that untranslatable French word that alliterates the orgasm. "Only one of my snakes likes to enter me, and that is Hercule, the python. It is an extraordinary sensation. That and no more. It doesn't move me as the very sight of your warm throat does when you undo your collar."

Aube de Tournelle was essentially a political being. Her husband, Admiral Count de Tournelle, was condemned, as all exiles from France think of such absences, to govern the French Gibbon Islands in Micronesia. This post had been his punishment by the Popular Front government of Léon Blum, recently out of office, for undue support of the Croix de Feu movement, France's fascists, who had narrowly failed to take over the country in 1932, at about the time that Hitler's Nazis were being successful in Germany.

Aube's father was a rich scrap-iron merchant from Clermont-Ferrand, and the marriage would provide for the admiral's eventual retirement in a way which a grateful French state could never afford. He had special tastes, even for a sailor, and it was part of the success of Aube's marriage that she managed to send him something "special" on his name day, his birthday, at New Year, and occasionally in between. Her most recent find was an aging black singing lady from Martinique, with a lower lip like a coal scuttle, whom she had sent out by P&O, steamer, second-class, to enliven the feast of Pentaecost for him in Micronesia.

Madame de Tournelle's predilections had always been for power rather than sex. Not that she neglected to use the latter in pursuit of the former. At least three of the ministers in the current government of Édouard Daladier were her lovers.

He had met her on the occasion of his birthday party, when she was standing with two of her chief rivals, the Countess de Portes, the mistress of Paul Reynaud, the finance minister, and the Marchioness de Crussol, the mistress of Daladier, the prime minister. Before the duchess presented her son to them, she briefed him as to their identities.

They asked him about Spain.

"You must ask Marshal Pétain about the new Spain, since you have sent him there as your ambassador," said Don Juan. "My Spain, alas, no longer exists."

"You speak of us as if we were the government of France," laughed Aube de Tournelle.

"You have the effulgence of true power, mesdames. One is dazzled," he said smilingly.

Aube laughed delightedly, but the other two were not quite so amused. For between them they were wearing enough diamonds to fill Cartier's window. Aube, on the other hand, wore no jewelry except the simplest of black velvet chokers around her neck, from which carefully graded pearls made a delicate fringe. Her dress was of black, with a high neckline and puffed sleeves. Turning to take a glass of champagne from a passing waiter, she showed him her back. She was naked right down to virtually the last vertebra of her spine. Don Juan had never seen a more beautiful back and neck in his life. Her head was crowned with very short, softly curling platinum-blond hair, from a bottle, no doubt, for it was then the fashion, but lovely just the same.

Don Juan looked at her with such a guileless, unfeigned admiration that both Hélène de Portes and Jeanne de Crussol found themselves smiling as the duchess led her son away for further introductions.

"It's perfectly true what they say. He's the best-looking boy in Paris," said Madame de Portes.

"The first time that doubtful title has *not* been held by a pederast in living memory," said Madame de Crussol. "Cocteau will be furious!"

"Can it really be that he is also so intelligent? Those eyes of his look as if they had already forgotten more than many cabinet ministers have ever known," said Madame de Tournelle.

"They did not look as if they would soon forget you, Aube, dear!" said Madame de Crussol.

"Will they have to, Aube, dear?" asked Madame de Portes.

"What with health and agriculture and armaments already in your life, Aube, can there also be room for love?" asked Madame de Crussol, mentioning the portfolios of Aube's ministerial lovers.

"If what one hears about him is true, he should be given that portfolio. I, for one, would lay down everything to help him," said Aube.

"That you would lay down, one has little doubt," said Madame de Crussol rather coarsely. "But what *exactly* does one hear?"

"That he was thrown out of his English school for deflowering the maids. Of course, you know that he has fought for two years for the Republicans. They say he interests himself in painting and has extraordinary talent, and not by any means only for painting. That is what they say. Oh dear!" concluded Aube, watching Don Juan's progress across the room. He was dancing with Germaine D'Albret, a woman of thirty-seven who for nearly two decades had enjoyed the reputation of being the most beautiful and the most heartless woman in France.

"She will destroy him, that one," said Aube. "Just look at her. She is pretending not to notice she is dancing in his arms and that together they look like two gods down from Olympus for an evening's slumming."

Everyone in the room watched them. Don Juan held the gossamer beauty in his arms and was grateful to his mother for the dance lessons she had insisted he take. Germaine D'Albret was so dauntingly lovely that she alone among the women at that party left him virtually speechless. He was horrified to remember afterward that the only subject he had managed to raise was tennis, and that was in error. She had asked him if he liked weekends in the country, and he had said, "'Anyone for tennis?' I'm not sure." She had stared at him silently as if he had said something obscene.

When he returned her to her table and friends, he felt, for the only time that night, like the seventeen-year-old youth he was. Germaine was extraordinary, of that he was certain. She was also beyond his reach. What had not occurred to him was that she might be the one who would decide to do the reaching.

But Don Juan now turned to Aube for his next dance. It was a slow fox-trot. By the time it was over, he knew that he had only to call upon her and she would be his. He liked that she didn't care if the whole room sensed her physical invitation to him. He was, after all, the prize of the evening. He left her with decorum and took both Madame de Portes and Madame de Crussol onto the dance floor thereafter.

Within a week he and Aube were lovers. He fitted her in among his other commitments, and she fitted him in among her cabinet ministers. She even thought of dispensing with them and abandoning politics, but he dissuaded her. Apart from the utter beauty of her back, her role as a power behind the scenes fascinated him. There was a sameness about their relationship that he never had time to find boring.

Her dresses all undid behind, and whenever she desired him she would turn her back, seeking his loins with her neat little buttocks, which were surprisingly muscular. When she felt him to be ready, she would bend forward while he undid the dress. She was always entirely bare beneath it except for her panties. These she liked to have ripped apart just before he entered her.

"I feel like a package being torn open and experienced 'fresh,'" she explained. "It is most agreeable. And only a peasant woman would wish to wear such a garment twice."

Don Juan loved the perfect patterns her back made as it arched and writhed its way through her pleasure.

She was quite unsentimental, and the instant she had stopped shuddering and shouting, "Don't stop. Don't cease. My God, what beneficence!" and unsheathed him again, it was time for talk. And talk was always political. One conversation in particular he would always remember.

She had leaped, still a little convulsed, upon her bidet. Closing her eyes, the better to feel the cool depth charge of the vertical douche, she announced:

"France *must* breed, my friend. It is the only way!"

Don Juan was lying on her huge gondola bed, watching her idly through the open bathroom door.

"But you have no children, Aube," he said reasonably.

"I was not created for that. I know the church would not agree.

But when half a million curés worldwide are giving of their essence every night to their bed linen, who are they to say that it is every woman's duty to breed?"

"I see. Some are more breedable than others. Do you want admirals and cabinet ministers to die out as a race?"

"Be quiet, my little one. This is serious. I am speaking of France. We must find a way to make the bourgeois, the peasants, and the workers of France have babies."

"How do they avoid it?" asked Don Juan curiously. "Birth-control devices are impossibly difficult to get here."

"It is Madame Bidet and Madame Douche who are the killers. Just as Madame Guillotine was for the aristocracy in the Revolution. That and 'leaving by the back door.'"

"Leaving by the back door?" queried Don Juan.

"Since I like to bend so much, it is not a habit I want you to get into, my friend. Suffice it to say that the peasant girls all do it. It is outrageous when France needs children so badly. Where will the men come from to fight the Bolshevik horde? Or the Boche if he decides to invade again?"

"The Boche? Surely Germany lost as many men in the Great War as you?"

"Evidently. But Hitler gives the *Mädchens* medals and money for getting in pod. The children don't even have to be legitimate. You can hardly get on a German bus these days, they say, for bulging bellies."

"So what are you doing?"

"I am getting 'health' to spread the use of special seats on trams and trains for pregnant women. To stop the men grumbling we have to add veterans to the notice. 'Reserved for pregnant women, and men mutilated in the war,' it reads. But we must do more. This cabinet is hopeless. It is, of course, the fault of Hélène and Jeanne, who fight incessantly for the personal advantage of Reynaud and Daladier. Hélène will not rest till Paul Reynaud is prime minister."

"Will that be such a disaster?"

"Not at all. But it depends on what Jeanne insists on for Daladier thereafter. He is not only prime minister at the moment, but also defense minister. Ordinarily it would hardly concern one who the defense minister is. But with France committed to the idiotic foreign policy of those perfidious English, war is in the offing, my cabbage, one cannot deny it. If he remains at defense, one worries for the safety of France."

"Aube, I know that the rumor was that the Germans had bought half the cabinet and the general staff. But surely that's all nonsense?" asked Don Juan.

"Not entirely. They may have bought Hélène de Portes. Not with money, perhaps, but the German military attaché is moving into a certain intimacy there. I personally consider our top generals, Gamelin and Georges, to be worth fifty divisions to the Germans if there is a war. But Jeanne thinks Gamelin is a genius. Stupidity can be as treasonable as treachery sometimes. Colonel de Gaulle will be here for dinner tonight. He will tell you."

"The one who wrote the book on tank warfare?" asked Don Juan.

"Exactly. The Germans regard him as the new Clausewitz. I am surprised that with your many 'other interests' you should have read it."

"No. But it was much discussed in Spain. The German Condor Division there used his ideas against us rather effectively. But you can hardly compare our rabble to the French army."

"The French army, my friend, is a matter of calling to the colors two million conscripts. You can inspect the French army in the cafés and on the Métro. Will they fight for this Republic?"

Don Juan would long remember what he thought of as "the sermon on the bidet." It was to prove prophetic.

Germaine D'Albret, one must admit it, fed Don Juan's ego with such monstrous doses of flattery that he was to feel some shame mixed with much remembered pleasure when their short, blazing affair was over.

The Princess D'Albret was of lineage so ancient that she had the leopards of England, the lion of the Beauforts, the bears of the Orsinis, and a complete bestiary of heraldic creatures in her quarterings to keep company, quite naturally, with more than a sprinkling of the lilies of France.

The Prince D'Albret, her father, had married Irma von Lowe und Taxis, only daughter of the great Darmstadt steel magnate. Their death together in one of the earliest fatal automobile accidents recorded in France had left Germaine, their sole heiress, so immoderately rich that it is accurate to say that the limits of her imagination were the only disciplinary factor in an entirely self-indulged life.

Her *hôtel particulier* on the Place Vendôme made Don Juan's mother's establishment on the Avenue Foch seem understaffed and modest by comparison. A fortune fed by her coal mines in the Saar, her textile mills in Lyons, her railway in South Africa, and her still-important holdings in the German steel industry made it possible for her only to *wish* something and it was invariably so. She sometimes wished so many things simultaneously that the administrative abilities of her "men of affairs" were strained. At her chateau on the River Oise (one of many) they had only recently completed arrangements for the entertainment of men which were, in their way, unique.

They corresponded, these arrangements, to a fantasy she had entertained about Don Juan after his birthday. She guessed that few women at that gathering would not want him as their lover. At first he would sample the cream of what was available. By the time he had satisfied his curiosity a little, perhaps jaded his palate, she would be ready to carry him off as her trophy, with some chance of exclusivity. Always assuming that once obtained he still interested her.

When her invitation to stay the weekend on the Oise came, the was surprised. He had thought she found him callow. Remembering her extraordinary beauty with awe, he read and reread her rather remarkable letter of invitation.

My Dear Don Juan,

Your grandfather and I are old friends. At this time of crisis in our European affairs, he has asked me to gather together for a Friday-to-Monday a small group of men from several countries whose mutual interest is the maintenance of peace.

The purpose of this gathering is to relax together and exchange views in pleasant surroundings. It is not in any sense, be reassured, a business meeting.

It occurred to us both that, representing the younger generation as you do, having the evident sympathy for the left that you have, it would be of interest to hear your views.

I have thought of you often since your birthday, when I believe I heard you express an enthusiasm for tennis. Please bring your rackets.

It would be pleasant if we could go down together on Friday morning in my car. It would enable us to get acquainted on the tennis court before the older gentlemen arrive in the evening, and we all have to tax our brains.

Please let me convey to you, dear Don Juan, my most distinguished sentiments.

Germaine D'Albret

Before accepting, he telephoned his grandfather in Barcelona. They had corresponded since the time he had spoken to him from Andorra, but only in a desultory fashion. Restoring production in his

Spanish factories had been the old man's chief preoccupation since the end of the civil war.

"You are calling me about Germaine's invitation," said his grandfather when he came on the line.

"Yes. D'you really want me there?"

"Certainly. You know, of course, who the other guests will be?"

"No. I've been asked to bring my tennis things. I hope she hasn't asked Borotra or any other Wimbledon champions."

"With Germaine that is quite possible, but the other guests are old friends of mine. Bruckner from Essen Steel. Ciano's friend Roffi of Montecatini. Laval, Lord Brasenose of Imperial Metal, Charlie van Damien from Pittsburgh, and others. Not refined people, not intellectuals, but people who make things happen. A strange gathering, even for Germaine."

"I'm not coming, Grandfather. I shall disgrace you."

"On the contrary, you will disgrace me if you don't come. Sometime soon I have to form an opinion about your character. If you behave like a clown you can't hurt me. Only yourself."

So Don Juan accepted the invitation, but with misgivings. Had his grandfather instigated the whole thing as a test? To see if, after his experience with the Spanish Republicans, he had become less radical? To measure how he handled himself in the club to which, as his grandfather's heir, he was born, that of the robber barons of Europe? That they were all simply pawns in a little game of Germaine's never occurred to him.

The green Bugatti in which she collected him was as polished and shining as a Fabergé egg. He really saw her now properly for the first time. At the birthday party she had trailed an aura of glamour to which everyone else, simply by the way they regarded her, contributed. She was the incomparable Germaine. The continued perfection of her skin was attributed to transplanted glands not of monkeys, but of children from the colonies. This and other calumnies added to the manna she shed all around her.

But seeing her in the summer sunshine waving to him from behind the wheel of her two-seater, a simple silk kerchief containing her naturally blond hair, she looked as wholesome as an advertisement for malted milk.

On the way down he was able to study her face at leisure. She had a high brow above a perfect Grecian nose, the nostrils of which were delicately flared like those of a creature that depends on its sense of smell to detect danger. Her lower lip was slightly rounder and larger than the upper lip. It was, on such a face, an infinitely promising lip. Her eyes were a pale, cool blue, the color of amethysts held up to the light. They were not eyes that often smiled, for they had, rather, a habit of staring in a disconcerting, unblinking way. When she really laughed, her body seemed to commit itself to the total act of being amused, from her toenails to the crown of her head.

Don Juan noticed long, strong fingers in her elegant chamois driving gloves. Her breasts and back, her belly and her thighs he could only guess at through her thick driving coat. But he guessed from the memory of holding her in the gossamer silk and lace dress she had worn at his party. It was an athletic body, entirely innocent of fat.

Her driving of the car, the delicate but assured way her feet acted on clutch and accelerator, her hand gently gliding the gearshift between the soft crescendos of double-clutching, taking the engine back and forth through its five gears, made him acutely conscious of her body. Rarely, unless they faced an obstacle like a traffic policeman, did she drive under eighty-five miles an hour. On the open road the Bugatti cruised blithely at a hundred and ten. But such driving demanded silence and concentration, as if she and the car were wrapped in an act of love. Don Juan, vicariously excited, was content with silence.

Only as they passed the gatehouse of her chateau, where the gatekeepers bowed low, their hats in their hands, did she speak.

"Put your hand on my heart, Juan," she said.

Surprised, but excited at the prospect, he slipped his hand into her driving coat, only to find her quite bare. Under compact little breasts whose rigidly erect nipples gave evidence of her excitement, he could feel the urgent drumming of her heart.

"Do you wish me to leave you alone with your car for a while?" he said, smiling.

She gave her total laugh, so that he worried that they would hit a tree.

"It's true, it makes me almost *jouisser* when I drive like that. No, my heart is telling me that we must play tennis at once. You have been considering the possibility of a naked Germaine, correct?"

"I first considered it when I danced with you. I find it as I imagined it," he said, caressing her bare belly under the coat.

"Good, then you are ready for the game," she said.

The chateau is approached along the banks of the River Oise by a drive that is lined by poplars. It is not an ancient edifice, having been rebuilt during the Second Empire according to plans drawn up by Haussmann. It is full of conveniences not available in Germaine D'Albret's older, more famous chateaus. On this sunny July day it looked at its best, the building grand and elegant if not beautiful, the garden verdant and glorious by the limpid Oise.

The ornamental parterres with their topiary and statuary lined the river banks, while the drive, after pausing at the huge gothic front door, skirted the edge of the castle, going first to the stables and garages, above which many of the staff had their quarters, and then on to the grass tennis courts.

Germaine drove the Bugatti straight to the tennis pavilion, got out of the car, and took off her driving coat. An aged groundsman scurried away like a startled rabbit.

"There are very few sports for which I care to wear clothes," said Germaine, looking like Diana, the goddess of the hunt, her bare body tanned uniformly by the sun. "A swimming costume I find intolerable. A horse, its back bare between one's naked thighs. A high-spirited stallion, naturally. I find that extraordinary. To ski naked, when the sun is high in the sky. Marvelous. I am a nudist at heart. Unfortunately, I cannot stand the sight or company of other nudists."

"Oh, good," said Don Juan with relief, retrieving the tennis rackets and balls from the Bugatti's rear. "My figure is hardly Greek."

"What nonsense, Juan. I expect you to look like Michelangelo's David. People who actually go in for nudism tend to resemble raw liver on a butcher's slab."

Don Juan hesitated, wondering why. Her body, long-legged and spare, the breasts high, slightly upturned, and small enough, as he had felt, to fit in the palm of his hand, was that of an athlete. It would be beautiful to watch in action.

"My grandfather is not due here till this evening?" He asked the question ruefully.

Germaine gave her laugh. "Late this evening. What are you ashamed of? A birthmark?"

He took off his clothes and threw them into the car. She had walked, already, onto the court, and he followed her, feeling the pleasure of the grass under his bare feet. When they paused to toss the racket for sides, she looked at him with her staring, considering look.

She saw a young man who was, in the classic sense, almost perfectly made, except that his forearms and shoulders were unusually well muscled. Both were barefoot, and he stood a complete head taller than she. Reaching out with her racket, she gently lifted his balls on its rim.

"Michelangelo was much less generous to David. Curious how touching, how appealing, that is in repose. Yet rampant, it becomes a weapon, exciting entirely different emotions."

They played tennis.

She had a serve very nearly as hard as that of any man Don Juan had ever played. Her net game, too, was good. She won the first set easily, five-one. He won the last game, however, having at last got used to the curious slapping sensation of running naked.

With his newfound confidence, he managed to serve properly and hard. The bob of her breasts as he started to make her move around excited him. Although he lost the first game to her service, he won the second and third. As he began to assume mastery of the court, moving easily from a net game back to hard drives against her backhand, she became covered with a sheen of sweat, breathing deeply from her exertions.

In the fourth game of the second set, he served with increasing force, sensing that even when she could get to the ball she barely had the strength to return it. He wondered if this would dismay her, and saw, as she stood legs apart, waiting for his next serve, that upon the inner swellings of her upper thighs the nectar was spreading from her loins. He meanwhile was so rigidly erect that it pained him as he ran and jumped.

Before the end of the game she lay down on the grass, stretching out her open legs toward him, moving her hips, feeling the soft grass with her rump and fingers, beckoning him with an arch of her back.

"This is the only way I can win this game," she murmured as he entered her.

The other guests arrived, for the most part, around ten o'clock that evening. Don Juan went down to meet his grandfather, taking a late supper alone with him in the suite which Germaine had assigned the old man.

They talked of family first. The news from Long Island. The continuing dementia of the unfortunate duke, now returned to his castle with Garcia.

"Whom God makes mad He often spares from other sickness," said Don Juan's grandfather.

"It makes what is known as His infinite mercy more puzzling than usual," said Don Juan. "They tell me Nationalist Spain is enough to make the pope anti-clerical?"

"That is true. However, one should try not to take it out on

God. Tell me, do you now know the complete guest list?"

Don Juan told him.

"It is very curious. She has asked a raffish group. Immensely powerful, but raffish. Maynard Keynes, Monnet, Schacht, are not on her list. A serious woman would have attempted to ask them to such a meeting. As it is, I shall not hesitate to transact a great deal of business here." Don Juan's grandfather beamed.

"I should have liked to meet Keynes," said Don Juan. "Since the capitalist system seems to be surviving, it would have been instructive to hear its greatest living advocate."

"Are you still an anarchist?"

"I believe I am. Temperamentally. Morally, I'm not up to it. One wonders if unbridled capitalism is not anarchy without the moral content."

"Unbridled capitalism, my dear Juan, we will not see again. The Wall Street crash has seen to that. But I should have thought that bridled capitalism might just prove anarchic enough for you?"

"You may be right. In any case, I feel intensely apolitical at the moment, Grandfather, if that's any comfort to you."

"It is, my boy. You are in your learning years. Listen a great deal. Make love whenever you can. It purges the body of ill humors. Keep all your political options open. These are not times for hasty decisions or irretrievable loyalties."

"It sounds like a certain prescription for going to hell, Grandfather."

"I shall be there to welcome you. Are you afraid?"

"No. Not yet."

Don Juan slept alone that night, not even knowing where his hostess's rooms might be in that labyrinthine castle. Since what had started on the tennis court had been continued in the swimming pool outside the dining room, and repeated until dusk, he slept dreamlessly, undisturbed by those gentle fits of lust that normally woke him in the night.

He breakfasted with his grandfather in his suite, and they received a note telling them that lunch would be at two P.M. Cars, horses, tennis, the billiard room were offered as diversions during the morning. The decided to go riding and met Roffi of Montecatini at the stables. The Spaniard and the Italian greeted each other with the warm backslapping embraces of men who have drunk and whored and plotted together. Roffi was a wiry man with, Don Juan thought, that simian look of quizzical intelligence which reminded one of portraits of Voltaire in the later years.

A groom rode ahead of them to show them the best rides through the woods.

"How is Mussolini?" asked Don Juan's grandfather. "Now that he has Albania and Abyssinia, what next?"

"The duce is insatiable, no doubt," said Roffi.

"I'm not talking about his sex life. That is understood," said the old Spaniard coarsely. "What country will he next invade? Yuguslavia, Greece, France perhaps?"

"I think you misunderstand his role. He wants new acquisitions. But he will take what Hitler leaves over," said Roffi. "Italy is about to be a client state. The relationship of a jackal to a tiger."

"Speaking of relationships," said Don Juan's grandfather pleasantly, "who do you think is really behind this unusual gathering Germaine has arranged?"

"I had assumed it was you," said Roffi, genuinely surprised.

"So had I," murmured Don Juan.

They all looked at each other quizzically and laughed.

The dining room at the Chateau D'Albret faces south toward the Oise and is modeled very loosely on the Hall of Mirrors at Versailles. That is to say it has mirrored panels on three sides of the room. Gilded rococo motifs separate the panels and climb to the ceiling, where there is an immense painting of phony bucolic life by the painter Boucher after a theme by the philosopher Rousseau. This dates from the original castle. The third side of the dining room opens through a series of French windows onto a pond once ornamental but turned into a practical swimming pool by Germaine D'Albret. Huge semi-opaque curtains draw across the French windows at midday, excluding the sun from the dining room but silhouetting to some extent any persons who may be moving around the pool.

Into this dining room filed the Princess D'Albret's guests for luncheon that day. A majordomo presided over a staff that outnumbered the guests by almost two to one. Footmen stood behind every chair, and these were, to Don Juan's way of thinking, very oddly arranged. The table was not large. Of the eight invited industrialists, six sat facing the curtained windows, while two sat at the ends of the table. Only Germaine and Don Juan sat with their backs to the window, but they could, of course, see the curtains in the mirrored panels facing them behind the other guests.

Don Juan had stuck close to his grandfather during the greetings in the salon outside the dining room. There were no women guests, and Germaine arrived only at the last moment before lunch was announced, so that he had ample leisure to examine the faces of these powerful men his grandfather insisted on calling rogues, almost to their faces.

Few urges and emotions so clearly mark the face, Don Juan reflected, as the acquisitive instinct. A feral watchfulness in the eyes. The mouth serving its role of trap, biting off emotion, issuing siren songs to the weak and impressionable. Sensuality of the "I must have it, give it to me" variety was there, too. They were an unlovely group. Lord Brasenose, a tiny sparrow of a Yorkshire industrialist with an appropriately bulbous nose. Bruckner, a cadaverous, balding Hanoverian. Laval resembled a flea-market dealer whose five-o'clock shadow grew almost as one watched it. He had quite recently been both premier and foreign minister of France, and expected to be so again. One guest failed to fit into the prevailing mold. He was an American lawyer friend of Don Juan's grandfather, a good-looking, burly, hearty man called Allen Dulles.

The moment they were all seated at table, Germaine made an announcement.

"Gentlemen. You may feel that I have been selfish in not inviting feminine company to join us at lunch. However, for the last course there will be sixteen odalisques and a number of charming Moroccan boys in the pool outside from whom to choose. Other calmer pleasures can be arranged. In the meantime I need your advice."

Germaine paused. Outside the curtained windows, the voices of young women could be heard over occasional splashes and laughter. Sometimes their shadows appeared tantalizingly against the curtains, a fine pair of hips or a soft lurch of a breast in movement. The industrialists found themselves in the unique position of theatergoers who have to complete their own "overture" before the curtain can go up.

The silence that followed while they gazed collectively at the curtain had to be broken again by Germaine.

"Will there be war?" she asked.

"Hitler doesn't want war," said Bruckner dutifully, admitting by implication that the actions of Adolf Hitler were the only likely *casus belli*.

"The dog does not wish to be punished for raiding the larder," said Brasenose. "If he takes Poland, having swallowed first Austria and then Czechoslovakia, there will be war. We and the French have guaranteed Poland's frontier."

"He will march into Poland, everything points to it," said Don Juan's grandfather.

"Does anyone think there will not be war?" asked Germaine.

Only Laval thought it could be averted. That France would come to see that Poland was dispensable. That the British might make a token declaration of war, but would soon conclude a peace.

"The British will naturally not fight for long without allies," he concluded. "Even America is unlikely to join her. Kennedy, Roosevelt's envoy in London, and Bullitt, his envoy in Paris, are both anti-British."

"So you conclude," said Germaine, "that there will be war, but not very much war?"

There was a murmur of agreement. She asked her second question.

"I believe almost everyone here has, as I do, interests on both sides of the fence. What is to be done to safeguard those interests while hostilities last?"

"I think our American friend, Mr. Allen Dulles, is the person who will give you the best answer to that question," said Don Juan's grandfather. "Throughout our civil war the American Telephone and Telegraph Company served both sides with admirable impartiality."

The conversation turned to the value of holding companies in Switzerland, the almost certain neutral among the European nations. Mr. Dulles promised to add the solving of the princess's little problem to many similar ones he was to handle in the ensuing years.

Don Juan was fascinated to realize that while the *terrine de viande Mirasol* was slipping down their throats, eased on its way by good Bollinger champagne, a Swiss-based cartel had virtually come into existence.

While a delicious *salade de poisson ravigote* appeared, hand in hand with a pleasant Sancerre, Don Juan's grandfather made a number of deals to sell the very best of the new French tanks, the R-35, to Yugoslavia, Turkey, and Romania.

With the *filet de boeuf jardinière*, a Chambolle-Musigny added fire to the spirit of the marketplace around the table, and French 25mm antitank guns, American Curtis P-36 fighters, Martin and Douglas light bombers, Chance-Vought dive-bombers, were sought, offered, and sold. Only Bruckner, to whom several men present appealed for German Stuka dive-bombers for their clients, refused, lending credence to Brasenose's certainty that Hitler intended to use every last one of them against the Polish army and then "on us."

The meal came to a crescendo with the *pêches aux framboises Antoinette* and a superb Latour *blanche*. What they needed, everyone agreed in a chorus of amiable accord, was a series of limited wars.

Clean wars, short wars, wars that must naturally, whenever possible, be won by the "right." However, parliamentary democracy seemed to Don Juan to be unexpectedly popular among these moguls. Bruckner thought parliaments corrupt by definition. Laval, always pragmatic, found them essentially impractical. But the others felt they provided, when stable, as in England and America, a good climate for business. Dictators were convenient because of their predilection for war, but they showed a regrettable tendency to ideological rashness.

And then the flushed faces of the eaters and drinkers and buyers and sellers fell into expectant repose. The curtains to the swimming pool were being opened by the footmen. The last course of this memorable meal was on view to the diners.

Don Juan could see the girls in the mirror. A few stood or sat around the pool, shinily oiled against the sun. The rest were playing with inflated balls in the pool. They were varied as to coloring—indeed, one looked Indian with the big, tight melon breasts of her race, and two were black, with the very delicate features of Central Africa. All were naked. Not one that Don Juan could see looked much over eighteen, and most looked younger. They stared in through the windows as the curtains opened, peering into the shadowed room at the diners.

Germaine had not risen from the table. No man present was so ill bred as to move before his hostess, and she had called her majordomo to her side and whispered to him. At his signal the curtains now closed again.

"Gentlemen. I opened the curtains so that you could see what was there and reflect for a few minutes on whether or not you want to take an odalisque with you to your siesta. God knows, I am not forcing them on you. They have none of them yet started work as courtesans, although naturally they will unless any is fortunate enough to have one of you adopt her, as it were. They are all the freshest that can be obtained. None speaks any Western European language. They are Estonian, Turkish, Hungarian, Nilotic, Circassian, Rajahstan, Siamese, Polynesian, and Yemeni Jewish. None can read. They have no idea who you are. I have had them collected for their beauty and variety. All are willing. That goes without saying. But some may be sad. You see, they are all virgins."

It can have been a rare sight indeed to see any single one of the men present dumbfounded, but the sight of them collectively gaping at Germaine D'Albret almost made Don Juan laugh out loud, loathsome as he found her announcement to be. But she was speaking again, clearly enjoying the sensation she had caused.

"Before you leave to select whatever pleases you, I wish to ask Don Juan for his reaction to our conversation. He represents the youth who will have to fight the wars you so blithely propose. He is also in much the same situation as myself, since he is, I understand, his grandfather's heir. Don Juan?"

"You give me this cue at an unenviable moment, Germaine. The pack has the scent. I am not a moralist, but I do have ideals. You are pirates, all of you. But since my experience of the civil war, I realize that there are political parties with high-flown ideologies every bit as rapacious as you. At least your acquisitiveness is individual and warm-blooded. Their life-denying dogma is often as cold as ice. I have always known that my grandfather is a *condottiere*. Because I cannot be like him doesn't mean I don't respect him. He is as honest a man in his way as any I know, and far from being a hypocrite. No, the real monster here is Germaine, with her Neapolitan ice cream of virgins. Her cynicism about our sex, gentlemen, is total. She has chosen girls who will submit to you, speechless if you hurt them, as you will be speechless to say a kind word to them. Her reading of all of you is that you are simply beasts of prey. She may be right. I hope she is not."

He had risen to his feet. Germaine looked up at him as amazed as the men had been when shown the girls.

"I am going straight back to Paris, Grandfather. Will I see you there?"

"I'll come with you, my boy. Thank you, Princess, but *this* is not to my taste. If you had offered yourself, it would have been different. You are not only beautiful, but *vicieuse*. That is more in my line. Excuse me."

"You Judas! You camel's crack! You unmitigated shit, Juan!" shrieked Germaine. "You pompous bastard! Who are *you* to suddenly be 'holier than thou'?"

"A lover of women, Germaine," said Don Juan over his shoulder as he left the room.

As they drove past the chateau on their way to Paris, Don Juan and his grandfather could see the swimming-pool terrace—Bruckner and three others with large bath towels, and the girls of their choice emerging rather timidly from the pool. The German stooped to dry the little fair-haired girl (the Circassian? Don Juan wondered). The last they saw, he was lifting each of her breasts to his mouth with the towel. She stood quite still, looking at his bald head like a paralyzed rabbit.

"You are a remarkable boy, Juan," said his grandfather. "Before you are through, the princess will offer you her very life on your terms."

Don Juan stared at his grandfather in amazement.

"D'you think I did that to attract her the more?"

"Didn't you?"

"Absolutely not."

"While my things were being packed she came and implored me to intercede for her. She has never been treated like that before. I suspect it excites her beyond anything."

"Grandfather, I'd rather we talked about the war. Will France expel me as an alien if that happens?"

"I don't know. But you will keep in touch with Mr. Dulles in New York and with Maître Barass here in Paris. I will speak to them both. A return to Spain, I'm sorry to say, is as yet out of the question."

They talked of Don Juan's future as a painter and as duke, when he should come into his inheritance. Only as they were entering Paris did the old man return to the subject of the princess.

"It would not have displeased me—had she been younger, naturally—if you had seen your way eventually to marrying the princess. It would have made us the most powerful family in Europe."

"It is true," Don Juan mused aloud, "that she is a woman with an extraordinary imagination. She brings to sex what Diaghilev brought to the ballet. Consummate theatricality."

"So you do not dislike her?"

"Put it this way, Grandfather—I hated the play she was offering us today. It was the theater of cruelty, and that is not to my taste. But there are pieces of theater, I suspect, with which she could still tempt me."

"Then I will tell you what she had planned for you this evening. She called it the Cesare Borgia game. You will recall that Cesare Borgia was the illegitimate son of the pope?"

"Yes, he married a child princess of France."

"Indeed, she was thirteen when they delivered her to the Borgia. He had a wager with the pope, his father, that each time he possessed her on the wedding night, he would give a great shout and a horseman waiting in the courtyard below his bridal chamber would ride post to his papal father with the news. Five riders set out that night. I forget what the wager was, exactly. A principality, perhaps, or a monopoly—the Borgias were very fond of monopolies."

"A trusting pontiff. He should have known how boastful Italians are in these matters!" said Don Juan. "But what variation of this game was in Germaine's mind?"

"Why, if all of us had decided to deflower one of her exotic menagerie this afternoon, it would have left at least eight virgins for you tonight. More, perhaps, because the little Moorish boys were there in case the Englishman, Brasenose, preferred them. She had constructed a small green baize theater in the billiard room. She hoped that you might have entertained us by popping them all after dinner on a bed that resembled a billiard table. The blood of each virgin on the green baize would confirm the score. We were to wager, like the old pontiff, on how many you would achieve. I must confess I was curious."

"Never would I have consented to that. Never," said Don Juan vehemently.

"Puritanism, my boy? Or still that aversion to cruelty? Please tell me. I am anxious to understand you."

"I am not given to introspection, Grandfather. But I will try. The soul of woman is what intrigues me. Her collective soul. I do not comprehend it as good or evil, it manifests itself as both. I see it, that soul that women carry around in common, as the one great metaphysical obsession of my life. As some people search for a nirvana, an ultimate obliteration of self in a oneness with the life force, so I feel impelled to find the meaning of my life, indeed all life, in woman, through woman. Physical relations with individual women are for me an adoration as well as a quest. The banality of treating those extraordinary separate cosmoses that each and every one of those girls of Germaine's represents as if they were a cross between an engineering problem and an athletic feat is nauseating. Worse, it is, for me at least, sacrilege!"

"It is one of the great griefs of my old age, Juan, that I shall not, in the nature of things, be likely to see how your life unfolds. The challenge you have given yourself with this metaphysical quest of yours seems to me more terrifying than the pact Faust made with the Devil. The anti-Christian Prince of Darkness is, after all, a predictable old thing, rather like myself. But Woman—there is a genie that should be kept securely in her bottle."

Don Juan's grandfather was right. The Princess D'Albret continued to issue many charming and amusing invitations to Don Juan, and she never again referred to his defection at the virgin lunch. He himself enjoyed inviting her to the theater. That fall they went to see *Cyrano* and *Madame Sans-Gêne* at the Comédie Française.

"If you had not been born beautiful," said Germaine to Don Juan after they had seen *Cyrano de Bergerac*, "I can imagine that you might have developed very much like the long-nosed one. That is to say, in your spirit."

With Mireille he went to listen to that adorable *diseuse* Lucienne

Boyer at her club in the Rue Volney and to Maurice Chevalier at the Casino de Paris.

Aube he took to see Jean Giraudoux's *Ondine*, and to the Théâtre Montparnasse to see *Phèdre*.

On the third of September came the declaration of war by Britain and France which formally started World War II.

He had spent the night with Mireille. The British declaration was expected, and he tuned the radio to the BBC.

The English announcer said that unless the German government gave satisfactory assurances by eleven A.M. that it would withdraw its troops from Poland, "a state of war will exist between our two countries."

"Papa and all the other communists are so confused," said Mireille in her lovely voice. "The Hitler-Stalin Pact has numbed their senses. It's as if I asked my snakes to imagine they have legs."

By the time Aube arrived at the Avenue Foch for a small dinner party he was giving for émigré Spaniards in Paris, it was known that France was also at war. The Spanish party were gleeful. Perhaps the Fascists would at last get a taste of their own medicine. France, after all, had beaten Germany in 1918.

But Aube was glum. She asked to be excused before the end of dinner, and Don Juan knew that what was known as the Cabinet of the Mistresses was far from unified about the war. They still hoped it might just go away. He ordered her a cab. The address she gave was in the Place du Palais Bourbon. It was Reynaud's address. The plot to replace Madame de Crussol's Daladier with Madame de Porte's Reynaud was reaching its final stage. Aube had recently confided in Don Juan that only Reynaud, supported by Hélène, had the energy to prosecute the war. If that failed she would have her own candidate. But whether health or armaments she refused to divulge. The Phony War, as it was called, had started.

In the winter of 1939–40 the French army faced the German army, fresh from its triumph in Poland, across that monument to military wishful thinking, the Maginot Line. Scarcely a shot was fired in anger for seven months.

During these months, however, activity continued in other areas. Colonel de Gaulle besieged the commander in chief, General Gamelin, Daladier, in his role as defense minister, Reynaud, and eighty of the principal military and civilian figures in France with the need for armored divisions supported by coordinated air power and much else. The wretched colonel was only too aware that the

Germans were using *his textbook* to do just this. Only Reynaud paid any attention, and he lacked the power as yet to act. The Germans themselves, who had tried out their version of de Gaulle's theories, which they called *Blitzkrieg,* on the hapless Poles, could not believe that the French high command had continued the World War I policy of tanks divided up among infantry units to be used mainly in support of foot soldiers.

The Germans trained assiduously to meet a French army that didn't exist, except as a number of men rather reluctantly under arms. An army which they assumed had radios, whereas it didn't. Even General Gamelin had no radio. It took twenty-four hours for new orders to reach divisional level at the front. An army that they assumed had coordinated air support, already developed in Spain. Whereas it didn't. An army that, for all their intelligence told them to the contrary, must be influenced into using tanks as de Gaulle had suggested. Not only was the French army not prepared to follow de Gaulle's ideas, it believed against all logic in moving tanks by train. Nor had anyone considered the need to send gasoline trucks with them to refuel them. Indeed, Don Juan's grandfather and others were allowed to sell half of France's tank production in those months to other states. Finally, the Germans believed that the French would show the courage and patriotism they had manifested in 1914–18. In the event, when the German onslaught came, about a third of the French army turned and literally ran for home. The long preparation of the Germans before their final attack in May 1940 was, therefore, unnecessary. But when it came it was thorough enough to destroy the French, Dutch, Belgian, and British armies in Europe in three weeks. In just over a month from the opening of the German attack, France sued for peace, asking for an armistice.

During those deceptively peaceful months until May, Don Juan threw himself into his work at the Beaux-Arts. He went to lectures by Matisse and Fernand Léger and by Paul Colin, the *affichiste.* He started to move out of the confines of the colored drawing, in which he was already amazingly proficient, into the realms of pure color, color rhythm, and the counterpoints of shapes and kinds of light. He learned to make his own paints from pigments, his own canvases from sisal and hemp. At the École des Arts Décoratifs he started to study the techniques of woodcuts and copperplates.

The joy this work gave him was such that, in addition to Mireille and Aube and Germaine, he had dozens of happy encounters that came about because the women around him sensed his energy, his sense of wonder at the world his artist's eye increasingly revealed to him.

Typical of these encounters was the time when he took ten of his canvases to a cinema theater where they were to be shown in the foyer. The girl from the management who helped him hang them was plain and dumpy, but behind rather thick glasses she had eyes the color of gentians. As they struggled to hang one of the canvases, he saw in her face an inkling of the passion she probably had to save for her dreams. He was reminded of Henrietta's old American friend H. L. Mencken, who had written that "there is a special place in heaven for the man who winks at a homely girl." But as he sensed the promise of her womanliness he did not need the gift of heaven to desire her.

"Mademoiselle," he said. "I am going to say something you may find impossibly impertinent. I would like to be your lover now, this afternoon. To express to you my joy at your being the woman you are. If you only allow me to kiss those extraordinary eyes, it will be enough to make this day utterly memorable. What do you say?"

When she had recovered from her surprise, she said, "Yes."

Her lovemaking moved him more than that of Aube or Germaine. But she lacked Mireille's vision of the world. In that sense, poor girl, she was myopic. She saw only Don Juan. Gently he disengaged from her, leaving her always the memory of an afternoon, like a pressed flower in an old book.

Daladier lost the premiership in March, bringing Reynaud to supreme power but leaving the former prime minister still holding the ministry of defense. For Aube de Tournelle's part in this partial putsch, she was punished by Madame de Crussol, who caused the exiled Admiral de Tournelle to be recalled to Paris for reassignment. In the meantime, Don Juan and the cabinet ministers concerned had to make themselves scarce while Aube saw to the creature comforts of the old salt.

Mireille went on a tour of the provinces in April with part of the Foire d'Orsay. So Don Juan, who was trying to finish enough canvases to send to America for Henrietta to organize a one-man show, now found himself on one of his periodic fasts from love. He dined at home nightly in the house on the Avenue Foch, working incessantly when he was not at his classes. Germaine occasionally came by to make love to him, always bringing with her some new and piquant fantasy. But he made her understand that by May he hoped to be free to play; in the meantime he intended that work must come first.

The French press and radio were heavily censored at that time, as always, and carried no real news of the developing battle after the attack began on May 9. Although by May 26 the total defeat of the Allies on the continent was already assured, no one in Paris had any idea that this was the case. Nor was this surprising. The French government of Paul Reynaud still had trouble getting any accurate reports from its commanders, who, denying themselves radios and faced for the first time with the pace of modern war, were usually whole days behind in their grasp of actual events on the front.

The evacuation of 350,000 men from Dunkirk was announced by the BBC as if it were a victory. Don Juan, who listened to the British radio because of its superior objectivity, was astounded.

Soon thereafter there was a telephone call from Germaine.

"You have heard that those *salauds* of English have left us on our own?" were her first words.

"They seem to have saved their army. It was on the radio."

"Have you heard how far into France the Germans have gotten?"

"The papers talk only of rectifications of the front, of shortening our line now the battle in Belgium is over. The BBC, however, let it slip that the Germans may have taken half a million Allied prisoners in Belgium. It sounds very serious for our side."

"My dear, yesterday I was leaving to drive to Laon to see Letitia de Moeurs. She telephoned to say the Germans were entering the town. It's only twenty miles away! I'm in the middle of closing the chateau. Meanwhile, the servants say that our troops are running, *running* down the road toward Paris without their arms."

"Do you need any help with closing the chateau?"

"No, but I'd like you to talk to Aube de Tournelle and find out what exactly is expected to happen. One does not want to be caught in a siege of Paris."

Don Juan finally reached Aube at Chanel's. The *tout Paris* were all buying traveling clothes, at which the illustrious Coco was thought to excel. The admiral was with her, dressed in rather sporting mufti, and Don Juan was introduced as the son of the celebrated duchess.

"It is good to see you, Admiral. How do you view the war at this point?"

"The British have ratted on us. That is evident," said the admiral, gazing with undisguised admiration at an aging *vendeuse* with a pronounced limp and a cane.

"But the front before Paris—do you think it will hold?" Don Juan asked this of the admiral and Aube both, hoping the latter would answer. But Aube avoided his eyes.

"It can only be a matter of time before the marshal assumes his destiny," said the admiral. "There will be an honorable peace very soon."

"Marshal?" Don Juan was bemused.

"Many of us are coming to agree with Laval, with Baudouin, with the new commander in chief, General Weygand, that Marshal Pétain, France's greatest living hero, must save us now," said Aube brightly, but with a taut look of strain on her face. "Even Reynaud begins to see it. Hélène de Portes herself feels an armistice with the Germans is for the best. But it will take the marshal to get us the best terms."

"Then there is no need to leave Paris?"

"On the contrary, Paris will be totally empty when the Germans get here. We are leaving and taking French civilization with us," said Aube, sounding like one who speaks of fighting on to the last.

"Where will you go?" Don Juan caught himself asking this momentous question as if he were politely inquiring about holiday plans.

"To Bordeaux. We always go to Bordeaux," said the admiral, recalling that the disasters which every fifty years or so rendered the French capital up to its enemies had made of this migration a norm.

"How long have we got? Here in Paris?" asked Don Juan.

"I doubt if the government will be here after the fifth of June," said Aube, looking fixedly at Don Juan now, her eyes filled with tears. The admiral supposed she was crying for France.

"Nothing to cry about, my rabbit," he said. "We will rebuild a better France when the marshal takes over. For myself, I cannot wait for La Gueuse * to die. Do you like that smart linen traveling coat, Aube?" The admiral poked the old *vendeuse* in the back as if he were testing the quality of a tempting fowl and pointed out the coat he liked. Don Juan kissed Aube's hand and said goodbye.

Germaine had already contacted the Wagons-Lits Pullman Company and ordered her train when Don Juan called her with the news. Three trucks arrived in Paris next day with her clothes and her more important pictures from the chateau on the Oise. When on June 2, 1940, her train pulled out of the Gare de Lyons on its way south to Nice, via Lyons and Grenoble, it consisted of one first-class and two second-class carriages, the Princess's private-suite car, her restaurant car, a restaurant car (second-class) for the servants, and three freight cars, besides the locomotive. Virtually all of the rolling stock was part of Germaine's private property with which she normally conducted her European travel. However, it was unusual to go to the South of France in the summer. The train was normally used for taking her or her guests south in the winter months, when it

* France's Third Republic.

was fashionable to stay in one's house on the Côte d'Azur. Tourists were still rare. The word "tourist" then had the same social connotation in Europe as "immigrant" has always had in America.

The freight cars were full of the better furniture from the Paris houses of the duchess and the Princess D'Albret. They also contained the best of their paintings and sizable portions of their huge wardrobes. The administrators and servants, according to their ranks, occupied the first- and second-class carriages. The princess's dining room divided her part of the train from theirs. Her private-suite car consisted of a bedroom and a living room and had originally been designed for the Empress Eugenie, just before the fall of the Second Empire to the German invasion of 1871.

As Germaine and Don Juan sat in the elegant little dining room of the train, starting to eat their lunch and waiting for the train to leave the station, Aristide, the majordomo, hurried in, disturbing their enjoyment of a marvelous watercress mousse and some Bayonne ham. She had just announced that Baudelaire's *Les Fleurs du mal* was the one book she had bought for their amusement on the journey.

"Madame la Princesse," said Aristide, "the most mortifying thing is happening. A great crowd is gathering and insisting on sharing our quarters. So many people are finding difficulty in leaving Paris."

"You mean they have got onto the train?" Germaine was shocked.

"No, madame, the doors are locked. But they wish to climb through the windows."

"Fetch me the engine driver."

"At once, Madame la Princesse."

Two minutes later the train's engineer appeared, sweating profusely from the heat of the locomotive's steam furnace.

"Madame?" he asked, standing awkwardly in this grand little dining room with its gilt and plush.

"Why cannot we leave at once, my friend?"

"My stoker is not here. I heard they have called him to the colors. Which is ridiculous. He is of a reserved occupation, in the national interest. Meanwhile I am stoking myself."

"I will help you," said Don Juan at once, hating the exclusion of people from the train but knowing that it might never leave if the huge crowds at the barriers thought they could all get on.

When he regained Germaine's carriage five hours later, they were puffing steadily through the Nivernais countryside south of Melun. Don Juan was gray with soot all over except his face, which was partly black, except for where he had been covered by goggles lent him by the train engineer. Germaine was sleeping in the Empress Eugenie's neat little four-poster when she was awakened by Don Juan grinning down at her, his teeth showing very white in his black face, a Gauloise drooping from his lips. He spoke in the argot of the Paris workman.

"Are you going to give me a piece of pink ham *en croûte* now, woman, or do I have to wait till you've drawn me a bath?"

Germaine screamed with pleasure at this propitious game.

"You know you hate to bathe until you've had me, you brute," she whined. "You like to see all the soot and sweat you can wipe off on me, beast!"

Don Juan lifted her off the bed and held her with one hand supporting her buttocks, the other cradling her head. Leaning her against the bedroom partition, he entered her in a series of sweeping motions, leaving her body entirely each time, but driving deep with each stoke of her furnace. Germaine felt him so deep inside her that she wondered if she could long contain the flood that started to come almost at once, for somehow these stunning strokes plus the smell of coal and sweat above Don Juan's own familiar smell was all unbearably exciting.

Feeling the hot pumping of her good soup, he decided to await his own pleasure till she should give him his bath.

He stood after he had dropped her on the bed, hauling off his clothes, shouting for wine and bread and some cassoulet and his bath. Germaine played her role as best she could, scurrying to the dining room to get his food and drink, bringing no glass or plate but letting him tear at the good baguette of bread with his hands and drink the rough servant's *ordinaire* from the neck of the bottle. Then, with a little help from a twittering maid who glimpsed Don Juan's magnificent bareness through the carriage door, she managed to achieve a hip bath full of hot water.

He sat in the bath and allowed her to scrub him.

"I feel like one of those women in Lawrence's books," said Germaine. "Not Lady Chatterley, but one of the miners' wives. I have just been accorded late in life, and much to my surprise, an orgasm. Can it be morally right to have had this pleasure with the mindless brute whose back I must scrub each day, I ask myself?"

"You must think of it as socially just, woman," said Don Juan. "Now drops your tits into these suds and let me clap them around my upstanding principal."

They slept together till almost nine that night, clinging close in the swinging, rattling train, waking twice to make love to the rhythm of the steel wheels hitting the joint in the rails. Tucker tucker bang, tucker tucker bang, tucker tucker bang bang.

She awoke just before nine o'clock and went to the kitchen to carefully choose their dinner. She had never before felt so happy, and wished this enchanted journey into domesticity with Don Juan might go on forever. The cooks had neither quails nor woodcock, having to remind her of the month when she asked for them. Normally she would have scowled. Not on this occasion. They had, however, fat duck, plump capons, and some fine-looking geese. These last birds were carried live, having to suffer being stuffed each day to enlarge their livers. She ordered that the geese be killed instead for cassoulet on the morrow, and chose duck for dinner, telling them to cook it in the Norman way with apples, bread, cinnamon, white wine, stock, Calvados, and cream. It was to be a simple peasant meal eaten in bed on a tray. She asked for three ducks for each of them, since that was all they would be eating, and ordered just two bottles of Bordeaux, a simple Léoville-Poyferré that the shaking train could not too seriously bruise before they drank it.

When the meal was ready they brought it on a tray. She woke him delicately, speaking a shrill, girlish English, a language that, like most French women of her class and epoch, she had learned at school in England.

"Albert, beloved, we will be in dear Scotland in just a few hours. We have ordered a light meal. The sort of thing we expect our dear Scots gillies' sweet wives bring them after a hard day's stalking in the heather."

"Zis is far too rich a dish at zis hour, Vicky!" exclaimed Don Juan, supposing rightly that he was addressing Queen Victoria, and had himself, in his sleep, turned into her German consort, Prince Albert. "I vould haf preferred Sauerbrauten mit Spiegeleier und Pfefferkuchen. Mit Liebfraumilch or Nacktarsch or Peisporter."

"Albert, please. We are nowhere near amused. German wines all have horrid rude names. We hate them. Wife's milk, Naked Ass, or Pisspot, indeed! We ask you, Albert, dear, what kind of names are those for bottles of hock?"

"Names that put Chermans in ze mood, Vicky, dear," said Don Juan, tearing off a leg of duck and starting to eat salaciously.

"But Albert, we already have six boys and five girls," said Victoria/Germaine primly.

"You are wronk. It is fife boys and six girls. You should get Disraeli to tell you how to be counting instead of talking literature mit him and letting him flatter you, sayink, 'We authors, Ma'am,' et cetera."

"We asked that unfortunate Mr. Havelock Ellis the other day if there was any hope of someone inventing birth control someday soon. He put us onto Florence Nightingale. 'Ma'am,' she said"——Germaine pursed her lips into the shape of a squeezed persimmon——"'my advice to you is to blow the blighter!'"

"Blow? Vot could she haf been meanink, Vicky?" asked Don Juan/Albert, as if alarmed. "Maybe ze introduction of a bagpipe into ze zexual eqvation? No, zer is zuch a zing as being too Zcottish!"

Both Germaine and Don Juan were giggling a good deal by this time, and their mouths and fingers were covered with grease from the ducks, and they had taken long drafts of the Bordeaux wine to cut and complement the richness of the birds. Germaine lifted the sheet that covered Don Juan's loins, saying, "First we lift the kilt, says Florence Nightingale. A startled hare will be found regarding us from a thicket. Anoint it with a little duck's grease, add a soupçon of wine. Blow or suck according to taste."

And Germaine, abandoning her sketch, harried the hare with lips the like of which Prince Albert cannot have even dreamed. And yet again, what do *we* know?

They were subjected to long waits on sidings while trains loaded with troops trundled south. Watching one of these trains pass during the night, Don Juan wondered whom they were going to fight. Perhaps they were going to the North African colonies to continue the war from there, or perhaps Mussolini's Italy would invade the south of France? He remembered Signor Roffi's words about Italy's role in this war, that of jackal.

He had made a roster with two of the strongest of Germaine's footmen to help with the stoking of the locomotive's furnace. At four A.M. there was a knocking on the bedroom door to tell him it was his turn again. Germaine came with him, a silk scarf at her throat, but wearing a sensible trench coat, its lynx collar turned up against the cool night air.

The locomotive was a massive Pacific horizontal five-tube boiler, the monarch of French steam engines. Don Juan thought it seemed like some fabled beast at rest. From its great chimney snout a steady rhythmic jet of steam breathed a pale and swirling cloud against the clear June night sky. Somewhere behind them the guard tapped the wheels of the train with his hammer, sounding like a distant smith honing some heavy weapon. The sharp smell of axle oil and coal increased as they approached the cab of the locomotive. They found the engineer dozing in a sleeping bag by the tracks, the dinner pail Madame Engineer had prepared for him close by with a thermos of coffee in it.

"Please don't move, monsieur," said Germaine, seeing that he was about to struggle to his feet in deference to her presence. "We are waiting for the signals to change?"

"Evidently, madame. There is much troop traffic tonight."

Don Juan was intrigued at Germaine's mellowness that night. Staff were normally considered only in the most peripheral way by the Princess D'Albret. It was not that she was cruel to them, but, like his mother, she considered them to have been irrevocably cast in roles that would last a lifetime. Her own role, unaltered still, would last as long.

Far down the line, on the horizon past the signal box, a light was burning steadily brighter, and from its direction came the pounding rhythm of the train they were awaiting. When it passed them by, its windows dark with blackout, its gleaming coaches, glimpsed in the light from their locomotive, a bluish gray, the engineer looked at his watch and said, "That, at least, is normal. The Blue Train will be in Paris more or less on time this morning."

As they passed through the dimly lit stations of Auxerre and Avallon, Don Juan, stripped to the waist, stoked hard, feeding the fiery mouth of the open furnace with rhythmic thrusts of his coal-laden shovel. The engineer watched the line ahead, one hand always near the shining brass valves that controlled the locomotive. And the steam engine itself roared its special cacophony of sounds, the deep huffing breath of the used steam escaping in sharp bursts, the hard metallic thrust of the oiled pistons hurling the great steel wheels around and around, screaming and clicking against the jointed rails on the roadbed.

Germaine felt, as she stood on the footplate, her legs planted firmly apart to keep her balance, one gloved hand gripping the protective rail at the open side of the cab, the sharp counterpoint of her femininity to this huge masculine mass, this Moloch of power and thrust that took them all storming southward that night.

On rare visits to her shipyards and steel plants, she had been repelled by the noise and the uncompromising hardness of heavy industry. Its total masculinity of image and character was not so much repellent as entirely alien to her. On this night, however, she rode the locomotive as Europa might have ridden the Zeus bull, frightened but enchanted. The cool wind rushing by filled her hair, so that it trailed in the slipstream of the engine among the firefly sparks from the furnace. The enormous mechanical beast beneath her sent her its metallic pulses through the shivering footplate and up into the apex of her thighs. Watching Don Juan, his body gray-black again and soot-streaked with the streaming sweat of his exertions, she felt each thrust of his hard-aimed shovel as if her very bowels were the furnace.

She came, as women sometimes do, alone, with a small but ineffably sweet *jouisse* that glazed her thighs and warmed her whole body.

When Don Juan stopped stoking, she wiped his brow with her silk scarf and could not stop herself from saying quite loudly and joyously in his ear, "I love you!"

During the morning, as the train made its slow progress through Burgundy, between Autun and Chalon, they awoke again in their bed to find sunny vineyards outside the windows and their breakfast champagne cooling beside them.

"I must have coffee, too," said Don Juan, savoring a huge hunger that excess of love and stoking seemed to have given him. "D'you think they could manage some oysters, a few eggs done any old way, but poached in cream would be good, closely followed by, I believe, a huge *tournedo*, rather rare, and then, I think, something sweet—you, Germaine darling, with a little *mousse au chocolat* in your navel and a spoonful of pear-blossom honey to help me coax open your rose?"

While Germaine hurried off to the kitchen to give the orders for this lucullan breakfast, he lay abed thinking of her words from the night before. The Germaines of this world made their own rules. When you were not only unimaginably rich but also brilliant, too much was endlessly becoming available to you, too many new experiences, too many new people, for love, that often acquisitive emotion, to be of much relevance. He thought of those pathetic and dim-witted American heiresses Duke and Hutton, essentially suburban people bewildered by their unearned plenty, needing love as people need clothes, going through the vulgar motions of marrying to sanctify their copulations with mindless, titled studs. How splendidly different was Germaine. Since Don Juan had himself always counted on money he had never even thought to have quantified, he found himself quite indifferent to Germaine's wealth. He admired, without having any particular wish to emulate, the panache with which she spent it. Where money bought beauty and sensual pleasure, his motto was "Give me excess of it." But he knew that, with Germaine, surfeit could easily come, like the sickening virgins' lunch. On reflection, and this journey was wonderful enough for him to accord her that, he knew he could never love Germaine. She was simply, at this moment, his favorite leading lady in the unfolding comedy of his life.

At the end of the perfect breakfast, he lay, his head cradled upon her thigh, and gently opened the outer leaves of her rose. Before taking the spoon from the honey, he suddenly gave a great shout of laughter that made her abruptly close her thighs and pull at his hair in pique.

"What was that for? Aren't you enjoying your breakfast?"

"The best I ever had," said Don Juan, trying to regain his composure. "I was thinking of the *Romance of the Rose.*"

"That long medieval poem about one man's hunt for the pudenda?"

"Exactly. Two thirteenth-century poets, living forty years apart, taking over a century to describe one lover's approach to the rose, and taking twenty-one thousand, seven hundred and seventy-five lines of verse from setting out on the romance to reaching the consummation. And here we have made of it simply the apogee of an hour-long breakfast."

Germaine laughed her total laugh and opened again her thighs. The rose, open before, had returned to being a bud. He opened the petals gently with his tongue and contemplated it anew, watching the dew gather slowly around the stem.

"I remember that the poet said, 'The rose seemed so lovely to me that I wanted to explore it to its depths.' If he could, after all that, have persuaded the god of love to make him infinitely small so that he could dive in . . . I wonder, what then?"

"We would have had another twenty thousand lines about his journeys within!" interrupted Germaine languidly. "You poets do go on so. . . ."

Don Juan put into the place of the stamen some drops of hymetic honey and followed it with his tongue. Neither spoke again for some time, and when they did it was to invent another game.

Through to the Lyonnais he played Talleyrand to her Madame de Staël. He limped elegantly about, and she spoke volubly in an atrocious French Swiss accent. He told her he couldn't possibly make love standing unless she sent for a footstool for his shorter leg.

She decided at Vienne that she would be the virgin Empress Marie Louise, newly delivered to an impatient Napoleon who decided to deflower her in her coach while the honor guard and the attendant marshals of France and other notables waited without.

"The coach cannot have been any bigger than this bed," said Germaine. "The trouble in re-creating a proper idea of the event is the size of you, my darling. We have it on good authority that poor

Bonaparte had the smallest of weapons. I shall close my eyes, and you will have to use your little finger. In my virginal state it will be more than enough excitement for me."

Planning a late lunch, he stoked away on the locomotive as the train passed through Montélimar, Orange and Avignon. They were halted at the water tower just outside Beaucaire when he rejoined Germaine, who had been writing letters in the little living room. For some reason, he thought she looked sad as he greeted her, but they went straight in to a late lunch, where the cassoulet ordered the previous day made perfect fare for a man new to stoking.

Afterward they went to bed, and he read to her as they lay, their naked limbs entwined, but at peace. He chose from Baudelaire while she lay, her head on his breast, staring out the window at the first glories of Provence. The sunshine of the long summer evening showed them their train's shadow hurrying south. He read, and as he read, to his astonishment, she wept.

> "My child, my sister, dream
> How sweet all things would seem
> Were we in that kind land to live together,
> And there love slow and long,
> There love and die among
> Those scenes that image you, that sumptuous weather.
>
> Drowned suns that glimmer there
> Through cloud-disheveled air
> Move me with such a mystery as appears
> Within those other skies
> Of your treacherous eyes
> When I behold them shining through their tears.
>
> There, there is nothing else but grace and measure,
> Richness, quietness and pleasure.
>
> Furniture that wears
> The luster of the years
> Softly would glow within our glowing chamber,
> Flowers of rarest bloom
> Proffering their perfume
> Mixed with the vague fragrances of amber;
> Gold ceilings would there be,
> Mirrors deep as the sea,
> The walls all in Eastern splendor hung—

Nothing but should address
The soul's loneliness,
Speaking her sweet and native tongue.

There, there is nothing else but grace and measure.
Richness, quietness and pleasure.

See, sheltered from the swells
There in the still canals
Those drowsy ships that dream of sailing forth;
It is to satisfy
Your least desire, they ply
Hither through all the waters of the earth.''

She lay in his arms, listening to his heart, running her hands
over his body as if memorizing it. Night had fallen when they reached
the outskirts of Marseilles.

"Make love to me, please," she asked simply.

He did, knowing that it was not a time for words.

She did not herself come, watching instead his coming, using all
her considerable power to hasten it. Then without a word further, she
dressed and left him, as he had already guessed she would, leaving
him a letter.

The train's final destination was Nice, where Thomas Cook and
Son's faithful representative waited to take care of the duchess's
things and the princess's agents would doubtless do the same. He
watched her walking down the platform at the Marseilles station,
followed by her majordomo and her other hurrying servants. It
seemed unlikely he would ever see her again. He had no wish to open
her letter. If it contained a reproach that he had been unable to be
"in love" with her, he had no wish to read it. No envoi that it could
contain, he felt certain, could alter the inextinguishable memory of
her as a Woman. He wanted no other souvenir.

Don Juan helped stoke the locomotive on to Nice, and on the
way he threw her unopened letter into the furnace.

12
In the Fascists' Shangri-la

The tide of love, at its full surge is not withstandable. Upon the yielding spirit she comes gently, but to the proud and the fanatic heart she is a torturer with the brand of shame.

—Euripides

On June 20, 1940, Don Juan found that France had a New Order. "We, Philippe Pétain, Marshal of France," as he royally styled himself in his proclamations, had started to ordain what the life of the *new* France would be like.

"I was with you in the days of glory," he said over the radio. "At the head of the government, I shall remain with you during the dark days. Stay by my side. . . ."

The French, bewildered by defeat, listened to him. His words persuaded and reassured them. The marshal had saved France from communism and socialism, from the Jews and from the British. In a Europe controlled by a Pax Germanica, the good marshal would build a new, more virtuous France. The old slogan of the French

Revolution, "Liberty, Equality, Fraternity," was replaced by "God, Country, Family."

The South of France had for years been partially an English colony. Writers like A. E. W. Mason and E. Phillips Oppenheim and royals like the duke of Connaught presided over a British expatriate society that wintered in Nice and Cannes, Monte Carlo and Antibes. These people were now attempting to flee back to England, and the well-to-do from Paris flocked to rent the now-surplus villas of the hated English.

When the new Pétain government signed the armistice that left the Germans in control of over half the country, it was the occasion for a wave of rejoicing on the Côte d'Azur, which was exempted from German occupation. Poor Madame de Portes, who had done so much to help bring the disaster about, was not to join in the rejoicing. In the heavily laden car in which she and ex-Premier Paul Reynaud now fled to the south, a piece of luggage broke loose as they stopped at a crossroads, and broke her neck. Aube de Tournelle was forced to accompany her husband to his new assignment as governor of the French Atlantic Islands of St. Paul and Marmiton. She wrote a pathetic note to Don Juan before she left:

My dear friend,

Dreyfus on Devil's Island, Bonivard in Chillon, the count on Monte Cristo, Napoleon on St. Helena, none of them could have felt an iota of the misery I feel at this enforced exile.

Was it our fault? I ask myself this a hundred times a day.

The military accuses us, because that same pathetic, geriatric military that betrayed us rules in our stead.

But I think history may be kinder.

Poor Hélène. Poor Reynaud.

And Don Juan, whom will *he* now love? Not a Pétainist. Not a fascist. Please, not that.

We were, in our way, the real France. I cannot believe it will not someday be *our* country again.

I turn my back for you and wish I felt you still. Oh Juan, don't entirely forget.

Your Aube

Don Juan had picked up his mail from the office of Thomas Cook in Cannes. Besides the letter from Aube de Tournelle, there were letters from his mother and Henrietta, from his grandfather, and from Juliet Fitzjames. His mother's letter was, as usual, really from Henrietta.

Dear Juan,

You must get on the very next boat to the U.S.A. Europe is
clearly going to be *impossible* this season. Never has this country
been pleasanter, and I'm sure we could get you into Harvard.
Yale, we understand, is distinctly stuffy. Some people go to
Princeton, although it is in New Jersey.

We rather hope you saved the pictures from the Avenue
Foch. A cable from Germaine D'Albret was certainly reassuring.
Your mother says she supposes D'Albret has seduced you, or we
would never have had the offer of her train for the furniture.

Don't worry. She's precisely the kind of woman who should
be teaching you which end is up. Just stay away from the Juliet
Fitzjameses of this world until you're much, much older. Her
mother wrote us a most pathetic letter saying the poor girl *pines*
for you. On no account are you to go to England to see her. Come
here instead.

American universities are built side by side with girls'
colleges. Harvard has Radcliffe. The girls are called coeds, and
lead splendid modern liberalized lives. The kind of girl you ought
to marry someday when you've calmed down! So get Cook's to put
you on the very next boat, and cable us.

Mother and Henrietta

His grandfather's letter was, as usual, practical. But it also
expressed a certain euphoria on the part of the old industrialist.

Dear Grandson,

At last the moment for which Europe has been waiting. Since
Charlemagne, since Napoleon. A Europe united as a single trading
area. How long will the British be able to resist joining in such an
adventure?

Pétain and Franco are on the best of terms. Mussolini will
have to do without more than a token piece of France, and Herr
Hitler will take care of the communists in the East. The New
York Stock Exchange climbs steadily.

It is sad that with the future looking stable and the climate
for all our affairs looking so promising, you yourself should still
have to live under something of a cloud.

Let me first say that I take seriously your intention to be a
painter. My inquiries at the Beaux-Arts indicate that you will be a
very good one. In these times, even after you *succeed* it will be a
perfectly proper activity for you. A duke who is a good painter is
an oddity, but in such a family as ours, a certain distinction can
be added to our name. You will remember the case of Doña Emilia

Pardo Bazán, the Spanish Brontë, a lady of excellent family who was also a poetess and a dramatist of great renown. Made a countess in her own right for her work. No, there cannot be the slightest harm in your being a *good* painter.

So where are you to work and continue to learn?

In Spain? Out of the question for several years. Even I, with all my influence, could not save you. The details of your participation in the attack on your own castle as well as the affair with Perlmutter in the north are on your dossier. I have secured copies for our lawyers, and they all agree that *no one* could protect you here.

In England? If England does not surrender soon it will be bombed to bits by the Luftwaffe and invaded by the Wehrmacht. So, not at the moment.

In America? Your mother and Henrietta are very anxious to get you to go there. But although Henrietta writes enthusiastically about an exhibition of some paintings in a New York armory (of all places!), I personally have never heard of an American painter except Sargent, and he found it necessary to work much of the time in England, I believe. It sounds unpromising.

In Vichy France, as we must now call that part of the country reserved for the marshal's exclusive and benign rule, I can protect you. Laval—you will remember him from the D'Albret weekend—will be the real power there, and he is an old friend (I understand he, too, left before the "dessert" that day). The arts will, I believe, flourish under Vichy. One hears of almost no artists, writers, or actors going to join the mad de Gaulle in London. Only Mauriac. But be sure to stay out of Paris and the rest of the German-occupied zone in France. I have not the slightest doubt that the Germans, too, have access to records of your activities in Spain. With *them* I cannot protect you.

Finally, I recommend that you find yourself a place not too far from the Swiss frontier. I believe that the major European earthquake is over, but one never knows; there can be aftershocks.

I am sending you a letter of unlimited credit. You do not seem to be a spendthrift like your dear mother.

Your father is quite unchanged and is now entirely bedridden. Garcia sends you his respectful greetings.

Grandfather
Barcelona

Don Juan saved the letter from Juliet Fitzjames till last, as one saves a special treat. He had written to her twice during the hectic summer, talking of the affairs of France and avoiding mention of his own activities except at the Beaux-Arts. Her letter contained a photograph of a young woman he just recognized as Juliet. She was wearing a thick Fair Isle sweater and a tweed skirt which effectively disguised her figure. The photograph, being black-and-white, told nothing of her complexion, but it showed a face that so spoke of intelligence that he noticed the beauty of it second. Not that it was great beauty—the jaw was perhaps a little too square, the nose a little bit snub—but he remembered her coloring and the soft auburn hair. It was still the photograph of a girl who excited no desire in him, only a liking so strong that it amounted almost to a yearning. Her letter was that of a bright schoolgirl.

Dear Juan,

I know that you really think of France as your home much more than Spain. So you must be terribly sad at what has happened.

Oh, Juan, I'm so happy. Mummy says you can come and stay with us if you want to. They say it's still possible to leave the South of France. I made Mummy cable your Aunt Henrietta to tell her we were inviting you. I do so hope you can come.

Giles is a full-fledged RAF fighter pilot now. [The next bit of the letter had been cut out by the British war censor.]

. . . so I hope when you next see me to be a Wren. I did so want to go up to Cambridge first. But everyone says it's much better to go to University *after*. Perhaps we'll be able to go together when the war is over. I dream of that.

It is very hard, Juan, to love someone for so long at a distance. Particularly when so many awful, terrifying things are going on all around us. I found a poem the other day which perfectly expresses my feelings about it. It is by G. K. Chesterton. I have a small flat in Holland Park, London, now, quite near the Campden Hill in this poem.

> *For every tiny town or place*
> *God made the stars especially;*
> *Babies look up with owlish face*
> *And see them tangled in a tree;*
> *You saw a moon from Sussex Downs,*
> *A Sussex moon, untravelled still,*
> *I saw a moon that was the town's,*
> *The largest lamp on Campden Hill.*
>
> *Yes; Heaven is everywhere at home*
> *The big blue cap that always fits,*
> *And so it is (be calm; they come*

> to goal at last, my wandering wits),
> So it is with the heroic thing;
> This shall not end for the world's end
> And though the sullen engines swing,
> Be you not much afraid, my friend.

Consider yourself kissed, you wicked, adorable Spaniard, and if you don't send that long-promised photograph soon, I shan't leave you my stamp collection in my will!

Love and lots of scrumptious wicked kisses,

Juliet

Don Juan's impulse was to get on the next boat to England after reading Juliet's letter, but the support for his painting from his grandfather had also moved him.

He had always feared that the old industrialist would ultimately dismiss his ambition to be an artist as trivial and unworthy. Now that he had his full support, it seemed both ungrateful and stupid not to follow his advice, which was also, of course, his wish. Nor did Don Juan have any real desire to leave France and start traveling once again. Above all, he wanted to settle down and *work*, to follow the patterns and inspirations which were developing in his art. He opted for Vichy France as his temporary home without sharing any of his grandfather's enthusiasm for the new regime. But the French capacity for self-delusion and myth-making going on all around him was too fascinating a black comedy to be missed, or so it seemed at first.

Traveling at a leisurely pace up the Rhone Valley toward Savoy and the Swiss frontier, he stopped frequently to talk to all sorts and kinds of Frenchmen he met in restaurants and bars, on buses and trains. To the doddering octogenarian marshal who had presided over the most abject surrender in French history they almost all accorded something very near to worship. *"Soyez notre bon Dieu, Monsieur le Maréchal,"* said a headline in a woman's magazine. Don Juan assumed at first that this must be a lunatic fringe, but as he scanned the papers, he realized that the whole of intellectual France was pro-Pétain.

Here was a regime passing strong antifeminist, anti-Semitic, antilabor edicts (the parliament had been indefinitely suspended by Pétain), a regime that ranted on about return to the soil, Joan of Arc, and bringing the church back into control of education, abolishing secondary education altogether. All this with the total support of the French Academy (except Mauriac), of nearly all the luminaries of the French theater and cinema, led by Sacha Guitry, Maurice Chevalier,

Danielle Darrieux. Writers like Céline, Fabre-Luce, Brasillach, Gide. Even Cocteau, Duhamel, and Giraudoux were not opposed, and André Maurois, though abroad at the time, was pro-Vichy.

In Annecy, that beautiful little city set by its almost ornamental lake high in the Savoyard Alps, he was taken to lunch by a real-estate agent to whom he had gone for help in finding a suitable place to settle down and paint. The radio always seemed to be on at that time in France, relaying the constant stream of "good news" from the new capital at Vichy. As he examined photographs of a series of houses around Annecy with "copious lofts suitable for conversion into studios," they heard an item which made Don Juan stare around at the other diners to see if anyone was laughing.

Paul Claudel, considered France's greatest living poet, was reading his "Ode to Marshal Pétain."

"*Monsieur le Maréchal, voici cette France entre vos bras et qui n'a que vous et qui ressuscite à voix basse.*

"*France, écoute ce vieil homme sur toi qui se penche et qui te parle comme un père. . . .*" *

No one laughed. Indeed, everyone kept a respectful silence until the ode was over.

"What a great poet," said the real-estate agent. "He expresses what is in the heart of France."

Don Juan had been about to ask whether the agent thought Paul Claudel could possibly be serious, but thought better of it. He found himself looking at a photograph of a long, lush valley, at the head of which stood a small chateau. In such a place he would be able to escape this madness.

"It is rather isolated," warned the agent. "The Val Romanée is marvelous farming land, but you would have only peasant farmers for neighbors, and perhaps a curé."

But Don Juan had all but made up his mind. Within a week he had seen it, found it eerily beautiful in its lordly, commanding position above the valley, and bought it.

In this perfect little medieval chateau which Don Juan now turned into a studio, he was, for the first time in his life, quite alone. It would have been easy and ridiculously cheap, in that summer of refugees and record unemployment, to find himself a servant. But he

* "Monsieur le Maréchal, here between your arms is France, who has only you and who with a low voice resuscitates.

"France, hearken to this old man who bends over you and speaks to you as a father. . . ."

was determined to prove to himself that he could live for a time without any other human being, that in the interest of his art and growing pride in himself as an adult man, he must try to relate to the physical and unyielding world around him and do without, for a short time, at any rate, the props that women had always provided in his life.

The story of his stay in the Val Romanée is that of his failure to do any such thing. At first he listened, sometimes intently, to the ambient sounds around him. The creaking of the old chateau's rickety beams, the distant sounds of the peasants at their haymaking. The lack of a woman's voice was, for him, like a stage pause that goes on forever. Food or wine without a woman with whom to share it tasted curiously unseasoned, bland, boring. Don Juan was a passable cook and enjoyed the activity, but with no one to share his efforts he virtually gave up eating.

Sleeping alone was, at this stage of his life, almost as painful as the experience of a junkie denied his fix. He lay in his deep feathered mattress imagining the bodies of all the young women then asleep in the Val Romanée below and literally aching for them.

In the end he surrendered to his nature.

When he announced the party he was giving for his neighbors in the valley, they were as surprised as they were alarmed. Since his arrival, they had seen him abroad working at his canvases. He bought farm produce from them sometimes, and occasionally and politely asked for access to their fields so that he might set up his easel.

The women and girls, who from the start had thought him exceedingly handsome and attractive, had been chagrined to notice that he never looked in their direction. Since such behavior seemed extraordinary in one so young, a number of rumors started to circulate about Don Juan. The first was that, being a foreign nobleman, he was too proud to notice peasant girls, however pretty. But no one could accept this. Then one of the worldlier of the farmers, noticing that Don Juan addressed himself only to menfolk, suggested that he might be a pederast *(un pédé)*. It was not long before this suggestion had become a rumor, and the rumor had, in turn, become an accepted fact.

Their reaction, therefore, to his invitation for a rustic ball in aid of the war charities was bewilderment, because they wondered how he would behave to them under these sociable circumstances. They could not know, of course, of his struggle with his sensual self, nor that he had now decided to let it reign once more.

It was spring when Don Juan decided to break his fast. During the long winter of 1940–41 his spirit had felt so bleak that his canvases had lost almost all color, like the landscape in the valley. A spare, crabbed line etched out his pain in hundreds of drawings, where the trees and buildings and the muffled people going about their winter work in the snow seemed all to echo France's shame. A shame the peasants of the Val Romanée were actually far from feeling.

At about the same time, Don Juan heard, listening illegally to the BBC in London, Churchill's defiant challenge to Hitler: "We will fight on the beaches . . . We will never surrender." Meanwhile every person in the Val Romanée gathered by the radio to hear the grand old man of France:

"Your life will be a hard one," said Father Pétain. "I shall not rock you to sleep with words of deceit. I hate lies—they have done you so much harm in the past. But the earth—the earth does not lie. It remains your refuge. This earth is our homeland. A field that goes fallow is a piece of France that has died. . . . Do not expect too much from the state, which can give only what it receives. Rely on yourselves for the present, and for the future, rely on your children, whom you will have brought up with a sense of duty."

He might have added, "go forth and fructify!" but he did not need to. They had understood him, and as the spring came, the leaves, the lambs, the calves, the tender shoots, the budding clover, the sap rising everywhere, the girls, their winter shrouding clothes cast off, their neat print dresses showing the promise of their strong little bodies, all saw to it that each kind would multiply according to its fashion.

At such a time Don Juan's party made the perfect celebration. With a neighborly tact, he ordered much of the feast from the wives of the region, paying good money for *pâtés vacherins, chaud-froids,* beef tongues in aspic, cold beef *en croûte,* and many other good things. Since the peasants were already selling to the growing black market in the cities, the prices they charged him were high indeed. Don Juan was determined, as he went from farmhouse to farmhouse ordering and preparing, that he would wait until the night of the party before making his choice of the superb peasant girl who would crown this bucolic feast for him. He therefore, with a final effort, avoided their often enticing eyes and lips and saved the slaking of his desire till the great day.

Edwige Donnay had seen the Spaniard, as they all called him, on the first day he had arrived at the little chateau. Her mother had been hired, with some other local women, to clean up the place before he arrived, and she had gone to help with the work. They were still busy washing the walls when the two trucks arrived with his furniture and his paintings. None of them had ever seen furniture or pictures like these in their lives. An average farmhouse in the Val Romanée had a three-piece suite, a dining-room table, perhaps a dozen wooden chairs, a well, an outside privy, and, as a great luxury, a radio. But here were frames of gold, chairs covered in damask; every object seemed like a treasure.

But the Spaniard, who arrived after the furniture, was by far the most remarkable sight of the day. Edwige had never seen a man remotely like him. Almost a head taller than most of the men in the valley, he had a tan to his skin that made him look as if, even in winter, he were in contact with the sun. Everything about him suggested strength and life, but without the slightest hint of restrained violence, so common in males that seemed as masculine as he. His eyes, which were of the most beautiful and unusual color, their deep greenish brownness suggesting the forest itself in high summer, were turned upon everyone and everything, seeming to record and caress at the same time.

From that moment he was the subject of endless discussion among the women. Although by the time the party was being prepared Edwige's father had, in agreement with the rest of the men, pronounced him a *pédé*, to be tolerated as a personage who was bringing business to the neighborhood and, whatever his predilections, giving him credit for keeping them to himself. Knowing he was coming to inspect the rabbit pâté they had prepared and the secret cake which was to be the Spaniard's presentation to the curé in honor of his name day (which date he had diplomatically chosen for this feast), Edwige and her mother nevertheless tried to look their very best.

Edwige saw him coming down the path past the cow pasture on his bicycle. She had boldly decided not to wear her brassiere, knowing that her breasts were considered the finest in the valley—so much so that the curé himself had suggested the brassiere to her mother, wishing to calm the stir she made among the men in her summer dress.

"He is here, the Spaniard!" she shouted to her mother, who was waving her hair with hot tongs for the occasion.

"It needs absolutely for you to talk to him!" shouted back her mother in the rich patois of the region. "Offer him some *marc*. No, no, that is your father's privilege. Offer him some camomile tea, offer him a spoonful of that plum preserve, not forgetting the glass of water with it!"

"Shall I use my christening spoon? The silver one?" shouted Edwige.

"Of course! What else?" shouted her mother.

He was at the door. Edwige felt her whole body blushing as she went to open it for him. She curtseyed without looking at anything but his shoes, the way she'd been taught to do with the curé.

"Is your mother in?" he asked.

"Her hair," she said, wondering why she said it.

"Perhaps I'd better come back later. I've come to see the cake and choose what we're going to write on it for the curé."

She looked up into his eyes and saw that he was taking her in not quite in the same way as the local men looked at her, seeing mainly *woman,* not bothering, unless they were a close relative, about her as a *person.*

"You're Edwige?"

"Yes, monsieur. How did you know?"

"The curé told me. He tells me about everyone. We play chess, and I have been painting him in his soutane and cleric's hat. I tell him he reminds me of a wise-looking raven in that garb. It doesn't seem to displease him. May I come in?"

She suddenly felt at ease with him. He talked like a Paris news announcer but with a much nicer voice. He didn't seem to expect any formality.

"Maman will be down in a minute. Would you like some jam?"

"Thank you. I would."

She brought him the preserve on the spoon, with a glass of water. He took the spoon with a hand that was as unlike any hand she had ever seen as was his furniture unlike any other in her experience. Very long muscular fingers sprang from a hand whose palm looked as soft as her own breast. Her eyes followed the spoon as he put it into his mouth, taking it in two mouthfuls, the second seeming to clear the spoon of the preserve with a single muscular thrust of his tongue. She saw this as if the spoon, her christening spoon, were an extension of her own body, as if his mouth were on her lips or her breasts. She spoke, looking at the whole man before her, quite involuntarily.

"How you are beautiful," she said in her dialect, and heard her mother on the stair behind her as she spoke. Covered with shame at her utterance, she ran out of the kitchen into the yard and went and hid herself in the hay barn among the chickens.

The party began at six o'clock on a Saturday night in May 1941. The war seemed far away, if indeed it still existed. Britain had not been crushed; the news everyone had waited for six months to hear had not come. Although Japan was already on the warpath in Southeast Asia, America still slept. In the Val Romanée the real world seemed to end with the Alps that surrounded them.

Trestle tables covered with gleaming white cloths and heaped with food, wine, and cider stood in Don Juan's orchard. Horse-drawn carts brought the guests, three or more families sharing a cart, everybody dressed in Sunday best, some of the men in stiff suits and celluloid collars, but with the colorful sashes of the region tied around their waists and hats. The women in their regional costumes, under each skirt of which they wore their wealth in petticoats, their hair tied in ribbons or elaborately curled. The weathered faces of these good people were rosy with the warmth of the day and the amount of their unaccustomed clothing, and they walked into the orchard like children on the first day of school, a little awkward, greeting old friends with vigorous handshakes.

Don Juan spent the first hour of the party with the curé, being introduced to everyone, talking in turn to the elders of each family. The men eyed him curiously, wondering if he could really be a *pédé*, or whether, like the priest, he simply chose celibacy out of some kind of odd Spanish vocation. At the end of the hour he led his guests up to the small ballroom of the chateau, where he made the surprise presentation of the cake to the curé, following it with a graceful speech that melted all the women present, although none fully recognized its exact meaning at the time.

"Monsieur le Curé, good neighbors and friends, I am grateful that you have all come to help me celebrate not only our good priest's name day, but the coming of spring. I look forward to living among you and enjoying with you a good harvest this summer. Never, my friends, have women seemed lovelier to me than do those of the Val Romanée here this evening. In a moment the music will begin, and I hope to dance with every woman in this room. I have but one question to ask you before they start the music." He looked about the room before he completed his question. "Where is Edwige Donnay?"

The guests, surprised at his sudden interest in women, were amazed that he should have sought out one particular woman in this way. Everyone looked around to see if the girl was there, and Monsieur and Madame Donnay rushed up to the curé in evident distress. He listened to them quietly and then said to Don Juan, with a courtliness that was natural to him, "She was shy, monseigneur. She is at home."

"Then may I go and fetch her?"

"Of course, monsieur," said her father, confused but flattered. "I will come with you."

"That isn't necessary, monsieur. It is only a mile away. I'll take a cart. Meanwhile, please start the dancing."

On Don Juan's signal the concertina and accordion band, imported from Annecy for the occasion, started to play, and everyone surged forward to start the dancing. The curé, whose feelings of benevolence toward Don Juan were at that moment almost bound-less, calmed the excited and confused Donnays and sent his host on his way to collect Edwige.

Don Juan, who had spent the previous night thinking of a dozen ways in which he would like to make love to Edwige, had been genuinely disappointed not to see her. His eyes had taken in many other promising girls—indeed, such was his need at this moment that every woman younger than a grandmother and older than a mere girl looked infinitely desirable. But Edwige, Edwige of the marvelous breasts and the extraordinary blush, of the cornflower-blue eyes and the heavy, gamboge-yellow hair, her, above all, he wanted.

The girl herself, feeling deflated and bored, sat listening to the radio with her older sister in the Donnay farmhouse. The sister had a baby, whom she presently suckled while they listened to a program of folk songs. They didn't hear the cart in the drive or his knock on the door. Edwige simply looked up to find him standing there, dressed very simply in a pair of dark trousers and a clean silk shirt, open at the neck. He greeted her sister, she supposed, but her surprise prevented her from comprehending what he said. She realized to her horror that she was wearing her nightdress and an old pair of plaid slippers. But she knew she couldn't run off again as she had before.

"Monsieur?" she managed.

"I was saying that yesterday you gave me no time to reply, 'But how you are beautiful,' in return."

"Oh," she said, sure that her heart's pounding must be heard aloud.

"Please, hurry and get dressed and come to my party."

She ran up the stairs two at a time, action being so much easier than words. "A minute only!" she shouted down.

"But how she is pleased now," said the sister, smiling comforta-bly up at him.

"Will you come too? You can bring the baby," he said.

She shook her head and laughed.

"Edwige you will have alone for the ride to the chateau. As a cow needs a fifth teat she needs me!"

"Where is your husband?" he asked.

"In Germany, with the others," she said sadly, referring to the nearly two million absent Frenchmen, prisoners of war or working in German factories.

He waited until they had reached the road and the old horse simply began following its nose to the chateau and the other horses. Edwige had sat very quiet beside him, not speaking, wondering about him, thinking him as strange and improbable as a fate conjured up in a teacup, watching his head of a god in the still twilight, prepared now for almost anything and ready, womanlike, to summon up an infinity of giving if only he would tell of his need. When he put the reins between his knees she felt herself already melting, knowing that it was going to happen now. He had turned to her, looking into her wide, childlike countrywoman's eyes, and she found herself opening her lips to receive his, wanting to open every last part of her body to receive him, to absorb and hold him, but able only to make her tongue an urgent metaphor for her rose, yet longing for all the rest to follow.

When he at last finished kissing her, he asked, "Can you come to me in the morning? We will have breakfast together."

"After the milking? At five-thirty. You will be asleep!"

"Yes, but the doors of the chateau are never locked. You can wake me."

"I will do it," she said simply, giving herself over wholly to her happiness.

Their arrival, even in the middle of the dancing, even though most of the men were by now rather drunk and noticed comparatively little, caused a small sensation. Edwige understood that he could dance with her only once, and that he did immediately, but she floated around the room in a way that every woman there knew could have been inspired by no *pédé*. They saw him meet their eyes now, indeed, search out their eyes. Each woman knew that as he approached to dance with her, her face, her figure, her laugh, her voice, her tread, her scent were part of the total considered woman he held in his arms. In the months and years that followed, they discussed him, trying to define the impression he gave. But it eluded them. Edwige, who loved him, came nearest to the truth.

"He was the bull, pure. Without horns, without menace," she said, adding, "But alas, in the end just as dangerous."

In the morning he was awakened by her breath on his mouth, breath smelling of apples. Then the soft surge of her breasts caressing his face as she entered the bed and pressed her body to his. He awoke to explore a maze of enchanting smells. The fresh milk smell from her hands, the cidery smell of her hair, the sharp, sharp musky smell of her desire.

"It has been a very long time," he said, knowing how inadequate he would be.

"I take you there straight, my beauty," she whispered.

She lay back for him, opened herself up for him, thrust up her thighs, her whole hips for him, and taking her at her word, he knelt between her legs, teasing her rose for an instant so that she swung her breasts to and fro with pleasure. Now he was ready to thrust, feeling the warm viscous flow of her. But she urged her hips higher.

"Not there, beauty," she said urgently. "I *must* remain virgin. Lower, there, there. The back door. It is to me all equal if you me make hurt! I you adore!"

In fact, to his dismay she gave a single shout of pain, but then he felt her urgent little fingers at work under his belly and saw her lose herself; and giving himself up to the pleasure of being inside this glorious woman, he broke his fast.

Much later. Lying still. Only their fingertips touching. He asked her the questions which made him feel for the first time in many years like the merest schoolboy.

"You will give your virginity to your husband?"

"Of course," she said, adding anxiously, "Is it that it gives you pain?"

"No. It is for *you* that it must be painful."

"A little. The thing important is to feel your pleasure *inside* me. In there. In my mouth. Not important where. It is my desire simply to you enclose!"

"But your pleasure?"

"Is already great. You did not see? You did not feel?" Her voice was anxious. She could not imagine that any other man in the world could have made her feel so intensely.

This, then, he thought, is what Aube meant when she spoke of "leaving by the back door" as a means of birth control among the peasants.

"You have no bidet at the farm?" he asked.

"There are. You fill them with a kettle. It's not very practical."

He introduced her to the bidet in his bathroom, laughing at her as she pretended the jet gave her too much pleasure to be used for mere hygiene.

"Do you confess what we did to the curé?"

"Of course. But it is an entirely small sin. Two Hail Marys. I have never heard of more."

"Poor Marshal Pétain. I see what he's up against, asking you women all to stay home and have babies for France."

"Oh, the Father Pétain has no children. But I'd *like* to make a child! When I will be married."

"You have a fiancé?"

"Not exactly. Maurice. That's his name. A neighbor. A friend, what. Since we were children."

"Where was he last night?"

"He is with the army."

"A prisoner?"

"No, the Chasseurs Alpins. They are at Grenoble, I think."

Don Juan remembered the French had been allowed by the Germans to keep a small standing army "for internal order."

They could hear the arrival of the women who were to clean up the chateau after the party. Edwige's mother would be among them. Edwige herself was supposed to join them. She hurried downstairs and was collecting dishes when they entered the chateau.

Don Juan, who went to help gather the dozens of empty bottles, heard Edwige's mother say, "You have the air of the cat that caught the mouse, my girl."

"She has the air of someone who owns the chateau," said another woman snidely.

But poor Edwige was soon to discover that she was very far from having an exclusive hold on Don Juan.

In retrospect, that summer seemed to Don Juan like a veritable pastoral symphony. Snow never entirely left the peaks of the surrounding mountains. These distant sentinels of retreated winter watched over the fecund valley while its hay and clover grew more lush, while corn and barley and oats and vegetables of every kind covered the patchwork quilt of little fields and the big mushroom-colored Swiss cows with their sad, suspicious faces wandered through the pastures ringing their little bells.

Letting his intellect go fallow that summer rather than try to cope any longer with the actual world where the Germans were already killing literally millions of Russians in the wake of Hitler's invasion of his strange ally, Don Juan attacked paper and canvas in a frenzied attempt to catch the meaning of the natural world around him, with its eternal, bucolic verities.

In the whole nineteen years of his life so far Woman had seemed to him the symbolic embodiment of the cosmos here on earth; she was the living ark of some mysterious covenant between mankind and nature. That summer he tried to further reconcile what he already knew of Woman with the budding world around him, and in that quest he came upon a startling inconsistency, or so at first it seemed.

His painter's eyes and intuition, rather than his intellect, were his tools, his antennae, in this quest. Among the many girls and women who almost vied with each other to be his lovers he looked always for echoes and harmony with nature. He drew, for instance, a plump girl of eighteen, the daughter of a tanner, lying half-asleep in the deep, rich clover where he had just made love to her. The very-pale-pink ordered smoothness of her thighs, flowing like those of a she-Gulliver above the little clambering, spiky mauve, white, and green flowers of the clover, were the purest of counterpoint. He could see them in no other way. He looked down at his own slightly hirsute flanks, the sharp angles of the muscles in his own calves. His man's body was much more at one with the things growing around him, with the bark and earth and sticks and leaves and beasts hunting and listening and fearing in the forest, than was hers. He, his whole being, was far more feral than she. Beyond her rose, just now being assaulted by a minute grass snail which he had placed there to gently waken her, lay the endlessly reserved host of her mystery.

He knew something of the valley's history now from the curé. A Celtic settlement before the Roman occupations that had given the valley its name, the region had a number of caves which showed something of the paleolithic people from whom succeeding neolithic and Celtic tribes had inherited the valley. There was a particular cave to which Edwige had taken him. It was vast and full of bats. Curious drawings of men hunting a creature he supposed to be the European bison were scratched in the soft pumice stone.

In another part of the cave there was clear evidence of the sleeping platforms of women. Edwige herself had not noticed this, for, giggling, she took him to see the drawing of a woman with breasts far larger than hers before whom there were three male figures kneeling in apparent worship.

"How the world has changed!" She laughed. "It is called La Cave de Vénus after her."

But he was looking at the ridge of pumice on which they had stood. Because the overhanging rock was low here, there was no bat dung underfoot, and he was extraordinarily moved to see the shape of a sleeping woman worn in the stone, the deep indentation for the hipbone making the gender of the long-gone sleeper unmistakable.

He had asked a reluctant Edwige to lie there, putting her hip where another woman, some tiny remanant of whose genes she perhaps shared, had lain as recently as seven thousand years ago. Perhaps more recently.

As he looked at the tanner's daughter lying in the clover, the scene in the cave came back to him like a kind of vision. Woman, soft woman, largely hairless woman, relatively unmuscled woman, enclosing within her the mystery of creation and birth, guarding the element sacred to her, namely fire, had borne for aeons the primacy in sapient mankind's astonishing ascent. Only when her hunting, ferocious mate had turned his vast energies to inquiring and inventing had she entered into her long subjugation. She kept her secret still. Knowing it, but her will to express it withered to something prehensile. Like her voice, shrill when demanding, unconvincing, often, even to herself. She had, he believed, set herself apart from the rest of the natural world long before man. But, in one of nature's endless contradictions, what she had kept of her instinctive nature had long outlasted what he had been able to keep.

The tanner's daughter, brushing the tickling snail from her little rose with an ancient curse, looked at her dreaming lover, the strange "Spaniard," and wondered to whom he would ever "belong." Poor Edwige was crazy to think it would ever be someone in the valley. She was dimly aware that the world beyond the mountains had gone insane. He was a bit of extraordinary flotsam sent their way by that insanity. Like the Roman army that had once passed through the valley.

Don Juan corresponded with the outside world that summer and winter. Letters that took an endless time traveled to Long Island, and answers came back. To his grandfather he sent a portfolio of his best drawings and watercolors with a request that he have them criticized during his next visit to Paris. Direct correspondence with his professors at the Beaux-Arts was considered too dangerous. Dulles had advised that he do nothing to draw the attention of the Germans to himself.

With Mireille he had exchanged postcards. She was traveling with a circus now, and they were due in Annecy in the spring of 1942. She hoped to see him. Her father, she said, had disappeared. Don Juan guessed that along with all the other known communist ex-members of parliament or trade-union officials he was being held in a Vichy jail, if he had not actually been executed.

From Juliet there was only indirect news in Henrietta's letter.

She was now an officer in the Wrens, the female branch of the Royal Navy. In a postscript to the same letter, Henrietta relayed the much-delayed news that Giles had been killed in the Battle of Britain. Don Juan wrote, care of Henrietta, to Juliet and her parents, telling them that he cared, that he wished there had been time to know Giles. After writing it he wondered whether it might be *his* duty to fight the Nazis too. The image of killing the men emerging from their tents with the machine gun came back like an instant nightmare. He put the thought from him, buried it deep and at once.

One early morning in February of 1942, Edwige, shivering with cold, crawled into his bed and warmed her hands on his sex.

He was instantly awake and looked up at her, kneeling astride him under the warm tent of his *plumeau*. The room was dark except for the flickering lantern that she had brought with her from the cow shed.

"I want you to do *everything* this morning," she said seriously, with only a hint of her usual laughter in her voice.

"Everything?" he exclaimed in mock fear, not really paying attention, absorbed in a game they both called "milking the milk-maid."

Like all lovers who are used to one another, accustomed to each other's nuances of pleasure and excitement, she started what was one of their customary rituals. She made of his sex what she called a marinade, holding the tip of it to her welcoming rose. Usually she waited until the last second before her own pleasure took off before, bending forward like a jockey, she took him into her southern entry. Then she always settled back to ride him with great whooping shouts, as if he were a beast in a rodeo. He used to clasp his fingers behind her neck when she did this, making her weaving breasts brush his chest with her large pointed nipples.

On this occasion, however, she hardly bent forward at all, but simply impaled herself, breaking her own hymen with a single downward thrust. If it hurt her, and it must have, he could not tell, but she shouted so loud and rode him so hard and came with such vast convulsions that he slowly slipped from control of himself and came. When they lay breathless and soaked with sweat afterward, he said, "You must douche, do something!"

She did indeed go to the bidet, and after a while came back with a sponge to wash the small quantity of blood from his body, and at once went to sleep in his arms, purring, he thought, like an exceedingly smug cat.

. . .

Since December 7, 1941, the day of Pearl Harbor, the United States had been at war on the side of Britain and Russia against Germany and her Axis allies. Relations between the U.S.A. and Vichy France were virtually at an end. From then on, Don Juan had to correspond via his grandfather in the full knowledge that every word he wrote was being surveyed by the censor. The war was inching in on his Shangri-la.

Since May of 1941 the official food ration per adult had been eight and a half ounces of bread a day; eight and one-half ounces of meat and two and a half ounces of cheese a week; nineteen ounces of fat, seventeen and a half ounces of sugar, seven ounces of rice, and nine ounces of flour a month; and two packets of cigarettes and a liter of wine every ten days.

The black market which helped circumvent this ration for the rich, and make it scarcer still for the poor, bred a whole new bourgeoisie in France that has stamped its character on the country ever since. Be that as it may, the immediate, and in some ways welcome, effect of all this for Don Juan was to bring Edwige's intended, Maurice, back from the army to work on his father's land. Vichy had decreed that ever more acreage should be put under the plow.

In April 1942 Don Juan was preparing to make his first trip out of the valley, to Annecy to meet Mireille, when a small delegation called on him. Led by the curé, it included Monsieur and Madame Donnay and Edwige. All wore their Sunday best as if some ceremony were about to take place. Don Juan, who was cleaning his palettes, a particularly messy job, had to ask them to wait in the never-used drawing room while he washed. He found them there, sitting uncertainly on the very edge of his mother's Louis Quinze chairs beneath some of the less important family portraits that he hadn't stored, looking both tentative and distressed. Taking their cue from the curé, they all rose when he entered the room.

"Monseigneur," said the curé, speaking to Don Juan formally, as he knew a grandee of Spain should be addressed. "I have news of the utmost importance to you. This young woman tells us she expects your child."

Don Juan suffered a feeling of intense self-reproach. He realized that he had been both reckless and stupid where Edwige was concerned. He had not seen her for more than two weeks, and assumed that Maurice's return meant that she had resumed her old relationship. While he had missed her in his bed, he had been relieved at this happy outcome for her; so many of the girls in the valley were still waiting for their loved ones to return. But now her action in dispensing with her own virginity explained itself, as it should have at the time. He looked at her, but her eyes were kept low, staring at the Aubusson carpet as if the pattern on it fascinated her.

"Please sit down," he said politely.

They all sat.

"You have never thought of marrying her?" asked the curé.

"It had not occurred to me, Father," said Don Juan. "I thought she was engaged to Maurice."

The curé looked at Monsieur Donnay.

"We had hoped for that," said the poor man miserably. "But now it is out of the question, naturally."

"You see?" said the curé, turning to Don Juan. "This is a tragic matter for this young person. Sin is always tragic. But in a community such as this, to have the child without marriage will be very hard for her. Such a huge punishment for a moment of illicit pleasure. What stupidity!"

"*Months* of pleasure!" burst out her mother angrily.

"Be quiet," said her husband. "One has no need for all that here."

"One waits to hear what monseigneur proposes to do?" said the curé, his normally kind, relaxed face looking very grim and serious.

Don Juan continued to stare curiously at Edwige. What had she supposed life married to him would be like? Living as mistress of this little chateau. Becoming, in time, his duchess. Reigning over the town house on the Avenue Foch, the castle in Andalusia. Did she know anything of all that? The curé clearly did, or he would not address him as he did on formal occasions. But the curé had no inkling of what Don Juan's life had actually been. The catalogue of his sins would certainly appall him.

"Father, while nominally Roman Catholic I have never been confirmed into the church," began Don Juan.

"A matter that could easily be corrected, my son!" interrupted the priest firmly.

"I was going to say that I would be prepared to propose this: I will make a general confession to you. I'm afraid I have no desire to be confirmed into the church at this time, but my confession will serve to inform you about me. If you still believe this marriage to be in Edwige's interest, I will consider further."

The curé accepted the arrangement at once. The girl's parents were privately relieved that the whole matter was going to be handled by the curé. Madame Donnay was embarrassed that the entire valley knew her daughter had gone each morning to the chateau. This essentially voluntary act and the airs Edwige had sometimes put on as Don Juan's acknowledged mistress-in-chief in the valley hardly put her in the category of a deeply wronged girl or someone with whom everyone would sympathize. Edwige herself knew that she had tricked Don Juan, and she knew that he understood how he had been tricked; she therefore burst into tears and begged Don Juan to consider that her life would be hell if he didn't marry her. Her parents led her, weeping, away.

"Shall we do this over lunch?" Don Juan asked the curé when the Donnays had gone.

"If it will help your memory, and since it isn't in any religious sense a confession, why not?" said the curé.

Over a simple meal of river trout caught locally, an endive salad grown in the chateau's garden, and a marvelous cauliflower cooked very slowly in onion juice and crowned with a cheese sauce, Don Juan attempted to recall the salient facts of his life. They both sipped slowly at a red Hermitage wine until suddenly the curé asked Don Juan to stop. He had just related the happenings in Jaén.

"Does it get worse?" asked the curé incredulously.

"It doesn't get better," admitted Don Juan.

"Then I do not wish to further spoil this delicious meal by keeping you in suspense about my decision. You could only make Edwige bitterly unhappy. You have led one of the most profoundly irreligious lives of which I have ever heard. If you had been a Protestant or a Jew you could hardly be a less suitable husband for that poor child."

Don Juan greeted these words with mixed feelings. He was relieved the curé found him unsuitable, but he was disconcerted that he seemed to the old man to be a kind of monster.

"My dear boy, if I call for a long spoon to eat with you, it doesn't mean I don't like you. I shall always pray for you. A little more of that cauliflower, please. The onion-juice marination is a brain wave. I must tell my housekeeper." The curé was clearly in deep thought as he finished off the Hermitage and polished the cheese sauce from his plate with his bread.

"What could you afford to offer the girl as a dowry?" he asked eventually.

Don Juan, who had been turning this very idea over in his mind, mentioned a sum.

"Frankly, that is too much. A sum like that would spoil their lives," said the curé. "Half that sum as a dowry and the other half to be invested in trust for the child. It will do for a start. The details can come later. A lawyer in Annecy will draw up a document for you."

"You don't think it will be too difficult for her to find a husband, since you mention a dowry?"

"If so many were not away in Germany, I would expect them to form a line for such a dowry," said the curé complacently. "But Maurice will be the first one to whom I shall address myself. If he can find it in his heart to forgive her, he will make her an excellent husband, that one."

"I see. D'you think he'll find it in his heart to forgive me?"

"That is another matter. One must never ask too much of human nature," said the curé authoritatively.

Thus a matter that in a metropolis would have enriched several lawyers was settled by the curé and a single lawyer in Annecy with one sole document to which all the parties concerned attached their signatures.

Maurice married Edwige the following week in a ceremony that the whole valley attended. Don Juan remained tactfully in Annecy, but the lawyer went as the curé's guest (officially), but actually to make sure that Maurice and Edwige fully understood the final agreement, which was only just completed in time. Under it Maurice formally adopted the unborn child that would bear his name. All claims on Don Juan or his estate were renounced by the pair, and the child was assured the largest patrimony in the valley. The dowry was paid in cash and the child's trust fund was made irrevocable, with the lawyer and the curé as trustees. Don Juan vowed to himself to be more careful in the future.

During his stay at Annecy he visited Mireille on the site of the traveling circus. Her non-act was still the same and provided a sideshow. She was now living with the ringmaster, a man called Bellin, and they invited Don Juan, together with some other friends, to dinner in their caravan after the show. Don Juan, who really had no taste for the circus, was relieved when the conversation turned at once to politics. He was starved for information on what was really happening in France. For the first time, he heard the word "Resistance."

"Who are they, these Resisters?" he asked after listening for a while.

"People like Papa," said Mireille. "Politically active communists."

"Since Hitler's invasion of Russia," said Bellin. "Not before! The trouble is that there are so many groups. In the occupied North of France alone, there are the FN, the Front National, led by communists but including people of all kinds. There are, for instance, a railwaymen's FN, a coal miners' FN, even a concierges' FN. Then there is the Organisation Civile et Militaire—many of those are civil servants of all parties or ex-servicemen. You have also the Liberation Nord, a socialist group, and perhaps the most active in killing Germans, the Francs Tireurs, the Trotskyites."

"One hears nothing of it in the valley where I live," said Don Juan, astonished. "The peasants, the curé, they never speak of resisting. Quite the reverse. They are always quoting Marshal Pétain as if he were God. 'The marshal takes care of the Boche,' they say, and seem quite content."

"But of course, my dear Juan. The supporters of the marshal and his armistice with the Boche are the peasants, the church, and the middle and upper classes," said Mireille. "The peasants get always richer from the black market; the church has grabbed back powers over property and education that have put the country back to before the Revolution, to the eighteenth century. Did you know that *women*, along with Jews and people of foreign birth, are now forbidden public office of any kind? In practice, of course, so many men are away that they have to use some women, but Jeanne, who is a teacher, was fired because she belongs to the left."

Don Juan looked across the table at Jeanne, a pale woman of about twenty-six with beautiful gooseberry-colored eyes and a rather angular, awkward body. A plain woman with a face redolent of a quiet, reflective intelligence, she had so far spoken little

"Fortunately for us 'unemployed,' there is much else to do in Vichy France these days," said Jeanne.

"Resisting?" asked Don Juan with a gentle smile.

"That is not a question one can any longer ask of a stranger," she said flatly.

"Because it is not safe to give a truthful answer, unless it is to deny it," added Bellin.

"Oh, you can trust Juan," said Mireille hurriedly. "He fought for the left in Spain. He's hopelessly compromised." She laughed as she used the word, looking reassuringly in Don Juan's direction.

"Is that true?" asked Jeanne, surprised that this good-looking youth, with his patrician manners and sometimes ironical expression, was truly of the left. Nor did he look old enough to have soldiered long in Spain.

"I was with the anarchist militia for nearly three years, but to tell the truth, I saw very little of the fighting," he said, looking her straight in the eyes, wondering about her, wondering why she seemed curious about him.

The talk turned to the French Nazis, to Déat, Doriot, Darnand, de Brinon, the politicians, and Luchaire, the editor of their paper, *Nouveaux Temps*. Everyone seemed to feel safe in hating these men, since even the Vichyites could not join them in wanting to see France become a mere province of Hitler's "Thousand-Year Reich."

"To me it is astounding," Bellin was saying, "that they have found more Frenchmen to volunteer for the French Legion that is fighting beside the Boche in Russia than General de Gaulle has been able to enroll to fight along side the British."

"No one trusts the British. That is evident," said Mireille. "And who is de Gaulle? Just another Third Republic general."

There was a general murmur of agreement from around the table, except from Don Juan.

"That is not accurate," he said. "I happen to know he tried very hard to influence both the generals and the ministers of the Third Republic to reform the French army. No one would listen to him. As a matter of fact, I quite often hear him speaking on the radio from London. I think he makes a great deal of sense."

"My poor Juan, he is a hopelessly right-wing figure," said Mireille. "And whom does he represent? At least the marshal is the legitimate choice of the National Assembly."

"You listen to de Gaulle on the radio?" asked Jeanne.

"Yes, I tune in to the BBC in London. It's the only interesting world news program I can get."

There was silence around the table when he said this.

"Here you are among friends," said Bellin kindly. "But do not tell people you do that, please. It is no longer safe. Even here in Vichy France. Remember that as a foreigner and one with a record of fighting for the left, you are very vulnerable."

"Thank you for the warning," said Don Juan. "But I am living hidden away from the world in a remote place. I hope the French government just forgets all about me."

"Where exactly *do* you live?" asked Jeanne.

Don Juan told her before he had time to wonder whether it was rash to have done so.

Back in the Val Romanée, Don Juan made a valiant attempt to return to the existence of hermit-artist that had characterized his first winter in the region.

He dined often with the curé and talked politics and comparative religion with the old man, arguing agreeably about both.

He sometimes saw the still-enlarging Edwige in the distance, but they both went out of their way to avoid each other. The other girls he saluted with the occasional kiss, but rarely did he take it further. To oblige his friend the curé, he started a project of designing fourteen panels, the stations of the cross, for the church. He painted these on wood and used one or two of the farmers as models. As he explained to the curé, it was hard to find an ideal model for a thirty-three-year-old Christ when there were so few civilian male Frenchmen of that age around.

"It would be marvelous," he said to the curé as they discussed the matter one summer evening over a bottle of good fresh Sancerre, "if one could only find a Jew to play the Christ, a Hasidic face with ringlets, a robust rabbinical scholar, if that isn't a contradiction in terms."

The curé looked surprised at this suggestion.

"People always criticize the church," he said, "for so often encouraging artists to paint the Christ in their own image. By that one means the image of their tribe or race. Black Christs in Africa, and so on. In general, I agree with the church's position in this matter. But what you say raises in my mind an interesting thought."

"You are being a little more Byzantine than usual this evening, Father," said Don Juan. "I've quite lost track of what you're talking about."

"It is not to deal in simplicities that one is called to the cloth," said the curé complacently. "Tell me, do you intend to continue your fast?"

"The sun perhaps has reached you through your tonsure, Father?" said Don Juan teasingly, poised as he was over a plate of *filets de truite Bercy aux champignons* made from a trout caught by the curé's own rod.

"It is the talk of the valley," said the curé, "and the lament of many girls, my housekeeper tells me, that you have lived in a state approaching grace since your return from Annecy. A fast, in you, more notable than giving up mere food."

"Ah, yes. That is so."

"I take it from what you say that you are not an anti-Semite?"

"Far from it. The only race I ever viewed with dislike were the Anglo-Saxons. But *they* have a way of making you admire or love them when you least expect it."

"I see. You have heard me say many times that I am Pétainiste.

The marshal has saved France. The Germans would never have signed so generous an armistice with any other leader. I am convinced of it. Perhaps almost as important, my parishioners are convinced of it. The stress on the family, the return to religion which the regime urges, is naturally most *seductive*, and I use that word advisedly."

"Equally, Father, you know that is *not* my view. But why do you use the word 'seductive'?"

"Because I have an uncomfortable feeling sometimes that we have been bought off, we of the church, with this policy. So that we will be silent when the regime carries out policies which, to say the least, are repugnant to any Christian."

"The persecution of the Jews?"

"My dear friend, this policy is no mere persecution. The truth cannot be other than that the annihilation of this unfortunate race is intended. Xavier Vallat—he is the commissaire for Jewish questions at Vichy—made a speech the other day in which he called the Jews 'unassimilable, a disruptive element.' He proclaimed the need 'to defend the French organism from the microbe which has produced in it a fatal anemia!' All over this country, Jews, even little children, even babies, are being deported to Germany. A train passed through Annecy station the other day in which Jews of both sexes and all ages were herded like cattle. People were horrified to hear them screaming for water, for food, to see them forced back into trucks filled with their own defecation—by French police, my friend. One does not suppose these Jews were bound for a free holiday in Germany. Nor for use as workers. The Boche is practical. Whom he wishes to work he feeds."

"How frightful! That is an even more dreadful story than anything that happened in Spain!" said Don Juan.

"It occurs to me that of all the people in the valley, you have the best means of concealing a Jew from the authorities. Perhaps he might consent to pose for the stations of the cross?"

"I would be glad to do it," said Don Juan eagerly, flattered and grateful that the curé should so far trust him as to make this proposal. It also helped salve, to some extent, his growing sense of guilt. For he was conscious of remaining a bystander when so many people like Giles were giving their lives for a cause he knew to be identical to that for which Inés and Colonel Perlmutter and so many other friends had died in Spain. A cause in which he still believed.

The Jew came in September. A family had been hiding him in Paris, where, because of the German occupation, they were all risking their lives in doing so. He was an Alsatian called Lamarre, and since

Alsace was now a German province, he could be deported as a *German* Jew instantly if caught in any part of France; such was the sovereignty the revered marshal had preserved for his country.

The curé brought him from Annecy, where he arrived by train, disguised as one of the few wounded French prisoners-of-war who were now trickling back from Germany. Don Juan had been fascinated to see his forged papers, which the curé had obtained from an organization in Lyons called Combat, at that time specializing in forging documents to help people escape both the German and French secret police. Combat, it appeared, was the beginning of a Catholic-led liberal and conservative resistance to both Pétain's Vichy government and the occupying Germans in the north.

Don Juan had prepared an upper story of the chateau, never normally used, for his guest. Since dismissing the maids who cleaned the chateau would have excited both comment and a natural resentment, he locked the door to the stair which led up to the story he was reserving for the Jew. He told the women he believed he had seen a headless, handless phantom there, whose image he turned into a most alarming illustration. After seeing it they were more than content to stay well away from that part of the castle. The noise the unseen guest was sometimes to make thereafter did nothing to calm their fears.

Yves Lamarre had been, before the war, a camera assistant working in René Clair's film unit. His late father before him had been a famous silent-movie director who had worked at the old Pathé Studios in north Paris. Yves had a lean, cadaverous face and very slightly protruding eyes, which gave him a misleadingly soulful appearance. Actually, he was a man who loved to tell stories, to amuse and entertain people. His ambition was to one day be a film director like his father.

It was at dinner in his new, rather sumptuous apartment on the night after his arrival that Don Juan broached the project of making him his model.

"If I were the curé," said Don Juan, "asking you this question, Yves, would probably lead me first through the whole history of Judaism. But I'm not up to all that. Tell me, are you religious?"

"I've been circumcised and bar-mitzvahed, if that's what you mean," said Yves. "But if you want to be converted into a Jew, I'm afraid the task's beyond me. You'll have to ask the curé."

"Would you consider posing as Christ?"

"Well, I was pretty good as a wounded *poilu* on that train. I made a fascist-looking old *ancien combatant* get up and give me his seat. You're joking, of course?"

"Look, please understand, you don't have to do anything while you're here that you don't want to do. But I'm painting the stations of the cross for the church. I need a man of about your age . . . perhaps you'd prefer to be the centurion?" concluded Don Juan doubtfully.

"The centurion? But that's a supporting role. No, I'll make a perfect Jewish Jesus. It's the star part or nothing. Wait a minute— does this show include a crucifixion?"

"Yes, it does."

"Well, if you're going to use real nails, I know a couple of French cops who'd be perfect for Barabbas and the other thief."

During the beautiful fall weather in the valley, poor Yves was never able to go out except at night, when he and Don Juan took long walks in the woods behind the chateau. They talked of many things, not excluding women. Yves was such a gifted raconteur that he was able to entertain Don Juan for hours with his stories of the frantic make-believe world that was already becoming, in French, a synonym for the improbable and the grotesque. "But it's *du cinéma*" were the words an amazed Yves used when Don Juan rather reluctantly related some of the bizarre adventures of his own short life.

It was not, however, in Don Juan's nature to discuss his romantic or sexual adventures. Admittedly he had seldom made men friends with whom such discussions might have taken place. Yet for him there was never an iota of locker-room titillation in such talk. Sex, in his eyes, was sometimes funny, but it could never be vulgar, for it was too important and sacred a part of his life for him to be able to bear having it made trivial.

Yves had a wife, who had escaped to the United States with their two young children. She was now in California, where friends in the movie colony had befriended her. He admitted to Don Juan that apart from a few whores before his marriage "to learn the ropes from," he had never since been with any other woman except his wife.

Don Juan was moved and, in a sense, made envious by what Yves told him. The older man described for him the ceaseless sense of loss he felt in being separated from this woman he considered his alter ego. Only in Henrietta's feeling for his mother had he ever before witnessed the felicities of people feeling they "belonged" to each other. He tried to imagine himself in such a situation. It was something, Yves suggested tactfully, that would come to Don Juan with maturity.

The very considerable task of painting the fourteen panels went on, with Yves warming himself from time to time by the wood stove after hours of posing his rather emaciated body in a loincloth. Don Juan found his figure perfect for the "crucifixion" itself, where Yves's muscles seemed to visibly stretch themselves as he grasped two bolts they had driven into the wall of the room Don Juan used as a studio.

Sometimes they listened to the BBC's overseas broadcasts while they were at work. Slowly the news was becoming a little better, giving some encouragement that against all the odds, the Allies might yet win. The British had defeated the German Afrika Corps in Libya and taken the whole of Abyssinia from the Italians. The Vichy French had attempted to cooperate with the Germans in using their protectorate in Syria as a base against the British, and lost both Syria and Lebanon for their pains. The Nazi invasion of Russia had been slowed to a crawl, and Moscow still had not fallen. The United States was beginning to fight back successfully against the Japanese in the Pacific.

It was while listening to a broadcast in the studio, at a time when the maids were not expected for their twice-weekly ritual of cleaning and scrubbing, that Don Juan and Yves became aware of somebody wandering about on one of the lower floors of the chateau. It could not, they decided, be the curé, because he always rang the big brass bell that hung outside the front door.

At once turning off the radio and giving Yves time to conceal himself in a small coffinlike chamber they had hollowed out of the floorboards against such emergencies, Don Juan crept barefoot downstairs to investigate.

Looking through the half-open door of the formal drawing room where he had interviewed Edwige's family, Don Juan saw a woman in a raincoat in the act of searching the room. This she did with apparent casualness, perhaps expecting to hear anyone who might come down the passage in time to be able to appear simply to be waiting in the empty room. But Don Juan saw her sliding open drawers and examining with more than cursory interest what kind of book he had on his shelves.

"Mademoiselle is an appraiser of antiques *and* a bibliophile, it would seem," he said suddenly from the doorway.

She almost screamed, dropping a book she had in her hand. As she turned to face him he saw that he knew her. It was Jeanne, the woman with the gooseberry-colored eyes, whom he had met in Annecy, *chez* Mireille.

"Monsieur frightened me!" she said accusingly.

"You are, if I may say so, a rather unexpected visitor yourself," said Don Juan, none too welcoming.

"Still listening to the BBC, I hear," she said.

"Are you a spy?" asked Don Juan, trying not to show the shock he felt at her words.

"Certainly!" She said it coolly, challengingly.

"Then you had better go and report me," said Don Juan, anxious to get her out of the chateau so that Yves could be moved before the police arrived to search the place.

"I shall. This valley seems to be a hotbed of subversion. The curé here is a known member of Témoignage Chrétien. They help Jews, you know. He also has contacts with Combat in Lyons. A turbulent priest, wouldn't you say?"

"You must be thinking of some other curé," said Don Juan, wondering how much of this was bluff. "Our priest is a staunch supporter of the marshal. He believes women belong in the home. I'm not sure that he would find spying an edifying occupation for a woman, either."

"Well answered, Don Juan. It's good to see you don't panic easily," she said.

They stared at each other. But her plain, rather bony face was smiling now. Not a mocking smile—if anything a rather admiring one.

"I work for a third group myself," she said. "It is called the Nettoyage des Administrations Publiques. We are trying to convert the civil service to helping with the Resistance. Like some of the others we are now in direct contact with London."

"Well, I hope you know what you're doing, mademoiselle," said Don Juan carefully. "I am a foreigner in this country and I steer clear of politics. If you are going to report me for listening to the BBC, the nearest police post is at Thorens, I believe. I do not wish to delay you." Don Juan held the door open for her.

She continued to smile as she walked past him and allowed herself to be escorted to the front door.

"It is to 'our people' that I plan to report you, my dear. We know what you are doing, who is upstairs with you. What we did *not* know was how you would react to an emergency. I would say you did rather well. Congratulations. One tip I will give you. Use earphones for the radio. Oh, and start locking your front door."

She shook the bewildered Don Juan's hand and, mounting a bicycle, rode off in the direction of the curé's house.

A week after this extraordinary encounter, the curé came to dine with Don Juan. The date was November 12, 1942. For several days France had been so inundated with rumors of a conflicting nature that even in the remote Val Romanée people felt alarmed and uncertain. Both the curé and Don Juan had radios, and the moment they sat down to eat with Yves, who had had more leisure to listen than the others, they all started to compare notes.

"While it is evident that the Allies have landed in French North Africa," said the curé, "I for one can form no clear idea about whether France will now fight the Allies—is fighting the Allies?"

"Pétain has sent Laval to Berchtesgaden to talk to Hitler," said Don Juan. "The Vichy radio itself announced that."

"Pathetic Vichy," said Yves. "As if Pétain could send *anyone* anywhere anymore. Vichy is finished. Hitler has summoned Laval, his puppet here, to tell him so."

"The BBC?" asked Don Juan.

"Exactly. At six this morning they were broadcasting that on their French service. Moreover, there was an unconfirmed report that the Germans are occupying the whole of what remains of France. They *and the Italians.*"

"I cannot believe that," said the curé. "The marshal will never permit it. We will fight first. You will see!"

There was an awkward silence. It was clear that neither Don Juan nor Yves thought Vichy would fight the Germans even though it still possessed an army and a fleet.

"According to an English-language broadcast I heard this afternoon," said Don Juan at last, "de Gaulle's Free French, as they call them, and General Juin's forces in North Africa are together going to help the British and Americans fight the Germans, who are landing in North Africa, to drive them out. It sounds like chaos. Poor North Africans. Do you think anyone has considered asking them?"

"We are speaking of the French Empire!" said the curé severely.

It was a gloomy meal. Both Yves and Don Juan tried to comfort the poor curé, whose sense of humiliation at his nation's plight was very great. They knew, too, that his trust in the marshal stemmed really from the fact that the hierarchy of the church had committed themselves totally to the Vichy regime, leaving only maverick priests like himself to hew strictly to where their consciences led them.

Before they had finished the *tarte aux pommes*, which had been

Yves's culinary contribution to the meal, the telephone rang. So low had Don Juan kept his profile among people who owned telephones (as the curé did not, for instance) that the unusual sound of its rhythmic clang seemed particularly alarming.

"Hullo, who is on the apparatus?" said Don Juan rather challengingly into the old-fashioned speaker on the wall outside the dining room.

"It is Jeanne, Don Juan. Can you get word to the curé? I will give you a number for him to call."

"He is here. I'll fetch him," said Don Juan, wondering how she dared used the telephone to communicate what was presumably Resistance business.

Don Juan fetched the curé to what the French called the apparatus, an apt term considering the archaic state of their telephone system. Shutting the door behind him, he returned to finish his meal with Yves while the curé spoke in privacy to Jeanne. When he returned he looked ever graver than before.

"The Italians have occupied Annecy. The Boches have given them the Alpes-Maritimes, Var, the Hautes Alpes, the Basses Alpes, Isère, Drôme, Savoie, and Haute Savoie. The whole rest of France is now occupied by the Boches. Jeanne and some friends wish to come here at once," said the curé, looking at Don Juan.

"To the chateau?"

"Yes. They want to install a radio transmitter here, if you agree."

"She said that over the telephone?" Don Juan was incredulous.

"No, we have had contingency plans for some time. She said they 'wished to come for the celebration of your birthday.' It means that with occupation forces in the town it is no longer safe to have their transmitter there. They will want you to learn how to use it. She is to be your outside contact here. There is, of course, great risk involved, but the technicians say that the geographic position of the chateau is ideal, both for broadcasting and for the difficulty of detection by the enemy." He paused over the word. "Yes, we must now call them the enemy. I have to telephone her your answer in a few minutes, Don Juan. Forgive me, my son, for imposing on you such a difficult decision."

"What about Yves, Father?" asked Don Juan. "Doesn't it expose him to extra risk?"

"We have been waiting to move Yves to Switzerland," said the curé. "Now that will become more urgent, although one hears that the Italians are less fanatical than either Vichy or the Germans on the subject of Jews."

"I doubt if they are less fanatical about clandestine radio transmitters," said Yves.

But he and the curé knew that their young host fully understood all the implications of the decision he was being asked to make. Don Juan never really hesitated to accept the assignment. Danger of this kind had always attracted him, and he trusted the curé. Jeanne, however, was an unknown quantity. She was not a woman who appealed to him sexually, which he thought was probably just as well. It was hard for him to think that the nerve-racking test she had imposed on him was necessary, and he was still slightly resentful of it, although he now understood better its purpose. On balance, he knew that he had been hoping for an opportunity to become "active" for the cause. There was unlikely to be a better opportunity than this.

He agreed.

In domestic terms, the immediate result of all this was a *ménage* (almost) *à trois.*

A truck, supposedly delivering firewood to the chateau, came that night with two technicians and Jeanne herself. The technicians installed the transmitter in one of the chateau's copper-domed towers. They then left, leaving Jeanne to instruct Don Juan in the procedures of radio transmission and to initiate him into the mysteries of the code by which communications was made with BCRA (Bureau Central de Renseignements et d'Action) in London. There Colonel Passy, de Gaulle's intelligence chief, and his staff evaluated all intelligence coming out of France and were starting to initiate and coordinate an increasingly military form of resistance to the occupying forces.

Next morning Jeanne breakfasted with Yves and Don Juan, and a new human equation had entered the household in the chateau. It seems doubtful that there will ever be a time when a woman, particularly a youngish woman, who finds herself living on terms of total equality with two male strangers is not obliged to "declare" herself. The "declarations" made both by her and by the males may be of the subtlest kind, but they are necessary just the same. In some cases, and this was one of them, the questions asked and the answers given are at least as important as the unsolicited "declarations" made.

Yves, unlike Don Juan, was attracted to Jeanne as a woman.

Socially and politically they had much in common. They were both of the left, but far from being communist. Their *formation,* as the French say, was from the middle reaches of the bourgeoisie, but being intellectuals, they tended to dismiss bourgeois values. In the French cinema, this attitude has always been a matter more of fashion than of practical politics, but it was nevertheless something of a bond between Yves and Jeanne. Individually both of them could relate to Don Juan without being concerned about his very considerable sophistication of mind and worldliness, to say nothing of his artistocratic origins. Facing him *together*, they presented more than a hint of class solidarity, that origin of class hostility, without, perhaps, intending to to be so.

Don Juan's relationship with Jeanne, she at once made clear, was one in which she would give the orders and he would obey without question. She did not impose this arrangement on him in an arrogant way. On the contrary, she explained it as being essential to their safety and that of many others who depended upon them. But whereas he had followed Inés as people do follow a natural leader, he had much more difficulty in accepting Jeanne's authority. He tried to rationalize this to himself as follows: She had chosen to recruit him, she had, quite unnecessarily, deprived him of some of his much accustomed freedom of action, and she was now imposing upon him a discipline. Jeanne was also one of the very rare women who appeared to have no interest in him as a man. That interest she had reserved for Yves, and Don Juan was forced to admit that he resented it. Not very much. But a pinprick of annoyance was there, and he disliked himself for feeling it. For he recognized that it stemmed from what old Father Lemoine would have called simply the "sin of pride."

On the night of November 27, the French navy scuttled its fleet at Toulon rather than let it fall into the hands of the Germans. At the same time, all over what had been Vichy France the French army, which had not fired a shot to prevent the latest occupation, was turned out of its barracks, like sheep being led to be shorn, and disarmed. In some cases, however, its officers managed to hand over sizable quantities of arms to the Resistance before the enemy closed in on them. Trucks came by Don Juan's chateau during the night, dropping off crates of arms, and Jeanne and Don Juan spent the whole of the next twenty-four hours working in eight-hour shifts of communication with London.

The months that followed were in some ways more monotonous than Don Juan would have expected, considering he now risked his life daily, communicating with London. Jeanne spent about half the week at the chateau and the other half traveling by bicycle and bus to meet with other members of the Resistance. Never at any time did Don Juan meet these people, and on the rare occasions that they came by the chateau, she ordered him to stay in what they now called the radio tower so that he could never be compromised by knowing them, even by sight.

He heard from the curé that Edwige had given birth to a boy, to be called Jean-Paul after the curé himself, and that Maurice was proving to be an admirable husband and father. Don Juan contrived to walk by Maurice's farm early one morning and saw Edwige coming home from the cow sheds, her marvelous breasts swollen with milk. She did not see him, and he stayed for a few minutes after she had gone into the house, waiting he was not quite sure for what. He had promised the curé not to ask to see the child, nor to speak to Edwige. But standing there in the shadow of the hedgerow, squinting at the farmhouse in the early-morning sun, he heard, at last, a baby crying.

Don Juan found that there were tears in his eyes. Hot tears such as a child sheds and he had not experienced himself since the day of his return from Ireland, hoping in vain that his mother would comfort him. He found himself wondering why he was weeping. Was it for the child he would never know, for the comfortable domesticity of Edwige with their son at her breast? Or was it for himself? For these moments of numbing loneliness which his nature and his life had reserved for him?

One night Don Juan became conscious that Jeanne had climbed the stairs to Yves's apartment. It had been a pleasant evening, in which the curé had participated, and they had listened to Yves explaining exactly how a motion picture was made, the importance of each piece of equipment; of how the director, like the conductor of an orchestra, must know each of his technicians' work, the better to direct them; and most fascinating of all, how a great director, such as Clair, handled his actors and actresses, how the art of directing thespians was a kind of seduction.

Don Juan, watching Yves and Jeanne, was not slow to see that his friend the would-be film director was using his beautifully told story as a metaphor for the drama of his own love affair with Jeanne. The curé had drunk deep of the good red Hermitage, of which Don Juan still had an abundance in his cellar, and missed the twin-tiered nuances of Yves's performance. They had all gone to their separate apartments, leaving the curé asleep by the fire. The old man usually awoke after an hour or so and enjoyed walking home alone, clearing his head in the night air.

The following day Jeanne went by bicycle to Annecy. The final arrangements for smuggling Yves over the border into neutral Switzerland were being made there.

Don Juan and Yves spent the morning in the studio, where the stations of the cross were all but finished.

"What do you think Jeanne's life was like before the war?" asked Yves suddenly.

Don Juan was surprised at this question. "But you are much closer to Jeanne than I," he said.

"She never talks of the past. You met her before I did. Through a mutual friend, I believe? I thought you might have some clue."

"None. She was a teacher, fired by the Vichy authorities for being a socialist."

"Might she have been married?"

"It's possible," said Don Juan. "I never thought of it. She seems so *single*, so independent, somehow."

"Will you keep a secret?" asked Yves. Then with a nervous laugh he continued, his words coming out in an unstoppable stream. "I have been so attracted to her. She has such strength, such a sense of herself. Like a spendid cat that can never actually *belong* to anyone. Or that is what I thought. Here we meet, I said to myself, in the middle of this frightful war. There will be a conflagration between us that neither will ever forget. It has nothing to do with my love for my wife, which is constant, or her love for her independence, which seems so evident. My friend, it was a disaster."

Don Juan, who was painting in the detail of Yves's feet, where the soldier hammering the nail appears in the pre-crucifixion scene, did not comment. He knew there would be more.

"I could not do it. And I wanted so much to do it."

"Could not? Because of your wife?" asked Don Juan.

"Because of my wife, because of my mother, who I pray is now safely dead and out of *their hands,* because, because."

"Did Jeanne understand?" asked Don Juan gently.

"She understood that I did not seem to want to make love to her. She dressed and left me, saying, 'It has been the story of my life as a woman.'"

"Is that why you asked me if she'd been married?"

"Yes."

"What a pity you aren't a Catholic, Yves. Then you could have done it and confessed it. If you believed that God absolved you, as they do, then how much more would your womenfolk forgive you." Don Juan said this with a smile; he was trying to lighten the atmosphere, to take away some of Yves's assumed burden of guilt.

"It is not for nothing that our Jewish brother Sigmund Freud invented psychiatry," he said. "You're right, all of us do so need the confessional." And Yves smiled.

"For what it is worth, I think it may have been something in Jeanne that stopped you," said Don Juan seriously, wondering if *he* could make love to Jeanne.

"My dear confessor, you are wrong." Yves laughed.

But whether or not Yves was being gallant, it was *he* who was wrong.

On February 5, 1943, Yves left the chateau concealed in a coffinlike box hidden under fifty or so crates of soda-pop bottles. Jeanne went straight to her room after he had left. Don Juan took her up some supper on a tray and put it on the floor outside, knocking and calling through the door to tell her it was there. He was on his way down the passage when he heard the door open. She called his name.

He turned and saw her standing there, holding the tray, her eyes red from crying.

"Thank you, Don Juan," she said, and then, as if triggered by something beyond her control, she started to cry again and hurried back to her room.

Don Juan followed her, closing the door behind him.

She had lit a wood fire under the great marble mantelshelf in the corner of her room. Now she sat huddled in front of it, hugging herself with her arms and shaking with the sobs she could no longer control. Don Juan poured her a glass of wine from the bottle he had brought her on the tray. He knelt beside her, taking a sip of it and smiling to show her he found it good. She looked at him through her reddened, blurred eyes, and she was, for an instant, infinitely dear to him. He was reminded of all the tears that women might have, probably had, shed on his account and that he had not been there to help staunch. And now she cried for another, and it was his turn to be there. He dried and kissed her eyes, and when the sobs returned he held her close to him as one holds a child. There was nothing he could *say* to make it better for her.

Speechless, he coaxed her to eat a little of the food he had brought her. And speechless she responded by simply staring at him now and then as if she were seeing him for the first time.

"I thought that, as far as women were concerned, you were simply a fucker!" she said at last.

Don Juan concealed from her how much this indictment appalled him. Finding her calm at last, he left her.

Confirmation that Yves had made it to the safety of Switzerland came a few days later. They were sitting side-by-side in the radio tower when the message came back from London in a routine "exchange of information" session.

Jeanne leaned her head on Don Juan's shoulder for an instant, then quickly withdrew it. He looked around at her and saw an expression of such smiling relief on her face that he laughed, and she laughed too.

"So I am free," she said.

"What?" He didn't understand.

"Now that he's safe, he's *hers* again. I'm free."

He found something superb about her rediscovered pride.

"May I kiss you in celebration?" he asked.

"Yes," she said, but her eyes were suddenly different, staring at him as they had done the night she had cried by the fire.

He kissed her on the lips, the eyes, the soft underpart of her chin, but she did not move. Nor did her eyes close.

"Doesn't that please you?" he asked. "It's not obligatory that it should. I hope I'm not *just* a fucker, or a kisser. But there really was something about you just then that made me want to kiss you very much."

She didn't answer for a moment, but stared at him, her eyes very fixed, as if they expected his face to light up with some revealing answer.

Then she asked, "Are you lonely?"

He considered. "At this moment in my life, perhaps I am. Usually not."

"With me it is permanent," she said.

He waited.

"Mireille told me about you. The lover of the *tout Paris*, of the boulevards, even of the fairs and the circuses. You couldn't have been lonely then. She said you were extraordinary in bed. Better even than her pet python. I could not bear the thought of you. But she said she trusted you. So in the end, here we all are. And you are not what I thought you were. Me, I am plain. Some people say I have fine eyes. But the rest of me I sometimes think was put together with leftovers after other, properly made, women had been sent out beautiful into the world. But you kissed me then as if you really wanted to. As *he* did the other night."

Again he waited.

"It is my fate, Juan, that I cannot respond. You kiss me. I like it. If he had made love to me I would have loved it. But he would have been disappointed. Because, me, I can but lie there, glad that it is happening. If I like the person, naturally. But they expect something of me. Kisses, sighs, the movement of my body, participation, you see. A man once pulled himself away from me—'You make me feel like a necrophiliac,' he said."

He kissed her hands, her bony, awkward hands with their red knuckles. Her smell was very clean and fresh and womanly. He liked her smell.

"Have you ever been with a frigid woman?" she asked.

"With Mr. Freud and Mr. Jung's phraseology I am both unfamiliar and slightly uncomfortable. They sound cabalistic and smack of alchemy in my ears," said Don Juan sincerely.

"Oh, frigidity is real enough," she said with finality.

Another message was coming through, and Don Juan opened up the code book. "Will you tell me more about it in bed tonight?" he asked as London transmitted: MARINER VERSE DEAL COAST SHORES PIECE OF STONE RAMSGATE SPAN . . . indicating the poem that held the code key. It amused and warmed Don Juan to the British that they could use nursery rhymes and doggerel for such deadly things as war codes. The war, seen from Britain, probably seemed like an amusing game. He almost expected to hear Springer speaking over the ether, saying, "You got it right, angel. Aren't you a clever puss?"

Jeanne was answering, "I'd like that. But you have been warned."

Don Juan thought he understood Jeanne to some degree, and up to a certain point, he did. Not for nothing had he spent his entire life considering the endless permutations of emotion and desire that enriched the sex which enthralled him.

He started out with an advantage given to few men. There was a quality of natural sympathy in him that women sensed and that made them tell him at least part of their feelings. What he often missed was what they themselves were unaware of, the buried feelings, the hidden, perhaps guilty, preferences or desires, needs or longings. It is the task of lovers such as Don Juan to help women find these things in themselves.

So he made a small experiment.

"There is a bottle of champagne in the cooling larder," he said as he left her in the drawing room that night. "Perhaps you'll bring it up with you." She stared after him.

When she arrived in the bedroom with the champagne, he opened it for them both with his usual courtesy, and they drank two glasses each quite quickly, without speaking.

She went to her room to get undressed, and came back in a cambric nightgown such as peasants wore. She found him in bed reading Le Cahier Noir, a Gaullist propaganda piece by Mauriac dropped into Vichy by Free French bombers attached to the British Royal Air Force. She slipped into bed beside him, finding him naked beneath the covers.

"Mauriac has such a wonderful talent for invective," said Don Juan. "Listen to this: 'So many, many of my countrymen are moved by this one elementary passion: fear. They will not admit it: and they are making a great fuss in praise of the marshal, and they keep invoking Joan of Arc; but, in fact, it all boils down to this one simple need: to save their privileges, to avoid a final reckoning. . . .' D'you think that's true?"

She lay beside him feeling the warmth of his body close to her, and better than that, the warmth of his human company, the pleasant mixture of threat and promise that she found in males she liked.

"It's particularly true in the cities and towns. A little less so in the countryside," she said.

"Here's another piece of his: 'Too many Frenchmen are giving the enemy a pretty ignominious spectacle of themselves—the French police, which is like the faithful watchdog of the black market profiteers, all these businessmen and all these men of letters who are being enriched by the Army of Occupation—they belong to an undying species. Already in 1796 Mallet du Pan wrote: "Everybody is trying by a thousand different means, and at any price, not to have to share in the general distress. People think only of themselves, themselves, themselves . . ."' I think as I read that how lucky I am to have friends like you and the curé at such a time," concluded Don Juan, closing the Cahier and turning out the bedside light.

She was silent, and he could feel that she trembled slightly beside him. He kissed her lips in the dark and found them, as he had expected, immobile. He caressed her rather meager breasts and found the nipples rising under the palm of his hand. Still she trembled slightly, but remained quite motionless. He ran his hand over her very flat belly and found her cleft to be welcomingly open, warm and viscous. But when he came to her rose she only murmured, "That tickles. I'm sorry. It's boring, but it *always does.*"

Without another word he took her. He raised her legs till her feet faced the darkened ceiling. Before entering her, he whispered, "Are you ready?"

"Do whatever you want, whatever you *do*. For me I shall be useless, but it will be good to know what Mireille meant when she said you were better than her python."

She means it, thought Don Juan.

He made love to her deep and hard, "with her sandals in the air," as the Greeks used to say. He bent her double and had her from the side, and behind, from underneath, and the other way around. He could feel the constant flow within her that proclaimed that whatever other effect he was having on her, he could not be hurting her.

Sometimes she murmured, "What are you doing to me?" But it was not a question that required an answer. No sign of climax did she evince. And he slept beside her afterward, waking her twice again in the night and finding her cleft as welcoming as ever, her body as motionless as always.

In the morning he woke to find her dressed and bringing his breakfast on a tray. She had made some baked eggs, a great treat with the rationing, and if the coffee consisted of acorns and chicory, it still tasted wonderful, the better for being brought on a tray. They spoke of work to be done during the day. She had to go for a rendezvous on the other side of Thorens with a woman who cleaned the police barracks and had been enrolled to spy for the Resistance.

"What did you *feel?*" He could not help asking, although he sensed that she hated questions.

"Don't ask me questions. Just use me. Whenever you feel like it. Whenever our work permits it."

That was how it was to be between them. She was the indisputable boss of the intelligence operation they carried on together, although she had started to train him to replace her in case one day she did not return. But in their life as man and woman, she assumed a very different role. He was not permitted to do anything personal and domestic for himself. Not a piece of sewing or pressing or washing or cooking. Doing all these things for him gave her real pleasure. She would wear a plain plaid skirt when they were alone together, without underclothes or stockings. Although never by any special sound or gesture did she show her pleasure, when he bent her over the kitchen table and had her there, he knew that such sudden, violent possessions did indeed give her a kind of ecstasy in her female soul, no less wonderful for her than the orgasms of other women. But of these feelings, or indeed any feelings, she never spoke to Don Juan. He kissed her often, believing rightly that in her heart she kissed him back.

. . .

The passing into law by the government of the Service de Travail Obligatoire (STO) was probably one of the most important events in France during the year 1943. It involved the calling up of all able-bodied young men below a certain age, including the young peasants, for work in German factories. These Frenchmen were to replace German workers who were now being called up into the army after the frightful losses that had followed the Nazi defeat at Stalingrad. Suddenly the Resistance had no shortage of recruits, and even the peasants who had lived rather well at their privileged occupation now faced the loss of their young men. The marshal had let them down. The combination of this feeling and the growing conviction that they were on the wrong side galvanized the French to oppose Vichy and the Germans at long last.

The next most important event for those in southeastern France was the Italian armistice with the Allies in September 1943, following the Anglo-American invasion of the Italian mainland. At a stroke of the pen Italy ceased to be an ally of Germany, and Nazi troops took over the garrisoning of the *whole* of France. All that Don Juan had seen of the easygoing Italian occupation forces was some soldiers who came up to the Val Romanée to help the shorthanded farmers bring in the harvest. Peasants themselves and homesick for their own land, they were immensely popular with the local people, particularly the women. Now they had gone, and German patrols came through the valley at regular intervals, including, ominously, a radio-detection vehicle. Warned of its coming, Jeanne was able to make sure that she and Don Juan ceased transmitting till it was well away from the area.

When Don Juan's task of creating the fourteen panels representing the stations of the cross for the church was completed, the curé ordained a special service of thanksgiving. Jeanne was, like so many of the French left, a defiant atheist in her Roman Catholic country, but occasions like these were always exceptions, and she accompanied Don Juan in joining the rest of the congregation for the service. The bishop of the Haute Savoie had been invited to unveil the panels, each of which had been covered with a cloth, so that this ceremony could take place before the service began.

Trestle tables laden with plates of food prepared by the peasants' wives, and wine and cordials given by the peasants themselves, were set up in the churchyard to be enjoyed after the service. It was here everyone gathered to await the arrival of the bishop.

Don Juan himself was the subject of something akin to stage fright. No one but the curé and Jeanne, and, of course, the now absent Yves, had seen the panels. These three, he felt, were too close to him in various ways to give objective criticism. But his concern over his art was quite taken away by an event that now occurred which seemed so bizarre that it made both him and Jeanne giggle nervously.

The copper towers of Don Juan's chateau could be seen beyond the bend in the road from the churchyard, and beyond this the mountain road that led to Annecy. From here the bishop's vehicle was expected to come, although what that would be at this stage of the war no one could guess. The curé thought perhaps a taxi. Before anything at all appeared, however, the wailing of police sirens was heard, and to Jeanne and Don Juan's horror, they seemed to pause outside the chateau, whose gate and driveway were invisible from where they stood. After a moment, though, the sirens started wailing again, and four German army motorcyclists appeared, escorting a huge open Mercedes staff car. In the back of this splendid vehicle sat the bishop next to a lady in a Bavarian felt hunting hat, resplendent with green and red cock feathers. In the front, sitting next to the driver, sat a general officer of the Wehrmacht in full dress.

The driver leaped out and helped the bishop from the car while the curé led his congregation in greeting their spiritual leader. Don Juan noticed that the general and the lady waited discreetly by the car while the bishop was introduced to the whole of the curé's flock, each person genuflecting slightly and kissing the episcopal ring. Then the bishop, a man with a face as empty as a pudding, with eyes like currants stuck indiscriminately on either side of a bulbous nose, raised his hands in one of those gestures that divines use so facilely when they wish to command attention.

"My children," he intoned, "I wish to introduce to you all my honored guests, Colonel General von Carlowitz and Frau Generalin von Carlowitz, who have been kind enough to transport me here today for this auspicious occasion. They are lovers of art, of France, and of the great church which must unite us all in these difficult times when the Bolshevik menace is at our door, when only the gallantry of the German armies and our boys who fight by their sides protect us all from the Russian hordes of barbarism and atheism."

Don Juan watched the curé's face while this speech was in progress. He saw that the old man had closed his eyes, as if very tired, and that his lips moved, perhaps in a prayer for the delivery of his church from fools and knaves. The people of the Val Romanée were so inured to speeches of this kind on the Vichy radio that they hardly heard what the bishop said. They did, however, stare hard at the

Colonel General, magnificent in his dove-gray uniform with its golden epaulets and scarlet and green facings, now unbuckling his sword and revolver and handing them to his driver in preparation for entering the church. Don Juan found his face interesting. It had the yellowish complexion of the North Germans, with alert, intelligent gray eyes and a sensitive mouth. When he removed his hat, a head of silky silver hair was revealed, hair which had not quite succumbed to the brilliantine and blew about in the breeze. His frau was a plump woman who must once have been very beautiful, but whose good features were now slightly blurred by being overfleshed; her eyes were brown, in striking contrast to her still-golden hair.

Inside the church everyone crowded in the center aisles while the bishop, with the curé and Don Juan at his elbow, toured the church, unveiling the tablets on the walls in strict order, from one to fourteen.

"Ah, yes," said the bishop of each one, intoning the obvious, "The scourging," or "Ah, yes, the crucifixion!" Then, pausing at each one, he blessed it with the sign of the cross and made an incantation in Latin that neither Don Juan nor anyone else present could understand. Then he and the curé went to the vestry to robe themselves for the serivce, and the congregation surged around the tablets, commenting and, on the whole, admiring them.

Don Juan found himself facing the general and his wife, who introduced themselves in perfect French with punctilious courtesy by their Christian and surnames.

"Otto von Carlowitz!" said the general with a slight bow.

"My name is Jean," said Don Juan, hastily making his name French.

"My wife, Irma von Carlowitz," went on the general.

Don Juan shook hands with them both.

"May I say that I think they are extraordinary, Jean," said the general's wife. "They have what in England they would call a pre-Raphaelite quality—one is reminded a little of Dante Gabriel Rossetti."

"Thank you," said Don Juan sincerely, since here was clearly a woman who knew about painting, and a German who wasn't afraid of praising an Italian Englishman.

"Remarkable," said the general. "The Saviour's figure is reminiscent of those Christs in Byzantine icons. It is a wonderfully authentic Levantine face. I do congratulate you. Is this the style in which you usually work? I mean, do you specialize in sacred art?"

Jeanne was now alongside them as they surveyed the carefully spaced and numbered paintings on the wall. Don Juan introduced them to her and then answered the general. "No, I used this style because I hoped it would make the story come alive for the people in the valley. The faces are their kind of faces. I wanted to do something a little Van Eyckish for the curé. My usual style is much freer, looser, sometimes abstract."

"Ah so, Van Eyck's altarpiece at Ghent, with those faces of the good Flemish burghers," said the general.

"Has it survived?" asked Don Juan innocently, wondering why Jeanne frowned at him.

"Happily, I believe it has," said the general.

But the curé had entered the sanctuary with the bishop, and everyone hurried to take their pews. Don Juan and Jeanne sat at the back with the general and his wife. Later, when the two Germans went to the altar rail to take the sacrament, Jeanne whispered to Don Juan.

"Ask them back to the castle!" she said.

"What?" Don Juan was incredulous.

"You can see they're crazy about art. Take them to your studio."

"Suppose they investigate me and find I'm a Spanish revolutionary?"

"They won't. The Nettoyage has changed your papers to show you as Francoist."

"What?" Don Juan was genuinely furious.

"We couldn't risk not doing so. Oh, I'm so sorry." She saw real anger on his face for the first time since she had known him, and it frightened her.

"How dare you do that without asking me?" he said aloud, making several people look around at them.

"My dear, your life could be at stake. They're shipping Spanish refugees either back to Spain or to the factories in Germany. Thousands have had to join the Maquis in the mountains."

"Well, I could do that, too," said Don Juan. "You've falsified my whole life without even asking me."

"Shh. Please. After the war everyone will know the truth. You're much too useful to us here. Besides, I need you."

He looked at her. Her face was scarlet and there were tears in her eyes. She's just afraid she's going to lose an agent, he thought. But she's taken too much for granted. And the idea of going back into "active" work for the cause with the armed Maquis Resistance seemed the perfect solution to ending a relationship in which he suddenly felt trapped, taken over. He was determined to tell her of his decision as soon as they got home.

There is a charm to bucolic banquets in France that puts everyone in a good humor. The French are at their very best when at table, Don Juan thought, as he surveyed the simple weathered faces of his neighbors, already flushed with wine, but all overflowing with unaccustomed friendliness for each other. The general mixed with the peasants and talked to them in his faultless French about crops and the prospects for a summer of good weather. He told them he'd heard that the Italians had helped out the previous year, and he hoped to be able to spare some men himself. They spoke to him respectfully, but glanced warily at his bodyguards, who stood watchfully by at the lych-gate of the church, their arms slung over their shoulders at the ready.

The Frau Generalin, as the bishop called her, talked to Don Juan and Jeanne while the curé and the bishop discussed matters ecclesiastical with the churchwardens. Don Juan was determined not to invite the Germans to the chateau. He saw only too well what was in Jeanne's mind. Here were Boches who were determined to seduce the local population with a little unaccustomed kindness. They seemed to have a real love for art, and it might be possible for Don Juan to make a genuine social connection with them. From such a relationship priceless information for the Resistance might eventually be gleaned. But Don Juan did not want to be a spy. He knew that "spying" was something incompatible with his nature. Clandestine radio work, he understood, was vital. It was as far as he was prepared to go in the spying line. Or so, for the moment, he thought.

"We stopped at the most delightful chateau just up the road," the Frau Generalin was saying. "It reminded me of those fairy castles in the Gustave Doré illustrations to the Baron Münchhausen stories. So romantic."

"It is Jean's," said Jeanne.

"Good heavens, is your studio there?"

"Yes," said Don Juan reluctantly, conscious that Jeanne was smiling at him.

"But my dear Jean, would you think it a terrible imposition if the general and I came and had a look at some of your other paintings?" asked the Frau Generalin. "We are collectors, you know. I am only here for a few weeks' holiday from my war work in Dresden, but we have already been able to buy one or two important pictures here."

"I'm not surprised, these are very hard times," said Don Juan.

But the expression on the German woman's face at this stinging remark made him regret it instantly. She was not his enemy.

"Please forgive me," he said quickly and as gracefully as he could. "The reflex actions of war. I do hope you will come and visit us?"

"Are you sure?" she said, about to turn to her husband.

"Quite sure!" he said, and smiled at her. He was wondering whether Rubens could have resisted her. He imagined the flowing voluptuousness of her naked; the pinky-blue shadows of her flesh where it folded, and it must fold a good deal. She would have a golden fleece, he thought, and watching her walk over to the general, he desired her. Jeanne noticed this and sighed. She had started something in which, it seemed, she was destined to be the loser.

In the studio at the chateau Don Juan was subjected to an unaccustomed but pleasant experience. Two genuinely knowledgeable people discussed his work with passionate interest and excitement. Two hours slipped by before the bishop's evident impatience caused the Germans to leave, but not before the general had conceived of the idea of having Don Juan paint his wife's portrait and she had responded by suggesting that they commission a matched pair of portraits of herself and her husband. Don Juan promised to consider the matter and let them know.

"I strongly advise you to agree, young man," said the bishop before they left. "These are very fine Germans. From one of the best Saxon families." Don Juan made no answer to the fatuous bishop. He and Jeanne and the curé relaxed and unwound with some wine after the excitement of the day, and discussed the proposed portraits.

"Is there not a terrible danger in having these Germans come here with the radio up in the tower?" asked the curé.

"On the contrary," said Jeanne. "Who would suspect a place the Boches frequent? How long each day can a portrait sitting take?"

"A few hours, usually," said Don Juan. "I can't imagine a German general being able to spare that."

"Being here is a rest cure for him. He's just back from a year on the Russian front," said Jeanne. "Listen, Juan, it's a heaven-sent opportunity."

"Let's keep heaven out of it," said the curé. "I understand Don Juan's reluctance. It is not the sort of work anyone *likes* to do. But if Jeanne thinks it can be useful, then surely there can be no question but that you must do it?"

Reluctantly Don Juan agreed.

At about this time the French police came through the valley, warning certain young peasants that they must soon leave for Germany under the STO Act. Among these was Maurice, Edwige's husband. He was given six weeks' notice so that he could make such arrangements as might be necessary concerning his farm. For out of the dowry Don Juan had provided for Edwige, he had bought himself nearly a thousand acres of the choicest land in the Val Romanée. He and Edwige had attended the service of thanksgiving, but they had kept out of the way of Don Juan. Only as the notables, Don Juan among them, started to walk up the road toward the chateau did Edwige allow herself to stare after them. She saw Jeanne slip her arm through Don Juan's, and at once she felt quite sick with jealousy. "Who is that woman with *him?*" she asked Maurice.

"They say she was a red schoolteacher in Annecy," said Maurice.

"I hate her!"

"Edwige!"

"I'm sorry, I can't help it," she said.

"You promised to forget all about him. You promised!" said the unhappy Maurice.

"How could I forget? I'm a human being. I have his child."

She burst into tears, and a red-faced, furious Maurice gripped her arm and hauled her along the road to their farm, acutely aware that literally dozens of their friends and neighbors heard her wails and guessed the cause.

Once he had her inside the house he took off his belt and beat her while her baby howled. He left her on the floor of the parlor in a spreading pool from a bloodied nose and her milk leaking through her torn blouse. Fortunately, her parents had seen Maurice taking her home and came by to see if she was all right.

Somehow the parents and the curé managed to patch things up between the young couple in the ensuing weeks. But for Maurice the knowledge that Don Juan would still be in the valley after he himself left for Germany was intolerable. In vain the curé assured him that Don Juan would never dishonor his agreement not to see Edwige. Although Maurice could not bring himself to say so to the curé, it was Edwige he distrusted.

Meanwhile, the sittings had started on a daily basis. The general's lady was to be painted first, because she had to return soon to her home near Dresden. On the first day she brought a number of dresses from which he could choose. He selected something rather Grecian which gathered under the bust and showed off her golden breasts to great advantage. Jeanne made a point of being there to help pin the dress as Don Juan wanted it, and then she and the general's wife talked while Don Juan made his preliminary sketches in charcoal.

Jeanne contrived on this and subsequent occasions to make the German woman understand that *she* had a proprietary right to Don Juan, that *she* was his woman. "Jean and I," she would say, or "As Jean is always telling me . . ."

While the general's wife was sitting, a German driver would wait outside the chateau in the staff car listening to the radio. One day he was astounded to hear "All mimsy were the borogoves, and the mome raths outgrabe" being repeated over and over again. Even if he had understood English it would presumably have puzzled him; as it was, he assumed it to be some obscure European dialect and switched to another channel.

Predictably, when the general came for his first sitting Jeanne left Don Juan alone with him. He came in uniform, but once at the studio he changed into a gray suit, allowing Don Juan to choose a tie from a selection he had brought with him.

"I'm rather surprised, sir, that you decided to be painted in mufti," said Don Juan.

"Although my whole career has been in the army, it isn't what I wanted to do, how I see myself." said the general. "I would like to have had the opportunity to be a patron of the arts. As a collector, if I could have afforded that, or perhaps as the curator of some important art gallery."

"Why the army then?" asked Don Juan, blocking in with firm lines the planes of the general's handsome skull.

"A family tradition. My native Saxony was not always the soft and cultured kingdom that Bismarck despised. It was once a great military power. My family's pretensions, if you will, date from those times," said the general, smiling.

Don Juan liked the smile and asked the general to keep it. He wondered what he had to lose in asking him what he thought of Hitler's ambitions for Europe. Nothing, he decided, and then had the inspiration to base the question around the general's known Catholicism.

"Will Herr Hitler's Thousand Year Reich be the bastion of Christianity the bishop described in his little speech, sir?" he asked.

"Christianity has great tenacity, my boy. Do not despair of it," said the general obliquely.

"If Germany were in France's place, what do you think the German people would do?" asked Don Juan.

"What did they do when Napoleon tried to conquer all Europe?"

"In the end the Germans and the other Europeans brought Napoleon to justice."

"So they did. But what did they do to France?"

"Ah, yes," said Don Juan, curiously excited at the direction this conversation was taking. "To France they gave the most magnanimous peace in history, at the Congress of Vienna."

"Exactly. The Treaty of Versailles in 1918, on the other hand, imposed on Germany intolerable burdens. The Kaiser, who was, with others, responsible for the war, suffered little or nothing. I visited him at Doorn, where he still lives. It's a great deal more comfortable than St. Helena, where the British sent Napoleon, I can tell you."

"Do you have much hope for a just peace?" asked Don Juan, sensing that he dared.

"Both Irma and I pray for it, wherever we are, together or apart, each morning, each night. We have a son in Italy and another still in Russia."

On the next occasion they met in the studio, Don Juan, encouraged by their first talk, asked the general a far tougher question.

"In France, since the fall of the Third Republic we have heard a great deal about the international Jewish conspiracy which is supposed to have been responsible for so many of our ills. Do *all* the Germans really believe that?"

The general did not answer. But before leaving he looked hard at Don Juan's face. "Is the mystery of the anonymous Jean that he is a Jew?"

Don Juan swallowed hard.

"Perhaps," he said.

"Brave of you to say that, but I think not," said the general. "Still, you may have discovered why I wish to be painted in mufti. Let's talk of pleasanter things next time."

But there was not to be a next time. The following day Maurice was due to leave for Thorens to report to the police. He decided to go to the chateau to speak to Don Juan man to man and express his fears about Edwige. The rich Spaniard was, after all, about his own age. No one to fear. He found the general leaving, the front door still ajar. In the front hall he saw Don Juan's retreating figure running up the stairs. A woman's voice was calling from above.

"Has the general gone?"

"Yes."

"He stayed so long."

"The drawing went so well. I've started painting already. He wanted to see the colors of the face blocked in. He's really very interested, you know."

Maurice was about to call after Don Juan when the woman's voice said, "I'm going up to the radio tower. London asked us to get through early."

"I'll be there in a minute. I've just got to wash the brushes first," said Don Juan's voice.

Now Maurice was not quite sure what he had heard, but the word "radio" stuck in his mind. That and the word "London." He wanted time to think this over, and meanwhile Don Juan had disappeared somewhere on the first-floor landing. Maurice went into the drawing room, that frighteningly formal room Edwige had described to him. He looked around him at Don Juan's haughty Spanish ancestors in their gold frames and wondered whether all this gilt and grandeur was what she had hoped for her child. Or did she simply long for the tall young man upstairs to whom the good God seemed to have given so much more than his fair share: money, looks, and talent? It really seemed monstrously unjust that the foreigner should occupy this castle from which he could behave, had behaved, toward the girls in the valley like one of the hateful aristocrats before the eighteenth-century revolution. As if he had the *droit du seigneur.* The right to have first go at a peasant's virgin bride. Exactly what he had done to Edwige, now he came to think about it, and then simply paid a little money to get rid of her. While thinking these thoughts, Maurice heard steps again on the stair. He saw Don Juan cross the hall and lock and bolt the front door. Maurice did nothing to attract his attention, but waited for him to go upstairs again. Then he followed.

Ten minutes later Maurice tiptoed hurriedly across the hall, and, making for the kitchen, let himself out by the back door. He thought he had heard enough to know what he could now do to rid himself of Don Juan.

A German officer telephoned the chateau next day to say the general's wife would not be coming for her sitting. Nothing more. Finding time on his hands, Don Juan went to find Jeanne. She was in the kitchen putting the finishing touches to the garnishing of a large trout which that gifted fisherman, the curé, had given them, before putting it in the oven.

"Do we have time before it is cooked?" he asked.

"You have time," she answered, smiling.

"I want you naked on the bed," he said.

"In broad daylight? It will not be a pretty sight." She laughed her slightly bitter laugh, but let him lead her running up the stairs.

He threw his clothes off, letting them fall in a heap, and then with tremendous urgency he helped her undress.

"The trout will take a little while, Juan," she said, laughing more genuinely this time. But he was already kissing her, tracing her whole angular body with his mouth. And then she did something she had never done before—she raised her thighs and, using her hands awkwardly, drew him into her.

The trout must have been a crisp fish indeed, and still he probed deep inside her, each thrust now making her head turn from side to side, faster and faster, and then suddenly he felt as if an earthquake were taking place below him. Jeanne, finding herself blinded, her eyes unable to open, losing control of her whole body, tried for one more moment to stop the dam within her from breaking. She held on to Don Juan as if she were drowning and shouted to him as though he were far, far away to "hold on to me, don't let me go! Oh no! Hold on to me, please!" And then she sank into a spinning, surreal oblivion where *he* seemed to be everywhere around her, below her, above her, inside her, above all inside her.

Afterward he went and rescued the smoking fish and then came back to bed. They slept in each other's arms and then did it again, and it was the same, again later that night, and it was the same. In the morning she bicycled to Annecy.

They picked her up in the late afternoon walking by the lake at Annecy, under the clipped plane trees, wheeling her bicycle. She took a long look at the distant Mont Blanc, so beautiful in the evening light, and wondered if she would ever see it again.

Don Juan received no message from her next day. Nor was there any further word from the Germans. He broadcast this news to London and told them he would broadcast no further until he had word from her. They agreed.

The cleaning women came the next day. One of them brought a sealed envelope from the curé. It was unsigned and said simply, "Go!"

He hurried upstairs and changed into his strongest walking shoes, put on the hardest-wearing shirt and corduroy pants he had, stuffed his pockets with as much money as he could find in the house. He took the code books and burned them in the kitchen stove, and he left a check for the cleaning woman in the kitchen and walked out by the back door. But they were just arriving to arrest him.

13
Don Juan Visits Hell

I am here, more than that I do not know, further than that I cannot go. My ship has no rudder, and it is blown by the wind that blows in the undermost regions of death.

—Franz Kafka, *The Hunter Gracchus*

For the first time in his life Don Juan was grateful for the experience of Deerhurst. It was not that the prison in which he now found himself was really much like the famous public school, but the smell of fear and pain it exuded was familiar, and he had been, to some degree, inoculated against it.

For what happened on his arrival, Jeanne had prepared him. The hours of being leaned, hands supporting body at a forty-five-degree angle, against a wall and occasionally beaten with rubber truncheons were standard French police procedure. If the Gestapo was in charge of this operation, he heard no German voices. The warders who took his clothes and gave him a suit best described as hempen pajamas, who searched him at regular intervals, using a cunning and painful device to peer into his anus, these people were a mixture of French types: a Provençal, a Corsican, and some local Savoyards.

He was eventually confined alone in a cell which resembled a none too commodious tomb. It contained a wooden pallet-bed and a bucket and nothing else whatever. It had no window, but a light, encased in a steel grill, burned night and day. The door had the conventional peephole through which he could be watched.

Don Juan thought mostly about Jeanne. Occasionally he heard the muffled sound of distant pain and wondered if it was hers. He was immensely grateful that she had told him nothing, knowing that she had enough information to be worth torturing. He occupied his mind ceaselessly in trying to organize a point of view that would make it possible for him to resist them when they came to question him. He rehearsed what he knew.

The radio activity to London. That was undeniable. They would have found the radio.

The code books. They were burned. But the codes would have been changed anyway.

Jeanne's other activities. Of these he knew nothing. No names. No faces.

All he knew was that the curé was also involved because of Yves, but he honestly believed that the curé's principal role was as part of an occasional chain of decent Catholic priests who were making it their business to help the Jews and perhaps other fugitives. He could not imagine that he was party to the bombings and assassinations with which the Resistance now harried their enemies. The curé's was the traditional and proper role of the church lending sanctuary to fugitives, particularly those fleeing injustice. Perhaps *they* knew about the curé? Of that he couldn't be sure. So there it was. There was no lie he could tell to protect Jeanne because he knew nothing *they* did not already know. But he could lie to protect the curé. And would. "Death, *compañero*, is such a little thing," they'd said in Spain. How ironical that he might have to face death now to save a priest. But of course, in Don Juan's estimation of himself there lay his final and most important line of defense. He knew that if he failed the test of resisting, there would be no further point to his life. Content in this conclusion, he waited.

If there was any shred of mercy in what followed, it came from the fact that the Gestapo and the French police needed information fast. There was to be virtually no waiting. At an hour that felt like four in the morning or thereabouts, Don Juan was taken from his cell, along a long passage, down a flight of stairs, the smell of urine and unwashed bodies reminding him of Deerhurst, and into what looked like a miniature gym, except that it contained, among other more ominous paraphernalia, two desks set side by side. Behind these sat two men in plainclothes, although the plainness of the clothes themselves was very distinct and different.

The man on the left, as Don Juan was forced to face them, was a man of wispy, deceptively mild mien, gray of face, pale of eye, a man who looked as if God had forgotten to color him. He wore a nondescript suit. On the right was a chunky man with an almost scarlet face inflamed around the nose and neck with a still-lurking acne, although Don Juan judged him to be in his early thirties. His short black hair sprouted from his head like the nap on an uncared-for carpet. His hands could have been those of a carpenter or a butcher.

"Sit down, Juan," said the red-faced man in a French flavored with the broad vowels of Provence.

Don Juan's guards brought a chair, and he sat.

"We have here papers which indicate that you were born in Spain. You are the heir to a dukedom. Your grandfather is one of the most important industrialists in Spain. You were, of course, a supporter of the Nationalists. You have been a guest in this country much of your life. Yet you have allowed yourself to be involved with the crime of consorting with the enemies of France, working with a revolutionary person, plotting violence against us and our German associates." The red-faced man read from a note clipped to a dossier in front of him, which he then passed to the wispy gray man. Only when he finished speaking did he look up at Don Juan, as if to see what the person described in the dossier looked like.

Don Juan, aware that he had been asked no direct question yet, waited. He was impressed with how the Nettoyage had changed his record to read Nationalist. They had made no other, unnecessary, changes. He saw that the wispy gray man was reading through the dossier and was wondering if he was German when he spoke in a curiously high voice.

"These documents may or may not give a true picture of your identity," he said. "The important thing is whether you are prepared to tell us all you know of the woman Jeanne." His accent was clearly Germanic.

"Yes, I am," said Don Juan, content that he knew nothing that could hurt her.

For ten minutes they ran through the banal facts of Jeanne's life. Her birth, education, socialist affiliation, record as a teacher, et cetera. All a matter of public record. The red-faced man asked most of the questions. Finally they came to her relationship with Don Juan.

"You were lovers—is that why you permitted the radio to be put in the chateau?" asked the wispy gray man.

"No," said Don Juan after an instant's hesitation. He doubted they knew for *certain* that he and Jeanne were lovers. To be sure of it might give them an advantage.

"You *were* lovers!" said the red-faced man. "I put it to you that she seduced you. After all, she is much older than you are. Perhaps you have an infantile preference for older women. I suggest that she made you put the radio into the chateau, perhaps threatening to expose to your family in Spain that you had fathered a child among the peasants in the valley? Here is a case where, if you are honest with us, you might simply be deported to Spain with a warning. But you must tell us every last detail about her. You must write down at once the name and description and whereabouts of every person with whom she has, to your knowledge, been in contact."

He put pencil and paper in front of Don Juan.

"There is none," he said simply.

"Not true. We know, for instance, that you first met her when the circus was in Annecy."

"But that was a purely social occasion."

"Write down who was there," said the red-faced man.

"I assure you *they* had nothing to do with the radio, with anything clandestine. Just an old girl friend from Paris. She was living with the ringmaster. They gave a party, and some other people whose names I never knew brought Jeanne. That is how I met her. I don't believe she even knew the circus people herself." Don Juan told this elaborate but plausible lie to try to protect Mireille from guilt by association. It was clear they already knew of the circus connection.

"Never mind about the circus people," said the wispy gray man impatiently. "Write down the names of all her contacts in this region. Everyone who knew her."

"Well, naturally the cleaning women who came to the chateau, people who lived in the valley, would have known her. I'm not entirely sure which. None of them knew anything about the radio."

"I don't think you understand, Juan," said the red-faced man, speaking slowly and distinctly. "If you cooperate with us, it can be back to sunny Spain in a week. If you don't you may not live a week. In fact, after a few hours with us, you will hope you don't. D'you comprehend me?"

"Yes," said Don Juan, fascinated by the red-faced man's obvious weariness. The menace was there, that he didn't doubt. But there was something more. A curious reluctance.

"We are waiting," said the wispy gray man.

"I have told you all I know," said Don Juan carefully, weighing his words. "As you must know, it is not customary for clandestine groups gathering intelligence and transmitting it by radio to allow any single person to know anything or anybody unnecessarily. My role was simply to house a radio and to operate it. Jeanne is the sole person involved I have ever seen or whose name I know. As far as I can tell, she herself knew no one else, but received her information from someplace where messages were left. A kind of mail drop, perhaps."

The red-faced Frenchman laughed and the German smiled briefly.

"Do you love this woman?" the German asked unexpectedly.

"No," said Don Juan.

"Then why are you making this childish attempt to protect her?"

"I am telling the truth," said Don Juan.

"Very well, bring her in," said the German.

The red-faced man got up from his desk and left the room by another door. Don Juan spent the waiting time trying once again to organize his thoughts. If they had already gotten Jeanne to confess, there would be little point in a confrontation between them. They already had enough evidence on both of them to follow their normal procedure of intense but brief torture to see if any other scintilla of information was to be gained, followed quickly by execution. They were busy people. He had to assume she had not confessed and hope he would find some way to continue to shield her. That he would soon die a violent death he now regarded as fairly certain. He simply hoped he could meet it with dignity.

When the red-faced man brought her in, Don Juan was so horrified that he found himself crying; he tried to hold back the tears, but they streamed down his face. She was naked and filthy. By a steel collar around her neck the red-faced man held her upright, for she could hardly stand. Her head had been shaved and her body was covered with small burns that had not yet scabbed and were blistered or suppurating. Don Juan was now able to take in some of the grim apparatus with which the room was furnished. In the corner was a large old-fashioned bath. Beside it, lying limp on the floor, was a hose with a brass nozzle. Hanging from the ceiling a few feet away were a series of huge butcher's hooks and some chains. Jeanne was taken to one of the latter and attached by her collar to the end of the chain. This forced her to remain standing or have the collar cut into her neck and jaw. Her hands were free, however, and she used them to gingerly ease the tight collar from the lesions it had caused on her neck. She did not at first see Don Juan, because the red-faced man propelled her directly to the chain, and only after he attached her could she look around the room.

When their eyes met, she saw her lover weeping openly. She looked at him with infinite tiredness through those eyes, with their curious gooseberry color, that were once her only claim to beauty. Now they were ringed with darkened, puffy flesh, and at the corner of one she had a huge yellowing bruise. She did not speak, although it seemed as if words were trying to form on cracked lips that she tried to moisten with her tongue.

Like some grotesque bath attendant, the red-faced man busied himself with filling the bath from the hose. Then he came and stood beside Jeanne, taking one of her bony hands in his huge, meaty paws.

"He told us that he doesn't love you," said the German in his high voice. "But we shall see." He nodded to the red-faced man.

The Frenchman took Jeanne's index finger and snapped it between the knuckle and the nail, causing her to give a strangled shriek, a sound that her poor mouth had difficulty emitting.

"She has seven more fingers and two thumbs, Juan," said the German. "Unless you write down the names of her contacts at once, my colleague will break them one by one."

"Of course, at once," said Don Juan. "But it would help me to think if you let her sit down and took that damned collar off her."

The German, no doubt influenced by Don Juan's tears, was convinced that they had made their point. He signaled the red-faced man to comply with the young man's request. A minute later Jeanne was sitting, cradling her broken finger with her other hand, staring hard at Don Juan in a puzzled way. The German watched her as Don Juan wrote the name Darnand. The red-faced man, watching over Don Juan's shoulder, hit him the moment he saw what he had written, hit him hard with a clenched fist to the side of the head, sending him sprawling to the floor.

Darnand was the name of the French torturer's probable boss, the head of the Milice, Vichy France's SS. Don Juan looked up from the floor at the German. He had grabbed the sheet of paper and looked at the name. Now he turned to Jeanne.

"Can you speak, Jeanne?" he asked.

"Yes," came her voice, hardly recognizable and low.

"He knows nothing, does he? He really does have no names? Is that correct?"

"Correct," she managed to say.

"I thought you showed strangely little concern when he started to write. But he is a very foolish young man to play games with us, isn't he? Tell me, do you love him?" The German's voice squeaked slightly on the question.

Jeanne made no answer. But her face now showed a new anguish. "Oh, no. No, no." She got the words out in a slow staccato way. They were not a denial, not in any way, but rather a plea.

Don Juan did not at first comprehend what had happened.

"Strip him. Then use the bath first," said the German to the red-faced man. "Remember, Jeanne, anytime you care to talk we can stop this," he added.

Once stripped, Don Juan found himself manhandled to the bath by the warders and his head thrust under the water by the red-faced man. He had time to take a deep gulp of air, but his ears soon started to sing and his chest felt as if both lungs and heart were balloons stretching and stretching until only the iron grille of his rib cage held them from bursting. The moment his head was released and some air came back into his mouth and nostrils, he sucked frantically for life, only to be thrust down again. This went on and on. Now his ears and temples and eyes all became pressure points in the screaming agony of his imploding head, while his chest told him that he had to open his mouth, there was no other way to end the thing. And so in the end he did. Oblivion came with the water as he gulped it down into his lungs.

The man with the red face, feeling Don Juan's body relax, hauled him out by the hair and threw him on the floor at Jeanne's feet like a fish slopped out on a slab. He stooped and massaged Don Juan's back with practiced hands, bringing the water up from his lungs, forcing him to breathe again.

As consciousness came back to Don Juan along with the pain of retching up the water, he found himself staring at Jeanne's long feet, noticing that the toenails had been torn from each toe, the raw, swollen stubs of which lay close to his face. This will go on till we are both dead, he thought. There is no other way. He managed to inch his head forward and touched one of her mangled feet with his mouth. It was the nearest he could manage to a kiss. A savage kick from the red-faced man flopped him over on his back.

Don Juan looked around him. The red-faced man was speaking

to the German, but he could hear no words. He moved his head and saw Jeanne's face. She, too, was talking, but he could hear nothing of what she said. She seemed to be screaming mutely, but no one was touching her. Then the red-faced man came and held her and directed her gaze at Don Juan. Why was she screaming? He turned his head and saw the German standing between his legs. With the well-polished pointed toe of his shoe, he raised Don Juan's sex, flopping it over and across his thigh. Then he started kicking him in the balls. Don Juan had time to lash out with his feet, but the two warders caught his legs and held him till he fainted from the atrocious pain.

A week later Don Juan found himself in a hospital. His hearing had returned, but at first there was nothing he wanted to hear. The room of pain was a dim memory. Only Jeanne's face screaming soundlessly and the hideous shiny, pointed toe remained vividly in his mind. He was dimly aware, because of the repeated agony of it, that someone came regularly and put a catheter in his swollen penis to relieve him. They also changed the dressings that swathed his whole genital area. The person was a male orderly of some kind, in a white coat. Slowly it came to him that he was in the private ward of a hospital.

It must have been one evening—Don Juan was conscious only of its being dark outside the window—when a man in the uniform of an officer in the Wehrmacht came to talk to him. He was fair-haired and rather boyish-looking.

"Don Juan," he said formally. "I am Lieutenant Claus Brandt, from the headquarters of General von Carlowitz. Do you understand me?"

Don Juan nodded. The general's name signified nothing to him, but he understood what was being said to him.

"This is a German military hospital. You are in the custody of the German army. It is a temporary matter, and the general sends you his compliments. He hopes you are feeling better. The doctors are very pleased with the operation."

"Operation?" Don Juan's hand went involuntarily to where his balls lay swathed in lint. They were undoubtedly still there.

"Yes, there was danger that your testicles would have to be removed altogether. Happily, if only for cosmetic reasons, they have been saved by a German surgeon here who is one of the best in his field."

"Cosmetic?"

"Perhaps I should have said psychological reasons," he said with a smile. "We all need our balls to feel whole men, yah?"

"Oh, yah," said Don Juan, not knowing whether to laugh or cry.

"The general is anxious for you to return to your chateau in the Val Romanée as soon as possible. The Frau Generalin is waiting to return to Saxony. You are doing a portrait of her. Are you prepared to complete it?"

Don Juan concentrated very hard on this thought. His thinking processes had been suspended for over a week. His mind had refused to concentrate on past, present, or future. It had opted for an unfocused limbo. The chateau. Ah yes, that and the whole Val Romanée scene came back. The curé, particularly. But something wasn't coming back, and he strained to think what it was. The mutely screaming Jeanne was an image all on her own. He now haltingly put her into the context of his recent life, finding her in the chateau and recalling the radio itself. But Jeanne. What of her?

The young lieutenant was waiting for his answer. Something about a Frau Generalin.

"Where is Jeanne?"

"She took her own life. Apparently she was deeply implicated with acts of violent terrorism against our forces."

"May we talk again tomorrow?" said Don Juan after a long pause. He wanted to be alone with his memories of Jeanne. He didn't want to consider anything else at the moment, and he sensed that with this pleasant, rather naive young German, he had a certain amount of leeway.

"Of course. Tomorrow morning, then. Perhaps by then you will be able to give me an answer?"

Don Juan nodded and closed his eyes.

Her reservoir of love to give had been so deep. How painful it must have been for her that she could barely find words or gestures to express it. She had shown him that she loved him in so many ways that it had really not mattered. From the morning when she first brought him his breakfast until the last moment, when, to try to protect him in the room of pain, she had been forced to forgo her last chance to tell him in words. She had not needed to. He hoped she knew that. Her every thoughtful act and wish he had interpreted as the caresses she could not, for some reason, give. It gave him terrible pain that she had heard from the lips of the wispy gray German that her Don Juan did not love her. In a sense, he adored her as one of the bravest of her sex, not only because of the way she had faced torture and death, but for the way she had been when he met her, facing that most difficult of lives: surviving as a plain woman and not despairing that she would find her chance to love. She had found it. Sublimely. It enhanced and humbled him to know that.

He arrived at the chateau at dusk. Riding with Lieutenant Brandt at his side in the back of the general's chauffeur-driven staff car, he gazed silently at the white Christmas-card Val Romanée. The wheels in their snow chains made a tinkling sound, and the clear mountain air brought the noise of cowbells as the animals stirred in their barns, restless before the evening milking. Don Juan believed his senses had taken on a heightened perception. I am not dead. I am not dead. That negative affirmation of his renewed life was his own voice yelling silently, exultantly, in his mind, oblivious of everything else except the smell, sound, taste, and sight of being alive.

The curé was at the chateau to greet him. The two cleaning women, old Claire and even older Marie-Josée, had polished and scrubbed everything, and there were roaring fires in the principal rooms. Don Juan was still very weak. He had his dinner with the curé sitting by his bed, while the old women fussed around. There were instructions about changing the dressing on his wound, and they had done this for him before the meal, clucking over the still-livid scar at the base of his testicles.

"They say," said Don Juan, trying to make light of it when the women had gone, "that I have had the most thoroughgoing free vasectomy it is in Hitler's power to provide."

"Are you sure that it is final, my son?" asked the curé sympathetically.

"I think so. This is hardly the moment to go seeking the opinions of the great medical minds of Europe. But Father, think of Jeanne. What a little matter this is beside that."

"I have said two masses for her already. D'you think she would mind if she knew?"

"No. And I'm so glad that you have. Your French atheists all lose their nerve at the last moment. Look at Talleyrand. I'm sure if she'd had the chance she might have wanted it."

They ate peacefully for a moment, glad to be sharing each other's company again.

"There is one question, Father, that I haven't dared ask anyone," said Don Juan at last.

"What?"

"Did she talk? Torturing me was to make her talk. And here I am safe. Hearing the answer to that terrifies me. But I must know."

"No, she hanged herself in her cell. I thought you knew."

"They told me she'd committed suicide. Not whether she'd talked. Did she?"

"Absolutely not!"

"How can you be sure? Please believe me. I would never judge her. But I have to know for certain."

"No one has been arrested that I know of. I am still here, for example."

"Father, you are not giving me a definite answer."

"I cannot. I wasn't there. But I can tell you I am certain that she killed herself because she was afraid she might break. God will forgive her. Of that I am certain."

"Then why have I been released?"

"The young lieutenant, he didn't tell you?"

"To finish the portrait of the general's wife. Does that make any sense?"

"Yes. I have been to see the general and his wife. It makes perfect sense."

"What?" Don Juan was astonished.

"They asked me to go. The staff car collected me. Enough questions, my son. Simply have faith in God. I don't know what you have done to deserve it, but He seems to be watching over you. Now try a little more of Claire's cassoulet."

They nursed him, and after a week he was able to take most of the dressing off and walk about again, although he was still not free of pain. The general's wife came the same day. She was very silent at first, changing discreetly behind the screen in the studio into her Grecian evening dress. He sensed that she was taut, like someone bursting with a secret.

Nervously she took her three-quarter-face pose, and then suddenly it came. She turned to him.

"I'm so sorry," she said. "We are both so sorry. What can we do—she is dead. And you?"

"I'm feeling a bit better, thank you," said Don Juan formally.

"I'm so sorry," she said again. "This frightful war. It has turned some of our people into beasts and lunatics."

"The French are about the same. Your beasts and lunatics and theirs work so harmoniously together."

"Oh, Juan, I have a terrible confession to make to you." She had come over to him and taken his hands in hers. The beautiful face set in the fat face stared at him through gentle brown eyes. Not gentle, he corrected himself, *sentimental* eyes. And then an appalling thought occurred to him. Could it have been she who had overheard something about the radio and reported it to the Gestapo? If not she, who had reported them?"

"Confession?" he said suddenly, his voice very hard.

"I couldn't do anything else. We prayed to St. Jude for guidance. But we had to curry favor with the Gestapo."

He saw it all. They had some problem of their own. Some trifling problem with the Gestapo, and for that Jeanne had died. He pulled back his hand to hit her.

"No, please. You must listen." She had turned, ducking away from him. He grabbed the back of her dress and raised his hand again. One stinging moment of pain for all Jeanne's pain. That was all he intended, but he felt impelled to do it.

"We will pay for them, Juan. They weren't your best. We chose carefully."

"What are you talking about?" said Don Juan, letting her go.

"The three pictures. It is we who took them."

"Is that your confession? It wasn't you who told the Gestapo or the Milice?"

"No, no. Of course, if the general had made that discovery, it would have been his duty to arrest you. But it was not us. It was some jealous peasant. I was distraught. I prayed for guidance."

"Then what is all this about three pictures?" Don Juan was mystified.

"When you were arrested, the general had the Gestapo keep him informed about your case. They told him at once that they believed you to be involved only with the radio. Serious enough for you to be shot, by the way!

"But Jeanne, they thought, was a key to many other people. So they concentrated on her. There was nothing we could do for her. But for you we saw a chance. I had noticed some of the wonderful and erotic drawings and paintings of some of the local girls that you have stacked over there. It gave us an idea. The general is on friendly terms with only one important Nazi. Goering. Art is the common interest, of course. And those paintings are erotic art of a very high order. My husband was due to confer with him in Paris. He took three of the paintings as a kind of bribe and asked him to intervene in your behalf so that my portrait could be completed. By itself, it might not have been enough, but Goering, on being shown your dossier, discovered he knew your grandfather, whom he admires as a friend of Germany. You are to be deported as soon as my portrait is complete. As a Nationalist, you will not mind too much, I'm sure. In fact, if you'd prefer to go sooner—"

"I'd like to finish the portrait," said Don Juan hurriedly. "And thank you both for everything." He bent to kiss her hand, brushing it gently with his lips. She stood very still and raised the back of her hand to her own lips in one of the oldest courtly gestures of European women. Then she took up her three-quarter-face pose once again. Her Wagnerian bosom betrayed, as it rose and fell, that she was physically excited. He concentrated on his painting.

He calculated that it would take three more sittings to complete the portrait. For the second of these she arrived in a great state of suppressed excitement.

"Why didn't you tell me you were a Republican in Spain?"

"Because the Resistance had my papers altered. It might have implicated someone in the Nettoyage."

"The Spanish are sending a Guardia Civil officer in plainclothes to collect you. He will be here tomorrow. It appears your grandfather can do nothing. They even say you were involved in an action in which many German volunteers were killed."

"That's true. It was at the very end of the war. Looking back, it was unnecessary. But I really didn't understand that at the time. Until too late."

"I wish I could go with you to Switzerland. Away from this hellish war. Because that's what you must do."

She was standing in the studio in her stout German tweeds, under which she wore green stockings. Her golden hair was plaited and wound around her head.

"Switzerland?" Don Juan felt a kind of paralysis of the will.

"No other way. And now. Tomorrow will be too late."

"But won't *you* be implicated for warning me? You and the general?" Don Juan found himself suddenly bereft of logic, longing only to stay in the chateau until the last possible moment, to have to take no further decisions.

"Oh, Juan," she said, "what have they destroyed in you, those fiends?" And to Don Juan's considerable embarrassment and surprise, she sank onto her knees before him and gently undid his fly. As if she were taking priceless jewels from a Fabergé egg, she coaxed his wounded balls into the palm of her hand and kissed the now-healing scar. For the first time since the torture, his sex saluted a woman, hurting him in doing so, like an athlete returning, on still-wounded muscles, to the fray.

She looked up at him. "Juan, there is only one way you can protect us. The general and me. We must seem to be your victims. You must tie me up to a chair and assault me. Your going to

Switzerland must seem to be the result of your having committed an enormity. Not because you had been warned the Francoists in Spain were after you. I will change into my Grecian dress. You must go and fetch some rope and a rod."

"A rod?" Don Juan was bemused. What she suggested made sense up to a point. But there was something about her relish for the charade that disturbed him.

"The sort of thing you put in a geranium pot. But a light walking stick will do."

When he returned she was in the Grecian dress. Her hair was unplaited, falling over her shoulders like a gilded tent. She resembled Brünnhilde about to launch into an aria. Carrying an armed wooden chair, she bent over the back of it and clutched the front legs, as if testing its strength for a sustained assault of her weight.

"It will do," she said, turning to him and putting her arms on his shoulders. "And because you must hurt me a good deal if this is to look authentic, I must first give you the kiss of my forgiveness." Her kiss was wet, her breath very slightly stale and hot.

"So!" she said, breathing very deeply. "Now you must do everything as I say. Tear first my dress. . . . So! Yah, now more. My breasts must come loose. . . . So! A few bites on the nipples. Harder. . . . So! Now you slap the breasts, great swinging slaps. . . . So! Now the cheeks of my face you slap. . . . So! Harder the slaps. . . . So! Now I bend over the chair and you tie my hands to the front legs and my ankles to the back legs. Tighter, much tighter. . . . So! Now you pull up my dress and tear off my corset, use a knife—any knife—a palette knife. . . . So! Now you take the walking stick and beat my buttocks."

"I can't do that," said Don Juan.

"Please beat me, please, Juan. I've been longing for this. Think of the guilt I feel. To have you, of all people, beat me, it is only just. Please! First you gag me. Then possess me! I shall want to scream. But the general's driver downstairs mustn't hear me."

Don Juan gagged her with a clean paint rag. Then, facing her, he broke the walking stick on his knee. Taking his palette, he painted the most fearful and realistic stripes across her behind. He knew her strangled voice was pleading for blows, begging for assaults of all kinds, and her musk poured down her inner thighs, leaving glistening rime on the tops of her green stockings. Not wishing, after all these invitations, to abandon her entirely unserved, he slipped gingerly into her and, finding that he was himself again, continued long and hard enough to leave her enormous painted rump still twitching in its own semi-detached delirium, while the studio parquet was as redolent of musky liquor as the Black Forest floor is of pine needles.

He put on thick mountain boots and the warmest clothing he possessed, and filled a rucksack with food from his larder. He had always kept large reserves of cash hidden in various parts of the castle against wartime emergencies. This he stuffed in with the food. After checking that the German driver was in the front hall keeping himself warm by the fire there, he made his way down the back stairs and out by the old servants' entrance. He walked fast toward the nearest trees at the foot of the mountain.

Almost all night he walked under a cold, ringed moon, finding the going easy on trails that ran within sight of the road. As dawn broke, he moved deeper into the forest and made himself a shelter of bracken in which to sleep. He lit a fire for warmth, but kept it small.

The next night he followed the road again.

On the following day a spotter plane droned overhead. He rightly guessed it was hunting for him. But the forest on the mountains was so thick that Don Juan was at risk only when he crossed roads.

On the third day he found himself within sight of Lake Geneva. Switzerland lay on the other side. He knew that the land border was very heavily guarded on both sides, and so he decided to try to find a boat on which he could cross the lake. The next night he managed to get within a quarter of a mile of the shore, and spent the day concealed on the roof of a barn where he could watch the activity on the lakeside.

In the winter weather the mist from the lake took time to clear in the morning sun. But when it did, Don Juan, from his vantage point, could see a chateau hotel with a restaurant terrace out of doors. The place appeared to be frequented by a few Germans during the day, and he watched them coming and going with their girl friends. There was a boathouse that did not seem to be in use. Shipping, except for a German patrol boat, was very sparse, although he noticed that the service across the lake between Évian-les-Bains, the nearest town to Don Juan's hideaway, and Lausanne, over on the Swiss side, did seem to be operating quite regularly. Don Juan lay there noting everything that might be useful to him and formed a plan.

When night fell he made his way toward the chateau hotel. Giving a wide berth to houses with barking dogs, he made for a small wood on the edge of the chateau hotel's property. Where the wood met the lakeshore, he found himself a hundred feet from the boathouse, which looked closed on all sides save that which faced the lake. Here the edifice protruded into the water some six feet. Don Juan stripped off all his clothes and started to swim in the freezing water for the mouth of the boathouse. It took only a couple of dozen fierce strokes and he was there. Inside, much to his relief, he found a boat. Designed for an outboard motor, it had neither oars nor mast for a sail, nor could he find in the boathouse any sign of a motor. The door into the chateau hotel's garden was locked, and he was about to give up when he saw that some planks had been left resting on the crossbeams of the boathouse roof. Deftly, quietly, he pulled these down, and after some further searching, found some rope. Out of these materials he fashioned two crude, thick oars attached by rope to where the missing oarlocks should have been. Very slowly he edged the boat out into the lake and rowed to where he could pick up his clothes. He dried himself briskly and dressed quickly. A quarter of an hour later he was almost out of sight of the dim lights on the French side, and found himself swallowed up in the rising mist.

He rowed for four hours before his hands were so blistered and sore that he had to stop and tear strips from his shirt and wrap his bleeding palms in the material. Then he rowed on, terrified in the pitch dark that he might be traveling in a circle or that the currents might be taking him back to the French side.

When dawn came, it was to bring him an eerie visual conundrum. The jagged tips of the Dents du Midi, sentinels of the Rhone Valley on the French side, showed above the pervasive fog, but neither coastline of the lake could he see. Then a sound like that of a water mill puzzled him. He seemed to be approaching it. Suddenly out of the mist, and barely twenty feet away, a paddle steamer appeared, churning the water into a heavy wake that rocked Don Juan's small boat almost into capsizing. No one seemed to have noticed him until, looking back at it, he heard a shout. A soldier in field gray and wearing a German helmet was watching him and shouting to others to come and see. He was speaking German.

Minutes later the paddle steamer had returned, located Don Juan, and started to lower a boat.

The steamer flew a Swiss flag aft, but there was the puzzle of the soldiers' uniforms that Don Juan felt certain were German. He was very tired, too tired to resist but too tired to face the tortures, the rigors of waiting to face death all over again. When the lowered boat had still not hit the water, Don Juan dived into the lake. As he pierced the deathly cold, clear surface of the lake, he thought of how he had opened up his mouth to try to drown in the torturer's bath. Now he swam down, down into the increasingly icy depth of the lake.

Opening his mouth at last, he tried to suck the water into his lungs. It poured in, compressing the air it met and making him gag. He found that the air trapped in his body was giving him buoyancy, and he was too numb in the intense cold to try swimming deeper. Like a cork his body started to be impelled up, up to the surface, till his head bobbed once again into the air.

14
The Politics of Treachery

This is the excellent foppery of the world, that when we are sick in
fortune, often the surfeits of our own behavior, we make guilty of
our disasters the sun, the moon, and stars; as if we were villains on
necessity, fools by heavenly compulsion, knaves, thieves and
treachers by spherical predominance, drunkards, liars and adulterers
by an enforc'd obedience of planetary influence; and all that we are
evil in, by a divine thrusting in.

— Shakespeare, *King Lear*

In the Switzerland where Don Juan found himself when
he fully regained consciousness the clock seemed to have stood still.
At no time in his young life had Don Juan ever been in such a place.
The prison-camp atmosphere of an English boarding school followed
by the Breughel-like nightmare of the Spanish Civil War, Phony War
France, and the creeping malady of the occupation all excluded a
state of normality that Don Juan had heard tell of, but never yet
experienced. The Swiss had it, this normality, and clung to it
tenaciously. They behaved, in relation to the rest of Europe, as a

single healthy doctor might who found himself locked into a ward full of patients afflicted with a serious epidemic whose bacillus was both infectious and contagious.

Don Juan awoke in a private room of what appeared to be a hospital run by nuns. He was dressed in comfortable pajamas, and a young novice in crisp white apron and shining, well-scrubbed cheeks came regularly to take his temperature, or with trays bearing simple but delicious meals. On the first day he was there no one questioned him and the nuns refused kindly to answer his questions except to tell him, reassuringly, that he was safe and should rest. They spoke the singsong French of Suisse Romande. A doctor came in the evening and made a thorough examination of him. The scar tissue on his testicles was still very evident. They pronounced him physically fit but emotionally exhausted, and possibly in need of psychiatric care. He was asked his religion, and answered Roman Catholic automatically. The doctor advised an early confession, to cleanse the soul. Don Juan wondered if he was referring to his attempted suicide. Meanwhile a Mr. Allen Dulles was waiting to see him.

Dulles was a name in Don Juan's lexicon of his grandfather's people. Filed after Cook, Thomas, travel agents, came Dulles, Allen, lawyer with Sullivan and Cromwell, New York, a man who had obviously enjoyed the Princess D'Albret's little party, but had the discretion to leave before the *bonne bouche,* as the French so accurately call the ultimate treat at a meal. Grandfather had since referred to Dulles, from time to time, as a sort of litmus of which way things were going to go in Europe.

Now, as this big man was led to his bedside, he carried an aura of bonhomie and extravert confidence about him.

"Don Juan!" he said, extending a large hand. "Congratulations on your escape!"

"Mr. Dulles," replied Don Juan cordially. "We've met before in France."

"Ho, ho, ho," huffed Dulles. It was a kind of jolly laugh, a cross between that of a Santa Claus and that of a man who has just heard a locker-room story. "Surprised you remember anyone but the hostess . . . that terrific Princess D'Albret!"

"My grandfather often mentions you, sir," said Don Juan.

"Yes, well, of course. I am not exactly lawyering just now. But your grandfather is a very dear friend. We've hunted in couples, he and I, ho, ho, ho! He tells me that you yourself carry being a chip off his old block rather far!"

"What news do you have of my grandfather, sir?"

"Fit as a fiddle, last time I saw him. He really is extraordinary for his age. Puts it down to a steady diet of flamenco dancers. Says they're better than a tonic to him!"

"Did he speak of my father?"

"Yes. Just the same, Juan, I'm afraid. No change there. What a tragedy it is. Particularly for your dear mother. I have mail for you. Couldn't risk sending it to France. But I had a hunch you'd be with us pretty soon."

Don Juan took, with great pleasure and anticipation, a wad of letters that Mr. Dulles passed him.

"Hunch?" asked Don Juan curiously.

"It's no great secret that although officially I'm on the American delegation staff here, I'm really running my own little show. In daily contact with London, rather as you were till very recently. The BCRA, de Gaulle's outfit, whom you talked to every day by radio, report to the British Secret Operations Executive, which is in contact with our OSS. Godawful alphabet soup, isn't it? To cut a long story short, I heard you were involved over there. And we got the news the krauts had you in the bag. Apparently Goering, of all people, wired your grandfather. Anyway, as you probably know the Nationalists won't have you at any price except to lock you up. Even as we speak, the Swiss are a bit upset because the French and Germans say you aren't a political escapee, but a refugee rapist."

"Well, that isn't true!" exclaimed Don Juan, thoroughly alarmed.

"Okay. I figured it probably wasn't, but tell me about it. As I always say to our guys when they come in from the field, 'Make a story out of it.'"

Don Juan did, and Allen Dulles's "Ho, ho, ho, ho's" were loud and long. He had lit his pipe and sat there beside Don Juan's bed swirling smoke like a priest waving his censer, and heaving as the laughing sailor at the carnival does when a coin activates his manic hysteria.

"That general sounds interesting to me," he said at last. "You'd be surprised how many of them have found their Christian consciences now the war is going against them."

"I liked him," said Don Juan simply.

"Look, I'm going to try to fix things up with the Swiss," said Dulles. "I don't *think* they'll hand you back. But they might lock you up as a public menace. They have generals' wives here, too. Ho, ho, ho."

Don Juan liked Mr. Dulles. He was not his idea of a master spy, but then he was American, and with Henrietta and H. L. Mencken as his sole guides on that bewildering country, Don Juan did not find it altogether surprising that one of their spy masters should behave as if he were running for election as the president of a Rotary Club. It was, after all, probably as good a cover as any other, conceivably better.

His mail was copious. Most of it over a year old and sent via his grandfather, Thomas Cook's operation having receded from the shores of continental Europe for the duration of the war.

From Henrietta and his mother a dozen letters told of literary lunches in New York, war-bond drives, and the inconveniences of being cooped up in fortress U.S.A. for so long. The last one in date order was clearly a rare letter *actually* written by his mother.

Dear Juan,

The principal penalty of this war, for those of us over here, is that it looks now as if we will *never* get rid of Roosevelt. It is also becoming impossible to get good *help*.

It really is too bad of you not to write more often. But they do say that things in France are *difficile*. Even under dear old Pétain. What a poppet that old man was. D'you remember telling him you were going into the church? News of your last winter in Paris still reaches us. It appears that D'Albret was quite dotty over you. She writes from Argentina. Too pathetic her letter was. Fully expects to die of boredom there. Has taken to narcotics but finds them to have a disagreeable effect on her complexion. I could have told her. I live almost entirely on crustaceans these days—so good for my figure, but the *despair* of Boris and Valéry. Who threaten to start a restaurant here in New York!

While it is true that the city is in desperate need of a good restaurant, they know that this defection would *kill* me!

Henrietta seems to have gone slightly mad. She has taken a job with the State Department in Washington. She says one has to *do* something. Very hard I should have thought in a place like Washington. Blazingly hot in summer, worse than Singapore they say. All right in peacetime when Congress only sits for half the year, but poor Henny was there all through this last summer. I can't imagine how she bears it. Women really have made appalling sacrifices in this war. I only hope they get some recognition for it.

Do think to write to your poor miserable mother.

September 1943

14a East 63rd Street, New York

From his grandfather there were a number of missives, mainly about investments, the movements of blocks of shares, the condition of the estate in Andalusia and the factories and mines. His holdings in Germany were a matter of great concern since the Allies had bombed most of them. One letter was more personal.

My dear boy,

The doctors say that your poor father is starting to deteriorate physically. A specialist in geriatric problems has told me that he believes there cannot be many more months left for him to live. Since living for him has, for many years, meant great suffering, I cannot say I am sorry.

It is indeed a tragedy that as you are about to succeed to the great estate and dignity that is your right by birth you cannot also take your rightful place in the "club of nobles" here in Spain.

The country is, as you know, once again a monarchy. But without a king. Many of us are now in favor of the Bourbons' coming back when Franco dies. I am coming to the conclusion that fascism is not an ideal "climate for business." A constitutional monarchy, like that of Britain or Sweden, is really best.

If such a thing could happen in Spain, you, with your flexible political views, and the power you will inherit from me, could play an important role. Try, now that you are grown up, to cause no further scandal. Keep your peccadilloes within bounds. I hear from Henrietta and your mother that you have a rare "innocent" friendship with a charming Scottish girl of impeccable family. Congratulations. Pursue it. Find yourself a wife of your own rank. I am prepared to spend a very large sum to gain you a pardon here in Spain.

Remember we need an heir, to ensure the continuity of your great name.

Your Grandfather

From Juliet there were some twenty letters. Most of them were chatty accounts of her life in the Women's Royal Naval Service, the Wrens. She wrote them, she said in one letter, knowing he would probably never get them, but just in case. The most interesting of her letters described the revolution in women's lives that the war had caused in England.

Dear Juan,

. . . You would have thought that boarding school would

have prepared me for life in an entirely feminine organization.
But of course then we were children, unsure of ourselves and,
being British, discouraged from thinking of ourselves as women
till we were eighteen. I sometimes think we were brought up
as sort of counterfeit boys. All those team games, and uniforms
to make us look masculine. Both utterly against our every
instinct.

I mean I pined to wear marvelous feminine clothes all
through my teens, to have diaphanous nighties and lacy step-ins
and outrageous dresses that showed off the shape of my bot and
gave more than a hint that I actually have a decent-sized bust.
So imagine my horror when, the moment I'm old enough to turn
into Mata Hari or Theda Bara and vamp it up all over the place, I
get thrust into another uniform. At least I've got the consolation
that they've now called up all women, without children, up to
about forty, and the older ones have all been drafted into
factories.

I have one relative, my gin-bottle aunt I call her, who has
spent her entire life in the Monte Carlo casino or playing bridge
here, guzzling pink gins by the dozen. She was about forty and
looked sixty. Now they've got her working in a factory eight hours
a day. She complained that the foreman pinched her bottom the
other day, but I'm not surprised. She looks marvelous now.
Something like a real person.

It's a shame I can't tell you about my job because it's madly
exciting and I adore it. The trouble is that we women are
expected to run it exactly as the men would if they were here. We
have *their* rank system and *their* organization. For *us* there must be
a better way to work as a group, and after the war I'm going to
give it some thought.

Perhaps you, who are, I hear, such an expert on women, will
have some ideas! Oh, Juan, I do so wish we could see each other.
There are lots of rather nice men in my life these days. But in the
back of my mind you lurk, like a pike fish in the shallows,
waiting, one day, to snap me up. Listen to me. Some optimist,
aren't I?

Poor Daddy and Mummy have still not got over Giles's
death. They went to the palace to collect his decorations from the
king. It seems to be a small consolation that we have the right to
descend through the female line. The fact that that nearly always
means the family were originally royal bastards doesn't seem to
worry anybody. But of course it all puts a huge responsibility on
me. Because when Daddy dies, I'll have to run the whole thing.

Damn this war. I wish you'd been the first person to whom
I'd ever given any of myself. But they do say that virgins wither

away with disuse, and we wouldn't want that. So forgive me, if
you care.

With love from
Juliet

Don Juan considered whether he cared. He found ridiculously
and illogically that he did and knew he would never tell her so. He
knew, too, that she wanted him to care. Then, considering the whole
of his strange relationship with Juliet, he was amazed. It reminded
him of Poe's poem about Annabel Lee—"*She* was a child and *I* was a
child, In this kingdom by the sea, But we loved with a love that was
more than a love," et cetera. He knew that it was she who had made
a legend out of him in her own mind. As for him, she remained the
little girl in the Tate Gallery tearoom, altogether charming, in a
childlike (not childish) way, and he was curious to see the woman she
had become. He *cared*, perhaps, because he would have liked to pick
up their relationship where it had left off, to have himself lifted the
veils of innocence, one by one, until she, trusting utterly in him, had
let him accompany her in the initial search for her womanhood.
Juliet pure might, he thought, have led him nearer to that female
grail which he instinctively sought, and which always eluded him.

Through Dulles's good offices Don Juan remained in the hospital
and underwent an exploratory operation conducted by a leading Swiss
specialist to see if his ability to produce sperm, as distinct from semen,
could be restored. The consensus of the doctors was that the damaged
area was still too affected by the damage done, but that, with time,
his body might restore tissue which would make a reconnection of his
progenerative organs to his purely sexual ones possible.

"It is not unlikely that you may, one day, be able to father a
child. But it would be very unwise to count on it. Surgery will be
needed. Meanwhile your sex life should be perfectly normal," said the
Swiss doctor, a medical man so antiseptically clean-looking that Don
Juan could picture him scrubbing his nostrils along with his teeth.

He was removing some stitches with the help of the nun with
the well-scrubbed cheeks who tended to Don Juan's private ward.

"What do you mean by 'normal'?" asked Don Juan. He was
acutely aware of the little nun. He kept on seeing her rosy body
through her voluminous white habit. He imagined her dimpled
bottom between rather large hips and tried desperately to shut other
thoughts of her from his mind, for already his organ was lifting itself
off his thigh and waving about as if undecided whether to go for a full
erection.

"Normal is different for everyone," said the doctor. "There are those who consider once a month normal. There are some who need it morning, night, and noon, every day of their lives. Just like regular meals. But I see we have an opportunity here for a clinical masturbation. Sister—some Vaseline, a little lint."

"Are you saying that whatever *was* normal for me can now be repeated?"

"Quite so, but I want to see how the ejaculatory muscles are working. It is hard to tell how much they have been damaged without witnessing an orgasm."

The nurse-nun smeared a little Vaseline the length of Don Juan's member. She then crossed herself, kissing her thumb, as nuns do, and went and stood by the washstand with her back to the proceedings. Don Juan looked past the doctor and, to his surprise, met her eyes as she watched him, in the washstand mirror. He could see that she reddened, her shiny cheeks becoming cherry-red, but she met his gaze and did not lower her eyes.

"You have a fiancée?" asked the doctor.

"Yes," Don Juan lied, knowing what he was going to say.

"Then be thinking about her and your marriage bed, when the great day comes."

Don Juan considered the nurse-nun, the delicate nape of her neck just visible. Her hair under her wimple would be short, but very soft. Her shoulders had a gentle slope to them where the hands of a man standing behind her could reach down and scoop up her breasts. He could not think of actually possessing a nun. His mind refused to imagine her further, and anyway her eyes were now all he needed. They watched his hands as they traveled up and down his member, and he saw that hers had gone forward to hold the basin as if she were supporting herself. Her mouth was open slightly now and he saw her measuring her breathing. But staring as if at an illusionist's legerdemain.

The doctor had taken a steel gauge and placed it by Don Juan's member, with a foot or so to spare, to measure the "leap" of the ejaculation.

Don Juan saw that her white-shrouded hips had started to move, making a gentle circular motion. He saw, in his mind's eye, the rosy bottom, mirror image of her flushed cheeks, and he came. Her mouth he saw suddenly open at the sight and her eyes close tight.

"Most satisfactory!" said the doctor, making a note and putting away his measuring tape. "The lint, Sister! Please bring the lint!"

Don Juan took the lint from her and mouthed a little kiss, smiling with his eyes. She fled from the room.

"They are very unworldly, these poor nuns," commented the doctor, shaking his head, and took his leave.

A driver collected Don Juan next day to drive him to Berne for an appointment with Allen Dulles. He had only the clothes in which he had walked from the Val Romanée, but Dulles was his grandfather's friend, and judging by the urgency of the invitation his appearance would not be held against him.

The spy master lived in an attractive house on the Herrengasse with a spectacular view over the mountains of the Bernese Oberland. He arrived in time for lunch and found himself to be the only guest. A lucullan meal with wild strawberries and German champagne to finish it off put Don Juan in an excellent mood. He was impressed at anyone who could get wild strawberries in February, particularly in the desperate year of 1944. He asked how it was done.

"Our people in the Balkans are endlessly resourceful. It seems that there is this valley in Rumelia where spring comes remarkably early."

Don Juan thought this answer wholly improbable but was too polite to say so. The mystery remained. That the man at the hub of a network plotting the downfall of a tottering but still puissant Reich should have claimed that his wild strawberries ripened in the winter could not merely have shown an ignorance of horticulture. It created a second mystery where the first had already seemed extraordinary enough. Don Juan decided that this must be a classic intelligence ploy.

Lunch had been spent in a delightful discussion of the charms, felicities and wonders of Madame de Staël, whose residence at Coppet had been visible from Don Juan's hospital window.

"It is remarkable that she should have been the absolute center of the intellectual opposition to Napoleon, and yet neither in World War I nor in this war has any similar giantess appeared," said Dulles.

Don Juan considered this and was amazed to find it true.

"The eighteenth century really was a vintage time for women. Why do you think they are so much less powerful now?" he asked.

"I think they may have sacrificed influence for power. And because they're stuck with *us*, thank God, power over themselves is all right in its way, but not at all the same as power over men. They actually had power over us, to some extent, in the eighteenth century because they exercised it through the application of *influence!*"

"Speaking of influence, sir, what is the reaction of the Swiss government to my being here?" asked Don Juan, who had long since assumed that Dulles had no business to discuss.

"They've given you a month."

"What?"

"The deposition of the Frau Generalin is most convincing. I've seen it. They're demanding extradition."

"How ghastly." Don Juan could think of no country contiguous to Switzerland that was not in German hands. He was trapped.

"No, not at all," said Dulles. "A month gives us plenty of time. We can fix you up by then and you can be back at work."

"Work?" croaked Don Juan.

"In France." Dulles did not appear to notice Don Juan's horror as he enlarged on his plan. "I thought we'd fix you up with a good Spanish cover. Sales manager for the Cordovan Shoe Corporation. It's a real company. Belongs to your grandfather. We'll change your hairstyle, have you use brilliantine. Get you some abominably cut off-the-peg suits made in Spain, pointed shoes, loud socks, that sort of thing. A Swiss shoe company here will train you in the niceties of shoe retailing, all about welts and stitching and so on. Then some of my guys will put you through a sophisticated radio course. Teach you how to defend yourself, kill people neatly, stay alive. I'm afraid we can't promise you much more than a year at it, two at the outside, and the war will be won. But you should have a bit of fun while you're at it. And it's better than rotting in a Swiss jail."

"That's the alternative?" Don Juan was angry. Not so much at Dulles, who was just doing his job, but at fate, which had so boxed him in. That this was being done with his grandfather's connivance amazed him. But once again perhaps the old man thought he really *had* raped the Frau Generalin. Being put into France, as an already wanted man, was like being sent to Deerhurst, another test of character, another kind of punishment. But still it was strange because of what the old man had said in his letter.

He didn't see Dulles until just before his departure. Indeed he had not expected to see him at all, for the guide who was going to take him over the frontier near Vallorbe was already with him in the safe house where he was resting up before the journey.

Dulles arrived with a rather charming German woman whose name Don Juan never caught. He had the impression that they were on their way to dinner somewhere and had just stopped by to wish him luck, but Dulles's face wore a serious expression, and he took Don Juan aside the moment he arrived.

"I hate to give people bad news when they're on the verge of going into the field," he said, "but I really have no alternative. Don Juan, your father is dead. I am so sorry. I just got word from your grandfather. I suppose we could try to postpone your departure . . ."

"It's not necessary," said Don Juan at once. "I hardly knew my father. He had suffered from a terrible affliction for many years. It is a release for him. That's all." Don Juan concealed nevertheless that he was shocked at the news, but there would be time to think of its implications later.

"All right!" said Dulles, clearly relieved. "Now there's one other thing your grandfather asked me to tell you. If all goes well, the American government has agreed with him to help seek your reinstatement with the Spanish regime."

"So that's the deal you made with him?" Don Juan was amused. "It happens that if Franco asked me back personally I'd have to say, like Rhett Butler in that great talkie of yours, 'Frankly, Franco, I don't give a damn!'"

Dulles didn't laugh.

"I shan't tell your grandfather you said that, Duke," he said. "Now let's go have a drink with that pretty lady and get you on your way."

If Don Juan's return to France came sooner than he had expected, he was nevertheless glad, once again, to be actively doing something to help fight the fascist forces of Germany and France. Trained now in advanced radio operating, and the minutiae of the Spanish shoe trade, he was slipped over the frontier near Vallorbe with two large suitcases of samples, in one of which was a disassembled transmitter. During the next months, often in a state of acute anxiety about his cover, he set diligently about the business of selling shoes. His itinerary had been designed for him with a view to taking him to strategic areas where he could observe and report back. At no time was he put into contact with the French Resistance. This was partly for his own security, in view of what had gone before, and partly because he was being used to double-check information the Resistance had fed through London. Don Juan had soon realized during his briefings that Allen Dulles did not entirely trust the British, and that the Free French of de Gaulle, and the Resistance groups in France, starting to come under their coordination and control, were even more suspect.

For the first time in his life Don Juan frequented whores. Since they had the closest, in every real sense, contact with the German soldiery he was provided with adequate funds to be the big spender at brothel parties. Traditionally all prositution in France was supervised by the state. It was really all that there was left for the French prefectures to do, since nearly all other power had passed into the hands of the Germans.

In briefing him on the best ways of gaining information in these places, Dulles proved to have been quite astute in the cover he had chosen for Don Juan. Holding a Spanish passport, he was described in it as a card-carrying member of Franco's fascist Falange. He could, therefore, when mixing with the *Herrenvolk*, represent himself as most sympathetic to Germany and her aims for "World Order." Moreover, because his grandfather controlled the quite real shoe company he represented, it had been possible to make virtually every detail of his cover check out. Thus if a German said he was going to Spain on leave (they sometimes did) Don Juan was able to provide addresses where his supposed "family" lived, in the secure knowledge that specially briefed Dulles agents would act out their roles if need be. He often wondered what pair of Spanish actors had been enrolled to play the mother and father of the ace shoe salesman.

From Lyons to Bordeaux, from Calais and Le Havre to Lille, Don Juan crisscrossed the country visiting shoe stores during the day and living it up in the evenings at bars and bordellos. Broadcasting his reports was, of course, the most hazardous part of his work, and for this he developed a special technique.

By mid-1944 the Germans and their French allies had radio-monitoring trucks dispersed all over the country in their attempts to crack down on the transmitters of the Resistance. To have broadcast from the hotels and inns where he stayed would have been too dangerous, for while he could probably get off his message before the area in which the inn lay could be pinpointed, there was always the possibility that if his name appeared consistently on the guest lists of hostelries that were in suspect areas, then the Gestapo might start to zero in on him.

So he made it his business to seek out, in every town he visited, a woman who kept shop alone. Not difficult in that year when most of the men had been shipped off to work in Germany or on the western defenses. The courtship was brief and in his character as an ostentatious spender and businessman rogue. Lunch at the best restaurant in town, a gift of black-market food, an assurance that he was the most discreet of men who, in any case, would soon be gone, a suggestion of how charming he might be able to make a brief interlude in wartime drudgery for the woman—while she, in return, could save him from having to spend a few nights in a cold, impersonal hotel.

Most of the time this ploy worked. Don Juan saw to it that the woman did indeed have a memorable interlude. He explained his occasional absences, when he went to the bars and bordellos, as business entertaining. And while she tended her shop during the day he broadcast from her house.

With the whores he was enormously popular. Since he took care never to take more than the smallest amount of drink himself he was always both alert, for information, and entertaining, to allay suspicion and make everyone with whom he came into contact relax and talk.

With his unerring sense for pleasing women it never occurred to him to have any but the most perfunctory sexual relations with the prostitutes. They had never inspired him with the slightest desire. Even his relationship with Berthe had been that of lonely youngsters keeping each other's courage up in a strange land. Instead he talked to them about food and tobacco and produced both. Together he and the whore would sit and eat and smoke. A trivial sexual service from her would be handsomely paid for and sometimes extravagantly praised if he felt the poor girl was insecure because of her lack of beauty or technique. The best-looking, most accomplished prostitutes in France were often the live-in mistresses of the German officers and NCOs, leaving somewhat poorer fare in the establishments themselves. But finally all Don Juan's encounters with these ladies always ended with a great deal of cozy, gossipy chat about their girl friends (many, of course, were lesbian), and about their plans for survival. Survival depended on the movement of German troops, which meant business being good or bad. It was ultimately a key topic for the women, and as a result, Don Juan was often able to send a remarkably clear picture of troop movements to his American control in London.

In April 1944, the Allied air raids were already seriously disrupting what remained of normal French life. While the targets were factories and railroad yards, military concentrations and the fortifications the Germans called the Western Wall (built to repel Allied landings on the west coast), neither the Royal Air Force nor the U.S. Army Air Force seemed able to avoid devastating centers of population. Le Havre, Rouen, Nancy, Épinal, Dijon, and many other places, including industrial areas of Paris, were devastated, and the victims were largely civilians, many of them women and children.

It was during this period that Don Juan found himself in Paris again for the first time since his departure on the train with the Princess D'Albret. He had an appointment with the shoe buyer at Printemps, the big department store, and he took him to lunch afterward at Maxim's, long since unfashionable and essentially an expense-account restaurant. It therefore served his purpose in flattering Monsieur Mornet, the buyer, without seriously risking that Don

Juan would be seen by anyone he knew. Surrounded by German officers, black marketeers, and their women, Don Juan talked convincingly of the prospect of a change in the fashionable height of heels in women's evening pumps, and deceitfully of his pleasure at being able to entertain in this remaining temple of French culture.

"This place has kept a wonderful standard of elegance," agreed Monsieur Mornet, sipping his outrageously expensive Cognac.

"Extraordinary," Don Juan echoed, wondering what the waiters, who must have remembered the great days of the restaurant, thought about the clientele they now served as efficiently and obsequiously as ever. Next to the humiliation of having to be a spy, the task of a waiter, under these circumstances, must come close.

"I believe I see Secretary of State Darnard over there. It is really wonderful how he keeps things going with the Boches," said Mornet, lowering his voice slightly as he said the offensive word and then realizing that his host, in spite of his faultless French, was a foreigner and might inform on him for this tiny gesture of resistance. So he added, "The Anglo-Saxons, one must add, have burned their boats with the French people after these awful air raids. Laval has been proved right—a constructive collaboration is indispensable if the Germans are to be able to defend us."

"Who is that lovely girl over there?" asked Don Juan, watching the animated features of a young woman basking in the total attention being given her by a group of German officers.

"She is the Luchaire girl. Corinne. One admires her father as a journalist. He is the most eloquent voice of the decent French right. She is what passes for a movie star these days. But hardly a Garbo. I liked the hauteur, the sense of hidden vice, in the Swede. This one plays to the crowd. It is not interesting," concluded Monsieur Mornet with a grimace.

Don Juan looked at the Frenchman curiously. Like so many of his people, he resembled a weathervane. Don Juan had long understood why the French, who, in the last analysis, liked nobody but themselves, nevertheless secretly preferred the Germans to the "Anglo-Saxons." They felt "culturally" superior to the Germans although socially more degenerate, hence perhaps their almost universal willingness to adopt fascism in 1940. In the Anglo-Saxons they sensed the competition of a more vibrant culture than their own, and although few yet admitted it, a richer, still-developing language. By linking the Anglo-Saxons with the Jews they believed they could pin the label of "conspiracy" on their rivals, as in times of trouble, since the twelfth century, so many French-made disasters had been firmly attributed to the scapegoat Israelites. He could vaguely imagine that this restaurant would soon be filled with Americans and this man would be mouthing the same equivocations. The lovely Corinne was the French person he preferred in this context. Men were her universe. As long as they spoke the language of admiration, she didn't much care what tongue they used.

Never before had Don Juan felt so alone as on that day in the city where so much of his life had been spent and where nearly all his friends had once lived. He walked about Paris that night covering huge distances on foot in the mild spring weather. Standing outside his sometime home on the Avenue Foch, he saw it was being used as some kind of service club by the Germans. He took a bus out to the Batignolles district, which was the last address he had for Mireille. It had come on a postcard, before he'd left the chateau, with the news that she was once more alone. He knew he didn't dare ask if she was there, but he wanted to go and look at the house on the ridiculous chance that he might just see her walking in the street and have time to kiss her cheek and hear her voice, her marvelous voice.

The grim apartment building which corresponded to her address was all blacked out when he arrived, and he went and sat in a rather unfriendly café opposite, looking around at the people congregated there, wondering why he'd come on this quixotic visit to nowhere in particular. She was not in the café. There was no one who looked remotely like her. He sat at the bar and started to order drink after drink, feeling like a man in an inviolable bubble gazing bleakly out at a world that soon, mercifully, receded, so that he had no exact idea where he was anymore.

He never left his bar stool in all this time, keeping his bearings only by the geography of the bar. The door out, behind him to the left. The body of the café, behind him to the right. A mirror in front of him, behind the bartender and the rows of bottles of Ricard and Byrrh, seemed to give him a cinema-screen image of what was going on behind. A wailing sound intruded on his consciousness. He knew he'd heard it before, but apart from a sense of menace he couldn't quite place it. People seemed to leave the café in a hurry, but many stayed. Then there was a great deal of banging as if an inordinately noisy party were going on upstairs. People were hiding under the tables. Don Juan wanted to ask the bartender what was happening, but he had disappeared and the mirror was crumbling, sending the bottles spinning about like ninepins. His head swooned, it was hard to hold it still, and he found himself falling.

The jar of hitting the floor must have sobered him a little, because he got up and recognized that the whole café was partly disintegrated and that dust was settling on everything and everyone in a way that reminded him of the scene in Seville. There was a great deal of screaming now, but he could pay attention to nothing but the small avalanche of acid bile rising in his throat. He just made it through the door, spewing up on the sidewalk, retching for what seemed like a quarter of an hour. Long before he had finished, his head was clearing enough to recognize the crumping and staccato sounds of antiaircraft fire, and the intermittent whine and subsequent ear-numbing explosions of bombs.

He looked across the road at the blazing apartment building that might or might not contain Mireille. Sober enough now to walk straight and know what he was doing, but by no means sober enough for normal caution or judgment, he threaded his way between the debris on the street, where hot shrapnel fallen from the artillery barrage still glowed, and inspected the front of the burning building. The top two stories were ablaze. The foyer was littered with debris, but serviceable. He walked in and inspected the little rows of bells. Mireille's name was there, sure enough. It was a fourth-floor apartment. He walked up the stairs. From the second story some people were carrying an old woman, who appeared unhurt and more worried about her *minou* than the air raid itself.

"Have you seen him?" she asked Don Juan as he passed. "He's a gray Persian. I thought he was in the apartment."

"I regret I have seen no cats, madame," said Don Juan carefully and politely, continuing on his way upstairs.

The steps to the fourth floor were blocked by so much plaster and brick that he found himself scrambling up a crumbling slope, gripping the banisters in order to finally achieve the landing. The heat was intense, and exposed electric wires sparked like fireworks, while water poured in a steady stream from the fractured central-heating system. Don Juan edged his way along the passage, feeling more sober, and more aware of his rashness, with every step. He found the door of her apartment and tried to open it, but it was jammed by the subsidence of the building. He kicked through the panels and hurled himself against the door till it cracked.

Forcing his way through, he saw at once that the outer, curtain wall was burning and that the room was quite full of smoke. He ran back to the burst pipe, soaked a strip torn from his shirt, and masked himself with it. He found no one in the living room, kitchen, or bedroom of the mean little apartment, but when he tried to open the bathroom door he found it jammed as the front door had been.

Almost blinded, and choking from the smoke, he finally got the door open. Mireille must have been about to take a bath, for she lay choking on the floor huddled in a terrycloth robe. Although trapped by the jammed door she had been spared the worst of the smoke for the same reason.

The upper part of the building was beginning to collapse by the time he got her out into the street. She was still speechless with coughing, but her legs were obeying her. He felt her reluctance as he almost dragged her away from the blazing building. Suddenly he heard her voice behind him.

"The snakes, Juan!"

"We'll come back tomorrow!" he shouted back.

But she had wrenched her hand from his and stood watching the building as on floor after floor the flames burst through the windows. When eventually he persuaded her to move, her body was rigid with grief and shock.

For the next three days Mireille stayed with him at his cheap hotel, the Atlantic, near the Gare St. Lazare. They slept together, but did not make love. She talked about her python as if he had been more than an occasional lover, but a friend with many winning ways she missed more than she could have imagined possible. He tried to comfort her, to talk of other things, but she remained inconsolable.

On the third day Don Juan had an appointment with a director of his company who was visiting Paris and staying at the Hôtel Georges V, where they were to meet at half past noon. He had been warned that when this director came to Paris it would be with instructions from Dulles. The other reason was, of course, to make sure that he was still really under their control. All too frequently when agents were discovered by the enemy, they were given the option of being taken over or shot.

It was April 26, 1944, a day of astonishing news. Marshal Pétain was in Paris for the first time since 1940. He had come as head of the French state to join Cardinal Suhard at Notre Dame Cathedral in a memorial service for the many killed by the Allied bombing of Batignolles. Curious, Don Juan watched the cheering crowds following the marshal's car on its way to the Hôtel de Ville. He was sorry that Mireille had elected to stay at the hotel, listlessly reading the paper, and still occasionally subject to spontaneous bursts of weeping. This amazing spectacle might have brought her back to the real world.

The old man appeared on the balcony of the Hôtel de Ville to shouts of applause from an enormous crowd of Parisians. He seemed more gaunt, more bent than the already old man to whom Don Juan had professed an interest in the church. People sang the "Marseillaise" and waved tricolors. Don Juan felt the infection of the crowd. The marshal was their history. He had actually won a battle against the Germans in World War I. He was, in a sense, a monarch without a crown, the only legitimate leader they had left, and their cheering helped to disguise for them, as well as the Germans, that the emperor had no clothes.

"Mesdames, messieurs," he said in his high, sibilant, old man's voice. "I cannot talk to each one of you individually—it's impossible, there are too many of you—but I did not wish to visit Paris without greeting you, without recalling myself to your memory.

"Moreover, these are unhappy circumstances which have brought me here. I have come here to console you for all the misfortunes that reign over Paris. They make me very sad."

Does he mean the Allied bombing? Don Juan wondered. Or his own police, his own specially formed murder and torture gangs that, at Hitler's request, he formed from all too many willing Frenchmen, and who now preyed like vultures on his people. Perhaps he is too old, too hardened in the arteries, to comprehend reality anymore. Like France itself.

"But this is a *first* visit I am making you," the marshal went on. "I hope I shall be able to come easily to Paris, without having to warn my guardians. I shall come happily. But today I am not making an *entrance* into Paris, merely a little visit of gratitude. I think of you very often.

"I find Paris somewhat changed, for it is now four years since I have been here. But you can be sure that as soon as I can I will be back and then it will be an official visit. So I hope I shall see you again soon."

The cheers of mesdames and messieurs were still echoing in Don Juan's ears as he approached the Georges V just in time for his appointment.

Don Juan had been trained not to walk into traps. A recognition password was one way. But how *exactly* to avoid each potential trap was left to his own initiative, using his own imagination. In this case he stopped at a telephone kiosk in a *tabac* opposite the hotel. He called and asked for Señor Hector Lopez. He was connected and a voice came on the line.

"Lopez on the apparatus," said a voice in Spanish. "Who is this?"

Don Juan gave his cover name. "I'm a bit late," he said. "The manifestation in behalf of the marshal delayed me. Very moving it was!" he said in as flat and classless a Spanish accent as he could achieve. That he had always spoken French-accented Spanish was one of the problems of this encounter.

"It's room four-ten," said Lopez. "When you get here come straight up. How long will you be?"

"About ten minutes. Is your friend with you? Annabel . . . I can't remember her other name."

"I'll tell you when you get here. Just come straight up," said Lopez, and put down his receiver.

Don Juan went straight out and got a taxi to the Place Vendôme. He walked to the Opéra and took a Métro to the Place Péreire. All the way he checked if he was being followed. He went into the Brasserie Péreire and made a call from the booth in the lavatory, having first checked that there was an exit into an alley behind the *brasserie.*

He telephoned Mireille at the Atlantic.

"Where are you?" she asked.

"Are you feeling more cheerful?" he asked in return.

"Oh, much. Where are you, Juan?"

"Why do you care?"

"Oh, don't say that. I know I've been boring. But I've snapped out of it now. I'm lonely. I feel guilty for taking so long to get over my loss. I want to . . . demonstrate that to you. There's always so little time these days. Oh, Juan, please come back to the hotel quickly. I want to do *everything* with you. I want to let you hear my voice again. Please."

"Wonderful. Splendid, Mireille. After the war, perhaps."

She shrieked as he hung up.

He took a taxi to the Gare du Nord and then the first train to Rouen. It left at two-thirty in the afternoon.

Once on the train, although he remained hidden behind his newspaper, he had time to think. For the last couple of hours, he had been *reacting,* like a beast in the jungle, to every scent of danger the wind bore him. Now the train was in motion. No one seemed to be watching him. He had time to think of Mireille. Her last postcard had come to Switzerland. Via his grandfather and Dulles. Which in itself was odd. Although she knew about his family. He might have given her that address. He really couldn't remember. Other things about her came back. She had been political. Their Annecy meeting introduced Jeanne. Everyone there had been left-wing. All anti-Pétain, anti-German.

But the German torturer had said something. "Never mind about the circus people." Why had he said that? Surely dissidents, licensed to travel, were dangerous. Unless they had been creatures of the Germans, posing as left-wing Resistance. What had happened to Mireille's father?

Don Juan looked around the railroad carriage. It was crammed with eight people all sitting face to face in the narrow space, a ninth standing at the doorway to the corridor. Don Juan had one of the window seats, by the other door. Opposite him sat a young woman with a baby. There were a couple of Ukrainian prisoners and a German soldier escort. The former would be going to work on the Western Wall, and could be distinguished by the prisoner uniforms they wore. They chatted amiably with their escort in German. Apart from a very old man in a French veteran's beret the rest of the people, sitting, were French women. The man standing at the door was a member of the Regiment of France, a force raised to protect the French government from the Resistance. Don Juan saw no immediate danger from his companions.

Don Juan returned to considering what had made Mireille work for the fascists. Her father might be the answer. His life might have been the bargaining chip that had bought her allegiance. She had never mentioned the ringmaster while they had been together at the Atlantic, but she had said her father was still in jail, that Pétain was slowly starving his communist prisoners to death. He had taken that as an expression of her opposition to the regime. But now he remembered something else she'd said. He tried to reconstruct the conversation in his mind's ear.

"Where have they got them?" he had asked out of personal curiosity, for it was unlikely that Dulles didn't already know.

"At Le Puy. The conditions are indescribable. Deaths there occur as much from disease as from executions. His daily ration was a small piece of bread, a bowl of turnip, and six watery spoonfuls of soup."

"Was?" he had asked.

"Now it is a bit better," she had said, adding, "You know Billoux?"

Don Juan did not.

"Billoux is with my father in Le Puy. A leading communist deputy under the Third Republic. He wrote to Père Pétain and offered to give evidence against Daladier and Reynaud, at their trial. In return for better conditions or being freed. My father refused to do that. He deserves to survive more than most!"

Don Juan knew that in intelligence work one was often left

guessing at the real story. Intelligence was not a science, but a game. And as in poker, if your opponent lost, nothing obliged him or her to show you their hand. He felt no resentment against Mireille. He knew that if she had betrayed him it was unlikely to have been for any trivial reason. Nor did it occur to him that she might hate him personally for not giving her all his love in 1939–40, when she had been prepared to give all hers.

He turned his mind from this examination of the past to his prospects for the future. Apart from a considerable sum of money, without which he never traveled, he had been forced to abandon his baggage together with the radio, all left with Mirielle at the Atlantic. His control would expect him to make contact after the meeting with Lopez. Loss of contact would mean that he was probably in enemy hands or that he had defected. He was now following the procedure laid down for the situation in which he found himself. He was making for a safe house in Rouen where he knew one of Dulles's agents to be. There he would be interrogated, await further orders, and probably be given a new cover identity.

Don Juan became aware that the train had been sitting on a siding for a considerable time.

"Where are we?" he asked his companions in the carriage.

"Just outside Mantes," said the soldier in the doorway.

He looked at the girl opposite him. She had just put her baby to her breast and had spread her legs very slightly, completely absorbed in the sensation and, thought Don Juan, presumably the emotion, of giving suck.

She was less than beautiful, with a pale freckled face and mousy-colored hair, but her guileless eyes were an unusual, almost duck's-egg blue, and they betrayed her totally. Now that she looked at her baby they were infinitely gentle and trusting. But the instant she glanced up at the people around her, they were as wary as those of a wild creature.

"Are you going as far as Rouen?" Don Juan asked her.

Most of the other people in the carriage were talking, and she didn't appear to hear him. He watched her eyes closely to see if this was really the case. After a small interval she gave him a scared, curious glance. He trapped the glance by repeating his question, and smiling encouragingly.

"Baby and I are going home!" she said, her voice a little too high-pitched, as if she were not quite certain how loud to speak.

"Where is home?"

"Châtillon-sur-Risle. But baby's never been there yet. Have you, Pierre?"

He leaned forward to look at the baby, thinking of Edwige's child, his own son, far away in the Val Romanée. He noticed how Pierre kept his eyes tight shut, as he sucked, occasionally kneading her plump breast with his tiny fist.

"No one knows I'm arriving," she said unexpectedly, laughing out loud, as if this were a joke. "Papa's going to be so surprised!"

"The baby's papa?"

"No, no. Papa. My papa." She laughed again, looking at Don Juan as if she expected him to see the funny side of her papa's surprise. Don Juan smiled at her gently as if he understood and were amused. He realized that she was slightly "simple" and understood her fear of the people around her. The normally intelligent person was probably always challenging her with words or thoughts which were beyond her. If she were actually retarded she probably wouldn't be aware of or care that she was missing something. But that was not the case. The baby, till it grew, he supposed, was an ideal companion, its needs and her capacities being perfectly matched.

In the distance the sirens were wailing, proclaiming another air raid. They'd heard them in the distance while the train had been moving. Now he guessed they must be those of the town of Mantes, nearby. He looked out the window at an engine shed where a locomotive was being slowly revolved on a huge turntable. Some rolling stock laden with coal stood on another siding, and beyond that he could see a steel-wire fence skirting a wood of remarkable oaks, huge and gnarled. The remains perhaps of Tabatha's primeval forest? The European oak took many centuries to grow to such proportions. To his amazement one of the trees started to burn.

For only a fraction of a second did he remain wondering whether the White Goddess was giving him a sign. The thought amused him and he was smiling when the noises came to him, and the locomotive on the turntable seemed to open like a huge steel flower, slowly, at first, blowing a distended bubble of flame into the air.

Some people in the corridor shrieked.

"Keep back from the windows," said the Regiment of France man, rather fatuously, since the windows, although crisscrossed somewhat with tape to protect from blast, were in reality capable of ripping people indiscriminately all over the carriage if they blew in.

But everyone stood up, crowding toward the door. Everyone except Don Juan and the woman with the baby. Don Juan let down the window in the outside door, thus enclosing some of the glass. Fires blazed among the rolling stock, and the bombs were still exploding at those terrifyingly predictable intervals that are one of the chief terrors of air raids. The whine before the bang is like the guillotine in slow motion. He looked out and saw two fighter-bombers wheeling in the sky; they were coming back for another run.

"Let's get out of here," he said to the young mother.

She looked up at him, paralyzed, not with fear but with the effort to understand what was happening. He had opened the door. Now he grabbed the baby from her breast, knowing she would follow the child, if not him. In the same movement he jumped the six feet to the ground, holding the baby high as he went, and rolling painfully across some sleepers as a result. Leaving the shrieking baby for an instant on the ground, he turned to the mother, half-catching her as she leaped blindly after her baby.

A water tower was exploding down the line, right next, he could see, to their train's locomotive. The planes were shooting cannon and tracers now, pretty orange flames spurting from the leading edges of their wings as they came. He scooped up the baby and started to run.

Now came the staccato sound of the train behind him being ripped open by cannon shells. He glanced, momentarily, over his shoulder to make sure she was following him and saw she was and that the train was blazing from end to end. So difficult is it for the human mind sometimes to comprehend horror that he actually wondered why their opening shots should have hit the oak if they were capable of such devastating accuracy. He thought that before he allowed his mind to register, through the transmissions of his eyes and ears, the spectacle of several hundred people burning to death in what looked like a series of ruptured sardine cans. The planes then banked, heading straight up into the sky, as some rather ineffective anti-aircraft fire started laying a barrage over the railroad yard.

The mother reached Don Juan, grabbing the baby, as hostile to his holding him as a female animal is to any stranger touching her young. Her breast still hung out of her dress, and she pressed the baby to it before turning and looking for a long time at the train. Don Juan touched her shoulder, anxious to get himself away from the railroad yard, where some twenty or more railroad workers now surrounded the stricken train and police were arriving. He didn't want to risk having to show his papers.

"Goodbye," he said. "The police will take care of you."

But she thrust her hand into his, gripping it tightly.

"You mustn't leave us," she said. "I'm so grateful to you. Please don't leave us."

"Well, we must leave here. I'm in a great hurry to get to Rouen," he said.

Hand in hand he led her to where one of the bombs had blown a gap in the steel fence.

It was almost dark in Mantes by the time they arrived on foot. He found out that her name was Lise and tried to discover a little more about her travel plans. It appeared that from Rouen there was a bus to Châtillon-sur-Risle. Meanwhile she had no money and no papers, having left everything on the train. He offered to lend her money and take her as far as Rouen with him and put them on the bus to Châtillon-sur-Risle. She accepted this arrangement as a matter of course. There was always a person, usually male, to whom she had looked for decisions, for guidance, and for protection. In Paris it had been her Uncle Louis, a butcher in the Seventeenth Arrondisement. On the way into Mantes she chattered about her uncle and aunt, having either not fully understood what had happened on the train or somehow shut it out.

"He used to come into my bedroom and fiddle with me. You know," she said, giving her laugh after the word "fiddle," as if she thought what he'd done was most amusing.

"But my Aunt Marie, she got very angry. If she caught him doing it, she'd come and hit me and say horrid things to me, as if it were my fault. Last Saturday he came back home all drunk and acting very silly, pinching me and that. She shouted at him and he shouted at her. My goodness, it went on and on and woke baby. Then they went to bed, but baby cried and cried. I couldn't stop him."

Don Juan waited for her to go on. They had just passed the cathedral church and seen a sign to the bus station. He walked as fast as he could without actually pulling her along.

"Baby must have been frightened," he said, thinking this was the point of the story.

"Yes," she said. "That's right. That's what I said. But Uncle Louis got furious with poor little Pierre and came into my room and took him out of his crib and shook him, to try to stop him from crying. But he cried more, and I, I was so afraid I attacked Uncle Louis. I mean I hit him."

Once again Don Juan waited almost a minute, until they had actually come in sight of the bus station, before realizing he must ask a supplementary question if he hoped to learn the outcome of the drama of the lecherous butcher.

"What happened after you attacked him?"

"Oh, he had to go to the doctor and Aunt Marie said I would have to take baby home to Papa."

Don Juan decided to be inquisitive enough to clear up all the outstanding mysteries in this little story.

"Why did he have to go to the doctor? Did you hit him that hard?"

"No, but I used my scissors."

"I see," said Don Juan, slightly shaken by this news, although not entirely surprised. "Is he still alive?"

"Oh yes!" said Lise, laughing a great deal at the thought that he might not be.

"And why doesn't Papa know you're coming back?"

"They were afraid to tell him in case he said I had to stay. Papa is Uncle Louis's older brother."

"Do they get their supplies of meat from Papa's farm?"

"Yes, how did you know that?"

"Just a guess. And where is Pierre's father?"

"We don't know."

Don Juan decided that the mystery of where any Frenchman had disappeared to in the last few years was so common as not to be worth further inquiry. Besides, it really didn't seem to be any of his business.

They were fortunate to get the last bus to Rouen that night. It is not a particularly long journey, and they were in the city before midnight, but too late for Lise to get a connecting bus to Châtillon-sur-Risle.

The safe house Don Juan sought was in the cathedral close. Indeed, it was above a bookshop that catered to the ecclesiastical trade, selling sacred-music sheets, tracts and books of philosophical and religious interest, the two subjects being not necessarily in conflict for some French Catholics. Its whereabouts had been so carefully described to him that he could easily find it in the blackout.

He knew that Lise was best delivered to a convent for the night, since she had no papers and could not be put in a hotel. He was thinking this and that there was bound to be some priest in the environs of the cathedral who could direct them to a convent when he found himself looking down the street where the safe house was located. There were no street lights, but in the bright summer moonlight he could see plainly enough. Half the street had been reduced to rubble. To Lise's bewilderment and distress, because the baby had started to cry, Don Juan hurried back and forth making quite sure that the rubble represented where the bookshop had been.

He took Lise across the cathedral square to a restaurant which was still open. They sat and ate a miserable meal, at which Don Juan asked the owner to join them, buying some expensive wine to ensure that his invitation was accepted. For a moment he resumed his role as Spanish traveling salesman.

"Good of you to join us, monsieur," he said as the restaurateur came with an overpriced bottle of Burgundy. "That will do us good, after what we have been through. Madame and I were lucky to escape from that train bombed in Mantes today."

"But they believe the death toll was stupendous!" said the landlord, as if he were seeing ghosts. "The radio says it is impossible to know how many people were on the train."

"I can well believe it," said Don Juan. "We both lost all our things. I wonder if you know of a neighbor who has some diapers. Otherwise perhaps I could buy some napkins on madame's behalf."

The restaurateur was full of sympathy and hurried off to telephone his wife.

"My wife is bringing some over," he said on his return. "She uses them for dusting these days, but she is sure she has some clean ones. Is monsieur German?" he asked politely.

"Spanish. I'm on business here. Although it becomes more difficult all the time with this bombing."

"Those damned Anglo-Saxons!" exclaimed the restaurateur. "You know they almost bombed the cathedral two days ago? Is that a military target? We have asked the cardinal to appeal to the pope. Even among the English and Americans there must be some Christians."

"No, no," said Don Juan pontifically. "They are Protestant!" It was the kind of statement a Frenchman expected of a Francoist Spaniard. He saw this one smile.

Madame arrived with a diaper, and she and Lise went off to the ladies' room clucking over Pierre, who had fallen asleep and was annoyed to be awakened.

"There used to be a good religious bookshop across the square. Was that affected by the bombing?" asked Don Juan as if making conversation.

"No, it is completely gone. It is most ironic."

"Ironic?" Don Juan was puzzled.

"Yes, it appears it was a nest of terrorists."

"Resistance?"

"That is what they call themselves. But whom are they resisting? It is the British bombers that are killing the most Frenchmen today. And the irony is that the police arrested them and they were shot last week. If they'd waited another day or two the Anglo-Saxons would have bombed them to death and saved us taxpayers the cost of the bullets."

"But they were Frenchmen?" Don Juan managed to sound astounded.

"Yes, monsieur, I'm afraid so. One only was American, they say. They shot him too, naturally."

"You are right," said Don Juan, forcing a smile. "Very ironical!"

That night he spent on a bench in the bus station while Lise slept on the restaurant owner's couch curled up with Pierre. He gave out to her hosts that he was staying in a hotel.

Don Juan woke in the early hours, rather chilled now the warming effects of the heavy Burgundy had worn off. Shivering, he wondered what he would do after he'd put Lise on the bus in the morning. He was at grave risk wherever he went in France. His identity, the only one for which he had papers, would be circulated to all police throughout a country which was now a maze of checkpoints, and where police came into cafés and onto buses and trains, as a matter of routine, asking for identification. It was what he had dreaded while sitting in the train outside Mantes.

Reflecting on Lise's soft, warm little body and rather wishing he could lie with it, he started to walk. It occurred to him that her father might be prepared to shelter him for a few days. After all, he had saved her life. He assumed that the reason she'd been sent to Paris was that Châtillon-sur-Risle was so near the coast. Few people doubted that the Allies would soon invade, and then this whole area of Normandy would become a battleground. He really had nothing to lose by taking her home to her father and conceivably something to gain, for the nearer he was to the invasion point the better.

In the morning, to her delight, he accompanied her on the bus. They rode through the bright, spring-girt Norman countryside; she smiling as contentedly as a girl finding herself on a successful blind date; he feeling increasingly ill with every kilometer the lurching bus traveled, not travel-sick but fevered. She told the bus driver to drop them off outside her father's farmhouse that lay on the near (Rouen) side of Châtillon-sur-Risle, and she used her by now howling baby as a means of persuasion.

Her mother answered the door. An explosion of surprised, relieved emotion. "Uncle Louis telephoned," she cried. "He was so afraid you were on that train! Papa has been half a dozen times to the police to try to get information. Now he is at the other farm feeding the beasts."

Lise's mother, ushering them into the house, wept with relief and with the excitement of seeing her grandson. But Don Juan, who was wishing someone would ask him to sit down, was surprised to sense in the older woman's voice and manner an underlying fear.

Lise's own delight at being home was total until she noticed Don Juan's sickly, sweating face.

"Monsieur Jean," she exclaimed, using the name by which he had introduced himself. "How ill you look. Me, I'd lie down if I were you."

"I'd like that," said Don Juan, longing only to lie flat and close his eyes and be warm.

He found her mother looking at him closely. She was a comely woman with a face marred by warts. Now she came and put a hand on his forehead.

"My God!" she exclaimed. "We must put him in the cottage, at once. Lise, there are some warm sheets in the linen cupboard. And get extra blankets. Monsieur Jean, you must go straight to bed. We will call a doctor."

Don Juan was following her, the focus of his eyes becoming increasingly blurred. But at the sound of the word "doctor" he pulled himself together enough to say, "Please, madame. No doctors. I have a horror of doctors."

She looked at him curiously and then she said, "All right, Monsieur Jean, but just tell us if you change your mind."

From the moment they left him in the well-warmed bed he slept. It was a balmy May day outside, but he awoke shivering and then, before he could stop himself, started to vomit. He staggered out of the bed and found a basin. Half an hour later he collapsed back into bed and became unconscious. When the women came to bring him some lunch they were horrified. For the next two days they nursed him through bouts of vomiting and raging temperatures, changing his sheets and wrapping him in warm towels. Monsieur Dupuis—for that was the family name—came to visit him on the first night with the intention of thanking him for saving his child's life, but found Don Juan speechless.

"One asks oneself why he does not want the doctor," said Monsieur Dupuis to his wife.

"It is odd," agreed Madame Dupuis. "Between us, he has an enormous quantity of money with him. Lise emptied his pockets so that she could clean his suit. So it cannot be a question of that."

"Besides, one would have gladly paid, for heaven's sake!" said Monsieur Dupuis. "I am still not quite sure, from Lise's account, what exactly happened. But there is no question that she was on that train on which all those people died."

"If that one does not hold down some nourishment soon, we may have to call in the doctor," said Madame Dupuis.

"I have a strange feeling that he came here looking for a refuge," said Monsieur Dupuis. "It would have been so easy just to put her on that bus. The money he'd lent her was a trifle."

"It's possible," agreed Madame Dupuis. "Another man might have taken her to his hotel bed with him. He must have known Lise wouldn't have refused. It is extraordinary that she should have found someone so honorable to look after her."

When Don Juan's temperature started finally to recede he was so weak he could scarcely lean on his elbow. He lay, his utterly evacuated body feeling strangely hollow and brittle, focusing on the beamed ceiling and the strawberry-patterned curtains on the windows. Lise came in and sat on the bed, stroking his hair.

"You look a little better, Monsieur Jean," she said. "Are you ready to eat something?"

Don Juan's stomach and throat were so sore from retching that the prospect of starting that cycle again dismayed him. He shook his head and managed a smile at her, for she looked at him as if he were a child.

"Little Pierre always leaves some over. He's a greedy boy." She gave her laugh. "But I'm a good milker." She laughed again. "That's what Papa says about his cows, you know," she concluded, staring at his face and tracing the contours of it with her fingers.

Then without saying anything else she undid her blouse, loosing her breasts. There were pads of cotton wool inside her brassiere to absorb her leaking, and she mopped both nipples to see which breast seemed still to have most of what little Pierre had left over. Then she gave Don Juan her left breast, expressing a little of the milk to wet his dried lips first, then inserting her nipple.

"Suck, Monsieur Jean, suck, suck."

Don Juan tested the unfamiliar, sweet liquid, but when his lips felt the familiar spongy feeling of her nipple, it seemed to revive him and he sucked. After a while she gave him the other nipple. It was then he noticed a rhythmic movement of the bed and saw that she had thrust her hand between her thighs. As he sucked he felt life coming back into his own loins and saw her eyes closing, their duck's-egg-colored irises just visible between the half-closed lids. She shuddered for a moment or so and then withdrew her breast, buttoning herself up again.

"Well, Monsieur Jean. I hope you feel better. I know I do," and she laughed delightedly.

"You are forgetting the *bonne bouche*," he said.

She looked puzzled.

He reached for her hand and put her pleasuring finger to his lips, taking a tincture of the musky taste on his tongue.

"The end of a perfect repast," he managed to say. But he really preferred the musk to the sweet stuff. Milk had never been his favorite drink. But he did keep it down, and from that moment his recovery began.

The same evening Monsieur Dupuis came and brought some *eau de vie* with him in case his guest felt revived enough for it. He didn't.

"Monsieur Jean," said the farmer, rather formally, "René Dupuis. Please let me first express the deepest gratitude of my wife and myself. It is an honor to have you under our roof. I hope you will stay as long as you can."

Don Juan looked up at the russet-cheeked Norman peasant with his tobacco-stained mustache, his breath smelling of wine and *eau de vie*, but his eyes clear enough, a countryman's eyes all crinkled against the sun.

"It is I who am grateful," said Don Juan. "I owe you my life."

"I don't know that you were in that much danger." Monsieur Dupuis smiled. "But it is true that my wife was concerned that you did not want a doctor. Monsieur will forgive me, but you have been unable to communicate with anyone for over a week. Would you not like me to telephone someone for you and tell them you are all right? Your family perhaps? Or your business associates? Somebody, after all, must be very concerned about you."

He is suspicious that I have made no such request, thought Don Juan.

He said, "I was more or less on holiday when we were caught on the train. Mixing pleasure with a little tourism. I was not due back in Spain for two weeks. But I will telegraph tomorrow. Please don't trouble yourself."

The older man looked him in the eyes.

"Monsieur, we live in very difficult times. People can no longer tell themselves the truth, let alone others."

Don Juan guessed that his host might have something to say about Lise. If this was so he wished to make it easier for him.

"If it's about Lise, I think I understand about her."

"We have two sons, you know. They are both working in Germany. The STO. But they are perfectly normal. She was born in a leap year. The harvest, it was no good either. But we love her, you understand?"

"Yes. I understand. And the baby?" Don Juan knew this was what the man really wanted to tell him about, but found it hard to put into words.

"A German. A sergeant who was billeted here. In this cottage. He was an excessively ugly man. None of the local girls wanted to go out with him, although they all went with the other German soldiers, from time to time. Why not? They are human. The sergeant took Lise to Rouen one day in his truck. He bought her clothes. He took her to a hotel and made love to her. When he came back with her she said she wanted to stay with him. What could we do? No one had ever praised her or loved her except us. She was entirely happy. When he was on duty she just waited for him to come home. Like a bitch with her master's slippers. He used to take her into the town. He trained her to kiss him and fondle him in public to show everyone, including his own soldiers, that he had a woman who wanted him. In a way he was more pathetic than she."

"D'you think he really loved her?"

"As a matter of fact I am certain of it. Otherwise we would have sent her away to my brother's in Paris long before. But he was posted to the Italian front. He writes me letters for her sometimes. She cannot read, of course. We have written to him about the child and he has expressed a wish to marry her after the war. It is a rare thing, that, as you must know. But we were friends, all of us. He was a good man. A farmer like me. From Bavaria. Mixed farming, some Riesling wine grapes. It would not be a bad life for her. And you know when she is with kind, understanding people she gets much better."

"I can well believe it," said Don Juan. "You sent her to your brother's place to have the child?"

"This is a small town. All our lives we must live here. If she can really go and live in Germany after the war, why should we face criticism and disgrace here?"

"Does anyone know she's here?"

"No. No one who knows her saw her get off the bus. You would be surprised at how many people have been obliged to hide, sometimes for years. A man I know keeps a couple of Jewish children. No one ever sees them. Of course, his farm is remote. They can show their faces to the sun each day. Do you wish such sanctuary, Monsieur Jean? It is just a guess. Don't be offended."

"For a while, yes, I would," said Don Juan.

"I have another farm. It is in what we call the Risle Valley, about five miles away. I have grazing for beasts there, by the river. There is a farmhouse. Not much furniture. There are three thousand acres, some of them marsh. If you keep away from the road, no one need know you are there. Would that suit you?"

Monsieur Dupuis had an old Renault truck for transporting

animals and hay. Because he was one of the most important peasant farmers in the region in terms of acreage and production, the prefecture allowed him a gasoline ration from his own pumps. One night soon after their discussion he drove Don Juan over to the Risle Valley farm. It had no electricity, but Don Juan liked the soft light of the oil lamps and loved the old building with its exposed beams weathered by centuries of wind and rain without, and human dwelling within.

"It is about seven hundred years old. From the epoch of the Plantagenets," said Monsieur Dupuis, showing him around.

"When Norman dukes were English kings." Don Juan smiled.

"Don't let anyone tell you those were the good old days," said Monsieur Dupuis. "We think these times are terrible. Can you imagine your farm being a yearly battlefield for a hundred years?"

"But surely life on a farm was simpler then, more complete?" said Don Juan, thinking that the lush countryside beyond the kitchen door would have struck Inés as the "effortless Acraria" of her dreams.

"The work that eventually kills a farmer," he said, "that most of us die of, you know . . . the work is endless; when we grow more or less the same crops as they, raise more or less the same beasts. But they had to *make* everything they wore, everything they used in the way of implements, as well. And on top of that, every year, the ravaging hordes of English. Taking crops and beasts. Raping all the women. No, my friend. This is a trying time for France, but she has seen worse."

Don Juan spent the rest of May in a quiet love affair with Nature, that goddess Inés had so adored. He bathed in the river every morning and let the sun dry his naked body afterward as he lay in the deep clover, under the poplars, and watched the dragonflies and the kingfishers working diligently at their feeding in the shallows. On his host's behalf he watered the beasts, and checked the fences where they were grazing. On rough children's sketch blocks he did hundreds of drawings of natural minutiae. He drew flowers and mushrooms and insects and frogs and minnows and moths and molds and leaves, living and dead, and vegetables and fruit and berries and mice and water rats and hedgehogs and rabbits and hares, hiding with their leverets in their forms, and owls and hawks and hedge sparrows and jays and doves. He drew the cows, the Charolais and the Guernseys and the Holsteins, and on one single day when she came down with her father in the early morning, and left after nightfall, he drew Lise.

He sat her in a corner of the hay barn where the sun came through an upper window and lit her in a slowly moving halo of light. Little Pierre lay contented at her breast. Don Juan drew her, consciously, for the curé in the Val Romanée, a small offering for his Lady Chapel.

"Just think about your baby and his life," he said to Lise, preparing the child's watercolors and crayons which were all M. Dupuis could find him.

"That's what I *am* thinking about," she said.

Watching them, making them tangible and plastic on his page, Don Juan thought that they represented the most puissant symbol in the history of humans' worship of deities made in their own image. Venus and Cupid, Mary and Jesus. Goddesses whose sons' fate was to kindle love in human hearts. The reassuring image of woman, the eternal mother, writ large, with man the small suckling child, his sweet sex infinitely peaceful and unthreatening. How sad that the cold cult of virginity had shaped the myth. For the curé then he drew Lise, a sweet Venus, and her baby, merely the father of the unknown man. It was the best he could do.

Don Juan was awakened early next morning by a sound. It seemed far away, but he knew it at once. It was war. Come once again to France. He walked naked out into the orchard behind the house and stood, his bare feet in the cool dew. A soft breeze stirred the crystalled cobwebs in the pear trees and the sky was the color of a smoky pearl.

Like ordered armies of insects the engines of war droned overhead. Within ten minutes, as he watched amazed, several thousand aircraft seemed to have their comings and goings, and distant guns were firing in the rhythms and at the intervals that marked their different species. It was a dawn song of death.

As he went indoors to make himself his breakfast he heard the rattling sound of tanks moving at speed on the distant highway.

He spent the day trying to pin everything in that place into his memory, bitter, in a way, that he must soon move on. He wondered, now the test was come, how his class at Deerhurst were acquitting themselves on the beaches. By any law of averages at least a couple of them might be there, fighting, and perhaps dying, while he calmed the restless cattle, bringing some succulent bales of hay to distract them from the unaccustomed noise. He wondered who. Manley-Cohen, perhaps a chaplain to his battalion if he'd followed in his father's footsteps. Or Portarlington, leading a platoon of Guardsmen. There would be men like Whitticker, noncommissioned officers most of them. He reflected that a British army had driven the Germans from the Egyptian border to the gates of Rome in the last couple of years. Then there would be the Americans. He tried to visualize the American fighting man. An image of General Pershing leading square-jawed soldiers in Boy Scout hats came to him from pictures of World War I. And then he remembered Marny Perlmutter. That was what they'd be like. He saw thousands of Americans in football helmets with a general, not unlike Perlmutter, shouting at them as they were about to hit the beaches: "I'm a linesman. I tell you, all games are decided up front. Get up front, you guys. Go eat those bastards and spit out their socks."

Don Juan laughed at his fantasy and was still smiling when Monsieur Dupuis arrived. The Frenchman gave what news he'd gleaned from the radio. There were many rumors. One was that there were thousands of ships disgorging tens of thousands of men from landing craft. The Boches had expected them much farther north on the Pas-de-Calais, but the radio said they were landing in the Baie de la Seine between Point Barfleur and Deauville. Tanks and trucks full of Germans moving southwest had clogged the main road through Châtillon all day.

"Well, we must wait and see what happens, monsieur," said Don Juan, hoping he would be able to stay as long as possible in that beautiful place, reluctant, for once, to take a step into the future. But something told him that the immediate future held nameless, difficult-to-imagine horrors and that they would come to him soon enough. Monsieur Dupuis had the same, perhaps more specific forebodings. People already talked of "liberation" in the town.

"It is not a matter of the Germans or the British being here. France will not so easily be liberated from this war," he said grimly before driving home.

Two weeks later a squadron of Tiger tanks moved onto the farm during the night. Don Juan heard them coming and walked down to the pasture in the half-light, where he hoped to see and not be seen. The fighting had been coming nearer each day, and Monsieur Dupuis had transferred most of the grazing cattle to his home farm on the main road near the town. Don Juan watched one tank move into the orchard, crushing some of the trees, but using the rest for camouflage. Two other tanks drove into the hay barn, tearing through part of the old wooden wall. Their guns swiveled to cover the distant road that led west. A fine, light rain had started to fall.

Don Juan decided he had been a spectator long enough.

Having taken many long walks in the countryside, he knew the lie of the land along which the Allied column, for which the German tanks must be waiting, would have to come. He ran along a muddy path that followed the river for about two miles; then, skirting some woods, he climbed toward the road, listening carefully as he went. Soon he heard the sound of distant human activity. His eyes, now very accustomed to the dark, made out the glow of cigarettes, and soon, walking silently in the soft loam at the side of the field, he could see a row of trucks parked off the road, and the low murmur of English voices came to him with the sound of a warm wet wind disturbing the branches of the hedgerow.

There would be sentries posted, covering this field. If they hadn't seen him yet they soon would. "I want to speak to your commanding officer," he suddenly shouted, in his English public-school accent.

There was complete silence; then a sentry ahead of him said, "Advance and be recognized."

Don Juan walked forward, his hands raised, and found himself looking up the muzzle of a rifle with a fixed bayonet. A British Tommy wearing a helmet, camouflaged with leaves and twigs that made him look like a pagan reveler, stared at him suspiciously.

"What's the password?" he asked.

"I have no idea. I'm an Allied intelligence officer. I'm unarmed and I need urgently to speak to your commander."

A sergeant had joined the sentry. Without further ado he searched Don Juan for arms or grenades.

"What did you say your name was, guv'nor?" asked the sergeant.

"Don Juan," he said, unwilling to add his title and full name. "Of the American OSS," he added.

"All right, Don. Got any identification, have you?" asked the sergeant.

"Hardly—the Germans mightn't have liked it. Look, I've got information on the enemy's positions forward. I'd like to see your commander."

"Fair enough, Don," said the sergeant. "Just wait here and I'll see if the old man's awake. Keep an eye on him, Bill," he said to the sentry.

Something less than a Whitticker, this NCO, thought Don Juan as he waited.

After what seemed a very long time a British captain appeared.

"Well, hullo, hullo. Who exactly are you? Don somebody? The sergeant said something about OSS. That's a Yank outfit, you know."

"Captain, I have something very simple and important to report. I assume you are about to advance along the valley of the Risle. I can pinpoint three Tiger tanks that are waiting for you and their exact locations. Are you interested?"

The captain had only to listen to Don Juan's voice to be instantly interested. Someone who spoke the king's English, even if he appeared from nowhere in the middle of the night looking like a gypsy, had to be taken seriously.

"Name's Clive Poulson. Come on back to my HQ. We're having a spot of brekker. You can radio your chaps from there if you like. Got to be sure you're not a Hun in disguise. Meanwhile we'll get the Brylcreem boys to plaster those tanks."

So it came about that the British bombed the lovely farm of Monsieur Dupuis, by the river, knocking out two of the tanks and causing the other to flee. When Don Juan passed by, marching with Captain Poulson's Headquarters Company, he tried not to look at his home of the last two months. The barn was still burning, and the Plantagenet house, which had survived the Hundred Years War and seven centuries, was now a shell of smoldering timbers.

The captain said that Châtillon-sur-Risle had been evacuated by the Germans, who were falling back on a line in front of Rouen. Don Juan was anxious to see the Dupuis family before going through the long procedure of making contact with the OSS and getting his further orders. He had made contact with his "control" via the British divisional HQ. To his enigmatic code sign, "Annabel," someone had answered with the name "Lee," the name that the man in the Hôtel Georges V had not known. He'd been told to wait at Châtillon-sur-Risle, where an American liaison officer was coming to pick him up.

It was the first time he'd seen the little town itself as they marched through the throngs of cheering people waving tricolors, the men mostly wearing armbands proclaiming themselves to be in the Resistance army, the FFI—French Forces of the Interior. Some of the women and girls came forward and kissed the British Tommies and gave them flowers. Many people seemed already drunk, and half the crowd had bottles or glasses in their hands.

"Are you leaving some troops here?" asked Don Juan of the captain as they approached the *mairie*, where FFI figures were standing on the balcony, brandishing a huge French flag and a makeshift British Union Jack.

"There'll be one of our supply platoons here shortly. But we're leaving garrisoning to the frogs," he said. "God knows what they're up to. One hears terrible stories of their being pretty frightful to the collaborators. Kangaroo courts and all that. Still, it's nothing to do with us! Excuse me, we have to do the honors here. . . ."

"Company!" yelled Captain Poulson. "Company, eyes right!"

The British troops looked smartly right at the mayor and the other worthies clutching the flags and dressed in their tricolored ribbons and sashes, while Captain Poulson saluted.

Don Juan fell behind the British troops as they marched out of the town on their way to Rouen. He walked down to the Dupuis house, noticing that many of the French men were armed with rifles.

Although a few were drunk, they all seemed to be involved in some purposeful activity, shouting a great deal, knocking on doors. He supposed that after years of inactivity being once again their own masters must be an extraordinary sensation.

Outside the Dupuis house a large crowd had gathered; some forty women of all ages and a few youths, some older peasants, and a dozen armed men wearing the armbands of the FFI. They seemed excited, like a crowd waiting for a show.

Don Juan started to run, making for a side entrance to the house that led round to the back. But two youths with guns headed him off.

"Where are you going?" one of them shouted.

"I live here," said Don Juan. "I'm an Allied officer!"

They were too quick for him, and one of them swung the butt of his gun at Don Juan's solar plexus, winding him and making him double up.

Some of the FFI men hurried over to look at Don Juan, who was still speechless with pain and trying to regain his breath.

"He tried to get in the back way!" said the youth excitedly. "D'you think he's a Boche?"

Even as he spoke the crowd started screaming and shrieking taunts:

"Collabo!" "Traitor!" "Mother of a whore!" "Shit-eating friends of the Boches!"

Don Juan looked up and saw they had brought out Monsieur and Madame Dupuis, who both looked pale and stunned with fear. Madame, who had most of her hair hacked off, wept openly, her teeth chattering. The women aimed punches and kicks at her while Monsieur Dupuis was dragged by his handcuffed hands so that he stumbled and was pulled along, his knees scraping in the gravel.

"Is this the New France?" yelled Monsieur Dupuis. "Just take *me*. Leave the women, for God's sake."

But now there was another howl from the crowd, and this time it was the most hideous sound Don Juan had ever heard. It was like the baying of hounds about to tear their prey to pieces. But worse. For the animals kill from a pure instinct, uncomplicated by sexual cruelty. This cry held a lust for pain and fear.

It was Lise. Almost unrecognizable, but certainly Lise. They were thrusting her out of the house. It was Lise, stripped naked, clutching her baby, her head entirely shaved. Don Juan himself wanted to scream with horror at the sight of her face. Her eyes swiveled and her lips were set in a rictus grin of pure terror.

Don Juan pulled an identification pass the British had given him from his pocket and showed it to the FFI men. But as he suspected, they were not really soldiers. They had probably received their armbands and their guns only that morning. The pass meant nothing to them. But they sensed from his French that he wasn't a Boche. So when he pushed forward they reluctantly gave way for him.

The women were holding a mirror up in front of the wretched Lise, shouting, "Pretty, aren't you, German whore?"

Don Juan's rage gave him extra strength, and he used every blow and chop Dulles's people had taught him on the crowd around the girl. They fell back howling with pain and surprise. Then he grabbed Lise and started to run with her toward the town. He waved his pass in his other hand, shouting, "I am an Allied officer. She's under my protection!"

But some rifle-swinging youths were ahead of him. Their faces were red with drink and they were charging.

Don Juan made for the orchard at the side of the farm, but felt the tug of her hand leaving his, as she fell. He turned to receive the blow of a stone in the chest. They were all hurling stones at her, and she knelt huddled over the baby whimpering and wincing at the cutting, jabbing stones. Don Juan threw himself over her, shielding her, and yelled at them to stop.

The men ran forward now, trying to prize him off their prey with their rifle butts. But when he resisted them, they made a sport of it, laughing and shouting their excitement as they then jabbed and swung their guns at him.

He not only heard, he could feel, not painfully then, but as in a dream, his arm break, his collarbone snap, his upper leg crack under the hail of blows. There was the smell of the crowd's fetid, vinous breath and of Lise's milk. The sound of a convoy of trucks came to him just before he succumbed to blackness.

Ever afterward there was one brief incident that Don Juan remembered before finally becoming conscious that he was in a hospital in England.

Perhaps an hour after the lynching, he somehow revived while a cheerful Cockney medical orderly was putting his limbs in splints. Don Juan was lying on a stretcher, looking up at a number of peering faces. Among them a very concerned-looking American officer.

"Are you the liaison officer?" Don Juan managed to ask.

"Yeah. Listen, don't try to talk, fella. Just relax."

"What happened to the woman?"

The American shook his head gravely. "But the baby'll be okay."

"If you can call growing up to be a frog okay, eh, guv'nor?" said the medical orderly to Don Juan as he started to give him an injection that sent him to sleep for a very long time.

15
Juliet

One ceases to be a child when one realizes that telling one's trouble does not make it any better.

—Cesare Pavese

They had put him into a civilian hospital. In a private room. Slowly, as for a child just born, its sights and sounds became real for Don Juan and ceased to have a merely insubstantial dreamy quality. First when he became aware of anything, it was always of pain. In his legs, arms, and chest. The nurses came and gave him regular injections. They wore starched white aprons over dark-blue dresses, and black stockings. Upon their carefully pinned-up hairdos ridiculous little white starched caps were perched. Long before Don Juan started asking himself questions like where or why or how, in relation to his own situation, he found himself visualizing the bodies of these young women under the provocative shell of these tight, neat uniforms. They were utterly unlike the Swiss nun-nurses with their rather asexual shapeless white coveralls, white stockings and shoes. These brisk temptresses with their cheery smiles and soft complexions, their little watches pendant beside their fountain pens upon their well-starched bosoms, would have been surprised to know that they peopled a very seraglio of passion and libidinousness in Don Juan's torrid, drug-fueled dreams.

He was largely encased in plaster. His left arm broken as well as his left leg. His chest plastered where they had reset ribs that had punctured one lung. Scars healing where the lung injury had necessitated surgery. But at first he simply took in these facts, bore the pain as best he could, and comforted himself with fantasies about the nurses. And slept.

One day he awoke to find a young woman watching him. There was something familiar about her face, but he couldn't place it exactly. She wore a dark-blue uniform with gold buttons, a stiff collar and black tie. Upon her head there was a rakish tricorne hat over her auburn hair. The hat gave her a nautical air. Her eyes were the color of polished chestnuts, and her cheeks reminded him of faintly bruised peaches. She looked as if she had walked in cool wind and rain all her life, and the sweet flush it gave to her skin never left her. She had not noticed that he was awake because she was talking to one of the nurses.

He had never, since his sojourn in the hospital, tried to form a sentence of his own. A nurse would ask him if he needed a "bottle" and he would nod, or a doctor, probing his chest, would question him about pain, when he found that he could manage monosyllables. A padre had come round several times to ask him if he was RC or C of E, and he had just shrugged. The same person had offered to write a letter for him, but Don Juan did not yet wish to consider whom he might wish to write to, or, indeed, who there *was* to write to. So he simply shook his head. Now this beautiful naval woman, as he thought of her, was sitting beside him, and he wanted to speak. To ask her name.

The doctor appeared on his regular round, at that moment, with his usual retinue. Matron, sister, staff nurse, and nurse hovered behind him, each in her own degree, each wearing a different combination of starchy apron and Victorian lace headgear. Florence Nightingale was one eminent Victorian whose work endured. Don Juan saw the woman by his bedside rise to her feet.

The matron, a galleon of a woman, introduced her to the doctor. "Second Officer Fitzjames—Dr. Knatchbull. She wants a report for the American Embassy, Doctor. She's acting as liaison."

"Well, after we've had a look at him I'll give you an opinion."

"Shall I wait outside?"

"No, no. It's all right. Has he talked at all yet, Sister?"

"Monosyllabic, Doctor," said the sister.

The doctor, helped by the nurses, now checked Don Juan's various plaster casts, his charts and his pulse. Don Juan knew for almost certain who the beautiful naval person was, but could scarcely believe that the little girl in the Tate Gallery tearoom, the child-woman in her nightie he had sat up and talked to in Brown's Hotel, with her brother Giles, should have turned from so sweet a cygnet into so glorious a swan. Speech was something to which he was so unaccustomed now that it had to be planned like a leap over a difficult ditch. He could not be certain exactly where or how he would land.

"Juliet?" he blurted out suddenly.

They all stopped what they were doing and seeing that he was looking at Second Officer Fitzjames pushed her toward him.

"Juan!" she said. "Good God, you recognize me!"

He was planning his next leap so eagerly that it didn't come out very well.

"Beautiful! Gloriously beautiful! Not Titian nor Botticelli could have."

"You're Juliet, I take it?" asked the doctor.

Juliet's eyes had filled with tears. She nodded, not trusting herself to speak. The tears rolled down her cheeks and dripped onto her uniform.

"His mind wandering, would you say?"

She shook her head indignantly. The doctor turned to Don Juan.

"Good to see an old friend, eh, Duke? Your bones are going together nicely, I can tell you that. How d'you feel in yourself?"

"Glad to see Juliet," he said simply, smiling at her, his own eyes moistening at finding her here, after so much hell. Then to his horror, and uncontrollably, he started to cry, as a child cries. He turned his head away in shame, but he couldn't move his limbs. Sobs came wracking up from his chest, and he felt his voice howling like that of a baby, utterly beyond his control. He heard the doctor say, "Oh, good. Splendid. Juliet, d'you know him well?"

"In a way," she said, her own voice choked.

Don Juan heard the doctor say to him, "Let it out, old boy. It's a form of aftershock. Nothing to be ashamed of. Juliet will stay with you for a while. Nurse is going to be very near. I'll see you later."

"Juliet, I'm going to have to talk now. I feel bursting with words." He choked the words out.

"Talk. I've waited to hear your voice again for nine years."

"That tricorne hat is so smart, but can you let me see all your hair?"

She took it off, hauling out what seemed like a dozen hairpins to do so.

"How could you have become so much a woman and I not have been able to imagine it? That *bon Dieu* does marvelous work!" said Don Juan. But his tears still flowed.

"What is it, Juan?"

"People, dead people, lost people, miserable people, trails of them behind me. When I close my eyes I see their faces. Edwige, someone I dismissed from my life. It seemed right at the time. But I see her face. Jeanne, a woman who was screaming last time I saw her. Lise, a pathetic creature, but warm and human and utterly innocent, as innocent as an animal caught in a trap. But because she's my own species I can't bear to think of her in pain . . . and see her pain again and again. It won't go away."

"Was she the one with the baby?"

"You know?" He was surprised.

"Yes, Mr. Dulles ordered a report."

"The Dupuis? Did they kill the Dupuis?"

"No, they are in prison."

"Thank God. Would a deposition from me in their behalf help?"

"It might."

"Juliet, I can't grasp how you come to be here, to have known about me, about everything."

"Another time I'll tell you. Right now I'd like to hear about the last nine years of your life. . . ."

And so he talked. Hiding nothing of moment that had happened, he let it all pour out. The faces of the living and the dead wept and reproached him, crowding at the attic door of his memory, shouting their competition for his chagrin, his pity and his guilt. He allowed himself in those moments, as he babbled to Juliet, to feel with Teresa, and Edwige, and Berthe, and Blodwen, and all the others, the sometime devastation of their loneliness. He howled aloud, mouthing *their pain,* exorcising little of his own; but, in the end, managing somehow to close again his attic door.

Half an hour later, he was interrupted by the nurse.

"How is he?" she asked Juliet.

"Exhausted, I think" said Juliet. "Juan, I'll be back tomorrow. I think they want you to sleep."

"There can be no question of that," he said. "Unless . . ."

"Unless?"

"You kiss me. Oh Lord, I've wasted so much time talking about me. But I do feel better." He smiled sleepily.

She kissed him lightly on the forehead. At once she felt his mouth seeking hers. She glanced around, for an instant, at the nurse, who smiled back, shrugged, and left the room. Then Juliet kissed Don Juan on the mouth. He tasted of toothpaste and smelled, very faintly, of ether. It was nevertheless the most moving and memorable of kisses, an she wanted to linger over it. But she drew back and looked at him. He had closed his eyes and seemed, indeed, to be falling asleep.

"Please come again tomorrow," he said.

Next day he was expecting her. The ward sister had told her on the telephone that now he had started to talk he was full of questions it was hard for the nurses to answer. About the war, about the governance of France, but most of all about Second Officer Fitzjames.

"I am unlikely to live through this day, the doctor tells me, unless I am kissed often and often by the luscious Fitzjames," Don Juan announced as she came through the door with a bundle of mail for him in her hand.

"Golly, Duke, but you do have a nerve," said Juliet, kissing his cheek but avoiding his mouth.

"If you're going to call me that, I shall call you Lady Juliet and we'll sound like characters out of a Trollope novel."

"Read your mail, Juan. I've got to go to the office. I'll be back later." She stooped and kissed his mouth quickly before heading for the door.

"Hey," he shouted. "I've just remembered your last letter that I got in Switzerland."

"Yes?" She waited, holding her breath slightly.

"For the first time in my life I'm jealous."

"You don't really have any need to be. But I am delighted to hear it!"

And she left him, smiling her way along the passage between the bustling nurses.

He sat there using his one unplastered hand to sort through the mail when it came to him that he still had received not the slightest explanation of how Juliet had come back into his life. In a sense she had for so long lurked in the recesses of his mind as the girl who . . . "one day . . . when the time is right." And here she suddenly was, a fact of his everyday life. Like the nurses and the doctor. How the hell had she got there? What heaven that she had.

There were a good many letters from people like Dulles saying,

"Congratulations. We're glad you made it." No explanation as to what had happened in Paris, he noticed. But Paris had fallen now, that much he had gleaned from the sister. He wondered what had become of Mireille, and of her father. Perhaps he was now in de Gaulle's government. There was a letter from Don Juan's grandfather enclosing a note from the curé. It had come via Dulles.

Dear Grandson,

The enclosed letter from the curé has moved me very much. The Germans told the press here that you were guilty of the rape of the Baroness von Carlowitz. It was put a little more delicately than that. "A criminal assault" was the phrase used. But Goering called me to tell me the facts of the matter. He said he had some pictures of yours that were evidence of psychotic tendencies, whatever that may mean from a man like Goering!

However, there was the deposition of the baroness which I was shown, and that seemed conclusive evidence. You can imagine my anger and shame. I was in touch with Allen in Switzerland and he told me he'd seen you and that you had given a satisfactory explanation of the rape (which amounted to a denial) and at the same time volunteered to do *more* work for his side. This was the first time I'd heard, naturally, that you were working for the Allies. I was still convinced by the baroness's deposition, but glad that you had decided to expiate your offense by working, in the field, for Allen. It was at the time of your father's death, and I sent you the news through Allen, together with my hopes for your rehabilitation in Spain.

I finally got the curé's note in April. The post has been abominable between France and Spain. It came at a terrible moment for me. As you will now know, if you have received this letter, we discovered a German agent working in my office, a person who was privy to some of the things we were doing for Allen. This put you, among others, in great danger. At the same time the curé makes it clear that you were *totally innocent* of the offense the baroness alleged, although he says that you committed the sin of adultery. Seldom have I read of a mere adultery with more joy. Please forgive me for doubting you.

At the time of writing I just received the dreadful news of your disappearance and probable capture by the Germans. I have prayed to God for your deliverance. So surprised must the Deity have been to hear from me that He may indulge this old sinner. If He does my gift of thanks may have to be my soul!

Your loving grandfather

The curé's letter was brief.

Monseigneur,

While the cure of your grandson's soul has not been entrusted to me I have had the honor and pleasure of his friendship.

Quite recently he was publicly accused of an abominable offense by a woman who is a believer. She tells me that your grandson is innocent of the crime of which she accused him, although she herself has confessed to the sin of adultery with him. In this confession to me she absolved me from secrecy where and when, at my discretion, I could help clear your grandson's name from the obloquy his supposed crime must bring.

Since her motives in accusing your grandson were not without justification, helping to preserve both his liberty and his life, I must call upon you to keep this matter a secret from the civil and military authorities and, naturally, the press.

The time will, doubtless, come when I can absolve you from this secrecy so that your grandson's name may be cleared. The lady's action can then be represented as a hoax, which is no more than the truth.

Her sin must be kept confidential, since she has confessed and received absolution. Don Juan's sin and his life, which is being lived in defiance of God's Will, is a matter of great concern to me. It would give me the greatest joy, since I began my mission, to bring him to the church.

For the fact that he has never been confirmed, you and his whole family, must bear a heavy responsibility, Monseigneur.

Yours, in Christ,
Ortolan

From Henrietta and his mother there was a letter from Washington, D.C.

Dear Juan,

We have written the moment we heard that you had arrived in England. The news of your fearful injuries has shocked us both a great deal. Allen Dulles wrote us a charming note full of praise for you.

Mr. Dulles has explained that it may be some time before you can respond to us. Please don't worry about that and concentrate on getting well. We will be *rooting* for you as we say here.

Since we hear there is *nothing* to eat in Britain we are sending you a huge bundle of food. Hope you like peanut butter. It is the only American delicacy your mother cares for, apart from shad roe.

We have taken a house temporarily, in a charming but rather rundown section of Washington called Georgetown. Our life is simplicity itself. Just Boris and Valéry and a staff of three. This city is trying to get used to the idea that it is the center of a world power, possibly *the* world power. It is rather as if such a fate had overtaken Bordeaux, but the excitement of it all is intoxicating. Your mother has consented to winter here, which makes me very happy because now we can start doing a little entertaining again.

I have a fascinating job at the State Department, where anti-de Gaulle feeling is high. I try to exert some Francophile influence.

The first moment it is possible to cross the Atlantic again, we want you to join us. Dulles's people should be able to arrange it. Meanwhile, think of nothing but getting better.

Your loving mother,
and Henrietta

When Juliet returned, he was alseep again, the letters scattered across the bed. She sat down and looked at his face in repose and loved it. The rather high brow, the dark long lashes under the sharply defined, sweeping eyebrows that made a kind of bow above his nose. A mouth that had not changed since she had first found it in her dreams as a girl. His body, normally strong and muscular and spare, now touchingly weak with leg and arm and chest all encased in plaster. She wondered if she had taken too much for granted when she had maneuvered herself into the position of being his "guardian and friend" with the intelligence community to whom she reported. Another nagging worry was whether he would regret his flood of confession to her if they became close. She did not dare let herself project her imagination as far as their being lovers. It was all going too dangerously well, it was too perfect to be true. She must remain cool or, defenseless as he was, he would feel abducted.

"Juliet!" he exclaimed, waking. "I just left you in my dream and here you are, looking rather overdressed. Of course, I was plasterless in my dream, so perhaps it's only fair."

"I'm glad you've stopped being curious about me professionally," she said.

"That's not fair. I am, I am. It's just in a way you've always been there at the back of my mind. It is amazing that you are here. But then again it is such a wish fulfillment that I'm loath to question it. But tell me."

"Well, first I report to people who report to Mr. Dulles. Then I have been working for British naval intelligence all through the war.

Codes, radio, using my French. They seconded me to the Free French when they set up their Bureau Central de Renseignements et d'Action here. One day, while I was working there, I came across your name. I got myself assigned to be your control for a time when you were working with poor Jeanne—you know, the Gaullists have given her a posthumous Croix de Guerre; they're trying to find family to give it to. Anyway, when we heard you were wanted for raping a German general's wife you became something of a legend in the office. Mr. Dulles told us it wasn't true about the same time we sent you back into France, but this time, of course, you were reporting to his people. 'Wild Bill' Donovan's OSS here.

"BCRA made a lot of jokes about your reentry into France. 'Trains packed with panic-stricken German generals' wives left Paris for Germany today!' was one crack on the bulletin board. Everyone thought Dulles a crazy man. He was just far too successful to be anything else. And sending you in again seemed madder than most of his stunts.

"It was very hard for me, all this. I never admitted to anyone I knew you or they'd probably never have let me keep contact with you. But of course I cared more about what happened to you than anything. It was like listening to a terribly real radio serial about part of your own life. Anyway, I appealed to my bosses at naval intelligence to transfer me, preferably to some job which would put me in contact with Wild Bill's OSS. I had to pull a few strings. My uncle is one of the Sea Lords, so it wasn't too hard. Dulles appeared in London and my uncle arranged a dinner party. Allen really is a charmer. In the end I had to tell him my heart belonged to you. He took it very well, and when news came through that you were alive, but in a very bad way, he arranged for me to be your debriefing officer. Here I am."

Don Juan looked at her quizzically for a long minute.

"All right," he said. "Debrief me. Let's get it over with. Then we can just talk about us."

The debriefing took a couple of weeks. There were reports that had to be made and supplementary questions Don Juan had to be asked. During the course of it, Don Juan was saddened to hear that Mireille had been arrested by the new French government and was awaiting trial as an informer. Her father had apparently disowned her and was part of the new all-party administration.

The British and the Americans had meanwhile crossed the Rhine, and the end of the war in Europe was in sight.

By "Victory in Europe" day Don Juan was being taken from his casts one by one. But by that time he and Juliet had become, in a complex but not disagreeable way, lovers. She visited him almost every day, bringing small items of food or drink, books or materials for his drawing (Sister forbade painting as both dirty and smelly). They caressed each other covertly. She, her velvet palm slipped beneath the covers. He, his toes gently tickling her upper thigh, probing beneath what she called her "blackouts"—the long black panties British naval women wore to douse the curiosity and passion of sailors who climbed ladders to their aft. She sometimes sat so close to him that they would breathe in concert, concentrating on each other's physical presence so intently that she, suddenly shaking with relief, would bury her head in her hands and feel herself engulfed by sensation as if they had, in fact, been one.

The walls of his little private room were meanwhile covered with drawings in charcoal, in conté crayon, in pen and ink. There were sketches that made some of the nurses flush scarlet. They depicted the starch-and-black-stocking-wrapped houris of his dreams bursting from their aprons, their hair escaping wildly from their lace caps. There were also disciplined still-lifes reminiscent of his drawings of nature in the Risle Valley, which encompassed the objects of hospital life, like instrument trays, but counterpointed with the life-filled masses of flesh of the healthy, sapient nurses. Juliet had helped Don Juan elect for life, and inevitably women, lovely women, were his celebration.

He thought he was going to like England this time. He had put from his mind the horrors of his English public school. The England he sensed, through the medium of the women around him, was, for a young and not unattractive foreigner such as he, Elysium.

And all those Englishmen, from the overbred scions of ancient Norman lineage, with their passion for uniforms both civil and military, to the horny-handed descendants of the Saxon yeomanry with their toothbrush mustaches and their porkpie hats—salt of the earth they all might be, but it was seasoning on a pretty bland dish. Every one of them sitting in his little drawer in the national dresser. Between top drawer and bottom drawer an endlessly tiresome series of subclasses—upper middle, middle middle, lower middle. . . . And all of them smugly despising each other in a language of sterile vilification for fellow countrymen that few societies can ever have equalled: N.O.C.D. (Not our class dear), U and Non-U, Upper Middle Class Twit, The Working Class Can Kiss My Arse, Not Quite a Gentleman, Terrible Cad, Awful Bounder, Fellow's a Counter Jumper, Class Solidarity, et cetera, ad nauseam.

As Don Juan saw it, being exempt from this hierarchy, by virtue of being foreign, made him, like a joker in the pack, able to stand in anywhere. In the grim hierarchy of English society every man, it was true, had available a pool of women of his own class from which, in theory, to choose.

The foreign Don Juan was a rather undesirable mate for marriage (Mummy would say he was "odd"), but acceptable to every woman who wished to have a "fling" for that reason. He was, from his point of view and theirs, gloriously outside the system.

Further, if the nurses at the hospital were anything to go by—and he knew them, in wartime, to be drawn from every walk of life—there was certainly female "life" to be celebrated in each of those class stratifications. No group of women he had met anywhere seemed so full of promise to a keen student of that marvelous sex as did the roses of England. In a slightly different context a current war song had it:

> Bless 'em all,
> Bless 'em all,
> The short and the plump and the tall . . .

Don Juan's thought exactly.

Some weeks before his release from the hospital the Juliet who now, like Winston Churchill in his letters to Roosevelt, described herself as a Former Naval Person (for she had been demobilized) brought, as a last act of liaison duty, an official from the American Embassy to see Don Juan.

Money was discussed. Don Juan had been accruing a salary from his American spy masters since he had left Switzerland. There was also to be a special gratuity. In all a fairly large sum in 1945 England. He surprised them by refusing it.

"Spying for money is something I have never thought of doing," he said simply. He knew it sounded smug, because he had never *needed* to earn money. But he couldn't help it. Whitticker and Inés and Jeanne were all in his mind when he did it.

Then there was the question of a promise made before he had left on his mission in France. But the Spanish government was still balking. While it was not clear in 1945, as it later became, that Franco's power in Spain would last for decades more, Don Juan had been anxious to assure himself some future national status more solid and acceptable than that of stateless Spanish political refugee. The American official now confirmed an open-ended promise to admit him to the U.S. as soon as he should wish to go.

The Former Naval Person had gotten into an entirely proprietorial view of her relationship with Don Juan by now. He had said nothing about their future, but Juliet had supposed his hesitation to be chivalrous, prompted by his uncertain prospects. She had enchanted Don Juan by talking a great deal about her home in Scotland, her parents, her dogs, her dolls (now in dignified retirement), her horse (waiting for her impatiently). He longed, after so much wandering, to find himself again in a real home. So he encouraged her to talk about it. Her father, Lord Stow and Lauder, apparently lived for his books. "Mummy" was the family organizer. With only a staff of six to run a fifty-two-room castle and a thirteen-thousand-acre estate, she had to be. But now the war was over, "help" would be easier to find.

"If you're good at the Plantagenets, Daddy will positively drool over you," said Juliet. "Please don't admit to Mummy that you're not keen on hunting or shooting, she'd never understand. She's president of the Society for the Defense of Blood Sports!"

"It sounds a great deal cozier than my castle," he said reflectively, wondering how Garcia would receive him if he were to return now. If he brought a duchess, not unlike Juliet, he thought, then the old man would probably skip about and throw his hat in the air. The image made him smile.

"A penny?" she said.

"I was thinking of the castle in Andalusia. I wonder if I'll ever see it again."

"Juan, you will come, won't you? You are coming to stay? I've dreamed of taking you home for so long."

"Thank you. I look forward to being in your home—because it's part of you. I suspect a rather important part," he said.

"All the time we've known each other there have been waits," she said. "Sometimes I think I can't bear it any longer. Will we never be 'complete,' I wonder? But if we somehow last the course I feel it's going to be so special between us that it will last forever."

He hated the word, and she knew it. But then, unexpectedly, she laughed.

"After all that I must tell you *when* we're inviting you."

"I'll be out of here in two weeks," he said, not quite understanding her.

"I'm inviting you to come in three months' time. If you say you're off to America or something, I'll quite understand, but I've promised Mummy I'll take this short forestry course. I have to be both Giles and me for them now. Oh Juan, please wait and then you can bring all your painting things and stay forever. Oops—that word again."

Don Juan smiled. His fantasy of English women en masse, standing thousands deep outside the hospital, returned. He wanted to go to Juliet's house; he particularly wanted Juliet herself. But he wondered why any of these things needed to be mutually exclusive. Now it seemed they need not.

"I know you're going to be quite hideously wicked while I'm away," she said. "It's not that I mind. Just that I want you to get it over with. But if you care for me at all I want you to promise me one thing."

"If it's in my power. And I'll tell you if it isn't."

"Promise me that while I'm gone you'll never sleep with the same girl twice."

"Supposing I only meet one girl I can persuade to sleep with me?"

"We used to call a question like that 'fishing for compliments.' I won't grace it with an answer."

"All right, I promise."

"If I think you've betrayed me and spent two nights, or a night and a day, with the same rotten woman, I warn you I'll kill you."

"You are a clever Former Naval Person," he said.

"To fall for you is hardly clever, my darling," she said. "But it's a folly I plan to temper with some wisdom."

The U.S. Embassy, in a valedictory act, as he officially left their service, had found him a London mews house to rent, with a studio upstairs.

The day after he moved in there he gave a thank-you party for all the nurses and their boyfriends. It was not exactly a saturnalia, but it might as well have been to read the press reports the next day.

It was inevitable that the British press would sooner or later catch on to the possibilities for good copy of an anarchist duke in their midst. Don Juan's party was announced in advance in the newspapers without his realizing it. The caterers that had been recommended by the embassy were probably responsible, but, in any case, the result was dozens of gate crashers, mainly newpapermen who came to glimpse the romantic figure the left-wing *Daily Mirror* dubbed "The Forgotten Hero." They must have tried pumping the embassy for details, because his exploits in France were described as "one of the great untold stories of heroism in the war." Which meant they'd been told nothing except that he'd been awarded American decorations. The right-wing *Daily Express* asked whether Britain could afford to harbor self-confessed anarchists who had participated in the atrocities of the Spanish Civil War even if they were dukes and had done dirty work for the Americans.

The *Daily Sketch* (then known as "the woman's own") had a picture of Don Juan beside a picture of his mother (taken in her twenties after being presented at the British court) and half a column of name-dropping and slightly inaccurate genealogy.

All the journalists got very drunk and many of them ended the night in odd corners of Don Juan's house locked in various amorous positions with nurses, having first telephoned in lurid descriptions of Don Juan's little party to their rewrite men.

The result was that a sometimes bizarre but pleasantly varied flood of invitations began to come in from all but the most pompous and respectable corners of the English social scene.

In 1945 Britain was still under the illusion that she had won the war. There was a great deal to celebrate. Every man and woman who had served had gratuity money, from a grateful government, to burn. Food was rationed, Scotch scarce, and beer watered, but making love, dancing, and generally celebrating were free and plentiful. Don Juan went to a party practically every night and hardly ever slept alone. The uncomplicated bounce and joy of British girls, particularly the so-called wellborn, was all he had imagined. Sex, for them, was simply one of the celebrations of being alive. They were completely innocent of self-analysis. Few had ever heard of Freud or Jung. In a class that had been functionally agnostic for more than a generation they were quite free of feelings of guilt. Nancy Mitford wrote the good news that sex could be "Utter, Utter Blissikins" long after most U English girls in 1945 had found every reason to stop rationing it.

When the time came to join the Former Naval Person in Scotland, Don Juan was thoroughly looking forward to domesticity and even thought fleetingly that constancy might have its attractions. He had enjoyed himself but had hardly touched a canvas or done a drawing, and the revolving door he had made of his bed had finally satiated him physically while making him feel spiritually arid.

She met him in Edinburgh early in the morning, off the overnight train, and drove him south toward Kelso and the English border.

Outside the town they kissed, and he loved the taste of her mouth. The passion of her kiss was intense. Her mouth made of his lips a whole territory of exploration, her tongue suggesting in subtle ways the promise of the whole Juliet. But he wanted to have all of her, not just bits and pieces. Coming up in the train he had had a feeling of foreboding, that staying in the castle with her parents would be awkward and frustrating, that their whole love affair might founder on a myriad of little social difficulties.

"The plan is this," she said at last. "Straight to Kelso! It's a little town on the Tweed, near the border. Very ancient and beautiful and special. I have a cottage there that Daddy was going to give Giles for his twenty-first. Poor Daddy. In the end he gave it to me. It's on a very quiet stretch of the river. We'll spend a week there discovering if . . . " She paused.

"If?" echoed Don Juan.

"If after all this waiting . . . "

"Yes, of course." Don Juan smiled, and, finding her hand, kissed between the thumb and forefinger, kissed the soft, the very tender palm. "I'm glad they didn't have you wielding axes in that course," he added.

"They did. I used gloves!" she said. "Please don't interrupt, Juan. Then we'll go and stay at the castle—"

"Forever?" he interrupted, smiling.

"More or less." She laughed. "Darling, all this is only if my lord duke approves the plan. Do you?"

"My dear Lady Juliet," said Don Juan, putting on the air of an eighteenth-century fop. "I am excessively obleeged to you. 'Pon my soul if I'm not."

"Juan!" Juliet was slightly hurt.

"Penalty for reminding me I'm a duke. No, I love your plan. Drive on quickly."

They approached each other on their first day in the Kelso cottage with a mixture of caution and passion that seemed to perfectly suit the extraordinary quality of their relationship; the trust born of a hunch about each other which had fathered, in both of them, a myth about their destiny to be together.

She led him through the very green garden of the cottage, full of rambling roses just starting to die and scatter their petals, the weeds overgrowing the paths, and into an old Jacobean kitchen with big copper pots for making jam and low beams and a huge fireplace. An old woman with frizzy gray hair had made a very Scottish meal of bannocks and ham and tomatoes, with some rhubarb pie to follow.

She looked at Don Juan, after Juliet had introduced her as Mrs. Drummond, as if he were a cross between the Prince of Darkness and the young Lochinvar.

"Ye have only to call me, Lady Juliet, if ye need anything,

anything at all," said Mrs. Drummond, half-backing out of the cottage, staring at Don Juan.

She paused at the door.

"His grace would make a grand laddie. D'you no think so, Lady Juliet?"

"Yes, Mrs. Drummond," said Juliet patiently. "He certainly would. I don't think I'd want to trust him to the bussers, though, do you?"

"I would no mind being a busser m'self if *he* were the laddie," cackled Mrs. Drummond.

"Goodbye, Mrs. Drummond!" said Juliet firmly.

"Just pullin' yer leg, Lady Juliet. You ken that, don't you?"

"Goodbye, Mrs. Drummond."

"Oooh hooo! Oooh hooo!" laughed Mrs Drummond as she retreated down the drive.

"I hate to think of the stories she'll tell in the pub in Kelso tonight," said Juliet, laughing. They were standing facing each other across the kitchen, she beside the lit fireplace, he with his back to the door.

"Who is the laddie?" he asked, taking off his coat and tie.

"A king for a day. They have a different one each year. They all ride out after him and gallop about all day. He has attendants and everyone honors him," said Juliet, taking off her coat and staring at him.

Don Juan remembered Tabatha Truscott and the little girls.

"The bussers are female gifts for his great day?" he asked, thinking how marvelous Juliet would be as his busser.

"Ay, the bonniest girls they can find him is the idea."

"If you were his busser, what would you do?"

"Anything his heart, his mind, or his imagination could desire."

"Would you need to kindle his imagination?"

"I hope not."

"I can see that if he were going to die at the end of the day . . . At one time, he did die I take it?"

"Oh yes."

"And if a busser like you came to him in the morning, as now, he would want to have all of you before he rode out on his last ride. If I were he I'd want you warmed by fire and cooled by water, 'my lovely pagan busser.'"

"I'm yours, laddie," said Juliet. "Be a little fierce with me, this first time, as if it were the only time ever. . . ."

He took off her blouse and skirt swiftly, kneeling on the warm slate floor of the kitchen. He devoured with kisses and his tongue each part of her as he released it from her clothes. She closed her eyes and made little ejaculations of contented sound at the feel of him.

"Oh, laddie. I should have been a virgin for you," she gasped as he held her sex tight between his fingers and lowered her bare back onto the tiled floor. "For ritual and my pleasure's sake, punish me. Just a little. Purge me from ever having been with anyone else. Beat me just a little. Not too hard."

She turned a marvelously rounded but firm rump, and he slapped it three times hard with the palm of his hand.

As he did so, her whole body shook with excitement and she swung around quickly, opening her thighs, thrusting to find him, her legs reaching for him like arms, holding his waist tight as he sank into her. She had that quality not given to every woman in that each thrust of his body seemed to fill her with feeling. Each thrust caused her fingers to tighten or caress, her thighs to surge in meeting him. Each thrust made her say or shout or whisper an entirely separate and distinct sound for the sensation, the pleasure it gave her. Each thrust was a unique event building slowly into a tumultuous whole. When she came, Don Juan had to hold her tight as one holds an epileptic, for fear she might hurt herself in the fire.

He carried her up to the bedroom on the floor above, kissing her breasts and face all the way, for her spasms continued and her mouth and hands sought him frantically. There was a large, man-sized bath in the bathroom, as there usually (mercifully) is in British houses, and he plugged it and put her in, turning on the cold tap and climbing in after her. She shuddered from the cold water and screamed pleasurably as he entered her again, making love hard and at once so that she became frantic again and the cold, splashing water surged back and forth. Finding the soap, he covered every exposed part but her face with it and slipped around so that she sat astride him. Now he bucked her like a Brahma bull, soaping her breasts and thighs the while. She screamed so loud now that her head flicked from side to side till it became almost a blur above him, and the soaked tresses of her auburn hair would have blinded her if she had been capable of opening her eyes for an instant.

It was at this exact instant that Mrs. Drummond appeared in the doorway.

"Lady Juliet, are you a'right?"

"OOOOOOOOOOOOH!" shouted Juliet, trying to open her eyes. Don Juan lay still, turning off the tap with his toes.

Slowly Juliet regained herself and leaning on the edge of the bath opened on eye on Mrs. Drummond.

"Mrs. Drummond. Will you get the hell out of here. How dare you! Christ!"

The old woman looked appalled.

"I never heered anyone scream so. I thought he was killing you."

"Mrs. Drummond, if you hadn't been listening in the garden you'd never have heard me. Your cottage is a mile away! Now get out!"

"I jest never heered anything like it. I thought the fella was killing ye," grumbled Mrs. Drummond as she retreated hurriedly down the stairs.

"Golly, she makes me angry!" said Juliet. "Nosy old bitch."

She still sat astride Don Juan. They looked at each other then, and laughed and laughed.

"Can you imagine what she's going to say now in the Kelso pubs?" she asked.

"I thought she was goin' to drown the pair wee fella," he said, doing a rather imperfect imitation of poor Mrs. Drummond.

Juliet wiggled her bottom where she had Don Juan imprisoned.

"She still intends to," she said.

He gave a great buck, but she hadn't ridden to hounds all her life for nothing. She stayed in her seat until she took the next fence, and then he slid over her and, holding her gently in his arms, kissing her face very tenderly, he took a long soft hour to keep her hovering in and out of her bliss until finally with a great heaving, splashing spasm he took his own reward.

They went and curled themselves up together in her bed afterward and slept for hours.

So, with occasional walks in the hills, and long talkative walks they were, and long hours of loving each other, in and out of bed, the week passed. On one occasion they visited the hill, covered with ruins, where once a city stood and where once the king had died each year. To be grieved over by his bussers? They wondered about that. Don Juan doubted it.

"The harvest is glorious. It must be reaped. After the winter, which is a sad time, in a way, there is always the joy of another harvest. The laddie once harvested is just another seed bearer, like the grain itself, to be turned under the plow. I think that's how it was."

At the end of their week of loving, they drove to her castellated home, actually part Norman castle and part Scottish-baroque palace. Like many such buildings it had been built over a span of seven centuries and parts of it were a collage of textures, in brick, flint, gesso, cow plaster, and seasoned oak.

He liked her parents immoderately. He wished they had been his. The countess could, in his opinion, have run any major enterprise, say Imperial Chemical Industries or a small nation, to perfection. Her kitchens produced food so delicious and so varied that for the rest of his life it remained a yardstick when it came to matters of the palate. Her prewar sauce cook had gone into semi-retirement in the castle, where he was now asked to prepare only one meal a day, but to confer each morning with her so that he might lend his inspiration and ingenuity to any or all dishes she planned that might catch his interest.

No detail missed her attention. Among the dozen silver chafing dishes at breakfast containing porridge, kedgeree, kippers, kidneys, sausages, bacon lean or fatty, tiny baby lamb chops pink or crisped, eggs scrambled or *en cocotte,* sugared ham and hot fresh bannocks— among these were always butter, salt or sweet, and three different thicknesses of cream, and, of course, tea, China or Indian, and slightly chicoried French coffee with or without hot milk.

What lucullan arrangements she was able to contrive for the four other meals of the day can be left to the imagination.

The earl was, perhaps inevitably, fat. He was also dying slowly from muscular dystrophy. A charming table companion, he had a fund of good anecdotes dating mainly from the fourteenth century or earlier, with an encyclopedic knowledge of what medieval people ate and drank. He was an enthusiastic critic of his countess's efforts in the kitchens, telling Don Juan that his one quarrel with the English was their curious aversion to discussing food, as if it were an unmentionable bodily function. He treated each meal rather as a benevolent theater critic greets the "first night" of friends. He grieves if something goes wrong, but is forced to say so. His congratulations were always couched in such felicitous terms that it was an incentive to one and all who created for his table.

When he was not in the dining room he was in his library. There he would sit by the hour reading and making notes, cataloguing, writing to booksellers and other libraries all over the world. If Don Juan and his daughter visited him he would sit and share with them some verse or prose, sometimes reading in the Old French and translating if it was too obscure for them.

There were nearly always six or more guests in the house, usually of the countess's inviting, or friends of their daughter. Malcolm, the butler, was a young man, just back from the war, who had inherited the job from his father, and he was the perfect chief of staff to the countess's inspired general.

Into the routine of this household Don Juan settled as if he had lived there all his life. He was given a room in which to paint, but much of the time he spent exploring the mind and soul and body of the Former Naval Person.

For him, in those happy months, "she made the sun to shine," greeting him each morning with the unconstrained delight of an eager cocker spaniel, her brown eyes alive with pleasure at the sight of him; merely hugging him, if in public; but, if alone, fondling him, pressing her hand to where she could feel the immediate response of his familiar flesh.

They kept the rules of the house and never slept together at night, making love only in a kind of deliberately rationed way when they were out for walks in the woods or down in the meadows, by the glen. There, childlike, they played private games, as nymph and satyr, Niebelung and Rhinemaiden, Bottom and Titania, Lady Jane and John Thomas. However the game started, at the end they looked at each other and loved the sum total of each other as "one entity," as if seeking to pin their melded but ephemeral happiness and hold it still and forever outside the continuum of time that blew with the breeze around them, or trickled away with the stream in the glen.

"When we finally share a bed again," she said, "I think I shall miss ants in my pants!"

She had, in his experience, a unique capacity to be *naturally* physical and communicate with him on an intellectual level at the same time. If it was raining and they knew they would be alone in the large, comfortable room that had once been her nursery, whiling away the afternoon by reading to each other—at such a time her hands and her body never stopped loving him, caressing him, and being in gentle contact with him. So that they read together in a state of heightened awareness and communication.

As if to make paragraphs of physical sensation in their mental life together, they developed an absolutely shared sense of the moment when a book or sketch should be abandoned and he or she, by opening a button or merely putting their fingertips upon the object of their sudden, all-excluding desire, could lose themselves in passion and, after a tender while, satiated, return by degrees to the world of their shared imagination.

One night there was a memorable dinner party at the castle. Memorable because of a very special guest. In general there were several dinner parties each week, and the guests varied from the local county set, politicians, or friends from other parts of Scotland or England passing by, mostly the countess's guests these, to, more rarely, a don from Oxbridge, a French historian, a collector of books or an antiquarian, these usually friends of the earl.

On this occasion the "very special guest" was an antiquarian bookseller of international renown, who had fled from his native Germany back in 1938. His name was David Berncastler.

When the earl introduced Don Juan to Mr. Berncastler before dinner he committed that most British sin—he failed to explain who Mr. B was and what he did. In polite British society Don Juan realized this was a matter to be slowly discovered by indirection but never by a direct question. So, while a distinguished Roman Catholic theologian arrived and he and an elderly Swede, who was introduced by a mumbling earl as Professor Um Er (his host had forgotten his name), Don Juan and Juliet found themselves sipping white port with Mr. Berncastler and setting about the detective game.

"You are not the theater critic who has cracked the problem of Ibsen?" asked Don Juan.

"Absolutely not. What problem?" Mr. Berncastler was puzzled.

"No, no, Juan. Mr. Berncastler is here to advise Mummy about bees. He's the world's greatest authority. Maeterlinck is out the window since Mr. Berncastler's theory."

"Lady Juliet, I assure you I have a horror of bees. I believe I am most frightfully allergic to their sting." Mr. Berncastler was alarmed.

"Oh dear. It must be another Berncastler." Juliet sighed.

"There cannot be many," said Don Juan.

"I am David Berncastler, the antiquarian bookseller, and I believe I am the only one in the London telephone directory," said Mr. Berncastler.

"Ah, an antiquarian bookseller. You're a friend of Daddy's!"

"I hope so." Mr. Berncastler smiled. "And I'm not on bad terms with the countess."

"I'm sorry. I hope you don't think us awfully rude, but Daddy never tells us who people are. Juan here is Spanish and we sometimes play an oblique, silly game to try to find out."

"I don't think Lord Stow mentioned your name," Mr. Berncastler said to Don Juan. "But you must be the Spaniard who is trying to introduce bullfighting to Scotland?"

"Touché." Juliet laughed delightedly, and introduced Don Juan properly.

"If you want to know why I am here I shall tell you," said Mr. Berncastler. "And even if you don't want to know! You see that paper parcel over there sitting on the sofa table behind Lady Stow?"

"Oh dear, it looks like a bomb," said Juliet.

"In some ways it is. And it's been ticking since the twelfth century."

"What is it?" asked Juliet.

"A Batcherian hymnbook. Really a folio containing quires, or sheets of papyrus."

The earl, who was sitting now, because of his disability, motioned to them to join him. He spoke to Mr. Berncastler in a gruff voice he used when he was particularly moved and excited.

"David," he said. "My dear fellow. Will you open up our treasure for everyone to see?"

David Berncastler hurried to comply. He seemed elated by the earl's sense of the occasion.

"I feel," he said, "as if I should first assure you that there is nothing up my sleeves."

He then deftly undid the paper, revealing a transparent plastic box containing what, to Don Juan, looked like a French mille-feuilles pastry. Hundreds of stuck-together pages, enclosed partially in a leather binding. They looked stuck together because they seemed to congeal in the center and splay out somewhat at the sides.

"It is hard for us all to get excited about it if you don't explain," said Lady Stow to her husband.

"It contains clues to the nature of an important religion of which we know nothing."

"The Batcherians of the Jura region of France and Switzerland," said Don Juan, suddenly remembering the connection in which he'd heard the name.

"I'd prefer it if you called it a heresy rather than a religion," said Father Cox, the Roman Catholic priest.

"Very well," said Lord Stow. "It contains details of a heresy for which the population of the region were massacred in the twelfth century."

"By whom?" asked Juliet.

"By the church," said David Berncastler. "Or rather on orders from the church."

"Why?"

"There is a theory that they were very similar to the Albigenses of the Languedoc and the Bogomils of Bulgaria," said Father Cox.

"You mean they were butchered because they were buggers?" asked Juliet.

"Juliet! Really!" said Lady Stow. But all the men laughed except Father Cox, who gave a thin-lipped smile.

"Well, that's where the word comes from, isn't it, Daddy?"

"Certainly," agreed Lord Stow. "We don't really know what, if any, connection there is between the Batcherians and the Bogomils, but if we can decipher this book we may find out. Tens of thousands of families died because of the belief those pages reflect."

"Have you acquired the book through Mr. Berncastler?" asked Professor Knud. "I think rumors of its existence have been around for many years."

"David," said Lord Stow, "perhaps you'd be kind enough to explain something of the history of the book? The bibliography—"

"David shall tell us at dinner," said Lady Stow firmly, taking Father Cox's arm and leading the party in to dinner.

Once seated at the head of his table, secure from some of the problems of his infirmity, Lord Stow settled comfortably into the role, natural to him, of guiding conversation among guests he knew and understood. "Without Mummy," Juliet had said, "no party here would ever get going. But once it's going, Daddy's in his element. He loves to talk, and he's not a bad listener." As the guests started on a mock turtle soup, with subtleties more pleasurable than mere sherry lurking in its amber depths, Lord Stow decided to introduce David Berncastler properly.

"Before David tells us how he traced the labyrinthine history of my little book—you'll forgive that possessive 'my' as a collector's foible—I think David will let me introduce him properly for the benefit, at least, of Juliet and Don Juan. David is the Maigret, the Holmes, the Peter Wimsey of antiquarian booksellers. If you were to have the good fortune, as I have, to have visited his charming house in London you would see several thousand volumes in his library. You would be forgiven for thinking that this is his stock, what he has to sell. Not at all. These books are almost entirely bibliography. One catalogues the books in the possession of, say, Lord Chesterfield about the time he was writing his celebrated letters to his son. It is in itself of enormous interest because it gives us a picture of the 'furnishing' of Lord Chesterfield's mind. Another may give us particulars of the books Benjamin Franklin took home from Paris when he returned to America. Yet another may list the specially commissioned volumes in the possession of the Duc de Berry in the thirteenth century. In this way David is able to trace a book as it has changed hands, perhaps been rebound, or subsequently inscribed and annotated. A book like the Batcherian hymnal will, of course, have been hand-copied by scribes for everyday use, for it was used long before the invention of printing. There must have been many copies. But when the massacre of the believers took place you can well imagine those who oversaw the pogrom made sure that all their literature was destroyed with them. But one, obviously, was hidden and has survived. Now, David . . . "

"Before I start on that , it occurs to me, Lord Stow, that there is probably one other copy," said David Berncastler, smiling and looking at Father Cox.

"In the Index Librorum Prohibitorum," responded Father Cox. "Possible."

"Oh, certainly," said Lord Stow, "but available for a little scholarly comparison, Father. What do you think?"

"Very unlikely. The proscriptions of almost a millennium are not relaxed easily. I personally am doubtful whether they should be. Sects and cults continue to multiply, almost all of them evil."

"Good heavens, Father, you're not referring to the Kirk or the Church of England?" asked Lady Stow.

"Not exactly," said Father Cox with his thin smile.

David Berncastler started to tell his story. The libraries of the Valois and the Medici came into it. Don John of Austria and the Battle of Lepanto were factors in the movement of a library. The book was always listed by title, but never "described" in the catalogues. It was part of a library bought by a Greek scholar from Smyrna (Izmir) in Turkey, and eventually found its way to Stamboul. Every step of this progress David Berncastler had traced, having just returned from France, where he had cross-checked some of his sources.

"I know that this is probably a fool's question," said Don Juan, "but how will you ever discover the secret of the book as long as it remains a congealed mass of papyri? It has been that for most of its long life, I take it, or one of the catalogues would have described it."

"That is an excellent question, Duke," said David Berncastler. "To which at the moment we lack the answer."

"Mounting the papyri is a technique recently developed, and most of the experts have been scattered by the war," said Lord Stow. "It is our most urgent task to find one."

"Where is Arthur Cranston?" asked Professor Knud.

"Dead," said Lord Stow. "Peterson, the American, is somewhere in China, no one knows where. Dr. Kohlner, who is the best, is in East Berlin and can't get out."

In the aftermath of that dinner party Don Juan thought about the earl's problem a good deal. The old man, himself, seemed to become more introspective than before, and there were signs of an increase in the momentum of his illness. It became harder for him to feed himself, and to hold a book steady he had to secure his shaking hands against some solid surface. It would not be long before his slow foot-dragging walk would give way to a wheelchair. Don Juan knew that he longed to unravel the secret of the hymnbook before he died. It was a final task he had set himself.

One day the countess asked Don Juan to come and help her dead-head the flowers in the rose garden. The Former Naval Person had started to put into practice what she had learned in her forestry course. Don Juan himself had contracted to prepare for a one-man show in a small but important little gallery in Edinburgh and had been spending a great deal of his time painting and preparing in the sunny room they had given him to use as a studio.

"Juan, you know that having you stay here is a delight for all of us. Since Giles's death we've missed a young man in the house."

"It is like a haven for me, Lady Stow. I'm sure you know that. I've led such a peripatetic life these last years. It's an immense luxury to be in a home."

"Has Juliet told you anything of my husband's illness? I know he hasn't, because he hates talking about it."

"She has told me that the prognosis is not good. I'm so sorry to hear that. At least Lord Stow's mind is so active that life remains interesting to him."

"Twelfth-century life!" said Lady Stow with a smile not wholly innocent of regret.

"My father was mentally unbalanced for twenty years, Lady Stow. If he had been able to concentrate on the twelfth century one could have reached him there. Fathers had sons then, too. But I think you exaggerate?"

"Yes, I do. He's sometimes marvelously here. He loves this place, and he has a great sense of family and continuity, which I suppose you'd expect in a historian," said Lady Stow.

Don Juan waited, knowing for sure now what was coming.

"Has he spoken to you about Juliet? No, I was sure he wouldn't, although I've asked him several times. He wants to see her married before he dies. It's another of his 'before I die' ambitions, like deciphering the hymnbook."

"What are my intentions?" Don Juan asked himself aloud.

"Duke, I'm sorry to put you through this. But we would like to know. Juliet is obviously devoted to you, but she has refused to discuss it. She said something that hurt and shocked me: 'I don't want to feel like a prize heifer that's got to breed to justify her existence.'"

"She said that to her father?" Don Juan was surprised.

"No, she said it to me. She dishes it out to me because she knows I can take it. That's the way it is between daughters and mothers sometimes."

"But she knows he wants her to marry and give him an heir, preferably male?"

"Yes."

"Lady Stow, isn't it enough that she can inherit as countess in her own right? Not every peer can by any means, I understand. There are years before she needs marry. Lord Stow's line isn't threatened."

"Is that your answer?"

"D'you think Juliet *wants* to get married?"

"Of course. D'you suppose she wants to spend the rest of her life making love in haystacks?"

"Lady Stow, Juliet is the only girl I have ever thought of marrying. But I must admit it was a *future* prospect. I see that the matter is more urgent. But there is a problem in my case, a medical problem."

"A medical problem? You look the picture of health." Lady Stow was astonished.

"I hope I am. But it concerns having children."

"I see." Lady Stow's mind immediately flew to hemophilia, but that passed only through the female line. Still, twenty years of madness in Don Juan's father was scarcely promising; perhaps that was his concern.

"If I go to Edinburgh and consult a specialist, I could have him send you his report. It is just possible that it may be favorable and that I could have children. If so, I'll ask Juliet to marry me at once. I take it I have your permission?"

"Of course, of course. But have you never discussed this children problem with her?"

"We've never discussed marriage, Lady Stow. May I ask you to keep all this just between us until we have the report?"

"Naturally, but what will you do if it is unfavorable?"

"I shall leave at once."

"We shall miss you," said Lady Stow sincerely. But in the rule book by which she lived her life and by which Don Juan was consciously playing his hand there could be no other outcome.

Don Juan had so facilely grasped at his means of escape that he felt the shame even as the words *medical problem* passed his lips. His glib arrangement to go and discover what he, more or less, already knew filled him with self-disgust. He justified it to himself afterward as having been a reasonable ploy to escape a commitment which was being forced upon him at point-blank range by the countess.

Both Lady Stow and Don Juan were quite unaware that Juliet and her father had discussed the same matter, but in very different terms. A week before the encounter in the rose garden Juliet had lent the earl her arm for the slow and painful constitutional he made each day, keeping carefully to the level grass paths that made their geometrical patterns among the newly clipped topiary. The task of clipping had been neglected during the war and the now demobilized head gardener and Don Juan had spent a week developing harmonious and sometimes surprising shapes from the box bushes and the yew trees. Here and there a griffin or a phoenix would guard a cornered hedge, or a halcyon survey a mirrored pool, daring the dragonflies to disturb the ordered clouds sedately journeying there.

"One half-expects a creamy unicorn to come trotting by," said Juliet admiring her lover's handiwork.

"Isn't Don Juan's presence here strange enough?" asked her father.

"Wonderful, Daddy, not strange," she replied, surprised.

"*Both*, I would venture," said her father. "One is full of wonder that something so strange should have happened."

"I don't understand you," said Juliet defensively. "I've always wanted Juan. Ever since we took him out from Deerhurst. I think he was always intrigued about me. No more, certainly. Not until we met again. If you're saying that it is strange that he should then have decided he wanted me, I don't think that it is very flattering."

"Of course he wants you, darling. That's not the point. Listen— a sainted virgin, preferably the Blessed Mary herself, is reputed to be the only woman who can tame a unicorn. Lovely, precious, intelligent but less-than-sainted daughter, do you not find it strange that you believe you can tame Don Juan? I mean unicorns may have seemed a potent threat to women, but surely the Don Juans of this world are far more so?"

"Who said anything about taming him, Daddy? All I want is to love him and be loved in return. I believe I am."

"Darling, that is less than honest," said her father reprovingly. "Don't you want him to 'forsake all others, cleaving only unto you,' as the church puts it?"

"Yes. I do want that."

"Juliet, you astonish me!"

"But he's not a unicorn, Daddy. He's a here-and-now man. An extraordinary man, certainly. Who's led an amazing, sometimes terrifying life, the memory of which he shuts up in some cupboard in his mind the way they closed Pandora's box. It's true that he believes, with a fearful resignation, in his daemon, as he calls it. Some fate that impels him to search out in women something like a holy grail . . ."

"Holy?" Her father was smiling.

"My words, not his," said Juliet hurriedly. "We think of holiness as something coldly spiritual, ecstatic perhaps but quite unearthly. No, I think it's a sublimely profane holiness he sees in us—if that isn't contradictory . . .?"

"It sounds pagan certainly," said her father encouragingly. "Not necessarily contradictory."

"I think he believes we contain, all of us women, a universal female soul that is actually of itself the *deity* and that through our heightened ability to love—to love totally, sacredly and profanely— we have the power to redeem men."

"Did he tell you that?"

"Not exactly. But I have put together what he has said, particularly when he was sick in hospital. He hates looking inward, you know; being introspective seems to frighten him, I do believe."

"I'm not surprised," said her father. "If I were the Flying Dutchman condemned to pace perpetually that ever-heaving deck; to see, over and over sun follow storm, zephyr follow calm; tired in the marrow of my bones with the predictability of it all; aching, and this is the extra and cruelest curse, aching for harbor—if I were he, I don't think I'd be able to bear a scintilla of introspection. What could it show but a void more terrifying than my own known fate?"

"Don't say that, Daddy. You make it sound truly dreadful. He's not condemned like that. I know you'll think me girlish and silly, but I believe that my love *will* redeem him, and then we'll have a lifetime for me to help him banish his ghosts."

"Darling, you're wrong," said her father. "The truth you won't face is both better and worse, I believe, than you've been able to accept."

"Worse?" she asked her father sharply, a tinge of irony in her voice. "What can be worse than having to wean him away from the rest of womankind? But I believe that he loves me so much and that I love him so completely that it can be done. And you don't need to tell me that it's a woman's daemon always to believe that. As surely as she forgets the pain of childbirth."

"I see you're more realistic than I thought," said her father, smiling at her wryly.

They walked silently for a moment or so, looking together at the image of a placidly unfolding sky in the reflecting pool. The earl was the first to break the reverie into which they had both fallen.

"It is perhaps a symptom of my sickness that I feel encouraged to prophesy. I think what I see in the future is woman being redeemed at last."

"From love?" His daughter was incredulous. "Who wants such a redemption?"

"Not from love freely given and taken, certainly not," he replied carefully, "but from possessive love, yes. That is the fate I mentioned which seems better than you imagined. It appears to me that if Don Juan is ever to be redeemed it will be on the day that women no longer feel the need, if they love him, to possess him exclusively."

"I'm sorry, Daddy, but you simply won't do as a prophet," laughed Juliet. "The nature of woman in the twelfth century you know so well hasn't really changed. We haven't changed biologically. How can our needs have changed?"

"Don Juan is your lover, Juliet. That is a fact, is it not?" asked the earl.

"Yes, Daddy, I'm afraid it is." Juliet's voice was suddenly childlike as she made this admission to her father out loud. It had been tacitly accepted as true between them, but out loud she feared it. The fear was that it would change her relationship with her father in ways complex and subtle that she would instinctively have preferred not to occur.

"Do you take precautions? I'm not being inquisitive about how— only is it a fact that you do?"

"The navy was full of good advice. Yes, I do."

"And you say that the nature of woman hasn't changed. I think it has. But then, perhaps I'm misunderstanding what you mean by nature?"

"I don't think you are!" she said.

"Then what of innocence?" asked her father, gently.

"I'm sorry I lost mine. Wish I'd been able to give it to Juan." She said it with real regret.

"But lost it is, darling. Do you lose sleep over it? Do I? Does your mother?"

"No."

"Don't belittle that change. It is fundamental. More so perhaps than the invention of the wheel. It will, I believe, be Don Juan's fate to trace the revolution your sex will achieve in a unique way, woman by woman. Until the day he finds a woman with the same choices as he, the same reflexes, perhaps the same drives. The question is, will he then find himself free of his quest and be content, or will Don Juan have finally found hell?"

To this prophecy and this question Juliet made no reply, no comment. But after a little while the earl found that his daughter was crying. He squeezed her arm, as he hobbled along, to show he shared her pain.

But when, with ample time to think out what he was doing, Don Juan found himself still prepared to go through with the charade of the medical consultation he was forced into a little unwonted introspection.

Peering inward always frightened Don Juan. In his search for the eternal woman in all women, he was conscious of a dedication of soul and mind. In this quest, as yet just begun in the perspective of a whole life, he felt an almost religious vocation. But that his religion was essentially sacrificial was something he preferred not to dwell upon.

No human soul who contemplates his uniqueness and conscious of the prison formed by the gristle, blood, and bone of his own body can fail to feel both awe and fear. If you add to those natural and universal feelings, mainsprings as they are of most metaphysical conviction, the certainty in Don Juan's mind that his was an immutable fate, a treadmill he had neither demanded nor, necessarily, deserved, then his reluctance to consider his innermost reasons for acting as he did is more understandable.

Yet in Juliet he knew he had the woman whom he must be able to love, as other men loved, or be forced to admit an essential lack in himself.

So he asked himself, "Do I *love* Juliet?"

The answer was as rich a tapestry of yeses as had been inspired in his consciousness by any woman he had ever known. *Yes*, both her beauty and her blemishes move me in my entrails; in the tear ducts of my eyes I am moved just to think of her physical existence in the same space and air I occupy. *Yes*, her goodness and honesty and even her occasional deceits are all equally dear to me. They are part and parcel of a standard of behavior with which I feel utterly in tune, even if I cannot always achieve it myself. *Yes,* she is in every way the perfect sexual counterpoint to me. I need a caress and she is tender. I need to feel engulfed by her quite uninhibited desire and she leaves my bones picked clean, my rivers emptied while she carries away what she has of me to lie close and satiated till I come again into my own. I am in the mood to be tender to her and she responds gentle for gentle, her sighing commentary a muted symphony of soft requited-ness. Will I sense her impulsive ache to be mastered as I was lately mistressed? She is then the incredulous, half-apprehensive city opening its gates to a victor for whose occupation, for whose total possession she has secretly yearned. *Yes,* she is the one with whom no words are needed for precious and vital things to be said and understood. *Yes,* her sense of what is funny is so exactly synchronous with mine that it does not merely double the quality of our laughter but quadruples it, the perceived sharing of fun being of itself a special extra joy. As the sonnet said, "Let me count the ways." But they are uncountable. For with her they keep appearing anew, like felicitous gifts on days that are not birthdays.

"Yes, I love Juliet," he said to himself with certainty.

But did Don Juan love Juliet to the exclusion of other women, to the exclusion of the possibility of continuing his quest? Could Don Juan live his life like an inspired astronomer whose telescope is tied to viewing forever a single star? Even though that star were the incomparable Juliet, he knew the answer to be no.

No, because of a girl half-seen in a dream, golden-bodied, tawny-haired, smelling of violets, the color of her eyes, and singing lieder softly to his navel in a husky contralto voice while her petaled hands made his mind melt and his thighs thrust. *No,* for a woman so *vicieuse* and funny that life with her could be played like a game of checkers with long periods of watchful speculation, occasional pain, but much laughter when the moves are right and the going good. *No,* because of the woman with whose inspiration and vision his art and love could meld into painting more extraordinary than his lonely talent had yet attempted. No, for the handsome Nubian, tall as a Watusi, with drums in her legs, the scent of myrrh between her thighs, and a close-cropped head so touchingly female, so full of sunny African laughter that he would long to linger as her slave, filling her cup and learning her song. These and many others, *the soon and future women in his life,* crowded into his imagination and begged him to say *no.*

No, I cannot give my life to Juliet, he thought. Knowing she would not ultimately settle for anything else but the dedication of his life, his physical and emotional and sexual life, to her.

The question arose in his mind whether he could bear the pain of leaving her before the attrition of time had changed their feelings, before some accident of fate had moved him on. Then he realized that the Countess's intervention *was* the hand of fate for Juliet and for him.

He rehearsed, in detail, why this was so.

Suppose, he considered, I went to Juliet and said, "I am unlikely to ever be able to give you a child. Do you mind?" What would her answer be? Almost beyond doubt: "It makes me sad. For I would have liked not only your children, but mine as well." But that she would have insisted on their remaining together was certain. As sure was he of the steadfast quality of her love as he was resigned to his own inability not to go on dividing his own loving among all the future women he would surely encounter.

The honest thing for him to say to her was simply "Don't you see who I am? That marriage and happiness forever are just not what fate has written for us?"

She, being woman, he reasoned, perhaps speciously, would never accept so ephemeral a reason as fate for abandoning the attempt to break the pattern of his life. Given the chance she would fight for the *them*, the Juan and Juliet duality, she already believed to be strong enough to withstand the forces of heaven and hell, those potent abstractions that presumably controlled the workings of fate.

In going to the doctor and causing him to send the countess the inevitable findings, he was giving Juliet the news that he had found his love for her too weak a thing to challenge his fate. It would be, for her, the signal of her failure to do what she believed she alone of womankind could achieve—the taming and the changing of Don Juan.

It would be quite simply the end between them.

That it was as constructive an end as Don Juan could imagine, he justified to himself, because it would leave him on perfectly good terms with his host and hostess. Any end, he knew, would in the short term be devastating to Juliet. Perhaps to invite her contempt for him was the best way to salve her pride.

In this way, and with these thoughts in his mind, he made his decision.

Once made it was in his nature to abandon introspection and to look ahead once more. But the loss of Juliet, already accepted, was like a blight on his days. It filled him with a sense of perhaps irreparable loss and a doubt he had never felt before. The doubt that amounted to a fear that he would never find her like again. That doubt gnawed at his resolve during the next weeks. Juliet's own actions alone finally caused him to put it aside and accept the fate he had molded for himself with his usual optimism.

The trip to Edinburgh to see a specialist, recommended by the local general practitioner, was made in the ancient family Lagonda driven by Malcolm the butler. Don Juan talked to him about his "war." Malcolm had served in the Argyll and Sutherland Highlanders, rising to the rank of sergeant. Don Juan liked him. He had a pawky Scottish humor and a lively intelligence.

While he was being examined by the doctor, Don Juan's mind concentrated on the hymnbook. If the earl was to be disappointed in Juliet's marriage, perhaps he could help him solve the riddle of the Batcherians. He knew that his grandfather was heading a Spanish trade mission to Britain, arriving in London during the next few days. He was not sure whether Allen Dulles was now back in America or not, but he rather assumed he was.

"Not a chance without surgery, and very little chance *with* it, would be my guess," said the doctor.

"Would there be any further hazards in the surgery?" asked Don Juan.

"There are always hazards when you use the knife, Duke," said the doctor. "You're functioning sexually. I wouldn't risk it."

That night Don Juan went to the Former Naval Person's rooms when the rest of the household had gone to bed. He went because he knew now for how short a term she would be his. The doctor's report would come to the countess when all the tests were complete. But the result was already conclusive.

Because it was not in their relationship to misunderstand each other's motives, she knew that he was not simply breaking the "rules" they'd made together, that there was something else.

He came into her bed that night like a tired and frightened child and laid his head on her breast. She held him tight and waited, feeling his tears warm on her flesh. When he spoke it was of the Flying Dutchman, the Ancient Mariner, the Wandering Jew—how he felt, like them, an actor on a stage he could never leave without dying, playing a role of which he grew increasingly weary.

"And what of your *will?*" she asked. "Any free person can use his will to force himself off the treadmill his environment and upbringing creates for him. You mustn't let your exile become a sort of moving prison."

For the first time, she had misunderstood him. And in that instant he came to terms with his aloneness.

"My darling," he said gently. "You, for whom birth and

education, natural love and loyalty, have built as gracious and beautiful a prison as any mortal could hope to live in, could you, would you, have the *will* to break out of it?"

She knew now for sure that it was *they* that were at stake, and that in that perilous single file that humans walk, along the cliff face of the reality principal, he had stumbled but recovered himself. She, on the other hand, who had walked in such perfect, almost inhumanly perfect, step with him for so long had suddenly, herself, stumbled. There is no way in that particular single file that any walker can look behind and help another. Each person must be surefooted for himself alone or the whole line is endangered.

But in her panic that he was slipping away from her she tried to haul him back and hold on to him with her physical love. She made love to him like a tigress, igniting him with a ring of imaginative and wanton fire. She rode him like a Valkyrie, galloping into battle. Dazed with her passion, he could only respond with the mounting ecstasy she was raising in his body, trying desperately to let go, to float with her, away from reality into their recurring dream and idyll. And then she said it:

It was a declaration of her utter and complete love of him, of her hope at this very instant she might be taking his life into her and creating new life—"I so much want to have your babies!"

Don Juan was taking the train to London next day, having told his hosts that he had business there and would be back in a few days' time.

Juliet bade him a grave farewell in bed when they woke in the wee small hours. As she kissed him awake she said, "I'd like to have 'This is the property of Juliet Fitzjames—trespassers will be prosecuted' written there."

"That's rather a long message."

"That's right. They'd only be able to read it if you got excited," she giggled, settling down to her task.

He left her smiling at him from amid her pillows, one arm raised and placed behind her head, the breast beneath it tugged up and peeping at him over the sheets.

He came back and gave it a small valedictory kiss and went.

Malcolm drove him to the station at Berwick, where he picked up the London train from Edinburgh. Before they parted, Don Juan had a short conversation with Malcolm.

"Between us, Malcolm," said Don Juan, "I'm hoping to see if we can't get Dr. Kohlner out of East Berlin for the earl."

"So that he can mount the pages of his wee book?"

"That's right."

"Och, that'd be a grand thing to do. Whenever I take him his dram of whiskey into his library I see him look at it like, from time to time. It just sits there in its wee box tantalizing his lordship."

"If I telephone the castle and ask for you, it'll be about this. So keep it to yourself. I don't want to raise false hopes."

"Anything I can do, your grace, just call me."

"Malcolm, please forget about 'my grace.' It makes me feel like an archbishop. I'll be in touch."

In London he went to the offices of his former bosses. Dulles, he knew, was not going to be there, so he saw a man called Frank Wisner who seemed to control a great deal of the intelligence work now being directed at the countries under Russian communist control. He was cordial and clearly wished to be helpful.

"If you know Dr. Kohlner is at the university, what can we do to help?" he asked.

"What I want to know is, will he come to the West? If he does, I'm prepared to offer him a considerable sum of money to work on an important antiquity."

"A considerable sum?"

"Ten thousand pounds sterling."

"If you're living in a country where a packet of cigarettes will buy almost anything, that is a fortune, Duke. Why so much?"

Don Juan explained the circumstances.

"What you need is a good free lance," said Frank Wisner. "I couldn't justify risking one of our people on this, but I could give you a name. And it shouldn't be hard to find out whether he wants to come west."

Two days later they knew. He did.

Meanwhile, Don Juan's grandfather had arrived in London and was staying at the Savoy Hotel. Don Juan saw him between his rounds of official duties as head of the trade mission. On the first occasion they talked of family and family finances, about the chateau in France, and about the continuing problem of getting Don Juan back into Spain. U.S.–Spanish relations were still far from friendly. The Western democracies still hoped to unseat Franco by isolation. The old man admitted that his own mission was semi-official, backed by business interests in Britain and Spain, and regarded by Britain's Labour government rather coolly.

On the second occasion they had lunch in the Savoy Grill, one of the few restaurants in London where you could get a square meal in the immediately postwar era. Don Juan started by making an announcement.

"I have decided to go and visit my mother and Henrietta in America."

"Good, good," said his grandfather. "And how is it going with the lovely Fitzjames girl? I saw a picture of her in the *Tatler* the other day. Everyone takes it in Spain. I really compliment you, my boy. For a Britisher she looked as if she might have some of the fire of a . . . of a flamenco dancer."

"I think she has! But you have the advantage of me with flamenco dancers."

"Have you asked her to marry you yet?"

"I've discussed it with her mother. I believe they're going to be against it. I'm still not quite sure."

"Against it? Have they any idea how rich you are?" asked his grandfather, incredulous.

"There are other factors."

"Not British, eh?"

"No, not that, Grandfather. I'll write to you about it when I know for sure. Meanwhile, I want to do something for the earl. I want you to understand that I am unlikely to marry Lady Juliet. That this thing I want to do I will do with my money, but in practical terms I need your help. Your power and influence spreads across frontiers. I want to get a man out of East Berlin. The Company"—he said the name his grandfather used for American intelligence—"tells me he's prepared to come. They've given me the names of people who are prepared to do it for money. Will you have *your people* oversee it for me?"

"The names they gave you?"

Don Juan told him.

"The best people for this! I have used them often. How long are you here in London?"

"Till this is settled."

A week later, just before his grandfather left for Spain, they met again.

"They proposed all sorts of elaborate plans," said his grandfather. "These people are children. They tend to overcomplicate. I told them to keep it very simple. So here it is. You have to find them a good five-hundred-foot landing strip in Scotland—level, dry, you know. You cable me the exact map reference using the detailed one-inch-to-the-mile survey maps they say you can get here for the whole country."

"I know. So, I cable you the map reference and . . .?"

"I cable you the estimated time of arrival. It will be at night. Date, et cetera. You prepare a flare path."

"Seems beautifully simple. A plane lands, off gets Dr. Kohlner, and plane flies back again."

"Wrong," said his grandfather. "Plane lands, off get Dr. Kohlner and the pilot. You leave the pilot at the nearest railroad station. Dr. Kohlner you take to the castle."

"The plane?"

"The RAF will, I hope, miss it coming in at night, under radar level. But a return journey is risky. A dead pilot costs more than a plane. So you write it off. You can afford it."

"Thank you, Grandfather."

"Will you look for an American wife?" asked his grandfather before they parted.

"I'm sure Mother is already working on it," said Don Juan, laughing.

Don Juan telephoned Malcolm that evening and asked him to meet him off the sleeper at Edinburgh, next morning.

"I'd best put you on to Lady Stow, sir," he said.

"Wait a minute, Malcolm. I think I know what Lady Stow is going to say, but I need your help. I think we're going to be able to solve the problem of the wee book."

"For that I'm your man," said Malcolm.

"All right, let me talk to Lady Stow."

When she came on the line, Lady Stow sounded both agitated and embarrassed.

"Duke, I am so sorry to tell you that Juliet has taken the news, which I had to break to her, most dreadfully to heart," said Lady Stow.

"I'm not at all surprised," said Don Juan.

"We've had to move all your things to the George Hotel in Edinburgh," she said. "Both my husband and I are mortified at her behavior."

"I quite understand, Lady Stow. I take it the results you have received indicate no hope of my having children?"

"Didn't you know? Oh, this is too frightful," shrieked Lady Stow.

"Please be calm, Lady Stow. I was supposed to telephone the doctor, but haven't had time."

"He says you are quite—what is the word—impotent? No, that's not quite it."

"It will do," said Don Juan. "I would like to borrow Malcolm's services for a few days. It is very important, Lady Stow."

"Malcolm! Good gracious. You're not going to steal him away altogether?"

"No, Lady Stow. I'd like him to meet me tomorrow in the car. Please trust me."

"I do, my dear boy, I do. He'll be there. You can't tell me anything, I suppose—it's too hush-hush?"

"Better that way, Lady Stow!" said Don Juan.

"I think I can guess. I shall go to church and say a prayer."

"Please do," he said.

He and Malcolm spent the next morning acquiring maps of southeastern Scotland. They eventually found a spot between Teviothead and Selkirk that looked promising for their purposes, and set out on a reconnaissance. After two days' hard searching they found the ideal place, a hidden plateau. They checked and double-checked the map reference and then sent a cable from their inn at Selkirk. Twenty-four hours later they received an 0200 hours rendezvous time.

In the meantime they prepared mounds of bracken in lines which, when lit, would guide in the plane. Since the landing place was on heathered heath two miles from sight of the nearest road, their main worry was rain. The landing strip itself had good drainage, but the long approach path was doubtful. They couldn't risk having the Lagonda bogged down in mud, so they left it concealed just off the hard-surfaced road and camouflaged it with bracken.

"If he's a wee old man who can no walk too well, I'll carry him on my back," said Malcolm.

Don Juan hoped in that case that he was exceedingly wee, because Malcolm was only about five feet six inches himself.

At 0145 hours they lit all the mounds of bracken. A light rain was falling, and they used a little gasoline to make sure each one blazed. They heard the plane long before they saw it, but when it finally loomed up out of the black night the landing seemed childishly easy.

To Don Juan's relief Dr. Kohlner seemed to be a healthy sixty-year-old who looked more like a retired football coach than an antiquarian. The pilot was quite young and American.

"Seems a real shame to have to ditch her," he said of the abandoned Dakota as they followed Malcolm, who carried a powerful torch to guide them. Don Juan was about to ask the cost of his aircraft when they heard a plane flying low overhead. It circled and started to fire flares that lit up the whole area.

The four men pursued their elongated shadows over heather

made even more purple by the color of the flares. The plane had left the scene before they reached the car.

In the far distance they could hear the insistent ringing of a police car's bell. Malcolm had the Lagonda moving so fast that they were halfway to Teviothead, traveling at a hundred and ten miles an hour along a twisting hillside road, by the time the police reached the dying bonfires on the heath and the eerily abandoned Dakota.

At six in the morning they dropped off the American pilot at the station at Berwick on Tweed. Then they drove north to the castle. Once into Scotland again, it became daylight, and Dr. Kohlner seemed delighted to see the beauties of the lowland countryside about him. Malcolm was driving more sedately now, and Don Juan talked quietly with the German in the back of the car. He handed him a check for five thousand pounds.

"The other five thousand you will receive as soon as the work is complete."

"Thank you," said Dr. Kohlner. "Did you know that I had seen the hymnbook when I was in Stamboul during the war?"

"No. It was in the hands of a Greek?"

"Alex Parasheles."

"Didn't he want you to mount it?"

"He was afraid that what we would discover inside would not be interesting."

"It was more valuable as a mystery?"

"Exactly, like a woman."

"A strange analogy."

"I hope that in this case he was wrong."

While Malcolm took Dr. Kohlner into the castle, Don Juan waited for him in the car.

He saw a determined, flushed-faced Juliet striding out of the front door to confront him. He got out of the car and went to meet her, putting out a hand which she deliberately avoided.

"I just came to say goodbye to you, you bastard," she said. "Did you think that your nasty little doctor's note would have made any difference to me if I'd known you really loved me? Poor Juan, you *are* the Flying Dutchman, aren't you? You just don't know how to do it. How to love. No amount of sensibility—and, I'll grant you, you have that—no amount of being a fabulous lover—and of course you are, you should be, you've made a career of it almost—none of that can make up for an empty place in you somewhere. You simply can't sustain a human relationship, can you? The permanence of it—and, perhaps, damn you, the very glory of it—frightens you. Still, thanks for getting the little old doctor out for Daddy. That, at least, was an unselfish act. Goodbye!"

The countess came to see him the day after he had settled properly into the George. She brought the earl's thanks in a letter.

Personally, she was distraught. Partly she felt guilty that she, with her demand for declarations by Don Juan, had precipitated a rift which she knew had made her daughter desperately unhappy. Nor could she reason with her daughter, who, guessing the part her mother had played, threw it in her face. Her mother, she declared, wanted a marriage and an heir. Well, she was quite right, and that was what she would eventually get if a man capable of fathering a child ever asked her.

Don Juan read Lord Stow and Lauder's letter after the countess had gone. It was short because the writing of it must have caused him great physical difficulty. Don Juan was touched that he had not dictated it.

My dear Don Juan,

I knew when you first came to stay with us that we wouldn't be fortunate enough to keep you for long. Remembering you as a boy, I wondered, before you arrived, if you'd changed. But why should you? I have not changed, and Juliet, who has always loved you, hasn't changed. I wonder if she would have loved you were you not who you are? For women the impossible wish of taming the untamable is often as strong as our male need to tread where no other foot has trod, the kind of instinct that drives me to solve the riddle of the hymnal.

No thanks of mine can ever be adequate to describe my gratitude for your initiative in bringing Dr. Kohlner here. We will let you know every detail of his progress and what it reveals.

Sincerely and gratefully yours,
Stow and Lauder

On this and other matters the countess kept in touch. She came to Edinburgh once a week to shop and have her hair done and would either lunch with Don Juan or at least visit him at work. At these times she made her reports.

One was that Juliet had been going out with a neighboring landowner, whose property bordered theirs. He was currently the colonel of a lowland regiment stationed at Jedburgh, nearby. They had a love of horses in common, and she'd known him since her childhood, when he'd taught her and Giles to ride.

The day of the opening of Don Juan's one-man show came and was far more successful than he had dared to hope. It showed that in the cultural backwater that the Scottish capital still represented, before the Edinburgh Festival had even been thought of, his work might seem avant-garde, but was thought to be, as one critic put it, "so vivid with life, that he seems able to make even a doorknob palpable, and when it comes to his people I expected them to burst from his canvases and grab me by the sleeve if I dared to turn my back on them!"

The countess, to Don Juan's surprise, did not come, but Juliet did, with her colonel, a handsome man with a face left vacant of something, perhaps humor. The Former Naval Person looked beautiful in a curiously heightened way, as if she had finished off a little too much wine at lunch. She greeted him effusively, introducing the colonel as "absolutely the end of my rainbow. This is it! Made in Britain by master craftsmen. The traditional model. As advertised!"

They toured the exhibition with Don Juan, and the Former Naval Person showed how keen a student of his work and style she had been. Before they left she pressed an invitation into his hand. "Don't open it till we've gone," she murmured. "Oh, that's *your* line, isn't it?" she added, and left the gallery, the colonel smiling apologetically and trailing after her.

He didn't have to open it to know its contents, and in a fit of sudden bitterness and grief, for her, for him, for what they had had together and what she had dreamed of for them—in that mood of loss and resignation he tore up her invitation without looking at it.

Her engagement party was front-page news in *The Scotsman*, so Don Juan couldn't miss it. Every great name in Scotland seemed to have been there, even a couple of British royals. He was intrigue to see that Portarlington had been one of the guests and was glad that he had survived the war.

He supposed he had heard no more from the countess because she was now involved in that greatest of maternal enterprises, preparing daughter for wedding.

Thomas Cook, now nationalized by the Labour government, made all the arrangements for his flight to New York, routing him from Prestwick, near Glasgow, via Gander in Newfoundland, an eleven-hour journey. He was making what he hoped were indestructible packages of his drawings, on the evening before the trip, when Malcolm appeared at his door.

"The earl heard you were leaving the country, your grace. He couldn't let you go without you hearing the meaning of the wee hymnbook. I ken well," he added in a tone of personal understanding, "that you might not wish to come to a dinner party with her ladyship's fiancé and all his friends, but in my opinion, if you'll forgive the personal allusion, you're a big enough man to handle that. His lordship will be that stricken if you don't come. He sent me himself."

So Don Juan went.

The dinner party included as extraordinary a mixture of people as can ever have sat down in that odd, strawberry-gothic dining room, which, now that the castle is opened to the public, is such a feature of the guided tour. There was the Herr Doktor. There were the regimental officers in their scarlet monkey jackets and miniature medals; Father Cox, the man of Rome; David Berncastler; and a number of Scottish divines both high and low—and, of course, wherever pederasty or the cloth did not preclude it, their lady wives.

Before dinner there had been a drinks reception in the great hall for the colonel to be formerly introduced to the earl's tenantry as the future consort of the Former Naval Person. The courtesies completed, the tenantry had withdrawn from the house party and other special guests had followed a magnificent haggis, held aloft by Malcolm, in to dinner.

Don Juan was embarrassed to find himself on the right of the Former Naval Person, the colonel, of course, being on the countess's right. Juliet talked to him enthusiastically about his good fortune in going to New York in time for Christmas. She had always heard that it was the perfect season for that fantastic city, et cetera.

He wondered how he could have allowed himself to come and take part in this charade. He didn't wish to look at her carefully contrived vivacity, he couldn't bear to hear her talking, as if her life depended upon it, about trivia. He, who knew about the real world. She, who'd been there with him.

He found himself watching as he turned dutifully, every ten minutes or so, to his left and then to his right, kindling or rekindling each time a conversation just unimportant enough to last about ten minutes. He watched during this stream of platitudes, this continuum of banality, a single lovely woman's face.

Framed in a lion's mane of coppery-colored hair, she had gray-green eyes set in a slightly freckled, tawny face. She was one of Malcolm's assistants. Not a regular parlormaid, or he'd have recognized her, but probably someone brought in from the village for the occasion. She had a particularly attractive walk, her carriage held very erect but with a spring in her stride as if she were preparing to do something amazing in the gymnasium. Her body under that black dress and that apron pinned so tantalizingly near to where her nipples must be . . .

Don Juan felt a kick on his ankle so hard that he almost cried out. It was followed by a fork being jabbed into his thigh by the Former Naval Person. He had to hold her wrist under the table to stop her furious jabbing.

That the earl chose this moment—the savory plates were just being cleared from the table—to tell his assembled guests about the hymnbook was fortuitious indeed for Don Juan. If the Former Naval Person had had a sharp knife to hand, he would have feared to turn his back on her. But as it was, she hissed, "I loathe you!" at him and settled down, a fistful of walnuts in one hand and the nutcracker in the other, to listen to her father.

The earl, if he lacked other attributes of his caste, certainly had a sense of occasion. He told them that he would not simply relate to them a set of dry facts; that could wait for the paper he hoped to deliver before the Royal Society (applause). Instead he wished to tell them a story. . . .

"If we look back to what it was like to be medieval man, we have," he said, "to think what it would be like to once again really *fear* God, to believe in a Hieronymus Bosch hell or a Sistine Chapel heaven. To go cowering and credulous to confession, to buy remission of sins for hard-earned coppers. To believe that black cats contain the souls of demons. In a world like that, where God was *real* and the Devil quite as *real,* but a good deal more in evidence, in those days to defy the settled order of belief needed incredible courage; and if a few of you came to the same defiant conclusions then you felt that there was safety in numbers. In such a way grew those aberrations of the Christian faith that, before Martin Luther made of protesting a durable religion, they called heresies.

"Now, I have said that this is what men felt. It is impossible to do more than guess the feelings of women in the matter. In the first ten or more centuries of the Christian belief, what women thought was not of the slightest importance. They bred, they bore. They toiled and they spun, and if some of them were as lovely as the lilies of the field it did them very little good. Women, to quote a learned 'divine' of the time, were baskets for the bearing of children. No more!—and they could hardly be less. It was as if the Christians in Rome, remarking on the fearful profligacy in the final days of the pagan empire, had blamed it on what they often called the natural lewdness and viciousness of women. Christianity, that clammy hand which descended on the Mediterranean world, was the offspring of Judaism, which still today has so little place for women that they are merely spectators at its rituals. Of the bestial treatment of women by Islam one prefers not to speak in mixed company.

"In all three great monotheistic religions, woman is the person who tempted Adam. She it was who, in league with the serpent, sent man from paradise. She it is, according to them, who is recurringly unclean to men." He turned to acknowledge his wife's reproving cough. "I say nothing, my dear, that you cannot hear read out to you in church.

"Medieval woman had heard so much of this that she had started to believe it herself. In the place of the comfortable mixed society of pagan gods and goddesses of her ancestresses, where she had her honored place, she was faced with God the Father, God the Son . . . and a host of male demigods in the form of masculine apostles. Their male plenipotentiaries on earth, the priests, forbade women almost everything that might give them joy—sex except in the strict service of procreation, theatricals, singing, dancing, or any form of education. In those early Christian days there were no Lady Chapels in the churches. The Marian creed had yet to be invented. The mother of God, like Fatima, the daughter of the Prophet Mahomet, were, and *are*, thought of as two extraordinarily fortunate women. The male connection, in both cases, being the ultimate benediction.

"Picture yourselves, then, in the twelfth century. You are in the Jura region of what is now France and Switzerland; the feudal world is then still in existence." A smothered giggle came from the maid with the copper-colored hair, silenced only by a thunderous frown from Malcolm. "The peasants live lives much like that of the Indian villager today. Tending the soil and the crops and animals by day, sleeping with the animals by night in a one-roomed hut. The church, whose bells summoned them to every celebration of the year, of their lives, was then the center of their existence. Of his crops and earnings a man gave a share to the lord of the manor for the doubtful protection of his sword. To his priest he gave another share, to ensure his place in heaven. From what was left he fed himself and his family. His wife, whom he could chastise, under God's law (for in such matters there was no other), he brought to bed each year, or near enough, with sons to help him in the fields or daughters whom he could sell or barter to the highest bidder. She was a piece, this wife, with the twenty-acre field he also farmed, and if he was a good or sensible man he so husbanded her. If he was not, death could be her only release from hell on earth.

"If you lived in the manor, or in the castle, or even if you were a merchant in the town, your life was much better, of course, but not in its essential relationships much different from the peasant's. To the sweet tyranny of the church bells you were equally subject. Matins, evensong, high Mass, Lent, Easter, Pentecost, christening, nuptials, and burial service . . . not to forget that all-important Christian service, the churching of women, in which ceremony, still in the prayer books, a woman was *cleansed* after what, to the priestly male minds of the time, was the essentially unclean business of giving birth to children. Only if she was cleansed of the 'evil' inherent in that mysterious carnal act could the priests admit the woman to their 'mystery' of eating the miraculous body and blood of their Lord at the communion table.

"In such an atmosphere in the Jura at that time, the idea of an ultimate Christian purity began to form among the men.

"Since women were so often ritually unclean, since their favors, such as they were, could only be bought from their fathers on an interminable lease, for their fathers were not anxious to have them back . . . for these and other reasons it seemed to many of the men that God had really meant love to be an all-male affair. Why else had He made man in His image? Why else had He ordered the world so that poetry and art, government and church, peace and war, everything, indeed, except the trivia of the age, were men's things in a male world?

"Now you must remember that in the twelfth century the world had, almost within living memory, suffered the most fearful disappointment. The one thousandth year of Christ's birth had passed and with it had *not come* the widely promised Second Coming, the end of an imperfect world and the beginning of a perfect one. Thousands of pagans had been converted in the ninth century against the 'promise' of this event.

"People everywhere wondered how they had erred. What had gone wrong? In the Jura men found this an additional reason to believe that Christ had shunned the company of men who were essentially impure, who had polluted themselves in women, often for the sole and pointless purpose of having children. For if the purity of men would summon the Second Coming, then what need would this last happy generation of men on earth have for children?

"This was, my friends, the heresy of the Batcherian Church.

"Christians in the Jura, both priests and their male congregations, were swept up into this idea as if it were a divine revelation. The fashion for this notion moved from court to court across Europe. Of course, like more recent Christian cults from Calvinism to Christian Science, it found pockets of adherents everywhere, but met many more who were strictly opposed to it as an idea. It was in the Jura, however, that it developed into a formalized religion, took possession of the very churches themselves, made of pederasty a licensed pleasure, since in loving another man, they reasoned, a man loved God's image of Himself.

"In Rome the church saw the danger of this heresy. If it were to succeed widely it meant the virtual end of the human race. Nor were they so sanguine about its appeal to Our Lord as a good reason for His Second Coming.

"I will not dwell on the measures Rome took to stamp out the heresy, for they have little to do with the story I am telling you. Suffice it to say that they started with exhortation and failed; they tried anathematization and excommunication and failed. Finally they ordered the total genocidal extinction of the Batcherians, and they were far more successful even than Hitler appears to have been with the Jews.

"That the Batcherians resisted until the final massacres started is part of the evidence we have discovered in this hymnbook.

"The Batcherian church, which they loved, they called—how ironic it sounds—the White Lady. Whether they called it that because the image of woman as an object of love was suddenly politically expedient or whether, as in the intimate sexual conversation of homosexuals, there is always a tendency to give the passive lover, in this case the church, the feminine gender, we cannot be sure.

"What is certain is that these hymns are songs of praise, as romantic and beautiful as the Song of Solomon in our Bible, which they rather resemble. They are songs of unrequited love. The Christ was expected and has not come. The Batcherian church has made a promise (all churches do), but it will not, or perhaps it cannot, keep it. That is the kernel of unrequited love, surely?

"Today a man meets a woman. He desires her. Her very existence in the same space and world as he may seem like a promise. If she spurns him, for whatever reasons—she is married, in love with another, does not desire him—then he is the victim of unrequited love.

"But at the time of the massacre of the Batcherians, the idea of such an unrequited love for a flesh-and-blood woman was patently ridiculous. Love for man or a church perhaps. Both had the power or choice. Woman had no choice and no status, was more important than a cow, but frequently less valuable than a good horse.

"And so it seems a kind of ironic miracle happened. As the Batcherians were slaughtered and every evidence of their heresy put to the fire, those who would keep the faith with their idea of the pure homosexual ideal learned the songs in this book by heart. For the book itself was too dangerous to possess. To talk of their adherence to the anathematized cult was as perilous for them as it would be to preach Keynesian capitalism in the Red Square of Moscow today. So they sang these songs. Wandering from court to court, they sang of an unrequited love for a White Lady, knowing that there were those among their listeners who understood their true meaning and sympathized. But the tunes were catchy and the words often sublime. They became the hit songs of their day.

"Generations passed, and the singers, who were among those they called troubadors, transformed the lives of the courts and cities they visited by introducing the idea, the marvelously romantic notion, of unrequited love.

"It was the end of what we still call the Dark Ages, so named, perhaps, because during their murky passage women were virtually absent from the pages of our history books, except as martyrs.

"Now women became the ideal of purity. The White Lady was for succeeding generations the unattainably pure. The lady for whom knighthood and chivalry were invented. Her father might still give his daughter in marriage at his whim, but the whole world knew again what it had almost forgotten: that her valuable love was only hers to give.

"Consequently, woman's whole estate changed. If man, imperfect man, had now to prove his worthiness of her, then she surely became entitled to own property, even, in his absence, to rule in his name. In civilized Christendom only the French resisted the logic that women might rule in their own right, inventing Salic law to bar the inheritance of women or through women.

"Elsewhere the emancipation of women has been part of the wider enlightenment. And today I am enormously proud that my daughter will succeed me here.

"Such things are in a small way the consequences of the misplaced faith that was locked away in this hymnbook." So the old earl finished with a smile of satisfaction his homily on his wee hymnbook.

The guests at the dinner table burst into spontaneous applause. Some (such as Lady Stow) because they thought he had spoken far too long and were relieved that he'd finished. Others because they feared he might have gone on to speak of the church and women in the modern world, and the divines high and low and the man of Rome had already found little enough for their comfort in his dissertation. Their clapping was polite and very brief indeed. But the women at the table clapped long and loud, led by the future countess . . . and joined, to Don Juan's huge pleasure and amusement, by the maid with the copper-colored hair.

The countess insisted that Don Juan spend the night and leave early, Malcolm having volunteered to drive him to Edinburgh and collect his things and then on to Prestwick in time for his plane. He was given his old room and retired at the same time as the rest of the house party after all the other guests had left. He lay in bed thinking about the girl with the copper-colored hair, wondering if she was Malcolm's particular girl. He must have just drifted off to sleep when he felt a series of hammer blows on his head and shoulders.

Juliet, quite frighteningly beautiful and angry, stood by his bed lithe and naked, looking like a cat that has caught up with her prey and is considering, in her own good time, the pleasures of the kill. He made to hold her wrists, but took a four-fingered gash on his cheek.

He leaped at her, holding her as a boxer hugs his opponent, to be out of range of the more powerful blows, only to feel her biting him on the shoulders and the neck hard enough to draw blood. And then her groin found his and her bites had turned to kisses and she consumed him with her body, yelling and sobbing, moaning and laughing, and in among it all shouting in his ear with every thrust of her body, "I hate you. I hate you. I hate you!" When they were done she left him without another word, slamming the door behind her.

In the plane the next day he managed to find a seat where his torn face was next to the window. He watched Scotland and her Western Isles recede, and his plane took him toward the New World and, as someone in the Company had explained to him, the New Woman.